Xi-Bootis

A

Planetfall Secundus

By Michael Robert von Blucher-Altona

25-December-2025

Copyright @ 2026 by Michael Robert von Blucher-Altona

Library of Congress Control Number: 2025926400

ISBN:
Hardback	978-1-7644482-0-8
Paperback	978-1-7637277-9-3
Kindle	978-1-7637277-8-6

This is a work of fiction. Names, characters, places and incidents either are the product of the author's imagination or are used fictitiously, and any resemblance to any actual persons, living or dead, events, or locales is entirely coincidental.

First published 2025

Books by Michael Robert von Blucher-Altona

ForkBraid
Book 1: ForkBraid   -   The Price of Peace
Book 2: ForkBraid II   -   The Cost of War
Book 3: ForkBraid III   -   Just Rewards

Golden Age
Book 1: Golden Age   -   The Unexpected Conflict
Book 2: Golden Age II   -   The Great Explosion
Book 3: Golden Age III   -   The Outer Satellite
Insurrection

Xi-Bootis
Book 1: Xi-Bootis A   -   Planetfall Secundus
Book 2: Xi-Bootis B   -   Planetfall Primus

Xi-Bootis – A – Planetfall Secundus

is set prior to

Golden Age II– The Great Explosion.

This book portrays the events from the discovery of the

homeworld of the Mimasian Thols, called,

(Secundus / Homwol / Vale, depending on the species),

which orbits the Star, Xi-Bootis A, (Cathol),

including first contact and colonisation,

up until the book,

Golden Age II – The Great Explosion.

If you have already read The Great Explosion,

it will help to enhance your understanding of the both

this novel and the next novel.

A home is not simply a place.

It is the culmination of memory, hope and the will to endure.

A people scattered through time and space may forget its shape,

but not the pull that it exerts on their hearts.

When they finally return,

they are not the same as they were,

nor is the world that awaits them.

Yet the meeting of hearts and land is always worth the journey.

Roberta Nummus, April 1st, 3470 AD.

Table of Contents

1. New Worlds.

In the deep void of the solar system's outer reaches, cradled among the Jupiter Leading Trojan asteroids, drifts Hector, not a world, but a dream hollowed into rock. Once a massive, lopsided rock tumbling in the silence of space, surrounded by a myriad of smaller rocks, Hector has been carved, shaped and re-spun into a cathedral of human tenacity.

Three hundred and seventy kilometres in length, one hundred and ninety-five in diameter, an ancient potato turned into a cosmic Eden. Its interior, a cylinder three hundred kilometres long and one hundred and fifty wide, slowly turns at zero point one one rpm, creating a little over one standard gravity, via centrifugal force.

Midway down its length, a central circular sea, thirty kilometres across, lies like a sapphire eye, fed by six magnificent long seas, each one hundred and twenty-five kilometres in length and thirty wide, branching out like veins of life.

Between these watery arms stretch lush landstrips, flanked by mountain spines rising four thousand meters high, a terrestrial homage sculpted into an alien sky. Far above, a brilliant central illuminating light beam, suspended seventy five kilometres overhead, never sets, engineered as an eternal dawn.

At the great junctions where each sea meets sea, three radiant capitals bloom: Hector Alpha, the mind of law; Hector Beta, its bustling trading heart; and Hector Gama, the soul of its society. Each is a jewel set upon a sea-girt isle, each humming with the pulse of millions.

Far at the cylinder's ends, two vast spaceports, each a twenty kilometre gateway to the void, anchor the station's cosmic commerce. And despite its open axis, Hector's rotation and mass hold its atmosphere firm, centrifugal force pressing it against its inner living surfaces. A miracle of engineering masquerading as magic.

The spaceports were each twenty kilometres wide, with the same diameter as the interior of Hector. Their atmospheres are contained by precisely the same centrifugal force. Between these immense spaceports and the main interior of Hector was twenty kilometres of Hector's crust. Vitrified and fused solid, as with the whole crust of Hector, impervious and resilient against the void.

From Hector's raw materials, other giants were born: Ganymede Prime, Callisto Prime, Europa Prime, Io Prime, Amalthea Prime, and a whole fleet of other O'Neill Cylinders, Stanford Toruses, and Bernal Spheres, scattered like pearls across Jovian, Trojan and Saturnian space. But Hector remains first, the heart and hearth of Jupiter's Leading Trojan asteroids. A hollowed asteroid turned beating metropolis, a monument not to conquest, but to endurance and the unyielding will to call the deep void of space our home.

Hector was not the first of these new hollowed-out worlds. Humanity had started work on three at the same time, not long after the turn of the twenty-second century: Hector, Patroclus and Menoetius. Both Patroclus and Menoetius were the two largest of Jupiter's many Trailing Trojan asteroids.

The smallest, Menoetius, the moon of fellow asteroid Patroclus, came online first. At one hundred and four kilometres in width and the same again in length, it was half the width and far less than one-third the length of Hector. Menoetius was completed and brought online far earlier, in the year twenty three ninety.

Patroclus was larger than Menoetius, but not by much. One hundred and thirteen kilometres in width and the same in length. Patroclus was completed and came online two decades after Menoetius in the year twenty four ten. At the time, both hollowed-out asteroids were considered Humanity's greatest engineering achievements in space habitats. That was, of course, until the completion of Hector.

The Great Reveal came in the mid-twenty-sixth century and with it, the true history of the solar system was unveiled. The Great Disaster of twenty one forty two was shown to be a War, the Mimasian War, an unintended conflict that led to the need for what became known as the Great Conceal.

A subspecies of Humans, the Martians and a completely alien species, the Thols, were revealed at the same time. This led to the decade of Great Confusion as the two histories sat side by side. The cover-up of the Great Conceal gave way to the unveiling of the Great Reveal.

At the end of the decade of Great Confusion, Hector was completed and brought online and with its sheer majesty, it dwarfed Menoetius or Patroclus that had come before it. Hector was, at that time, the greatest engineering marvel Humanity had ever produced. There was only one other hollowed-out world that could be compared, and that was not created by Humanity at all.

Suspended in Saturn's shadowed hush, the great icy sphere Mimas turns, a colossal sanctuary forged not from cold rock alone, but from the aching dream of exile and rebirth. At three hundred and ninety kilometres in diameter, it looms in space just like any other ice moon, its surface star-pocked to mislead the gaze of passing craft.

Cleverly crafted lies had been woven to protect Mimas throughout the Great Conceal. Mimas was an independent sovereign colony that held supremacy over the Saturnian Demarchy, yet did not wield its sovereignty over the Demarchy that came with it. Mimas. The mysterious technological powerhouse that held the solar system in both awe and trepidation. All became unveiled during the Great Reveal.

Within Mimas, however, lies an entire world: a serene interior globe, likened to an enormous fish-bowl, some three hundred and fifty five kilometres across, its lands caressed by gentle arcs of light from the eternal artificial plasma fusion sun suspended at its very heart. Its concave horizon was the reverse of any naturally occurring world.

Gravity here is a lover's whisper, zero point four gs, born of rotation, pulling softly against skin and soul, inviting both to linger, to float, yet belong. Three circular seas, equatorial, northern and southern, glimmer like jewels set into the inner crust, their tranquil waters reflecting mountain ranges that ring the poles like solemn crowns.

From those mountainous caps, island peaks pierce the sky, forming both barriers and beacons. The southern ringed mountain cradles the capital, nestled among its crags like a candle in a lantern, casting the laws of civilisation outward into this rotating cradle.

Martian Humans, lean and flame-hearted, live side by side with the enduring Thols of Mimas, whose original home world, Homwol, lay long lost across the vastness of the deep void of interstellar space. Together, they shape a culture rooted in survival and the sanctity of a shared sky. And as Mimas turns, steady and eternal, its people look both inward and outward at once, back to Saturn's ghostly sheen and forward into deep, unending time.

Created by the Thols of Homwol well over six million years ago in the distant past, now home to Thols and Martians alike. With the Great reveal, so too came the knowledge of the Martians and their close friends, the Thols. A handful of Earth's people, both the mundanes living within Mimas and the psychic Council of Shadows members, had hidden and protected them across the centuries.

Most had forgotten Humanity's first hollowed-out world. It was far smaller than Hector, far smaller even than either Patroclus or Menoetius. It was a forgotten world that people did not want to remember.

It was a world that showed Humanity's shame, Humanity's inhumanity and cruelty. It was a reminder of genocide! It was Eros, the Tomb within the Rock, in its high halo orbit in Earth's Trailing Trojan point. A constant reminder of Humanity's inhumanity to its fellow Humans.

Located at Earth–Sun Lagrangian Point 5, Eros, a vast hollowed-out asteroid colony shaped like a potato, measuring twenty miles in length and six miles across. Inside, a massive cylindrical cavity stretches eighteen miles long and four point seven five miles wide, rotating at point five revolutions per minute to generate a centrifugal force of just over one standard gravity.

The interior landscape featured six land strips arranged symmetrically around the circumference, separated by a system of interconnected artificial seas. A central circular sea two miles wide, two longer seas, each six miles long and one mile wide, were directly linked to the central sea.

There were also four shorter seas organised in two pairs, each five miles long and one mile wide, set apart by one mile of land from the central sea. The seas and land strips repeated around the interior, spaced one hundred and twenty degrees apart, with central mountain ranges running the length of each land strip, peaking at fifteen hundred meters tall.

Eros hosted two docking hubs positioned at the north and south poles of the interior cylinder. Each hub consisted of a one-kilometre-diameter by one-kilometre deep disk, featuring six external docks for small local craft and two internal docks for larger vessels, accessed through six immense petal-shaped docking doors.

Eros's internal illumination inside was provided by an artificial plasma sun that travelled along its central axis, suspended two point three seven five kilometres from the interior surface. This artificial sun bathed the colony in steady light that drifted from north to south over twelve hours. Then there were twelve hours of night before the artificial sun started its twelve-hour journey once more.

The capital, Eros Central, the Citadel, as it was known, sat at the confluence of the central circular sea and the two long seas. Spanning one square kilometre, the city was crowned by its tallest structure, the Central Spire, which rose fifteen hundred meters toward the central axis. The Citadel's eight other spires only reached a mere thousand metres in height.

Eros was home to six point five million inhabitants, predominantly Earth humans, alongside sixty thousand cetaceans, including dolphins, porpoises, and dwarf sperm whales, thriving in the vast aquatic habitats, its artificial seas. Eros was, at one time, a paradise.

A brilliant shining gem, yes, but one that was more than two hundred times smaller than Hector!

That was the Eros of old. Eros the City within the Rock. Eros the World within the Rock!

Eros the World within the Rock was brought online in the year twenty ninety eight AD.

Eros the World within the Rock was murdered in the year twenty one eighty two AD.

Unfortunately for the paradise that was Eros, the World within the Rock, it was also the first target in the First Horridian War. Six and a half million people, sixty thousand cetaceans and a whole world would be murdered all because of the greed of one man.

The High Prince of that time, Godric von Horridian of the Six Jovian Realms, slapped Eros with eight cold-fusion missiles, each with two-megaton thermonuclear warheads. Eros fractured, and through those fractures, its precious air and water bled out into space. The void vampire fed well that day!

People don't like to remember acts of genocide; people don't even like to think of them. People don't like to think that Humanity was capable of such atrocities. Some, however, did remember. Some people, however, can never forget!

Roberta Nummus was one of those people. Roberta Nummus remembered Eros and its destruction as she gazed out over the vast expanse of the interior of Hector. It was ironic that Eros presided over the first Great Explosion, not the destruction of Eros itself, no.

The first Great Explosion was Humanity's rapid outward colonisation of its own solar system. The irony was in the fact that Hector was now in Eros's role, presiding over the second Great Explosion. Humanity's rapid, albeit more controlled, outward colonisation of the nearby star fields.

Roberta Nummus had seen the rise and fall of Eros, from paradise to tomb. Eros, the World within the Rock, the paradise, now for thirteen centuries, Eros has been, Eros the Ossuary of Stone, the Tomb within the Rock!

Eros was now a monument forevermore, a permanent reminder of Humanity's propensity for evil and people did not like to remember it, as it reminded them that they all had that same propensity, that darkness within.

Roberta Nummus had seen it all. Roberta Nummus was born in the year twenty eighty. It was now the year thirty four fifty and Roberta Nummus was thirteen hundred and seventy years old. For all intents and purposes, Roberta Nummus was immortal!

Roberta Nummus looked out through the long, thick, clear, crystalline plasteel observation windows. The observation lounge was fifteen kilometres from Hector's main interior living surface and the gravity here was lower at only point eight gs. Beyond those long windows, the air was thin, an unbreathable seventeen percent of one atmosphere.

The sky stretched onwards to the other end of Hector, three hundred kilometres distant. Sixty kilometres above, the interior illumination beam shone brightly along the central axis of Hector. Beyond that, there was the other side of Hector, a hundred and thirty five kilometres away.

It was an extraordinary sight, one that Roberta Nummus and native Hectorians were used to. For newcomers from Earth or Venus and Mars, well, vertigo was common and the sight of an inside-out world took a lot of getting used to.

From fifteen kilometres above the inner curvature of the vast rotating cylinder, the world bends gracefully upward on all sides, an endless ring of green valleys, rivers, and sparkling lakes sweeping toward the zenith in a soft, surreal arc. Above, instead of sky, there's land, sunlit forests clinging to the upper walls, distant cities glittering like constellations in a dome of Earth turned inside-out.

The central axis, veiled in a gentle haze, stretches like a gossamer thread through the heart of the habitat, strung with fixtures that mimic the passage of day and night. It's a view both impossible and intimate, as if standing within a giant, living kaleidoscope, cradled by a horizon that wraps around the very soul.

Roberta Nummus lamented, all those centuries ago, Eros had been like this. Just very much smaller.

As Roberta Nummus stared out into the vastness of Hector, her cup of warm coffee in hand, a cappuccino, white with one sugar, as her first Wife, Elaine Haynes, now more than twelve centuries past, had liked it, a voice behind her drew her attention.

"Fleet Admiral Nummus?", the voice queried urgently.

Roberta turned around and found herself looking at a young Midshipman, "Yes, that would be me."

"Ma'am, this communique just came in", the Midshipman replied, adding, "I do apologise for disturbing you on your day off, Ma'am, but your Lieutenant Adjutant said you'd want to read this."

Roberta nodded, "If my Lieutenant Adjutant says it's important, then he's probably right", she replied as she accepted the communique.

While Roberta read the communique, the Midshipman enquired, "Ma'am, if you don't mind me asking, why don't you have neural augments like most of the senior brass?"

Roberta looked up from the communique and asked, "What do you know about me, Midshipman?"

"Only what everyone else knows, Ma'am. That you are essentially immortal", he replied.

"Yes, it is kind of hard to hide that one isn't it?", Roberta asked rhetorically before noting, "Neural augments don't work on me. My brain chemistry is different and quickly rejects the augmentation."

The Midshipman nodded and then asked, "Is there any message that I can convey back to your Lieutenant Adjutant?"

"Yes, tell him that this is excellent news, Midshipman. The original homeworld of the Thols, Homwol, has been found", Roberta replied, noting, "This is the best news I've heard in over a century."

"Original homeworld, Ma'am?", the Midshipman enquired.

"Yes, Midshipman. Did you think Mimas was the Thol's original homeworld?", a rhetorical question, "It's not. Mimas is just the generation ship that brought the Tarlaks and Thols to our system."

The Midshipman nodded and enquired, "Tarlaks, Ma'am?"

Roberta frowned and asked, "You've not studied history, have you,

Midshipman?"

"No, Ma'am. I've never really studied history", the Midshipman admitted.

Roberta gave the Midshipman some advice, "Read up on the Mimasian War of twenty one forty two. That is an order, Midshipman. Just to give you a quick rundown, though, the Tarlaks arrived in a generation ship, Mimas, over ninety thousand years ago. That generation ship was constructed by the Thol's ancestors well over six million years ago. Now, the Tarlaks enslaved the Martians when they arrived. We defeated the Tarlaks in the Mimasian War and freed the Martians and the Thols. Okay?"

"Yes, Ma'am, I've got that", the Midshipman replied.

"Good, Midshipman. Good. I was serious about you reading up on the Mimasian War. I will be expecting a detailed report from you on the subject, due this time next week. Is that understood?", Roberta replied with further instructions.

"Yes, Ma'am. Understood, Ma'am", the Midshipman replied, before enquiring, "The Thol's original homeworld, Homwol. Which star system was it located in, if I might ask, Ma'am?"

"The Xi-Bootis binary star system. Xi-Bootis A Secundus to be precise", Roberta informed him.

"Ma'am, the Xi-Bootis system is only twenty two light years from Sol. Might I enquire as to how it took us so long to find it?", the Midshipman asked.

"You know your stars, Midshipman?", Roberta questioned once more rhetorically, before replying, "Then you will know that within twenty five light years of Earth, there are over one hundred and sixty star systems containing over two hundred and twenty five individual stellar objects. We may be an interstellar species with dozens of colonised worlds, but there are a lot of stars and a lot of planets out there. It just takes time, Midshipman."

"Yes, Ma'am. I hadn't thought of it like that. I guess we can't be everywhere all at once", he replied.

"Yes, Midshipman, and that's just the way it is", Roberta agreed.

"Now, Midshipman. Tell my Lieutenant Adjutant that I'll be there shortly. I just need to finish my coffee first and finish my reminiscing. Now on your way", Roberta replied before turning back to the view through the long observation windows.

The Midshipman then turned and left the way he'd come.

Roberta Nummus entered her command centre in the Citadel of Hector Alpha's main central spire. Built in the same design as the old Citadel of Eros, it had nine spires. The central one was three thousand metres tall, the other eight surrounding it, a mere fifteen hundred metres in height. Each of the three Citadels was built to the same blueprints.

The spires reached into the sky, thin shining cones of plasteel, clear aluminium and astcrete that defied Hector's centrifugal forces. The upper levels were so high that the interior was pressurised to maintain one atmosphere of pressure. They were like shining gems poking out of the landscape, equidistant apart.

"Admiral, I didn't expect you back so quickly", Lieutenant Adjutant Harrison Sharkmore noted.

"Are you kidding me? My day off or not, finding the ancestral Tholish homeworld is simply far too important", Roberta responded.

The Lieutenant nodded and then noted, "Admiral, I took the liberty of reassigning Midshipman Leonard Mitchel to your team permanently."

"Leonard Mitchel?", Roberta questioned rhetorically and then she asked, "Is he a descendant?"

"Yes, Ma'am. He's a direct descendant of Lina Mitchel. I've sent the confirmation data to your data tablet", Lieutenant Sharkmore replied.

"Good work, Lieutenant. Lina has so many descendants now, it's getting harder and harder to keep track of them", Roberta Nummus admitted.

"Will he be receiving your specialised training, Ma'am?", the Lieutenant queried.

"He's on my team, Lieutenant, of course he will", Roberta replied.

"Now tell me, Lieutenant, have you notified the Tholish Matriarch of the discovery of their original homeworld? The discovery of Homwol?", Roberta enquired.

"Admiral, I thought you might want to do that yourself", the Lieutenant replied, smiling.

Roberta smiled back with a chuckle, "Too right I do, Lieutenant, good call."

Roberta checked her data tablet and checked the genealogical data on Midshipman Mitchel. It was confirmed that he was indeed a descendant of Roberta's long-deceased adopted Daughter, Lina Mitchel.

Thoughts of Lina flooded Roberta's mind and the tears began to well. An attentive Lieutenant Adjutant Sharkmore expected this and passed Roberta a box of tissues. Roberta accepted it with a thankful nod. Time heals not the wounds of loss; it just makes them distant, yet they remain painful upon one's remembrance of them.

Roberta then checked the data on Xi-Bootis A Secundus and there it was, a perfect image of a world not unlike the Earth and yet very different. Just as the Tholish histories portrayed it, Homwol, in all of its glory. A single large continent on an otherwise ocean-covered world. There were islands and smaller land masses scattered here and there, but just the one continent, Masula.

It did look somewhat different. The Masula Valley that ran eastwards from the high Western Mountains, with its mighty Masula River, appeared to be somewhat broader. Roberta smiled, of course, six million years of plate tectonics and crustal movement.

The huge Masula Continent was slowly, inexorably being pulled apart by tectonic forces. Six million years, it was to be expected and yet still, the continent was unmistakable; it was most definitely Masula. This world was Homwol!

Even its star was perfect, a small yellow G-type Sun that the Thols had named Cathol.

Roberta Nummus smiled her broadest smile in many, many decades.

And yet there was more. It was as if the universe was throwing in a complementary set of steak knives. The Xi-Bootis system had a second and third habitable planets. The first of these, Xi-Bootis B Primus. A tidally locked eyeball world not unlike the tidally locked eyeball world of Proxima Centauri, Twilight! A world long since colonised and tamed.

Like all eyeball worlds, the side facing its small orange K-type Sun, named Cythol, by the Thols, was a hot, parched desert wasteland. The opposite side, by contrast, was covered in a vast frozen ice cap. And along its terminator, the region of constant twilight, was a planet-girdling ocean full of thousands of islands of various sizes and shapes. Some large, some small. The coasts and islands of this terminator zone on Xi-Bootis B Primus would, in all likelihood, be habitable. It was in the cards!

The second of these bonus worlds was a super Mars analogue: Xi Bootis B Primus Quasi. It was a strange world, not quite a moon, not quite a planet in its own right. It orbited its star, Xi-Bootis B, just inside the path of a Saturn-sized gas giant designated Primus Major. Primus Major itself was also unusual: a co-orbital world, sharing the same orbital path as the primary habitable planet, Primus, but leading it by sixty degrees like a cosmic pacer.

Primus Quasi wasn't gravitationally bound to the gas giant, but from the perspective of Primus Major, it appeared to be: looping lazily across the sky, always nearby, like a false moon. In truth, it was just another tidally locked eyeball world, following its own path around Xi Bootis B, a trick of orbital dynamics making it appear to be a satellite, when it wasn't one at all.

Roberta Nummus made three quick decisions.
First, Roberta Nummus sent confirmation of the discovery of Homwol personally to the Tholish Matriarch at Mimas. The communique was formally worded, but it was difficult to hide Roberta's sheer joy and happiness, her excitement at sending the Tholish Matriarch the incredibly good news. It was sent off via tight-beam laser comms even before the hour was out.

The second decision Roberta Nummus had made was to recommend, or more correctly, order, research teams to be dispatched to both Xi-Bootis A Secundus and Xi-Bootis B Primus as a matter of urgency. There were things that needed to be known. Earth and Mars, so far, were the only worlds found to have sapient, fully sentient life. Beyond the Earth's system, Sol, only the Tholish homeworld was recorded as having sapient life in the past and now it had been rediscovered.

Another world that had sapient life and not just one species either, there were five: Thols, Carlins, Tarlaks, Harricks and Chitten. A lot could have changed in six million years and all of those species may well be extinct!

Did Xi-Bootis A Secundus still have extant Thols and Carlins?

Did Xi-Bootis A Secundus still have Tarlaks living on Homwol and were they still a threat?

What of the other sapient species, the Harricks and the Chitten?

And the bonus world, Xi-Bootis B Primus, did it have sapient life as well?

Too many questions, not enough answers and Roberta Nummus wanted to know. She quickly roped in her own impatience at not having any answers.

The third decision that Roberta Nummus had made was that when a fleet of interstellar colonial push ships was sent to colonise the Xi-Bootis system, she would be the one to command it.

Roberta put in her application right then and there, first, before anyone else could consider it.

2. New Life.

Ordering research teams to be dispatched to both Xi-Bootis A Secundus and Xi-Bootis B Primus as a matter of urgency was one thing; actually getting all of that politically approved was another. Roberta soon found out that her priorities and the priorities of the Earth's Interstellar Alliance Colonisation Committee, situated within Hector, were not in alignment. Roberta and her Tholish friends considered this urgent.

The Thols needed to know if their cousins, the Indigenous Thols and their ancient friends, the Indigenous Carlins, were still extant, still alive. Roberta agreed with their stance entirely. The Colonisation Committee, however, considered it to be of *"lower to mid-level priority"*, to be scheduled in due course, as *"funding permitted"*. It was exasperating.

It was over a year before sufficient funding was *"found"* and another six months before an action team was put together. By the time the research team and all of their equipment had been assembled, another year had passed.

Finally, three years after Roberta Nummus had put in her recommendation, her order, the two research teams had been dispatched to Xi-Bootis A Secundus and Xi-Bootis B Primus.

Roberta had checked through the expedition details. As always, too little, too late, overstretched and spread thin, but at least the research teams were on their way.

Bureaucracy!

Five years had passed since the discovery of the Thol's ancestral homeworld and the latest reports had trickled in from the research teams in their orbital stations high above Xi-Bootis A Secundus and Xi-Bootis B Primus. For the most part, all observations and sampling were performed by class seven A.I. stealth drones, with whisper-quiet propulsion systems.

The researchers rarely went to the surface themselves. If they did so, they were supposed to be accompanied by Colonial Marines. However, they didn't have any Colonial Marines with them, as their budget had not allowed for it. A handful of researchers had bravely gone down to the surface of Secundus in Tarlakand. That was their one and only surface excursion and it was detailed in their reports.

The Mimasian Thols, who had designed the stealth drones, had assured everyone that their stealth drone technology was not only inaudible and undetectable to Humans, Martians and Mimasian Thols alike, but that they would also be undetectable to their Indigenous Thol cousins and the Indigenous Carlins, assuming they were both still extant, both still living species.

Roberta read through the reports on her data tablet while sitting in her usual seat in her command centre. Roberta switched on the command centre's main screen and linked it to her data tablet.

"Gather around, people", Roberta called out and her team all quickly approached and gathered around, watching the screen.

"These are the latest reports from Xi-Bootis A Secundus and Xi-Bootis B Primus", Roberta announced, noting, "These are the most important reports I've read in centuries."

Roberta continued, "You all know me, so you'll understand why I'm showing you these reports from a tactical threat assessment perspective. And yes, there are threats on Secundus!"

Roberta brought up some stealth drone video on the screen.

On the screen, two flying objects could be seen in the distance. The researchers were on the first and final surface excursion. As the two flying objects approached, the stealth drone began sounding the alarm. The researchers all looked up and scanned the skies. They were far too late.

The two objects, now easily identified as Tarlaks, with their mighty wings and angry Gorilla-like Gargoylish features, swiftly swept in and grabbed a researcher with their long, gangly arms. While they lifted the hapless researcher aloft, another pair of Tarlaks swept in from another direction and grabbed another researcher and took him into the air.

Panic and pandemonium ensued as the remaining researchers fled back to their shuttle to take shelter. From the safety of their shuttle, behind the shuttle's locked airlock doors, they watched as the Tarlaks played with their prey. They'd fly high into the air and drop their victims, only to swoop back in and, at the very last moment, catch them by the legs and lift high into the air once more.

It was as if they were enjoying it, knowing that their victim's friends were watching from the safety of their shuttle. They did that several times, before finally allowing their victims, the captured researchers fall to their deaths.

Then they flew away with their prey, the researcher's bodies, freshly caught meat!

"Those were Tarlaks", Lieutenant Harrison Sharkmore noted, before asking, "Aren't Tarlaks meant to be extinct?"

"They are extinct, Lieutenant. At least in our system, but that is Xi-Bootis A Secundus, Homwol, the ancestral homeworld of the Thols and there, Tarlaks are most certainly still alive", Roberta explained, before commanding, "Lieutenant, take note. When we do finally leave to colonise Secundus, all of our military personnel need to be trained in how to take down Tarlaks. I want you to set up training simulations. The Tarlaks are just one of several aggressive species that we might encounter."

"So noted, Admiral", the Lieutenant replied.

Sub-Lieutenant Leonard Mitchel noted, "Ma'am. Tarlaks are big; they're strong, but it's grappling strength. Their hands are designed for grasping. Tarlaks have six-fingered hands, with their fingers grouped in three pairs like a Thol's hand. They can't form a fist and they can't punch. They have hollow bones like Thols as well. Strong for flight, sure, but they can't take a punch. They're no match for a trained martial artist, especially one armed with swords."

"How do you know all of that, Sub-Lieutenant?", Roberta enquired.

"You once asked me to study the Mimasian War, Ma'am. We actually have a lot of useful information on how to defeat the Tarlaks in hand-to-hand combat", Sub-Lieutenant Mitchel reminded her.

Roberta nodded, "Lieutenant Sharkmore, make use of Sub-Lieutenant Mitchel's knowledge when setting up your Tarlak combat training simulations."

"So noted, Ma'am", the Lieutenant replied as he gave the Sub-Lieutenant a polite nod.

Another voice piped up, "Admiral, what the hell were those researchers doing in Tarlakan?", Special Operative James Reas enquired.

Roberta looked up a Special Operative Reas. He was a descendant of Gideon Reas and Freyja. Knowing his ancestry, James Reas had studied the Tholish histories.

Roberta replied, explaining, "They weren't in Tarlakan, they were in Korland, confirming drone observations that the Korland region was abandoned. Sadly, they were wrong and hadn't considered roving Tarlak hunting parties."

James Reas replied with further information, "Based on the Tholish histories, nowhere south of the Southern Mountain Range is safe from Tarlaks. Tarlakan connects via passes to Slaver Land in the east and to Korland in the west. For anyone going to Secundus, the Tholish histories should be a mandatory read. Especially considering that the Tarlaks consider that everything that's not Tarlak is food."

"So, noted Mr Reas, so noted", Roberta replied, enquiring, "You got that, Lieutenant?"

"Yes, Admiral, so noted", Lieutenant Sharkmore replied.

"Just so you know, Admiral. Korland in Tarlak means Land of Corpses", James Reas informed her.

"Nice to know, Mr Reas, nice to know", Roberta replied.

Roberta Nummus was quiet in thought for a moment before announcing, "I don't want anyone telling the Martians or the Thols about Tarlaks still existing on Secundus. Not yet, anyway. Both species have suffered at the hands of Tarlaks in the past. I'll make an appointment with the Mimasian Embassy and tell them myself."

"So noted, Admiral", Lieutenant Sharkmore confirmed.

"Now, that was the bad news. Tarlaks are still alive. The good news is, so are the Indigenous Thols", Roberta informed everyone as she played another surveillance video.

The video showed Thols flying between the branches in the canopy of tall trees. Trees so high that one could not see the ground far below. They had great creamy coloured leathery wings and they soared from the branches with gravity-defying ease. Spaced well apart in the forks of massive tree branches were nests made from lesser tree branches woven tightly together with vines.

The nests looked like broad bowls with an even larger bowl upturned and placed over the top like a canopy. Thols dropped over the sides of their nests into flight, while other Thols flew up between nest and canopy, folding in their mighty wings at the last second to enter them.

Sub-Lieutenant Mitchel straight away noted, "They look just like our Mimasian Thols!"

"Almost, Sub-Lieutenant", Roberta corrected, explaining, "Our Mimasian Thols are all alabaster white with creamy wings. They also have the same uniform height, five feet tall. The indigenous Thols on Secundus reportedly ranged from around four feet ten to six feet two. While their wings are still creamy white, their skin isn't quite alabaster white. Their skin has slightly deeper tones and shades, a ruddy complexion."

One of Roberta's other team members, Ensign Maria Young, commented, "Admiral, I suspect that the Tholish Matriarch will be wanting to see that video."

"I believe you're right, Ensign", Roberta agreed, adding, "Lieutenant Sharkmore, make sure that the Tholish Matriarch gets a copy of this video and the report that's attached to it. It is fascinating reading."

"Yes, Ma'am. I have that noted down", Lieutenant Sharkmore replied.

"Most of the other reports from our researchers above Secundus are concerning other species. Our stealth drones have observed a few animal species, notably Sleimorps, Fern Dragons and Wyverns. They have also observed a dangerous, sentient, ant-like insectoid species, the Chittens. If you thought Tarlaks were dangerous, well, based on the Tholish histories, even Tarlaks avoid the Chittens. Of the other sentient species on Secundus, we have video of the Carlin-folk. Unfortunately, our researchers have yet to observe the Harricks. They appear to be nocturnal and skittish, like Cryptids", Roberta informed them before playing the next video.

The video displayed a small village with around seventy or so houses. Each house sat on a fair-sized plot of land. Each plot of land was surrounded by dry stone walls. Within each plot were crops, broad fruit trees and houses made of timber and stone. Goat-like animals grazed on bluegrass that grew both on the ground and on the rooftops. Carlin children played around the houses and climbed the fruit trees.

Cobblestone paths led into the village, allowing access to the houses. Surrounding the village were communal crop fields of a blue-grass grain. On the outskirts of the village, Carlin-folk gathered, trading goods with the Indigenous Thols. The Thols and Carlins each conversed in their own languages and they both seemed to understand the other. It was obvious that Carlins could understand Tholish and the Thols could understand Carlinish.

"It's just as our Thols have always said. On their homeworld, they and the Carlin-folk always got along", Special Operative Reas noted.

"Different environments. The Thols live in the high tree canopies and the Carlins live in the valley. They don't have to compete, so they cooperate with each other", Sub-Lieutenant Mitchel replied.

"Yep. It looks like Thols and Carlins have been cooperating for over six thousand millennia and yet we Humans have only just managed to cooperate for one", Roberta commented dryly, noting, "They make us look downright uncivilised."

Special Operative Reas noted, "The Thols call their homeworld, Homwol. According to their histories, the Carlin-folk call their world Vale. One means the trees, and the other means the valley. That is their only disagreement, as far as we know."

Ensign Maria Young noted, smiling, "Oh my God, the Carlins, they look just like cats!"

"Cats?", Roberta queried.

"Yes, Admiral. Look at them. They walk on the pads of their feet with their heels off the ground. They have cat's tails, cat's ears, cat-like noses, cat's eyes, cat's whiskers", Maria rattled off a list, then she looked more closely, "Oh my God! They even have six breasts, just like a cat!"

Sub-Lieutenant Mitchel chimed in, "Hairless cats, with blue stripes. The Carlins have no fur or hair."

Special Operative Reas noted, "The Tholish histories tell us that Carlin women give birth to litters of kits."

"As much as the Carlins might look like cats, we should keep in mind two things. They walk upright and most importantly, they are a sentient species", Roberta reminded them.

"Admiral, I do believe that the Tholish Matriarch will want to see this video and the associated reports", Lieutenant Sharkmore suggested.

"Absolutely, Lieutenant. Make sure you send her a copy", Roberta agreed.

"It's on my list, Admiral", the Lieutenant replied.

"The other reports I have are largely written reports", Roberta informed her team, noting, "They are from Xi-Bootis B Primus. You will all be interested to know that Primus is another world with sentient life. That in itself was quite a shock. Of all the worlds we've colonised and visited, we thought that only Earth, Mars and the lost homeworld of the Thols, Homwol, had sentient life. Now, we have a fourth world, Primus. And Primus is one hell of a weird world."

Ensign Young enquired, "Admiral, what's so weird about it?"

"Well, Ensign. Our Earth life comes in the form of flora, fauna and fungi. You know, plants, animals, and fungi. That same pattern existed on ancient Mars before the Tarlaks destroyed its biosphere. That same pattern seems to be predominant on the Tholish homeworld as well. Primus, however, is different. It has flora, fauna and fungi, but in the reverse proportions of what you might expect."

Sub-Lieutenant Mitchel chimed in, questioning, "So, Admiral, does that mean the dominant life forms are fungal and that plants and animals are more niche?"

"Yes, Sub-Lieutenant", Roberta confirmed, noting, "And the sapient species on Primus are neither plant, animal, nor fungi. They are a mixture of all three. The researchers had to create a completely new taxonomic kingdom for them. They called it Floravitae. Fungal and Floravitae lifeforms are the dominant lifeforms on Primus. That is what makes Primus so different, so unique."

Roberta put two reports on the screen side by side, while noting, "Meet the new sapient species. The Chantrieri and the Simianthus."

Lieutenant Sharkmore queried, "Admiral. No video? Was there a problem?"

"Yes, Lieutenant. Our whisper-quiet stealth drones work so very well for life as we know it, but not so much for life as we know it not", Roberta replied cryptically and then she explained, "Both the Chantrieri and the Simianthus are able to *'sense'* our stealth drones. When you read these reports, you might get a feel for why."

Chantrieri Species
Chantrieri sapiens obscurus,
Chantrieri sapiens aureus,
Chantrieri sapiens lucidus.
Common name: Petals.
Chantrieri Sapiens – Anatomical & Biological Overview
(Applicable to all three subspecies: obscurus, aureus, lucidus)

1. Vision

The *Chantrieri* possess smooth, unsegmented eyes composed of millions of minuscule photo-bio-sensors. These function similarly to a compound digital retina, granting them exceptionally acute and dynamic vision across a wide spectrum of wavelengths, while maintaining an uninterrupted ocular surface.

2. Auditory Perception

External ears are absent. Instead, sound is captured via their cranial petals, large, sensitive appendages that act as acoustic reflectors. These petals transmit vibrations to internal membranous structures, which interpret sound as a form of vibrotactile sensation; effectively, the *Chantrieri* feel sound.

3. Breathing

The *Chantrieri appear to absorb atmospheric gases directly through the pores in the skin, especially around their shoulder region. Oxygen appears to be the primary gas required for respiration, although elevated carbon dioxide levels are essential for Chantrieri spore production and budding processes. It should be noted that Xi-Bootis B Primus carbon dioxide levels are currently around eight hundred ppm.*

4. Feeding Strategies

The *Chantrieri* possess a complex, multi-modal feeding physiology:

4.1 Primary Method:

Nutrient absorption via facial tendrils. These tendrils function similarly to proboscises, capable of extracting sustenance from water, mineral-rich soils, and organic substrates like flower nectar.

Used by all three subspecies.

4.2 Secondary Method:

Dermal absorption. Submersion in water allows nutrients to be osmotically absorbed through the fibrous integument.

Most common in aureus; present but less prominent in lucidus; not observed in obscurus.

4.3 Tertiary Method:

Photosynthesis. Subdermal chromatophores convert solar radiation into chemical energy.

Dominant in obscurus; present in aureus; not observed in lucidus.

5. Reproductive Mechanism

Reproduction is sexually dimorphic and mediated via fungal-like microspores. Males produce these pollen-analogue spores, which are transferred to receptive structures on the female abdomen during a pollination ritual. This process triggers the budding response in the female's reproductive cycle.

6. Gestational Period

Approximately three months. It can be longer if more than one bud is present.

7. Birth Process

Offspring develop externally via **abdominal budding**, resembling the reproductive mechanism of *Hydra* species. Upon reaching maturity, the bud detaches to become an independent juvenile organism.

8. Infant Nutrition

Neonates are nourished via **paired, nipple-less mammary glands**. These glands exude a nutrient-rich solution directly through the porous, fibrous skin. The offspring's immature facial tendrils absorb the fluid directly, bypassing any oral ingestion.

9. Defecation

Disposal of bodily waste appears to be the reverse of nutrient absorption.

Bodily waste is expelled through the skin in the buttock region, where it either dries and flakes off or dissolves when immersed in water. The process appears to take place once per day and produces no measurable odour.

10. Communication

The *Chantrieri* language remains untranslated. Leading hypotheses suggest **pheromonal signalling**, **bioelectric fields**, or **telepathic cognition** as likely modalities. No phonetic language has been detected, and their communication may be non-localised or multisensory. Martian analysts recommend initial contact via telepathic means, with potential future use of Universal Sign Language (USL).

11. Conflicts

Neither the *Chantrieri sapiens obscurus* nor the *Chantrieri sapiens lucidus* is aware of the existence of the other. The *Chantrieri sapiens aureus*, on the other hand, being the seafaring subspecies of Chantrieri, is known to both.

The *Chantrieri sapiens aureus* have been observed raiding the Simianthus Islands and using the Simianthus as a *'rich food'* source. They do this by composting the corpses of their victims and ingesting the resultant remains through their facial tendrils. They do find resistance from the Simianthus and this results in casualties on both sides.

Domain	Kingdom	Phylum	Class	Order	Family	Genus	Species
Eukaryota	Floravitae	Petalarthra	Chantrierimorpha	Chantrieriformes	Chantrieridae	Chantrieri	sapiens obscurus (dark)
Eukaryota	Floravitae	Petalarthra	Chantrierimorpha	Chantrieriformes	Chantrieridae	Chantrieri	sapiens aureus (golden)
Eukaryota	Floravitae	Petalarthra	Chantrierimorpha	Chantrieriformes	Chantrieridae	Chantrieri	sapiens lucidus (light)

Simianthus Species
Simianthus sapiens floridus.
Common name: Blossoms.

Simianthus Sapiens – Anatomical & Biological Overview

1. Vision

The *Simianthus* possess smooth, purple or blue-lidded, segmented eyes that appear almost mammalian, complete with sclera and pupils; however, they are composed of millions of minuscule photo-bio-sensors. These function similarly to a compound digital retina, granting them exceptionally acute and dynamic vision across a wide spectrum of wavelengths, while maintaining an uninterrupted ocular surface.

2. Auditory Perception

External ears are absent. Instead, sound is captured via their cranial petals, large, sensitive appendages that act as acoustic reflectors. These petals transmit vibrations to internal membranous structures, which interpret sound as a form of vibrotactile sensation; effectively, the *Simianthus* feel sound.

3. Breathing

The *Simianthus breathe through a surprisingly Human-like nose. Oxygen appears to be the primary gas required for respiration, although elevated carbon dioxide levels are essential for Simianthus spore production and budding processes. It should be noted that Xi-Bootis B Primus carbon dioxide levels are currently around eight hundred ppm.*

4. Feeding Strategy

The *Simianthus* consume food through a *surprisingly Human-like mouth.*

5. Reproductive Mechanism

Reproduction is sexually dimorphic and mediated via fungal-like microspores. Males produce these pollen-analogue spores, which are transferred to receptive structures on the female abdomen during a pollination ritual. This process triggers the budding response in the female's reproductive cycle.

6. Gestational Period

Approximately three months. It can be longer if more than one bud is present.

7. Birth Process

Offspring develop externally via **abdominal budding**, resembling the reproductive mechanism of *Hydra* species. Upon reaching maturity, the bud detaches to become an independent juvenile organism.

8. Infant Nutrition

Neonates are nourished via **paired, nipple-less mammary glands**. These glands exude a nutrient-rich solution directly through the porous, fibrous skin. The offspring absorb the fluid directly via their mouth.

9. Defecation

The *Simianthus* appear to defecate in much the same way as Earth mammals.

10. Communication

The *Simianthus* language remains untranslated. Leading hypotheses suggest **telepathic cognition** as a likely modality. No phonetic language has been detected. Martian analysts recommend initial contact via telepathic means, with potential future use of Universal Sign Language (USL). Their untranslated language, possibly telepathic, may play a role in the complex social hierarchy described below.

11. Gender Dimorphism and Sentience

The Simianthus exhibit extreme sexual dimorphism, once leading researchers to classify them as three separate species. Genetic analysis has since confirmed that they are, in fact, a single species.

Males are brutish in form, with coarse, simian-like features and a subservient role within their society, displaying limited independent reasoning. They respond instinctively to perceived threats against females, often acting on the females' direction to attack.

Simianthus females occur in two distinct phenotypic variants:

11.1 Purple variant

The most common, with a large crown of cranial blossoms and a single central chest blossom, refined facial features, and predominantly purple colouration. This variant manages family settlements as a Matriarch. They have Human-level sentience.

11.2 Blue variant (rare)

Much rarer, with far fewer cranial blossoms, a more refined humanoid facial structure, and bluish skin tones. Their function remains unclear; observational data suggest they do not maintain fixed homesteads but instead travel between settlements, leading to theories that they may serve as "*Super Matriarchs*". When present in a settlement, the settlement's Purple-variant Matriarch always becomes subservient to the Blue-variant.

Simianthus settlements typically centre on a purple-variant Matriarch, attended by ten to twelve subordinate males, plus younger individuals of both sexes, with female young in the minority. Housing is constructed from carved fungal sheeting sourced from local fungal forests, and agriculture focuses on cultivated fungi species, samples of which have been collected for study.

12. Location

The Simianthus live on the islands of the largest archipelago in the Terminator Ocean. A remote archipelago containing many islands, some quite large, collectively known as the Simianthus Islands.

13. Conflicts

The Simianthus are aware of the other native sapient species, the Chantrieri. Storms occasionally wash deceased *Chantrieri sapiens obscurus* and *lucidus* individuals onto the beaches of their islands.

Chantrieri sapiens aureus, the seafaring subspecies of Chantrieri, has been observed raiding the Simianthus Islands and using their inhabitants as a '*rich food*' source. They do this by composting the corpses of their victims and ingesting the resultant remains through their facial tendrils.

Notably, when raids occur, the Blue Matriarchs direct the Purple Matriarchs in deploying their males for defensive actions, though Chantrieri attacks remain a significant threat.

Domain	Kingdom	Phylum	Class	Order	Family	Genus	Species
Eukaryota	Floravitae	Petalarthra	Simianthimorpha	Simianthiformes	Simianthidae	Simianthus	sapiens floridus

Ensign Young quickly finished reading first, "Both the Chantrieri and the Simianthus possess eyes that technically behave like the biological equivalent of a digital retina. I cannot imagine what the world looks like to them. It must be like seeing through a pair of digital scanners."

Sub-Lieutenant Mitchel noted, "Yeah, but I don't think that's the cause of the detection problem. It's their hearing. They don't have ears, they have those '*petals*' things. They are both acoustic and vibration sensors. I bet that they can feel our stealth drones. It doesn't matter how whisper-quiet their propulsion systems are. They can literally feel the vibrations that they make. Even the vibrations of the drones simply flying through the air. They can *'feel'* the drones!"

"And that is the leading hypothesis, Sub-Lieutenant", Roberta agreed, but also noted, "Once they feel the drone, they can bring their eyes to bear on target and see the subtle ripple effects in the air from the drone's propulsion systems and the heat that they give off. They don't see the drone, but they know that something is there. They just don't understand what it is."

James Reas chimed in, "Which makes it very difficult to observe them without being detected. That is why they haven't provided any videos. They've been using the stealth drones at the extreme range of their systems. Far enough away to not be detected and yet still observing from a distance."

"Bingo, Mr Reas!", Roberta confirmed, noting, "These *'Floravitae'* sapients are the strangest things that our biologists have ever seen."

"Now, guys. We don't have any video of the *'Floravitae'* sapients; however, we do have video of the fungal forests and fields. You can watch those anytime you like", Roberta informed them.

"Fungal forests and fields?", Ensign Maria Young queried.

"Yeah, they have what look like Shimeji mushrooms thirty five feet tall and what look like King oyster mushrooms as big as Baobab trees. All growing in clusters with other smaller varieties, the likes of which we've never seen before", Roberta explained, noting, "There are whole meadows of what look like Enoki mushrooms growing like grass, with colourful Button mushrooms popping up like flowers everywhere."

"Are all of Primus's forests and fields fungal, Admiral?", Sub-Lieutenant Mitchel enquired.

"Not all. Mainly in the south", Roberta began and then stopped, "Now, this will sound strange. Primus is an eyeball world, so its rotation matches its orbit perfectly. So, even though it's technically wrong, the hot side of the planet has been designated north and the cold side designated south."

"They do the same thing with Twilight, Admiral", Special Operative James Reas noted.

"Yes, they do. Now, where was I? Okay, on the *'southern'* coasts and the Terminator Islands, the fungal forests and meadows predominate. Very few other kinds. On the *'northern'* coast and interior, the fungal forests are not so prevalent and where they are, they give way to fungal meadows. There are other, more *'common'* kinds of forests and meadows in the *'northern'* region. The kind that, although alien, we might consider normal", Roberta explained.

"Admiral, are any of these fungal forms edible?", Ensign Young queried.

"Actually, yes, Ensign. Our researchers have been obtaining samples using their stealth droves. There are more than a few edible varieties", Roberta confirmed.

Special Operative James Reas's communicator began buzzing for his attention. He answered the call.

"What! Oh my God! Now! It's happening now! I'll be there as soon as possible", then he hung up.

"A problem, Mr Reas?", Roberta Nummus queried.

"Ah, no, Admiral. My Wife, Simone, has just been taken to the hospital", Special Operative James Reas replied.

"Hospital?", Roberta questioned with concern.

"Yeah, the hospital. It's not a problem, though, just her waters have broken and the baby is coming a couple of weeks early", Special Operative James Reas explained.

Roberta turned to her Lieutenant Adjutant, "Lieutenant, clear my schedule for the rest of the day. I'm taking Mr Reas to the hospital to be with his Wife. Everyone else, the files are on the network server. Make yourselves familiar with them."

Roberta placed her hands on Special Operative Reas's shoulder, "Well, come along, Mr Reas. You have a baby on the way", and then she led him out of her command centre.

Roberta Nummus waited patiently outside the delivery room at the local hospital. Special Operative James Reas had already gone in to be with his Wife, Simone. Roberta had known James all of his life. James was a scion of Folcrom Tafazah and a descendant of Gideon Reas and Freyja after all.

Roberta was there when James joined the Colonial Marines. Roberta was there when James started his training as a Special Operative. Roberta was at the wedding when James married his Wife, Simone. Roberta knew that Simone was pregnant and it was a surprise for her as well when the little one decided to come into the world early.

It was Thursday, November tenth, in the year thirty four fifty five and almost eleven thirty pm at night. Simone Reas's labour had been long and difficult, but finally the baby was out and its lungs were loud and healthy. Roberta Nummus had fallen asleep in her chair with her data tablet sitting loose in her lap. She had been reviewing the research reports for a fourth or was it perhaps the fifth time.

Roberta Nummus startled awake and looked up as a head poked out of the delivery room door. It was a nurse beckoning her into the room. Apparently, the happy couple wanted her to see their new baby. Roberta secured her data tablet, stood up, yawned and stretched, and then walked into the room.

The first thing Roberta did when she saw the newborn baby was start to cry. She always found these moments emotional. Especially when she had the privilege of being right there when one of her newborns entered the world. Roberta considered them all to be hers.

The descendants of her adopted daughter, Lina Mitchel and the descendants of her closest friend, Freyja, the third Wife of Gideon Reas. If only her own Wife, long-deceased Elaine Haynes, could have been there as well. Sometimes life for an immortal could be overly emotional, often sad and lonely; times like this made up for it.

James gently took the baby from his Wife, Simone's, arms and carefully handed it to Roberta.

"We're going to name her Angelique", James informed her before asking, "What do you think?"

Roberta carefully took the newborn baby into her arms and smiled, "Well, she does look like a little angel, so Angelique sounds like the perfect name."

Roberta smiled, tears still streaming, "She has that newborn baby smell. She's beautiful."

After a few long moments, Roberta gently passed newborn Angelique Reas back to her Mother.

James enquired, "Do you tear up when all of us Freyja descendants are born?"

"Of course, I do, James. When I'm present for their births. All of Freyja's descendants. All of Lina's descendants. All of them. I was there when you were born as well, you know", Roberta admitted.

"How many?", enquired Simone.

"Too many to count, Simone. Too many to count", Roberta smiled as she sat down on the edge of the maternity ward bed.

Roberta took out a handkerchief, wiped her tears away and smiled, "When you're an immortal, it's moments like these that remind you that you're alive. So many memories lost in time. Not really lost, mind you. I never forget anything. Still, it's good to be there when a new life enters the universe."

3. Jovian Send Off.

The year was now thirty four seventy AD; it was early morning and Roberta Nummus once again looked out through the long, thick, clear, crystalline plasteel observation windows. Fifteen kilometres from Hector's main interior living surface, looking out through those long windows into the thin Hectorian air, thin at least at this altitude.

Roberta tapped her foot gently to get a feel for the gravity in the observation lounge. Yep, still point eight gs. Hector was, as always, a rock-solid world. Roberta Nummus's eyes scanned the beautiful cylindrical horizon of the interior of Hector and smiled. The view was always spectacular.

Roberta's time inside this hollowed-out world was growing short. Hector bent gracefully upward on all sides before her, the endless ring of green valleys, rivers, sparkling lakes and the blue azure waters of the Hectorian Seas. This was, or at least had been,

Roberta's favourite place. Roberta sipped her still-warm coffee, a cappuccino, white with one sugar, thinking back to her first, long-deceased Wife, Elaine Haynes. Soon, her mind wandered to her second, long-deceased Wife, Celestia. Memories flooded in. Roberta, as an immortal, had a lot of memories, eidetic memories that Roberta could never forget.

"Ah, hum. Fleet Admiral Nummus?", a young female Midshipman, drew Roberta's attention.

"Yes, Midshipman. That would be me", Roberta replied.

The Midshipman passed Roberta an envelope, "This came through from Cis-Lunar Space, Ma'am."

Roberta opened the sealed envelope and silently read the communique it contained, "Woo hoo, my new command is ready! I've been waiting twenty years for this moment!", she exclaimed.

"New command?", the young Midshipman queried.

"Twelve interstellar colonial push ships, Midshipman. This Admiral is officially colonising Xi-Bootis A Secundus", Roberta excitedly informed her.

"Congratulations, Fleet Admiral", the Midshipman replied.

Roberta corrected her, explaining, "That would be High Admiral, Midshipman. High Command has decided to promote me."

"Congratulations again, High Admiral", the Midshipman replied with a genuine smile.

"Yes, although now I'll have to go and see my tailor", Roberta responded with dry humour.

"Tailor, Ma'am?", the Midshipman enquired.

Roberta smiled, "Yes, Midshipman. I need to have a star sewn on top of my five stripes", then she paused before adding, "Dismissed, Midshipman."

The young Midshipman saluted and then quickly walked away.

Within days, things were changing. There was a distinct transition at Roberta's command centre. New people were coming in and old people were moving out. Not all of them, of course, only those that were transferring to the interstellar push ships.

A new Fleet Admiral was slated to take over from Roberta Nummus. He, of course, was still in transit from a military colony in Cis-Lunar L-Four. Roberta Nummus and her team would be on the lead push ship and on their way long before he arrived.

Travelling to Xi-Bootis A Secundus along with Roberta Nummus were: her old Lieutenant Adjutant, now Commander Harrison Sharkmore, Sub-Lieutenant, now Lieutenant Commander Leonard Mitchel, Special Operative James Reas and Ensign, now Lieutenant Maria Young, along with a handful of others who had volunteered for the colonisation mission. They all met at the transport ship that was taking them to the Ganymede L-Four shipyards, in the Jovian Realms, where the twelve interstellar push ships had been constructed and were now waiting.

Roberta commented in amusement, "Back in the days of the Horridian Wars, those shipyards were enemy territory, churning out enemy destroyers, cruisers and dreadnoughts. Now, they work for us."

Special Operative James Reas commented, "I think you can thank High Prince Leopold, the Great Reformer, for that one. Before he passed away in the twenty-fifth century, he divested his shares in the Horridian shipyards and sold everything to the Dumas family."

Roberta laughed, "You don't need to tell me that, James. I was watching it all unfold from Mimas at the time as the Mimasian Administrator."

Simone Reas, James's Wife, noted, "It really is funny how things work out."

Simone's and James's now fifteen-year-old Daughter, Angelique, added, "There is only one true constant in the universe, Mother. Everything changes, nothing stands still for long."

An eight-year-old Johnathon Reas asked, "Mum. Is Aunty Roberta really nearly fourteen hundred years old?"

"Shoosh. Johnathon! You're being rude", Simone gently scolded.

"It's okay, Simone. Little Johnathon is just being curious", Roberta replied, before turning to Johnathon, "Yes, little Johnny. I'm thirteen hundred and ninety years old. Which means, as an Aunt, I have so many greats in front of that title that even I've lost count."

Johnathon Reas responded, "See, Mum. Aunty Roberta is really, really old", and then he noted, "And, Aunty Roberta, I'm not little, I'm eight years old!"

Roberta smiled and ran her hand through Johnathon's hair, "I do apologise, Johnathon. I didn't mean to upset you."

"Good, Aunty Roberta. I don't want to be on bad terms with my future Wife", Johnathon replied with a smile.

"Say what!", Roberta Nummus exclaimed.

Simone Reas face-palmed herself as her Son, Johnathon, explained, "Now that we've established that you're ancient and that you aren't really my Aunt. So when I'm all grown up, I'm going to marry you."

"I am so sorry, Roberta", Simone apologised.

"No, Simone. Don't apologise", Roberta replied, before noting, "Johnathon Reas, I am far too old for you. And besides, by the time you're all grown up, you will have had a dozen girl friends and won't even remember me."

"You're wrong, Aunty. I won't forget you", Johnathon assured her.

Johnathon's Sister, Angelique, stepped in, "Little Brother, Aunty Roberta's previous spouses were both Wives. You know, they were girls. Maybe Aunt Roberta isn't interested in boys."

Johnathon Reas simply replied, "People change."

Simone gently took hold of Johnathon's ear and started leading him away towards the transport ship, "I'm so sorry, Roberta. Johnathon can be so incorrigible at times."

"It's okay, Simone. Your Son will grow out of it. I'm certain of it", Roberta assured her.

Angelique Reas smiled, "My little Brother is so embarrassing!"

Commander Harrison Sharkmore looked out of the viewport at their transport ship. It was a typical mid-range transport, more than capable of taking them from Hector in Jupiter's Leading Trojan Republic to the Jovian Realms and the Ganymede L-Four shipyards.

Hell, it was capable of flying all the way to the Belter Nations or the Saturnian Demarchy. What caught the Commander's eye, though, was the ancient Tristar Interplanetary Stealth Ship docked at the transport's mid ventral docking hub.

"High Admiral Nummus", the Commander formerly addressed Roberta, "If I may? Why do you keep that old junker?"

Lieutenant Commander Leonard Mitchel chimed in, "Yes, Admiral. I've often wondered that myself. That old Tristar must be, no offence, almost as old as you."

"Commander Sharkmore, my ship, the Dark Angel, is not a junker", Roberta assured him, before noting, "And actually, Lieutenant Commander, the Dark Angel is five years older than me. That Tristar was a twenty seventy five model."

"Then why do you keep it, Ma'am?", Lieutenant Maria Young enquired.

"Ah, Lieutenant, you mean apart from nostalgia?", Roberta replied.

"Yes, Ma'am", Lieutenant Young replied.

"Believe it or not, that ship is the most practical ship I've ever flown. They simply don't make them like that anymore", Roberta explained.

"Admiral, the Dark Angel is almost fourteen hundred years old", Commander Sharkmore noted.

Special Operative James Reas laughed, "Shall I tell them, Admiral?"

"By all means, James. By all means", Roberta replied.

"Guys, there is not a single component on the Dark Angel that is more than ten years old", James Reas informed them, explaining, "That ship has undergone a complete overhaul and refit every ten years since the Admiral stole it. That's a hundred and forty refits all up."

"Stole it?", Lieutenant Young questioned.

"Ah, yeah. I kind of did. It was a long time ago. I was a lot younger back then. Kind of impetuous and psychotic at the time", Roberta admitted.

Special Operative James Reas continued, "The Dark Angel has the latest drive systems, the latest weapons systems and the latest computer systems. Even the hull was originally a titanium plate hull. If you check the refit logs, that was recast as a single-piece polyceramalloy hull nearly five centuries ago."

"Yes, it was, James", Roberta confirmed, adding with a wry smile, "And no, you can't have her."

"A shame, really. I've flown that ship. The Dark Angel's a sweet ride", James replied.

"Yes, she is, James. Now let's get aboard that transport, we'll be leaving before the hours out", Roberta Nummus commanded.

They all boarded the transport and were soon on their way to the Ganymede L-Four shipyards.

They were three days out from Ganymede L-Four when eight-year-old Johnathon Reas started to complain. Whenever he went to find his Aunt Roberta, she was always nowhere to be found.

"Where's Aunty Roberta's cabin?", Johnny Reas asked, noting, "I can't find it anywhere! It's not even listed on the ship's passenger listing."

Angelique Reas rolled her eyes, "You're looking in the wrong place, Little Brother. Aunt Roberta's cabin is on her ship, the Dark Angel. She doesn't have a cabin on board this ship."

"How do I find it? How do I find her ship?", Johnathon enquired.

This time Simone Reas rolled her eyes, "You don't. All of the ventral docks are off limits to all but the ship's crew and military personnel."

Johnathon Reas snorted, "How am I going to get to know my future Wife, if I can't find her?"

Simone had had enough of her Son's nonsense, "Johnathon Reas! You are only eight years old, so you can get that silly notion out of your head!"

Little Johnathon let out a low growl and snarled back, "I won't be eight forever, you know!"

As Little Johnny stomped off down the corridor, Simone noted, "My Son is incorrigible!"

"Mum, Johnny will grow out of it. Give him a year or two", her Daughter, Angelique, assured her.

As Johnathon Reas disappeared around one corner, Roberta Nummus appeared around another from the opposite direction. Roberta just managed to glance as Little Johnny disappeared.

"Did I miss anything?", Roberta enquired.

"Oh, no, Aunty", Angelique replied, before adding, "Just one of Little Johnny's little rants."

"I have no idea what to do with him. I'm at the end of my tether", Simone admitted, before remarking, "Ever since his declaration back on Hector, he's done nothing but talk about you."

"He's just infatuated", Roberta replied with a smile, "What Johnathon needs is a distraction and I may have just the thing."

"A distraction?", Simone queried.

"Didn't you guys notice that our transport ship has changed course?", Roberta asked.

"Ah, no. How would we know that?", Simone enquired.

"Okay, right. I forgot, you guys can't feel the ship's manoeuvring through its deck plating the way I can", Roberta commented, before explaining, "We're not heading to Ganymede L-Four anymore. About three hours ago, we altered course for Ganymede L-One. I've just received official notification. Our twelve interstellar push ships have moved to a new staging ground at Ganymede L-One."

Simone responded, "Ganymede L-Four, Ganymede L-One? Does it matter?"

"Not really, Simone. It's the other communique I received just after the course change alteration", Roberta informed her before commenting, "High Prince Wilhelm has requested my presence at his palace on Ganymede Prime."

"That's in the main colony zone, at Ganymede L-Five?", Angelique queried.

"Yes, it is, Angelique", Roberta confirmed before offering, "If you like, Simone, your family can come with me. Meeting the High Prince might be just the distraction Johnathon needs."

"Why does the High Prince want to see you?", Simone asked.

"High Prince Wilhelm is one of my fan boys, Simone. He and Little Johnny", Roberta explained, before noting, "Before he became the High Prince of the Four Jovian Realms, he kind of had a soft spot for me. A bit like young Johnathon."

"I've never met Royalty before", Simone noted and then asked, "Can we go with you?", she asked, double-checking.

"Of course, I'll just bring you along as a surprise", Roberta replied with a wry grin.

While the transport ship continued to Ganymede L-One, Roberta detached her ship, the Dark Angel, from the transport's mid ventral dock and flew to Ganymede Prime in Ganymede L-Five. Roberta had four passengers with her: Special Operative James Reas, his Wife, Simone, and his Children, Angelique and young Johnathon.

As they flew to their destination, Roberta and James instructed Angelique in how to fly the Dark Angel. Roberta made the instruction session official, logging Angelique's flight time as official flight training. The Dark Angel, although ancient, was heavily upgraded and, as a Tristar Interplanetary Stealth Ship, Angelique would acquire a class five pilot's license at the end of her training.

With Roberta's instruction, Angelique docked the Dark Angel at external docking port thirteen, its usual docking port, at the northern end cap's main docking ring at Ganymede Prime. This particular docking port was used exclusively for the Dark Angel and the docking bay was marked accordingly.

Across all of the centuries, it had been that way. Ever since the twenty-second century, no one had the balls to change it. It was considered very bad luck to alter its status, an unwritten rule. It was Roberta Nummus's docking bay.

Simone made sure that Angelique and Johnathon were dressed in their finest clothes. For her part, Simone wore a beautiful gown that she would only ever wear on special occasions. This was, of course, a very special occasion.

Much to Simone's chagrin, her Husband, James and Roberta Nummus, both dressed in full tactical body armour, complete with weapons. Roberta, for her part, was literally armed to the teeth with more swords, knives and other assorted weapons than could be counted. Roberta was also carrying a heavy, high-powered, rapid-fire pulsed laser canon that was probably as old as her ship.

"Are we having an audience with the High Prince or are you going to commit regicide?", Simone inquired, wondering why they were both so heavily armed.

"Been there and done that", Roberta noted with a grin, before explaining, "High Prince Wilhelm has insisted that I turn up fully armed as I was in the old days of his ancestor, High Prince Albert. Apparently, Wilhelm wants a selfie or two. To be honest, when I attend the High Prince's palace, this is how I'm usually dressed. It's a thing, a historical thing. It's just expected of me."

"And my Husband? James doesn't need to partake in this charade, does he?", Simone questioned.

"Your Husband, James Reas, is a Special Operative, Simone. Wilhelm will expect him to dress the same as me", Roberta explained.

Simone shook her head, "It is absurd!"

"Agreed, but then so are most of the High Princes of the Jovian Realms", Roberta Nummus noted.

Roberta Nummus and her entourage entered the High Prince's throne room. With Roberta in the lead, Simone Reas, her Son, Johnathon and Daughter, Angelique, behind her and Simone's Husband, James Reas, following closely behind.

Roberta noticed the High Prince's entire ministerial cabinet was seated to their left, and to her right were seated the higher-ranking Nobility. There were several Princesses amongst them. High Prince Wilhelm sat on his ornate, yet comfortable, gold-gilded throne. They all stood as Roberta Nummus entered and bowed to her, before retaking their seats.

Not much had changed in eleven hundred years, although the Four Jovian Realms were now a Constitutional Democracy. The power of the High Prince was quite limited. That was the result of the Second Horridian War over eleven hundred years ago. A War the Horridian regime of High Prince Heinrich had lost, before he and two of his Brothers, Wulfric and Valdamar, fled into exile.

Heinrich's youngest Sibling and Son, Leopold, the Great Reformer, had, as his name suggested, made a great many reforms. High Prince Leopold had curtailed the power of the High Princes who followed him. He had even made it unconstitutional for the Four Jovian Realms to instigate or wage War unless it was in self-defence. It was a constitutional amendment that could not be changed.

Roberta stood there before High Prince Wilhelm, her guests on her right, Johnathon, Simone, Angelique and James Reas. Both Roberta and James were wearing full tactical body armour and fully armed. Roberta even carried her heavy pulse rifle. A weapon so heavy, it rightly belongs on an armoured personnel vehicle or a starfighter. There were few in the throne room who could even lift it.

"Wilhelm, why am I here?", Roberta questioned before the High Prince could speak, "You know I hate pomp and pageantry."

"Oh, Roberta, please. You are going away to some distant star system and I might never see you again. Please allow me some pleasures in life", Wilhelm replied.

Young Johnathon Reas added helpfully, "Xi-Bootis A Secundus. That's twenty two light-years away."

Roberta glanced at Johnathon, "You might want to add a 'Your Majesty' in there somewhere, Johnathon. Unlike myself, you're not on a first-name basis with the High Prince."

Young Johnathon Reas frowned, but at least he didn't snarl, although he had considered doing so.

High Prince Wilhelm looked at Johnathon Reas, "Johnathon, now that I know your first name, you can call me Wilhelm."

Before Roberta could introduce her guests, young Johnathon announced, "I'm Johnathon Reas. This is my Mum, Simone and my Sister, Angelique. My Dad, James, is over there on the end. Dad's a Special Operative, that's why he's all dressed up in body armour."

Simone and Angelique curtseyed. James bowed slightly.

"Great, introductions are over. Now, Wilhelm, why am I here?", Roberta questioned again.

"Roberta Nummus. Do you have to go? You could stay here and sit at my side, you know. My offer of marriage still stands", Wilhelm replied with a hopeful smile.

"Wilhelm, this is the sixth time you've asked me and the answer is the same", Roberta replied, shaking her head, before explaining, "The purpose of a royal Wife is to produce heirs to the throne, Heirs and spares. I am an immortal and cannot provide you with an heir. Choose one of those pretty young Princesses you have sitting over there", she gestured to her right.

Several Princesses smiled at Roberta's rejection of marriage. They were still in with a chance.

Young Johnathon interjected, "You can't have her anyway. When I'm all grown up, I'm marrying Aunty Roberta."

Wilhelm smiled and then he laughed, "Is that so, young man?"

Simone pinched the bridge of her nose before apologising, "I'm so sorry, Your Majesty. My Son, Johnathon. He has a fixation with Roberta at the moment. I'm sure he'll grow out of it."

"No, I won't, Mum!", Johnathon insisted.

High Prince Wilhelm got up from his throne and approached Johnathon.

He crouched down, "Young man, your Aunt Roberta has rejected me six times. Perhaps, you'll have your chance", and then he ran his hand through Johnathon's hair.

"You see, Mum. Even the High Prince says I will", Johnathon commented.

High Prince Wilhelm stood back up, "Minister of Royal Protocol. Please record that young Johnathon Reas is hereby granted the right to have an audience with me upon request, anytime he should ask. I like this young man. His attitude is quite refreshing and his taste in women is excellent."

The Minister for Royal Protocol took down some notes, "Yes, Your Majesty."

Simone's face took on an astonished look.

Then the High Prince announced, clapping his hands, "Okay, it's time for photos", before enquiring, "Special Operative, James Reas. Where is your pulsed laser rifle?"

"Your Majesty? Do you mean like the one High Admiral Nummus has?",
James Reas replied, "If that is the case, I don't actually have one of those. That is
a bespoke weapon."

Roberta chimed in, "Wilhelm, if you'd let me know that was a requirement, I
could have lent James, Aurange Sheergibbon's pulsed laser rifle."

"Oh yes. I guess that one's on me", Wilhelm admitted, noting, "I forgot there
are only two of those."

The High Prince noted almost matter-of-factly to Johnathon, "You know, your
Aunt Roberta once beheaded an ancestor of mine. Chop, chop, rip and off she
went with his head as a trophy. Then, when his Son, Godric, became High Prince
and started the First Horridian War, your Aunt Roberta ended the War with an ice
pick. One of those ice picks in her utility belt."

"Wilhelm, is this an appropriate discussion for an eight-year-old?", Roberta
asked.

Johnathon quickly stepped in, "How did my Aunt Roberta do that? Stop a War
with an ice pick?"

Wilhelm continued, "Oh, well, she stuffed it up Godric's nose and
lobotomised him. Turned Godric's brain to mush. If Roberta had not done that,
I would not be the High Prince. That not only ended the First Horridian War, it
changed the line of succession."

It was now Roberta's turn to pinch the bridge of her nose.

High Prince Wilhelm gestured to James to stand beside Roberta. Then the
High Prince stepped in between them. He placed his left arm over James's
shoulder and his right arm over Roberta's. Several of the High Prince's Ministers
began taking photographs. Those would hit the news feeds even before the
audience was over.

The High Prince was well-known and famous. Roberta Nummus was also well-
known and famous. Now poor old James Reas, Special Operative, was going to be
well-known and famous as well.

Wilhelm put his arm around Roberta's waist, "I want this photograph to be
personal", he announced.

"Really, Wilhelm. I'm not really comfortable with this at all", Roberta
protested.

"Oh, Roberta. It's just a photograph", Wilhelm protested dismissively.

And that was how the rest of the audience with the High Prince went.
Wilhelm insisted on having photographs taken with Simone, Johnathon,
Angelique and James. Roberta Nummus was popular, very popular. They all
wanted their photographs taken with Roberta Nummus, the legendary immortal
who'd beheaded one High Prince and ice pick lobotomised another.

Several Princesses, who were each hoping to become the High Prince's Wife, also wanted their photographs taken with Roberta Nummus. One of them even thanked Roberta personally for turning Wilhelm's offer of marriage down. She was apparently the frontrunner for his affections. All Roberta wanted to do was retreat to her cabin on board her ship, the Dark Angel.

After all of the photographs were taken, Angelique Reas enquired, "Why is the fleet leaving from Ganymede L-One? It was scheduled to leave from the shipyards in Ganymede L-Four."

"Oh, that. Well, two reasons actually", Wilhelm replied, explaining, "The first reason was for the boarding of passengers. There are twelve thousand colonists and the facilities at Ganymede L-One are far superior. Far more efficient, or so I'm told."

"And the second reason?", Angelique queried.

"Ah, that's a historical thing", Wilhelm replied with a smile, explaining, "After the Second Horridian War, the then High Prince, Heinrich and his Brothers, Wulfric and Valdamar, left the Jovian Realms for exile at the Dwarf World, Eris. Their push ships left from Ganymede L-One."

"So, we're going into exile? Is that what people think?", Angelique questioned.

"No, not at all, young woman", Wilhelm countered, explaining, "It's just that the mere presence of Roberta Nummus in this system has been a deterrent to war for well over a thousand years. Roberta could turn up anywhere, anytime and end someone who had those intentions. We'd all rather she stayed here amongst us than fly out to the Xi-Bootis system."

Young Johnathon asked, "What happened to those exiles?"

"Oh, young Johnathon. They're still out there at Eris. We have stealth surveillance drones keeping an eye on them, but they seem to be content to stay where they are", Wilhelm informed him, noting,   "Their society is like a time capsule. All of the technology is stuck in the twenty-fourth century."

"So there are two Horridian Dynasties?", Angelique queried, adding, "One here in the Four Jovian Realms and the other one out there at the Dwarf World, Eris?"

"Three, Angelique", Roberta chimed in, noting, "The Trailing Trojan Principality is a Horridian Dynasty as well."

"Yes, quite, although the Horridians out at Eris adhere to their old ways. They are a regime that has not changed in over a thousand years, whereas the Dynasties back here are all Constitutional Monarchies", Wilhelm confirmed.

Angelique nodded in understanding.

Young Johnathon, although surrounded by beautiful young Jovian Princesses, only had eyes for his Aunty Roberta Nummus. He was infatuated with Roberta and that was not going to change.

The remainder of the audience with High Prince Wilhelm ended with hors d'oeuvres, canapes and drinks. While the Reas family found it all surreal and exciting, Roberta found it exhausting. Roberta had been trained and honed, fine-tuned as a weapon and although her neural conditioning had long ago been eliminated, fitting into *"polite society"* was more of an effort than fitting into a *"meat grinder"*.

When they finally returned to the Dark Angel, Roberta stowed away her weapons, changed into a more casual uniform and slumped into her Captain's chair.

"Thank the Gods, that's over", Roberta stated to no one in particular.

James Reas changed out of his tactical body armour and quickly joined Roberta on the bridge.

Angelique Reas wasn't far behind and took up the pilot's station.

Simone Reas had found the Jovian wine a tad too strong and decided to sleep it off in her cabin. While at the audience with the High Prince, Simone had gathered contact details from some of the younger, prettier Jovian Princesses and invited them to visit should they ever find themselves at Xi-Bootis A Secundus. Simone was determined to break her Son, Johnathon's, obsession with Roberta.

Young Johnathon had eaten way too many hors d'oeuvres and sweets and went to the cabin he shared with his Sister. Jonathon was horrified to find smudged lipstick kisses on his cheeks where several of the younger Princesses had kissed him. Johnathon Reas had considered that unwanted attention.

Roberta checked the Dark Angel's fuel status and then requested, "Take us out, Angelique. Detach the docking clamps. Take the Dark Angel to a safe distance from Ganymede Prime and then punch in a course for Ganymede L-One. Lock in on the lead push ship, the Artemisia's beacon. I've had enough pomp to last me a lifetime."

4. Outward Bound.

Once the Dark Angel had arrived at Ganymede L-One, Roberta instructed Angelique to dock at the Artemisia's central external docking port on its ventral hull. The Artemisia did have internal docking bays, but Roberta would never use them. Docking clamps were one thing; internal docking bay doors were another.

Roberta's mind was always tactical and she could never bring herself to dock the Dark Angel in an internal docking bay. Angelique, as instructed, positioned the Dark Angel for the appropriate docking port and then activated the docking computer interlock. Within minutes, they were docked and ready to board the interstellar push ship, Artemisia.

While Simone and her children made their way to their cabin, Roberta and James made their way to the Artemisia's bridge.

"High Admiral on the Bridge", one of the bridge officers announced.

"At ease, people. "No need to make a fuss", Roberta announced, before inquiring, "Captain Wolf, what's the status of my fleet?"

"Ready and waiting, Admiral", Captain Wolf replied, noting, "We have been awaiting your arrival."

"Noted. I take it all of the other push ships have their colonists on board?", Roberta questioned.

"Yes, of course, Admiral. The other eleven push ships are all fully loaded. One thousand colonists each. We, ourselves, have taken on board eight hundred colonists and we just need to pick up those two hundred Thol colonists from Mimas", Captain Wolf responded with further information.

Roberta Nummus nodded, "Notify the other ships to prepare for slipstream to staging point Alpha. We'll meet them there after a quick detour to the Saturnian Demarchy and Mimas."

"Very well, Ma'am", Captain Wolf replied as he nodded to his Communications Officer to pass on the order for slipstream preparation.

Roberta turned to James Reas, "Special Operative, James Reas. You might want to have your Daughter, Angelique, on the bridge before we slipstream to Saturn. We'll want to add that to her pilot's training."

"Yes, of course, Admiral. I should have thought of that myself", James Reas replied.

Three hours later, all of the push ships had performed their systems checks and were ready to slipstream to staging point Alpha, fifty astronomical units from the Sun. The flagship, Artemisia, of course, had a detour to make before joining the other ships.

"Admiral Nummus, the other ships are ready for slipstream", Captain Wolf announced.

"Excellent. Make sure that they're leveraging Jupiter's gravity well and magnetic field for this first jump. Let's not waste any power if we can avoid it", Roberta replied.

"That is the plan, Admiral", Captain Wolf noted in reply.

"Make sure that they triple-check their slipstream exit point parameters. I don't want any entanglement disasters at our staging point", Roberta recommended.

"Ma'am, that is standard procedure", Captain Wolf informed her.

"Yes, Captain. It is, but with this many ships and colonists involved, I don't want anything going wrong. Is that understood?", Roberta explained.

"So noted, Admiral. I'll have that passed on to the other ships immediately", Captain Wolf replied, as he gestured to his Communications Officer.

"Angelique, please take a seat and use the ship's scanners to monitor the space in front of those push ships", Roberta instructed.

"Yes, Aunt Roberta", Angelique replied as she took a seat and started adjusting the ship's scanners.

"Angelique, we're going to be leveraging Jupiter's immense gravity and rotation. That generates frame-dragging events. When those occur within a magnetic field, which Jupiter has, and it has a very powerful one at that, it generates spacetime anomalies. Now, if we pulse the right spacetime anomaly, with precisely the right electromagnetic pulse, we get our useful slipstream", Roberta explained.

Her Father, James Reas, chimed in, "Now, each push ship will pulse their chosen spacetime anomaly with almost the same frequency, but each will be slightly offset from the others. The results should leave the slipstream exit points in a tight cluster, yet far enough apart that there won't be any mishaps."

"What if two or more push ships use the exact same frequency?", Angelique questioned.

Her Father replied, "Then their slipstream exit points will overlap and we'll have disastrous collisions at our staging point. Everything has to be coordinated perfectly."

Roberta stepped back in, "This is just one method. We are leveraging Jupiter's gravity and magnetic field to save a shit ton of power. This method works with any rotating planetary-sized gravitational mass that has its own magnetic field. For planets that don't have a natural magnetic field, we can use an artificial electromagnetic dipole, either set in the planet's L-One zone, which requires the use of offset parameters or, where possible, equator-girdling electromagnetic dipoles. There is a whole field of science dedicated to this technology. If you want, I can run through the math with you later."

Angelique nodded, "Perhaps, Aunt Roberta, when I've got my head wrapped around this part first."

Roberta Nummus commanded, "Captain Wolf, we'll go last. Give the other push ships the go-ahead for slipstream", and then she turned to her Niece, "Keep a watch on those scanners, Angelique."

Captain Wolf nodded to his Communications Officer, who transmitted, "All go for slipstream. Repeat. All go for slipstream."

As Angelique watched the scanners, she detected a short, precise pulse of electromagnetic energy targeting and otherwise invisible point in space. Then, a few seconds later, the push ship would lurch forward and simply vanish. One by one, the eleven push ships vanished into the void.

Angelique looked confused, "I could see that they were targeting precise points in space. I could detect their precise electromagnetic pulses. I did not see any slipstreams or wormholes; the ships just vanished. How is that possible?"

"You can't see the slipstream, Angelique. They're not visible to the naked eye. Our ship's systems have to show us the funnel and its gravitational gradients", Roberta explained.

James smiled and gave off a small chuckle, "The two guys who first cracked slipstream travel, Varakhan Utana and Peter Swann, had I.Qs hovering above and below three hundred, respectively. Varakhan Utana worked on the hardware and Peter Swann worked on the maths and computational logic. This slipstream technology was originally discovered during the Second Horridian War and then locked way for more than two centuries. The two Psi Corps operatives involved, Folcrom Forkbraid and Folcrom Selene, who commissioned the research, were horrified that it might end up being used in another Interplanetary War."

Angelique nodded, "I can see how that might have been an issue back then. Those were scary times."

"Okay, Captain Wolf, it's our turn. Takes us to Saturn", Roberta commanded, before turning to Angelique, "This time I want you to watch the bridge's main screen, Angelique."

Captain Wolf turned to his Helmsman, "Go ahead on slipstream to Saturn, Helmsman."

The Helmsman went through his checklist, "Frame dragging event detected. Spacetime anomaly is in alignment with our intended destination. Pulsing the anomaly in five, four, three, two, one, go!"

The bridge's main screen displayed a funnel-shaped graphic, with a series of converging lines tracking towards the narrow end, each line pulsing with movement as if charting a gravimetric flow. The entire construct appeared to be slowly rotating. The lines were a distinct red colour, as if a warning that stated, "*Do not touch.*"

"Extending our long-range scans into the slipstream funnel", the Helmsman noted and then after several long seconds, "Confirmed. The targeted exit region beyond the slipstream's exit funnel is clear."

Captain Wolf ordered, "Helmsman, go for slipstream. Keep us centred in that pipe."

"Aye, Captain", the Helmsman replied and the Artemisia lurched forward into the funnel.

Once over the funnel's lip, the sides of the slipstream tunnel showed definite spatial distortions. The walls of the slipstream tunnel were a kaleidoscope of colours and distorted, swirling lights. Colourful orbs would flit into existence and then simply vanish just as quickly.

The visual effects of the experience were both psychedelic and surreal. Minor turbulence was noted in the slipstream tunnel as well, but nothing that the Artemisia's inertial dampers couldn't handle. It felt like a lifetime, an eternity and then the exit funnel came into view and they were quickly over the lip and back in normal space.

The ship's chronometer displayed a transit time of precisely two minutes and ten seconds, although everyone thought it felt like much, much longer.

The screen display changed and ahead of the Artemisia was a smallish ice moon. They were now in Saturnian Demarchy space, just outside of the Mimasian borders and gently flying under the ship's own inertia towards their destination, Mimas. The home of both Martians and the Mimasian Thols.

"Well, that went well", James Reas noted, adding, "Angelique, if our history is correct, the first time this was done, it was on a ship named the Solstice and half the crew ended up tossing their lunch."

"Almost correct, James", Roberta noted, adding, "It was the Martian Defence Force Ship Solstice, later, the Starship Solstice and only the three pregnant crew members vomited. Although the rest of the crew was nauseated by the effects. They had some inertial dampener issues on their first run."

"There were pregnant women on a Warship?", Angelique questioned incredulously.

"Well, the ship wasn't strictly a Warship to start with and the crew members were somewhat complicated. Two of those pregnant women, Zuawalo and Zeealas Pod, were Security Officers and also the First Officer, James Murphy's, Wives. The other pregnant woman, Nyaliep Pod, was an Engineering Assistant and also Varakhan Utana's Wife. Besides the Pods, two of the other crew members were a Husband and Wife team as well. Zuawalo's and Zeealas's Mother, Zyaliep Pod, was also a crew member. I knew the Solstice's crew very well back then. They were all wonderful people, much more like a family than a crew, really."

Roberta was quiet for a moment after that. She remembered the crew of the Solstice very well; they had been her friends after all. Such was the curse of immortality. Her friends passed on while Roberta always remained behind, with harsh and lonely memories.

Roberta's silent reverie was broken by the detection of an approaching transport ship from Mimas.

"That would be our Thol colonists coming out to meet us", Roberta noted.

Captain Wolf enquired of his Communications Officer, "What class of transport is that, Lieutenant? I'm not familiar with its design."

The Lieutenant replied, "It's old, Captain. Very old. It looks like an old colonial interplanetary troop transport. Its designation is CTT-VC-999. That ship dates all the way back to the Mimasian War, Sir."

Roberta Nummus stepped in, "Mimas has a thousand of those troop transports. They were all left behind on Mimas after the Mimasian War. The Mimasians have modified them for general multipurpose use. If you check that transport ship's maintenance logs, you will find it's in good operational order."

The Lieutenant checked the Mimasian transport's maintenance logs, "Confirmed, Captain. The CTT-VC-999 is extremely old, but very well-maintained."

"The Mimasians have a simple philosophy: waste not, want not. They recycle and repurpose everything. Both the Martians and the Thols are technological wizards", Roberta explained.

Angelique, who was still on the bridge, sitting at the scanners, noted, "Aunt Roberta, just how many Thol colonists were we expecting?"

Roberta replied, "We are expecting two hundred Thols. Why do you ask?"

"It's just that I performed a routine scan of that Mimasian transport ship and it came back with four hundred and sixty life signs. So I accessed the transport's manifest", Angelique replied, before dropping the bomb, "They have on board a pilot, a co-pilot, eight Martians and four hundred and fifty Thols. They also have a lot of supplies on board. Far more than needed for a simple passenger drop-off run."

"Captain Wolf, query that transport ship and find out what the hell is going on", Roberta commanded, noting, "We have just enough berths for two hundred Thols, no more and no less."

"Yes, Admiral", Captain Wolf replied, before turning to his Communications Officer, "Lieutenant, put me through to the CTT-VC-999. I need to talk to that ship's Captain."

"Aye, Captain. Putting you through now", the Lieutenant replied.

The transport's pilot appeared on the bridge's main screen and Captain Wolf questioned, "Captain. We are expecting two hundred passengers. You have over four hundred and fifty aboard your ship. Please explain?"

"Stand by, Captain. This is well above my pay grade", the transport pilot replied.

Another face appeared on the bridge's main screen. It was a female Thol.

The Tholish woman smiled with her perfectly Angelic features and announced with trills, clicks and subtle, soft barks, "I am Ytryan. I have been assigned the Matriarch of the Thol colonists. How may I help you, Captain?"

Captain Wolf politely bowed before enquiring, "Ma'am. Might I enquire as to why you have over four hundred and fifty passengers and such a massive amount of supplies? We were expecting to take on board only two hundred colonists."

Ytryan replied quickly, with clipped trills, clicks and barks, "We had so many of our people clamouring to go home to our original homeworld that we needed to accommodate more Thols. They are ever so homesick and want desperately to go home, to Homwol. So, we made a change to our plans. There are now four hundred and fifty Thols and eight Martian colonists. As well as the Human pilots."

Roberta Nummus stepped in, "Ytryan, we only have two hundred berths. We cannot possibly take on an extra two hundred and fifty-eight colonists."

Ytryan smiled and then bowed before trilling back, "Roberta Nummus, you honour me with your words. Please allow me to explain the current situation?"

"By all means, Ytryan, please explain?", Roberta agreed.

Ytryan trilled, clicked and barked softly, "This transport ship has been modified. Only two hundred of my people will board your push ship. The remaining passengers and crew will remain on this transport. We have stowed away enough supplies to last us at least two years."

Roberta interjected, "I am familiar with that class of transport. Modified it may be, but it is most certainly not slipstream capable."

"That is correct, Roberta Nummus", Ytryan admitted with a trill and a click, before explaining, "We will dock our transport to the Artemisia's central dorsal docking port. Once our allotted colonists have disembarked and boarded your ship, our transport ship will remain docked."

Roberta quickly caught on and queried, "You want us to piggyback your transport ship through a slipstream tunnel to your homeworld, Homwol?"

"Yes, Roberta Nummus", Ytryan confirmed with a quick trill.
Roberta turned to Captain Wolf, querying, "Captain Wolf, is that even possible?"

The Captain replied, his face showing serious doubts, "For a smaller vessel like the Dark Angel, sure, not a problem. For a transport ship of that size, I don't think so. I very much doubt that our docking clamps will be adequate enough to piggyback something that big through a slipstream tunnel. The gravimetric shear will rip that transport straight off from the docking port and take a large section of our hull with it."

Roberta shook her head, "I'm sorry, Ytryan. We can't take the risk. We can only take the two hundred colonists that were allocated berths aboard this ship. No more and no less."

Ytryan frowned, something that looked so out of place on a Thol's Angelic face. Most people believed that Thols couldn't frown, that they were perpetually happy and always smiling.

"Roberta Nummus, we have considered the load-bearing capacity of your push ship's docking clamps. We have also considered the slipstream tunnel's gravimetric shear. Our transport ship has been modified accordingly", Ytryan trilled, clicked and barked in reply, before explaining, "Our transport ship's ventral hull has been significantly modified. It is lined with mag-lock grapples that extend and lock onto your push ship's outer hull. This has all been simulated and found to be a viable solution."

Roberta looked at Captain Wolf, "What do you think, Captain?"

Captain Wolf rubbed his chin, "We'll need to see those mag-lock specifications. Hell, I'd want the complete specifications for that transport ship. Run everything by our engineers and run our own simulations. If Matriarch Ytryan is right, we could have a viable solution, but we need to do this by the numbers."

Roberta nodded and then turned back to the screen, "Ytryan, did you get that?"

"Yes", Ytryan trilled and clicked, "You want our transport's complete specifications to run your own simulations."

"Correct, Ytryan. I keep forgetting just how clever you guys can be when you get together with our Martian friends", Roberta replied, before agreeing, "If our simulations pan out as a viable option, we'll give it a go."

"The results of your simulations will match ours, Roberta Nummus", Ytryan replied, clicking and trilling, "You will see. You will agree. Very clever we are, as you well know."

Roberta nodded to Ytryan and requested of Captain Wolf, "Captain, let the fleet know that we'll be delayed due to unforeseen circumstances. Tell them that it's nothing to worry about."

"Yes, Admiral", Captain Wolf replied as he gestured to his Communications Officer.

Just as the Tholish Matriarch, Ytryan, had stated, the results of their simulations matched the results of the Thol and Martian simulations. Roberta thought to herself that she should have known better; after all, she had lived inside Mimas with the Martians and the Thols for over four centuries. Then again, there were well over a thousand lives at stake and Roberta Nummus was ever cautious.

Two hundred Mimasian Thols disembarked the transport ship, CTT-VC-999 and made their way to their assigned berths on the interstellar push ship. The remaining Thols and other passengers aboard the transport all strapped in for the slipstream transit.

Captain Wolf had his bridge crew triple-check that the transport ship was locked to the Artemisia by both his push ship's docking clamps and the transport ship's mag-lock grapples. The transport ship, CTT-VC-999, was locked firmly in place.

The Artemisia's Helmsman notified the Captain, "Sir, the Artemisia is ready for slipstream."

"Angelique, I want you watching the bridge's main screen again when we go through the slipstream", Roberta instructed her Niece, "It's pretty much the same as our last jump, just this time we'll be leveraging Saturn's gravity well, rotation and magnetic field to save on power."

"And that works for every planet, Aunt Roberta?", Angelique queried.

"Almost every planet. The planet has to be rotating and have a magnetic field, either natural or artificial", Roberta clarified, noting, "So it won't work on a tidally locked planet. It won't work on Mercury or even Venus either; they both rotate far too slowly. There is a minimum limit when it comes to planetary mass as well. The Dwarf Planet Ceres, for instance, sits just above that lower limit."

Captain Wolf announced, "Ready for slipstream, Admiral Nummus."

"Make it so, Captain Wolf", Roberta confirmed.

Captain Wolf turned to his Helmsman, "Go ahead on slipstream to staging point Alpha, Helmsman. Place our exit funnel safely this side of the fleet's position and we'll cruise in under our own inertia."

The Helmsman went through his checklist for the second time, "Frame-dragging event detected. Spacetime anomaly is in alignment with our intended destination. Pulsing the anomaly in five, four, three, two, one, go!"

The bridge's main screen displayed a familiar funnel-shaped graphic, with its series of converging lines pulsating with movement, charting the gravimetric flow towards the narrow end. As with the previous slipstream, the whole structure was slowly rotating.

Once again, the Helmsman noted, "Extending our long-range scans into the slipstream funnel", and then after several long seconds, "Confirmed. The designated targeted region of space beyond the slipstream's exit funnel is clear."

Captain Wolf ordered, "Helmsman, go for slipstream. Keep us centred in the pipe and remember, this time we are piggybacking a transport ship."

"Aye, Captain. Will do", the Helmsman replied and the Artemisia lurched forward into the funnel.

The Artemisia slid over the slipstream funnel's lip, and the spatial distortions began once more. The kaleidoscope of colours, the distorted, swirling lights and colourful orbs became visible again.

The turbulence was far more than minor this time around and the Artemisia's inertial dampers strained under the ungainly load she was carrying, but they held. Then, after what felt like an eternity, the Artemisia slipped out of the exit funnel and they were back in normal space. The ship's chronometer displayed a transit time of precisely two minutes and ten seconds, exactly as expected.

The screen display changed and ahead of the Artemisia was a small fleet of eleven other interplanetary push ships. They had successfully transited from Saturn to staging point Alpha and were now coasting under their own inertia towards their colonisation fleet.

Roberta shook her head and chuckled, "Always trust the Thols. They always know their shit!"

The Artemisia coasted through the formation of eleven colony push ships and slowed to a halt just beyond them. One by one, the other colonial push ships lined up behind the Artemisia, forming a single linear formation. Angelique was on the bridge watching the scanners with great curiosity.

"Aunt Roberta, why is the fleet forming up in a line?", Angelique enquired.

Angelique smiled knowingly, "Well, you've seen one slipstream technique, Angelique. Now you're about to see another one", and then she turned to Angelique's Father, "I'll let you explain it, James."

"No problem", James Reas replied, "Well, Angelique. The previous slipstream technique is kind of like travelling from one suburb to another in the same city, using a light rail system. Now, we are going to use a technique that's more akin to travelling from one city to another by high-speed rail."

"So, slipstreaming from planet to planet is like a short hop, but slipstreaming from star to star is a much longer jump", Angelique caught on quickly, but then questioned, "Dad, there's no planetary mass out here to leverage. So, how is this going to work?"

Her Father chuckled, "Angelique, the Sun is one big stellar mass, it's rotating and it also has its own magnetic field."

"So, we're leveraging the Sun itself?", Angelique asked.

"That is correct, Angelique", Roberta confirmed.

James Reas continued, "Interstellar slipstreaming is a bit different. Planetary masses limit us to jumping from one planet to the next within a solar system. It's all about the mass. You can't slipstream from Ceres to Eris, for instance, but you can slipstream to Jupiter and from Jupiter to Eris. Of course, once you're out at Eris, well, Eris doesn't have enough mass to slipstream back. You'd only get around thirty astronomical units or so closer to the outer planets."

"And that's when you'd need the third technique, which you will learn about later", Roberta added.

"So, if a planet's mass limits how far the slipstream can go, then that has to apply to stellar masses as well?", Angelique asked.

"Correct again", Roberta confirmed, noting, "Stellar masses have far greater range, but that range is not infinite. It is still limited by mass, stellar mass."

James chimed in, "Our Sun's mass enables us to slipstream as far as twenty five light years into the stellar field. If we need to go further, we'd have to make multiple slipstream jumps from one star to the next and so on, in the direction that we want to travel."

Roberta stepped in, "Just within twenty five light years, there are over one hundred and sixty stellar systems. That's over two hundred and twenty five individual stars. So, we have had plenty of stars to keep us busy exploration-wise."

James continued, "That's one of the things that makes interstellar exploration a slow process. There are a lot of stars out there in interstellar space and slipstream travel is not a magic wand. I wouldn't even call it faster-than-light travel. It's more like boring a tunnel through spacetime itself."

Angelique nodded in understanding, "So the more massive the star, the further you can slipstream, the more stars are within range?"

"That is the gist of slipstream travel", Roberta confirmed.

"There is more to it, though. Within a solar system, planetary gravity wells are smaller and more compact, so you can find frame-dragging events and spacetime anomalies far more readily. With stars, that's a bigger problem. You need to first calculate where to look and it's usually in a line between the star you're leaving and your destination star", James explained, before noting, "Not far ahead of us is just one of those anomalies and we'll be using it to jump to the Xi-Bootis system."

"All colonial push ships have reported readiness for slipstream jump", Captain Wolf announced.

"Okay, so we're all lined up and ready to go", Roberta commented, but quickly double checked, "Captain, make sure our twelfth man remembers to close the tunnel."

Captain Wolf turned to his Communications Officer, "Lieutenant, remind the last ship in our chain to close the slipstream tunnel after they exit at our Xi-Bootis staging point."

"Aye, Captain. Sending the reminder now.", the Lieutenant replied.

Roberta noted, "I should have mentioned this earlier, Angelique. In an ordinary one-ship jump, our slipstream drive system automatically triggers the closure of the slipstream after exiting it with a single, short em pulse. In this jump, twelve ships are using the same slipstream tunnel one after another, so the em pulse is disabled in every ship, except the last one in the chain. The last man closes the tunnel."

"What happens if we accidentally close the tunnel?", Angelique queried.

"Heavens forbid, Angelique. Eleven push ships would be disintegrated in transit, along with all of their crews and passengers", Roberta responded, adding, "There are two main modes of operation. In single ship mode, the em pulse is sent. Whilst in chain mode, the last ship in the chain triggers the slipstream's closure. It's automatic depending on the mode being used, yes, but we always check. It's better to be safe than sorry."

Captain Wolf announced, "Everything is set. All safety checks completed. Ready when you are, Admiral Nummus."

"Make it so, Captain", Roberta commanded.

Captain Wolf turned to his Helmsman, "Go ahead on slipstream to Xi-Bootis, Helmsman."

The Helmsman went through his checklist, "Frame dragging event is holding steady. Spacetime anomaly is in alignment with our intended destination. All push ships in our slipstream chain are online, ready and waiting. Pulsing the anomaly in five, four, three, two, one, go!"

The bridge's main screen displayed a funnel-shaped graphic once more. This time it seemed larger somehow, as if it was scaled up by an order of magnitude or more. The series of converging lines tracked towards the narrow end. Each line pulsated with movement, charting the gravimetric flow. The entire construct slowly rotated.

The Helmsman performed his usual checks, extending the Artemisia's long-range scanners into the slipstream funnel,   "Confirmed. The targeted region of space beyond the slipstream's exit funnel is clear."

Captain Wolf ordered, "Helmsman, go for slipstream. Keep us centred in the pipe. Monitor all subsequent push ship entries."

"Aye, Captain", the Helmsman replied and the Artemisia lurched forward into the funnel.

Once they were over the funnel's lip, the sides of the slipstream tunnel started displaying spatial distortions. The walls of the slipstream tunnel became a kaleidoscope of colours and distorted, swirling lights, with colourful orbs appearing and then disappearing just as quickly.

The now-familiar psychedelic and surreal visual effects continued as they traversed the slipstream's length. The turbulence was minor as the Artemisia's inertial dampers worked to smooth the transit.

A barely audible Helmsman noted, "Second push ship entry", then about fifteen seconds later, "Third push ship entry", followed fifteen seconds after that, "Fourth push ship entry.... Fifth push ship entry.... Sixth push ship entry.... Seventh push ship entry...."

The Helmsman continued reporting the entry of each and every push ship as it entered the slipstream. His voice was distorted and almost inaudible. It sounded drawn out, stretched thin like taffy. It had an almost colourful quality to it. They were literally seeing sounds! And then after an eternity had ended, the Artemisia shot out of the slipstream's exit funnel and back into normal space.

The ship's chronometer displayed the transit time, two minutes and ten seconds. One by one, the other eleven colonial push ships exited the slipstream funnel and continued coasting under their own inertia towards a nearby star system.

A double star system appeared on the bridge's main screen. Ahead of the colonisation fleet, suspended in the inky black void, hung two piercing points of light, the Xi Bootis Stars, A and B, like twin beacons igniting the interstellar gloom. Xi-Bootis A, a yellow G-Type dwarf star, slightly smaller than the Sun and Xi-Bootis B, an even smaller orange K-Type dwarf star.

It was a beautiful sight to behold.

Xi Bootis A, the brighter of the two, blazed with a sharp, yellow-white brilliance. It wasn't just a star, it was a presence. A needle of searing light, far too intense to be mistaken for anything distant or ordinary. Even at this vast distance of one hundred astronomical units from the system, it shone far more fiercely than Venus ever had in Earth's night sky.

To its side, just over nineteen degrees across the sky, Xi Bootis B burned a dimmer, orange-white, still unnaturally bright, a silent sentinel trailing its companion. Smaller, softer, and tinted with the warmth of a dying ember, it lacked the raw intensity of its sibling but remained unmissable, a second eye watching the deep void.

The two stars hung in a shared stillness, close enough to seem like a double star, yet impossibly far, the twin hearts of a binary system, beating light across centuries of distance. Around them, the sky was dark and clean, the local dust swept thin by their stellar winds.

Nothing competed with their brilliance. The rest of the cosmos was likened to a whisper and the Xi Bootis system was a roar.

From this vantage point, the stars offered no warmth, only light and a sense of presence. But they pulled the gaze like gravity, drawing every eye on the bridge toward them, as by simply watching them, you could feel the weight of the system's ancient rhythm. Ahead of them, Xi-Bootis A, their destination.

Roberta Nummus smiled with relief. They were now all in Xi-Bootis space!

5. Planetfall.

Angelique Reas enquired, "They look so small. Bright, but small. How far are they, Aunt Roberta?"

Roberta replied, "This staging point is one hundred astronomical units out from our target star. If the Xi-Bootis system were a single star system, we would have come out much closer, say fifty astronomical units, but as we are dealing with a double star system, we are erring on the side of caution."

"Aunt Roberta, this far out, exactly how are we going to leverage anything to slipstream into the system?", Angelique questioned, "I can't imagine our fleet flying in through normal space. Wouldn't that take a dozen years or longer?"

"Too right it would, Angelique", Roberta confirmed, noting,   "Assuming you're using plasma drives. Even with an ionic-assisted fusion drive, you're still looking at a good six or seven years. This far out, we have nothing we can leverage to slipstream into the system. So, my Darling Niece, we will be using that third slipstream technique that I mentioned earlier."

"Our third slipstream technique?", Angelique questioning.

"Yes, and this technique is the one that makes true interstellar travel possible", Roberta confirmed.

Angelique's Father, James, chimed in, "Planet to planet, not a problem. Star to star, also not a problem, but once you get to that destination star, that's where you have the problem. No one wants to spend years flying through normal space. Our third technique solves that problem."

As Angelique nodded, Roberta announced, "Which reminds me. Captain Wolf, I want every one of our push ship systems checked and scanned. We've just performed an interstellar slipstream jump and I want every system checked and double-checked."

"Aye, Admiral. I'll have my Communications Officer spread the word", Captain Wolf replied as he gestured to his Communications Officer.

"Excellent. Tell the other Captains I want their system status reports on my desk by zero-eight-hundred tomorrow morning", Roberta commanded as she turned back to her Niece, "Angelique, tomorrow you'll get to see our third technique in operation. Some homework for you. Do a few searches on our network and read up on it, yeah?"

Angelique nodded and replied, "Yes, I'll do that, Aunt Roberta."

Her Father, James, chimed in, "Remember that I said that we can slipstream from Jupiter to Eris, but we can't slipstream back. Eris simply does not have enough mass to make that possible. This technique solves that particular problem."

Roberta then interjected, "This technique also uses up a huge percentage of our power reserves, which is why we use it only when we absolutely have to."

Angelique nodded once again.

Roberta Nummus was on board her ship, the Dark Angel, which was still docked on the colonial push ship, Artemisia's, central ventral docking port. It was zero-eight-thirty in the morning and Roberta had just checked through all of the colonial push ship status reports. Every ship was ready to go. The final one hundred astronomical unit leg was before them and it was all just waiting on Roberta's go-ahead. Roberta smiled. They were nearly there. Roberta got up from her desk, left her cabin and then crossed through the docking port on her way to the Artemisia's bridge.

When Roberta arrived at the Artemisia's bridge, she found the Tholish Matriarch, Ytryan and a Martian waiting outside. The Martian was female and just a little tall for a Martian; her hair and skin tones were also not so vibrant, like gold that had lost just a small fraction of its lustre. Her eyes were the dead giveaway, though; they were not the usual Martian emerald green, they were a very definite blue. She was a hybrid.

The Martian hybrid's telepathic voice entered Roberta's mind, *"I am Wynessa, Roberta Nummus. The Martian representative. They won't let us in. They say civilians aren't allowed on the bridge."*

The Tholish Matriarch, Ytryan, trilled, clicked and softly barked, "I am the Tholish Matriarch, Roberta Nummus. I am honoured to be in your presence. This situation is highly embarrassing."

"It's okay, guys. It's just our rules and procedures. I'll sort it all out for you", Roberta replied, adding, "Just follow me in."

As Roberta passed through the door into the Artemisia's bridge, she announced, "Admiral on the bridge and I've brought a couple of honoured guests."

"Captain Wolf. I've checked all of the status reports. We are all good to go for our final slipstream jump", Roberta informed him.

Ytryan walked closer to the bridge's main screen. Most of the bridge crew had never seen a Thol before. Ytryan was of short stature at five feet tall. Although she stood out with her alabaster white skin and white-blond hair. Her great leathery wings, creamy in colour, were neatly furled against her back. Ytryan looked magnificent, with facial features that made her look like an Angel descended from heaven.

Her prehensile tail with its rounded, prehensile manipulator tip was held above the ship's deck. Ytryan's feet were bare, showing her six toes in her people's configuration, three pairs, the outer two being opposable. Her hand showed the very same configuration, but with long, slender, almost delicate fingers.

Ytryan's Angelic features and purple eyes glowed with both intelligence and wisdom. Ytryan was a Tholish Elder and now she was a Tholish Matriarch, yet the simple white tunic she wore made her seem unconcerned with the trappings of wealth, power and privilege.

Ytryan stared at the screen, her purple eyes wide open in wonder.

She pointed to the brighter of the two stars, Xi-Bootis A, "That one there, that one. Is that Cathol?", she asked, trilling and clicking, her voice full of emotion and barely held back tears.

Roberta confirmed, "Yes. That one is Cathol and the other one is Cythol."

Ytryan's excitement grew, her tears began to well, "Roberta Nummus. I need data. Please scan this entire system. Please tell me everything. I must know."

Wynessa, the Martian hybrid, transmitted, *"Ytryan is worried that this is all a dream. That none of this is real. It has been well over six million years since the Thols of Mimas have seen their home system. Ytryan is concerned that the four hundred and fifty Thols that she is responsible for will all be disappointed. It is a serious concern for Matriarch Ytryan."*

Roberta nodded in understanding before giving a command, "Astrometrics. Information please. List the details of the Xi-Bootis system, starting with the lesser component, Xi-Bootis B. From the outside in and save the cherries for last."

The Astrometrics Officer, Lieutenant Peter Barents, began listing off the Xi-Bootis B system's details, "These are from last night's detailed scans", he began.

"Xi-Bootis B, the minor component star is spectral class K-Four-V, an orange dwarf star, much smaller than Sol, significantly cooler and less massive, at point six eight solar masses", Lieutenant Barents listed off.

The Lieutenant continued, "There are planets in two orbital zones around Cythol. The second orbital zone contains a Neptune-sized planet, designated Xi-Bootis B Secundus, with seven moons of about the same size as the moons of Uranus. The first orbital zone is somewhat unusual and highly atypical. There are three co-orbital worlds in that first orbital zone, the Primus zone."

As Ytryan listened intently, the Lieutenant continued, "The largest planet, designation Xi-Bootis B Primus Major, is a Saturn-sized planet. It has one known massive moon, Primus Major Alpha, which is slightly smaller, yet more massive than Mars, a Mars analogue world with a thin, barely breathable atmosphere and minor life forms. It is a fixer-upper."

The Lieutenant paused before continuing, "There is also a quasi moon, designated Primus Quasi, orbiting within the first orbital zone very closely to Primus Major. Primus Quasi is a world in its own right. A super Mars analogue, it is tidally locked to Xi-Bootis B and is, in fact, habitable. The cherry in this system is another co-orbital world, simply designated as Primus, which trails sixty degrees behind Primus Major. It is a Trojan world and is habitable. Primus has multiple sapient life forms."

Ytryan smiled and nodded, trilling, "So far, everything matches our recorded histories. Our people never made contact with the people of that world. They were significantly different from us."

Lieutenant Barents continued, "Yes, Ma'am. Xi-Bootis A, the major component star, is a spectral class G-Eight-V, a yellow dwarf star, slightly cooler and less massive than Sol, at around point nine solar masses. This star, Cathol, has three major orbital zones with known planets and an outer asteroid belt."

"The closest planet to Cathol is a Venus analogue and will likely be terraformed sometime in the future. The furthest planet from Cathol is a Jupiter analogue, designated Xi-Bootis A Tertius, with four large moons, none of which are habitable. Tertius has two sets of Trojan asteroid fields, sixty degrees ahead and behind it in its orbit. The heavily populated asteroid belt is farther out beyond Tertius.", the Lieutenant reported.

Ytryan noted, smiling and trilling, "That was the world where Mimas originated. It was a smaller outer moon before my people turned it into a generation ship. Further detailed scans will show it has a great many smaller moons."

Lieutenant Barents smiled, "Ma'am, you will be pleased to know that the cherry in this system is Xi-Bootis A Secundus. A true Earth analogue, with a single large continent, that has a tectonic rift valley running from west to east. The homeworld of the Thols, Secundus, has one large moon, slightly larger than Earth's."

Ytryan smiled an even broader smile, confirming with glee, "Secundus is Homwol, my people's homeworld. That continent is called Masula and that moon, we call it Luns, our Tholish word for Silver light."

Lieutenant Barents added, "Ma'am, I should note a couple of things. That rift valley on the Masula continent is probably somewhat wider than you might remember. On the opposite side of the planet from your continent, Masula, there is also a fair-sized archipelago of Islands. Those islands are volcanic in nature and have been dated to around four or five million years old. They will be new to you as well."

"Yes, understood, Lieutenant. It has been well over six million years. Much will have changed", Ytryan trilled and clicked, the happiness showing on her Angelic face, which was wet with her tears of joy.

Without warning, Ytryan opened here arms wide and embraced Roberta Nummus. First, Ytryan's arms wrapped around her and then her arms were followed by her great leathery wings. Roberta found herself encased in the warm embrace of a Tholish double hug, a true privilege if ever there was one.

"Thank you, Roberta Nummus, for bringing us home", Ytryan trilled, clicked and softly barked.

Wynessa smiled almost coyly, her eyes showing her attraction to Roberta and transmitted, *"Ytryan is very grateful. She thanks you on behalf of her people, but then again, you already know that, Roberta Nummus."*

Ytryan's hug lasted far longer than Roberta had anticipated and when it finished, she had to wipe tears from her eyes. Something that Ytryan herself was doing. Roberta quickly regained her composure.

"Angelique, please make sure that you are at the scanner station. You will find our transit to Xi-Bootis A Secundus very interesting", Roberta recommended to her Niece.

"Yes, Aunt Roberta", Angelique replied.

"Helmsman. When we transit to Secundus, make sure that you clearly enunciate each step. I want my Niece to learn everything she can from this experience", Roberta commanded.

"Yes, Ma'am", the Helmsman replied.

"Captain Wolf, notify the fleet that we are ready for transit to Secundus. Target our exit funnel just outside of Cis-Luns L-Five. We'll coast in under our own inertia", Roberta commanded.

Captain Wolf turned to his Communications Officer, "Lieutenant, coordinate the fleet. Our final slipstream will be in fifteen minutes."

Captain Wolf turned back to Roberta, "Admiral, since our Tholish friends are returning home, might I suggest that Matriarch Ytryan give the final command for transit to Secundus?"

Roberta Nummus looked at Ytryan and smiled, "When we're all set, Matriarch Ytryan, you'll get to give the final command."

Ytryan's purple eyes brimmed with tears once more.

The fifteen minutes to their final slipstream passed quickly. Roberta Nummus took Matriarch Ytryan's hand in hers. The Tholish Matriarch had only recently been appointed to her position and was clearly anxious. The former Matriarch still presided over those Thols who remained on Mimas, back in the Sol system.

Ytryan, by contrast, now bore the weight of leading those returning to their long-lost homeworld. Homwol, the home of all Thols. To say she was nervous was an understatement.

"Whenever you're ready, Ytryan", Roberta informed her.

"I don't know what to say", Ytryan trilled and clicked, there was even a nervous squeak.

"Just keep it simple, Ytryan. Remember, you are taking your people home", Roberta assured her.

Ytryan smiled, yes, it was that simple, her people were going home, "Captain Wolf", she announced, "Please, take my people home."

Captain Wolf bowed slightly and nodded to Ytryan, "Yes, Ma'am", and then he turned to his Helmsman, "Lieutenant, initiate our slipstream and enunciate the procedure for young Angelique Reas. I suspect that she may become a Helmsman one day."

"Aye, Captain", the Helmsman replied.

Angelique interjected, "I'm going to become a Special Operative like my Mother and Father."

Captain Wolf nodded in reply before instructing his Communications Officer, "Lieutenant, inform the fleet that we'll go first. They are to follow in an orderly fashion upon our departure."

The Artemisia's Helmsman announced, "I am bringing the Gravitic Displacement Drive online now. It will take just a few moments."

Angelique's Father, James Reas, noted, "The Gravitic Displacement Drive creates a quantum singularity ahead of the ship. That provides us with our gravitational well, artificial though it may be", and then he chuckled, "Like most things, the Gravitic Displacement Drive was originally designed as a weapons system back during the Mimasian War of twenty one forty two. After that, the technology was hidden away for over five centuries. Psi Corps again, of course!"

The Helmsman chimed back in, announcing, "Quantum singularity detected. I am now bringing our Spin Dizzy online and applying rotational parameters to the quantum singularity."

Jame Reas noted, "The Spin Dizzy pulses the quantum singularity and starts it rotating."

Angelique nodded in understanding, "So, that's how we get our rotating gravitational well."

"Yes", her Father, James Reas, replied.

The Helmsman then announced, "We have our rotating quantum singularity. I'm now bringing the Electromagnetic Field Overlay Generator online."

James Reas stepped back in, explaining, "The Electromagnetic Field Overlay Generator wraps the quantum singularity in an artificially generated electromagnetic field. The whole construct will rotate and create the spacetime anomalies that we require for slipstreaming into Xi-Bootis A Secundun space."

As Angelique Reas nodded in understanding, the Helmsman announced, "Spacetime anomalies detected. Our ship's A.I. system is scanning the anomalies to determine which one we require."

Then there was a long pause and finally, "We have a candidate anomaly. I am now locking the candidate spacetime anomaly's coordinates into the targeting array. We are ready for slipstream, Captain Wolf."

Captain Wolf turned to his Helmsman, "Go ahead on slipstream to Secundun space, Helmsman, on Matriarch Ytryan's mark."

Roberta Nummus took hold of Ytryan's hand once more, "You're on again, Ytryan."

Tholish Matriarch, Ytryan, trilled and clicked, "Take us to Homwol, take us to Secundus, Helmsman."

The Helmsman went through his checklist, "Aye, Ma'am. The frame-dragging event is stable. Our chosen spacetime anomaly is in alignment with our intended destination. Pulsing the anomaly in five, four, three, two, one, go!"

The Helmsman performed his usual checks, extending the Artemisia's long-range scanners into the slipstream funnel, "Confirmed. The targeted region of space beyond the slipstream's exit funnel is clear."

Captain Wolf ordered, "Helmsman, all go for slipstream. Keep us centred in the pipe."

The Artemisia lurched forward into the funnel. Once they were over the funnel's lip, the sides of the slipstream tunnel started displaying the usual spatial distortions. The kaleidoscope of colours began once more. Distorted, swirling lights, with colourful orbs, flickered in and out of existence. The now-familiar psychedelic and surreal visual effects continued as they traversed the slipstream's length.

Turbulence was significant and the Artemisia's inertial dampers strained to smooth their transit. And then just like that, the Artemisia breached the exit funnels and was back in normal space. What Ytryan and Wynessa had thought had taken a lifetime was, according to the ship's chronometer, two minutes and ten seconds of elapsed time.

Wynessa shook her head and transmitted telepathically, *"That was far rougher than our previous two slipstream jumps. I thought I was going to be sick."*

"Sorry about that, Wynessa. We probably should have mentioned that using artificially created gravity wells to induce slipstreams can be a little rough", Roberta replied.

Ytryan had not heard. She was staring at the bridge's main screen. The Artemisia was coasting under her own inertia towards Cis-Luns L-Five space. To the left of the bridge's main screen was the Secundun Moon, Luns. To the right of the bridge's main screen was the cherry, the true prize, the hope and the want of all Thols. Their homeworld, Homwol. Ytryan felt her knees go weak.

Roberta put her arm around Ytryan's waist and whispered, "Easy there, girl. I've got you."

"It's so beautiful", Ytryan trilled weakly, as her eyes welled with tears once more.

Ytryan and her people were home after all of those thousands upon thousands of millennia.

Ytryan swooned and Roberta swept her up into her arms and carried her over to a nearby chair.

Wynessa crouched down in front of Ytryan and reached into her mind, "*The Matriarch is okay, Ytryan is just overwhelmed with emotion. She will recover shortly.*"

While Ytryan was recovering from her fainting episode, Angelique enquired, "Aunt Roberta. What happens to the quantum singularity that we created? Does it just sit there forever?"

"Ah, no, Angelique. When our ship exited the slipstream, a pulse was sent back through it. It's an automatic procedure for this particular slipstream technique. The quantum singularity evaporates and then the slipstream closes", Roberta informed her, before asking,   "Any more questions?"

"Yeah, just one", Angelique replied, before asking, "Each time we travel through a slipstream, it takes us precisely two minutes and ten seconds. That's our perspective, our frame of reference. How do outside observers perceive that transit?"

Roberta instructed the Artemisia's computer verbally, "Computer. Slipstream transit times. Slipstream traveller and external observer perspectives."

The Artemisia's computer replied, "Complying. Internal slipstream frame of reference, time differential, T-Exit minus T-Entry equals two minutes and ten seconds. External frame of reference, time differential, T-Exit minus T-Entry equals three seconds. These are slipstream constants."

Angelique enquired further, "I don't understand why they are constants. Especially that last one. I mean, really, three seconds. Where does that figure even come from?"

Her Father, James, stepped in with a chuckle, "The two minutes and ten seconds is related to the folding of spacetime itself. When folded sufficiently, the rupture between two points in spacetime creates a slipstream tunnel that has exactly the same parameters every time. There is no deviation. It doesn't even matter what the actual distance is between the two points, either. The result is always the same."

"And the externally observed three seconds?", Angelique queried.

"Yeah, that one, Angelique, no one has an answer for that", her Father admitted.

Roberta stepped in, "Centuries ago, when the Martian Psi Corps released the slipstream drive technology, all sorts of tests were performed. The most famous ones were the Earth-Mars timing tests."

Roberta paused for a moment to gather her thoughts,"They set up a pair of quantum-entangled clocks, one on Earth and one on Mars. They were both set to the same precise time. Then they had a ship transit a slipstream from Earth to Mars. The internal transit time was the standard two minutes and ten seconds. Everyone expected the externally observed time to be somewhat longer. After all, it kind of does make sense, but no. The ship enters the slipstream funnel, traverses the slipstream and then exits the slipstream funnel at the other end. The test results were the same every single time, three seconds, no more and no less. They've repeated that same test between the Earth and the other Planets, even between Sol and Proxima Centauri. The results are always the same."

"And no one knows why?", Angelique questioned.

Her Father chuckled once more, "There are a lot of theories, Angelique, but none that have given us any concrete answers. Not yet anyway."

Roberta added with a smile, "Everyone expected the observed time to be longer than the transit time, but no, it was the opposite. It is completely counterintuitive and perplexing, but there you have it. Sometimes the universe has to throw us something really odd to think about. A puzzle to solve."

Ytryan was still sitting in the chair, staring at the bridge's main screen. There in front of her was Homwol, it was like a dream come true. Wynessa stood beside her. Even her eyes were wide open in wonder. One by one, the other eleven colonial push ships appeared on the screen and soon all twelve ships were coasting towards Cis-Luns L-Five. Twelve thousand colonists in all and this was just the first fleet. In the due course of time, there would be others.

Roberta had little time to sit around watching the bridge's main screen. She was all business and there was a lot of work to be done.

"Captain Wolf. How are our power reserves?", Roberta enquired.

"We are down to ten percent, Admiral", Captain Wolf replied.

Roberta turned to her Niece, "Angelique, please take note. Creating rotating quantum singularities with electromagnetic fields to drive a slipstream jump uses massive amounts of power. We used up ninety percent of our power reserves just on that one jump, which is why we use them so sparingly."

"Ninety percent!", Angelique exclaimed, "That's a lot."

"Yes, it is", Roberta replied, before turning her attention back to the Captain, "How long will it take us to recharge, Captain?"

"Ten hours at least, Admiral", Captain Wolf replied.

Roberta nodded, "Captain Wolf, notify the fleet Captains, I want complete fleet status reports on my desk before zero eight hundred."

The Captain nodded to his Communications Officer, "Lieutenant. The Admiral requires fleet status reports by zero eight hundred. Send out the word."

"Captain Wolf, I want all of our ore processing and manufacturing stations detached and on their way to Cis-Luns L-Four by the end of the week. I want them ready for operations", Roberta commanded.

The Captain started taking down notes on his data tablet, "I'll notify our Colony Operations Manager myself, Admiral."

"Excellent, Captain. Those stations won't have much to do without ore. We need to organise survey teams to Luns, asap. Once we have its resources mapped, we can detach all of our mobile mining stations and send them down to the surface", Roberta noted.

Roberta was all business and no nonsense.

"Captain Wolf, which of our push ships has our ore catchalls and electromagnetic mass driver?", Roberta enquired.

Captain Wolf checked his data tablet, "Our tenth push ship, Kappa, the Netis, has one catchall; it's stowed away in a disassembled state. Our eleventh push ship, Lambda, the Anuket, has our other catchall; it's also disassembled and stowed away. They're all stowed in externally attached docking pods."

"And our mass driver?", Roberta queried.

"Our twelfth push ship, Mu, the Hyperion, has our mass driver on board. Just the one. It's also disassembled and stowed away in external docking pods", Captain Wolf informed her.

Roberta nodded. "We can ferry ore to the orbital processing stations, using the mobile mining stations. However, that is woefully inefficient. We need our mass driver down on Luns and our catchalls in Cis-Luns L-Four as soon as possible. Otherwise, it will take us forever to build our mega-colony."

"Cis-Luns Colonial Central Command? Building a twenty-four-kilometre-long mega-colony is no easy feat, Admiral. Even if everything goes according to plan, it's still a five-year job", the Captain commented in understanding, "I'll have a word with our engineering teams. No promise, Admiral. I'll see if we have the catchalls and mass driver operational in a month."

"Do what you can, Captain", Roberta replied, before noting, "We have to build our second colony on the surface of Secundus as well. In the Masula Valley on the north side of the Masula River, smack dab in between the Carlin villages in the plains and the Indigenous Thol villages in those awfully tall Jula Jula trees to the north. We need to make first contact before we start on the surface colony and that has to go perfectly."

"True enough. We can't have any bad blood with the native sapients", Captain Wolf replied.

Ytryan approached them, trilling and clicking, "My people have studied the videos from your stealth research drones. We are quite fluent in all four languages required."

"All four languages?", Captain Wolf enquired.

"Yes", Ytryan trilled in reply, adding with a few clicks and soft barks, "Ancient Tholish and ancient Carlinish, but now we are also fluent in contemporary Tholish and Carlinish as well. As you Humans often say, we've got this."

Wynessa approached and transmitted telepathically, *"Where language might fail us, telepathy will succeed. Between the Mimasian Thols with their language skills and my telepathic*

Martian folk, we will ensure first contact goes well", and then she gave Roberta a reassuring smile that seemed so much more.

"You guys make it all seem so easy", Roberta replied; she was still quite concerned.

"Nothing is easy, Roberta Nummus", Wynessa replied, noting, *"And yet, we do it anyway."*

Roberta nodded and smiled back, "It is ironic. The original plan was to build the surface colony on those new volcanic islands on the other side of the planet. No indigenous populations live there, so first contact could have been put off for years."

Ytryan trilled and clicked, adding a few soft barks and a grunt, "We rejected that plan, Roberta Nummus, we Thols did. It would have put off the return of my people to our beloved Masula Valley and that was completely untenable. This plan is far bolder. It ends with cooperation and integration."

Roberta's smile broadened as she agreed, "Then we are all on the same page, Matriarch Ytryan. The easy way is not always the right way. Sometimes what seems hardest is worth doing because it turns out best."

Wynessa chimed in telepathically, *"Yes, Roberta Nummus. It also gives us another opportunity. The Indigenous Thols and Carlin-folk do not know about those volcanic islands. We can offer them our aid in colonising them, assuming that they wish to do so, of course."*

"Not to mention, Ytryan's people were once a space-faring people. We can offer them off-world opportunities as well", Roberta replied, but cautiously added, "But as you said, Wynessa, assuming that they want to do so."

Angelique and her Father, James, came to Roberta's side, joining Ytryan, Wynessa and Captain Wolf. They all watched the bridge's main view screen in wonder. An image of Secundus, the Tholish homeworld, was now magnified in its own window on the screen. Homwol was such a magnificent sight.

"So, Ytryan, is it worth it?", Roberta asked.

"Worth it!", Ytryan exclaimed with a trill and a click, "Most definitely worth it, Roberta Nummus!"

6. First Contact.

The Dark Angel made its way from the colonisation fleet at Cis-Luns L-Five to Secundus. On board the ship were Roberta, Special Operative James Reas and his Daughter, Angelique, the Martian hybrid Wynessa and the Tholish Matriarch, Ytryan. Their journey took only a few hours and with young trainee pilot Angelique Reas at the helm, they were soon in Secundun high orbit.

Angelique placed the Dark Angel in a geostationary orbit above the Masula supercontinent, directly above the Masula Rift Valley with its mighty river flowing west to east and its deep, broad lake.

"Good work, Angelique", Roberta commended, before noting, "You'll be ready for your class five pilot's exam before your sixteenth birthday."

Angelique smiled until her Father, James, brought her back down to earth, "Your piloting skills are still too raw for my liking, Angelique. I'd prefer you to have more experience, more hours under your belt before you take the exam."

Angelique frowned, but she didn't argue. Her Father was usually right and he always had her best interests at heart. When it came to her training, her Aunt Roberta was all encouragement, the good cop, while her Father played the role of the bad cop, always bringing her back down to earth and keeping her well grounded.

"I was reading the latest reports on Secundus yesterday", Angelique remarked as she set the Dark Angel to autopilot and activated its dynamic positioning module.

Roberta watched Angelique's handiwork with approval as Angelique questioned, "The Indigenous Thols and the Carlins all live in the Masula Valley. Why is that?"

The Tholish Matriarch, Ytryan, trilled, clicked and barked, "The mountains box the valley in on three sides and they are exceedingly high. In the east, there are high cliffs and the Eastern Sea with its reefs and shoals. It is not so easy for the Carlin-folk or Thols to leave. At least, not now or so it appears."

Angelique picked up on that last part and queried, "At least not now?"

Ytryan trilled and clicked, "It was different in the past. All those millions of years ago, when my people lived here, we lived side by side with the Carlin-folk. We were technologically advanced and together we flew the local space lanes of this system."

"So, back then, you could just fly over the mountains", Angelique understood.

"Yes", Ytryan trilled in confirmation, adding with clicks and soft barks, "We even had transport tunnels under the mountains. Those connected us with the lands to the north, south and west."

Angelique nodded before asking, "Then what changed?"

"He came", Ytryan trilled softly, as if in fear of conjuring something truly awful, before continuing, "The evil Emperor Ahriman! He came at first like a whisper in the dark. A disembodied evil, infecting and possessing one mind after another. Taking hosts of ever higher rank. He always took Thols as hosts, something about our wings and our ability to fly."

"I'm not familiar with your people's history before their awakening after the Mimasian War", Angelique admitted.

"Few are, young woman, few are", Ytryan trilled and began to divulge the Mimasian Thol's history.

"We didn't see what was happening until it was far too late", Ytryan trilled and clicked, noting with sadness, "We could not stop it. He was too powerful. All we could do was hide our Matriarch Yarule, her Husband, Yanis, her younglings and the royal court in cryosleep pods, hoping that they could be awakened after the evil was dealt with. That did not work out as intended."

"Yeah", Angelique understood, "Your entire royal court ended up in our system."

Ytryan nodded, commenting with trills and clicks, "Before the coming of Ahriman, Homwol looked very much as you see it now. It was beautiful. Scores of millennia after his coming, the deserts in the southlands had expanded to cover that whole region. The northlands, once green and fertile, were turned into an over-exploited wasteland. The westlands became a polluted, fetid swamp. Homwol was dying. Its biosphere was collapsing. No Carlin or Thol lived outside of the valley at that point. Outside of the valley were all wastelands and only the Tarlaks could survive there."

"He made the Tarlaks, didn't he? The evil Emperor?", Angelique queried.

"Oh, yes", Ytryan confirmed, trilling and clicking, "The Tarlaks were once us. Ahriman bred them into existence, selecting for traits that he desired. When that was too slow, he resorted to genetic manipulation. He took his creations south of the mountain, into Tarlakan, southwest of the Shar wastelands. There, he perfected his creations and named them after that region. Tarlaks!"

Ytryan continued recounting the history of her people, "The outlands beyond the valley were long devoid of Carlin-folk and Thol before the biosphere began collapsing. Ahriman trained his Tarlaks by setting them loose and hunting down all Carlin-folk and Thols outside of the valley. He preferred us all to be contained. Boxed in and controlled. We were all of us, his Slaves!"

Ytryan pointed to a large island, a subcontinent, below the Shar wasteland and Tarlakan, "That Island is called the Isle of Sorrows. It was once a bustling hub of Carlinish civilisation. When Ahriman was finished, it was full of ruined towns and cities. He would ship Carlin-folk from the valley to the Isle of Sorrows to be hunted down by the hundreds and the thousands."

Ytryan pointed to another southern land to he east of the Shar wastelands, "Korland. In the tongue of the Tarlaks, it means Land of Corpses. It was said that you could not walk there without tripping over the bones of the dead. It was another Tarlak hunting ground."

Ytryan pointed to another southern land, to the west of the Shar wastelands, "Slaverland, literally the Land of the Slaves. That was where Ahriman kept his Carlin Slaves. His workforce."

Roberta chimed in, "All of the lands south of the mountains, except the Isle of Sorrows, are off limits. The Tarlaks still live there and to them, everything that is not Tarlak is prey, as in food."

Ytryan nodded, trilling and clicking, "Yes. All, except the Chittens. They fear the sapient insectoids."

"Why is the Isle of Sorrows the exception?", Wynessa asked telepathically.

Roberta replied simply, "There are no Tarlaks on that Island. It seems that they can't reach it."

Ytryan trilled and clicked, "The Tarlaks are big, yes, but they are also heavy. Even with their great wings and their hollow bones, they cannot fly across the Sorrowful Straits. It is simply too far for them."

Wynessa smiled and transmitted, *"So they cannot fly over the Southern mountains and they cannot fly across the Sorrowful Straits. They are just as boxed in as the Carlins and the Indigenous Thols."*

Angelique agreed, "That sounds like a very good thing to me."

Angelique enquired, "Matriarch, you said that the biosphere was collapsing. Is that the reason why the evil Emperor left?"

"Yes, young Angelique", Ytryan trilled in confirmation, "He could see that the world was dying around him, so he had my people build him a generation ship, Mimas, out of one of the smaller moons of our big gas giant. The Carlin-folk were used as workers. My people were used as the designers and the engineers."

Ytryan smiled as she trilled and clicked, "He did not know of my people sequestering our Matriarch, her family and the royal court, still sleeping in their cryopods within that generation ship, nor did he know of our histories being sequestered there as well. We hid them in the very places that he would never have thought to even look."

"Which was?", Angelique questioned.

"Embedded deep within the rock wall of his throne room, right behind his throne. Ahriman had two thrones, his main throne in Mimas's Southern Central Mountain, which is where the cryopods were hidden. His secondary throne was in Mimas's Northern Central Mountain, which is where our histories were hidden. That particular mountain was an emergency escape ship with its own ion drive."

"He only took his Tarlaks, didn't he?", Angelique questioned.

"Yes, young one. When the generation ship was completed, he had my people explain how to operate it to his higher Tarlak castes, his engineers. Then the remaining Carlin and Thols aboard were cast out into space", Ytryan trilled and clicked.

"Wow! He sounds so unpleasant!", Angelique exclaimed.

"*In the extreme*", Wynessa agreed, "*When Ahriman arrived in the Sol system, he straight away destroyed the Martian biosphere and enslaved the surviving Martians. There had been billions of us. When he was finished, we were less than a few million. My people were his Slaves for over ninety thousand years. I cannot imagine how long he enslaved the Carlins and the Thols. It must have been much longer.*"

"It was far, far longer", Ytryan trilled and then she smiled once more, trilling and clicking, "After his leaving, Homwol appears to have healed itself. The fool simply did not understand that it was his very presence that was killing the world."

"And a good thing too. The various Matriarchs back on Mimas, for centuries, had been really concerned that when Homwol was found, it would be a dead world devoid of all life", Roberta noted, adding as she pointed to the screen, "That is one beautiful planet."

Roberta brought up a closer image of Secundus on the screen and highlighted a section of the Masula Valley with a small laser pointer.

"The valley has this majestic river, the Masula River, flowing from west to east. It eventually flows into this fair-sized lake, the Masula Lake and then the outflow continues to the Eastern Sea. Everything is named Masula, the continent, the rift valley, the river and the lake, which will make things easy to remember", Roberta explained.

"Okay, now both sides of the river have rich, fertile soil, which is covered in vast bluegrass meadows. That is where the Carlins have their villages and their shared crop fields. Their main staple crop is called masuli grain and it's kind of like rice with a blue tinge to it. As an agrarian society, they do grow other food produce as well. Their villages are quite picturesque. Large plots with lots of dry stone walls and cobblestone paths, kind of like in northern England. Their houses are made of stone and timber with sod roofs", Roberta informed everyone.

"It sounds idyllic", Angelique noted.

"Except for the predators and they do have quite a few of those", her Father, James, interjected.

Roberta smiled and moved the pointer to the north, "The Indigenous Thols have their villages high up in the Jula Jula forests of both the southern and northern mountain ranges. They live in large tree nests with overarching canopies.

They don't have any villages in the western mountains; there are just too many predators in that region and it makes hunting and foraging woefully dangerous. The western mountains will be off limits to our colonists."

Ytryan smiled and then trilled, "That is where we will build our tree houses. In those northern Jula Jula forests amongst the Indigenous Thols."

"If our first contact all goes well, Matriarch Ytryan", James Reas reminded her.

"Okay, now in between those beautiful bluegrass meadows and those immensely tall Jula Jula trees in the northern forests, we have rolling hills running from the mountains to the Masula river. These hills are largely covered in bluegrass meadows, but there are a lot of forest stands scattered everywhere. The lowland forest stands grow larger and thicker towards the mountains and then they thin out and become smaller towards the river where the Carlin-folk live. They are made up of a different tree species from the mountain Jula Jula forests. Predators do live in those forests, dangerous predators", Roberta informed everyone.

Roberta highlighted a large, squat hill surrounded by bluegrass meadows midway between the Carlin villages and the Thol villages.

Roberta continued, "That is where we are building our first colony. The bluegrass meadows make it look like good land, but it isn't. The soil is shallow, acidic and of poor quality. The only thing that will grow there is the bluegrass and even that struggles. Underneath the shallow soil is solid basalt. It's not much good for anything other than building on. I doubt very much that the Carlins or Thols can use it."

Ytryan noted, trilling, "The basalt can be quarried for your buildings."

"That was the general idea, Ytryan", Roberta confirmed.

Ytryan smiled and added with a few trills and clicks, questioning, "How deep is that basalt?"

"It is deep, very, very deep", Roberta replied.

"If it is deep enough, you could grow Jula Jula trees there. They need very deep basalt for their roots. Their seeds dissolve the basalt and sink into it", Ytryan commented.

"Perhaps we might grow one or two to make the Indigenous Thols feel at home", Roberta replied, but noted, "That, however, will not be up to me. The colonists will make those decisions."

"What about our own agriculture, Aunt Roberta?", Angelique questioned, adding, "We can't have the colony dependent on imports from Cis-Luns space."

Her Father, James, chuckled, "I think we've got that covered, honey. We will definitely be planting our own crops."

"Yes, we do", Roberta agreed, noting, "There are lands to either side of our chosen site and to the south that are good crop lands. We will produce our own crops there and share the harvests with the Carlins and the Indigenous Thols. I'm sure that they'll find our foods as fascinating as we find theirs."

James stepped back in, "The main thing is that we complement the available food supply. We don't want to be competing with the locals. We want to augment the food supplies with more options."

Angelique nodded, "Well, that sounds smart. We all cooperate and everyone benefits."

"That is the general idea", Roberta agreed, before commenting, "Though we do have backup sites."

Ytryan trilled a quick query, "Backup sites?"

"Well, yes, of course, Ytryan", Roberta replied, explaining, "If our first contact does not go well, we will need backup sites. Of course, if it does go well, then the backup sites become future colonies once the main colony is fully developed."

"Where will the backup sites be?", Ytryan enquired with quick trills and clicks.

"Well, we can't use any of the lands south of the Southern Mountain range, or, for that matter, the lands beyond the Western Mountains. The Tarlaks down south are bad enough, but over in the west, in the Swamps of Larg, there are dangerous things over there we have yet to even classify", Roberta replied, commenting, "We've chosen uninhabited and abandoned lands."

"Which ones?", Angelique enquired.

"Well, there are those uninhabited volcanic islands, we're calling those the Antipodes Islands", Roberta noted, adding, "Then there are the lands to the northeast and northwest of the Northern Mountain range, which Ytryan will be interested in."

Ytryan nodded, trilling in reply, "There will be Jula Jula forests on the other side of the mountain range. My Indigenous cousins may want to join us when we open up those lands for colonisation."

"And, of course, there's the Isle of Sorrows. Uninhabited and abandoned. A whole sub-continent", Roberta reminded them.

Wynessa was curious and she wanted to be certain, "*So those lands have no sapient life at all?*"

"Well, not entirely, Wynessa", Roberta replied, qualifying her previous statement, "There are no Carlins, no Thols, no Tarlaks and no Chittens."

"Harricks", Ytryan trilled, noting, "There are Harricks everywhere. Except perhaps on those new, Antipodes Islands."

"*And they don't qualify as sapients?*", Wynessa transmitted, questioningly.

"They do, Wynessa", Roberta admitted, before requesting, "Ytryan?"

"Harricks are everywhere, Wynessa", Ytryan trilled and clicked, "They are sapient, yes, at least the males are, but they are uncontactable. They hide in the shadows and are very rarely seen."

Ytryan frowned and trilled, "I don't like to speak ill of sapient species, but the Harricks tend to live like Earth rodents. The ones that live and feed off Human detritus."

Angelique almost laughed, "You mean like rats?"

Ytryan shook her head, "They are sapients, but, yes, they live like Earth rats."

While they were talking, the proximity alert caught James Reas's attention: "Our first transport ship has arrived."

Roberta nodded and checked her ship's chronometer, "Right on time. Send them down to the colony site. Will join them later after we've let the locals know we're here."

James sent a message over the Dark Angel's communications, "Transport ship, proceed to colony site Alpha. Repeat. Transport ship, proceed to colony site Alpha."

"Acknowledged", the reply came back and they all watched the bridge's screen as the transport ship flew ahead of them towards Secundus.

Roberta picked up her data tablet and sent a detailed flight plan in a data file to Angelique.

"That's an odd flight plan, Aunt Roberta", Angelique enquired.

"It is", Roberta agreed, explaining, "You'll be piloting us just above the tree tops where the largest cluster of Indigenous Thol villages is. Then you'll be flying low over the Carlin villages in the lowlands of the valley. There is no way that they won't see us. After that, you'll fly to colony site Alpha, with our altitude gradually increasing so that the locals can see exactly where we are going."

Angelique nodded, "We'll be clearly visible. I recommend that we stay above the colony site until we're certain that they've seen us and are on their way."

"That is my intent, Angelique. Make sure they see us. They're both sapient peoples and they will be curious. They will come to us", Roberta explained.

Angelique began piloting the Dark Angel precisely as Roberta had instructed.

The Dark Angel followed the first transport ship from their fleet towards the surface of Secundus. They passed through the thick cloud layer towards the Masula Valley and their designated colony site to the north of the majestic Masula River. As they approached from the east, the rift valley opened up beneath them.

As they passed over the Eastern Sea and the Masula River estuary, the tall mountain ranges to the north and south became clearly visible. They were tall, enormously tall. Too tall and dangerous to climb, or for a Thol or Tarlak to fly over, nor were there any mountain passes. Ytryan, the Tholish Matriarch's, eyes flicked from north to south and back again, sheer joy and happiness on her face. This was her homeworld, her people's homeworld.

The Dark Angel continued flying in the transport's six, following it as they crossed the outflow from the Masula Lake and altered course slightly northwards. They crossed inland from the lake on its north bank. There were broad, bluegrass meadows far below them.

Gradually, small forest stands appeared in the bluegrass meadows as they flew further to the north. These forests of gnarled and twisted trees gradually grew larger and more numerous as the terrain below them turned into rolling hills.

Their destination was a broad, almost flat-topped hill. It was covered in the same bluegrass as the meadows they'd flown over, although these particular meadows appeared patchy and stunted.

Their transport ship landed in the centre of the hill, a perfect touchdown. Angelique piloted the Dark Angel in a broad circle around the hill. On its flanks were a combination of tree stands and bluegrass meadows. Both of which looked healthier than those on the hilltop.

High Admiral Roberta Nummus sent a quick command to the transport, "Transport Alpha Zero One. No one leaves the ship until after successful first contact. Repeat. Transport Alpha Zero One. No one leaves the ship until after successful first contact."

"Copy that, Dark Angel", the transport's Captain acknowledged.

Roberta turned to the others, "If our first contact goes badly, we'll move onto our secondary site."

"Which secondary site, Roberta Nummus?", Ytryan enquired with trills and clicks.

"Our secondary site is just northeast of here on the other side of the mountains, Ytryan", Roberta informed her, noting, "We'd still be close to the Indigenous Thols and Carlins, just not in the valley."

"Over in the Eastern Sea, we passed over some good-sized islands. Why not one of those? The one labelled as Big Rocky Island looked good", Angelique enquired.

"It was considered, Angelique, but rejected. The valleys on the other side of the mountains to the northeast are far larger and also closer to the Thol villages", Roberta answered before requesting, "Now, take us over those Thol villages. We need to let them know that we are here."

"Yes, Aunt Roberta", Angelique replied.

Angelique flew the Dark Angel to the north. The patchwork of bluegrass meadows and stands of forest started to change. There were fewer and fewer meadows and the number of forest stands grew until they were the predominant feature.

The stands of forest merged into one mass of tangled, gnarled trees that from above looked almost impenetrable. Roberta had pointed out on the view screen trails through the meadows that led into the forests. The Thols could fly over these forests; the Carlins could not. They had trails, probably hunting trails in the forests.

The terrain changed abruptly, becoming more mountainous and the forests quickly changed. The gnarled and twisted trees of the lowland forests disappeared and before them was a line of trees that made the mind boggle. These trees were tall, impossibly tall. The lines of trees faded into the distance to both the east and the west.

These were the Jula Jula forests that lined the mountain ranges. The three mountain ranges encircled the Masula Valley to the north, south, and west and these immense forests grew on their flanks, on both sides.

Ytryan's excitement grew; she trilled and clicked, her Tholish colloquialism taking over, "I alone of my people, am first to see these I trees am, in six thousand millennia and longer. These be the Jula Jula forests, old, dreamed of and oft told, but not seen, never seen, until now, this very moment."

"But you do have Jula Jula forests inside Mimas", Angelique questioned.

Ytryan smiled, trilled and clicked, "Young one, those trees are not the same as these behemoths. Jula Jula trees we call them, yes, but they are not the true Jula Jula trees that you see before you."

Wynessa chimed in telepathically in her usual Martian way, *"The Jula Jula trees inside Mimas are a lesser related species. Not the same as these. Some of these trees are over five hundred feet tall."*

"Yes", Ytryan trilled, noting, "The basalt here runs very deep indeed. The seeds sink deepest and the roots grow strongest, so the trees grow the tallest."

Angelique flew the Dark Angel up over the tops of the Jula Jula forests towards their designated target. Red dots appeared on the bridge's main screen. Each represented a Thol nest, each with its family of Indigenous Thols. The dots first appeared in small clusters.

They were Thol villages and then as they approached their target zone, the clusters of dots grew far more numerous until they were completely overlapping, with multiple layers.

A low spot in the trees appeared before them, although it was only about a hundred feet lower. It was easily a mile across, probably more. Below them were clusters of structures nested amongst the bows of the mighty Jula Jula forest trees. The structures overlapped significantly. The largest of them all was in the very centre.

Tears streamed down Ytryan's cheeks, "Behold, the Tholish High Council", she announced, trilling.

Roberta requested, "Computer. Life signs?"

The ship's computer replied, "Thols. Indigenous. Approximately fifty thousand within a two-kilometre radius. Would you like a more detailed scan and analysis, High Admiral Nummus?"

"Detailed scans to log, Computer. I'll read them later", Roberta instructed.

"Compliance", the Computer replied.

Instinctively, Angelique lowered the Dark Angel into the low spot within the forest. As she did so, everyone could see that the low spot was unnatural; it was carved out of the trees as a very large communal space. As they watched, they could see scores upon scores of indigenous Thols watching them. Many appeared scared. Many others appeared curious.

Some were more than brave, dangerously so, flying up to the Dark Angel for a closer look. One even shot an arrow at the Dark Angel and then, noting that it had no effect, flew back to a nearby tree. The Dark Angel hung there, hovering within the centre of the low spot, surrounded by frightened and curious Thols. The Indigenous Thols had never seen a spaceship before and had no idea what it was.

Ytryan spoke into the communicator; her voice was soft and gentle, yet loud enough to be clearly heard, echoing across the Tholish Capital. Ytryan spoke in perfect Indigenous Tholish.

"We come in peace. Be not afraid. We come with the open arms and the open wings of friendship", Ytryan trilled, clicked and softly barked, "Please follow us south to our meeting place, midway between this place and the Carlinish villages. We will await you there for our first meeting."

Ytryan repeated her message five times to make sure it was well heard and understood. Ytryan had spoken in the Indigenous Tholish tongue and Wynessa, the Martian hybrid, had translated it telepathically to those aboard the Dark Angel.

The Dark Angel hung there suspended above the Tholish Capital for several more long minutes.

"Angelique, good job. Now, please take us to the Carlinish villages, we have more locals to say hello to", Roberta instructed.

"Yes, Aunt Roberta. Locking in our course now", Angelique replied as she flew the Dark Angel away from the Tholish Capital and turned the ship south once more.

As the Dark Angel flew above the tops of the Jula Jula trees once more, Ytryan trilled and clicked softly to Roberta in almost a whisper.

"I have concerns, Roberta Nummus", Ytryan trilled and clicked, noting, "One of the Indigenous Thols shot an arrow at our ship. Weapons are very un-Tholish. It was never our way. Are these Native Thols warlike?"

Roberta sighed softly, "Not warlike, Ytryan. The Indigenous Thols hunt. They eat meat."

"No, Roberta Nummus. Thols are vegetarian. We do not eat meat", Ytryan protested.

Roberta placed her hand gently on Ytryan's shoulder, "Your people, the Mimasian Thols, are vegetarian. The Indigenous Thols here on Homwol are not. They are omnivorous."

Ytryan frowned. She had never heard of such a thing.

"What does this mean, Roberta Nummus?", Ytryan asked.

Wynessa chimed in and squeezed Ytryan's hand gently; she transmitted, *"It has been more than six thousand millennia, Matriarch Ytryan. Your cousins have changed. They live off the forest and what it provides them. It is the dictate of survival. They are not farmers, Ytryan, they are complex hunter-gatherers with a communal governance."*

Roberta added gently, "Ytryan, these are not the Thols your people once were. They have survived the collapse of Homwol's biosphere and its rebirth. They have evolved."

Angelique chuckled dryly, "The Thol that shot that arrow reminded me of Cupid in a funny sort of way. He looked so Angelic and yet he is a hunter."

The terrain beneath the Dark Angel changed from Jula Jula forest to lowland forest and eventually to blue grass meadows with scattered stands of lowland forest once more. As they flew over the colony site on its low flat hill, Roberta noticed some of the nearby forest stands were quite large; a few of them were five or six kilometres across. Roberta made some mental notes. All of those small forests had dangerous predators living in them. Her colonists would need to be cautious around them.

Before long, the small stands of lowland forests became sparse and then they finally gave way to the fertile plains of bluegrass meadows that lined the banks of the mighty Masula River. There were red dots displayed on the bridge's main screen. They all appeared in clusters, each cluster representing a Carlinish household plot, each cluster representing a Carlinish village. Instinctively, Angelique adjusted course slightly to what appeared to be the largest of the Carlinish villages.

As they approached the village, the first thing that they noticed was the large crop fields of masuli grain. The village was surrounded by the masuli grain fields on the north and south, with a broad dirt road leading up to the village on its east and west sides.

There was a wide area where the two roads met the village; they were covered in cobblestones. The two roads traversed the village from the outside to its very centre. At the centre of the village was a large open circular area covered in cobblestones, a village centre and smaller cobblestone paths radiated out into the village from that point. The cobblestones were a combination of basalt, blue stone and granite. Materials not found locally. They must have been quarried elsewhere and brought to the villages by some form of transport. That indicated a substantial local trading system.

The household plots were quite large, almost all the same size and they were all surrounded by neat, well-kept dry stone walls. Most of the entrances to the plots were from the radiating cobblestone paths. They were mostly accessed via a single stile, allowing one to simply step over the five-foot-high dry stone wall, although a few did have actual gates embedded in them.

Each household plot had a single house in the centre made of a combination of stone and timber. There was no one style. A few were sprawling single-level dwellings. Many were two-level dwellings and a handful were even trilevel dwellings. The one common theme was their roofs, which were all sod covered with a thick growth of bluegrass. Goat like animals grazed both in the plots themselves and on the dwelling roofs.

Ytryan informed the other with trills and clicks, "Those goat-like animals with the blue stripes and flesh tendrils on their chins. They're called Gudongs."

Angelique noted curiously, "They have four eyes."

Ytryan smiled, trilling and clicking in reply, "Many predators in the bluegrass meadows. Blue stripes to hide, four eyes to see and two sharp horns to defend. They provide the Carlins with meat, milk, cheese, and hides for both clothes and parchment."

The other common feature of the Carlin's household plots was the fruit trees. The houses were generally surrounded on three sides by very large fruit trees. Carlin children were playing on the ground around the houses and in the fruit trees themselves. The children all looked up at the Dark Angel in wonder. Some of them ran into their houses. The fronts of their houses had pastures of bluegrass, while at their rear were well-developed vegetable gardens and what looked like chicken coops.

Ytryan smiled, trilling and clicking, "The Carlin-folk have not changed. Those fruit trees are Chillic fruit trees and Bell Nut fruit trees. Those chicken coops are for Zrrakil, although they call them Thrixan. They provide the Carlins with both meat and eggs. So many kits. The Carlins always have so many kits. Too many to manage."

"They're children are called kits?", Angelique enquired as she completed her third circuit of the village before hovering above its centre.

"Yes, young one, they call their younglings kits", Ytryan confirmed.

Angelique smiled and noted, "I know that I shouldn't make comparisons, but they really do look like cats. Upright walking, hairless, sentient Cats. They are absolutely beautiful!"

"Yes, well, Angelique. You will be keeping that observation to yourself when we make first contact", Roberta noted and Angelique nodded in reply.

Ytryan felt saddened and a single sorrowful tear ran down her cheek, "The Carlins don't appear to have changed much at all. They were always largely hard-working agrarian people. My folk, the Thols of old, we were an industrious space-faring species. We helped them build their metropolises on the Isle of Sorrows. We even took the Carlins into space with us. And now, my cousins, once Thols of great technological innovations, are little more than hunters and gatherers. How far have they fallen? It is heartbreaking!"

Roberta put her left arm around Ytryan, "Cheer up. If our first contact goes well, over time, we'll uplift them. They can join us in the stars like the Thols of old."

Angelique stepped in, "It's not their fault, Matriarch Ytryan. When the biosphere collapsed, those best positioned to survive and maintain their lifestyles and traditions would have been the agrarian societies like the Carlins. Your people, being much more advanced, would have actually been at a severe disadvantage. The Carlins didn't have that far to fall. Your ancient kinfolk had much further to fall. This is the result."

Ytryan smiled at Angelique and trilled, "Yes, such wisdom from one so young", she stated.

Angelique adjusted the bridge's main screen to show a three-sixty panoramic view of the village two hundred feet beneath them. There were now several hundred people crowded into the village centre.

There were even more in the main roadway and radiating pathways. Others were out of their houses and in their yards. The ratio of Carlin kits to adults was extraordinary. All of them were staring up at the Dark Angel as she hovered above them.

Roberta turned to Ytryan and asked, "How good is your modern Carlinish?"

"About as good as my ancient Carlinish, considering that no Mimasian Thol has spoken to a Carlin in well over six thousand millennia", Ytryan trilled and clicked in reply.

Wynessa squeezed her hand and encouraged her telepathically, "*You're new to this, Matriarch Ytryan. You're the new matriarch to four hundred and fifty Mimasian Thols. You would not have been chosen if it were beyond you. You've studied both ancient and modern Carlinish, even Indigenous Tholish. You can do this.*"

Ytryan spoke into the communicator once more; her voice was soft and gentle. Below her in the village, it was loud enough to be clearly heard, echoing across the Carlinish village. Ytryan spoke in perfect modern Carlinish, although her trills, clicks and soft barks were still present and audible.

"We come in peace. Be not afraid, our sweet Carlin friends. We come with our open arms and the open wings of friendship", Ytryan trilled, clicked and softly barked, "Please follow us north to our meeting place, midway between this place and the Tholish villages. We will await you there for our first meeting."

As before, Ytryan repeated her message five times to make sure it was well and truly heard and understood. Ytryan had spoken in the modern-day Carlinish tongue and Wynessa, the Martian hybrid, had translated it telepathically to all those aboard the Dark Angel.

The Dark Angel hung there suspended above the Carlinish village for several more long minutes.

"Angelique. Please take us to our chosen colony site. Keep us high enough to make sure the Carlin-folk can easily see where we're going.", Roberta instructed.

"Yes, Aunt Roberta. Locking in our course now", Angelique replied as she flew the Dark Angel away from the Carlinish village, turning the ship north once more.

Angelique flew the Dark Angel back to their chosen colony site at an altitude that would make the ship clearly visible for scores of miles in all directions. Once they'd arrived at their destination, Angelique set the Dark Angel to hover directly above their transport ship.

"Aunt Roberta, we are now hovering above our designated colony site", Angelique announced, before commenting, "Awaiting further orders?"

Her Father, James, smiled, "You'll make an excellent pilot, Angelique."

"Actually, Father, I will make an excellent Special Operative", Angelique replied.

Roberta stepped in, "Angelique, we hover on station until we detect the approach of our guests. When they're all close enough that they can't miss us, then we'll land."

Angelique nodded and replied, "Hovering on station."

As the Dark Angel hovered, Matriarch Ytryan approached Angelique, "Your Aunt was right to recommend not referring to the Carlin-folk as cats or even resembling cats. It would upset them."

Angelique replied, "Yes. I will refrain from making any cat-like comparisons, Matriarch."

Ytryan nodded and added with trills and clicks, "You find them attractive, the Carlin-folk? You said they were absolutely beautiful?"

"I do, and yes, they are, Matriarch", Angelique confirmed.

"You might not want to express that to them. Especially not to their womenfolk", Ytryan advised.

"I can't compliment them on their beauty?", Angelique enquired.

Ytryan tilted her head slightly, "The Carlin-folk have certain biological imperatives."

"Biological imperatives?", Angelique queried.

"Assuming that they haven't changed", Ytryan trilled in reply, explaining,

"When the Carlins come of age, they usually bond with a member of their opposite gender. That bond is permanent and it drives them to procreate, which in most cases results in the birth of kits, seven months later."

"Okay, so what does that have to do with me?", Angelique asked in a very confused tone.

"Carlinish women, in order to have their pleasures and not have kits, will often sleep with other Carlinish women", Ytryan trilled and clicked in reply.

"Not a problem, Matriarch Ytryan. I'm a Human, remember", Angelique replied.

"That might not matter to a Carlinish woman. If you compliment her on her beauty and if she finds you just as attractive, you might find yourself in a very delicate situation", Ytryan trilled and clicked, with a huge smile on her face.

Angelique's eyes opened wide in shock. Her face went bright red.

Roberta leaned over Ytryan's shoulder and recommended with a smile and a small laugh, "No complimenting the Carlinish women, no matter how beautiful they may be."

The Dark Angel hovered above their colony site for three days before the Carlins and the Indigenous Thols arrived. Roberta thought they would have arrived sooner, but she saw their numbers and she understood why they'd taken so long. There were so many of them.

From the north flew thousands of Thols and from the south marched thousands of Carlins. The Thols carried finely crafted compound hunting bows. The Carlins carried a mix of hatchets, long bows, spears and short swords.

Roberta rubbed her forehead. This did not look good.

Roberta sent a message to their already landed transport ship, "Transport Alpha Zero One, place your ship under full lockdown. Repeat. Transport Alpha Zero One, place your ship under full lockdown."

"Copy that, Dark Angel", the transport's Captain acknowledged.

Special Operative, James Reas, commented, "It's not as bad as it looks, Admiral. By our standards, they're both primitive peoples behaving cautiously. You or I would do the same in their circumstances."

Roberta nodded and turned to Angelique and teased, "You're in luck, Angelique. I haven't seen any Carlinish women amongst our guests", which caused Angelique to blush.

Roberta then instructed, "Angelique, when our guests cross the two-mile mark, land the Dark Angel just ahead of our transport ship."

Roberta then whispered to James, "Full tactical body armour and weapons. Just in case."

The Dark Angel had touched down fifty metres east of the transport ship. The two spaceships were facing each other. Androids from the transport ship alighted and set up a triangular table in the central space between them. The table had seating for five along each side. One side faced the bow of the Dark Angel. The north side was for the Indigenous Thols, while the south side was for the Carlins.

Angelique had ordered a swarm of stealth surveillance drones released to observe the proceedings. They were military surveillance drones, unseen and armed, but with weapons designed to disable and not harm. They were armed with pulse stun guns and needle guns, their needles dosed with sleeping agents. The drone's onboard A.I. systems had been instructed to protect and serve in *"gentle"* mode.

Roberta was the first to step out of the Dark Angel. She wore full tactical body armour and carried her usual array of weapons. A kukri sword was fastened horizontally to her belt at her back and her Katana, the Harōingu, or the Harrowing, in English, was slung in its scabbard across her back. Roberta did not expect to use either. If push came to shove, she would rely on the pulse stun gun holstered at her right hip.

Special Operative James Reas stepped out next. He was wearing his own tactical body armour and carried the same weapons as Roberta, minus the Katana. Instead, on his left hip, he wore a long Sabre.

The beautiful Martian hybrid, Wynessa, stepped out next, her golden-toned skin almost glowing in the light of morning Sun, Cathol, which had risen to its ten o'clock position.

The lesser Sun, Cythol, was already way past zenith, adding its eerie orange light to the scene. Wynessa wore little more than a simple white tunic, as was the Martian way. Wynessa smiled fondly at Roberta, a smile that caught Roberta's eye.

Following Wynessa came the Mimasian Thol Matriarch, dressed in her official robes of resplendent white, cream and gold. The last to step out of the ship was Angelique Reas. She was dressed in simple jeans, with a shirt and jacket, nothing fancy. The Dark Angel's ventral portal closed automatically behind them.

The Indigenous Thols to the north dropped out of flight less than fifty metres away. The Carlins marching from the south stopped at about the same distance. Both sides looked at the two spaceships, especially the transport, which was by far the largest construct they had ever seen. Their gaze fell upon the five unusual figures standing between the smaller spaceship and the table.

Murmurs arose from both sides. From the north in native Tholish, while from the south in native Carlinish. The murmurs were not quite close enough for Ytryan's keen hearing to pick up cleanly and so she turned to Wynessa.

Wynessa let her mind reach out, spreading like ripples in a pond. She perceived the minds of the Thols and Carlins as golden orbs of thought and memory, all threaded and woven into consciousness.

Ever so slowly and gently, Wynessa skimmed the surface of their minds.

"They are confused. Very confused. They don't understand why a wealthy Thol stands amongst us sky people. The Carlins are using the term star walkers to describe the remainder of us. The Thols are using a slightly different term, star striders. They both use the term Mardhin. They find me particularly strange. They seem to think they've encountered Humans of Earth descent before, but not Martians. They've labelled me a Golden Mardhin!"

"Mardhin?", Matriarch Ytryan questioned, trilling and clicking, "It is not a word in ancient Tholish or Carlinish, not one that we've detected before in our studies of their modern tongues."

Roberta had a strange inkling, star walkers, star striders, the Mardhin.

Council of Shadows operatives, perhaps?

Could it be?

Had the Council of Shadow Operatives jaunted out this far with their psychic teleportation abilities?

How long ago had this happened?

Were they still here?

Roberta Nummus said nothing.

The Council of Shadows was a hidden, very occult branch of the Psi Corps.

Not even the Psi Corps knew of their existence. They had only appeared once in history at the time of the Great Reveal, which had led to the Decade of Confusion and then vanished once more as if they'd never been. They were a thing of myth and legend. Something Mothers told their children to keep them from being naughty. Roberta knew them well; her second Wife, Celestia, had been one of them.

Five of the Indigenous Thols to the north leapt into the air and quickly flew over, landing no more than thirty feet away. They were all male. Two carried hunting bows slung over their right shoulders, their quivers slung over their left. They stood on both sides of the three who appeared both unarmed and ornately dressed. Two of them carried what looked like staffs of office.

No sooner than that had happened, five Carlins ran across from the south. They ran on the pads of their feet. Like felines, their ankles were well above the ground. Digitigrade walkers with legs like coiled springs, they covered the intervening ground with incredible speed. Two of them were armed with a hatchet on their right hips and a short sword on the left. Three of them were unarmed and wore simply tunics, leggings and hooded cloaks made of soft leather.

Matriarch Ytryan trilled, clicked and softly barked in perfect Carlinish, a language both native species understood and could speak. Wynessa telepathically translated Carlinish to English, so that Roberta, James and Angelique could follow. The translation was almost seamless, a continuous stream of conscious thought. Martian telepathy at its finest.

"I am Ytryan, Matriarch of the Thols of Mimas. This is my companion, Wynessa of the Humans of Martian descent. These are my other companions, High Admiral Roberta Nummus, Special Operative James Reas and his Daughter Angelique Reas, Humans of Earth descent", Ytryan introduced them all.

As Ytryan made her introductions, Wynessa, Roberta, James and Angelique said hello to their guests.

The Indigenous Thols and Carlins all stepped back several steps as they heard the greetings.

The Indigenous Thol in the centre of his group spoke, trilling and clicking, "You speak like us with words, yes, yet you look like the Mardhin. Dressed differently, yes, but the Mardhin nonetheless!"

The Carlin in the centre of his group added in Carlinish, "The golden one speaks like the Mardhin with her mind, yet she is so different. She is not Mardhin at all!"

Wynessa continued to translate as Roberta raised her hands with her arms open wide, "We are not Mardhin. The Mardhin are star walkers, star striders. We use starships", she gestured to the transport ship and the Dark Angel, adding, "We three are Humans from Earth. Wynessa is a Martian Human from Mimas and Matriarch Ytryan is a Mimasian Thol, also from Mimas. We are not Mardhin."

"Not Mardhin", the Indigenous Thol leader mouthed.

"Not Mardhin", the leader of the Carlins agreed.

The Indigenous Thol leader introduced his group, "I am High Chancellor Yuntark of the Tholish High Council. To my left is Councillor Yindrarl and to my right is the Keeper of Ways, Yorsal. Our other companions are simple hunters. They protect us, just as your armed ones protect you."

Ytryan replied, trilling and clicking, "High Admiral Roberta Nummus is both our leader and our protector. However, she does not speak Carlinish or Tholish. As I speak all of the required languages, I speak instead. Wynessa and I will translate for them when they speak."

The Carlinish leader pulled back his hood and introduced himself, "I am Elder Kelyarn. On my left is my Wife, Keegali and on my right is my Daughter, Kitty."

Both Carlinish woman pulled back their hoods as Kelyarn introduced them. Angelique did her best to hold a straight face. The Daughter of the Carlinish Elder, a people who greatly resembled upright walking hairless sentient cats, was named Kitty.

Kelyarn noted, "Our companions are also hunters. We brought them along for the same reason."

Kitty noticed the amused look on Angelique's face; she tilted her head left and then right before smiling and remarking, "Your Daughter is very pretty, Special Operative James Reas."

Angelique blushed; she had been told not to compliment Carlinish women, yet no one had told the Carlinish women not to complement her.

At the request of Ytryan, their guests all took their seats. The Carlin and Thol hunters remained standing, so Roberta and James did the same. As everyone else sat down, Ytryan activated the table and a holographic globe of Secundus appeared above its centre.

Ytryan trilled and clicked while Wynessa translated telepathically, "This is Secundus, the world you call Homwol or Vale. Our own worlds are a very long way away in the distant stars."

The Indigenous Thols and Carlins stared at the image in wonder. They had never seen their world displayed in such a manner before. They found it both perplexing and enlightening, all at the same time.

"How did a Thol end up in the stars?", High Chancellor Yuntark enquired, trilling and clicking.

Ytryan frowned and replied with trills and clicks, "It is a long story. My people, the Mimasian Thols, left Homwol many millennia ago."

"How many millennia?", Yorsal, the Keeper of Ways, enquired with a quick trill and a click.

Ytryan answered, trilling, "More than six thousand millennia."

The Indigenous Thols and Carlins all looked shocked.

Yorsal, the Keeper of Ways, noted in reply, "Our own recorded history only goes back two millennia."

Ytryan smiled, trilled and clicked, "I did say it was a long time ago. It was back when the Tarlak Emperor ruled Homwol with an iron fist."

Kelyarn replied, "We all know of the Tarlaks. It was the Mardhin who helped us defeat them and drive them from our valley."

Yorsal, the Keeper of Ways, noted, with trills, clicks and soft barks, "That was eleven hundred years ago. The star striders came. They blocked the Tarlaks from entering our valley and then they helped us to eliminate those that were left, root and branch; we slaughtered them all."

Keegali stepped in, "Before the Mardhin, the Tarlaks raided our valley at will. Their favourite prey was the Thols. They would catch them and eat them."

Councillor Yindrarl smiled as he admitted, "We Thols were no match for them. Our Carlin friends came to our aid as best they could, but they could not fly and take on the Tarlaks in their own element."

Kitty noted, "Yes, we can run fast and jump high, but not fly, but we do have steel weapons."

Roberta stepped in and Ytryan translated, "The Tarlaks are still across the Southern Mountains in Tarlakan. They have no access to this valley."

All of the Indigenous Thols and Carlins nodded in understanding.

The High Chancellor commented, "When the Mardhin left, they said they'd keep watch over us and that one day, they would walk amongst us once more."

Kelyarn added, "It is said that they have a place in the Mardhin Plateau, high above the far Western Jula Jula forests, but none will dare to go there. The Chittens, the Sleimorps and the other forest denizens are far too dangerous."

Ytryan nodded as she moved the meeting along by pressing a button under the table. Two compartments opened. One in front of the Indigenous Thols and another in front of the Carlins. Each compartment contained two scrolls.

Ytryan trilled and clicked, "The reason for us coming here is on those scrolls. Please open them. Start with the one on the left."

Elder Kelyarn and High Chancellor Yuntark opened the recommended scrolls. They rolled them out and spread them across the table before them.

Ytryan trilled, clicked and barked softly, explaining, "This scroll contains an image of Homwol/Vale from far above the clouds", and then she gestured to the holographic image of the globe above the centre of the table, "When you project a globe into two dimensions, you get such maps."

Ytryan continued, "Homwol/Vale is different from most worlds. It only has one single huge continent, Masula, a smaller subcontinent, the Isle of Sorrows and a handful of islands. The Human homeworld, Earth, has seven continents spread across its surface. Other worlds have more, some less."

Wynessa chimed in telepathically, *"My homeworld, Mars, has a single land mass, mainly in the south and in the Northern Ocean, a single subcontinent, Elysium. However, Mars is a smaller world, with much smaller oceans and seas."*

Elder Kelyarn and High Chancellor Yuntark kept flicking their eyes from the holographic globe to the maps rolled out before them.

High Chancellor Yuntark noted with clicks and trills, "We know only of our Masula Valley."

Elder Kelyarn queried, "What are those islands, over to the west?"

Ytryan trilled and clicked, "Those are the Antipodes Islands on the other side of Homwol/Vale. They did not exist when my people were last here. They are relatively new. Please, open the next scrolls."

Both Elder Kelyarn and High Chancellor Yuntark rolled up the first scrolls and placed them back into the table's compartment. Then they took out the second scrolls, unrolled them and spread them across the table before them.

Ytryan explained with trills and clicks, "This is the same projection as the first, but it is not an image; it is topographical. You will notice the labelled lands, labelled in both Tholish and Carlinish. Those are the old names from times long forgotten."

Elder Kelyarn read the labels to the south, "We know the name Tarlakan."

High Chancellor Yuntark agreed, "Yes, the homeland of the Tarlaks!"

"Yes", Ytryan confirmed, trilling and clicking, "While your peoples have been confined to the Masula Valley, it appears that the Tarlaks have been confined to the four lands south of the Southern Mountain Range."

Yorsal, the Keeper of Ways, held his hands out wide, "Thanks be to the Mardhin for their aid."

The Elder's Daughter, Kitty, enquired, "What are those red dots?"

Ytryan replied, clicking and trilling, "Each red dot in the Jula Jula forests is the location of a Thol village. The more clustered the dots, the closer the villages. The red dots on either side of the Masula River are the Carlin villages. Those scattered dots to the southwest of the Shar Wastelands are the Tarlak villages in Tarlakan."

"And the golden star?", Kitty tapped the map, noting, "That is where we are."

Ytryan confirmed with a trill and short clicks, "Yes, that is where we are."

"And the silver stars", Kitty's Mother, Keegali, enquired.

"Those are safe locations for possible future villages", Ytryan informed them all, noting, "The Antipodes Islands are uninhabited and only have forests and plants. The other locations on the Masula Continent were long ago abandoned. No one lives there but the Harricks."

Angelique chimed in, as Ytryan translated, "My people and the Martians would like to build our own village here on this hill. With your permission, of course."

Roberta smiled, her Niece had brought up the main point of discussion, she added, while at the same time, Ytryan translated, "Assuming that you allow us to build our village here, later, perhaps in some years from now, we will build new villages outside of this valley. The lands those silver stars represent are good lands, good for Carlin, Thols and Humans alike. We can all share in those lands and any new villages."

Opening up new lands beyond the mountains, the Carlins and Thols had never dreamed of such a thing. Their eyes opened wide with all of the possibilities.

"This land you want is worthless. It has sad soil, not fit for planting", Elder Kelyarn commented.

Ytryan explained with trills and clicks, "That is why the Humans want it. Neither Carlin nor Thol can use it. Here, the Humans will build their village, their homes. For their crops, they will use the fields beyond this hill. Those fields are not perfect, but the Humans have ways to make them work."

Angelique stepped in, noting, "And when our crops are harvested, we will share the produce with both Carlin and Thol alike."

Once Ytryan had completed her translation, an excited Kitty commented, "We can trade our produce for yours. We can try your foods and you can try ours."

Elder Kelyarn agreed as he rolled up the scroll and placed it back into its compartment, "That will be mutually beneficial."

High Chancellor Yuntark rolled up the scroll and replaced it in its compartment as well.

Roberta announced as Ytryan translated, "The scrolls are yours. They are a gift. They are made of materials that will last for many centuries and even longer."

Kitty frowned and her Carlinish whiskers drooped, "Gift! No! We are not yet friends. We must barter", and she took a pouch from her belt and opened it onto the table.

There were many glass beads with holes drilled through them. There were polished semiprecious stones, also with a hole drilled through them. There were also diamonds; most were small, but some were larger.

Kitty explained in her Carlinish way, "The beads are worth one. The river stones are worth ten beads. The small, clear stones are worth ten river stones and the bigger shiny stones are worth twice that."

Kitty turned to her Father, "How much are those maps worth, Father?"

Elder Kelyarn thought for a moment and then replied, "Each map has a very high value and is easily worth one of those big stones."

Kitty pushed two of the larger diamonds across to Angelique and replaced the other barter bead and stones into her pouch.

Angelique reacted instantly and picked up the two diamonds. She reached out and took Kitty's right hand in her left before dropping the two diamonds back into Kitty's hand.

"No, no, Kitty", Angelique told her, "The maps are gifts! They do not require any payment. A gift is freely given to a friend and should be freely accepted by that friend."

Kitty placed her left hand over Angelique's right hand and replied, "As you are my friend, Angelique. I also give you a gift. Please accept my two stones as my gift to you."

Wynessa's telepathic translation made it clear that what had started from the Carlinish perspective as a barter was now elevated to a personal gift, friend to friend. Angelique had to accept the diamonds.

Angelique turned to Wynessa and thought, "*I must decline. I cannot accept such a valuable gift.*"

Wynessa shook her head, "*You have no choice in this matter, Angelique. You have made Kitty your friend and the maps are gifts of great value to the Carlins. If you say no, you will sever this new friendship. You will insult the Daughter of their village Elder."*

Angelique turned back to Kitty and replied, "Thank you", before placing the diamonds into her pocket.

Roberta whispered quietly to James, "They use a similar system to the sixteenth-century Europeans. Venetian glass beads actually had real value back then."

High Chancellor Yuntark noted dryly, "Every exchange with the Carlin-folk is transactional, even their gifts. First, it is trade barter, later it is reciprocal friendship gifts. The result is always the same. Always transactional."

Elder Kelyarn's reply was measured but harsh: "As opposed to yourself, who would receive gifts of immense value and yet, accept them without recompense as neither trade nor an exchange of gifts."

His Wife, Keegali, noted, "A barter in trade is balanced. Reciprocal gifts given freely by friends are also balanced. Would you have this world out of balance, High Chancellor?"

Their Daughter, Kitty, remained calm, gently holding her new friend's hand in hers. Angelique realised at that point that Kitty was not going to let go. Kitty even moved her chair a little closer to her.

High Chancellor Yuntark was severely embarrassed. He was right about the Carlins, but he was also wrong to accept the valuable maps without offering gifts of their own. His face turned from its white complexion to a shade of pink.

Turning to the Keeper of Ways, Yorsal, the High Chancellor enquired, "Keeper, did you bring any barter stones or gifts?"

Yorsal took his pouch from his tunic. He opened it and took out a single item. It was green and had been carved into a dodecahedron.

Twelve facets reflecting the twelve fingers of typical Tholish hands. Its facets were numbered in High Tholish, the Tholish Tongue that only the Keepers of the Ways used. It was made out of a rare green diamond.

Angelique's Father, James, looked at it with fascination, wondering how they managed to carve it. Yorsal passed the dodecahedron to Yuntark.

Yuntark then passed the dodecahedron to Ytryan, stating, "In friendship, I offer you this humble gift. It reflects our gratitude for the knowledge that your gifted maps provide us. They are truly invaluable."

Wynessa sent a telepathic caution to Ytryan, *"You must accept this gift. To refuse would be an insult of unimaginable proportions."*

Ytryan trilled and clicked in reply, "I humbly accept your gift, High Chancellor, although I suspect it outweighs the value of the maps by several orders of magnitude."

Yorsal chimed in, trilling, "No, Ytryan, Matriarch of the Mimasian Thols. Those maps are priceless to us."

Kitty noted in awe, "Those are rarely ever seen. They are worth ten times the large, clear stones. Twice that in some places."

High Chancellor Yuntark looked at Ytryan, "Matriarch Ytryan. You have stated that the Humans wish to build their village here. What about your Mimasian Thols? You have not mentioned where you wish to build your village, nor how many of you there are?"

Ytryan trilled, clicked and softly barked in reply, "There are four hundred and fifty of us, High Chancellor Yuntark. We are Thols, Mimasian Thols, yes, but Thols nonetheless. Our desired home is in the Jula Jula forests, in the tall trees. That is where we wish to build our villages. With your permission, of course."

The High Chancellor nodded, "You are Thols. Smaller than us, paler than us, but Thols nonetheless. You may build your nests amongst ours in our villages, or if you wish, build new villages. That choice will belong to your people."

Ytryan bowed slightly and trilled, "Thank you, High Chancellor Yuntark."

By this stage, Kitty had moved her chair right up next to Angelique's. She was still holding her hand.

"Your hands are just like ours. Four fingers and a thumb. Not so different at all", Kitty noted.

Kitty then began inspecting her hair and Angelique allowed her to do so, not wanting to upset her.

Kitty then leaned in very close and gently sniffed Angelique's neck. It was making Angelique very uncomfortable, but as this was their first contact, she allowed it.

Wynessa sent Angelique a telepathic message, "*It's a Carlinish thing. Their sense of smell is orders of magnitude more sensitive than ours. I could not even quantify it. Kitty is fascinated by you. She likes your scent, the way you smell. Kitty is becoming quite enamoured with you, Angelique.*"

Kitty leaned in even closer, her whiskers were raised and her tail was swaying rhythmically. Kitty's eyes closed and she nuzzled her face into Angelique's neck; she began to purr. Angelique allowed her to do so.

Eventually, Kitty stopped purring and looked up, smiling, "Mother, I like my new friend, Angelique. Can we invite her home? I wish to sleep with her."

Wynessa's translation stopped dead in its tracks. Wynessa and Angelique both looked at each other in shock.

High Chancellor Yuntark rolled his eyes, "Elder Kelyarn, must your Daughter display her promiscuity at this table. This is simply not appropriate. The Human girl is not even a Carlin."

Roberta quickly asked, "What's going on?", as Ytryan translated.

Elder Kelyarn replied matter-of-factly, "Your cross-species relationship taboos do not apply to us Carlin-folk, High Chancellor. As long as the couple are both consenting, there is no problem."

Keegali quickly chimed in and explained, "Among we Carlins, we have certain biological imperatives. Once a Carlinish woman reaches the age of the quickening, if she sleeps with a male Carlin too many times, they will bond with that male. The bond is for life and every time they are intimate, kits will follow seven months later, always. The quickening comes on between the ages of eighteen and twenty one."

James enquired, "And just how does that explain your Daughter's request?"

Keegali's whiskers drooped slightly as she explained further, "It is a dangerous time at Kitty's current age. To avoid premature bonding, young Carlin women will sleep with other Carlin women instead. Even after bonding, a Carlin woman will often choose to sleep with another Carlin woman to have her pleasure and avoid bringing forth kits. Amongst our people, it is a very common practice."

Kitty asked Angelique, curiously, "Do you not find me attractive, Angelique?"

Angelique was slow to answer, thinking carefully, she finally settled on, "Kitty, you are very beautiful, absolutely beautiful, but I am still far too young."

James chimed back in and clarified, "My Daughter won't reach our legal age of consent for another month. Until then, she can not consent to such a request."

Kitty smiled and questioned, "And after the age of consent, the choice is hers?"

James replied honestly, "Yes. That is what the age of consent means. It is a Human legal issue."

High Chancellor Yuntark questioned, trilling and clicking, "Surely your species does not allow cross-species relationships?"

Matriarch Ytryan replied, trilling, "We Mimasian Thols have no laws against it, but then again, there has never been a Mimasian cross-species relationship in our history. They just don't happen."

Wynessa's telepathic reply was somewhat different: "*We Martians have no experience with cross-species relationships. I myself am a hybrid of my Martian Mother and my Earth-descended Father. However, whether descended from Earth or from Mars, we are the same species, just different subspecies.*"

Roberta chimed in, noting, "I don't think we have any specific laws against sapient cross-species relationships. Our existing bestiality laws only forbid mating with lesser, non-sapient species. With consenting sapient cross-species mating, I don't actually know the answer. I would need to check with our legal advisers. It is something that we have never come across before."

James stepped back in, noting, "Even if it were legal and Angelique was over the age of consent, you also have to consider that in our culture, women sleeping with other women is not so prevalent. It does happen, yes, but it's not the norm. It's not as prevalent in Human society as it may be in Carlinish society."

Kitty's tail stopped swaying and her whiskers drooped. Her ears flattened and she lowered her head. Kitty looked completely deflated.

Angelique automatically wrapped her arms around her, holding her tight and stated, "You are still my friend, Kitty. Please don't be sad. I don't want you to be sad."

James Reas enquired, "I don't understand how a Carlin-Human tryst would even be considered."

Keegali simply replied, "Do you not find we Carlin-folk attractive?"

James replied, "Of course, we do. Both you and your Daughter are very beautiful, but that doesn't mean that we want to take that into cross-species intimacy. I don't think we'd even think of it."

Keegali nodded, replying, "We Carlin are driven by our senses, by scent. Our Kitty finds your Daughter's scent alluring and wants to experiment, wants to experience her intimately. For we Carlinish women, that is a very natural thing."

James also nodded, "Please understand, Keegali, we Humans may not respond in the way that you might think."

Kelyarn chuckled and commented, "Our sense of hearing is as strong as our sense of smell. Even now, I can hear my Wife's heart beating faster. She also finds your people, your scent, alluring. Both you and the High Admiral. To a Carlinish woman, your being a different species simply provides her with a free pass to intimate pleasures without the price of bringing forth kits. That in itself is quite alluring."

Keegali whispered to her Husband, before gently biting her lower lip, "Kelyarn, please, not now. You are embarrassing me", her blue stripes were becoming visibly iridescent.

Kelyarn laughed out loud, "Special Operative James Reas, even now, my Wife, Keegali, wants to grab you by your breeding pole and drag you off to her sleeping mat. This is quite normal for a Carlinish woman."

Keegali's blue stripes became even more iridescent; they even began to glow, a sign of deep embarrassment in Carlins, "Kelyarn!", she exclaimed, before turning her face away from the table.

James remarked, "Elder Kelyarn, with Humans, most married couples don't tend to stray from their partners. We tend to be monogamous."

Roberta decided at that point that they were getting sidetracked.

"These are unexpected developments and quite distracting, quite embarrassing in fact. Might I suggest that we get back down to our discussions?", Roberta informed them, noting, "And yes, Keegali, Carlinish women are very attractive; however, this is not the time or the place for that discussion."

The remainder of the meeting consisted of Ytryan explaining further ways that the Humans could help the Indigenous Thols and Carlins. Most of this involved things that neither species could have considered. They were completely unknown unknowns.

The Indigenous Thols usually only had one or two younglings at most. The Mimasian Thols had also had that same problem. Fertility issues. The Humans had developed Thol-specific fertility drugs to help with their fertility issues. Those would become available to the Indigenous Thols.

The Carlins had the opposite problem. They had too many kits being born in too many litters. This was biologically exhausting to the Carlin women, who died younger than they should have as a result. Humans could develop contraceptives to help Carlin women better manage their extreme fertility.

Then there were other advanced medical treatments. Humans could provide the Thols and Carlins with antibiotics, vaccinations and far better healthcare. Injuries would no longer lead to death through infection. Diseases would no longer kill. Human bone-knitters could heal broken bones. This was incredibly important for the Indigenous Thols.

Those Thols who had broken wings in the past could never fly again and would usually wither away and die within a year or two. There was no safety for them on the forest floor and once carried to their nests, they could never leave. The ability to heal broken wings was something that the High Chancellor really wanted.

As the meeting drew to a close, the Indigenous Thols and Carlins could see the benefits of having a Human village, with Human technology and medical assistance close by. They all agreed to the Humans' new colony and even offered to help build it. Ytryan had to explain the concept of Android workers, "*Metal Men*", machines that would do most of the work. Both Indigenous Thols and Carlins alike were also interested in joining the Humans in the future when they would create new villages beyond the valley.

When the meeting was finally over, Roberta gave them more gifts. A box of various Earth seed packets and instructions for the Carlins to experiment with. A box of various Earth fungal spores, mushroom packets with instructions for the Indigenous Thols to experiment with. The augmentation of Indigenous food supplies had begun even before the new colony had broken ground.

Once the Indigenous Thols had left, flying north once more, to their forest villages, Kitty confided in Angelique. It was a little-known secret that the Indigenous Thols were not to hear. Wynessa provided the telepathic translation.

"Their High Chancellor is not so smart", Kitty said, confiding, "When the Thols come to our village to trade. They usually trade at the village centre. Our people set up stands of produce and trade wares. The Thols bring in their goods with them by wing."

Kitty whispered, "Sometimes a Carlin woman will say to a Tholish woman, *'I have more goods at my house.'* Then they will both go to the woman's house and go inside. They will be there for a long time and when they come back out, the Tholish woman will have a new trinket, and the Carlin woman will have a new bracelet of barter beads."

Angelique smiled, understanding what Kitty was saying. Wynessa's face took on the rose gold hues of Martian embarrassment.

Kitty finished her story by stating quite clearly, "They weren't trading. They spent most of their time on a sleeping mat together. It was an arrangement. It happens more often than you might think."

Angelique and Kitty both laughed while Wynessa just shook her head. So much for Indigenous Tholish taboos against interspecies relationships.

When it was time for the Carlins to leave, Kitty had trouble letting go of Angelique's hand.

"I really like your scent, Angelique. Are you sure that you can't come to my house with me?", Kitty enquired.

"I'm not of age yet, Kitty", Angelique shook her head, "My Father would not allow it."

"Perhaps when you're older? When you are of age?", Kitty suggested, her voice full of hope.

"Perhaps, Kitty, but even then, I'm not sure. We are different species", Angelique reminded her.

Wynessa stopped translating and noted, *"You'll likely be off-world anyway, up at Cis-Luns L-Five."*

Angelique nodded, "Yes. More than likely. I may not be back until the colony is ready."

Kitty frowned, her whiskers drooped and then she smiled, "When you come back, you can find my place. In the village, our house is next to the village centre. It is the only house that has four levels."

Angelique smiled and replied, "Well, that should make it easy to find, at least."

Kitty took off her hooded Gudong leather jacket and handed it to Angelique, "A gift of love. No need to reciprocate. When you wear it, you will think of me."

Angelique accepted the jacket, but asked, "Won't you be cold, Kitty?"

Kitty grinned a wide, almost Cheshire cat wide smile, "I have another one in my pack at our camp."

Kitty wrapped her arms around Angelique and then leaned in and kissed her. Angelique hesitated at first, but then returned the kiss. After the kiss was over, Kitty ran back to her parents, her eyes welling with tears. Kitty was going to miss her new friend.

A single tear ran down Wynessa's cheek, *"Was that your first kiss, Angelique?"*, she transmitted as she wiped it away.

Angelique nodded and confirmed, smiling, "Yes. That was my first kiss", before she noted with curiosity, "Carlin tongues are cat-like. They're kind of bristly."

Wynessa smiled and laughed a small telepathic laugh.

7. The Colony.

Six weeks had passed and Kitty had not heard from Angelique. Each day, she went to the fourth-level sleep room of their home in their Carlin village and watched the skies keenly, hoping to see a Human spaceship.

Angelique's Father, James, had stated that Angelique would reach the age of consent in a month. It had now been two weeks past that time and Kitty was becoming anxious, sadder and more deflated by the day. Kitty's sadness was becoming visible for all to see; her blue stripes becoming paler by the day.

Her tail rarely swayed, her ears rarely raised and her whiskers were always drooping. The blue stripes on her face had taken on a dull, almost ashen grey pallor. Something that only occurred in Carlins when a great sadness had crept in.

Kitty was at the age where she was approaching the Carlin quickening, but also suffering from a great sadness, which could bring on the quickening prematurely. Keegali was concerned and she voiced those concerns.

"Kelyarn, we are going to the Human village", Keegali announced.

"Keegali, the Human village is two days north", Kelyarn protested, "Who will plant our vegetables?"

"Our older kits will plant them. Look at our Daughter, Kelyarn. She pines for Angelique, her Human friend. We must take her to the Human village", Keegali insisted.

As Keegali gestured towards Kitty, Kelyarn looked up from their garden at his Daughter. Kitty was sitting on a garden bench, he tail hanging motionless, her legs drawn up to her chest with her arms wrapped around them.

Kitty sat there, staring forlornly skywards to the north, scanning the horizon for any sign of an approaching Human spaceship. Kelyarn tilted his head to the side; even the blue stripes on Kitty's arms and legs had begun to turn exceedingly dull.

Kelyarn stopped turning over the soil and dropped his broadfork, "Keegali, tell our boys to take over from me. Tell the girls to look after our younger kits. We are going north to the Human village."

That was that, and by mid-morning, their packs were set, and their provisions readied. By midday, they were on their way. Kelyarn's belt had a hatchet slung on his left hip, a short sword on his right hip. He carried a spear with a sharp steel point, as both a hiking aid and for defence. Keegali and Kitty carried the same. The Human village was two days north and predators were abundant along the trails.

By mid-afternoon, Kitty had completely changed. The pallor in her blue stripes had begun to recede and her more usual blue colouration was reasserting itself. Kitty was excited and began to skip ahead, then running back on the pads of her feet, when her parents maintained their pace.

"Pace yourself, Kitty. It's a two-day hike and you don't want to tire yourself out or suffer leg cramps", Keegali advised her.

"Wise words, Keegali", Kelyarn agreed and he looked up at his Daughter, "Kitty, stay close. This trail can be dangerous. There are Kyrrax and wild Vort packs everywhere in the bluegrass meadows."

By the late afternoon, they'd reached their first campsite. Carlin hunters used the trails and they burned the bluegrass meadows back regularly to make it difficult for predators to approach unseen.

In the places where the bluegrass had been burned back the farthest, that was where Carlin folk prepared their camps. Those were the places where a predator would have to cover the maximum amount of open ground. They were safest.

Kelyarn set up their tent while Keegali built a small campfire. Their fare for the evening meal was jerked Gudong meat, rations, yes, but more than adequate. As Kitty and Keegali slept during the night, huddled together against the night's cold air, Kelyarn kept a careful watch.

Vale's yellow Sun Cathol had already set, but its lesser, orange Sun, Cythol, was still high above the horizon, with its eerie, distant glow. Vale's large moon, Luns, was full, adding its reflected silver light to the night.

Kelyarn smiled; it was a bright night and the predators were unlikely to approach. Just after midnight, Keegali awoke and took Kelyarn's place for the remainder of the night's watch.

Although it was a two-day hike to the Human village site, Kelyarn and Keegali had kept up a brisk pace. Their Carlinish legs, with their digitigrade gait, worked like coiled springs, covering the distance quickly. A distance that should have taken a two-day march, they covered in a day and a half. Humans had evolved as endurance predators; similarly, so had the Carlins. The Carlins had evolved on Vale as both endurance and ambush predators.

By the evening of the next day, they were on the outskirts of the Human village site. The Carlin hunter's trail continued further to the north, towards the dense forests and their branching hunting trails. Another, newer trail, only six weeks old, led up the low hill to their right. That was the broad hilltop where the Humans were building their village.

Keegali and Kelyarn set up camp for their second night on the trail. On the morrow morning, they would follow the trail up the hill to the Human village site.

The surrounding area was surprisingly quiet and it didn't take them long to understand why. Now and then, a Human spaceship could be seen rising into the sky and disappearing beyond the nighttime clouds. They were transport ships and they were very large. The following morning, when they awoke, they saw more

Human spaceships, only these were arriving.

They descended slowly and gently through the cloud layers as they approached the colony site on the hilltop. With their tent packed up and their campsite cleaned, the three travellers hiked up the trail to the hilltop. It was an easy task for Carlins, who walked on the pads of their feet.

Kitty was the first to reach the top of the hill, her youthful exuberance and young Carlinish legs propelling her forward with ease. When she reached the top of the hill, she stopped and stared in both surprise and disbelief. When her parents caught up to her, they, too, were surprised by what they saw.

Gone were the sick bluegrass meadows on the hilltop that grew poorly in the sad soil. The meadows were gone, the sad soil was gone. Before them, the hilltop had been cleared back to the bare basalt rock and the basalt itself had been levelled, scraped flat as if by a giant iron chisel in the hands of a God.

Across the hilltop, which was quite vast, they saw machinery and skeletal structures of Human buildings. Shiny metal men were working diligently and Human spaceships were offloading materials.

The entire hilltop was in the process of a transformation, an extreme transformation. As they stood there, a small Human vehicle approached them. They didn't know it then, but it was called a hover jeep and it moved far faster than a Carlin hunter could run.

When the hover jeep stopped thirty feet away from them, a Human stepped out of it. It was a Martian Human, a man with golden-hued skin, emerald green eyes and golden-yellow hair.

He was as tall as any Carlin, perhaps an inch or so taller. He wore an odd device, wrapped around his left forearm. His mind greeted them with both telepathic words and a broad telepathic smile.

"Greetings, Elder Kelyarn, Keegali and Kitty of the Carlin-folk. I am Wingtarla of the Martians of Mimas", he announced as he approached them.

"You know our names?", Kelyarn enquired.

"Yes, we Martians share our memories and experiences", Wingtarla confirmed, adding, *"I detected your approach last night when you set up camp during my evening meditations."*

Kitty smiled at seeing a Martian for the first time since first contact and asked, "Are you a hybrid like Wynessa?"

Wingtarla smiled warmly, transmitting in reply, *"Yes. There are no full blood Martians amongst the colonists and only eight hybrids. I'm the site foreman for the colony construction. I manage this site."*

Wingtarla turned to Kelyarn, *"So, what brings you here to our colony site, Elder Kelyarn?"*

Keegali's answer was quick and urgent, "Our Daughter, Kitty, has been greatly saddened of late. She wishes to see her new Human friend, Angelique Reas."

"Angelique Reas?", Wingtarla queried rhetorically, noting, *"The Reas family is off-world on the lead colony push ship, the Artemisia. James Reas works very closely with the High Admiral. His duties keep him quite busy, I expect."*

"Has Angelique reached the age of consent?", Kitty asked urgently, her longing driving her questions, "When can I see her?"

Wingtarla touched the device on his left forearm. A holographic screen and keyboard appeared.

"This is how I communicate with our machines", Wingtarla informed them, explaining, *"It's called a 'grip'. As a Martian hybrid, I am fully non-verbal, so I need this device to control the site and access our network databases."*

There was a slight pause before Wingtarla announced, "I have just checked our colonial records. Angelique Reas turned sixteen two weeks ago. So, yes, she has reached the age of consent. However, she is still a minor until she turns eighteen. Until then, she cannot travel alone."

Kitty heard the confirmation of Angelique reaching the age of consent and her heart lifted, only to be broken once more upon hearing that she was still a minor and could not travel independently.

Wingtarla picked up on Kitty's emotional distress automatically, *"May I approach?"*, he enquired.

Keegali was also quite aware of Kitty's emotional distress and replied, "Please do, Wingtarla."

Wingtarla approached Kitty and lightly placed two fingers of his right hand on her left temple.

After a dozen seconds, Wingtarla withdrew his hand, *"I see. You have developed quite an emotional bond with young Angelique Reas, which is interfering with your natural progression to your quickening. Young love can be quite disruptive emotionally."*

Keegali confirmed, "Yes. My Daughter has a yearning for Angelique Reas. A yearning that can only be alleviated by a direct connection. Kitty needs to see Angelique Reas urgently."

Wingtarla nodded in understanding, *"Please, accompany me to my hover jeep. We'll go to my transport ship and I will see what we can arrange."*

Wingtarla sat in the driver's side of his hover jeep while Kitty and her parents sat in the back seat holding their packs and other equipment. It didn't take long to approach the transport ship and when they did so, the port side internal docking bay doors opened wide. Wingtarla drove his hover jeep straight into the docking bay.

The internal docking bay was huge and full of construction equipment, none of which the three Carlins could comprehend.

Wide-eyed with amazement, Wingtarla led Kelyarn and his family through the transport ship's corridors to the bridge.

Once inside the bridge, Wingtarla requested that they sit down on the available seating, while he switched on the bridge's main screen.

"I do apologise for our chairs not accommodating your Carlinish tails, but our bridge was designed for Human crew members", Wingtarla commented, adding, *"Please make yourselves as comfortable as you can, while I bring up some data on the* screen."

An image appeared on the screen depicting the Secundus/Luns system with its Lagrangian points.

Wingtarla explained, *"On the left, that's your world, Vale. On the right, that's your moon, Luns. Those red dots joined by the yellow lines are called Lagrangian points. The one labelled L-Three on the opposite side of Vale from Luns is unstable. We can't really use it. The others, though, are very useful."*

"I'm not sure I understand?", Kelyarn responded.

Wingtarla nodded, *"I'm hoping it will make sense in a few minutes, Kelyarn. Please bear with me. The other two spots on either side of Luns, labelled L-One on the near side and L-Two on the far side, are gravitationally stable points. We can use those in the future. The other two, forming the vertices of those two triangles labelled L-Four and L-Five, are highly stable gravitational points. They are the gravitational sweet spots, so to speak; we will be using those two first."*

Keegali was having trouble following, "Gravitational sweet spots?", she queried.

"Gravity is the force that holds everything to the surface of a world, Keegali", Wingtarla explained, noting, *"Lagrangian points are the points where gravitational forces cancel out. In this case, the gravitational forces of Vale and Luns. Some of those points are more useful than others. Points L-Four and L-Five are the most useful; they're the sweet spots."*

All three Carlins nodded in limited understanding; much of what Wingtarla had said went straight over their heads. This was all new to them and the Carlin-folk had no knowledge of physics.

Wingtarla pointed to the L-Four point, *"That is where we place our ore processing and manufacturing stations"*, and then he pointed to L-Five, *"That is the place where we will be building most of our off-world colonies."*

It suddenly dawned on Kelyarn, "That's where you'll build your off-world villages."

"Yes! Precisely, Kelyarn", Wingtarla confirmed.

Wingtarla instructed the transport ship's computer via his grip, his instructions appearing on the lower portion of the bridge's screen.

"Computer. Image on screen. Lock onto Cis-Luns L-Five depiction. Link the screen display to the appropriate Secundun satellite for optimal visual feed displaying Cis-Luns L-Five. Zoom in on the L-Five region slowly over a sixty-second interval. Display the colonial push ships and the developing mega colony, Colonial Central Command."

The L-Five depiction on the screen spawned a new window and slowly over the course of a minute, the current infrastructure within the L-Five region came into view. Slowly, each object grew in size until the window showed the objects clearly. There were a lot of smaller objects flying around the larger objects on display. Too many to count. The entire region was a hive of activity.

Wingtarla pointed to a group of a dozen large ships on the right-hand side of the screen, "*Those are our twelve interstellar push ships. That is how we came here from our home solar system.*"

"They look so big", Kelyarn noted, before asking, "Just how big are they exactly?"

Wingtarla replied, "*They're a kilometre and a half in length*", before he pointed to the left-hand side of the screen, "*That large construction, when it's completed in five years, will be our main off-world colony. The mega-colony, Cis-Luns Colonial Central Command. It will be our largest off-world village, so to speak.*"

Keegali stood up and approached the screen, "Your interstellar push ships, they are much longer than our village is broad", before looking more closely at the colony under construction, "That thing dwarfs them. How big is your main off-world colony going to be?"

"*Keegali, that's a standard mega-colony. When it's complete, it will be twenty four kilometres long and four kilometres wide*", Wingtarla replied, smiling with pride; something a pure Martian would not do.

Keegali mouthed the words, "Twenty four kilometres long and four kilometres wide", and she felt her legs grow weak as the sheer size of Human-scale construction sank in.

Kelyarn stood up and quickly braced his Wife before her knees could give way.

He then helped her back to her seat, noting, "The sheer scale of that thing is daunting."

Wingtarla smiled and informed them, "*Over the next half century, the Humans will uplift your people technologically. There will come a time in the future where this will seem as normal to your people as a simple Sunrise or a Sunset, Kelyarn.*"

Kelyarn, Keegali and Kitty all stared at the screen in disbelief.

Wingtarla keys some more instructions into his grip, "Computer. Lock in on the Artemisia. Gradually zoom in and display on the screen. Separate window."

As Kelyarn's family watched the screen, another window popped up and slowly the colonial push ship Artemisia came into view.

"*That is where Angelique Reas and her family are currently living*", Wingtarla informed them.

"Can we go there?", Kitty quickly enquired.

Wingtarla replied with a telepathic smile, "*I was just about to explain that to you, Kitty. Our transport ships land in the morning and then in the evening, they fly back to Cis-Luns L-Five. I can arrange passage for your family to go to the interstellar push ship Artemisia, where the Reas family currently is.*"

Kitty smiled, her tail began swaying and her whiskers raised as she turned to Keegali, "Can we go there, Mother? Please, can we go there? I must see my friend, Kitty!"

Wingtarla checked the currently landed transport ships, "*The first available transport is offloading plasteel girders, I-beams, lengths of box beams and C-Box beams. If all goes to schedule, they'll be ready to return to Cis-Luns L-Five well before dusk.*"

Keegali enquired, "Just how far is Cis-Luns L-Five?"

Wingtarla replied, noting, "*Cis-Luns L-Five is as far away as Luns, just in a different direction. It's about four hundred and twenty thousand kilometres.*"

"I don't know, Kitty. That is such a very long way from here", Keegali told her Daughter.

Wingtarla saw the sad look appearing on Kitty's face and quickly noted, "*The transport ship will take you there in six hours. It is not a problem. I can arrange it.*"

Kelyarn was carefully studying the images on the screen, "We will go there. Six hours is not long and we do need to learn more about the Humans", he decided.

Wingtarla switched off the screen and told his guests, "*Now that we have that decided, let's go and get an early lunch, after which, I'll show you around the colony construction site.*"

On the way to the mess hall, they met with another Martian man, an engineer named Wootan. There was a short, silent, telepathic exchange and then they continued.

Wingtarla informed them, "*I've asked Wootan to make the arrangements for your transport to the Artemisia and to notify Special Operative James Reas and his Wife, Simone, roughly what time to expect your arrival.*"

Once at the transport ship's mess hall, they all sat down at a table and Wingtarla passed them menus of the available meals before remembering that the Carlins could not read English.

Wingtarla shook his head, "*Sorry, guys. My mistake. If you like spicy food, they do have a spicy Goat curry today, a Goat Madrasa, or if you prefer a vegetarian meal, they also have a mushroom version which is equally spicy.*"

"What is a Goat?", Kelyarn enquired.

Wingtarla tapped a few keys on his grip's holographic keyboard and a hologram of a Goat appeared in full colour, "*That is a Goat. I believe that they are very similar to your Gudongs.*"

Keegali looked at the hologram, "It looks like a Gudong, but it only has two eyes. A Gudong has four."

Kitty chuckled, "Gudong's don't have any hair either. Most certainly not on their chins. They have flesh tendrils and their skin has blue stripes."

Kelyarn looked at the hologram, "If it looks like a Gudong, it might taste like a Gudong and spicy is always good. We Carlins do love spicy food."

Wingtarla sent a telepathic message to the transport ship's cook ordering three portions of Goat curry and one portion of mushroom curry, "*Three Goat curries it is then. I'm a vegetarian, so I'll be having the mushroom curry*", he informed them.

Kitty and her parents were very surprised to find that Goats tasted similar to Gudongs, similar but not the same. They washed the Goat curry down with Goat's milk, while Wingtarla had green tea. Kitty noted that Goat's milk tasted similar to Gudong milk, but lacked its sweetness.

After their lunch, Wingtarla showed Kelyarn's family around the colony construction site. He explained to them that most of the work is performed by their Androids, their metal men. Driving them around the site in his hover jeep, Wingtarla parked in a more central position on the vast hilltop.

Wingtarla pointed to a series of buildings to the south, their frameworks of plasteel showing their early construction, "*Over that way, we are building housing apartments for the colonists.*"

Wingtarla then pointed to the east, "*In that direction, we are building the colonies' school. It's going to be made of stone, largely blue stone, basalt and moncrete, and built in what the Humans call the Gothic style of architecture.*"

The school buildings were also starting to take shape.

"School?", Kitty enquired.

"*That's where children go to learn, to study. Usually from the ages of five to eighteen, although they may go on into further, more advanced studies for an extra three to eight years*", he explained.

Pointing over to the west, where more plasteel frameworks were appearing, Wingtarla noted, "*Our airport, spaceport and warehouses will be over in that direction.*"

"*Over to our north will be our business district. That's where all of the shops will be, along with other businesses and other places of trade*", Wingtarla informed them.

Everywhere they looked, there were signs of construction. Construction machines and metal men were working everywhere, supervised by what looked like fewer than twenty or perhaps twenty five Humans. The whole process was proceeding at an incredibly rapid pace.

Keegali noted, "We Carlins don't have schools. Our kits are taught at home, more or less. We, Mothers, teach our Daughters and Fathers teach their Sons."

Kelyarn added, "Any specialised skill sets that we have are family-based and are all taught in the same way. Mother to Daughter, Father to Son. Iron working, timber and stone cutting are good examples, as are hunting, fishing, boat crafting, wheelwrighting and barrel making."

Wingtarla tapped the side of his hover jeep several times and then pointed to his transport ship in the distance to the west, "*Our technology is somewhat more complicated. No one person can know it all and to learn it can sometimes take many years.*"

"Can we learn these things?", Kitty enquired.

"*There is no reason why not, young Kitty. Carlins and Thols are just as clever as Humans, Martians or Mimasian Thols for that matter*", Wingtarla stated, noting, "*The only difference is that you haven't been exposed to our teaching and training methods yet.*"

Kelyarn replied thoughtfully, "That is something that we can discuss with your High Admiral. Human schooling may be useful."

Kitty looked down at her feet, then asked, "You've told us what will be in each direction, but what will be built here in the centre?"

Wingtarla smiled and replied, "*This is where the colony's governing council will be. A splendid, modern building of plasteel, basalt blocks, moncrete and crystal aluminium. It will be surrounded by parks and gardens, as well as recreational buildings, such as an aquatic centre.*"

Keegali looked around at the mayhem of construction and noted, "None of this was here six weeks ago. Just sick bluegrass growing in sad soil over blue stone. Your people move so fast. How long will it take to finish your village?", she asked.

Wingtarla smiled telepathically, again showing a hint of his hybrid pride, "*In three more months, it will be mostly completed. They'll be finishing off and landscaping in the final month and a half. Six months after breaking ground, it will be ready for the Human colonists to move in.*"

"Landscaping?", Kitty enquired.

"*Yes, Kitty. That is when they will be planting grasses, shrubs and trees*", Wingtarla replied, adding, "*The space between the four corners and the centre will be parklands. It will be quite beautiful.*"

"I can't see it, at least not yet", Kelyarn commented.

"*If you come back in four and a half months, you will be pleasantly surprised*", Wingtarla suggested.

Kelyarn became curious, "Where will you get your water from? This hilltop is all blue stone; you cannot possibly dig wells here."

"*Jump in my hover car and I will show you our water cistern*", Wingtarla requested.

Wingtarla drove them past the school's building site towards the far eastern side of the school. He stopped the hover car close to an enclosed area where metal men were working diligently. There was a conveyor belt carrying large, equally sized blue stone blocks from the site to another location.

Looking towards the other end of the conveyor belt, in the distance towards the west, was the school site. More metal men were unloading the conveyor belt and stacking the blue stone into neatly aligned rows for future use.

"Blue stone basalt blocks for our school", Wingtarla noted as he led them over to the enclosed area.

Kelyarn and his family watched as the blue stone blocks whizzed by; they were all uniformly cut. The conveyor moved the blocks with efficiency and precision. Wingtarla opened the door to the enclosed space.

A metal man approached them, "Danger! Danger! Please keep away from the cistern pit!", it cautioned in perfect Carlinish.

The three Carlin's eyes all opened wide when they heard it speak. They didn't know that the metal men could speak. It was somewhat of a shock to them.

"Yes, that is good advice. Do not get too close to the cistern pit. It is well over a thousand feet deep", Wingtarla informed them, adding, *"We are extracting blue stone blocks from the pit and using them for building material. We'll be using the hole to store fresh water when we're finished."*

He brought up a hologram using his grip and it displayed the narrow, circular pit opening. The pit shaft dropped down fifty feet and then opened up into a broad cylindrical chamber that must have been a thousand feet across. As noted by Wingtarla, the main cistern chamber was over a thousand feet deep.

Wingtarla noted, *"Basalt is not impervious to water, so we need to seal the entire inner surface. The end result will be a fresh water supply for the entire colony when it's been filled. We'll pump the water up the hill to the cistern from the river at the base of the hill. It will, of course, be filtered for purity."*

A flabbergasted Kelyarn noted in awe, "That is incredible", then he asked, "How do you cut the basalt? Our people use iron hammers and chisels. It is back-breaking work. Only the strong can do it."

"We have our ways, Kelyarn. Suffice to say, we cut the basalt with high-powered laser cutting machines and, of course, our metal men do all the hard lifting", Wingtarla explained.

"We know not of these things", Kelyarn had to admit.

Wingtarla nodded in understanding.

"It appears that you have water covered, but what will you do for food?", Kelyarn enquired.

Keegali chimed in, "Look at the size of that cistern, Kelyarn. I think they'll have their food covered."

Wingtarla led them back to his hover jeep and began to fly it around the sides of that vast hill. He flew his hover car away from the hill and maintained altitude. Wingtarla asked them to hold on as he banked the hover care while circling the hill in a counterclockwise direction.

"You see those Androids on the flanks of the hill. They're crafting broad steps into the hillside for orchards, berry fields and vineyards. If you look down at the lower slopes and base, they are being turned into crop fields for Rice, Wheat, Soy, Oats, Millet, Corn and Barley; just some of our staple grains. Other fields are being prepared for vegetable gardens. All of that sad soil, as you call it, we removed it and it's being processed and enhanced. By the time we're finished with it, it will be the most fertile soil in the valley and we'll use it for all of our plantings", Wingtarla explained in as much detail as necessary for them to understand

"When we came here for our first meeting with your people, we had no idea how much you could do in such a short amount of time", Kelyarn admitted.

Keegali looked at her Husband, Kelyarn, "When these fields are producing and we begin trading, food shortages and famine will be a thing of the past."

"Keegali, that is the general idea. We want everyone in this valley to benefit from our expertise", Wingtarla smiled in agreement.

A low buzzing sound emerged from Wingtarla's grip, "Wow. Time flies, as the Humans say. Your transport ship is ready", and then he turned to Kitty, *"You'll be able to see your friend in roughly six hours or so."*

Wingtarla flew Kitty and her parents straight to the waiting transport ship. When they arrived at the transport ship, there was a metal man waiting for them.

The metal man spoke in perfect Carlinish, "All preparations have been made. The Reas family have been notified of your approximate arrival time. We have prepared your cabin with bedding, protein bars and rations packs. The flight duration is approximately six hours and five minutes. We recommend using that time to sleep in preparation for arrival. The refreshment ensuite is at your disposal."

Wingtarla typed into his grip's holographic keyboard, "Thank you, Android Alpha Zero Three. Please accompany our guests during their flight. Return with this transport when it returns tomorrow."

Wingtarla said goodbye to Kelyarn and his family, *"Enjoy the trip. It should be an eye opener"*, as if what they'd seen already at the new colony site had not been.

8. Cis-Luns L-Five.

Android Alpha Zero Three led Kelyarn and his family to their cabin. The colonial transport ships were multi-purpose vessels. They were designed to transport cargo, equipment and supplies, but also passengers. The transport ships were currently hauling cargo and equipment and the passenger cabins were all empty.

The cabin that Android Alpha Zero Three led them to was a family cabin. It contained a fair-sized double bed and two double bunks capable of catering to a family of up to six. It also contained an ensuite with two wash basins, a toilet and a shower. All water on the transport ship was, of course, recycled.

There was a series of four thick, clear crystalline plasteel portholes along one wall, the ship's hull. Alpha Zero Three opened the cabin door and stepped aside for Kelyarn and his family to enter.

"We have been instructed to accompany you on your trip", Alpha Zero Three informed them, noting, "We may stay with you inside the cabin, or if you wish, we may stay outside the cabin by the door. We will be at your service upon request."

Keegali wasn't sure about having the metal man stay inside the cabin; it felt just a little creepy to her.

"Please stay outside by the cabin door, metal man", she instructed.

Kitty was curious and inquired, "How is it you speak perfect Carlinish?"

Alpha Zero Three replied, "We have access to the networks and with that access, the linguistics databases and language matrices. We are capable of fluently speaking every language recorded in those databases."

"Are you sentient? Do you have a soul?", Kelyarn enquired of the metal man.

"We are artificial, machine constructs with photonic neural networks and multiple-layered positronic assembly matrices. Android photonic neural networks mimic sentience only. Souls are an undefinable concept. We do not have souls as you would envisage them", Alpha Zero Three explained.

"*Soulless metal men who mimic sentience*", Kelyarn thought to himself.

Kitty had run her eyes over the double bed and the two double bunks, but her eyes caught the ensuite and she made her way curiously over to it. Looking inside, she found it completely unfamiliar.

"What are these things?", Kitty asked curiously.

Alpha Zero Three strode quickly to the ensuite and entered. The Android looked around the room and began explaining its fixtures.

"These are wash basins", the Android gestured to the wash basins set into the bench against the wall.

"Underneath the wash basins are storage cabinets. The tap marked with a red dot is for hot water. The tap marked with the blue dot is for cold water", he explained as he showed them how the taps worked.

Next, the Android gestured to the shower, "This is a shower. It is for bathing", and then he proceeded to show the operation of the taps and the water flowing out of the shower head.

"What is that thing?", Keegali enquired.

Alpha Zero Three replied, "That is a toilet. It is of a multi-species design", as he began his explanation, "This is the cover. You raise the cover, exposing the seat. A Human would sit there to urinate and/or defecate. Males often raise the seat to stand and urinate. You are Carlin-folk with tails similar to Thols. You would raise the seat and use the side foot attachments to squat for your urination and/or defecation. The foot attachments feature a non-slip surface for added safety. Male Carlins and Thols may stand and urinate as Humans do. It is considered good manners to lower the seat and cover when finished. Once the cover is lowered, the toilet will automatically flush and self-clean."

Kitty stared at the unfamiliar contraption, noting, "We have a small building behind our house. We use it for washing and", she paused, the blue stripes on her face glowing slightly iridescent with embarrassment, "urinating and defecating."

The Android replied, "Humans call that an outhouse. There are places where they are still used."

Kelyarn noted absently, "We mulch our defecations for use as fertiliser."

Android Alpha Zero Three replied, "There are places where the Humans still do that as well."

After Android Alpha Zero Three's explanation of the ensuite's facilities, he led them back into the cabin and showed them where to find plates, cups and cutlery. Alpha Zero Three also showed them the fridge. It contained bottled cold water and even cold Goat's milk.

After which, he proceeded to explain how to open the protein bars and ration packs. There eventually came a point where there was nothing left to explain and he walked over to the cabin door.

Standing in the cabin doorway, Alpha Zero Three noted, "We will wait in the corridor by the door. If you require assistance, please ask. We are here to serve."

Keegali quickly enquired before Alpha Zero Three closed the cabin door, "Are there Humans that live the way we Carlins live?"

"Yes. There are some Humans who prefer to live in ways similar to the Carlins", the Android replied.

As the cabin door closed, Keegali noted, "They are not so different from us, these Humans. There are some Humans who still use ways like ours."

Kelyarn smiled; it was an important observation, "There will be Humans who can relate to our people and the way that we live. There will be common ground between us."

Kitty looked out of a porthole. It was half a metre in diameter. The transport ship was lifting off. Kitty instinctively reached out to grab something and then began to relax as she realised that she could not feel the ship's movement at all. Neither Kelyarn nor Keegali could feel the ship's movement either. They did not know of things like inertial dampers.

"Look out of the windows. We are moving! We are flying!", Kitty exclaimed with excitement.

The transport ship flew swiftly and silently into the skies of Secundus. Kitty and her parents watched the view intently outside the porthole as the ship ascended. Soon, it was breaching the lower cloud layers. The Carlin family found the view both horrifying and exhilarating all at once.

The clouds outside the porthole grew thicker and thicker as they passed through layer upon layer of cloud. Then, without warning, they were above the clouds and the sky began to lose its blue colouration, becoming darker and darker the higher they flew until it became an eerie, inky black.

Kelyarn stood wide-eyed in abject horror. Keegali and Kitty both screamed at the sight. The inky blackness was everywhere, extending as far as their eyes could see and while they could still see the stars, they were small, faint and did not twinkle at all. Android Alpha Zero Three stepped into their cabin as soon as he heard the Carlin women scream.

Keegali turned to the Android with urgency, "Metal man. Where is the sky? Where has it gone?"

Alpha Zero Three replied, "The sky surrounding a world is different from the skies above them. Living worlds have atmospheres, air, which, depending on the constituent gases and particulate density, give their skies colour. Above the world is space, a vacuum. There is no air, there is no atmosphere and the particulate density is insufficient to scatter light."

The Carlins had no idea what that meant and Kelyarn enquired, "How big is this space, this vacuum, you speak of?"

"Suffice to say and for all intents and purposes, space is endless, only punctuated by stars, worlds, moons and other cosmological phenomena", Alpha Zero Three replied.

"Endless?", Keegali repeated, questioningly; her mind boggling at the thought.

"Yes", Android Zero Three confirmed, reassuring them, "Be not afraid, Carlin-folk. You are all safe inside this transport ship."

Android Alpha Zero Three stood in silent computational contemplation before switching on the cabin's forward wall screen.

The Android quickly linked the wall screen to the transport ship's forward optical scanner array and brought up an image of Cis-Luns L-Five. He set the central focus of the screen onto the colonial interstellar push ship Artemisia.

"The view from the portholes is not recommended. It can be both disorienting and frightening. Even some Humans react to it in the same way. Please focus on the wall screen and our destination, the interstellar push ship Artemisia. Our gradual approach to the Artemisia can be soothing on the nerves", the Android advised and then, before he left the cabin, he added, "Sleep is also advised."

Keegali turned her face away from the portholes and looked at the screen. The view was still strange, yet somehow both compelling, calming and almost soothing.

Kelyarn noted, "That metal man is right, Keegali. We should try to get some sleep."

Kitty had already climbed into one of the bunks, "I can see the screen from this sleeping mat. You can do the same from your sleeping mat as well."

Keegali smiled and agreed, "That is a very good idea, my little one. Although even the Human sleeping mats are so strange, so thick. Why are they so thick?", she asked rhetorically, not expecting anyone to answer.

They all climbed into their beds and watched the wall screen. The transport ship's A.I. detected this and began gradually dimming the lights. As they watched their destination approach, one by one, they fell into a sound sleep.

With one hour of flight time left, Android Alpha Zero Three entered the cabin. It was dark and Kelyarn's family were all still asleep. The screen still showed their destination, the Artemisia, although it was much larger now and took up a larger portion of the screen. Alpha Zero Three was silent and meticulous as he opened a compartment and a table and chairs slid out of the wall.

Android Alpha Zero Three placed three plates, three cups and three sets of cutlery on the table. He then proceeded to pour Goat's milk into the cups, adding just a touch of maple syrup to give the milk a slightly sweet flavour that the Carlin's preferred. It was something that Wingtarla had suggested.

He placed two protein bars beside each plate and opened three ration packs, emptying them onto the plates. They were creamy chicken curries, Filipino style. One by one, he heated the meals in a microwave oven recessed into the wall. Then, he waited as the lights switched back on and gradually illuminated the room.

As his prediction algorithms had suggested, Kitty was the first to awaken; "We have prepared your breakfast", he informed her before silently leaving the cabin.

A few minutes later, Keegali and Kelyarn awoke to find Kitty already eating, "Come, eat. Before the food gets cold", she beckoned, noting, "It's really, really good. The Goat's milk is almost like masuli-infused Gudong milk."

Kitty quickly finished her breakfast, noting, "This is another curry, similar to what we had for lunch yesterday. It kind of tastes like Thrixan, but it's not the same. The grain is kind of like masuli, but it's not quite the same either."

As Keegali and Kelyarn sat down to eat, Kitty got up and walked toward the ensuite, "I'm going to try the shower."

Keegali tried the chicken curry, "Kitty is right. Similar to Thrixan but not the same."

Kelyarn tried the accompanying rice, "It lacks the bluish tint, but tastes very similar to masuli, just not sweet."

Keegali agreed, "Similar but not the same", and then she turned her head to the cabin door, "Metal man", she called out.

Android Alpha Zero Three entered the cabin and Keegali enquired, "What are we eating?"

"We prepared creamy chicken curry, Filipino style, with rice and Goat's milk with a dash of maple syrup", the Android informed her.

Keegali smiled at the Android, a broad Carlinish smile complete with raised whiskers, "That was very considerate of you, metal man."

Kitty stepped out of the ensuite, wrapped in a towel, "Mother, you have to try the shower. It is like standing under warm rain. The water is so clean!"

Alpha Zero Three nodded before leaving the cabin, "We will leave you to prepare for our arrival. We will be docking at the Artemisia in forty five minutes."

Kelyarn and Keegali both prepared for their arrival at the colonial interstellar push ship, the Artemisia and then waited patiently, sitting on the side of their bed, watching the wall screen. Kitty, on the other hand, showed four more times. The sensation of warm water flowing over her body like rain was something that she really enjoyed. The young Carlin woman couldn't get enough of it.

The Artemisia seemed to grow larger by the second. The push ship was long, very long and totally incomprehensible to them. Both Kelyarn and Keegali were perplexed and asked the Android, Alpha Zero Three, to explain what they were looking at, to describe it to them, so that they could make sense of it.

"We are looking at the Artemisia's starboard side", Android Alpha Zero Three began, before pointing to one end, "That is the bow of the push ship. That is where the command and control is located, including the ship's bridge. High Admiral Nummus and Special Operative James Reas will be on the bridge."

Kelyarn and Keegali couldn't really follow what the Android was saying, but its commentary was at least something they could listen to as they approached the Artemisia.

Android Alpha Zero Three pointed to the section just behind the bow of the push ship, "That section is where the passengers are all billeted. It contains cabins, restaurants, food outlets, recreational facilities and a large promenade complete with a large observational sky dome."

Kelyarn curiously enquired, "How many passengers are on board that push ship?"

The Android replied, "Each push ship houses one thousand passengers."

Keegali was astonished, "One thousand Humans?", she queried for confirmation.

"On the Artemisia, the passenger breakdown is eight hundred Humans, two hundred Mimasian Thols and eight Martian hybrids. The Artemisia has a crew complement of two hundred. The Mimasian transport ship, CTT-VC-999, that is docked at the Artemisia's central dorsal docking port, contains another two hundred and fifty Mimasian Thols and two Human pilots", Android Alpha Zero Three gave them a detailed breakdown of the passengers and crew aboard the Artemisia and docked Mimasian Thol transport.

Keegali's eyes widened and her whiskers stood perfectly still, "That's a lot of people."

Android Alpha Zero Three acknowledged, "Yes", before continuing, pointing to the other end of the push ship, "That is the stern section. The engines, propulsion systems and engineering departments are located in that section."

"The section between the passenger section and the stern section contains special docking for mobile mining, orbital ore processing and orbital manufacturing stations. Some of the push ships also carry specialist equipment such as orbital ore catchalls and lunar surface magnetic levitation mass drivers", the Android continued with its commentary.

The final commentary was, "In that same section are a great many docking bays where transport ships and other ships are internally docked. The other eleven push ships contain one thousand Human passengers and two hundred Human crew", and then Android Alpha Zero Three went silent, its task completed.

As the transport ship approached the Artemisia for docking, the forward optical scanner feed stopped and the screen went blank.

"Please collect your backpacks and your other belongings and follow me to the docking portal", Android Alpha Zero Three requested.

Kelyarn, Keegali and Kitty did as instructed and followed the Android to the transport ship's port passenger docking portal. The docking procedure proceeded so smoothly that they couldn't feel the transport ship dock. Their transport ship had docked on one of the Artemisia's many starboard docking ports.

Android Alpha Zero Three led them through the transport's airlock system and into the Artemisia. The airlock doors closed securely behind them and they stood before one of the Artemisia's inner bulkhead entrance doors.

"We will leave you now. The door will open momentarily", Android Alpha Zero Three told them and then he walked back the way they'd come.

Kelyarn and his family waited for the door to open, wondering what would be on the other side.

There were quiet, almost imperceptible hissing sounds as the inner bulkhead door cycled to open. A Human would never have heard them, but Carlinish ears and hearing were so much sharper.

Each imperceptible hiss elicited small flinches of fear. Then the heavy bulkhead door slid to the right, disappearing seamlessly into the bulkhead.

On the other side was James Reas, his Wife, Simone, his Son, Johnathon, the Martian hybrid, Wynessa and wearing Kitty's gifted hooded Gudong leather jacket was Angelique Reas. Kitty squealed in delight and sprinted to Angelique, wrapping her arms around her. Kitty's eyes welled with tears and she held on for dear life, hugging Angelique tightly, not wanting to let go.

"Okay", Simone remarked, before introducing herself, "I'm Simone Reas, Angelique's Mother, this is my Son, Johnathon. I believe you know everyone else."

As Wynessa provided the telepathic translation, Keegali greeted them in turn, "I am Keegali, this is my Husband, Kelyarn and our Daughter, Kitty, is hugging your Daughter, Angelique."

Wynessa continued her translating, "You're wearing my jacket", Kitty commented, smiling broadly.

Simone interjected, "Angelique has been wearing that jacket nonstop since first contact."

Kitty's smile broadened even more at hearing that; it meant a lot to her, "I really missed you, Angelique."

"I missed you too, Kitty", Angelique replied, as they touched their foreheads together and looked deeply into each other's eyes.

Kitty leaned in and kissed Angelique, who hesitated at first, before kissing Kitty back in return.

Young Johnathon scrunched his face in disgust, "Peeyew, gross! Why is Angelique kissing the cat girl, Mum?", he was only eight years old after all.

It was a long, slow kiss and Simone reacted in complete surprise, "Okay, I wasn't expecting that", as she turned to James with a questioning look.

James looked at his Son, Johnathon, "Kitty is not a cat girl, Johnathon, she is a Carlin", before he turned back to Simone, "During our first contact, they became friends and quite close", he explained.

"They look just like cats on two feet, but with no fur", Johnathon continued.

Simone rolled her eyes and Keegali crouched down in front of Johnathon, "Perhaps, young man, your cats look like us Carlin-folk."

"Wingtarla expressed an urgency in your coming here, Kelyarn?", James queried.

Kelyarn gestured to Kitty and Angelique, who were now back to hugging each other, "Kitty and Angelique were the urgency."

Keegali stepped in, "Our Daughter, Kitty, has developed a strong attachment to Angelique. When Angelique reached the age of consent and did not come to visit us, Kitty became despairing and then fell into a very deep sadness from which we could not lift her."

Kelyarn added, "The blue stripes on her face turned grey as ash and the discolouration spread to her arms, torso and legs. It is a very bad thing for us Carlins and we had to bring her here to see Angelique."

"A bad thing?", Simone queried, asking, "That doesn't sound good. Just how bad is it?"

Keegali's whiskers drooped; "It is a very, very bad thing, especially at Kitty's age."

James caught on, "Is it related to Carlinish biological imperatives?"

"Yes", Keegali's Husband, Kelyarn, confirmed.

Simone's face took on a confused, questioning look.

Keegali did her best to explain, "When a Carlin girl matures, the quickening comes upon them. This usually happens at twenty one years of age, sometimes earlier at twenty. Rarely, it can come on at nineteen and even rarer still, at eighteen. The older the better, as the girl will make better choices in choosing her bondmate. At a younger age, nineteen or eighteen, we parents must help her. Once the quickening is reached, if the Carlin girl sleeps with a Carlin man, then over the course of two weeks, they go into the heat and their lifelong bond completes. Then, seven months later, their first kit will arrive. The first litter is always just the one kit."

Kelyarn stepped in, "To put off bonding, a Carlin girl will often develop friendships with other women. They do this for the purposes of mutual pleasure without the price of bonding and bringing forth kits. This is very normal for Carlins, although not all young Carlin girls require this. Kitty is one who does."

"So, Kitty has developed a friendship with Angelique", Simone noted in understanding, before enquiring, "Just, how old is Kitty?"

Keegali interjected, "Kitty is seventeen, almost eighteen and at a very crucial age. It is far more than simple friendship; it is a bond. For a Carlin girl, a deep sadness at this age can be very, very bad."

Wynessa quickly chimed in telepathically, "*Simone, read deep sadness as a deep clinical depression, a really deep depression that affects Carlinish biology and requires medical intervention.*"

Keegali nodded in agreement, "Yes, yes. If the deep sadness is prolonged, it can bring on the quickening and the heat prematurely, but without any male partner."

Kelyarn noted sadly, "When this happens, the girl will look seriously ill and the parents will seek a man to volunteer to bond with her", and then he paused, "Ashen grey stripes are not attractive to Carlin men and no man wants to enter a life bond to someone who looks so ill. No one would volunteer."

Simone turned to Wynessa, "You're quite knowledgeable, Wynessa. Is there an Earth analogue? Something familiar that can help us understand this situation?"

Wynessa was quiet in thought for several moments before she transmitted, *"Yes. There are the mustelids, weasels, ferrets and stoats. When the female goes into oestrus, she has a biological imperative to breed to come out of it. It ends with conception."*

"What happens if they don't breed? If they don't conceive?", Simone enquired.

"Persistent oestrus in mustelids leads to organ failure within two to three months. It is always fatal, unless medical intervention is provided", Wynessa informed.

Kelyarn pointed to Wynessa, "Yes, yes. We lost our eldest Daughter to the deep sorrows; we cannot lose another! We cannot! That is why we came to find Angelique."

"James, this is a life-threatening condition. We need to take Kitty to our medical centre. They need to perform some tests to make sure that she's okay", Simone recommended.

Keegali commented, "We think the worst of it has passed. Look at our Kitty now. Her stripes are blue once more and practically glowing with joy and happiness. Her closeness to Angelique has lifted her out of her deep sadness."

"No, Keegali. We should still take Kitty to our medical centre, just to make sure that she's okay", Simone insisted.

James agreed wholeheartedly, "Yes. That would be the wisest thing to do. Simone, show our guests to our cabin. Drop off their belongings at our cabin and meet me at the medical centre. I'll call ahead and let them know we're on our way."

Simone looked worried, "James, what will they use for a baseline? They've never seen a Carlin before; they'll have no baseline to work with."

"Simone, I suspect that Kitty will be their baseline. There's always a first", James replied.

When Simone arrived at the Artemisia's medical centre, with her children and Kelyarn's family, she found her Husband, James, already present, explaining the situation to the Doctor. The Doctor looked a little confused. Wynessa, who had been telepathically translating for everyone, came up with a very simple and very Martian suggestion.

"If permitted, I can show you Keegali's memories. You will be able to see the issue through her memory, through her eyes", Wynessa suggested, noting, *"Seeing is halfway to understanding and this is the most efficient way to see."*

Wynessa approached Keegali, *"Please, may I?"*, she asked.

Keegali nodded, giving her permission and Wynessa leaned in, touching her forehead to Keegali's. After less than fifteen seconds, Wynessa withdrew her mind from Keegali's and stepped back.

Wynessa turned to Doctor Morrow, *"With your permission, Doctor?"*, she asked.

Wynessa approached the Doctor and leaned in close, touching her forehead to his. It took less than ten seconds to transfer Keegali's memories to the Doctor and when completed, Wynessa stepped back.

Doctor Morrow stood there silently as his mind observed Keegali's memories. He saw through Keegali's eyes the deathly, ashen grey pallor of Kitty's stripes. How the young Carlin woman had looked, not three days earlier.

The Doctor looked at Kitty, her stripes now a vibrant blue and almost glowing, yet still, the image in his mind of that deathly, ashen grey pallor was still in his mind.

Doctor Morrow approached Kitty, "Indeed. Seeing is believing", he crouched down in front of her and took out a small penlight.

The Doctor shone the light in Kitty's eyes, noting how her pupils reacted. He put his penlight back in his shirt pocket and reached out, holding Kitty's hands. He looked at her blue stripes and ran his fingers over them. So vibrant now and yet that deathly ashen grey pallor, not so long ago.

Doctor Morrow stood up and turned to Wynessa, "Thank you, Wynessa. Keegali's memories put everything into perspective. Adding in that mustelid Earth analogue was very useful as well. I had no idea that Carlins could suffer from persistent oestrus. That is of great concern."

The Doctor turned to Keegali, "It appears your Daughter has suffered an adverse biological reaction, triggered by some form of separation anxiety. Deep clinical depression is indicated. We need to perform some blood tests and I'd also like to take a full body bio-scan. I'll have one of our radiologists go through the scan with a fine-tooth comb, looking for any other possible health issues."

Wynessa translated the Doctor's words telepathically as he turned to Kitty, "Young lady, please follow me and we'll start those tests."
Kitty didn't move. Apart from the fact that everything around her was unfamiliar and strange, she had no idea how Human doctors or medical procedures worked. Kitty was fearful.

"It's okay, Kitty", Angelique reassured her as she took her by the hand, "I'm coming with you."

Kitty and Angelique then followed the Doctor into the treatment section of the medical centre.

While Kitty's and Angelique's parents were waiting, Simone enquired, "Keegali, how many children do you have?"

Keegali replied, "We currently have ten kits. Kitty is currently our oldest kit."

Kelyarn noted with great sadness, "Keegali brought twenty four kits into the world. We lost all but ten."

"All but ten?", Simone questioned in shock.

Keegali was silent, but Kelyarn confirmed, "Yes. Keegali does not like to talk about it. No Carlin woman does. Younger kits are often lost to disease, infection, or even spoiled food. Fatal accidents, even broken bones, can cost lives. Some, a few, are taken by predators like Kyrrax or wild Vort packs. In the masuli grain fields, poisonous vipers can be a problem as well. As I said earlier, we lost our eldest Daughter to the deep sorrows."

Keegali stepped in with tears in her eyes, her voice faltering, "I've carried twenty four kits inside of me. All but ten are now gone. The deep sorrow took our eldest Daughter, our firstborn kit, from us. She was such a beautiful girl, so full of promise. Her laughter filled our household. All of our other kits loved her. We've lost so many kits, I cannot bear to lose another. It is too painful for me."

Simone wrapped her arms around Keegali and allowed her to collapse, crying on her shoulder.

"These deep sorrows. Just how prevalent is it in your village?", Simone enquired.

"Every household has lost at least one kit to the deep sorrows. Some two kits, some three kits, some even more", Kelyarn replied, remarking, "The deep sorrows are often brought on by the loss of siblings."

Simone gently dabbed at Keegali's tears with a tissue as Keegali commented, "A Carlin's life is a very hard life."

It was nearly an hour later when the Doctor came back with Kitty and Angelique. Kitty sported a small patch of cotton wool and a band-aid in the crook of her arm from the blood test.

Kitty ran to her Mother, "They took three small vials of my blood and put me in this big machine. It was so noisy, so strange."

Angelique explained, "They needed the blood for testing and the machine was a full-body bio-scanner."

Keegali nodded but didn't understand.

Doctor Morrow had an old-fashioned clipboard in his hand; he was flicking through pages and reading through the test results.

"Okay then. Kitty's interleukin levels are elevated, so there has been some form of inflammation, possibly an extreme immune response. Your neurotropic factor is very low; I would expect that from a recent depressive event. Your cortisol levels are elevated and your vitamin D levels are very low, stress indicators and negative mood indicators", the Doctor read off, more for himself.

"Hmm, your oxytocin levels are very elevated", he looked at Kitty and Angelique still holding hands, noting, "Well, that does make sense."

Doctor Morrow continued, "Yet, your dopamine, serotonin, endorphins, enkephalins and dynorphin levels are all quite elevated. Hmm, your glucose and insulin levels are as one might expect, so there are no signs of metabolic disorder. That is good."

"I'm no expert on Carlin physiology, but it seems to me that you recently went though an episode of deep clinical depression, triggered by separation anxiety, which subsequently put you under severe biological stress", Doctor Morrow pronounced, adding, "As I said, I'm no expert on Carlin physiology, but it does look like you are coming out of it."

Doctor Morrow continued, "There are some things that still concern me, though. This talk of persistent oestrus. If clinical depression in a Carlin of Kitty's age can bring on premature quickening and oestrus, that is a major problem. Persistent oestrus is a life-threatening condition."

"We are aware of that, Doctor. We lost our eldest kit to the deep sorrows", Kelyarn noted.

James added, "This problem of persistent oestrus appears to be an endemic problem in Carlin life."

The Doctor nodded, he did appreciate the problem, "While I do understand that persistent oestrus is a major problem in Carlin life, my primary concern at this moment is my patient, young Kitty."

James nodded, "Understood. I will speak with High Admiral Nummus about our concerns for Carlin health issues and outcomes. That is something we will need to plan for in the very near future."

"Exactly my point", the Doctor confirmed, "Now back to my patient. Kitty's clinical depression was brought on by separation anxiety. Literally the absence of Angelique. My concern is that when Kitty returns planetside to her home in the village, she will relapse and another episode will be triggered by Angelique's absence. I'm recommending that Kitty stay with us here on the Artemisia. We can then monitor her condition and ensure her health."

"That doesn't sound very practical, Doctor", Simone chimed in, noting, "The Carlin are a highly social, agrarian people. We can't expect Kitty to live on a spaceship, no matter how large it might be."

Kitty smiled mischievously, "Angelique can live with us in our house in our village. She can sleep with me."

Keegali frowned, "It is the same situation in reverse, Kitty. You can not expect a Human, who is used to living up here, to live in a Carlin village."

Keegali informed the Doctor, "Before the quickening, young Carlin girls form close bonds with other girls. It is for pleasure without bonding. It calms the body, steadies the heart and keeps the heat at bay until she is ready for a mate. When Kitty reaches the age of the quickening, the problem should resolve itself. Kitty's need for Angelique will diminish as her need for a bondmate exerts itself. It is our way."

Simone tapped Keegali's arm gently, reminding her, "That could be when Kitty is twenty one. Kitty is only seventeen, so we need to put something in place to cover those intervening years."

"Mum, why do parents have to make things so complicated. I can visit Kitty on the weekends. It is really that simple", Angelique suggested, reminding them,

"I'm sixteen and my class five pilot's license test is already booked in and only six weeks away. I'll be able to fly there myself."

Her Father, James, interjected, "Angelique, until then, you still need a qualified pilot with you and assuming you pass your pilot's exam, you are still under eighteen. You need either your Mother or me with you."

Simone smiled, "James, you could accompany Angelique. Fly down with her early on a Saturday morning and then drop her off at Kitty's village. Then on Sunday afternoon, you could then fly back down and pick her up."

James shook his head, "Logistics, honey. You're describing a four hundred and twenty thousand kilometre trip and that's one way. There and back, double that and then do it twice. It is simply not practical."

Johnathon chimed in, "And all for a booty call with her cat girl girlfriend."

"Johnathon Reas! Will you not! If you can't say something useful, you can just sit there and say nothing at all", Simone admonished.

Angelique and Kitty giggled amongst themselves.

"I'm so sorry, Simone. None of us could have foreseen that our first meeting would lead to this problem", Keegali apologised.

"No need to apologise, Keegali. It's just one of those things you find out about when it happens. Right now it's just another problem that we need to solve", Simone replied, still thinking of the problem.

Johnathon came up with a useful suggestion for once, "After Angelique has her pilot's license, you can fly down to the village with her, Mummy."

Kelyarn caught on and added, "You can both stay overnight at our house. That halves the trips."

"Okay, that's a start, but we're still six weeks away from that, assuming Angelique passes her pilot's exam", Simone agreed, noting, "We just need to bridge those six weeks", and then she turned to James.

"Okay, okay, I'll talk to Admiral Nummus. I can fly down to Secundus, drop off Angelique at Kitty's house and then spend the weekend supervising the colony's construction", he suggested, adding, "On the Sunday, I can pick up Angelique and then we can fly back. That will halve the trips as well, but I really don't know what supervision I'll be doing; my presence at the colony will be completely superfluous."

"We have a way," Kelyarn smiled broadly, "You could even bring your Son, Johnathon, to visit."

"Yes, yes," Keegali agreed, her whiskers twitching in thought, "We have younger kits, Johnathon's age. They will become good friends, playmates for him they'll be."

"Cool. I'll get to play with cat people", Johnathon blurted out.

"Johnathon Reas! Will you not!", Simone admonished, as she pinched the bridge of her nose in frustration.

Keegali's ears flicked up; she looked at Johnathon thoughtfully, "I like your

Son. He's a fine kit, very much like our own", and then she reached over and gently touched his cheek with a slight pinch.

Johnathon blushed and responded, "You're already married. When I grow up, I'm going to marry my Aunt Roberta."

Simone muttered under her breath, "Not this nonsense again."

"Marry your Aunt?", a surprised and amused Keegali queried.

James chimed in and explained, "High Admiral Roberta Nummus is our honorary Aunt. She is not related to us by blood."

Kelyarn laughed out loudly, his whiskers raised in amusement, "Very much like own own kits."

Doctor Morrow had stood there patiently while the parents worked out the logistics for Angelique's visitations; however, he also had some recommendations.

"Mr Reas. You should acquire a communicator for Kelyarn and teach him how to use it. Should Kitty relapse into another clinical depression, we can bring her here for emergency medical treatment", the Doctor recommended.

"That is a good idea, Doctor. I can arrange that", James agreed.

"Good then. Should Kitty or another young Carlin girl go into persistent oestrus, we do have a pharmaceutical solution, deslorelin acetate. It, of course, has never been tested on a Carlin; however, under clinical conditions, it could be attempted if necessary", Doctor Morrow informed them.

Kelyarn's ears picked up and his whiskers raised, "If it works, we never need to lose a Daughter to the deep sorrows ever again."

"That is the general idea, Kelyarn", the Doctor confirmed, before adding, "Now, I have a request. We have very little real information on Carlin physiology or biochemistry. Could I trouble you both to possibly provide us with blood samples and full body bio-scans?"

Simone assured them both that it was okay, "It's the same thing they did with Kitty. Very routine procedures. I can accompany you if you wish."

Kelyarn and Keegali both nodded in reply and all three of them followed the Doctor into the medical centre's radiology department.

James turned to Angelique, "They're going to be at least an hour, probably two. Take Johnathon and Kitty back to our cabin. We'll all meet up for lunch later at the Sky Dome restaurant. Say, at one pm."

Angelique nodded and led her Brother, Johnathon and her Carlin girlfriend, Kitty, back to their cabin.

Angelique opened the door to their cabin and Johnathon bolted off to his room to play computer games, slamming the door behind him. Angelique shook her head and rolled her eyes.

Johnathon always slammed doors; it was as if he'd never learned to close one. A habit his Mother had yet to break him of. The boy was incorrigible, but once inside his room, he would be content to play his computer games.

Angelique showed Kitty to her room and closed the door behind them. It wasn't a big room. Only containing a double bed, desk and chair, clothes closet and off to one side a small ensuite with toilet, wash basin and a shower.

There was a clear crystalline plasteel porthole above the bed. Angelique would often stare out at the stars and the new mega-colony, Cis-Luns Colonial Central Command, that was still under construction.

Kitty saw the ensuite and, without hesitation, stripped off her clothes, leaving them on the floor and made her way straight over to the shower. She could not resist the feeling of warm water flowing over her naked body like gentle warm rain.

Angelique watched with clear amusement while at the same time trying not to look at Kitty's naked Carlinish body with its six breasts arranged in three pairs. When she finally came out of the ensuite, she had Angelique's bath towel wrapped around her.

Kitty stood there watching Angelique for several long moments before dropping the towel to the floor. Angelique's face went bright red with embarrassment and she had no idea where to look. When she finally turned around to look at Kitty, she found herself staring at a perfectly humanoid body, but with distinctive alien feline features.

Kitty's eyes with their vertical slit pupils, her cat-like ears and even her small cat-like nose. Kitty's whiskers grew out from above her upper lip, which was slightly pronounced and padded. Her tail was long, thin and extremely expressive and, of course, her heels were well off the floor, giving her that digitigrade walking stance.

The most striking feature of all was Kitty's blue stripes. They covered her entire body from the top of her head to the tip of her toes and from the fingers of one hand to the fingers of the other. They were symmetrical, quite uniform and followed the curves of her body perfectly.

Kitty's blue stripes flowed down her throat to her torso and then formed intricate patterns and swirls. They spiralled around each of Kitty's six breasts and merged with her six areolas, which were also blue in colouration.

Kitty's blue stripes had a vibrancy to them, almost glowing with opalescence. Angelique found the sight of Kitty's Carlinish nakedness both alluring and intoxicating.

Kitty smiled and purred; it was loud and inviting. She strode to Angelique's bed, pulled back the bedclothes and climbed in, leaving her body clearly visible and inviting. Angelique stood there, frozen in both awe and shock.

This was new to her and she faltered, not knowing what to do. Angelique bit down lightly on her lower lip; she felt weak at the knees. Kitty slapped the bed gently multiple times while beckoning Angelique with an alluring, inviting smile and that ever-present purr of promise.

Angelique closed her eyes. Was this a dream? Was any of this real? What's happening to me?

Angelique opened her eyes. The vision was still there. Kitty was still there. It was all very real.

Angelique climbed into the bed beside Kitty, who then gently wrapped her arms around her.

Kitty rolled Angelique onto her back and then gently rolled on top of her, kissing her passionately.

It was Angelique's first time and they were both hot with passion, wrapped in each other's mutual embrace.

It was a good two hours later when they both reemerged from Angelique's bedroom, beaming with smiles.

After the medical scans and blood samples were taken, James and Simone led Kelyarn and Keegali to the Sky Dome restaurant. Wynessa followed closely behind, telepathically translating whenever translation was needed.

The Sky Dome itself was a huge, clear, multi-sectioned crystalline plasteel dome in the centre of the Artemisia's habitat section along its dorsal hull.

The base of the dome was lined with a promenade that included shops, entertainment venues and cafes. The dome itself offered incredible views of space outside the push ship and a clear view of the new mega-colony under construction.

As they walked out of the corridor and onto the promenade, the view through the Sky Dome caught Kelyarn's and Keegali's eyes. Kelyarn instinctively reached for the nearest wall. Keegali's legs began to give way as vertigo took over. Simone was quick to grab her by the arm and steady her.

"It's okay, I've got you", Simone reassured Keegali, advising, "The first time can be overwhelming. It's best to avert your eyes and try not to look at it."

Keegali and Kelyarn steadied themselves and followed that advice, following James and Simone over the restaurant.

The Sky Dome restaurant was a circular structure located at the very centre of the Sky Dome. A gently sloping walkway ran around the outside of the structure to its top, where a large open space was filled with carefully laid-out tables and chairs.

The outer edge of the space was surrounded by an ornate safety railing and a refreshments bar sat in the very centre. James led the group over to the table he'd booked for their lunch.

Keegali noted as she sat herself down in a chair that thankfully had an open space at her lower back that could accommodate Carlinish tails, "Everyone is looking at us."

"Yes, Keegali. They're just curious. They've never seen a Carlin before",

Simone explained, noting, "Neither had Johnathon or I, until your family arrived this morning."

Keegali nodded, just Humans being curious. Her neighbours would be too if the situation were reversed.

Carrying on from their earlier discussions about Carlinish biological imperatives, Keegali remarked, "Our coming of age, the quickening, the heat and our mate bonding must really sound awful to a people who have nothing like it."

"We have something similar, just not as intense. It's called adolescence. Teenagers go through growth spurts, have hormonal changes. They can even fall in and out of love almost weekly", Simone replied, noting, "It can take several years and be difficult for both the teenager and the parents."

"Not so different then", Keegali understood, "Just a different way to reach maturity."

"I guess so. There has to be a transition between childhood and adulthood", Simone agreed.

Keegali smiled and commented, "When Kitty reaches the quickening, her feelings for Angelique will calm down. They will become lifelong friends. When she finds her bondmate, she will become a true Carlinish Mother, run off her feet with more kits than she knows what to do with."

"That actually sounds daunting", Simone replied, wondering how they coped with so many children.

Keegali smiled and her whiskers raised, "There are always the nights. The mate bonding is special. When a young couple goes into the heat, they can be at it all night and even the next day, for up to four days. The bonding happens at the home of the girl's parents and the parents manage their excessive mating with special incenses, food spices and herbal teas."

"That, that, Keegali", Simone began to reply and then stopped, "I have no idea what to say. Young Human lovers can spend a lot of time in bed, but for up to four days! That really sounds excessive!"

Simone was trying to think of an Earth analogue and Wynessa stepped in, providing one, "*That sounds very similar to lions. When the female lion goes into heat, they can mate fifty times a day for as many as three to four days. If the male lion gets tired or has had enough, the lioness will bite his testicles to encourage him to continue mating.*"

Simone had to push the image of lions and lionesses mating and biting testicles out of her head.

Kelyarn laughed and pointed to Wynessa, "Yes! A Carlinish woman can behave in the exact same way."

Simone looked shocked and Keegali corrected her Husband, "Kelyarn exaggerates, we only give them a little nibble of encouragement. We are really quite gentle."

"We won't mention this to my Son, Johnathon", James recommended, noting,

"He'll start calling your people space lions."

Keegali, sitting next to Simone, giggled and reached out for her hand, entwining her fingers in Simone's, "Space lions. That is so funny", she mused, "The irony of that. We are probably the first Carlin family in space."

Spot on one thirty pm and Johnathon Reas came bounding over to their table, his usual energy unabated. Following casually behind him were Angelique and Kitty. They were holding hands and that was drawing looks from the other diners, curious looks.

"So, my boy, what have you been up to? Nothing naughty, I hope", James enquired.

"Dad! I've been playing video games", Johnathon replied, before smiling and remarking, "I think Angelique and Kitty were playing Twister. They were in Angelique's room with the door closed, but they sounded like they were playing Twister."

Simone reached for the bridge of her nose as Keegali queried, "What's Twister?"

"It's an Earth game. It's played by children and teenagers alike", Simone explained and then she leaned closer to Keegali and whispered, "They were definitely not playing Twister."

Keegali turned her gaze to Angelique and Kitty. They both wore broad, beaming smiles and Kitty's blue stripes were so vibrant and opalescent that she glowed.

Keegali giggled and whispered back to Simone, "You are correct. They were definitely not playing Twister", and then she gave Simone's hand a gentle, excited squeeze.

Simone looked back up at Johnathon and fibbed, "Yes, Johnathon. They were both playing Twister."

Johnathon smiled and laughed, "I knew it!"

Keegali chortled and giggled, knowing better.

James read out the menu and Wynessa telepathically translated the menu items into something the Kelyarn's family could relate to. One item caught their attention. It was called "*six-mushroom*" pie. It came in both family-size pies and individual pies.

Keegali was intrigued, "Wait! Please. What is a six-mushroom pie?", she curiously enquired.

Wynessa explained, "*It's a pie with six kinds of mushrooms*", and then she listed out the mushrooms: "*King oyster, white Shimeji, brown Shimeji, Swiss Brown, Portobello and Morel mushrooms. That's actually what I'll be choosing to eat.*"

An excited Kitty interjected, exclaiming, "Mother, that sounds just like your many-mushroom pies!"

"Many-mushroom pies?", Simone enquired.

Keegali laughed with a broad smile and raised whiskers, "It is a pie with six kinds of mushrooms. It is a Carlin favourite. Every Carlin family has their own recipes."

Kelyarn added, his smile equally broad, "They are mushrooms from our world, of course, and the pastry is made from masuli grain and Gudong butter, but they sound so similar."

Keegali noted, "Each Carlin family grows their own variety of mushrooms. Sometimes as many as twelve varieties. We can alter the flavours slightly by altering the variety of mushrooms."

Simone was hooked, "Okay then, six-mushroom pie sounds like the go."

"I'll order three family-sized pies", James agreed, commenting, "And if they are as good as they sound, I might order some more to take home. The individual variety."

As they ate their six-mushroom pies, they looked out of the Sky Dome into the distance on the Artemisia's port side. The new mega-colony, Cis-Luns Colonial Central Command, was under construction, its skeletal structure slowly being built.

It was like adding great lengths of duralium steel bones to a behemoth's skeleton. James informed them that it would be five years until it was completed.

Kelyarn had enquired about its size. He, Keegali and Kitty were all gobsmacked when they heard it truly would be twenty four kilometres long and four kilometres in diameter. They'd all thought that Android Alpha Zero Three had made a mistake when he'd described it. The three Carlin-folk stared in awe at the massive construction taking place. To them, it was simply mind-boggling.

When James added further details about the twenty-kilometre-long strip windows and equally long reflective mirrors, it started to go over their heads. For them to comprehend, James had to call up a holographic image using the data tablet he always carried with him to show them something similar on the same scale.

James showed them an image of the latest version of Cis-Lunar Colonial Central Command in Earth's Cis-Lunar space L-Five zone. Using that, he could better explain the hemispherical end caps, the long main cylinder with its land strips and strip windows and its long reflective mirrors. It was a lot for them to take in. The learning curve, naturally, was huge. The Carlin-folk had a huge amount to take in. A lot to learn.

After lunch, James ordered a dozen six-mushroom pies to be delivered to their cabin around dinner time. After which the Reas family showed Kelyarn, Keegali and Kitty around the Artemisia's promenade. They spent the next several hours trying coffee and different snack foods from the promenade's cafes and even had a look at the Human entertainment venues available.

At the end of the day, they all returned to the Reas family cabin. The six-mushroom pies were delivered on time and they had them for their dinner. Kelyarn's family stayed the night with the Reas's. Kelyarn and his Wife, Keegali, slept together on a sofa that folded out into a double bed.

Kitty stayed the night in Angelique's bedroom. Simone quietly took them aside and requested that they not make too much noise. She informed them that young Johnathon had heard them playing *"Twister"*. Kitty's blue stripes went from their current vivid opalescence to a shimmering iridescence, which signalled her extreme embarrassment.

The following morning, before Kitty and her parents left, Kelyarn suggested to Simone, "You and Keegali get along so well. You are becoming very good friends. When you visit our house, you should sleep with my Wife. You will both enjoy each other's company."

Simone blinked and had no reply. Keegali smiled, laughed softly and squeezed Simone's hand.

"No pressure, Simone", Keegali had told her, "No pressure."

Simone and Johnathon said their goodbyes and then, James and Angelique showed Kelyarn, Keegali and Kitty to one of the Artemisia's internal docking bays.

James Reas was a Special Operative and he had access to two fast ships. One was a Broad Head, Arrow Class Starfighter, which he deemed not appropriate as a civilian transport. Instead, he chose his Manta Ray Class Passenger Transport, which was capable of both space, atmospheric and even underwater flight.

The big transport ship that took the Carlin family into space covered the distance between Secundus and the Artemisia, four hundred and twenty thousand kilometres, in six hours, but it was not designed for speed.

James's Manta Ray was designed for speed and it covered that same distance in just over two and a half hours. Keegali and Kelyarn were amazed at how quickly they arrived home from their trip into Cis-Lunar space. Kitty was still overly enamoured with Angelique and barely noticed at all.

Kitty and her parents were dropped off at their house in their picturesque Carlinish village with its dry stone walls and blue stone cobbled laneways. Angelique said her goodbyes to Kitty, which took a considerable amount of time, promising to come back weekly. True to their word, Angelique and the Reas family kept their promise. Angelique was there for her weekend visits and Kitty's blue stripes continued to glow with their pure Carlinish opalescent beauty.

9. They're Not Like Us.

Six months after breaking ground on the basaltic hilltop, the Human colony was ready for the new colonists; it was ready for occupation. Houses and apartment buildings lined the southern section of the hilltop and along its flanks; arranged on small allotments in neat rows, with access provided by well-made streets. On the northern section of the hilltop were the shops, businesses and other commercial buildings. In the eastern section were the colony's school, water and power utilities.

The western section contained the aerospace facilities, including the engineering plants, the airport, the spaceport and the colony's warehousing. The colony's governmental buildings and recreational venues were in the centre of the hilltop, surrounded by beautifully designed parks and gardens, with ponds and fountains. A paradise ready for the new colonists.

Carlin hunters travelling north from their villages in the south to their hunting grounds in the thick, tangled lowland forests would look up at the flanks of the hill as they passed by. They saw the developing steps along the hill's flanks, the orchards, the grain fields and vegetable gardens.

Occasionally, they would follow the track heading east and up to the hilltop, staring at the new Human village in wonder. Never lingering long, they travelled to their hunting grounds and, upon returning home with their smoked meats, carried news of the developing Human village with them. The wonder of Human construction was spreading.

Most of the colonists currently living on the twelve interstellar colonial push ships were true spacers. They'd been born in space and they preferred to live in space. That was their way. They were constructing the new mega-colony, Cis-Luns Colonial Central Command, to be their home, the first of many O'Neil-style colonies to be built. It would take them five years.

There was, however, a good portion of the Human colonists who had chosen instead to live planetside in the newly developed colony. They numbered around two thousand and they waited patiently to be allocated housing and appropriate job positions, commensurate with their skill sets.

Amongst the Human colonists were the Mimasian Thols and Xi-Bootis A Secundus was their ancestral homeworld, which they called Homwol. So wondrous it was that Homwol had finally been located that two hundred Mimasian Thols applied straight away to return to their homeworld as colonists. They were the lucky ones who were able to get berths on the interstellar push ship, Artemisia. There were many other Mimasian Thols that were not so lucky.

The Mimasian Thols had converted an ancient, yet functional military transport to support another two hundred and fifty of their people for the twenty two light-year crossing to Homwol. That transport ship, the CTT-VC-999, was even now tightly docked and coupled to the Artemisia's dorsal hull. Two hundred Mimasian Thols quickly alighted the Artemisia and re-boarded the CTT-VC-999 to travel to the surface of Homwol along with the other two hundred and fifty of their kin.

The Human colony, simply named Hilltop, was now open for colonists and that was their first, temporary destination on Homwol. Their final destination was the Jula Jula forests to the north and it was there that they intended to build their homes amongst their distant cousins, the Indigenous Thols. The dream of all Mimasian Thols was to return home and yet, there were another quarter of a million more Mimasian Thols still living inside of Mimas, back in the Sol system.

The interstellar push ships held Human crews of two hundred. These were not colonists. Once the new mega-colony was completed in five years' time and all of the colonists had been offloaded, the twelve push ships were to return to the Sol system and take on board more colonists. The colonisation of the Xi-Bootis double-star system was an ongoing project.

Xi-Bootis A had a true Earth analogue planet, Secundus, called Vale by the Carlins and Homwol by the Thols; Indigenous species both. In addition to Secundus, there was a Venus analogue, a Hell world, for later terraforming.

There were four large Galilean-sized moons around a Jupiter analogue planet, all with useful resources, including a great many L-Four and L-Five gravitational zones and even a pair of well-populated Trojan asteroid fields. Beyond that world was a vast, heavily populated asteroid field.

Xi-Bootis B had even more possibilities. Its primary orbital zone was a co-orbital system unlike any other; never seen before in any other solar system.

There was a Saturn analogue world, Primus Major, with a Mars analogue moon, simply called Alpha, that was almost habitable; it just needed a bit of tweaking.

Then there was a quasi moon of Primus Major, a super Mars analogue world, Primus Quasi, that was habitable, but tidally locked to its Sun. Trailing Primus Major in its orbit was the Trojan world, Primus, another true, although tidally locked, Earth analogue. It also had multiple Indigenous sapient species.

There was also a Neptune analogue world with no fewer than seven large moons, more useful resources and their accompanying L-Four and L-Five gravitational zones. A sparse asteroid field existed between the primary and secondary orbital zones.

Many more colonists would be arriving from the Sol system. The colonisation process just took time. It was inevitable, unstoppable and simply had to be managed.

The rich resources of the Xi-Bootis system were an open invitation to those who would exploit it, which is why High Admiral Roberta Nummus was there. No government could prevent it from happening; they could only guide it and manage the outcomes. That was the High Admiral's task.

It was a little over four and a half months since the sojourn of Kitty and her parents to the interstellar push ship Artemisia in Cis-Luns L-Five. During that time, Angelique and her Mother, Simone, visited every weekend. There were even occasions when Angelique's younger Brother, Johnathon, accompanied them. Angelique and Kitty's relationship had deepened considerably, as had the friendship between Simone and Kitty's Mother, Keegali. Johnathon had become good friends with Kitty's younger Brothers as well. During this time, Kitty and her family learned English and the Reas family learned Carlinish. Over those four and a half months, they had all become quite proficient in each other's tongues.

The usual mode of transport from the Artemisia in Cis-Luns L-Five to the Carlin village was James Reas's personal transport. A Manta Ray class passenger transport, which was small enough to land within the boundaries of Kelyarn's and Keegali's family plot on a relatively clear patch of ground. Angelique now had her class five pilot's license and was more than proficient at piloting the craft.

Today, however, Angelique was piloting High Admiral Roberta Nummus's personal ship, a Tristar Interplanetary Stealth Fighter, the Dark Angel, and it was far too big to land within any Carlin family plot. Angelique touched down gently, the Dark Angel's whisper quiet anti-gravity thrusters earning their name, in the large circular village centre in front of Kelyarn's and Keegali's family plot.

Unlike James Reas's Manta Ray, which was skinned in a silver colouration, the Dark Angel's hull was skinned in a deep midnight black. A black so dark that it seemed to absorb and swallow any light that touched it. Half the village had watched it descend and now they surrounded the Dark Angel in fear, fascination and curiosity. They crowded into the village centre and even the plots that surrounded it. Angelique Reas was highly proficient at piloting the Dark Angel; it was the very ship that she had trained in.

The first one out of the Dark Angel's ventral airlock was Johnathon Reas. He bounded straight over to Kelyarn's and Keegali's family plot, waved to them, then jumped up onto the gate, rolled over it and, flipping about, landed squarely on his feet before bolting over to Kitty's Brothers to play.

Keegali had never seen anyone leap over their gate in such a fashion. Johnathon had cleared the gate in a heartbeat, in one quick, clean motion; he was almost Carlinish in his movements. Kelyarn opened their gate wide to let their guests in without having to leap it.

Angelique shook her head at Johnathon's antics and, looking around at the gathered Carlin villagers, addressed them in perfect Carlinish, "It's okay", she gestured to the Dark Angel, "This is just my Aunt Roberta's spaceship. It's a sweet ride", she told them.

The casual remark did little to dissuade their concerns and Angelique continued over to Kitty and her family, greeting them and then giving Kitty a warm embrace.

James, his Wife, Simone and High Admiral Roberta Nummus stepped out of the airlock and walked over to the gate and greeted Kelyarn and Keegali. Kitty had already led Angelique off to the house so they could be alone together, to catch up. They headed straight to the fourth-level sleep room.

Roberta explained to Kelyarn and his Wife, Keegali, in perfect Carlinish, "I thought I'd come with James and Simone today. I'm hoping to look around your plot and perhaps your house to get an idea of what a typical Carlin household is like. With that knowledge, we can better offer what we have to make things a little easier for your people."

"What kinds of things?", Keegali enquired in almost perfect English, wanting to get more practice in.

James fielded the question, explaining, "Fridges and freezers to keep your food from spoiling. Cleaner, more robust cooking stoves. Even composting toilets that can turn one's daily ablutions into high-grade fertiliser without any odour or the passing on of any diseases."

Keegali and Kelyarn both smiled, and Kelyarn noted, "I can show you our garden. We have been planting some of the seeds you gave us at our first meeting. Many of our Carlin families have."

"So Angelique has said. Angelique told us you've planted peas, beans, capsicums, chillies, radishes and potatoes, even corn. It will be interesting to see how they're growing", Roberta remarked, adding, "We have our own people who want to know what mushrooms you guys grow. They'd like to add some of them to our own fungiculture operations. Of course, we can share ours in return."

The discussions continued as they casually walked towards the house. Over by the house, Johnathon had set up a swing rope in a tall Bell Nut Fruit tree and was swinging from it as if he were Tarzan. Kelyarn's and Keegali's Boys were all taking turns with Jonathon.

Keegali cried out to one of her Daughters, a female kit about twelve years old, "Kayala. Keep an eye on your Brothers. Make sure that they don't get carried away and hurt themselves."

They walked around the house to the back of the plot and Kelyarn showed them his family's garden. There were a lot of native plants, vegetables and tubers of various kinds, some of which looked almost Earth-like and others, of course, which looked totally alien.

In the middle, amongst all of the native species were the peas, beans, capsicums, chillies, radishes, potatoes and two rows of corn. They were all growing based on the instructions they'd been given in written Carlinish.

Roberta was both stunned and pleased to see how well they were growing, of the native vegetables and tubers she noted, "Our botanists would love to see this, perhaps they could collect some samples and some seeds."

Kelyarn smiled as he replied in faltering English, "You gave us your seeds, we can give you our seeds. It is only fair, one exchange for another"; it was eminently practical.

As they walked back to the house, James pointed to their outside wash house, their outhouse, noting, "Angelique mentioned you can't use your outhouse after dusk. She said that it was far too dangerous. That predators sometimes came into the village at night."

The blue stripes on Keegali's face became dull, her ears flattened and her whiskers drooped, "Yes. Sometimes a pack of wild Vorts will come in along the roadways. Sometimes an old Kyrrax with bad teeth will climb the outer walls of the village looking for soft, easy prey", Keegali noted; her tone was deadly serious.

Kelyarn leaned in, his blue stripes dulling and his whiskers drooping, stating, "Most of our dry stone walls are five feet high. The walls around the village perimeter are much higher, seven and even eight feet high. Yet, a Kyrrax can climb them. For those four-legged predators, no wall is high enough to stop them."

Keegali added, "The Carlin-folk who live in the outer plots or along the roadways leading into the village. They will keep two, three, even four domestic Vorts to keep the predators at bay."

"Even then, each year a predator will succeed in taking a Gudong or, far, far worse, a kit", Keegali noted.

As James ran his eye over the Carlinish wash house, he noted, "If we build a covered walkway from your back door to the outhouse, it will prevent predation. We can include doors on either side of the walkway for easy daytime ingress and egress, which can be closed and locked at night. Then we just need to add ventilation windows along the top of the walls."

Kelyarn stood there in shock, "Such a simple solution. I should have thought of that myself", he shook his head, "I will get some stone and lumber, and start work on the walkway at the soonest convenience."

Kayala rushed up with Johnathon's swing rope in her hands, "Father, I took this thing down. My Brothers are getting far too carried away", she passed the rope to Kelyarn, "You need to hide it."

Kelyarn sighed, "Carlin kits and their Carlin kit chaos", he remarked, shaking his head.

They entered the house and made their way to the kitchen, the beating heart of any Carlinish home. Keegali provided them with refreshing Gudong milk to drink. Roberta carefully scanned the kitchen with her communicator, which recorded not just the scene but millimetre-accurate measurements.

"Apart from replacing your current toilet systems with clean composting systems, we can fit in a proper fridge in here to keep your food cold and a freezer for longer term food storage", Roberta noted, adding as she looked at their fired clay cooking stove with its grill and five conical cooking towers, each designed to support a pot or a pan, "We can replace your cooking stove with something that works in the same way, but is far more robust. Pressed iron stoves are always nice and rustic. I kind of like them myself as well."

"Pressed iron?", Keegali enquired.

"Yes. It's far stronger than fired clay and it transmits heat far better. Set up correctly, it can also help heat your house", Roberta explained, noting, "It will still burn wood or charcoal, so your cooking will still maintain its correct flavour profile."

Simone chimed in, "That's actually an elegant solution. It's a step up from your current cooking station and yet, not a step too far away from what you're currently using."

James stepped in, "All of our technology is powered by long-lasting batteries that last literally for decades. When they begin to run low on power, their battery management systems contact our maintenance departments."

That went straight over Kelyarn's head, "What would you require in exchange for these new things?"

"If you insist on a trade, Kelyarn, then not much more than botanical seed samples and friendship", James replied, adding, "We don't really need much. We are more interested in helping you and your people."

As they sat down around the kitchen table to drink their Gudong milk, a small female Carlin about four years old came into the kitchen and sat on Kayala's knee.

"Hey, little Kearill, are you thirsty?", Kayala asked.

Little Kearill nodded and replied, "Gudong milk, please."

Kayala passed Kearill her own cup of Gudong milk, "This one's my favourite. My little Sister, Kearill, she's only four. Aren't you, sweety?"

Kearill nodded as she looked around the table at the Humans.

Kayala then noted, "James and Simone have two kits, Angelique and Johnathon", before asking, "How many kits do you have, Admiral Nummus?"

Roberta smiled and replied, "A long time ago, I had an adopted Daughter. Her name was Lina, Lina Mitchel. There are more than a few of her descendants amongst the colonists up at Hilltop."

"Descendants?", Keegali enquired.

Roberta sighed and nodded, "Yes, descendants, Keegali. My Lina passed away many, many centuries ago."

Keegali's eyes shot wide open and she enquired, "Just how old are you, Admiral Nummus?"

James Reas did the math quickly in his head and stepped in, "Roberta Nummus is thirteen hundred and ninety years old."

"Thirteen hundred and ninety years old?", Kelyarn repeated questioningly.

Simone stepped back in and explained, "Our Aunt Roberta is the one and only Human immortal."

Roberta looked around the table at the shocked Carlin faces, "That which makes me immortal means that I can never have children of my own, my own kits", before her eyes landed on little Kearill.

Little Kearill finished drinking her Sister's Gudong milk, climbed down out of her lap and then climbed up on Roberta's lap. She leaned in close and placed her little arms around Roberta's waist.

"No kits. Immortals must be so lonely", the young Carlin kit commented.

Roberta smiled as a single tear escaped and ran down her cheek, "Yes, little one. Immortals do get lonely", she confirmed while absently stroking Kearill's cheek.

Kayala's whiskers raised and she smiled, commenting, "When you feel lonely, Roberta Nummus, come and visit us. Our little Kearill loves cuddles."

Roberta smiled and replied, "Only if little Kearill wants me to."

Little Kearill replied softly, "Yes, please. Johnathon's always too busy playing and Angelique only wants cuddles from my big Sister, Kitty", before she blurted out, "They sleep together on the same sleeping mat and have naked cuddles."

Roberta's eyes opened wide and she looked to Simone, who confirmed, "Angelique and Kitty are in a relationship. I'll explain it all to you later. It's a Carlinish thing."

Roberta thought back to the day of first contact, to the friendship that was developing between Angelique and Kitty and then thought to herself, "*Why didn't I see that coming?*"

Simone, Angelique and Johnathon stayed with Kitty and her family, while Roberta Nummus and James Reas flew back towards the Human hilltop colony to the north.

Roberta asked James, "When were you going to tell me, James?"

"It was a personal matter involving my Daughter, Angelique and Kitty", James replied, noting, "It also involved Kitty's personal medical condition and records. It was a privacy matter."

Roberta nodded, "Well, James, I kind of know now, don't I?"

James opened up a file on his data tablet and tapped it three times. The file automatically transferred to Roberta's own data tablet and she read through the document.

"Blood test results. Full body medical scans", Roberta noted as she read through the document to its conclusion, "Severe clinical depression at a crucial age in Kitty's adolescent development. Negative outcomes, including premature quickening and oestrus, leading to persistent oestrus and multiple organ failure, have been avoided. Persistent oestrus, well, that does not sound good at all."

Roberta read the final recommendation, "Angelique Reas is Kitty Carlin-folk's emotional and biochemical anchor. Their continued relationship is recommended with medical monitoring. Well, now, that is just fascinating."

James agreed, noting, "The Carlins have certain biological imperatives and we can unintentionally and adversely interfere with those. My Daughter has become Kitty's emotional and biochemical support. At least until Kitty goes through her quickening naturally in around three years."

Roberta nodded before making a decision, "James, make sure our medical department is aware of this. We need to keep a close eye on any other possible biochemical interaction with the Carlins."

"Doctor Morrow is already working on that. He has blood samples and full body biomedical scans from Kitty and her parents, so he's building a baseline for future Carlin medical needs", Jame replied, before noting, "We look at the Carlins and we automatically think that they're feline, but they're far more complex. They look like felines, sure, and they breed like lions, sure, but their biochemistry is very similar to mustelids, to ferrets."

Roberta nodded as she continued flying north.

Back in Keegali's household, Simone sat with Kayala and young Kearill at the kitchen table while Kelyarn and Keegali went about their daily chores.

"Kayala, your Mother mentioned losing her firstborn kit to the great sorrows", Simone mentioned.

"Yes. I was not yet eight at the time. Kearill wasn't even born", Kayala replied, then she frowned and her whiskers drooped, "It was a very sad time. Mother lost two kits in the span of less than three months. So very sad it was."

"Can you tell me what happened? Or is that something you can't talk about?", Simone enquired.

"Mother's firstborn was Krylla. She was a beautiful girl. When Carlin girls reach five years of age, we start helping our Mothers. Krylla was the firstborn and started by looking after her newborn Brother, Korval. He was a brand new kit, just born and to Krylla, he was so special. Krylla treated Korval like her own kit. No sibling bond can be greater", Kayala explained, she almost laughed, it would have been a sad laugh, though, "Krylla would have suckled him at her own breasts if she could have."

"And what happened to them?', Simone asked.

"I was eight, Korval was twelve and Krylla was seventeen; approaching the age of quickening", Kayala remembered, tears began to well, "The adults and older kits were planting the masuli grain in the fields. The younger kits were playing by the outer wall and the other kits were just all playing."

Kayala stopped and wiped her eyes, "Beyond the grain fields is a burnt zone. A buffer that we keep clear to deter predators from approaching. We are supposed to avoid that buffer zone; it is simply far too dangerous to be close to tall bluegrass. Korval, his Brothers and Cousins were playing stickball. They have a ball and they hit it really hard with a stick."

Simone understood, "We have similar ball games as well."

"A Cousin hit the ball very hard and it landed in the buffer zone. Instead of asking one of the hunters, who were all armed and watching for predators to retrieve it, Korval ran out after the ball", Kayala recounted, with freely flowing tears, she continued, "Mother and Krylla called out to him to come back. He picked up the ball and threw it to his Cousin and then he started walking back to us."

Kayala faltered and then continued through flowing tears, "A Kyrrax lunged out of the tall bluegrass. Its jaws clamped around Korval's head and its teeth dug deep. Korval's head popped! It just popped! We all heard it and we knew that he was dead. Then the Kyrrax dragged Korval's body back into the bluegrass."

"They never found his body. The hunters tracked that Kyrrax to a large stand of lowland forest northwest of here, where it disappeared and they could not follow", Kayala wiped the tears from her eyes, "Krylla entered the deep sorrows; her blue stripes turned a deathly ashen grey. Her quickening came on far too early and, along with it, the unbonded heat. She died within three months of Korval's death."

Angelique and Kitty were standing in the doorway that led to the stairs and had heard the last part of the story Kayala was telling.

"Mum, you must never speak to Keegali about this", Angelique advised.

Simone wrapped her arms around Kayala and let her cry on her shoulder before asking, "Why?"

Angelique and Kitty came into the kitchen and sat down while Angelique explained, "Carlin Mothers have so many kits that they don't have time to grieve properly. For every kit they lose, they have others that need their constant attention. So they can't grieve; instead, they push all of their grief aside and bury it, then force themselves to smile and carry on. Mum, a Carlin Mother, loses sixty to seventy percent of her kits and still has ten or more others to raise. Carlin Mothers simply cannot process grief the way we do."

Kayala had stopped crying and wiped her eyes, "Please don't speak to my Mother about this. It will upset her greatly."

Kitty agreed, adding, "Angelique is right. It would turn my Mother's blue stripes grey."

Angelique nodded in agreement, "Understood. I'll not bring this up again", and then she noted, "It certainly wouldn't have helped, not being able to recover Korval's body. I mean, no closure."

Kayala sat up and, with a wisdom belied by her twelve years of life, replied, "That is a Carlin Mother's lot in life. Many kits come into our world, many kits leave it and a Carlin Mother has no time to grieve any of it. No time at all."

Roberta flew her ship, the Dark Angel, past the Human hilltop colony, heading further to the north. Their destination wasn't the Human colony. Their destination was at the borders of the mighty Jula Jula forests farther north, where the indigenous Thols built their tree villages.

Where the tangled lowland forests met the tall Jula Jula forests, there was a sharp, abrupt delineation that stretched far off into the distance, both to their left and to their right as far as their eyes could see. The Jula Jula forests were vast, truly vast.

Sitting on a high grassy knoll surrounded by the thick, tangled lowland forests that lined the edges of the Jula Jula forests was the Mimasian Thol transport ship CTT-VC-999. It had flown up from the Human colony two days earlier.

A smaller, far more modern colonial troop transport was landed on the grassy knoll close by, near its port side. On the starboard side of the Mimasian transport was another colonial transport, an engineering transport.

The colonial troops had set up repulsor barriers around the perimeter of the grassy knoll to keep the local predators, Kyrrax and wild Vort packs, amongst other predators, at bay. Some of those local predators, a large species of what the Carlins called Fern Dragons, labelled Wyverns by the colonists, were man-sized and could fly. As a result, the colonial troops, armed with pulsed laser rifles, had taken up guarding positions within the repulsor barrier to ensure that any flying predators were kept well at bay.

There were a lot of Androids, all dressed as Humans, to avoid scaring the Indigenous Thols and they were busily unloading supplies. Of particular interest were the disassembled parts of what looked like elevator systems. These were stacked to one side on the grassy knoll within the repulsor barriers. It looked like there were six complete sets of them.

Some of the Androids had been harvesting local timber, vines and immense, thick leaves that grew in the local lowland forests. The Mimasian Thols had described in detail what they needed and how it was to be cut, graded, treated and prepared.

Those locally harvested resources had been stacked, ready for use, within the repulsor barriers. It was obvious that the current operation had been ongoing since well before the Mimasian Thol transport arrived. Perhaps for several weeks, as multiple supply drops had apparently been made.

"Busy as beavers our Mimasian Thol friends have been", James Reas noted as he looked over the grassy knoll, advising, "I don't see anywhere to actually land."

Roberta smiled and chuckled, "You're looking for a patch of ground, James. I'm just going to dock the Dark Angel on the CTT-VC-999's central dorsal docking port. It's as simple as that."

James shook his head, "Of course, why didn't he think of that?"

Roberta docked the Dark Angel perfectly, the inky black skin of its hull almost absorbing and swallowing Cathol's midday sunlight. Roberta left the Dark Angel's anti-gravity lifters running at their lowest level to mitigate any strain on the CTT-VC-999's structure. They were planetside after all and gravity could be a bitch.

"Let's have a look around and see what all this fuss is about", Roberta suggested.

Once on the ground, they met two Mimasian Thol colonists. Their English was laced with Tholish trills, clicks and soft barks. Yannick was in charge of the operation. His Wife, Yealah, was a clinical diagnostician; her purpose was to attend to any illnesses or injuries that occurred. So far, Yealah had used standard bone-knitters to fix the broken wings on two Indigenous Thols. Something that she had not considered when they first arrived on location.

As this was considered a dangerous place to be, both James and Roberta wore their full tactical body armour, complete with pulsed laser pistol sidearms, knives and machetes. Both carried kukri swords, sheathed and horizontally mounted on the utility belts at the backs. Roberta's Katana, the Harōingu, or the Harrowing, in English, was slung in its scabbard across her back.

Yannick and Yealah greeted them both and led them to a nearby hovercar before driving north into the Jula Jula forest. The trees were enormous. Many of the larger ones were close to five hundred feet tall, if not taller, with trunks easily sixty to eighty feet or more across at the base.

"I'm glad you're both armed", Yannick noted with a dryness, explaining, "The Indigenous Thols are far too tolerant of predators. We Mimasian Thols are not. We would have driven the predators away from the villages long ago."

"So wild Vort packs and Kyrrax hunt around the forest floor? Even here?", James queried.

Yealah stepped in, her voice full of concern, laced with trills and clicks, "Yes, even here, wild Vorts, Kyrrax, amongst other things. All Thols fly, as you know, but the Indigenous Thols seem rather uncaring about the ground predators. They're are apparently even Sleimorp packs in these forests."

"No, that can't be right. The Sleimorp packs hunt much farther to the west", Roberta corrected.

"So we thought too", Yealah admitted, noting with trills and clicks, "However, the locals have told us that Sleimorp packs can still be found hunting this far east."

James quickly enquired, "The Sleimorps? They look like an oversized hairless Velociraptor, don't they? Long, sickle-shaped talons on their hind feet. Grasping front hands with long claws."

"And a two-foot-long retractable bone-sword sheathed inside the skin of their tails", Roberta added.

"Yeah. That's an accurate description", Yannick confirmed, adding with trills and clicks, "They also have an almost sapient level of intelligence as well."

"Intelligent sub-sapient predators. Just what every Tholish woman needs running around under her home", Yealah added sarcastically, wondering, "Why on Mimas did we bloody well come here again?"

Yannick stopped their hovercar in front of the biggest tree that either James or Roberta had ever seen; well over five hundred feet tall and close to a hundred feet across the base of its trunk.

Yannick looked around and pointed out another, smaller tree in the distance, "You see that tree. It's a juvenile Jula Jula tree. Our trees inside Mimas were kind of like that one, somewhat taller, but very similar."

Yealah explained, trilling and clicking, "Juvenile Jula Jula trees are solid right through. When they mature at just under two hundred feet tall, they develop a hollow centre. That hollow centre grows as the tree grows."

Yannick drew their attention back to the huge tree in front of them, trilling and clicking, "The hollow in the centre of that tree is over forty feet across."

Roberta had lived inside Mimas for centuries. She had seen the trees that the Mimasian Thols built their tree houses in. They were ridiculously tall and broad across the trunks. Those trees were not Jula Jula trees, although they were a lesser, related species of tree. They were also not hollow in the centre. The sheer scale of true Jula Jula trees was staggering.

James Reas looked at the tree in front of them, asking curiously, "Why does that tree have a door in its trunk?", he was flabbergasted.

"We'll show you", Yannick chuckled, with trills and clicks, as he turned his hovercar's motion detectors on full and scanned the surrounding area.

Yannick and Yealah put on utility belts with holstered pulsed laser pistols and Roberta questioned them, "Mimasian Thols don't carry side arms?"

"Not ordinarily, but we know what lives at the base of these trees", Yealah trilled, clicked and softly barked, adding, "So, today, we all carry side arms."

Yannick added, trilling and clicking, "Nothing is showing up on the motion detectors, but keep your hands close to your side arms anyway. Kyrrax are ambush predators and Sleimorps, well, they're just really clever. They just know when to remain motionless."

Yealah mentioned, clicking, trilling, "We lost three Androids before the local Kyrrax understood Androids aren't edible."

Yannick chuckled with a trill and a bark, "No meat! It took three goes for the local Kyrrax to learn that", his face took on a grim look, "The Sleimorps, they just know the difference."

The doors of the hovercar opened and without any delay, they quickly walked to the base of the tree. The hovercar's doors automatically closed and locked behind them. Yannick unlocked and opened the door in the tree's trunk with one swift, clean motion.

Once inside the door, the lights came on automatically; Yannick closed the door behind them and locked it, trilling and clicking, "A Sleimorp can open doors. A Kyrrax, not so much."

They found themselves inside a tunnel carved through the tree's trunk. The door itself had been carved out of the first section sliced out of the trunk. The tunnel itself was thirty feet long and well illuminated.

When they entered the hollow at the end of the tunnel, the lighting came on automatically and they found themselves staring into a vast open space. It was easily forty feet across and when they looked up, they could see light at the very top, so the hollow was easily as deep as the tree was tall.

Around the walls of the hollow, there were a great many storage lockers carved out of the tree's trunk. Each one was covered by an ornately carved wooden door, the work of true craftsmen. In the centre of the hollow was an elevator, much like the disassembled ones they'd seen on the grassy knoll.

"This is the first elevator we've set up. We have another six more to install in the next six trees we colonise", Yealah informed them with trills and clicks.

"An elevator?", James questioned.

"Yes. Thols, Mimasian, or Indigenous can fly. Humans, whether Earthen or Martian and Carlins can not. Would you want to climb up a five-hundred-foot tree just to visit your friends?", Yealah trilled, clicked and softly barked in reply.

"Sorry, Yealah. It's just a lot to take in. I can see why they're needed", James replied.

Yannick gave Roberta and James a quick rundown of how Jula Jula tree housing worked, trilling and clicking, "Ninety five percent of the Indigenous Thols build their nests between three hundred and three hundred and fifty feet up. It's convenient for them. An easy flight up or down and if they feel like it, they can fly even higher. So most of the tree's *real estate* at that level is taken up by the Indigenous Thols."

"Our first elevator landing is at three hundred feet. Any Indigenous Thols who cannot fly because of age or injury will be free to travel beyond their nests", Yealah trilled and clicked, noting, "Before our arrival, such Indigenous Thols were completely nest-bound. They couldn't go anywhere."

Yannick continued, clicking and trilling, "The second elevator landing is at three hundred and fifty feet. For fifty feet above that, there are some Indigenous Thol nests. Mostly those who came to the village after all of the preferred *'real estate'* was already taken up. Some of us Mimasian Thols may build our tree houses at that level. That will be a personal choice."

Yealah chimed in, trilling and clicking, "The third elevator landing is at four hundred feet. We expect most of us Mimasian Thols will build our tree houses at or above that level. We don't want to overly intrude on our Indigenous Cousins."

Yannick trilled and clicked, "There is a fourth elevator landing at the four hundred and fifty foot level. We are going to turn that into a cross-species community gathering and recreation space."

Yealah smiled and added trilling, "The view of the stars above that level is truly glorious, it is amazing!"

Roberta summed up, "So Indigenous Thols on the lower residential level. Mimasian Thols on the upper residential level and a mixture of both on the middle residential level."

Yannick confirmed, clicking and trilling, "Pretty much. For this Indigenous tree village, at least and for any other existing Indigenous tree villages. If we start a brand new tree village, those rules won't apply. It will be all new tree *'real estate'*, and there will be plenty of room for all Thols, Indigenous or Mimasian, at every possible residential level."

They all stepped into the elevator and Yealah pressed the button for the third landing, trilling and clicking, "At each landing, there is a tunnel leading to the outer tree trunk. For each level, we've built three broad balconies and those are all connected via a spiral staircase that hugs the outer tree trunk. The staircases run around the tree's trunk clockwise, following the apparent motion of Cathol across the sky. That seems to be something the Indigenous Thols like, although south of the Masula River, it is apparently the reverse. All of the balconies have strong safety railings; we can't have our guests falling off the edge."

Yannick added, trilling and clicking, "Thols, Indigenous or Mimasian, can land on or launch off from the balconies as they see fit."

Roberta had watched Yealah push the button to the third landing and she enquired, "So, what's on the third landing exactly?"

"We are about to show you, Roberta Nummus", Yealah trilled.

The elevator stopped at the third landing. Roberta and James followed Yealah and Yannick through another tunnel carved out of the tree's trunk on its northern side.

A Mimasian Thol's features and dispositions were so angelic, it was as if they were being led by a pair of Angels. Eventually, they stepped out onto the broad balcony, labelled level three, balcony one. The view was spectacular.

Yealah led them toward the balcony's safety railing and pointed to an Indigenous Thol nest at a slightly lower level. It was a circular object, nestled in the fork of a massive tree branch. It didn't look like much; all that they could really see was its shape and the large, shiny leaves on its roof.

"Is that an Indigenous Thol nest?", asked Roberta, noting, "They look so different from your tree houses."

Yealah confirmed, trilling and clicking, "Yes, that is an Indigenous Thol nest. It's quite high up and relatively new. Those resin-coated leaves can't be much more than six months old."

Yannick went on to describe the typical Indigenous Thol nest, clicking, trilling and softly barking, "Usually, the Indigenous Thols build nests with a nesting bowl that's twenty to twenty five feet across. They then cover that with a roof, a canopy, that's twenty five to thirty feet across."

Yealah chimed in, trilling "They look like one nest with an even larger upturned nest over the top."

"They're made using extremely flexible branches and vines gathered from the lowland forests. That in itself is very hazardous work. We use our Androids to do that sort of work", Yannick trilled and clicked.

"They weave the branches together and bind them all with vines. The result is a really tight and structurally sound nest", Yannick continued, trilling and clicking.

"They stuff moss and mud mixed with tree sap resin into any gaps to stop the wind from getting in. That moss continues to thrive and over time, the nest blends into the background. That's another reason that we can tell that this one is quite new", Yealah added with a few trills and clicks, noting, "They weather-proof their canopies using large leaves from the lowland forests."

Yannick smiled as he trilled, "They process those leaves with a tree sap resin and then glue them in place. From start to finish, they can build a nest like that one in a week or two. The owners of that nest, Yorvick and Yarling, built it about three weeks before first contact took place. It is still very new."

"Now, that is very interesting timing", Roberta quietly noted.

"In between the walls of their nest and the walls of the canopy is a gap, which they use to enter and leave their nest. They usually fly up, fold in their wings as they enter the gap and simply climb into the nest. Some of them can get reckless; they'll approach the gap way too fast, fold in their wings at the very last second and let their momentum carry them into the nest. That is very dangerous. If they get distracted or their timing is off by even a fraction of a second, they can get injured, even break a wing", Yealah informed them with trills, clicks and a harsh bark.

Yealah continued, trilling and clicking, "An older Indigenous Thol that can't fly or one with a broken wing can only enter and leave the nest along the branch.

Their mobility is severely limited. Our balcony and elevator system should alleviate that. Usually, when they leave their nest, they just drop over the side and glide away."

"That's not all they drop over the side of their nests", Yannick trilled with disdain, noting with clicks and barks, "All of their rubbish and their daily ablutions just get tossed over the side. You do not want to be walking underneath that, trust me."

Yealah reached out and grabbed his arm, trilling and clicking, "Don't be so judgemental, Yannick. There's usually nothing on the forest floor except for Harricks and animals, and they never build their nests above another Thol's nest. Our Indigenous Thol Cousins live a cooperative hunter-gatherer, foraging existence."

James enquired, "How on Earth do they cook? Those nests must be a fire hazard."

Yealah trilled a quick laugh and then explained with further trills and clicks, "They generally use communal cooking hearths, situated on safe rocky outcrops and then they carry their cooked food back home. Although there are some more progressive Indigenous Thols like Yorvick and Yarling. They have a large flat stone and a baked clay hearth inside their nest. If you look at the very centre of their nest's canopy, you'll notice a clay weather cap above the smoke outlet. Yorvick was very interested in our tree house, by the way. Both he and Yarling flew up to watch its construction on several occasions. They were actually studying our construction methods."

James looked more closely and yes, there was a clay weather cap. There were even small wisps of smoke.

Roberta's eyes were drawn to her left. She'd noticed something in her peripheral vision.

Roberta turned to her left and exclaimed, "Now that is what I call a proper Tholish tree house!"

Roberta started walking in that direction. James, Yannick and Yealah followed.

Roberta stared at the tree house. There was a suspension bridge crossing the gap from the broad balcony around the tree's trunk to the tree house itself, connecting at its front porch. It was a typical Mimasian Thol tree house. Roberta had seen many of them inside Mimas; she had even stayed in one or two of them over the centuries that she'd lived there.

Yealah's and Yannick's tree house had three levels. The suspension bridge provided safe access for those who could not fly, directly to the front porch and door on the mid-level. The lower level was all utilities, bathroom, toilet, laundry and storage. In the middle level was the foyer, family room, living room and kitchen.

Inside the top level, there were the bedrooms. In typical Mimasian Thol fashion, there would be four bedrooms. A bedroom for the parents, a bedroom each for two children, which Yannick and Yealah currently did not have, and a spare bedroom for family guests.

The tree house was built in a typical Mimasian modular design. Each module, room, was built of the same materials as an Indigenous Thol's nest; just the modules, although similar, were different. They were all of the same basic circular design, but their sizes varied depending on their purpose. Each module was interconnected where the sides of the modules met.

The entire structure was tightly bound to the enormous tree branches around it by specially treated vines that were exceedingly strong and resilient. Vines treated in this way by the Mimasian Thols had a high tensile strength and breaking strain; they also did not rot.

Roberta stared in wonder, noting, "Guys, it's been a while since I've seen a proper Tholish tree house. Nothing else compares. Not even tree houses made by our own people."

Yannick gave off a Tholish chuckle, trilling and clicking, "All of the modern conveniences as well. There's no crapping over the sides of our nest."
Yealah rolled her eyes and trilled, "Our Indigenous Cousins will take on board our technology at their own pace, Yannick."

Yealah trilled and clicked, noting, "The inside is still being worked on, so it's not quite finished yet. When it is, you are most welcome to visit us; even stay overnight if you wish."

Roberta nodded, "I might take you up on that, Yealah. The best night's sleep I'd ever had was in a Tholish tree house back inside Mimas."

Yealah replied, clicking, trilling and softly barking, "High Admiral Robert Nummus. I must mention that we Mimasian Thols are currently divided. We are not all in agreement, now that we are all finally here on Homwol."

Roberta looked surprised. She had not heard anything about this. That Yealah had used her official title in full meant that the issue was serious, extremely serious.

Yannick saw her confusion and quickly stepped in; his words were precise and he clipped his trilling and clicking short, "When we came here, we all expected a thriving Thol society, much like we have back inside Mimas. None of us had considered that our Indigenous Cousins would be so primitive, just simple hunter-gatherers, foraging for their existence. It was quite a shock, I can tell you! We Mimasian Thols and our Indigenous Thol Cousins are just so very different!"

"It's not just physical differences either. I mean, we Mimasian Thols are all the same height, five feet. The Indigenous Thols vary from well under five feet to well over six feet. Our skin tones are all alabaster white; their skin tones vary from white to almost Human skin tones. We are vegetarians, they are omnivores, they eat grubs, insects and even meat. Our society is matriarchal; theirs is patriarchal. They even have religious dogma and ancient taboos. They expect us to follow their dogma as well.", Yannick explained, leaning in closer, "And their behaviour. They squabble, they argue and they fight amongst themselves more than Humans do! Many of us Mimasian Thols are just so disappointed! There are so many differences! They are not like us at all!"

Yealah chimed in, trying to minimise her trills and clicks for greater clarity, "Matriarch Ytryan is back at your Human colony in discussions with the leaders of our splinter groups, our factions!"

Yannick stepped in, trilling and clicking in frustration, "There are four factions! It is just so un-Tholish! Some want to stay here amongst our Indigenous Thol Cousins. Some want to wait, staying in your Human colony. They wish to build a new Mimasian Thol colony with your people at one of the secondary colony sites. They prefer a new colony with our Human friends; they do not want to live amongst the Indigenous Thols. The other two factions want to return to Cis-Luns L-Five, to the interstellar push ship Artemisia. One of those factions wants to live in the new mega-colony, Cis-Luns L-Five Colonial Central Command, with you, Humans. The fourth faction wants to return home with the interstellar push ships when they fly back to Sol. They are very disappointed and simply want to return to Mimas. It has become such a mess; we are so divided. Future Mimasian colonists will need to understand the true situation here."

Roberta sighed deeply as she replied, agreeing, "That is unprecedented. It's so un-Tholish! I have never seen Mimasian Thols disagree on anything. Not ever!"

James interjected, "And you'd know. You lived amongst them for four centuries."

Yealah nodded in agreement, her trills and clicks picking up with deep sadness, "We know that it is so un-Tholish. We also know it is very real. It is tearing our community apart."

Roberta rubbed her forehead, "You do understand that I cannot interfere. Your people have free agency to do as they wish. If they need help building a new joint Human Mimasian Thol colony at a secondary site, we will assist them, although that is a long way off in the future. They can stay in the Human colony in the interim. If they wish to live with my people at Cis-Luns L-Five, not a problem; they can do that. Those returning to Mimas, well, that is their choice. The interstellar push ships will return to Sol in five years."

James enquired, "And your choice, Yealah, Yannick?"

Yannick pointed to the almost completed tree house, "That is our choice. We are staying here with our Indigenous Cousins", he trilled.

Yealah trilled and clicked with more positive emotions, "We will live side by side with our Indigenous Thol Cousins. We will uplift them by example. They will watch us, they will learn from us and then they will choose what they wish us to provide them. Our Indigenous Cousins also have free agency."

Yannick wrapped his arm around Yealah and trilled happily, "Our faction is the largest. Most of those who booked passage have decided to stay here. Those who came on the CTT-VC-999 are a mixture of the other three factions. Most of those want to stay here, either in a new Human Thol colony down here or up at Cis-Luns L-Five Colonial Central Command."

Yealah agreed, trilling happily, "It is the smallest faction that wants to go back to Mimas", before noting, with a few trills and clicks, "We need more Martians to come here. Eight is not enough. We really do miss our Martian friends."

Roberta chuckled and replied, "I will send word back to Sol, but I suspect that the only Martians who will come out here will be the Martian hybrids. They have our Earthly wanderlust and the pure Martians don't."

"Just as long as they're Martians", Yealah smiled, trilling with delight at the thought, before she noted, "Their ancestors were once space-faring just as our Tholish ancestors were. Not so far nor as much as you Humans, but space-faring nonetheless."

As they casually talked, the sound of trilling, clicking and barking came from their right.

Yarling and Yorvick landed on the broad balcony, their heads dipped slightly in greeting before Yorvick trilled in their native Tholish. Neither Yarling nor Yorvick could speak English as yet.

Yorvick and Yannick trilled and clicked amongst themselves, while Yarling waited silently with what could only be described as a curious, enigmatic smile. She stared curiously at Roberta and James, not knowing what to make of them. To her, they looked like strange tailless Carlins, with hair and odd legs. Once Yorvick had finished speaking, he trilled something quickly to Yarling.

Yarling pointed to Yealah's and Yannick's Mimasian Thol tree house and trilled one word in fluent Carlinish, "Beautiful", before they both leapt over the balcony's safety railing and glided back to their own nest. Roberta and James watched as they both disappeared into the gap between their nest and its canopy.

"That was a quick visit", Roberta noted.

James smiled, noting, "It appears that Yarling approves of your tree house."

"You understand Carlinish?", Yealah trilled in surprise.

James smiled and explained, "It made sense to learn Carlinish. We do have Carlinish friends."

Yannick smiled and trilled, "The uplifting has begun. Yorvick wants to add four more nests to their existing nest. He just asked for my advice."

"Really", Roberta replied in astonishment.

"I'll fly down to their nest tomorrow and explain the technical details to him. He'll understand, our Indigenous Cousins are very fast learners", Yannick trilled and clicked in reply,

Yannick pointed to Yorvick's and Yarling's nest, trilling and clicking, "If we span the gap between the tree's branches at the back of their current nest with three or four long laminated, treated beams, then they can add on two more nests right there. That will form a nice triangle of nests. From there, they can add another two nests above the triangle, giving them five good-sized rooms. I'll have to make sure that it's all structurally sound, of course, but that's not a problem. It's just prudent engineering."

Roberta smiled broadly, commenting, "That was quick. I want this little project to succeed, Yannick. If it does, the other Indigenous Thols families will want something similar. Offer them help whenever they ask for it. This is a very important step. The credits will come out of the overall colonisation budget, so it's all covered financially."

Yannick and Yealah both nodded in agreement, with Yealah trilling, "We need to make friends here. As you said, Roberta Nummus, it is very important."

"Do we have any idea of which faction Matriarch Ytryan leans towards?", James enquired with curiosity.

"Our Matriarch, Ytryan, favours the concept of a new colony at one of the secondary colony sites", Yannick informed them, trilling and clicking, remarking, "Ytryan will stay in the Hilltop colony for now and when your people are ready, she will join them in opening up the new chosen colony site."

"I must say, I do find that surprising. Very surprising", Roberta replied.

"It does make sense", Yealah trilled back, noting, "It's the Indigenous Tholish High Councillors that pushed Ytryan into that direction. Whenever she meets with them, they only want to speak with her Husband. It has left Ytryan embarrassed and frustrated. She is our Matriarch and they unwittingly insult her."

Yannick trilled and clicked in explanation, "It's their Patriarchal leadership system. They see their women as bed partners and producers of younglings. Not as political personages in their own right. Matriarch Ytryan has received very little respect from the Tholish High Council since the day of first contact."

Roberta nodded, "I'm seeing the problem. At least Ytryan isn't going back to Mimas. Fortunately, we have three other secondary colony sites, but guys, that's not scheduled until the year thirty five hundred and those three sites are only provisional, pending further studies and investigation."

"Matriarch Ytryan is very patient and we Thols are quite long-lived. She will wait", Yealah trilled and clicked.

Yannick trilled and clicked, "Our Indigenous Cousins are so like us and yet they are not like us at all. It is complicated."

10. From Cat People to Space Lions.

It was a typical trading day in Kelyarn's village. The village centre outside of Kelyarn's plot was bustling, full of Carlin-folk and Indigenous Thols, each trading for the things that they wanted. The Carlins had set up trestle tables to show off their wares. The Indigenous Thols had flown in with their Gudong skin carry bags, which themselves had been crafted by the Carlins.

The commotion was not nearly as loud as one might have expected. Carlin and Thol alike were overly respectful of each other as they traded their wares, swapped their stories, and even shared their gossip.

Kitty and Angelique watched them from their shared sleep room on the fourth level of her family's house. They had a good view of the village centre, but it was still quite a distance away across her family's plot. Angelique quickly rummaged through her travel pack and pulled out a small pair of field glasses. She passed the binoculars to Kitty and showed her how to use them.

Kitty was surprised at how the binoculars made everything look so much closer. She kept lowering them to look with her own eyes and then raised them again to scan the village centre across the plot to the north. It was weird, truly weird, but then again, wasn't all Human technology weird?

Kitty's whiskers raised in both surprise and fascination. A broad Cheshire grin came over her face.

"There are at least six Humans here today and I'm pretty sure there are at least two Mimasian Thols. Their skin and hair are ridiculously white, really, really white and their hair is braided. Our Native Thols never braid their hair. They just let it hang freely in the wind. Their clothing is also very different. Our Native Thols don't mind if things just hang out", Kitty explained, almost laughing as she noted the last part.

"No way! Let me see", Angelique replied, holding her hand out for the binoculars.

Angelique scanned the village centre, "No way! I don't know who the Humans are, but those two Thols, I know them."

Angelique placed the binoculars down and jumped up, running off to find her Mother. Kitty followed her close behind.

Angelique ran to her Mother and grabbed her by the hand, dragging her in the direction of the front door, "Where are we going? What is so important?", she asked.

"Yannick and Yealah are here. You know, Ytryan's friends from the Artemisia. They're in the village centre. Quickly, Mum", Angelique replied.

Kitty and her Mother, Keegali, followed closely behind.

When they reached the plot's front gate, Simone immediately recognised Yannick and Yealah. She also noted that there were easily six to ten Humans wandering around the village centre, milling about with the crowd, but standing out like sore thumbs.

"Yealah, Yannick!", she called out.

With just a few quick flaps of their wings, both Mimasian Thols were at the gate.

"What are you guys doing here? We haven't seen you in ages", Simone enquired, her smile beaming.

"We were in the colony and heard that a group of Humans was going to come here, so we offered to come along to provide interpreter services. We do know both modern and ancient forms of Tholish and Carlinish, along with Human English", Yealah trilled and clicked in explanation.

Keegali, always the perfect host, commented, "You should come inside where you can catch up."

Yannick politely declined, trilling, "We can't today. We need to keep an eye on the Humans. Make sure that they don't accidentally cause an interspecies incident. Another time perhaps."

"Yes, the Humans have this uncanny habit of anthropomorphising everything", Yealah trilled and clicked, adding, "They keep referring to the Carlins as cat people. It is so disrespectful. We have to keep reminding them not to do that."

Simone chuckled, "I know what you mean. My own Son, Johnathon, sometimes refers to them as space lions, but he is only ten, so Keegali's family is fine with it. They all actually get along very well. This is Keegali and Kitty, by the way."

"That may be true, but not all Carlins are happy with it", Yealah trilled in reply.

"Okay, let's nip this in the bud", Simone suggested as she took out her communicator and spoke into it, "A.I., please locate all communication devices within the village that are registered to Humans. Once located, link them together for broadcast communications."

Within seconds, Simone's communicator was linked and ready for broadcast. She entered a message and set the status to emergency broadcast.

"Please turn towards the big house and look towards its front gate", the message read.

Communicators buzzed across the village centre and their Human owners all turned to look towards the big house and its front gate. They could all see their two Mimasian Thol interpreters, two Humans and a pair of Carlins standing at the gate.

Simone keyed in another message and broadcast it, *"Now that I have your attention. Please do not refer to the Carlins as cat people. It is rude, disrespectful and they really don't appreciate it. To avoid an interspecies incident, please refrain from using any term that equates the Carlins to cats."*

A series of replies appeared on Simone's communicators. Some of them said "*sorry*", a few said "*understood*", another couple said "*okay*", and one even said, "*my bad*".

"Don't you just love simple solutions?", Simone remarked.

Yannick and Yealah both nodded in agreement.

A woman with blue-rinse died hair approached them, "I was hoping to buy one of those beautiful Carlin jackets. You know, the ones with the hood", she looked at Angelique and Kitty, "Just like those", she pointed out.

Kitty, speaking in perfect English, replied, "Well, you can't have ours, but you can maybe make a trade for one out there", she gestured towards the crowd.

Angelique added, "Yeah, mine was a gift from my friend, Kitty. So I can't possibly trade it", and then she reached out for Kitty's hand and held it.

"Kitty?", the woman enquired, before whispering, "Isn't that a cat reference?"

Keegali explained, also in perfect English, "Our children are called kits. So Kitty is actually just a very popular Carlinish name. Nearly every family has a kit named Kitty. Mine is no exception."

"Extraordinary!", the woman exclaimed, before noting, "Your people and the Indigenous Thols don't accept our credits. They use these beads and polished stones."

Kitty nodded and explained, "Barter beads and barter stones. You can trade something you have for something that they have, or for barter beads and stones."

Keegali looked at the woman's jacket, "Your Human-made jacket is beautiful. Is it well-made? Very long-lasting?"

"Yes, all Human-made clothing is well-made and designed to last", the woman informed her.

"Good. Then you can trade. Just find a Carlin woman who is the same size as you and has a hooded jacket. Offer your jacket in exchange for hers and trade. It is a very simple system", Keegali explained, before adding, "Just remember to treat my people and the Native Thols with respect and they will be equally respectful with you. It is our way."

Angelique added, gesturing to her own Gudong leather jacket, "These jackets are made from Gudong hide leather. The Gudong leather has been waterproofed and softened. These jackets are incredibly warm and comfortable. I love mine, but then again, my friend Kitty did gift it to me."

"Thank you, young lady. I'll have a look around", she replied before moving back into the crowd.

It wasn't long afterwards that the lady with the blue-rinsed hair wandered back over wearing a nice Carlin-made, hooded Gudong leather jacket.

"Oh my God! This is so beautiful. It is so warm and comfy", the woman told them, her face beaming with a wide smile, before stating, "Your people could sell these in the Colony, you know. Make really good credits! Thank you so much!"

And then she walked off back into the crowd, perhaps to trade something else. Yannick and Yealah looked over at the crowd. There were a couple of other Humans now wearing Gudong leather jackets as well. Humans were learning to trade with the Carlins and the Indigenous Thols.

Angelique smiled and noted, "That lady is right, Mum, you know. People in the Colony would buy these jackets. There's probably a lot of Carlin-made things that Humans would buy. Not to mention Carlinish food products. I mean, who wouldn't like masuli-infused Gudong milk? And their Cheese!"

Simone was more realistic, "While you may be right, Angelique, the Carlins have no need of Human credits at the moment. Trade between our peoples hasn't really begun yet."

Yealah smiled and trilled, "Today has been a good day. Everybody is getting along fine. The Humans are making simple trades with simple gestures."

Yannick also smiled, trilling and clicking in reply, "Yes, today has been a good interaction and that is how I will write it up in my report later."

By and large, when small groups of Human colonists turned up in the Carlin village, their interactions proceeded with respect. A few colonists preferred to just walk along the cobblestone streets and paths, taking photos of the picturesque Carlin village. The colonists would wave at Carlins and Carlins would wave back. It was all very peaceful and polite.

The colonists soon learned that one day per week, the Indigenous Thols would fly from their tree villages in the northern forests to the Carlin villages in the south to trade with the Carlins. It was relatively easy to work out the day, just by watching the skies for the Indigenous Thols flying past the Human colony. Small groups of colonists would arrive on those days and attempt to trade with the Carlin and Indigenous Thols alike.

The problem, of course, was what to trade. The Carlins liked Human jackets, T-shirts and even underwear, which was something they'd never worn before. They just had to modify the underwear to take into account their long Carlinish tails. Although female underwear, such as bras, did not suit a Carlinish woman's six-breasted bust at all. So those were useless to the Carlin women.

The Indigenous Thols had no use for Human clothing at all, which did not take into account their wings or tails, in any way, shape or form.

What was traded to both Carlin and Indigenous Thols alike was jewellery, rings, bracelets and necklaces, even anklets. Of course, these items had to be traded for Carlin and Indigenous Thol wares.
The Human colonists had little use for barter beads and semi-precious barter stones in the Colony.

Those were simply traded for simple curiosity and kept as keepsakes with little value to them. One thing that was sought after was the larger, top-tier barter stones, the polished diamonds.

However, those were highly prized and sought after by both the Carlins and Indigenous Thols alike. They were also rarely traded at the small market level, being used more for big-ticket items.

One day, Kitty and Angelique were strolling through the village and they saw a Carlin woman wearing a Human T-shirt with three large Human letters written on the front of it.

"What does that say?", Kitty asked Angelique, as she could not read English yet.

Angelique smiled, noting, "It's just three letters that represent three words", and then she chuckled, "HFY, which means, Humans Fuck Yeah", she explained.

Kitty's whiskers raised high with both astonishment and amusement, as she laughed and replied, "I prefer CFY, meaning Carlins Fuck Yeah!", and then she grinned mischievously at Angelique.

Angelique smiled and looked deeply into Kitty's eyes with their cat-like, vertical pupils, "That sounds good to me", and then she grabbed Kitty by the hand and led her back to Kitty's house for some pleasant, personal, afternoon fun.

Later, Angelique had matching T-shirts made, with Humans Fuck Yeah on one and Carlins Fuck Yeah on the other, both in the three-letter format and spelt underneath; one for each of them.

It looked to be a typical trading day in Kelyarn's village, just like any other. The village centre, outside Kelyarn's plot, was starting to bustle. Carlin-folk and Indigenous Thols were beginning to gather.

The Carlins were setting up trestle tables for their wares and the Thols were descending from the skies, flying in from the north with their Gudong skin carry bags full of things to trade.

As usual, Kitty and Angelique were prepared to watch the proceedings from their shared sleep room on the fourth level of her family's house. Two pairs of binoculars sat on the windowsill.

Angelique had acquired a second pair for Kitty so that they could both watch out of the window at the same time. They had a good view of the village centre and their binoculars brought that view right up close, making it far easier to see everything.

Sounds caught Kitty's sharp ears and they perked up, focusing toward the window. That was where the sounds were coming from. Angelique was still asleep and Kitty gently shook her awake.

Angelique yawned and stretched, and then she too heard the sounds. They both scrambled out from under their sleeping covers and jumped up off their sleeping mat.

They quickly put on their clothes and they urgently made their way to the north-facing window. Almost in unison, they popped the lens caps off their binoculars and began to scan the village centre.

"Holy fuck!", Angelique exclaimed as she watched four hover buses coming down the village's main road from the east.

Angelique let her binoculars hang from their straps as she rubbed the sleep from her eyes.

"Kitty, get your Mum. Get my Mum as well", Angelique requested.

Kitty didn't need to; both Keegali and Simone could be heard running up the stairs.

"Johnathon was out watching the traders setting up for the day. He said hover buses were coming up the main road", Simone noted urgently as she entered their room.

"Kitty, give me long sight", Keegali requested, gesturing to her binoculars.

Kitty and Angelique both passed their binoculars to their Mothers.

As Simone and Keegali scanned the village centre, the four hover buses entered, drove straight into the very centre of the communal space and parked. Their anti-gravity lifters slowly lowered the hover buses to the cobblestones and then shut down.

"This isn't right", Simone said, commenting, "Visitors usually arrive using their personal hovercars and park them outside of the village by the side of the road."

Keegali continued watching, noting, "There are a lot of Humans coming out of those big things."

Simone put the binoculars to her eyes and looked again. Keegali was right, there were a lot of people.

"Oh my God. There must be a hundred and fifty colonists out there, at least", Simone told them, noting, "It looks like two people in charge of each bus. A man and a woman each. This looks like an organised tour group. I doubt very much that that would have been approved."

Simone passed her binoculars back to Angelique, who continued scanning the village centre.

"Keegali, they would have had to have gotten permission from Kelyarn. Some form of authorisation", Simone noted, asking, "Has Kelyarn authorised anything like this?"

"No, my Husband hasn't authorised anything like this. No one has come here, except you, Angelique and Johnathon", Keegali confirmed.

"Well, then. That makes these people uninvited trespassers", Simone noted dryly, adding, "And that is now a legal issue."

Keegali handed her binoculars back to Kitty and then asked, "What should we do?"

As Kitty and Angelique continued scanning with their binoculars, Simone started taking action. Simone took out her communicator and called her Husband, Special Operative James Reas, who answered almost immediately.

"Honey, we have a situation down here in the village centre", Simone informed him.

"What kind of situation, Simone?", James enquired.

"Oh, you know, tourists. Four hover bus loads of tourists, around a hundred and fifty, perhaps a dozen more", Simone replied with a dry tone, before adding, "They are not authorised to be here. They are all uninvited trespassers."

"Understood, honey. What course of action would you advise?", James enquired.

"At the moment, they're just unauthorised tourists. Colourful shirts, cameras and expensive watches. That kind", Simone smiled as she replied, before requesting, "I think we need some stealth surveillance drones down here asap. Just to keep an eye on the situation. We should record all of their faces for identification purposes and monitor the entire situation."

"Understood. I'll organise eight drones and have them dispatched straight away", James confirmed.

"Honey, as long as they're peaceful and well behaved, we should be alright", Simone advised, before noting, "They are all still trespassing, though and the company responsible has to answer for that."

"Understood, my love. I'll keep an eye on the surveillance feeds. I'll have a team on stand by just in case the shit hits the spinning turbine", James reassured her and then finished the call.

"Eight stealth surveillance drones are on their way", Simone informed the others.

"Mum. Do you have access to Dad's firearms data?", Angelique enquired.

"Yeah, I think so. I was a Special Operative before I married your Father and retired to have a family, so I probably still have access", Simone confirmed, chuckling, "I'm actually in reserve, so I can still be recalled to active duty at any time."

"Good, I think you should scan for firearms", Angelique advised her Mother, noting, "Those so-called tour guides all have suspicious objects under their jackets. I think they're shoulder holsters."

"Is that a problem?", Keegali asked as Simone looked through Angelique's binoculars once more.

"Possibly", Simone replied to Keegali, before noting, "Yeah, Angelique. Those bulges under their jackets do look suspicious. I'll check for registered firearms. They should all be low-jacked."

Simone checked with her communicator and after a minute, its A.I. assistant replied, *"Two registered pulsed laser pistols detected. Licensed to: Simone Reas and Angelique Reas."*

"That's just ours", Simone noted, adding, "We have them handy just in case of predators."

"Mum. I don't trust that result. Those are definitely shoulder holsters", Angelique was not convinced and requested, "Have your communicator scan for pulsed laser pistol power packs. If there truly are only two pulsed laser pistols in this village, it should locate just six. The ones in our pulsed laser pistols and our backup power packs."

Simone used her communicator to scan for all pulsed laser pistol power packs within a one-kilometre radius. When her commutator's A.I. assistant responded, she was quite shocked.

"Eighteen pulsed laser pistol power pack signatures have been detected within scanning range. Six are registered to: Simone Reas and Angelique Reas. The remaining twelve pulsed laser pistol power packs are unregistered", her communicator's A.I. assistant reported.

"Sweet Mother of God!", Simone exclaimed, noting, "There's up to twelve unregistered and unlicensed pulsed laser pistols out there in that crowd."

Kitty enquired, "Unregistered and unlicensed?"

Angelique responded, "Illegal, Kitty, illegal. It means they are illegal", and then she told her Mother, "It could be just the eight tour guides. Perhaps a couple of them have backup power packs."

"I don't know, Angelique. Civilians simply don't think that way", Simone reminded her.

As Angelique nodded in agreement, Simone approached a locked, metal box by the sleep room's wall. She ran her fingers over the combination slides and opened the box's lid. Simone pulled out two utility belts, each containing a holstered pulsed laser pistol, a K-Bar knife and two backup power packs.

"Angelique, put this on and remember your training", Simone told her Daughter, as she put on her own utility belt, noting, "You're about to learn how to protect and serve in real time."

Kitty looked concerned, very concerned. Her ears flattened about as much as they could and her whiskers drooped; her tail went deathly still. Her previous blue opalescence began draining from her facial stripes.

"My Dad's a Special Operative, Kitty. We are a military family and we are all trained", Angelique explained, noting, "Even Johnathon, although technically, his training won't start until he's twelve."

Keegali let out a shocked shriek. They all turned to the window and looked out at the village centre. The female tour guides, who Angelique had also determined were armed, had organised their tourists into four large groups.

All of which were milling around the gates to the private Carlin family plots. One of those four tour groups was outside of Keegali's gate. As they watched, the tour guide opened the gate, stepped inside and stepped aside, allowing the milling tourists to file in.

Both Keegali and Kitty bared their fangs and began to hiss and snarl, low growls of anger erupting from within them, from deep within their chests.

Simone shook her head with disgust at the tourists and at the sheer hubris of what they were doing.

"Angelique, we need to get down there right away", Simone commanded and headed for the stairs.

Angelique dutifully followed closely behind her. Keegali and Kitty followed, their growls growing more pronounced.

As they reached their front door, a loud bell started sounding. They looked to their right. Two of Keegali's boys were jumping up and down, pulling on a rope. The rope led up to the top of one of their taller Bell Nut Fruit trees, a huge one, probably one of the tallest in the village.

Kitty noted, her pupil slits narrow with intense focus, "It's the village warning bell. Everyone will hear it. Everyone will be coming."

Keegali snarled at the tour guide, "This is a private place. Leave now!"

Simone backed her up, "You are trespassing on private property. You came to this village uninvited. You are all trespassing here. It is time for you all to leave."

The female tourist guide waved her clipboard as if it were a badge of law, "We are an authorised tour group. With have explicit permission to be here. The mayor of this village signed off on it."

Keegali erupted in anger, "Gudong shit! You lie like a viper! My Husband is the village Elder and he has made no such arrangements."

Simone interjected, "Her Husband is the village mayor and I very much doubt that he has signed anything. No, Carlin has yet learned to read or write English. So, pack up your things and get the hell out of this village", and then she rested her hand lightly on her holstered pulsed laser pistol.

The tourist guide noticed and shot back, "Are you threatening our authorised tour?"

Simone rolled her eyes and spat back, loud enough for nearly everyone to hear across the whole village centre, "I am Reserve Special Operative Simone Reas. You will pack up your things and get the fuck out of this village now!"

Kelyarn came out from behind the house carrying a long pitchfork, "I am the Elder of this village and you have no right to be here. You will remove yourself from my plot and then you will leave our village. You will never come back! Any of you! You are not welcome here! Leave now!"

The tourist guide pinched the bridge of her nose and held out he clipboard,

"It's all been authorised. It's all been agreed upon. We have every right to be here."

Kelyarn's patience was wearing ever so thin, "Authorised with who exactly? Certainly not with us, Carlin-folk! You are not welcome here! You will leave now and never come back!"

"No, no, no! You don't understand. These people, my tourists, they've all paid for the cat people home visit package. It's all above board, I assure you", the tourist guide tried to explain.

Keegali looked at the crowd of tourists, "This woman speaks lies! This woman speaks falsehoods! You have all been cheated!", and then she turned to Kelyarn and gave him a simple nod.

Then Kelyarn roared. It was a loud, mighty roar like the roar of a lion. Its subsonic frequencies spread through the nearby tourists, eliciting fear. At first, they all froze, too terrified to move. Some of them even wet themselves.

One woman cried out, "They're not cat people at all, they're lion people!"

Young Johnathon Reas, now ten, stood beside Kelyarn with his arms folded across his chest and a smug look on his face, "Now you've all done it. You've just awoken the space lions. You probably should all leave before they sink their fangs into your throats."

Kelyarn glanced down at Johnathon in complete astonishment as the entire tour group turned around and fled, bolting for the gate so fast that they began tripping over themselves. Even the tour guide turned and ran, slipping and falling several times; her expensive, pristine pantsuit was now coated with mud and soaked in piss.

"You haven't heard the last of this", she screamed over her shoulder.

Johnathon shrugged, "It worked, didn't it?", and Kelyarn reached down and gently stroked the boy's hair, thinking to himself, "*Space lions*", he let out a soft chuckle.

Simone and Angelique followed the panicking tourists to the front gate of Kelyarn's plot. They turned to their right, just in time to see Kelyarn leap majestically over his plot's five-foot-high dry stone wall. As they looked around, other Carlin men were running to the scene. They ran down the cobblestone laneways, they ran down the cobblestone main road, they ran through family plots and leapt the dry stone walls. The tourists found themselves surrounded. The Indigenous Thols all took to the air and fled. They wanted no part in what might possibly follow.

"The Thols are all leaving?", Angelique questioned.

Kitty's reply was simple, "Thols have hollow bones, fragile. They cannot afford to get injured."

Simone ordered Kitty and Keegali, "Stay behind your dry stone walls. Pulsed laser pistols are really dangerous and there are twelve of them out there, so stay safe. We'll handle this."

The tourists were angry and were shouting at their tour guides. Many had purchased the *"Cat people home visit"* package. Others had purchased the *"Cat people trading package"*, which came with two hundred and fifty *"barter beads"*, supposedly worth one credit each.

Of course, there were really, really stupid tourists who'd purchased the *"Cat people deluxe package"*, which not only included both of the other two packages, but also included selfies with the cat people. The tourists were all angry and an angry mob never ends well.

"I paid for the cat people home visit package and now we find out that the cat people never authorised it. I want my money back", one angry woman shouted out, as others joined in.

One man shouted out, "I paid for the cat people trading package and none of the cat people will accept our barter beads. I want my money back", as others joined the chorus in revolt.

"You think that's bad. My wife and I paid for the cat people deluxe package, both of us. We've been completely ripped off. We want our money back as well", another screamed out.

The head tour guide shouted above the din, "There's been some kind of mix-up. I'm sure your credits will all be refunded. We just need to contact our head office."

Angelique shouted out, "Show me those barter beads."

A man who'd also paid for the cat people trading package approached cautiously and passed her a large pouch containing two hundred and fifty barter beads, each supposedly worth one credit.

Angelique opened the pouch and carefully examined the beads before passing them over the wall to Keegali. Kitty and Keegali both examined the so-called barter beads before passing them back.

Keegali announced, "Your barter beads are all fake. They are not artisan-made, neither Carlin nor Thol."

Angelique shook her head as she passed the man back his pouch and then she shouted loud enough for all to hear, "These are all counterfeit barter beads. Cheap plastic polymer beads. They are all fake, worthless."

The tourist crowd was quickly growing into an angry mob.

The head tourist guide shouted above the din, "You will all get your credits back. You just need to make a formal complaint at our head office back in the colony."

Someone in the crowd shouted out, "I'd rather take it out of your fucking hide!"

One of the female tour guides shouted, "We are just your tour guides. You need to take your complaints back to our head office. We just work for the company. We don't control it."

The mob began to chant. "Refund! Refund! Refund now! Refund! Refund! Refund now! Refund! Refund! Refund now!"

They were all angry and pumping their fists into the air.

One of the female tour guides panicked and drew out her pulsed laser pistol, pointing it at the angry mob. Then another and another, until all of the tourist guides had drawn their pulsed laser pistols. The angry mob went deathly silent. Their tour guides were targeting them. Simone drew her own weapon and nodded to Angelique, who drew her own pulsed laser pistol.

Angelique looked towards Kitty and Keegali and ordered, "Get down. Get down now."

Simone's voice cut across the silence, "Stand down! Stand down now!"

Angelique added, "You are all brandishing illegal, unlicensed pulsed laser pistols. Stand down now!"

Keegali looked over to Kelyarn, who was standing on the wrong side of their dry stone wall. She caught his eye and nodded a single decisive nod.

Kelyarn roared; it was far louder than anything heard before. All of the other Carlin men began roaring in unison. Subsonic frequencies spread across the village centre. The angry tourist mob froze in sheer, collective terror. Many pissed themselves and a few defecated in their pants.

Then, as one, all of the tourists turned and fled back towards the four hover buses, leaving trails of pee on the cobblestones behind them. They all quickly piled into the hover buses and barricaded the doors. All, except for four, a woman and three men who lingered outside at the closest bus to the Carlin traders, still sitting at their trestle tables, still displaying their wares.

The tourists guides all swung around in sheer terror and targeted Kelyarn with the pulsed laser pistols.

"Fuck!", Angelique exclaimed, shaking her head and noting, "Mum, Kelyarn has protected the tourists and placed himself and his people in the cross-hairs."

Keegali shouted out with concern, "Kelyarn!"

Simone took note of the four tourists who'd remained outside of the hover buses, "What do you think? Four pulsed laser pistols?"

Angelique nodded, "And all of them illegal", and then, without being asked, Angelique sprinted towards Kelyarn, sliding to a halt directly between him and the head tourist guide.

Angelique stared at the head tourist guard with piercing eyes like cold steel, "Stand down now, or I will drill a hole straight through your fucking heart", she commanded, mustering as much authority as her seventeen-year-old voice could muster.

Kitty was apoplectic and leapt over the dry stone wall, swiftly sprinting to Angelique's side.

"For fucks sake, Kitty. Not now. Get behind me", Angelique commanded.

Kitty fell in line behind Angelique and then Kelyarn grabbed her by the shoulder and shoved her forcibly behind him, thinking to shield her from harm.

"You're just a kid!", the head tourist guide laughed.

"My Daughter is a highly-trained kid from a military family. You might want to factor that into your calculations", Simone shouted out, wondering how this was going to end.

Mother and Daughter both shouted out in unison, "Stand down now. Place your weapons on the ground and stand down now!"

Without warning, the other four tourists who had not re-entered the hover buses drew their own pulsed laser pistols. They ran straight over to the Carlin traders and targeted them.

Their leader, a tall, burly man with a limp, shouted at the Carlin traders, "Give us all of your diamonds! We want them all now!"

The Carlin traders could not speak or understand English and they simply sat there, wondering what these four crazy Humans wanted.

"Mum, we have four thieves and robbers at my three o'clock", Angelique shouted.

Simone looked at where Angelique was standing. It was a perfect position to take down the thieves, assuming the timing was right.

Simone shouted out, "It's all about the location, honey, location, location. By the numbers, my girl, by the numbers!"

Angelique replied with two words, "Roger that!"

The leader of the four robbers demanded again, "Give us all of your diamonds! We want them all now!"

The head tourist guide looked confused. He was having a seriously bad day. He and his fellow tourist guides were apparently working for a company that had just ripped off a hundred and sixty customers. Their jobs, as it turned out, were all fake.

Everything was fucking fake, the paperwork, the authority, even the damned barter beads. They had all been hired as tour guides by a completely fake company and now they were all in deep shit! The pulsed laser pistols they'd all been issued, ostensible for predator protection, were all unregistered and illegal.

Did they even bloody well work? They had no idea!

Topping it all off, they had now gone from an armed standoff with an angry mob of their own customers to an armed standoff with two Special Operatives and the whole Carlin village. And just to make matters worse, four of their customers had infiltrated their tour to rob the Carlin traders of their diamonds.

Could this day get any worse?

The head tour guide spoke, "Ah, we're kind of having a fucked up day right now. Those four guys; they are not with us. They are on their own."

Angelique just shook her head and continued holding a bead on his centre mass, "You brought them here. You've drawn down with unregistered, illegal firearms on innocent civilians. That's kind of all on you. Now shut the fuck up and stand down!"

Simone shouted to Angelique, advising, "Stay frosty, sweety. Head on a swivel, my child! Stay alert!"

The leader of the four robbers turned to Angelique, "Shut the fuck up, you little bitch. We just came here for the fucking diamonds", and then he turned back to the Carlin traders and demanded again, "Give us all of your diamonds! We want them all now!"

Angelique eyed the four robbers through the corner of her right eye, while still maintaining a bead on the head tourist guide's centre mass, "You four fucking robbers must be a bunch of the dumbest fuck knuckles I've ever come across. I mean, do you all really have the collective intelligence of a squashed bull ant?"

Her taunt was working; the lead robber turned his attention to her, "What the fuck are you talking about, you little shit!"

Angelique smiled, she was still facing the head tourist guide while talking to the lead robber, "This isn't a huge trading fair, dick wad!", she stated, carefully explaining, "It's a small trade gathering. They don't actually have any diamonds on them, you moron! Those big barter stones are worth a hundred, two hundred, or even more of their little barter beads. They are only used for big-ticket items like land purchases or bulk grain purchases. They are far too valuable for this little trade gathering."

The female robber shouted back angrily, "You're just a lying little cunt!"

"Nope, that's the God's honest truth and by the way. None of those Carlin traders can speak or understand English. You are shouting instructions at them that they simply cannot understand. Who's the dumb cunt now, bitch?", Angelique replied.

Kitty chimed in, confirming, "My Angelique tells the truth. There are no big barter stones here."

Angelique thought to herself, *"Not now, Kitty. You're painting a target on yourself."*

The four robbers began to argue amongst themselves.

"What if she's telling the truth!?", the woman asked.

"Don't be ridiculous! Obviously she's lying", their leader replied.

Another questioned, "Have we come here for nothing?"; it was rhetorical and he exclaimed, "Fuck!"

The final robber stamped his feet several times in what appeared to be a tantrum and shouted, "Fuck! Fuck! Fuck!", before drawing down a bead on Angelique.

Angelique caught it all in the corner of her right eye. Angelique performed the splits, dropping as low as she possibly could.

Veeeee-wack! Veeeee-wack! Veeeee-wack!

Two of the high-energy pulsed laser beams passed by the top of her head, singeing some of her hair.

Angelique turned to her three o'clock, focused and in rapid succession let loose a deadly volley.

Veeeee-wack! Veeeee-wack! Veeeee-wack! Veeeee-wack!

The robber's third pulsed laser beam went wide to Angelique's right, missing her completely.

All four robbers collapsed to the cobblestones, their foreheads drilled through with neat little self-cauterised holes. They'd all died instantly.

Simone chided her, "Too fancy, honey. Always target the centre mass, just like your Father and I trained you."

The eight tour guides all turned around and watched in horror as the robbers collapsed dead to the ground. An adolescent teenager had taken them all down in one deft move. It was absurd! It was real! When they all finally turned back around to face Angelique, she was still standing there, still drawing a bead on the head tour guide's centre mass.

"Now, stand down, or I'll drill you all and put you down!", Angelique commanded firmly.

One of the eight tour guides, the female who'd led the tourists onto Kelyarn's plot, panicked and turned towards Simone. She fired her pulsed laser pistol once.

Veeeee-wack!

The superheated beam of energy passed by Simone, missing by millimetres, drilling into the blue stones of the dry stone wall behind her. The hole sizzled with latent heat as it dissipated its energy.

Simone had no hesitations and no qualms; she instantly reacted and fired.

Veeeee-wack!

The single pulsed laser beam drilled through the female tour guide's heart, leaving a neat, self-cauterised hole that went straight through her chest. She dropped to the cobblestones dead.

Simone apologised, "I'm sorry, guys, but I can't have crazy people shooting pulsed laser pistols around here like that. It's simply far too dangerous."

Johnathon Reas climbed up onto the dry stone wall and shouted, "You threaten the space lions at your own peril. My family will defend them!"

Simone chided her Son, "Get down, Johnathon, get down now, before you hurt yourself", and she turned back to Angelique, "Good work, honey. Now stand down, your Father will be here in three minutes."

Kayala, who had snuck out of the house with her little Sister, Kearill, to see what had happened, looked up at Johnathon, telling him, "Getting down, you silly kit. Your Mother is right, you will hurt yourself", before shaking her head and exclaiming, "Kits!"

Johnathon saw the concerned look on Kayala's face and, in typical Johnathon fashion, stated, "I am not for you, fair Carlin maiden. When I grow up, I will marry my Aunt Roberta. It is my destiny!"

Simone, Kitty, Keegali, Kelyarn and Kayala all rolled their eyes at Johnathon's antics.

Kelyarn started walking back to the gate of his plot and then he winced in pain. The stray shot that the robber had fired at Angelique had struck him. Keegali rushed to his side with concern. It was a through and through, having passed through Kelyarn's upper left shoulder. Kelyarn's body was pumped so full of adrenaline that he hadn't even noticed that he had a small self-cauterised hole in his left shoulder.

Simone was already on her communicator, "James, medical required. Kelyarn has a pulsed laser wound. A possible through and through."

"Roger that, honey. We have a medic on board", James replied.

While Simone kept a watchful eye over the remaining seven tourist guides, Angelique and Kitty collected their unregistered pulsed laser pistols and lined them up along the dry stone wall. Once that task was completed, Angelique rushed off to the house with tears streaming from her eyes.

Training or not, she had never killed before.

The Colonial Troops landed in their drop ship. James jumped out as soon as it landed.

"What a fucking mess, talk about clean up in isle three", James noted, looking at all of the bodies.

Simone simply pointed to the deceased tour guide, "Mine", and then she pointed to the four deceased robbers, "Angelique's; she's a little out of sorts over it."

James nodded, "You go and take care of Angelique. We'll take care of Kelyarn and this mess."

The fucked up day was finally coming to an end.

11. The Angels That Weren't.

It was nine o'clock in the morning and Yannick was reading reports on the integration of Mimasian Thols into the Indigenous Thol villages. So far, there were five Indigenous Thol tree villages into which Mimasian Thols had integrated and two brand-new tree villages inhabited by Mimasian Thols alone. Reading further regarding Indigenous Thol and Mimasian Thol interactions and it appeared that all was going well.

Yannick's and Yealah's tree house had been completed a year earlier and they had both settled in. Mimasian Thols would fly by wing to the hover bus terminus at the edge of the Jula Jula forest and then commute by hover bus to the Hilltop colony to the south for their work, returning at the end of the day the same way. The Jula Jula tree, in which Yannick's and Yealah's tree house was located, was the closest tree village to the hover bus service, so their flight was relatively short.

Yannick had helped two of his neighbouring Indigenous Thols, Yorvick and Yarling, to upgrade their nest. It went from being a single traditional Thol nest to one with five nest modules. The upper two nests were to be used as sleep rooms. One for Yorvick and Yarling and the other would be a sleep room for their future younglings.

The lower three nests formed a triangle. One of the new nests was used as a shared family space, while the other was outfitted as a bathroom, toilet and laundry. Yealah had even convinced them to install modern fixtures and conveniences, which Yarling absolutely loved.

Their original nest became their kitchen and dining room. Instead of their original flat stone and fired clay hearth, they now had a much safer, pressed iron stove for cooking and heating with a modern chimney system complete with a flue cap. Yannick could see Yorvick's and Yarling's nest complex from his small home office; it really was quite impressive. Yorvick and Yarling were highly progressive and adaptive Indigenous Thols, eager to make use of Mimasian Thol technologies.

A window opened up on Yannick's data tablet. The words *"Motion Detected"* appeared in Ancient Tholish, the Mimasian tongue. Yannick considered the window and its warning, probably a predator lurking around the base of the tree.

The warning in the window began flashing red with greater urgency.

A predator? Perhaps a lone Kyrrax? Perhaps it was a pack of wild Vorts or a pack of Sleimorps?

Then again, it could also be a hover car with visitors from the Human colony. Yannick tapped on the window with his stylus and then stared in disbelief at what he saw. He transferred the alert to his office's main screen and then connected his communicator to the closed-circuit camera surveillance system at the base of the tree, inside the tree's hollow and the tunnel leading between the two.

"Yealah, come here, my love. I think we have a problem", he trilled and clicked to his Wife.

Yealah looked at the screen, "What the hell!", she exclaimed, before trilling and clicking, "Why are there hover buses at the base of our tree? Three hover buses?"

"I have no idea, Yealah", Yannick trilled back, noting. "They appear to be full of people."

As they watched, a man stepped out of the closest hover bus. He walked over to the door that led into the tree and tried the handle. The door was, of course, locked. The man tried to force the door with his shoulder, which, being predator-proof, did not budge. A surveillance camera in a higher branch caught the look of frustration on the man's face. He then put his fingers to his mouth and whistled.

Another man stepped out of one of the other hover buses. He was carrying a small, heavy battering ram. The second man quickly joined the first and together the pair battered in the door that led into the tree's hollow. A clear case of breaking and entering; worse, that door was there to keep out predators.

"You have got to be kidding me!", Yannick exclaimed, trilling and barking, "That is illegal entry!"

"And property damage", Yealah added with a trill.

"We should get our side arms", Yannick trilled his recommendation.

"Yannick, they are only for predators", Yealah trilled a reminder.

"Yealah, sometimes the worst predators are Human", Yannick trilled in reply.

As Yannick and Yealah put on their utility belts with holstered pulsed laser pistols, they continued watching the camera feeds.

Someone in one of the hover buses shouted out, questioning, "Why are you battering down the door?"

The man holding the battering ram looked around and replied, "This door is not meant to be locked. It's a public access point. We are well within our rights to force entry."

Yannick clearly heard that through the speakers, "Public access point my arse!", he trilled and barked, then he requested, "Yealah, call the Colonial Marines. We have a problem."

As they watched, a stream of passengers disembarked the hover buses and made their way to the door. Yannick and Yealah stared in disbelief. There must have been over a hundred of them and they were nearly all carrying cameras. Many were wearing brightly coloured clothes and sunglasses. Tourists!

"What hell is going on here?", Yealah trilled and clicked as they watched this horde of Humans file out of the hover buses and into the tunnel that led into the tree hollow.

Yannick shook his head in disgust, it was a worst scenario, he trilled, "Idiotic Human tourists!"

Yealah blinked in surprise as she watched.

Once inside the tree hollow, the tourists began snapping photos of their surroundings before accessing the elevator system. Group after group travelled to the first residential landing and stepped out.

"Where are the Angels?", one woman asked.

Another tourist, a man, stated, "Yeah. Where are the Angels? We paid to see the Angels!"

What was apparently one of six tourist guides replied, "Everyone will get a chance to see the Angels, but you must all wait your turn."

"Will they pose with us for selfies?", another woman asked.

"Of course they will. It's all been arranged", another tourist guide replied.

The tourist guides led the tourists out of the hollow and onto the lowest of the broad balconies. Before long, there were a hundred tourists and their guides on the balcony. They were now three hundred feet above the ground and the balcony, not designed for such a heavy load, strained under their sheer weight.

The local Indigenous Thols at this level were coming out of their nests and they immediately started shouting at the tourists to go away in Native Tholish. A language that neither the tourists nor the guides could understand or speak.

Yannick and Yealah swooped down from their tree house, nearly one hundred and fifty feet higher up. They landed softly on the broad tree branches, their six-toed feet gripping tightly to the tree branches' bark. They'd landed on separate branches in front of the tourist guides, blocking any further access to the Indigenous Thol nests. So far, the tourists all remained safely behind the safety railings. However, there were only two of them and there were a great many more branches that the tourist might use. The tourists immediately began taking photos.

Yannick did not mince his words; he spoke in fluent English, his trills, clicks and even harsh barks, highlighting both anger and annoyance, "Leave now. You are all trespassing! This is a private Thol village!"

One of the so-called tour guides replied, "We are on an official tourist visit", before asking, "Why was that door locked? It should have been unlocked for open public access!"

Yannick rolled his head around on his neck in annoyance, trilling and barking back, "That door was locked to keep dangerous predators and arseholes like you out. You are all guilty of criminal break and entering and criminal trespass. Leave now, or you will suffer the consequences", he placed his hand gently on his holstered pulsed laser pistol.

Yealah barked and trilled, "This entire tree is a private village on Indigenous Thol lands. Just being in this territory uninvited is trespass. You will all leave now! The Colonial Marines have been called!"

One of the other tourist guides whispered to the one in charge, "This is a great show and all, but the punters want to actually visit the Thol nests. They want to meet the Native Thols. They want selfies!"

The tourist guide in charge replied, "It's all good. I've got this", and then he stepped over the safety railing and approached Yannick, walking along the branch.

As the tourist guide stepped over the safety railing, several of the tourists did the same and began walking along the tree branches. Yannick and Yealah both noticed.

Yannick thought to himself, "*Damnable idiots*", as the tourist guide got within whispering distance.

"Look, man. Just convince the natives to let our tourist group look around their nests", the tourist guide told Yannick, adding, "They can take a few photographs, take a few selfies and everybody is happy. We'll even cut you in on the deal. You can make pretty good money! Lots of credits!"

Yannick shook his head and barked harshly in reply, "Leave now, before this escalates!"

The tourist guide laughed, "We are not going anywhere, so you had better get used to it."

Yannick nodded to Yealah and Yealah trilled, clicked and barked in Native Tholish, "Get your bows. Nock your arrows. Protect your nests!"

One by one, the Indigenous Thol men went back into their nests. When they came back out, they were all armed with small hunting bows.

The tourist guide laughed again, "What? They're going to frighten us with their toys?"

Yannick rolled his head once more, trilling back softly, "Their arrows have poison-coated tips. They are quite deadly!"

The tourist guide replied, "Let's not get hasty. These are Thols. Thols are Angels, they're not violent. Why are you making them violent?"

"Are you a complete fucking idiot?", Yannick trilled back, "We Mimasian Thols may be Angelic, but these are Indigenous Thols and Indigenous are NOT Angels. They have the same propensity for violence as any Human and you have intruded into their village on their land. Leave now while you still can!"

One of the tourists who had climbed over the safety railing started walking along the branch, approaching an Indigenous Thol's nest. The nest contained four frightened Thols, parents with two younglings. Their Father loosed an arrow straight into the branch one foot in front of the advancing Human. A carefully calibrated and restrained action by the Indigenous Thol. The tourist quickly stepped back in shock, slipped and fell. The forest floor was three hundred feet below. There was a prolonged scream and then a dull thud.

The tourist guide exclaimed, "Holy fuck!"
Another tourist guide shouted out, "That's murder!"
Yealah responded with angry barks, "No. That is stupidity and misadventure. You are all illegally trespassing on Indigenous Thol lands and have criminally broken into their village. You should not be here. Whatever happens, it is all on you."
The tourist guide finally understood, these were not the Angels they thought they were.
"Get back, people. Get back onto the balcony. Stay inside the safety railing", he ordered.
The remaining tourists who had walked out onto the tree branches hastily retreated back to the balcony. Human shoes had little grip on the Jula Jula tree branches with their slippery bark. Three more tourists slipped and fell. There screams carried for several long moments, followed by three dull thuds of oblivion.
Yannick shook his head, trilling and clicking softly, "You illegally broke into this tree village. You are in charge. Every single death is on your head. Every single one."

The tour guide countered ridiculously, "You should have provided safety railings on the tree branches!"
Yannick shook his head, trilling, "Obviously, you're a complete moron", he stated, "You are trespassing. The safety railings around the balconies are for our invited guests, not trespassers. You were not invited here and in case you haven't noticed, Thols have wings; we fly, we don't need safety railings."
Yealah chimed in, trilling, "You should all get back behind the safety railings before you fall. Remember, you are three hundred feet from the ground."
The tourist guide sat down on the branch as a wave of vertigo passed over him.

Yannick's communicator buzzed for his attention. He checked the alert that came up. The communicator was still connected to the surveillance camera feeds. Yannick sighed deeply.
"Remember I said that that door was locked to keep the predators out", Yannick trilled and clicked at the tour guide.
The tour guide nodded. He remembered.

Yannick crouched down in front of the tour guide and showed him the surveillance camera's feed.

The tour guide went pale as a ghost, "What the fuck is that?"

Yannick stared into his frightened eyes, trilling and clicking, "It's a predator. It's called a Sleimorp. It's been attracted by the scent of death. Humans falling from three hundred feet to the ground create that kind of scent. And since you so kindly broke into our village, it has now walked straight in through that broken door. The very door that was meant to keep it out."

Yealah checked the other surveillance camera feeds and trilled with urgency, "Yannick, honey. There's a whole pack of them, at least ten and they're all coming in."

Yannick quickly trilled, clicked and barked, in Indigenous Tholish, "There's a pack of Sleimorps inside the tree hollow. Get inside your nests and keep your bows ready with arrows nocked."

Yealah quickly flew to the branch Yannick was standing. Together they grabbed the tourist guide and flew him back to the balcony, dropping him unceremoniously on the timber boarding, safely within the safety railing. The tourist guide, still pale with fear, nodded in appreciation.

The other five tourist guides and over one hundred tourists all stared at Yannick and Yealah, wondering what was going on. Yannick and Yealah focused on their communicators and the internal surveillance cameras. As they watched, the Sleimorps, all smelling the scent of fear, started staring upwards at the first-level landing. One by one, they started climbing the scaffolding that held the elevator in place.

Yealah looked at Yannick, a surprised look on her face, trilling and clicking in their native tongue, Ancient Tholish, "Is that even possible? Can they do that?"

Yannick replied with equal surprise, trilling back, "Apparently it is and yes, they can."

Yannick then told the head tourist guide, trilling and clicking, "The Sleimorps are climbing the scaffold, they're climbing up. Get everyone moving up those stairs", he gestured to the spiral stairs that wrapped around the tree.

To Yannick's and Yealah's surprise and horror, the tourist guide commented, "They'll only kill and eat a few of us, won't they? I mean, they won't just hunt us all down, will they?"

Yealah shook her head in disgust while Yannick explained the true horrors of Sleimorp pack hunting behaviour, trilling and clicking, "They will hunt and kill as many of us as they can. Then they will carry the corpses back to their den for storage."

Yealah chimed in, noting with trills and clicks, "They don't just eat fresh kills. They're carrion eaters. They actually prefer their meat well-rotted. Especially for feeding to their young."

Yannick trilled and barked harshly, "More Sleimorps will come. They could easily kill everyone in this village and the Human authorities would never find where they stash the bodies."

The tourist guide completely lost it, "Oh my god! Oh my god! Please don't let them eat me?", and then he pissed himself.

The other tourist guides turned away in disgust while the tourists all began to panic.

Yannick and Yealah start herding the tourists up the stairs to the next level.

Yannick shouted at them in English laced with trills and clicks, "Keep climbing. Don't stop until you reach the top."

Yealah enquired with a few short trills and clicks, "Just what do we do when the Sleimorps reach the top? We'll all be cornered with nowhere else to go."

Yannick tapped his holster, "For predators, remember. Our pulsed laser pistols are fully charged."

Yealah checked her communicator to gauge the Sleimorp pack's progress, "Sweet Mother of all things Holy, they're in the elevator and pushing the fucking buttons", she trilled and clicked.

"No, no, no. They're intelligent, but they're not that intelligent", Yannick trilled back.

Yealah shoved her communicator in his face, trilling and clicking, "Look, Yannick. See for yourself, they are in the elevator pushing the fucking buttons!"

The head tourist guide fled up the stairs towards the top of the tree along with all of the other terrified tourists. The other five tourist guides all scoffed, thinking that everything was being exaggerated and completely over the top.

Yannick scolded them, barking, "Get moving, that Sleimorp pack will be here in minutes."

One of the tour guides retorted, "Bullshit! What is a Sleimorp anyway?"

Yannick just shook his head and trilled back, "So be it. You're on your own."

As Yannick and his Wife, Yealah, herded the panicking tourists up the stairs, Mr "*What is a Sleimorp anyway?*", heard a series of odd clicks, whistles and shrieks coming from the tree's hollow. He looked down the tunnel that led to the hollow and what he saw made him piss his pants.

It looked like a dinosaur, specifically a hairless, featherless Velociraptor, only much bigger. Razor-sharp, retractable sickle-shaped talons on its hind feet clicked as it walked. Its long arms, with three-fingered hands and sharp, retractable claws, were held in front of it, retracted like a T. Rex, but far more menacing. Its long tail swished from side to side, with its two-foot-long bone-sword unsheathed and menacing. Its muzzle-like face was lined with fangs and the beast looked as if it was smiling with sheer delight.

Its eyes face forward and focused on Mr *"What is a Sleimorp anyway?"*, and then it raised its head, clicked, shrieked, made guttural, angulation sounds and then whistled. Three more Sleimorps stepped into the tunnel behind it.

Mr *"What is a Sleimorp anyway?"*, now knew exactly what a Sleimorp was; he did not like the look of it one bit. He bolted behind one of the other tourist guides and shoved them towards the tunnel. He actually thought that would keep the beasts busy; he was incredibly wrong.

The first Sleimorp lunged out of the tunnel, grabbed the sacrificed tourist guide by the head with its teeth and with a sickening crunch, bit it off and swallowed it whole. It then grabbed the body with its razor-sharp teeth and threw it against the tree's trunk. There was no surprise, no scream; the man had no idea what had just killed him; it was that quick.

The remaining four tour guides found themselves surrounded, being carefully herded by the four Sleimorps. Mr *"What is a Sleimorp anyway?"* had sacrificed his friend for nothing. Sleimorps didn't just eat freshly killed prey; they were collectors with long-term food storage in mind. All four Sleimorps raised their heads and began whistling, clicking, shrieking and making guttural angulation sounds.

Another four Sleimorps came out of the tunnel. The first Sleimorp focused momentarily on the Indigenous Thol nests. The tourist guides could almost hear its thoughts processing. Tree branches are dangerous, slippery. The Thols are armed. Bows and poisoned arrows. Thols can fly away. The risk was just far too high. A cost versus benefit calculation!

The first Sleimorp gestured to the stairs with a nod of its head. The four new Sleimorps began hunting the tourists, following them up the stairs to the higher levels. The first Sleimorp and its three companions looked from one to the other. They all looked as if they were smiling with absolute glee.

Mr *"What is a Sleimorp anyway?"* immediately shat himself.

They were all fucked!

Mr *"What is a Sleimorp anyway?"* tried to run towards a tree branch, thinking he could reach a Thol nest and maybe, just maybe, reach safety; he was wrong, very wrong.

The alpha Sleimorp lunged forward, forcing him to move the other way. It was quick, ridiculously quick. Another Sleimorp's unsheathed bone-sword ripped through his torso from behind and protruded out of his chest. Mr *"What is a Sleimorp anyway?"* was still alive as the Sleimorp carried him, still mounted on its bone-sword and stacked him unceremoniously on top of the man he'd just sacrificed.

Stacked and racked, Mr *"What is a Sleimorp anyway?"* slowly bled out.

The three remaining tourist guides all screamed. They all shat themselves, as the Sleimorps, smelling their fear, lunged forward and finished them off. One by one, their bodies were stacked and racked with the other two. Then the four Sleimorps raised their heads and began whistling, clicking, shrieking and making guttural angulation sounds once more. Then their alpha led them up the stairs to hunt down the remaining tourists.

The Indigenous Thols had watched their deaths with horror. There was little that they could do. They knew the Sleimorps. They were not to be trifled with and their hides were too thick for Indigenous Thol arrows to easily pierce.

Yannick and Yealah had heard the screams; they'd heard the Sleimorps communicating. They knew that they were on their way up. As the tourists continued to climb the stairs to the top of the tree, Yannick and Yealah hung back. They both flew out to strategic points along well-placed tree branches at the mid-level of the village and lay in wait.

The first four Sleimorps to come up the stairs were caught with a volley of pulsed laser fire.

Veeeee-wack, Veeeee-wack, Yealah shot the first Sleimorp, drilling it through its head. It staggered and fell, convulsing on the balcony deck.

Veeeee-wack, Veeeee-wack and Yannick dropped the second Sleimorp with equally precise shots.

The next two Sleimorps didn't dawdle. They rushed out too fast to shoot and leapt onto the tree branches. Yannick and Yealah launched themselves into flight, turned and fired.

Veeeee-wack, Veeeee-wack, Veeeee-wack, Veeeee-wack. Both Sleimorps, pulsed laser bore holes drilled through their chests, their footing faltered and they fell four hundred feet to their deaths.

Four Sleimorps down and six to go. Yannick and Yealah flew to another location.

By the time the tourists had reached the top of the tree, the remaining six Sleimorps had almost reached them. There were over a hundred tourists all gathered in the Thol's communal gathering space and the remaining Sleimorps were rapidly approaching on the stairs. Flying up from their previous ambush point, Yannick and Yealah caught two Sleimorps from behind.

Veeeee-wack, Veeeee-wack, Veeeee-wack, Veeeee-wack and the two Sleimorps had perfectly round, self-cauterising holes drilled through the backs of their heads. They both dropped, still twitching.

The alpha Sleimorp and another were almost at the top of the stairs and there were two more Sleimorps lurking about somewhere.

Pressing to the farthest end of the communal gathering space and all cowering in fear, two Sleimorps reached the top of the stairs, just as the elevator doors opened and two more Sleimorps stepped out. The elevator even made a surreal, bing sound as its doors opened.

The alpha Sleimorp smiled its fanged smile of glee, it raised its head and whistled, clicked, shrieked and made guttural angulation sounds once more. All four Sleimorps had their eyes focused on the tourists. A hundred prey just sitting there, waiting to be taken. The Sleimorps all smiled their hideous fanged smile. Too easy!

They moved slowly, methodically and began herding the tourists. One tourist tried to run, slash, a bone-sword took off her head and her body dropped to the wooden deck. There was no escape; they were already dead, time had just not caught up with them yet.

Another tourist tried to run, slash, another Human head rolled across the wooden deck, the man's body collapsing to the deck just like the woman's.

One of the Sleimorps was on collection duty, picking up and stacking the bodies to one side. Its movements were precise, methodical, moving and stacking bodies ready for future long-term storage. Another tourist tried to run, another woman, her head was severed just like the other two and her body meticulously stacked and racked. The Sleimorps weren't in any hurry. They had this!

There was a sudden rush of air and red dots appeared on the four remaining Sleimorps. They all looked around at each other in confusion. The alpha Sleimorp shrieked and whistled, gesturing with its head towards the open elevator doors. It knew something was wrong, but it just did not understand what.

Veeeee-wack, Veeeee-wack, Veeeee-wack, Veeeee-wack, Veeeee-wack, Veeeee-wack, Veeeee-wack, Veeeee-wack, Veeeee-wack, Veeeee-wack, Veeeee-wack, Veeeee-wack, Veeeee-wack, Veeeee-wack, Veeeee-wack, Veeeee-wack!

It was all over; the remaining Sleimorps lay dead on the communal gathering space's deck, riddled with neat little self-cauterised holes.

Colonial marines wearing aerial jet packs and full body armour landed on the deck. High-powered pulsed laser rifles trained on the dead Sleimorps.

"Make safe the village", Special Operative James Reas commanded.

James Reas remained at the Thol's communal gathering space while his men made safe the village. His pulsed laser rifle was still trained on the dead Sleimorps. He kicked them hard with his boot to make sure that they were all dead.

Yannick and Yealah both landed gently on the communal gathering space deck.

Yealah trilled, clicked and barked, "By all the Gods of the Greater Way, what took you so long?"

Yannick added, trilling, "We had to take down six of those things ourselves!"

"My apologies, Yealah, Yannick", James replied, explaining, "Some idiot businessmen back at the Colony kept objecting to us coming here. He said that we had no authority to interfere."

"No authority. We had over a hundred trespassers inside our village and they refused to leave", Yealah trilled and clicked.

Yannick stepped in, barking, "What the hell? They broke our door down with a battering ram!"

"The businessman said he had full official authorisation for '*Angel*' tours", James continued to explain, adding, "His '*official*' authorisation was fraudulent, forged. He is now under arrest."

Yannick and Yealah both shook their heads and Yealah trilled, "Twelve deaths, James. Twelve deaths. Someone has to be held responsible."

James quickly replied, "And they will be", he then addressed the surviving tourists, "You are all criminally trespassing on Indigenous Thol land and inside a private Thol village. You will all be hover-bused back to the Colony and criminal trespass charges will be filed."

Yannick pointed to the head tourist guide, trilling, "He's one of their so-called tourist guides."

James walked over to the man, turned him around and tied his hands behind his back with cable ties. "You, Mr Tourist Guide, are under arrest. Twelve deaths are hanging over your head. Not to mention criminal break and entry, and criminal trespass."

An Indigenous Thol approached them, clicking, trilling and barking in Native Tholish.

"What's he saying?" James asked.

"He's requesting that we leave the Sleimorp bodies. He says his people will eat them, that later their shit will help keep the other Sleimorp packs away", Yealah trilled.

James shook his head and chuckled, "Waste not want not. It's fine by me, although we will take two of their bodies back to the Colony for research, a male and a female. They have the highest level of sub-sapience we've ever encountered."

The next day, Yannick organised a new door for the tree village. Thick, solid and reinforced. It was installed to be "*battering ram*" proof. More doors were also added. Every tunnel through the tree had a door at both ends installed, with handle mechanisms that a Sleimorp could not open. It seemed like overkill, but after the tourist invasion and twelve deaths the previous day, it was deemed to be prudent.

12. The Gavel Comes Down.

The trading had been ruined for the day and the Carlin traders had all left. The indigenous Thol trading partners had left the minute that things turned ugly. The Carlin men who had responded to the ringing of the village's emergency bell all returned to their homes and their household duties.

The interloping colonists had been lucky. Many of the Carlin first responders were Carlinish hunters and they were big, strong and fast enough to run down a Kyrrax. They also doubled as the village's warriors during times of trouble. The Human colonists who'd live comfortable, sedentary lives would have been no match for them.

James Reas continued cleaning up the mess in the Carlin village centre. The seven surviving tour guides were arrested and later taken away in a prisoner transport. The five corpses were taken away by a morgue hover bus. The four hover buses, loaded with the tourists, were driven back to the Human colony by Colonial Marines.

The tourists had all been identified and would be charged on summons if the surveillance data showed any wrongdoing. Those tourists who had entered Carlin's household plots uninvited were most definitely going to receive fines for criminal trespass.

Keegali held Kelyarn's right hand with concern as the Colonial Marine Medic patched up his left shoulder. The medic mentioned that they had good baseline data for Carlins provided by some Carlin visitors to the interstellar push ship Artemisia, up at Cis-Luns L-Five. Keegali informed the medic that that was herself, Kelyarn and their Daughter, Kitty; that they were those visitors. The medic stated that it was a good thing that they'd volunteered to give the colonists baseline data for Carlins.

The medic first injected Kelyarn with a broad-spectrum antibiotic before injecting a local anaesthetic into the area at the entry and exit points of his wound. After that, the medic injected a regenerative growth compound directly into the wound itself from both sides.

Even with the local anaesthetic, Kelyarn winced in pain. Once the medic had strapped and immobilised Kelyarn's left arm with a harness, he told him that it should be all healed in around two weeks; just keep the wound clean and dry.

Kelyarn was fortunate; it was a through-and-through and had damaged nothing vital. It would just take time to heal. Kelyarn thought it could have been worse; it might have hit his Daughter, Kitty. That was Kelyarn's primary concern.

After James took over the cleanup, Simone quickly followed Angelique and Kitty. Simone knew that Angelique would not be handling her first kills well. Angelique was family-trained, but not military-trained. Angelique had not been hardened and conditioned, desensitised against the horrors that being a Colonial Marine, most especially a Special Operative, often entailed. How Angelique processed her first kills would either make her or ruin her and there was no telling which outcome it would be.

Angelique had rushed past the front door to Kitty's house, instead making a beeline to their semi-detached wash house in their back yard. That separate structure was used for washing cooking utensils, cutlery, plates and clothes. It was also where they bathed and performed their daily ablutions. Angelique felt sick and nauseous. It was the most appropriate place for her to go.

Angelique didn't make it to the wash house. She collapsed to her knees and within seconds was throwing up her previous night's dinner. Neither Angelique nor Kitty had eaten that morning. The arrival of the tourist hover buses messed up their entire morning routine. It did not take long before Angelique was dry retching. Kitty did her best to hold Angelique's hair out of the growing pool of vomit.

Angelique stopped vomiting several times, only for the process to begin again soon after. The dry retching continued and Kitty was growing extremely concerned, especially after she began vomiting up blood. After what seemed like an eternity, Angelique finally collapsed to her left side and rolled onto her back. Hair streaked with her own vomit, she cried uncontrollably. She was completely inconsolable.

Simone rounded the corner of the house and rushed to Angelique's side.

Kitty turned to Simone, exclaiming, "Angelique is vomiting up blood! I don't know what to do!"

Simone looked at the fresh pool of vomit and then looked back at Angelique. There clearly was blood in the vomit, bright red and fresh. There was also blood smeared on the side of Angelique's mouth. Simone's mind wandered back to when she was little more than Angelique's age, to her own first kill. Simone had only taken down a single terrorist, but Angelique had taken down four hardened criminals.

"Angelique will be okay, Kitty. The same thing happened after my first kill", Simone assured her, explaining, "Angelique's stomach is undergoing extreme gastric distress. The strain of dry retching has likely caused some minor blood vessel rupturing."

Simone grabbed her communicator, "James, send the medic to the back of Keegali's house."

"Roger that, honey. He's finished with Kelyarn and on his way", James replied.

Kitty held Angelique's hand while Simone stroked her face, assuring her, "It's okay, sweety. You're going to be just fine, my little love."

The medic arrived, took one look at Angelique and asked, "First kill?"

"Yeah, four of those corpses were hers", Simone informed him.

The medic knelt down beside Angelique and placed his neural medical scanner next to her temple. He ran the scanner from her temple, across her forehead and down to her other temple.

The medic checked the results of the scan, "Mrs Reas, your Daughter is undergoing some very heavy emotional trauma. She is suffering from post-traumatic stress."

Simone nodded in complete understanding, "I figured that."

The medic swapped scanners, switching to a more generalised medical scanner. He ran the scanner over Angelique's abdominal region. He repeated the process several times, just to make sure.

"Well, we have a case of dry retching strain. The blood has already staunched", he noted as he reached into his medical pack and took out a small vile of pills, "Antacid. Give her one every four hours for the next day. Wash it down with milk. The primary concern is post-traumatic stress. Bed rest, lots of bed rest. And plenty of fluids. Chicken broth wouldn't hurt. You know the drill: if in doubt, give the Colonial Marine Medics a shout."

"Thank you", Simone replied.

"My pleasure, Mrs Reas", the medic replied before heading back to his squad.

Once the medic had left, Simone asked for Kitty's assistance, "Okay then, let's get my baby upstairs."

Kitty and Simone helped Angelique up the stairs to the fourth-level sleep room, where she had been staying with Kitty. Once in the sleep room, Simone helped her Daughter undress and helped her onto the sleeping mat. Angelique was quiet and unresponsive.

Kitty left to get a basin of water and some washcloths. When she returned, they both gave Angelique a bed bath and then wrapped her up in warm blankets. Simone helped Angelique take one of the tablets and helped her wash it down with Gudong milk.

"Okay, Kitty, my baby girl needs some rest, lots of rest", Simone noted.

"I'll stay with Angelique. I'll make sure she's alright", Kitty replied.

"Okay, that's fine, Kitty, but Angelique needs rest. So no playing, just rest, okay", Simone instructed.

Kitty slipped out of her clothes in front of Simone, letting them fall to the floor and replied as she climbed under the sleep covers, "I'll just cuddle Angelique and keep her warm. Lots of cuddles."

"Just as long as my baby girl gets plenty of rest, Kitty", and she then went down the stairs to the kitchen, thinking to herself that Carlins had no hangups or inhibitions whatsoever with nudity.

Simone made her way back downstairs to the kitchen and found Kelyarn, his

Wife, Keegali and his Daughters, Kayala and Kearill, sitting at the kitchen table. She noticed the harness on Kelyarn's arm.

"How's the wing, Kelyarn?", Simone asked.

Kelyarn looked confused, "Carlins have no wings, Simone. It is the Thols that have wings."

"It's a Human thing, it means how's your arm, you know, your shoulder", Simone explained.

"My shoulder will be fine in two weeks", Kelyarn replied.

Keegali enquired, "How's Angelique?"

"Post-traumatic stress. Those four robbers were her first kills. That can kind of mess a person up. I think she'll be okay. She just needs some rest", Simone informed her, noting, "Kitty's upstairs looking after her."

Kearill climbed up onto Simone's lap and gave her a huge hug, "You need hugs", she told her.

Simone smiled and stroked Kearill's cheeks, "Thank you, Kearill, I actually do need a hug right now."

Kayala giggled, "Are you sure that Angelique will get any rest with Kitty with her?"

"Yes, I asked Kitty to let Angelique get some rest and she did agree to it", Simone confirmed.

Kayala commented, "I like Johnathon. I really do. He calls me his fair Carlin maiden, but then he says I'm not for him. I do not understand."

"Well, Kayala, you are a Carlin and my Son, Johnathon, is a Human, so you wouldn't be able to have any kits", Simone replied, adding, "Kits are kind of important to a Carlinish woman, so I understand. Like all Carlinish women, one day you will want kits. Lots of kits."

Keegali chimed in, "Remember, Kayala. After your quickening, you won't even think of Johnathon."

Kayala nodded, then asked, "Why is Johnathon so fixated on his Aunt Roberta?"

"Our Aunt Roberta is not a blood relation. She's an honorary Aunt", Simone noted, adding, "And Johnathon has actually been saying he's going to marry his Aunt Roberta since before he was four. If I remember correctly, the first words Johnathon spoke were Mum, Dad and Roberta, in that order."

Keegali's ears picked up, "Really! That sounds like something predestined, from before this life."

"Karma? From a previous life?", Simone questioned, "I hadn't thought of that."

"Could be", Kelyarn agreed.

Simone enquired, "Where is my boy, Johnathon?"

Kayala replied, smiling with her whiskers raised, "He's playing with my Brothers. They are all playing Space Lions. Johnathon says space lions are bold and fearless. He's so fascinating."

Kelyarn laughed so loud it made his shoulder wound ache, "That boy! He's just like one of our kits!", he exclaimed, "Surely he must have a Carlin in his bloodline somewhere", something impossible, of course.

Keegali added with own whiskers raised, "We love him as if he were one of our own kits, we really do."

Simone pinched the bridge of her nose and sighed. Her Son's antics were never-ending.

Simone then asked, "Angelique will need to eat soon. Can we make some Thrixan soup? It's the closest thing to Chicken soup that I can think of."

Keegali smiled, "Yes, of course, Thrixan soup is the perfect thing for Angelique right now."

Roberta Nummus's presence had been requested in the Human colony. She was now sitting in a conference room in the main colonial government building. There was no civilian government at present, nor was there any civilian judiciary. They were still quite some time away in the future.

The man who was ostensibly the Governor of the Human colony had no real power as yet. His government was still taking shape and in its earliest nascent form.

"So in the last two days, there have been two incidents: unauthorised tour groups. First, the 'Cat people tours' incident in Kelyarn's village, and the very next day, the 'Angel tours' incident in Yannick's tree village. What the hell is going on down here? I mean, seriously, what the fuck!"

James Reas informed the High Admiral, "Ma'am. It appears to have been a scam run by a Husband and Wife team. The tour guides involved all thought that they were working for legitimate tour companies with proper licensing and authorisation. Even the guy who financed them thought that they were legitimate businesses. They raked in nearly four hundred thousand credits before they both vanished."

Roberta shook her head in disgust, "That Husband and Wife team are responsible for seventeen deaths! Elder Kelyarn was shot! I want them found and brought to justice as a matter of urgency. And, S.O. Reas, legitimate businesses? How could anybody possibly believe business names like 'Cat people tours Ltd' and 'Angel tours Ltd' were legitimate businesses? It's a whole new level of dumbassery that I have never come across before."

"Yes, Ma'am. I can't agree with you more, but there you have it. It is what it is", James Reas agreed.

"I've read through all of the statements from those so-called tour guides, the ones that survived anyway. I'm flabbergasted. They all believed that they were working for legitimate businesses. Their statements are all first-person subjective, yet they're all consistent, so they do appear to be telling the truth", Roberta shook her head, "These people showed absolutely no common sense. None whatsoever!"

James agreed once more, "Yes, Ma'am. I can only assume that they are intellectually-challenged."

Roberta chuckled, "Intellectually-challenged. Now that's an understatement. At least they've provided us with good descriptions and photo-fits of that couple", before enquiring, "How's that going?"

"We used our A.I. systems to combine the photo-fits into a combined image. However, that couple does not appear to be in our databases", James informed her, noting, "They're not in the records of our colonists, nor are they in the records of our interstellar push ship crews."

"S.O. Reas, that is not remotely possible. Have Wingtarla or Wynessa scan their minds. Check that their memories match those photo-fits", Roberta suggested.

"Ma'am, I have already done that. The combined photo-fit image matches their memories", James replied, adding, "Wingtarla and his people are walking the village looking for them with their telepathic abilities. We also have a dozen undercover operatives working on the task. We will find them, Ma'am."

"Let's hope we do. The fact that they are not in any of our records means one of two things. Either they were stowaways in our fleet, which is highly unlikely, or we have unofficial colony ships in the Xi-Bootis system and you know what that means."

James nodded, understanding exactly what that meant, "Smugglers, criminals, pirates, terrorists, all sorts of nasty folk. Scammers could be the least of our worries. There must be unregistered ships out there somewhere in this system. Ships with unregistered slipstream drives."

Roberta nodded, noting, "And so early in our colonisation timeline. This is an unexpected development. Far too early for my liking."

"Angelique is suffering from post-traumatic stress. It was her first kill and without full training, so it was to be expected", James noted, adding, "Simone and I expect her to make a full recovery. Angelique is made of tough stuff. She is now recovering at Kelyarn's and Keegali's house. Simone believes that particular environment will speed her recovery along."

Roberta nodded and noted, "Four quick kills, all drilled through the forehead. I watched the surveillance video. Simone was right to rebuke her; nonetheless, her actions were impressive and likely saved half a dozen or more Carlin traders' lives. Let it be recorded that Angelique Reas is to be awarded an accommodation for bravery. We will make a trauma counsellor available upon request."

"Thank you, Ma'am", James replied, his face beaming with the pride he had for his Daughter.

"I cannot imagine how good an operative Angelique will be when she's fully trained", Roberta replied, noting, "Four kills without full training at seventeen, she will become an extremely valuable asset. When Angelique joins up, I'll make sure she gets the best instructors."

"Now, S.O. Reas, these four kills. Who were they? You have their bodies and yet, no identifications", Roberta questioned.

"Ma'am, just like our pair of scammers, these perpetrators are not recorded anywhere in our databases. No visual ID, no DNA, no biometrics. Nothing. We suspect that they came from the same place as the scammers, but that's only because they were involved in the same operation, the same scam", James admitted.

"That is not much to go on, S.O. Reas and that has me seriously concerned", Roberta replied, noting, "They may not have been involved in the tourist scam, but they did take advantage of it. We may have more than one set of interlopers out there in the greater Xi-Bootis system. I'll have our people start scanning for any signs of rogue ships. We need to find these arseholes before they cause any more problems. We already have two interspecies incidents and an attempted robbery."

Roberta shuffled the files on her desk into some semblance of order and then commanded, "S.O. Reas. Bring in our prisoners. I'll also be requiring Elder Kelyarn, Yannick, Yealah, Wynessa and our new bureaucrat, Governor Anderson. Our newly appointed Governor needs to be across this and also needs to understand how frontier justice plays out."

James opened the doors and everybody filed in. All of the prisoners were in handcuffs. Two Colonial Marines, acting as bailiffs, filed the surviving tour guides from the Carlin village incident, as it was now called, into the room and ordered them to sit at a table on the left.

Another pair of Colonial Marines, acting in the same fashion, led in the one surviving tour guide from the Thol tree village incident, as it was now called, and sat him down at a table on the right.

Alongside him was another prisoner, the businessman who had unwittingly financed the entire tourism scam. The four Colonial Marines, who were fully armed, took station along the wall, carefully watching over the prisoners.

Elder Kelyarn, Yannick, Yealah, Wynessa and Governor Anderson took seats at a table in the centre of the room, set slightly back from the two tables to either side. Kelyarn was still wearing his shoulder harness due to the injury from the pulsed laser pistol discharge.

"First, let me inform everyone present that we do have a Martian hybrid in the room. So understand this and understand it well. If you lie to me, Wynessa will know it and so will I", Roberta informed everyone in the room.

The head tourist guide from the Carlin village incident protested, "That is not legal! You can not have a telepath in a courtroom!"

"This is not a courtroom, nor is this a civilian trial. This is a military tribunal and you are here for summary judgement, not a trial nor a hearing", Roberta informed him bluntly.

"That is not how the law works!", he protested again.

Roberta rolled her eyes and shook her head, "Listen to me very carefully. You are on the outer frontier in a newly colonised star system. Here, right now, I am the law. No one else, just me. I have the power and the right to dispense summary judgement, up to and including execution. So, perhaps, just perhaps, you should keep your outbursts to a minimum."

The head tourist guide questioned reflexively, "Summary execution?"

"Don't piss your pants just yet. I'm not throwing anyone out of an airlock today", Roberta informed him, noting, "That is within the scope of my powers, by the way."

Roberta looked over to the table on the right, "I'm going to start with you, Mr Mort Baxter. I have read your statement. You have been most cooperative. Now, for the record, you say that you believed that the businesses, *'Cat People Tours Ltd'* and *'Angel Tours Ltd'* were legitimate, bonafide business enterprises. That you had no inkling that they were scams."

"Yes, Ma'am. The couple showed me the licensing, the authorisation documents and the signatures all looked legit", Mort Baxter replied.

"Mr Baxter, there's only one family of Carlin-folk who can speak and understand English. None of them has learned to read and write English yet. Shouldn't you have seen that as a red flag?", Roberta questioned.

"In hindsight, yes, but at the time, I thought they were legit", Mort Baxter explained.

"Well, sadly for you, Mr Baxter, everything that couple showed you was fraudulent. Now, for the record, please state how much you lost financing this fraud", Roberta asked.

"Twenty eight thousand credits", Mr Baxter admitted.

Roberta looked at Wynessa, who broadcast, *"Mr Baxter tells the truth. He is as much a victim in this as the tourists. He was duped."*

Roberta turned back to Mr Baxter, "When S.O. James Reas was organising a rescue mission to the Thol tree village, you interfered. You tried to have the rescue operation shut down."

"My apologies, Ma'am. I really thought that they were interfering in a legitimate business enterprise and had no business doing so", Mr Baxter replied, admitting his mistake.

Wynessa didn't wait for Roberta to ask and broadcast, *"His mind is clear. He is telling the truth."*

"Let it be recorded that for the crime of interfering in a legitimate military operation, I am fining Mr Mort Baxter two thousand credits, revoking his business license for twelve months and placing him on probation for the same period of time", Roberta announced.

Mr Baxter protested, "You can't do that!"

"I can and I have. Would you like me to double everything, Mr Baxter?", Roberta replied harshly.

Mr Baxter shook his head, while Roberta instructed one of the Colonial Marines, "Remove Mr Baxter's handcuffs and release him on his recognisance."

Mr Baxter was then uncuffed and shown to the door.

"Now, we get to the *'Thol tree village incident'*. I have watched the surveillance videos provided by Yannick and Yealah in great detail. I must say, Mr Jackson. The video clearly shows you battering down the front door to their Tholish tree village. Do you understand what that locked door was there for?", Roberta asked.

Mr Brent Jackson answered, "I didn't know at the time, but it was there to keep the predators out."

"Correct, Mr Jackson. Vorts, Kyrrax and Sleimorps can't open locked doors, nor can they batter down a solid reinforced door that is locked. However, when a pair of idiots uses a battering ram to shatter that door and smash it off its hinges, well, that kind of gave that pack of Sleimorps easy access to a smorgasbord. As the head tour guide of your group, you are one hundred percent responsible for every single death. The four tourists who fell to their deaths, your five fellow tour guides and those three tourists who were killed by that pack of Sleimorps; that is all on you. That's a body count of twelve."

"You can't be serious! You can't hold me responsible for all of those deaths!", he protested.

"Yes, I can, Mr Jackson. You see, it matters not that you were duped into believing that you had a legitimate job as a tour guide. The minute you battered that door down and entered that tree village, as the head tour guide, everything that follows on from your actions is entirely on you!"

"No, no, no, you can't. This has to be a mistake", he protested, before demanding, "I want a lawyer."

"Good luck with that, Mr Jackson. The nearest lawyers are in the Sol system, twenty two light years away", Roberta replied, before asking a rhetorical question, "Before battering that door down, did you perhaps look up at the surveillance cameras, wave and ask for someone to come down to, I don't know, assist you? Don't bother answering that, we have the videos, so we know you didn't."

"So you forced your way through a secured door, trespassing and causing property damage, which led to the deaths of twelve people", Roberta continued, stating clearly, "For the record, you are charged with Criminal Trespass, Criminal Property Damage and Criminal Negligence leading to what can only be described as Negligent Homicide. I have seen all of the evidence, so I have no qualms about pronouncing you guilty as charged. You will spend twenty years in incarceration. Here for three years and when we ship you back to the Sol system, the remaining seventeen years in the Jovian Cloud Penitentiary. You are also, hereby banished from the Xi-Bootis system, flagged never to return."

"No, wait! You can't! You can't be serious!", he protested.

"I am deadly serious, Mr Jackson. Twelve people died because of your actions. If not for the actions of Yannick and Yealah, and the timely arrival of the Colonial Marines, a lot more people would have died", Roberta told him in no uncertain terms.

"No, no, no!", he protested once more.

"One more outburst, Mr Jackson and I will have you spaced!", Roberta threatened.

Roberta looked at Mr Brent Jackson wandering about a question that needed answering, "Wynessa, I need you to peek into Mr Jackson's mind. We need to know why, on his tour, his tour guides didn't take pulsed laser pistols with them. That is a major difference between these two incidents."

Wynessa nodded to Roberta and proceeded to skim Mr Brent Jackson's mind.

After a long minute, Wynessa broadcast, *"It was an error in their perception, Roberta Nummus. They perceived that the Mimasian Thols and the Indigenous Thols were the same, Angelic. The indigenous Thols were not perceived as a threat, so they did not request any protection. They did not request any firearms."*

"Now isn't that very interesting. I spent four centuries living inside Mimas with the Mimasian Thols, who not only look like Angels, but their behaviour, by and large, is what I can only describe as Angelic. The Indigenous Thols, however, not so much. They may look the part, but behaviourally, they are much more like us Humans", Roberta explained, before noting, "Honestly, Mr Jackson, the Indigenous Thols clearly acted with restraint. They could have easily rained poison arrows down on your entire tour group and would have been well within their rights to do so."

Roberta turned to one of the Colonial Marines, ordering, "Take Mr Jackson back to his cell."

Roberta turned to the tour guides from the *"Carlin village incident"*, and noted, "Now, it's your turn. Mr Terry Hanson, you were the head tour guide in the Carlin village incident. So, why did your tour guides have pulsed laser pistols?"

"Our employers provided the pulsed laser pistols for our own protection. For predators and such", Terry Hanson replied.

Wynessa broadcast straight away, *"That's a half-truth. Provided they were, yes, but he's holding back."*

"A lie by omission is still a lie, Mr Hanson, and please remember that I hold the keys to the airlocks", Roberta responded, her voice almost jovial.

Mr Hanson gulped and quickly replied, "We requested the pulsed laser pistols for our own protection."

"You requested them", Roberta nodded, "Now, we are getting somewhere. Protection from predators, you say. Now that is very interesting. The floor of the forests under the Thol tree villages is far more dangerous than any Carlin village, yet your people requested firearms and Mr Jackson's people did not."

Roberta turned to Kelyarn, "Elder Kelyarn, is my assessment correct about the predator threats?"

Kelyarn stood up and spoke, "Yes, very correct. The floor of the Jula Jula forests has many predators, day or night. A Carlin village is safe from predators during the daytime and only sometimes sees any predators during the night."

As Kelyarn sat back down, Roberta replied, "That's what I thought, Elder Kelyarn", and she then turned to the head tour guide, noting dryly, "Mr Hanson, your tour was a daytime tour. This assertion that you needed pulsed laser pistols for protection from predators is pure nonsense. So, let's have the real reason, shall we?"

One of the female tour guides, who had been quiet, sitting with her eyes lowered, looked up and interjected, "It's cat people, Ma'am. We had the Cat People tour, not the Angel tour. The cat people are not Angels; it turns out they're Space Lions."

Roberta looked quickly at Kelyarn and gave him a look of apology, before confronting the tour guide, "I see, Ms Whinny Smith, it was another perception problem, was it? You perceived the Carlin-folk as the actual threat. You do understand, don't you, that that changes everything. You went to the Carlin village armed and prepared to use your weapons against the Carlin villagers."

Roberta shook her head, "And those pulsed laser pistols. How did you not see the red flags? Not one of them had serial numbers on them and that means that they were illegally manufactured. A pulsed laser pistol that is illegally manufactured cannot be registered, so obviously, they were unregistered."

Terry Hanson chimed in, "Our employers said that they were processing the paperwork. That the registrations and everything were pending."

"Pending is NOT approval, Mr Hanson", Roberta snapped back, noting, "Not a single one of you is licensed to carry a firearm, let alone concealed firearms. Tell me, did your employers provide any of you with any firearms safety and training at all?"

Mr Hanson replied, "No, Ma'am", and the others all followed, replying the same way.

"For the record, all seven of you are charged with the following. Possession of an illegal firearm. Possession of an unregistered firearm. Possession of a firearm whilst unlicensed. Possession of a concealed firearm without proper permits", Roberta announced, before smiling and noting, "And there is more. Drawing a firearm in a public space. Three counts each of threatening people with a firearm; that would be your customers, the Carlin villagers and, of course, S.O. Reserve, Simone Reas, and her Daughter, Angelique Reas."

Whinny Smith murmured, "That was the woman who murdered Karen."

"Self-defence is not murder, Ms Smith. I've seen the surveillance video. Karen Scilly drew and fired at S.O. Reserve, Simone Reas, first", and then she thought to herself, *"What an appropriate name."*

The image of Karen Scilly waving her clipboard around like a badge of authority while committing criminal trespass was still in Roberta's mind from her review of the video surveillance of the entire incident.

Roberta then continued, "Those are the eight major charges thus far. Let me add two more. When you entered the Carlin family plots, you crossed from a public space into private spaces and you did so without permission or invitation. So, that is criminal trespass, especially when you ignored repeated demands that you leave their land. You not only trespassed yourselves, but you held the gates open for the others to trespass, so we'll add, aiding and abetting the criminal trespass by others."

The seven defendants all looked shocked; they were now facing nine criminal charges.

"Fortunately, we have all of the evidence on the surveillance videos. You see, S.O. Reserve, Simone Reas, called in eight stealth surveillance drones from our Colony, knowing how quickly this was going to go south", Roberta informed them, noting, "If you had just left those damned pulsed laser pistols behind, you would only be facing the trespassing charges, but no, you took them with you."

The seven tour guides were all silent; they had a fair idea of what was coming.

"Elder Kelyarn is that Carlin village's Elder, effectively the village Mayor. You all completely ignored his explicit instructions to leave. Not just his own family's plot, but to leave the Carlin village entirely. Everything about your tour was fake. The tour packages, the counterfeit barter beads, everything", Roberta scolded, noting harshly, "In case you hadn't noticed, Elder Kelyarn is nursing a shoulder wound. He was shot. In addition to this, amongst your customers were four armed robbers, who, as robbers do, tried to commit daylight robbery. Those four armed robbers are now dead, as is one of your own. Now, just let that all sink in."

Terry Hanson protested, "You can't hold us responsible for those armed robbers. We didn't know what they were. To us, they were just more tourists, more customers."

"Mr Hanson. I am aware of that. I just pointed them out to try and get you all to understand, none of this would have happened had you not been there. More importantly, if you had not taken those firearms with you, you would only be facing trespass-related charges. As it is, those eight firearms charges cannot simply be ignored", Roberta explained.

All seven defendants looked deflated; they were about to receive frontier justice.

"For the record, I pronounce you all guilty of the charges previously announced. You will each spend ten years in incarceration. Here for three years and when we ship you back to the Sol system, the remaining seven years in the Jovian Cloud Penitentiary. I will advise the Jovian Realms that, on good behaviour, your sentence may be reduced, but to no less than five years. That will be the minimum sentence. You are also, hereby banished from the Xi-Bootis system, flagged never to return."

Roberta looked to the Colonial Marines and ordered, "Take them back to their cells", before looking at the room's surveillance camera and noting, "Both cases are now closed."

The Colony's A.I. systems automatically began collating and documenting everything.

While still looking at the surveillance camera, Roberta noted, "For the record, all of the tourists who trespassed into the Thol tree village or the Carlin private family plots are to receive fines of two hundred credits to be paid within thirty days."

"Now, we have another order of business for the day", Roberta announced, commenting, "We need to avoid any repeat of these incidents."

Governor Thomas Anderson replied, "While not disagreeing with your judgements, Admiral, I must query their harshness."

"Of course, you must, Governor", Roberta replied, explaining, "If you didn't question my judgement, I would be severely disappointed. Look, it's like this. Every new colony undergoes a period of innocence. Three days ago, we had no prisons, not here, nor up at Cis-Luns L-Five. Now, I have Androids carving out a prison on the western flanks of our Colony's hill, deep under the spaceport. It will, when completed, be able to hold up to one hundred prisoners. Up in Cis-Luns L-Five, all twelve interstellar push ships are being outfitted with Briggs. Now, we even have plans for a Stanford Torus Penitentiary in Cis-Luns L-Four. In two years, our colonies have lost their innocence, something I was hoping would take two decades, not two short years."

"So you made an example of them?", the Governor enquired.

James Reas chimed in, in Roberta's defence, "Harsh but fair."

"Yes, harsh but fair", Roberta agreed.

"Why are we keeping them here for three years, Admiral?", Governor Anderson.

"We don't have the means to send them back to Sol, Governor", Roberta replied, explaining, "When Colonial Central in Cis-Luns L-Five is completed, our colony fleet will be returning to Sol, all twelve interstellar push ships. The prisoners will return to Sol with the fleet, which is expected to occur in a little over three years from now. Until then, we are stuck with them."

"So, no one here can return to Sol?", the Governor questioned.

Jame Reas stepped in, "We have a communications runner, but it is not set up for passengers and certainly not set up for prisoner transport. It only has limited bunking for crew members."

"Yes, we do have our communications runner", Roberta confirmed, "Once a month, it slipstreams back to the outskirts for the Sol system to transmit our colonial reports. However, it only hangs around long enough to receive replies and for its primary power systems to recharge; then it slipstreams back again. It's essentially our monthly mail run."

"So, if we really needed to send someone back to Sol, we can't?", the Governor queried.

"We can, the communications runner does keep three bunks empty for military transfers", James informed him, noting once more, "Only for military transfers."

"Now, we need to get down to brass tacks", Roberta remarked.

Yannick noted, "I have spoken to High Chancellor Yuntark of the Tholish High Council, who has given me these signed documents. They are in Native Tholish."

Yannick took the documents out of his folio and explained their contents.

"This first document declares all Indigenous Tholish tree villages off limits to all Humans. The High Chancellor has carved out some exceptions. The Mimasian tree villages may choose their own limitations. Shared Indigenous and Mimasian tree villages, only Humans who have friends in the tree village or are invited are to be allowed in", Yannick explained, his English laced with trills, clicks and soft barks.

"That actually sounds fair", Roberta noted, adding, "Mimasian tree villages have their own agency and shared tree villages can still interact with our people, via the Mimasian Thol inhabitants. This is actually far better than I'd thought, considering the circumstances."

"Tell everyone the price to pay, Yannick", Yealah trilled and clicked.

"Yes, yes, there's always a price to pay", Yannick trilled, explaining with more trills and clicks, "The High Chancellor has seen our surveillance videos. He's really impressed and wants us to share our technology with his people."

"You showed him your surveillance videos?", Governor Anderson questioned.

"Yes, of course, we did, we must be fully transparent", Yealah trilled.

Wynessa chimed in, picking up on some tension in Yannick's and Yealah's voices, telepathically asking, *"What more did the High Chancellor request?"*

"The High Chancellor is horrified by the Sleimorps. He is demanding that we eliminate all Sleimorps from under the Thol villages", Yannick trilled, clicked and barked, adding, "He doesn't care how we do it either. Slaughter them, relocate them, drive them into the Western Mountain forests. He does not care. He just wants them all gone. Every single last one of them."

Yealah trilled, clicked and barked softly, "The High Chancellor took one look at our video, saw what were supposed to be animals, climbing our elevator support scaffolding and operating our elevator system, and that was it. Get rid of those beasts was his first demand. I don't really blame him, I mean, we've never seen sub-sapient animals act in such a way. They were uncanny, incredibly intelligent."

Roberta sighed, there was always a catch, "So noted, Yealah. Governor, this sounds like expensive business. The Northern and Southern Mountain ranges, where the Indigenous Thols live, are two vast regions. My people will work out the feasibility and logistics; beyond that, all discussions with the High Chancellor will be in your hands."

"So noted. When the feasibility and logistics studies arrive, we'll arrange the relevant meetings", Governor Anderson replied, adding, "I suggest keeping our laws in these matters simple. In this case, Indigenous Tholish villages are off limits to all Humans. For the Mimasian and shared Tholish villages, Humans may access via invitation only and absolutely no tours. Let's just keep it simple."

Everyone agreed and that became the first new law for the Human colony on Secundus.

Elder Kelyarn chimed in, "We need something similar for the Carlinish villages as well."

"Your suggestion, Kelyarn", Roberta requested.

"My village is by far the closest and largest Carlin village to this Colony", Kelyarn noted, explaining his proposal, "My village will remain open to Humans on an invitation and friends-only basis. Strangers who wish to visit will need to wait outside on the roadway. They may approach the closest households on the main entry road and wait respectfully for assistance. Again, absolutely no tours. For the near future, all other Carlin villages should be off limits."

Governor Anderson was taking notes, "I am fairly certain that we can codify that as our second new law. Is everyone in agreement?"

Everyone agreed and that became the second new law for the Human colony on Secundus.

"I know this is going to sound stupid, but we all know that some of my people are actually stupid, really stupid! I want to recommend that all Human visitors who visit Carlin or Thol villages be instructed not to call them cat people or angels. Let's have some kind of educational drive to teach our people how rude and disrespectful that is", Roberta recommended.

"We can put together some form of educational posts on our local news feeds", the Governor agreed.

Kelyarn chuckled, "Except for young Johnathon Reas. We love that boy like our own and when he calls us space lions, it's because he loves us too."

"I think we can allow personal carve-outs to the rule based on Carlin Human friendships", Governor Anderson agreed.

James Reas noted, "Our first two laws will need exception clauses."

"Exception clauses?", Yannick trilled.

"Yes, of course. If a Carlin or Indigenous Thol family wants some of our technological upgrades, we will need permission to install them. Professional access exceptions", James explained.

Yealah caught on quickly, trilling, "Also access for medical emergencies, upon request, irrespective of the status of the village, Carlin, or Thol."

"Okay, we can have a third law to carve that out. Access for legitimate profession and medical requests and interventions irrespective of village status", Governor Anderson suggested.

Everyone agreed and that became the third new law for the Human colony on Secundus.

Governor Anderson had some serious concerns about these new laws. He was also pretty sure that Roberta Nummus would have those same concerns, so he decided to voice them.

"Unfortunately, these laws will limit interactions between the Indigenous population and our colonists. We want our presence here to be both beneficial and uplifting. So I'm making some more recommendations", the Governor informed them.

"I wholeheartedly agree. So, Governor Anderson, your suggestions?", Roberta requested.

"Our school is free and open to all of our colonists, whether Human, Martian, or Mimasian Thol", the Governor reminded them, "Let's open up our school further, to freely include Carlin and Indigenous Thol children."

"That is actually a great idea", Yealah trilled excitedly, trilling further, "They can learn English to open up communications. Carlins and Thols are fast learners; their kits and younglings will teach their parents. Education is key."

Yannick trilled and clicked, noting, "We can teach them our history, our science and technology, and even our Culture. As my Wife, Yealah, just said, education is key."

James stepped in, noting, "We can even provide safe hover bus services to and from their villages. Carlin villages have large cobblestone areas at the edge of their villages, in the east and the west, where their main roads spill out into the bluegrass meadows."

Yannick added in with trills and clicks, "And my people can provide safe roadways under the Jula Jula trees", before noting, "We will need to eliminate the Sleimorps, though."

Governor Anderson proposed the new law, "Colonial education shall be provided free to all Carlin or Indigenous Thol families that want it and we will provide safe transport to and from the school."

Everyone agreed and that became the fourth new law for the Human colony on Secundus.

Wynessa chimed in telepathically, broadcasting, "*We need to open this up further. If the hover bus services bring Carlin kits and Indigenous Thol younglings to and from school. They can also bring Carlin and Indigenous Thol adults to and from our colony. We have limited ourselves from going to them, but we should be more open to them coming to us.*"

"Wynessa is one hundred percent right. We access the Carlin and Thol villages on their terms and that is the right thing to do. However, we should give them free access to our Colony, also on their terms. We provide the hover bus transport for their kits and younglings to come to our school and the parents can hitch a ride to our colony whenever they wish. They can come here or not, they get to decide themselves, no pressure and I bet that they will be curious", Roberta agreed with Wynessa.

Yealah noted a problem, "The Carlin-folk and Indigenous Thols use diamonds as barter stones. Diamonds from Homwol are disproportionately valuable to Humans. They come here with their barter stones, diamonds, and Humans will hoard them, taking them out of circulation. The indigenous economy will collapse."

James interjected with an idea, "All diamonds have chemical markers. Those can be used to pinpoint geographic origins, even planetary origins. We can ban our colonists from having Secundun diamonds in their possession. Make the possession of Secundun diamonds illegal for colonists."

"I don't know. I mean, we could do that, but would it work? Humans will just secretly hoard them", Yannick trilled and clicked.

"We'll need a carve-out there, too, James. You're forgetting, Angelique was gifted two large diamonds at first contact by Kelyarn's Daughter, Kitty", Roberta reminded him.

James nodded, "So noted."

"I do have a solution", Governor Anderson informed them, "But first let's codify our fifth and sixth new laws, shall we. Hover buses provided between our school and the Thol and Carlin villages will be open to use by Thol younglings,

Carlin kits and adults alike. Free access to and from the villages to the colony for all indigenous folk."

Everyone agreed and that became the fifth new law for the Human colony on Secundus.

"Now, I'm going to agree with the possession of Secundun diamonds being illegal for our colonists. An almost complete ban on that, with the exception of those diamonds held for research purposes and or historically gifted; they will be grandfathered in. To me, that's a no-brainer, we can't be wrecking the indigenous economy", the Governor announced.

Everyone agreed and that became the sixth new law for the Human colony on Secundus.

"Yes, now we've agreed, but what is your solution?", Roberta enquired.

"We'll implement a new policy", the Governor announced with a smile, "We can call it the Indigenous Species Visitation Incentive policy, ISVI. We inform our A.I. systems that we don't accept any barter tokens, not barter beads, nor barter stones, most especially not diamonds."

Kelyarn's transactional mind quipped, "And just how do our people pay for things if not by barter?"

"Kelyarn, in your villages or in the Thol villages, your rules will apply. You barter. No problem", Governor Anderson agreed, noting, "But here in our Colony, our rules apply. As an incentive for Carlin-folk and the Indigenous Thols to come here, we won't accept payment from them. We will give them goods and services for free. As an incentive. Consider it us paying for the Carlin-folk's and Indigenous Thol's valuable time spent here in our Colony. We are willing to pay them for their time."

Kelyarn laughed; the concept piqued his sense of humour. It was absurd, hilariously absurd.

"Sweet Mother of God, Anderson, that's not only radical, but it could become very expensive", Roberta noted.

"Obviously, Admiral. That's why I'm recommending that it comes out of your colonisation budget", Governor Anderson smiled.

They all had a quick vote and the Indigenous Species Visitation Incentive policy, ISVI, became law.

Roberta Nummus abstained from voting, as it was her budget that they were all messing with.

"Admiral, it is a justifiable policy, as it will lead to a much faster integration", Governor Anderson explained.

13. One Bond Begets Another.

The next day after the Carlin village incident, Angelique rested, recovering from her post-traumatic stress, brought on by her shooting of the four armed robbers, who'd arrived with the *"Cat people tour"*. Her bouts of vomiting had stopped, but she had become quiet and withdrawn.

Angelique's Father, Special Operative James Reas, had been called out to another incident at a Thol village that same day. It was yet another unauthorised tour, the *"Angel tour"*, that had gone horribly wrong.

Angelique was growing increasingly withdrawn and Kitty, who had stayed by her side, was getting anxious. Angelique's Mother was also growing very concerned, as was Kitty's Mother, Keegali, who'd noticed Kitty's blue stripes fading, showing signs of ever-increasing stress. Angelique's post-traumatic stress was, in turn, causing Kitty to become stressed and it was beginning to show. Even Kitty's little Sister, Kearill, had noticed; she'd curled up beside Kitty, cuddling her and would not leave her side.

The following day, Special Operative James Reas attended an early morning meeting with Admiral Nummus. That meeting was followed by the military tribunal of the tour guides involved in both incidents; summary judgements were delivered. The meeting that followed the tribunal led to the creation of seven new laws to prevent further incidents.

During these meetings, James Reas's communicator had been switched to *"do-not-disturb"* mode. When James checked his messages at the end of the final meeting, he found that his Wife, Simone, had been trying to contact him all morning. The messages seemed urgent and James called his Wife.

"James! Where have you been? I know you're busy and all, but we really need you here straight away", Simone told him.

"Calm down, Simone. Now, tell me the situation", James requested.

"Angelique is withdrawn, Kitty's blue stripes are starting to fade, Keegali and I are getting very concerned. So, I will not calm down", Simone chided, before demanding, "We need you here now and bring a trauma counsellor with you. Our little girl needs help."

"Okay, Simone. I'm on my way", James agreed and the call ended.

James started using his neural augments to look for a trauma counsellor, while noting to Kelyarn, "We need to get back to your village straight away."

Wynessa could see the concern on his face and asked telepathically, *"Is everything okay? Is there anything I can do to help?"*

"Not unless you know where I can find a good trauma counsellor, Wynessa", James answered.

Wynessa shook her head and transmitted back, *"Hello. I'm a Martian. We are natural-born counsellors. You can stop looking. You have a trauma counsellor right here in this room."*

James messaged Simone, *"We're on the way"*, and then put away his communicator, responding, "Okay then, let's get going."

Back in the fourth-level sleep room of Keegali's home, Angelique sat bolt upright in bed and began screaming; her body was sweating profusely, even though her skin was cold and clammy to the touch.

Kitty was startled at first, but then quickly sat up and automatically wrapped her arms around her. Kearill jumped up and ran downstairs looking for her Mother and Simone.

Simone, rushing up the stairs with Keegali close behind, swept little Kearill up in her arms, saying, "It's all okay, little cuddle puss", she reassured her as they entered the sleep room.

Simone passed Kearill to Keegali and Kearill smiled at her Mother, "I'm a cuddle puss, Mummy", before telling her, "Angelique is very scared."

Simone grabbed Angelique and enveloped her in her embrace, "It's okay, Angelique. I'm here, your Mother's here", she was cold to the touch and covered in sweat.

"I keep seeing them. Their faces. They all stare at me and then they're all dead", Angelique screamed, "Why are they staring at me, Mamma. I didn't want to kill them, Mamma!"

"Shh, shh, it's okay, my baby girl. You did the right thing. You really did. You save at least six Carlin lives, probably more", Simone reassured her.

"They won't go away, Mamma. They won't go away. I see them when I close my eyes. I see them when I sleep. I can still see them now!" Angelique cried out, screaming, "They're staring at me. Accusing me. Then they die, they all die with little holes in their foreheads where I shot them!"

Kitty watched her lover, frozen in terror, her blue stripes now the palest shade of blue they could ever be. So light, so pale, they were almost gone and her skin tones took on an eerie, almost Human appearance. Kitty began crying in sympathy for her friend, Angelique. Keegali automatically sat beside her and, still holding Kearill, she wrapped her arms around her Daughter.

"Angelique sees ghosts, Mother", Kitty whispered, her eyes wide in terror, "There are ghosts in her head, haunting her!"

"Not ghosts, Kitty", Keegali corrected, explaining, "Haunted memories. They can be just as bad."

There was the subtle sound of an aircraft outside Keegali's house and a Manta Ray-class passenger transport came into view beyond the window to the north. It landed gently in front of the house in Kelyarn's plot.

As soon as the Manta Ray's main hatch opened, Wynessa, who was not just a telepath but, like all Martians and Martian hybrids, was also a powerful empath, sensed Angelique's and Kitty's distress. Without being asked, Wynessa bolted straight towards the house, entering quickly and making her way straight to the singular point of emotional trauma.

Wynessa entered the fourth-level sleep room and ran to Angelique's side. Wynessa turned Angelique's face towards her and placed both of her hands on either side of Angelique's face; Angelique's brunette hair fell over her hands in messy strands.

While looking directly into Angelique's hazel eyes, Wynessa slowly touched her forehead to Angelique's forehead and carefully entered her mind.

Slowly, carefully, Wynessa traced the memories that were tormenting Angelique. There, deep within Angelique's mind, were a great many multiple, twisted and traumatic threads of thought, all entwined and looping continuously. Wynessa observed the looping threads of thought for many moments.

The faces of the dead, returning over and over again to haunt young Angelique. Alive as they approached Angelique's mind's eye, taunting and accusing, then changing to a deathly grey pallor with neat little holes in their foreheads.

It was like a scene from a horror movie, played over and over, continuously without end. They would not stop. Angelique's own feelings of shame and guilt had locked them firmly in place, and all the while those four hideous faces accused her, *"murderer!"*

One by one, Wynessa cut the threads of thought, breaking the loop, little by little, until the loop was no more. Then she followed the original thoughts from which they were derived and viewed the shoot-out from Angelique's point of view, as seen from her eyes.

Wynessa saw eight Carlin traders, the focus of four armed robbers. Angelique taunted them to draw their attention to her and not the Carlin-folk.

Her taunts worked and one of the armed robbers drew down on her. In rapid succession, Angelique, cold as steel and as sharp as a Katana, pointed and clicked, once, twice, thrice and then the final shot. The four armed robbers were dead in under three seconds.

Wynessa was stunned. Angelique was only seventeen years old, yet the cold steel of her movements and her deadly accuracy were uncanny. Wynessa froze Angelique's thoughts at that point and then redirected her mind towards the memories of the eight Carlin traders that she'd saved.

Now, those Carlin faces were what Angelique saw and not the faces of the four dead armed robbers. As a final measure, Wynessa redirected Angelique's thoughts of those four dead armed robbers into a null loop, from which they would be highly unlikely to reemerge.

Wynessa slowly withdrew her mind from Angelique's.

"What do you see now, young one?", Wynessa asked.

"The Carlin traders, eight of them. All alive and well", Angelique responded, feeling the guilt and shame she'd felt at killing the four armed robbers starting to fade.

"You saved lives, Angelique. You were at the right place, at the right time, to save lives", Wynessa reinforced.

It was a subtle, yet firm reaffirmation. Angelique's mind switched from guilt to acknowledgement of lives saved.

Wynessa sent a private thought to Simone, *"Your Daughter will be fine. It was her first kill and her feelings of guilt had ninety five percent of her thought processes trapped in a loop, repeating over and over. Reinforce her understanding that she saved eight Carlin lives that day and not to dwell on the four armed robbers, whose lives she took."*

Simone replied by thinking, *"Thank you, Wynessa"*, and Wynessa picked up the thought.

Simone gently turned Angelique's face to hers and then looked into her hazel eyes, "Honey, you saved eight Carlin lives that day. I couldn't do it. I was offside; I had eight tour guides blocking my view of those four armed robbers. It was either you took them down, or eight innocent Carlin-folk died. You did the only thing that you could do; it saved eight innocent lives, Angelique."

Keegali was pleased to see her Daughter, Kitty's, blue stripes reappearing as Angelique slowly began to recover, "You both should rest a little bit more, but before dark you should both wash", she smiled, "You both smell very bad", and then she passed Kearill to Kitty, "Our little cuddle puss will watch over you."

Kitty held Kearill in her arms, looked at her and queried, "Cuddle puss?"

Kearill nodded and replied, proudly, "I'm a cuddle puss!"

By the time Kelyarn and James entered the sleep room, it was all over.

James enquired, "How'd you sort this out so quickly, Wynessa?"

"I am a Martian, remember, James. Your counsellors talk you through trauma. We Martians, even we hybrids, dive deeper and redirect errant thought processes. It is so much more efficient", Wynessa broadcast, adding, *"Remember that. We Martians are natural counsellors."*

Keegali also wanted to understand, "Yes, but how? How did Martians acquire such abilities?"

"It was an adaptation to Tarlak Slavery and their barbarity", Wynessa broadcast in reply, explaining, *"The Tarlaks that destroyed my world and enslaved my people were not the same as the Tarlaks here on Secundus. They were far more sophisticated, divided into a caste system and technologically advanced. Their cruelty and barbarity were methodical. They enjoyed*

what they did to my people. We weren't just their Slaves, we were also their food! They taxed us in blood!"

"That sounds awful", Keegali responded.

"It was, so my ancestors adapted. More than ninety thousand years of enslavement and predation does that", Wynessa agreed, noting, *"We Martians share our memories with our family and friends. Especially so with Mothers and Daughters. I have memories from my ancestors who actually lived under the Tarlak enslavement. Our ability to handle and process trauma is an adaptation and there are times when we need to intervene in the minds of others. It is a very handy thing."*

Simone agreed, "A very handy thing, I'd say", before announcing, "Everyone who doesn't need to be here should head downstairs. The girls need to get some more rest."

As they left the sleep room and headed back downstairs, leaving Angelique and Kitty to rest, with Kitty's little Sister, the cuddle puss, Kearill, Wynessa sent a private telepathic message to Simone and Keegali.

"Angelique's post-traumatic stress is corrected for now, but she will need to visit me from time to time to make sure that it does not resurface in another form; that can and does happen. There is also another unrelated issue rapidly approaching", Wynessa informed them.

Keegali understood immediately, "Kitty's quickening is very close. Soon, my Kitty will seek to find her bondmate. Her bond with Angelique will weaken."

Simone understood as well, "It was only ever meant to be a temporary bond. Just long enough to keep Kitty stable as she approached her quickening."

Wynessa pointed out the part that the Mothers had both missed, *"Kitty is of Carlin kind, Angelique is of Human kind. Their bond, temporary though it may be, is unprecedented. Kitty will move forward and take her lifelong bondmate. Angelique is heavily emotionally invested in Kitty; she is in love. This quickening process will be very hard for her. It's the end of a nigh on three-year relationship."*

Simone rubbed her forehead, "Of course it is. Why didn't I see that? My Angelique will be emotionally upset. Really fucking upset."

Keegali took Simone's arm in hers and noted, "We have a thing for that."

"And I will also be available when the time comes", Wynessa added.

Keegali began explaining, "More than a third of Carlin girls need a temporary bond as they approach their quickening. It is far more common than you know and can last from three to four years. Normally, their bond partner is another Carlin girl of the same age, so they approach their quickening together. As their quickening pushes them both to find a mate and develop their lifelong bond, the temporary bond dissolves. It is a natural process. It is a beautiful thing for both of their Mothers to watch."

"Keegali, my Angelique is almost three years younger than Kitty, and she is not a Carlin girl", Simone pointed out.

"Yes, and we have a thing for temporarily bonded Carlin girls where the ages are mismatched", Keegali explained, noting, "This thing may help Angelique as Kitty moves beyond their temporary bond and seeks her lifelong bondmate. Kitty's choosing Angelique as her temporary bondmate was unusual, yes, but the dissolving of their bond can be managed in our usual Carlinish way."

"And I will be on hand if I am needed", Wynessa reassured Simone.

"So, Keegali, between you and Wynessa, you've got this, yeah?", Simone asked for confirmation.

Both Keegali and Wynessa replied with a simple yes.

As they reached the bottom of the stairs, Wynessa informed Keegali, *"If you ever need to ask me something quietly, without others hearing. All you have to do is think of me and then think of your question."*

"I can do that?", Keegali questioned audibly.

"Yes, of course, you can. Humans do it all the time", Wynessa confirmed, noting, *"Sometimes they do it without even meaning to. Their minds can be so chatty."*

Simone heard Keegali's odd question and tilted her head to one side, "You're explaining to Keegali that she can direct her thoughts to you, aren't you, Wynessa?"

"Yes, it is not something that people don't realise until it is explicitly explained", Wynessa confirmed.

"Keegali, you can have a full, complete conversation with a Martian, inside your head, completely private and no one would even know it. It can be very handy at times", Simone explained.

"I can see how it would", Keegali agreed, before asking, "Now, what will we be having for lunch?"

Wynessa smiled and transmitted, *"Many-mushroom pies, obviously."*

Before the month was out, things began to change. Kitty would awaken early, shortly after the rise of Cathol, their world's primary Sun. She would leave the house and wander aimlessly around the Carlin village for most of the morning, always returning for lunch at midday. Angelique would ask why Kitty hadn't woken her up so that she could come with her and the answer was always the same: she simply forgot.

Kitty's eyesight became sharper, more focused, her olfactory senses grew keener, her hearing picked up every single sound and her ears would flick from one direction to the next as if searching for something continuously.

"What's happening with Kitty?", Angelique asked Keegali.

"It's the quickening. It's taking her and she's searching for her bondmate", Keegali explained.

"Can't I go with her? Walk with her while she searches?", Angelique questioned.

Keegali held Angelique's hand, shaking her head, "No, little one. It does not work that way. The quickening leads to the wandering and the wandering is always done alone."

Simone enquired, "What if Kitty doesn't find her bondmate here in the village?"

Keegali sighed, her whiskers lowered and her face took on a concerned look, "If that happens, Kitty will wander further, to the other nearby villages. Kelyarn and I will have to step in and manage her wandering more closely for safety reasons. Kitty can not be allowed to leave our village alone at this time. There are predators prowling the trails between the Carlin villages. It can be very dangerous, so let's hope that she finds her bondmate here in our village."

Now Simone was concerned, "What if Kitty just wanders out of the village?"

Keegali smiled, replying, "Where the main road enters the village, for five houses on either side of the road and leading in, those families watch out for wanderers as we call them. They will stop Kitty before she can leave our village, for her own safety and then bring Kitty back to us. We all look after each other."

This went on for week after week, with Kitty becoming ever more distant. Angelique was becoming ever more anxious and deeply saddened by the situation. Keegali was receiving reports from the watchers of Kitty walking the main road to almost the edge of the village and was becoming increasingly concerned.

Simone was concerned for both Angelique's emotional health as well as Kitty's constant wandering. She was also fascinated and recommended drawing regular blood samples for analysis to build up an understanding of the biochemical processes involved. Keegali agreed, so long as it did not interfere with the overall process. When the blood tests came back, the situation became much clearer.

Kitty's gonadotropin-releasing hormone was running high, increasingly high. Her follicle-stimulating hormones were gradually rising, preparing her for her mating frenzy. Ovarian follicles were forming, ready for mating and conception.

Kitty's luteinizing hormone was also on the rise, as was a powerful form of oestrogen, called estradiol. Kitty was becoming increasingly primed for mating and conception. Angelique had also noticed an increased swelling in a certain private place on Kitty's body. The only thing that was required was a suitable bondmate for Kitty to breed with. If one could not be found, persistent oestrus could become a possible negative outcome; one that was to be avoided.

Unfortunately for Angelique, Kitty's oxytocin levels were also plummeting. Their temporary bond was rapidly collapsing. It was destined to dissolve and would very soon be gone. Angelique became increasingly despondent and depressed.

"Aren't you concerned about persistent oestrus?", Simone asked Keegali.

"Of course, I am concerned, we just have to give the process a little more time", Keegali replied, noting, "Kitty's future bondmate may have only just reached his own quickening. Kitty's wandering will have already triggered an appropriate partner to enter their quickening and they will find each other."

Simone shook her head, "This must be so harrowing for you, Keegali, both you and Kelyarn."

Keegali nodded, replying, "It is for every Carlin parent and it is every time a Daughter reaches their quickening. We just have to have faith in the process. There is nothing else to be done. Kitty will find her bondmate."

Then, just like that, Kitty spotted a young Carlin man in the distance across a family plot that sat between two cobblestone laneways. He, too, was wandering. Kitty was on her way back to her family's plot and the young Carlin man's path was going to intersect with Kitty's. They met and their eyes fixed on each other. They both began to sniff the air between them as they closed the distance.

"I like your scent", the young Carlin man noted.

"I like your scent too", Kitty replied as they slowly approached each other even closer.

Kitty and the young Carlin man began to nuzzle each other, "You smell so nice", Kitty noted, her eyes were closed and her whiskers fully raised, "I am Kitty, Daughter of Kelyarn and Keegali", she added.

The young Carlin man, his eyes closed and whiskers raised, replied, "You smell beautiful, Kitty", before adding, "I'm Kaymax, Son of Kortan and Krylta. I am a hunter."

"Such a nice name", Kitty replied and then, hand in hand, they both wandered back to Kitty's house.

Just like that, Kitty had found her lifelong bondmate. It was all about their scent; free will was not required.

The Carlin village grapevine was fast and Kelyarn knew that Kitty and her bondmate, Kaymax, were on their way. Kelyarn went upstairs and cleaned up the fourth-level sleep room in preparation for their arrival.

Keegali took Angelique by the hand and explained, "Kitty and her bondmate will go straight to the fourth-level sleep room. We'll prepare another sleep room for you on the lower level."

Angelique was devastated; she knew this was inevitable, but nonetheless, she felt miserable. When Kitty and Kaymax entered the house, they didn't say a word. Kitty led him straight up to the fourth-level sleep room. Their eyes looked slightly glazed over, as if they could see nothing else around them, only themselves.

Keegali was still holding Angelique's hand, she explained, "Their minds will fog over and their eyes will fully glaze. For the next ten days, they will sleep together, occasionally mating."

Kelyarn chimed in, "On the tenth day, they will fully enter the bonding heat. Then they will enter the mating frenzy. They will then mate continuously for up to four days. During this time, Keegali and I will attend to their every need."

Keegali noted, "At the end of this process, they will be bonded for life and Kitty will be with kit. After their final bonding, their mating will become far less dramatic."

Angelique immediately burst into tears and ran out of the house and into the back of the plot, with her Mother, Simone, following closely behind her. Everyone had expected this to happen. Wynessa was quick to follow after Angelique and Simone.

"Kelyarn, look after our Daughter and her bondmate, I will help with Angelique", Keegali stated.

When Keegali finally caught up to Angelique and her Mother, Simone, at the back of their plot, Angelique was tearful, crying and arguing bitterly with her Mother.

"We should never have come here!", Angelique screamed at Simone, "Everything is wrong. We should have stayed inside Hector or gone somewhere else. If we'd stayed there, none of this would have happened. I've killed four people. You killed one person. The girl I love doesn't even remember me!"

Every time Simone tried to reach out and hold her Daughter, Angelique slapped her hands away.

"Leave me alone! This is all your fault! We should not be here! We should never have come here!", Angelique screamed.

Even Wynessa held back, not wanting to interfere, at least not yet.

Keegali looked towards her youngest Daughter, Kearill, the infamous cuddle puss and she gave her a look. Kearill ran up to Angelique and wrapped her arms around her. Keegali then looked at her two other Daughters, Kreena and Kayala and they both walked up to Angelique and wrapped their arms around her.

Kayala kissed Angelique on the cheek, "Please don't upset, Sister. We all love you."

Angelique collapsed to her knees and cried. Keegali Daughters followed her, not letting go.

Kearill kissed Angelique on the other cheek, "I don't like to see you cry, Sister. Please don't cry."

Keegali whispered to Simone and Wynessa, "This is the beginning of the thing. They will smother her with love until the bond is almost dissolved. They won't leave Angelique's side, day or night."

"Until the bond is almost dissolved?", Wynessa queried telepathically.

"Yes, Wynessa. The night Kitty and Kaymax finally complete their bond is the night that the temporary bond finally dissolves", Keegali explained, whispering and elaborating, "On that night, I will hold Angelique as she falls asleep, smothering her with my own love, as if she were one of my own kits. In the middle of the night, Angelique's Mother, Simone, will take my place. When Angelique falls asleep, it will be with me, her temporary Mother and then when she awakens in the morning, it will be with her actual Mother. The temporary bond will be no more; it will have dissolved, although they will remain close friends."

"And that's it?", Simone enquired.

"Yes. This would normally be a sacred moment between two Carlin families. It is the Carlin way", Keegali replied, noting, "It is just as sacred with your family, Simone. You are my bond-Sister."

Wynessa watched with rapt curiosity before transmitting only to Keegali and Simone, *"It's their scent. Angelique can only sense it on a subconscious level. The Sisters have a scent that is so close to Kitty's that she can't tell the difference. Angelique is finding their scent soothing and familiar."*

"A Daughter's scent is like their Mother's and a Son's scent is like their Father's", Keegali added.

Kitty's Sister kits stuck to Angelique like glue. Wherever Angelique went, there was always at least one of Kitty's Sisters with her, insisting on holding her hand and trying to cheer her up. True to her nickname, Kearill hugged and cuddled Angelique at every opportunity. Kearill became Angelique's personal cuddle puss and was constantly by Angelique's side.

To Keegali's Daughters, Angelique was their Sister and her sadness required their constant attention. They wanted Angelique to be happy and so they lavished her with hugs and kisses, telling her that they all loved her and that she should not be sad.

At night, when Angelique slept, they crawled under the blankets with her so that she would not be alone. Keegali's Sons found it all amusing; they explained to Simone's Son, Johnathon, that it's a girl thing. It's just what Carlin girls do.

For ten days, this was the norm. A couple of times a day, Keegali and Kelyarn would take food and water up to Kitty and Kaymax. A couple of times a day, Keegali and Kelyarn would carefully guide Kitty and Kaymax down the stairs to the outside wash house. The couple's minds were fogged and their eyes glazed over; they could not do so on their own. During those moments, Keegali's Daughters would draw Angelique in another direction so that she would not see Kitty or Kaymax and become upset.

On the tenth day, things changed. Kitty and Kaymax no longer came downstairs. Their bonding heat had reached its maximum and their mating frenzy had begun. Every now and then, Keegali would check on them, peaking into their sleep room on the fourth level.

When they were exhausted from constant coupling, Keegali and Kelyarn would quietly go upstairs. The food they prepared was different now, lighter, in the form of cereals, soups and broths. They provided them with Gudong milk and water. Angelique's Mother, Simone, was fascinated by the process.

They no longer helped them downstairs to the wash house; instead, they took up basins of warm water and soft cleaning cloths. Always, Keegali had to check on the couple; they did not want to interrupt their coitus. Only the conception of a new kit could bring them out of the heat-bonding process.

Keegali's Daughter, Kayala, was very careful in instructing Kreena and Kearill in their care of Angelique. The temporary bond was gradually dissolving and she wanted Angelique to be as distracted as possible while that progressed.

The bonding process usually took from ten to fourteen days and on the fourteenth and last day, it was over. Keegali placed a special earthenware bowl on the kitchen table and burned some special incense in it. Kelyarn helped Kitty and Kaymax down the stairs and sat them down at the table, before returning upstairs to clean up the sleep room. After two weeks of bonding, it was a mess and needed cleaning and airing out. He, too, set up a special earthenware bowl of burning incense on a chest of drawers in the room.

Kitty and Kaymax looked exhausted, they looked drawn out, weak and ravenously hungry. Keegali fed them hot, spicy Gudong stew and boiled masuli grain. The newly bonded couple ate like they'd not eaten in days. Angelique's temporary bond to Kitty had almost completely dissolved and she felt miserable, refusing to leave her sleep room. Kayala, Kreena and Kearill held onto her tightly in their warm embrace while she quietly sobbed to herself.

After eating their first substantial meal in two weeks, Keegali led Kitty and Kaymax to the wash house. They needed to bathe. The family wash house had been upgraded; it now contained a shower and Keegali's favourite, a large, deep, claw-foot bath. Simone followed Keegali and drew a blood sample from Kitty. The blood sample was tested and the results came back quickly.

"Kitty's estradiol levels are right down. She is definitely out of oestrus. Her progesterone levels are quite elevated. If I didn't know any better, I'd say that Kitty is pregnant", Simone announced.

Keegali sniffed Kitty around her stomach region and then announced, "Kitty is with kit", and then she smiled at Simone, adding, "That is how we Carlins do it. A Mother can tell by the scent alone."

"Of course, your sense of smell is much more sensitive than any Human's", Simone replied.

"They are fully bonded now. When Kitty and Kaymax mate next time, there will still be heat, but it won't be this crazy. They will be able to manage it themselves. It is just the bonding process that is this long and messy", Keegali explained, noting, "They will stay in the upstairs sleep room until Kitty's kit is born and then they will look for their own plot, their own house. It is the cycle of Carlinish life."

Keegali also looked somewhat exhausted by the ordeal.

That night, Keegali entered Angelique's sleep room and her three Daughters were all looking concerned.

"Mother, Humans, they are not the same as we Carlins, Angelique still pines for Kitty", Kayala informed her Mother.

"I know. Human emotions are driven by different forces than ours. Now, take your Sisters to your room; you have all done very well. Tell Angelique's Mother to come here at midnight", Keegali replied.

Then Keegali disrobed and climbed onto the sleeping mat with Angelique, "I know you're still upset, little one, but when this temporary Carlinish bond with Kitty is dissolved, you will feel much better. Trust me, you will."

Keegali held Angelique in her warm embrace and began softly purring in her ear; it was almost a lullaby, soothing, relaxing, slightly intoxicating. Angelique slept the deepest sleep she had ever slept.

Around midnight, Angelique's Mother, Simone, entered the sleeping room. Keegali ever so gently let go of Angelique and slid off the sleeping mat. She stood up, disrobed Simone and gave her a deep kiss, which Simone was not expecting, but still returned.

"You take over now, Simone, hold onto Angelique all night and in the morning she will feel much better. The temporary bond will be dissolved", Keegali advised and then she smiled, noting, "They will still be good friends", before leaving the sleep room.

Simone climbed onto the sleeping mat and held onto her Daughter. Soon she was fast asleep.

The next morning, when Angelique awoke, she felt different. She stretched, she yawned and rolled over to face Keegali, only to find her Mother, Simone, was there. Angelique was surprised.

"Mum, what are you doing here?", Angelique enquired.

"Honey, I'm your Mother. Can't I just be here for you?", Simone replied.

"That's not what I meant. Last night, Keegali was holding onto me; now you're holding me. What gives?", she asked.

"Yes, I am. Keegali handed you over to me last night at midnight", Simone replied, explaining, "It's all part of their process for dissolving temporary bonds, apparently."

Simone rolled off the sleeping mat and stood up, "Mum, where are your clothes?", Angelique asked.

"Keegali undressed me last night. She said it was necessary, all a part of the process", Simone replied, before questioning, "Now, are you going to stay in bed all day, or are you going to get up?"

Angelique started to get up and Simone enquired, "Now, Angelique, how do you feel?"

Angelique was quiet for a moment, thinking, "I feel different. Good different, a lot less miserable."

"Oh, thank God for that, honey", Simone replied before wrapping her Daughter in a tight embrace.

Simone held the embrace for several long moments, not wanting to let go of her Daughter and then she slapped Angelique on the backside and said, "Good, now let's get dressed and get some breakfast."

"Mum!", Angelique protested the slap as Keegali's three Daughters all rushed into the sleep room and wrapped their arms around her.

Kayala, Kreena and Kearill all dragged Angelique out of the sleeping room towards the kitchen, "Wait, wait, my clothes. Let me get dressed first."

"Don't worry, honey. I'll grab them", Simone shouted out as they disappeared from the sleep room.

When Keegali's Daughters finally let go, Angelique was standing in the kitchen, naked and embarrassed, her face was bright red. Kitty was standing there at the kitchen table, equally naked, with her blue stripes positively glowing. Kitty rushed over to Angelique and wrapped her arms around her.

"I am with kit", Kitty told her and then she planted a long, slow kiss on Angelique's lips.

"Uh uh ah, none of that, Kitty", Keegali chided, "You know the rules. One bond ends, another bond begins. You need to grow into your new life bond. You have to wait until after your kit is born before you play with Angelique again."

"Sorry, Mother!", Kitty replied, before turning back to Angelique, whispering loudly, "It's a Carlinish rule."

Kaymax had stood up from the table, "I am so tired. My breeding pole is aching as well. I'm going back upstairs to get some more rest", and then he looked at Angelique, tilted his head and smiled, noting, "Humans have hair at both ends. Who'd have thought?", before going up the stairs.

"They do", Kitty confirmed knowingly.

Angelique's face took on the brightest shade of red she'd ever had in her life and she reached down to cover her private parts.

Simone came up behind Angelique and passed her, her clothes, noting, "You'd think that after three years of being around Keegali's family, that we'd be used to nudity by now."

Angelique quickly got dressed and noted, "I have this strange purring in my mind. It's kind of like when a song gets stuck in your head."

Kitty's whiskers twitched as she laughed, "That's my Mother's purring. Whenever we're upset, Mother purrs into our ears and the purring stays with us for days. It's really soothing, isn't it?"

"Yes, it kind of is", Angelique admitted, "It is really soothing."

Keegali smiled and placed two bowls onto the kitchen table and then ladled in some boiled masuli grain mixed with broth from her Gudong stew, "My boys have all eaten. They're all out playing with Johnathon."

Keegali put the ladle down, walked over to Simone, wrapped her arms around and kissed her tenderly on the lips, "You are my bond-Sister now, Simone. Your kits are my kits and my kits are your kits. We will love them all equally, both of us", and then she noted, "Don't be shy around Carlinish nudity. It's all very normal for us and besides, we Carlin-folk find Humans to be positively attractive. You are like us, Carlin-folk without whiskers or tails, and maybe just a little bit hairy"

Simone and Angelique sat down and began to eat. Kearill climbed up on Angelique's lap.

"Do you want some, Kearill?", Angelique asked.

"We all ate earlier while you were both sleeping", Kearill replied.

"Kearill, you're now seven. Don't you think that maybe you're just a little bit too big to still be climbing up on people's laps?", Keegali enquired.

"I'm still little, Mummy and I'm a cuddle puss", Kearill replied.

"Yes, you are. My favourite cuddle puss", Angelique agreed as she kissed Kearill on the cheek.

Kayala bit her lower lip gently, "I'm now fifteen. In three years, I'll be approaching my own quickening", she announced and then she asked, "If I need a temporary bond partner, will you be my bond partner, Angelique? Just until I find my bondmate."

Simone quickly stepped in, "Kayala, honey. Angelique has signed up for service in the Colonial Marines. So, she'll be leaving for Sol and her military training in a couple of months."

Angelique closed her eyes momentarily, "I'm sorry, Kayala. I could be gone for three to five years, perhaps longer."

Now Kitty gently bit her lower lip, "We'll all miss you, Angelique."

"I know, but I have to go there for my military training", Angelique explained, noting, "I will be back."

Keegali smiled, "Kayala may not even need a temporary bond partner. Only a third of Carlin girls do and there are a lot of Carlin girls nearby."

Kayala looked disappointed, but she understood. Humans had many responsibilities.

"Keegali, I did notice from these blood tests I've been taking from Kitty and checking, that the bonding heat breaks when the Carlin girl, in this case Kitty, becomes pregnant", Simone remarked, before asking, "Exactly what happens if there is no pregnancy?"

Keegali was quiet in thought for a long moment before replying, "I don't think that has ever happened in living memory. We Carlin-folk are so fertile, I simply can't imagine it."

Kelyarn was standing in the doorway, "It is very rare, but it does happen from time to time. The last time was in my grandfather's grandfather's time."

"And what happened?", Simone enquired.

Kelyarn closed his eyes momentarily and shook his head, "It was a very sad time. The couple remained in the bonding heat. It simply did not break. Their mating frenzy continued for more than ten days. They both died in the end from sheer exhaustion."

Everyone at the kitchen table went quiet.

Kelyarn continued, "It is very sad when the great sorrows take a Carlin girl. It is also sad when a Carlin girl can't find a suitable mate in her own village and has to wander the other villages to find one. But to find a mate and have such a thing happen? There simply are no words."

Angelique understood, she was smart like her Mother, "Persistent oestrus and organ failure due to mating-induced cardiac collapse", she murmured, "That's just horrible."

Keegali agreed, "Yes, it is, but that is an extreme example of Carlinish life-bonding going horribly wrong. It is so rare that only Kelyarn can remember an example of it."

"Kelyarn, Keegali, something to remember, as rare as it may be, if it happens again, we can break the heat bond with a simple injection of progesterone", Simone informed them, also noting, "We could possibly even correct the infertility issue that led to the problem in the first place."

Kelyarn smiled, noting, "Your people have so many things that our people could use."

There was a long silence before Angelique broke it with a simple question.

Angelique leaned in towards Kitty and cradled her head in her hands, curiously asking, "So, Kitty. What was it like? You know, two weeks of lovemaking?"

Kitty smiled and her whiskers picked up, "It was tiring, very, very tiring, but I only know that because I'm still very tired right now", she grinned, whispering to Angelique, "And quite sore down there. It will take me days to recover!", she pointed down to her private parts.

"So, you don't actually remember?", Angelique queried.

Kelyarn chimed in, "We never remember. It's two weeks of blank memory."

Keegali explained, "We parents look after the new couple. We check on them. We feed them. We bathe them. Sometimes we even just watch them. We don't remember our own mate bonding and they won't remember theirs. It is the way it is."

"So, one of the most important events in your lives and you can't remember it", Angelique asked, her face showing confusion and incredulity.

"Yes. We can't remember the bonding heat", Keegali admitted, but then she smiled a wry smile, "It is only the bonding heat, the very first time. We do remember every single mating after that. The heat is not nearly so intense, so strong."

Angelique smiled at Kitty and whispered to her, "At least you have something to look forward to."

Kitty just grinned knowingly in reply.

14. The Quickening Steel.

In the days and weeks that followed, Kaymax helped Kelyarn around the family's plot. The family's garden expanded with the introduction of various Earthly vegetables and grains.

Outside of the village walls, in the ploughed fields surrounding the village, there were experimental plantings of wheat, barley, rye, millet and rice.

Kaymax, as it turned out, was also an avid hunter, an expert in fact. Occasionally, he would go north with his Brothers to hunt along the tangled lowland forest trails. He always brought back smoked meats, including wild Gudong, amongst the many species that they hunted.

"We haven't had a hunter in our family for generations. Kitty's kits will never want for meat", Kelyarn had noted.

Kaymax and Kitty had been eyeing a plot of land with a nice, empty two-level house with a large attic sleep room. It had been empty for several years after the elderly Carlin couple that lived there had passed away.

There were a couple of other empty plots in the village, but this one was closest to the outer village wall and as Kaymax was a hunter, it was the plot that he preferred. Kelyarn had noted that the nearer a plot was to the village's outer wall, the more likely a Kyrrax or other predator would sneak in. Kaymax, however, countered that by saying that they would have three or four Vorts to keep any predators at bay. Kaymax was a hunter after all.

Simone had been compiling the results of Kitty's blood tests, taken during her quickening and bonding process, into detailed reports. These were then forwarded to Doctor Morrow up at Cis-Luns L-Five on the interstellar push ship Artemisia for academic review and further research. The actual preserved blood samples were sent up the slow way, via colonial transport ship.

Kitty's and Angelique's friendship remained strong, possibly too strong for Keegali's liking. Keegali was quick to remind them both that they should not engage in intimate play with each other until well after Kitty's kit was born. Kitty's and Kaymax's new mate bond was the priority and they needed to settle into each other, which, of course, took time.

The gestation period for a Carlin woman, as Kitty was now officially, was only seven months. Short by Human standards, but for the Carlin-folk, that was the norm. Long before the time that Kitty's kit was born, Angelique would be back in the Sol system, undergoing her military training.

It was not an ideal situation for either Angelique or Kitty and neither of them was looking forward to it. Their friendship had survived Kitty's quickening and mate-bonding process, only for them to be separated by duty and distance.

Twenty two light-years was a number, a concept, that Kitty, as a Carlin, could barely even comprehend. All Kitty really understood was that her dearest friend,

Angelique, would be somewhere unbelievably distant across the stars. It was unfathomable to her.

Simone and Keegali had been sitting in front of their house on Keegali's family plot, simply enjoying the Sunlight provided by Secundus's primary Sun, Cathol. Simone and Keegali had been watching Simone's Son, Johnathon and Keegali's kits all playing in the shade under the nearby Chillic and Bell Nut fruit trees.

Johnathon and Keegali's Sons were playing yet another version of space lions. Keegali's Daughters were watching them play while collecting fruit. Kitty and Angelique had been sitting with Keegali and Simone. Kelyarn and Kaymax were out back, repairing their Thrixan coups.

The Sun was warm and the air had a sweet taste to it, a consequence of the nearby Chillic and Bell Nut fruit trees, which were thick with ripe fruit. Simone's communicator buzzed for attention, so she took it out of her pocket and read the message. Simone shook her head and sighed.

"So much for me being retired", Simone commented as she switched off her communicator.

"Is there a problem, Mum?", Angelique enquired.

"It's the fallout from those fake tours a couple of months back", Simone replied.

Keegali enquired, "Fallout?", it was an English word she hadn't heard before.

"Yeah, fallout. What happens after something goes horribly wrong and those fake tours did go horribly wrong", Simone explained.

"So, Mum, what's the fallout?", Angelique enquired; she was eager to know.

"The two scammers who set up those fake tours and the four armed robbers you took down. We've received news from the Security Council of Sol, they've been identified", Simone informed the small group.

"That's a good thing, isn't it?", Kitty queried as she absently stroked her pregnant belly.

"Well, yeah, it is, except none of them were supposed to be here. They're all interlopers and that means we have rogue, unsanctioned colony ships in this system", Simone explained, remarking, "Our fleet of twelve interstellar push ships is not alone out here."

Angelique nodded; she understood, "Unsanctioned colonists always bring trouble with them."

Keegali's whiskers twitched, "Like those fake tours?"

"Yep. No unsanctioned colonists. No fake tours. No daylight robberies", Angelique confirmed.

"What's it got to do with your Mother's retirement?", Kitty questioned.

"My Mum retired to start a family, but has always remained in the reserves",

Angelique explained.

Simone stepped back in, "And now, with these *'interlopers'*, the Security Council of Sol has contacted the Earth Interstellar Alliance's military branch and that means the Colonial Marines."

Angelique nodded once more in understanding, "We don't have many Colonial Marines out here. So, Mum, have they placed you back on active duty?"

"No, sweety, not yet", Simone replied, explaining, "I've been stepped up from in reserve to on call."

Kitty, being a young Carlin woman, still fresh from bonding and having little to no concept of military matters, commented, "But aren't you retired. You have a family to look after."

Simone smiled and replied, "Kitty, honey. Once a Colonial Marine, always a Colonial Marine. We Special Operatives never really get to retire. The universe is too vast, the stars are too many and we Humans are spreading everywhere like a plague, spreading us very thin. Very thin indeed."

Angelique noted dryly, "It's a duty, Kitty. Just as your villagers living at the edges of the village have a duty to protect the wanderers during their quickening and your hunters have a duty to protect the village from predators. We have a duty to ensure that the colonisation of the stars does not become too chaotic, too dangerous. That's one of the reasons I'm going to become a Special Operative like my Mum and Dad."

Simone smiled and reached out, holding Kitty's hand reassuringly, "To keep everybody safe."

Angelique noted, "This planet, Secundus, and this entire system are very, very special."

"What's so special about our world, Vale?", Keegali enquired with curiosity.

Simone provided the answer, "Of the many dozens of worlds that we Humans have colonised, only six have been fully habitable worlds like this one. There's Earth back in the Sol system, Gaia, Odhinn and Twilight in the Alpha Centauri system and here in the Xi-Bootis system, your world, Vale, orbiting Cathol and orbiting Cythol, the world we call Xi-Bootis B Primus. That's only six out of many dozens."

Angelique stepped back in, adding more to the uniqueness of the Xi-Bootis system, "Of those six worlds, only three have indigenous sentient life. Earth, Vale and Primus. That makes Vale very special."

Simone nodded in agreement, "That's why everyone is so concerned about unsanctioned colonists. On the other worlds without sentient life, it's just Humans being Human affecting Humans. Here, it's very different. Everything that we do here has to be carefully considered, so as not to adversely affect either Carlins or Thols, or for that matter, the Harricks."

Angelique stepped back in, "I should mention Mars. Before the Tarlaks destroyed its biosphere more than ninety thousand years ago, it was also a fully habitable world with its own sentient species. The Martians. Mars, of course, has been terraformed, so it's back to where it was."

"That's a good point, Angelique", Simone agreed.

"What about the other dozens of worlds?", Kitty enquired, her curiosity had been piqued.

Simone explained, "Well, Kitty, worlds like this one are classified as class one worlds, rare and fully habitable. The next are the class two worlds. They are marginally habitable. Their atmospheres are thin but breathable. They have liquid water on their surface and they do have abundant life. We generally upgrade those, enhance them to be like Vale. Class two worlds are fixer-uppers. There are two of those in the Xi-Bootis system alone. One orbits Cythol and the other is a moon of Primus Major, which also orbits Cythol."

Angelique chimed in, adding, "The next class of worlds are the class three worlds. They generally have very thin atmospheres with low oxygen content. Pressure suits with oxygen tanks are required."

Simone then added, "Class three worlds can have life, although it's generally the lower forms of life if they do. Often, they're just barren rocks, like Mars was before terraforming. The class three worlds are shake and bake worlds; they require a lot more work to make them like Vale. Centuries of work in fact."

"So, what's a class four world like then?", Kitty enquired; she found this most interesting.

Angelique smiled and replied, "They're ocean worlds. They generally don't have any land above the ocean surface. They do have complex life forms, but they're all aquatic. They are generally kind of hard to live on, unless you can somehow create land or float colonies on their ocean's surface."

Simone chuckled, "Yeah, ocean worlds are tough. We use class four worlds as major water resources. If there's another planet in the same system that has insufficient water, we can use massive tanker ships to transfer water from one to the other. It takes a hell of a lot of time, but it has two results. The dry world gets more water and the ocean world ends up with less. That can mean submerged land surfacing, which then leads to reclassification; it becomes a habitable world in its own right. One process, two worlds. The ocean world gets dry land and the dry, desert world gets oceans and seas. It's a win-win for life."

"What about class five worlds?", Kitty asked, thinking the classification list was never-ending.

"Class five worlds are terrestrial worlds that are completely uninhabitable. Worlds like Venus, which was once a true hell world before we terraformed it. That's the last classification", Angelique informed her.

"Terrestrial worlds, like hell worlds or toxic worlds, require a whole other approach to terraforming. They usually require sophisticated bio-engineered organisms to convert their atmospheres. It literally takes many centuries. Xi-Bootis A Primus is a good example; it's a Venus analogue, a hell world. We will eventually terraform it, but that could be decades or even centuries into the future", Simone explained.

Simone's communicator buzzed once more and she took it out of her pocket and checked the new message, "The High Admiral, our Aunt Roberta, has ordered the quadrupling of the network communications satellites, the global positioning satellites and the surveillance satellites. That tells me that she is not messing about."

"Not messing about?", Keegali enquired.

"A fourfold increase in our communication bandwidth means we can communicate more data, much more quickly. A fourfold increase in our global positioning satellites means we have far greater global positioning accuracy. And a fourfold increase in our surveillance abilities means that any unsanctioned ship that lands will be seen, accurately located and swooped on by the Colonial Marines in a heartbeat. That's what it all boils down to", Simone explained in detail.

Angelique remarked, "That increase in network bandwidth will mean every Colonial Marine that has neural augments will have no trouble at all accessing data."

"Neural augments?", Kitty enquired.

"Show them, Mum", Angelique requested.

Simone moved back her hair and showed Keegali and Kitty a small patch behind her right ear, "That's one of my neural augments. I have another behind my left ear as well. With these, I can access and control any computer or device with an A.I. system. Although I turned mine off when I retired to start my family. I didn't think that I'd be needing them anymore."

"Does your Husband, James, have these as well?", Keegali asked as she gently touched the patch.

"Yes, he does. Although he hardly needed to use them down here", Simone confirmed.

Simone's communicator buzzed once more and she checked the message, "Argh! I knew it", she exclaimed, "Our Aunt Roberta has just asked me to turn my neural augments back on. I might need to get them upgraded as well. Great, well, there you have it. I am now officially on call."

"It's not Aunt Roberta's fault, Mum. She does have a job to do, you know", Angelique reminded her.

On the day that Angelique was to travel back to the Sol system for her military training in Earth Cis-Lunar Space, Special Operative James Reas arrived to pick them up in his ship. Angelique, her Mother, Simone, her Brother, Johnathon,

Keegali, Kelyarn and their Daughter, Kitty, along with her Husband, Kaymax, would all be travelling off-world to Cis-Luns L-Five, to the Artemisia, to see her off. It was, of course, Kitty's idea, as she wanted to be with Angelique until the very last second and her Husband, Kaymax, had never been off-world before.

When James's ship arrived, Simone was just a little shocked. It was not the sleek form of a Manta Ray Class passenger craft that was approaching from the north; it was a Broad Head, Arrow Class Starfighter, a gunship! James landed his Starfighter in the village centre just beyond the dry stone wall of Kelyarn's and Keegali's plot.

James alighted his ship and entered the gate, shouting out, "Are we all ready? Your ride's here."

Simone placed her hands on her hips and enquired, "Really, James? A gunship? What happened to your Manta Ray?"

"Orders, Simone", James replied quickly, explaining, "From now on, we'll be flying Broad Heads. Admiral Nummus says yours will be ready in two weeks."

"Mine? What do you mean mine?", Simone questioned.

James sighed, "Orders, Simone. All Special Operatives are being issued with Broad Head Starfighters, including those on call, like yourself."

"Our Aunt Roberta seems to be getting a bit paranoid, I think", Simone replied.

"Our Aunt Roberta is getting close to fourteen hundred years old. She lived through the Mimasian War with the Tarlaks, the First Horridian War and the Second Horridian War, so yeah, maybe she is a little paranoid", James commented, adding, "Maybe when our Aunt Roberta gets paranoid, we should probably take notice. She sees through a lens that we simply can't."

Angelique said her goodbyes to Kayala, Kreena and the infamous, cuddle puss, young Kearill. Kayala would be looking after her siblings while her parents were off-world. Then the group boarded James's Starfighter, the Sentinel Prime and Angelique piloted the ship into space at her Father's request. Even on her way to her training, Angelique was accruing flight experience and flight time.

The main screen on the bridge of the Sentinel Prime displayed the optical scanner's view from the nose of the Starfighter. Kaymax was wrapped in awe and could not take his eyes off the screen as the Starfighter rose above the clouds and eventually entered the deep, dark void of space.

Kaymax gasped in shock and Kitty squeezed his hand. Angelique looked up at Kaymax and smiled.

"It's okay, Kaymax. I've got this", Angelique told him.

"And yet, you are still a child", Kaymax replied.

Kitty squeezed Kaymax's hand for attention once again and he turned to her, "It's scary the first time", she told him, adding, "Maybe even the second time, but we are safe. We've been here before."

Kitty gestured to her Mother, Keegali and her Father, Kelyarn and they both nodded in reassurance.

"You see, Kaymax. We've done this before", Kitty reassured him once more.

James's Manta Ray Class passenger craft was sleek and fast, but his Broad Head, Arrow Class Starfighter, the Sentinel Prime, was so much faster. After a brief atmospheric ascent, the Sentinel Prime punched into the vacuum of space and hit a peak speed of Mach two hundred and thirty, crossing the four hundred and twenty thousand kilometres to Cis-Luns L-Five in about an hour and a half.

Once the Sentinel Prime had docked at an internal docking bay on the Artemisia and they'd entered the interstellar push ship proper, Kitty began to tear up.

"How long will you be away?", Kitty enquired, the concern in her voice was palpable.

Angelique was unsure herself and asked her Father, "Dad, when will I be back here?"

"Well, Angelique, you have three years of training ahead of you in a high gravity training cylinder", James informed her, noting, "After that, you'll be given a two-year post and that could be anywhere within a twenty five light-year radius of Sol."

Angelique and Kitty both frowned, so Simone stepped in, giving her Husband a dirty look, "Honey, I'll speak with Aunt Roberta and see if we can pull some strings. Maybe we can have you assigned back here on Secundus. You do have a rapport with the Carlin-folk."

At hearing that, Kitty's whiskers picked up once more and her blue stripes started to luminescence.

James noted dryly, "We can't actually guarantee that, Simone. We can make the request, but it is up to the Security Council of Sol and the Earth Interstellar Alliance military."

Simone had to agree with James, "That is true, sweety. We can only make the request."

Kaymax, in order to distract himself from his own nervousness, enquired, "What do you do in a high gravity training cylinder?"

Again, Angelique was unsure and looked to her Father, who replied, "Well, Kaymax, a high gravity training cylinder rotates really fast, so the artificial gravity generated at the main living surface is three standard gs. So, think of everything weighing three times as much as on Vale. But, because it's a huge rotating cylinder, there are other living surfaces with one, one point five, two, and two point five standard gs as well."

Simone carried on the explanation, "Angelique will go through six weeks of basic military training at one gravity. Then, when she completes that, the same training will be repeated, only at one point five gravities. That's basic training. So, once completed, after twelve weeks, Angelique will enter six weeks of special forces training at two gs. That is then repeated, assuming that Angelique wants to continue to complete Special Operative training, at two point five gs. So, that's twelve weeks of special forces training. So, together, basic training and special forces training take roughly six months."

James chimed in, "They need to give the recruits some recovery time between basic, special forces and Special Operative training, so there is a week's break between each."

"Yes", Simone confirmed, explaining further, "Assuming Angelique continues past special forces training, then she will enter the Special Operatives training program. Angelique will then spend the two and a half years living and training at three standard gravities. At the end of which, Angelique will receive her own neural augments, just like mine."

Kaymax wasn't sure he followed and asked, "You mentioned, if Angelique continues?"

"Yes", Simone nodded, noting, "If a recruit stops after basic training, they become a Colonial Marine. Training at one and a half gs is still tough work. After that, if the recruit continues, there are two special forces grades. Special Forces, F-Two-G, which means that they passed that level. Then there's Special Forces, F-Two Five-G, which means that they passed that level. Special Forces can be given neural augments upon request, but it isn't mandatory."

"And Angelique?", this time Kitty enquired.

"Well, assuming Angelique completes all three years, then she will be a Special Operative", Simone replied with a hopeful smile, "Then she'll receive her neural augments just like James and me. Eventually, she will be given her own ships."

Angelique smiled and noted, "I'll be really buff, like my Mum and Dad. Strong as an Ox."

James was quick to tell his Daughter, "It's not as easy as you might think, my girl. You will need to take supplements to help your body adjust and stimulants to help your body absorb and uptake those supplements efficiently. They do not taste very nice at all."

"That is true, honey", Simone acknowledged, noting, "They may even give you other injected serums to help your body adjust genetically."

"You mean like what happened with Aunt Roberta?", Angelique enquired with concern.

"No, no, nothing like that, Angelique. What was done to your Aunt Roberta was all experimental and highly illegal", Simone explained, noting, "Everything that's done during Special Operative training has been fully tested over the centuries. You will become so much more than you are now."

Kaymax looked at Simone and James, "So much more?", he questioned, "You both look strong, yes, even for Humans, but so much more? What does that mean? I do not understand."

James chuckled, "Show him, honey."

Simone furled in her left arm and asked Kaymax to hold her left forearm. Then she furled in her right arm and asked Kelyarn to hold her right forearm.

"Okay, my beautiful space lion friends. Try to open my arms. Try to pull them open", Simone instructed, chuckling and then she stood perfectly still in a rock-solid stance and braced herself.

Kaymax pulled one way and Kelyarn pulled in the opposite direction. No matter how hard they pulled, they could not pull Simone's arms out; they could not open them. Kaymax used both of his hands and Kelyarn followed suit. They tried once more and again, no matter how hard they pulled, they could not open Simone's arms. Her arms remained furled.

Simone smiled at Keegali and tilted her head slightly. Keegali began to laugh; it was funny, after all.

Keegali smiled at her Husband and Son-in-law, "Enough, boys. It seems my space lions are mere kits when compared to my Human Sister, Simone."

Kaymax and Kelyarn both gave up trying.

"And my Wife has been in retirement for eighteen years", James chucked.

Keegali whispered in Simone's ear, "I cannot imagine what your Husband, James, is like on the sleeping mat, if he is as strong as you, my Sister."

Simone laughed and replied, "That is my little secret, Keegali", and the two women laughed together.

James added dryly and seriously, "If you think Simone's impressive, you have never seen High Admiral Roberta Nummus in action. Our Aunt Roberta makes us two look like weak little children."

The group wound their way through the Artemisia's corridors, making their way to the Artemisia's communications hub. The Artemisia's communications runner, a slipstream-capable communications relay ship, was docked to a nearby external docking port. The communications runner was a fair-sized ship; it was nearly all slipstream drive, bridge, crew quarters, kitchen, hygiene facilities and not much more.

The communications runner's main task was to slipstream back to the Sol system, communicate with the Colonisation Committee and Security Council, situated inside the hollowed-out asteroid, Hector, in Jupiter's leading Trojan point and then slipstream back to the Xi-Bootis system. Faster-than-light communications was simply not a thing. The communications runner made the trip once per month, twice if necessary.

The Artemisia had two other communications runners as backup, should one of them break down or worse, go missing in the void.

Angelique had scored a berth on Communications Runner Alpha and would be travelling back to the Sol system with that ship.

On this communications run, it would be likely that the ship would not just travel to the edges of the Sol system to transmit and receive data; with a passenger on board, it would likely slipstream all the way to Jupiter to drop off Angelique at Ganymede Prime. From there, she would then have to travel to Earth's Cis-Lunar space on an inner system military transport. Passengers were rare on communications runners, and when they were, they were usually military passengers.

High Admiral Roberta Nummus was waiting for Angelique at the airlock to the Communications Runner Alpha; she was also there to see her off.

Before she could say a word, young Johnathon Reas rushed over, wrapped his arms around his Aunt Roberta and announced, "See, I haven't forgotten you at all, Aunt Roberta."

Simone pinched the bridge of her nose, "Johnathon! Must you?", she chided.

Roberta gently messed up Johnathon's hair, "Still not happening, little man."

Angelique said her goodbyes to her family and friends; when it came to Kitty's turn, they hugged for many long moments before they started kissing each other goodbye.

When they'd finished kissing, Angelique said to Kaymax, "You better look after my, Kitty Cat, Kaymax, she's really important to me", that was her pet name for Kitty.

Kaymax smiled and replied, "Of course, I will, Angelique. Your Kitty Cat is my Wife, she is really important to me too."

Goodbyes all said and with teary eyes all around, Angelique boarded Communication Runner Alpha.

Once Angelique had boarded the ship, Johnathon announced, "Lunch time. Can we have mushroom pies?", his Mother, Simone, herself with tearful eyes, pinched the bridge of her nose once again.

Once on board the communications runner, Angelique was shown to the crew's quarters. In the crew's quarters, there was a stack of three bunks set aside for passengers.

As Angelique was the only passenger, she chose the middle bunk, not because she particularly wanted that bunk; it was just that the lowest bunk seemed too close to the deck and the upper bunk seemed too close to the ceiling.

At the end of the bunks, which Angelique assumed was the foot of the bunks, were three built-in lockers. Angelique opened up the middle locker and placed her duffle bag inside, closing the door behind it.

Apart from the three passenger bunks, the crew's quarters had six other bunks, again in stacks of three. There was a single large table in the room and enough seating for up to nine people. Again, six crew and up to three passengers.

The conditions in the crew's quarters could only be described as cramped and spartan. The communications runner's Captain didn't even have his own cabin either; he also bunked in with his crew. The space on a communications runner was extremely limited.

The six crewmen of Communications Runner Alpha were far too busy to interact with Angelique; instead, they left her in the crew's quarters to her own devices. Angelique sat down at the large table and made herself *"comfortable"*, spending her time playing card games with a deck of cards that sat upon it. It was going to be one very boring trip.

Communications Runner Alpha leveraged Secundus's rotating gravity well and magnetic field to slipstream to the outer reaches of Cathol's solar system. Angelique felt a slight wave of nausea as the ship passed through the slipstream tunnel. That slight wave of nausea was gone in precisely two minutes and ten seconds.

They'd made their first slipstream jump. Angelique Reas was on her way back to the Sol system.

Angelique went back to playing card games for a while before deciding to lie down and get some rest. It was six hours later when another slight wave of nausea woke her up. Again, the wave of nausea was gone in precisely two minutes and ten seconds. They'd obviously made their second slipstream jump, leveraging Cathol's rotating gravity well and magnetic field to slipstream to the outskirts of the Sol system.

Angelique Reas was now in the Sol system, somewhere within the Kuiper Belt, perhaps thirty to thirty five astronomical units from Sol. The door of the crew's quarters opened and the communications runner's Captain Hans Barrow, walked in.

"Ah, excellent. You managed to get some sleep. I'm Captain Barrow", the Captain greeted, adding, "You might want to come to the bridge. Sitting around here in the crew's quarters can be boring, so follow me. You can see what we actually do out here to earn our keep."

Angelique nodded, stretched, got out of her bunk and followed the Captain to the ship's bridge.

When Angelique entered the bridge, there were two crewmen setting up their tight-beam laser communications array. Three other crewmen were working on checking their slipstream drive system in preparation for their next jump.

As they were expecting to jump deeper into Sol's gravity well, perhaps as far as Jupiter or even farther, to the Earth, they were busy checking that their power reserves were ready for using their Gravitic Displacement Drive.

In their current location, they could leverage the Sun's gravitational well and magnetic field for slipstreaming to other star systems within a twenty five light-year radius. However, slipstreaming inwards towards the Sun required the use of the ship's Gravitic Displacement Drive, Spin Dizzy and Electromagnetic Field Overlay. All of which required tremendous amounts of power.

"We'll be at full charge in six hours", one of the engineering officers informed the Captain.

One of the communications officers informed the Captain, "Ready on tight-beam laser comms to Hector, Captain. Locked on and ready to transmit."

The other communications officer noted, "We'll have a tight-beam laser locked on the Earth's Cis-Lunar L-Four region in five minutes, Captain."

"Nice work, team. Start transmitting our data packages to Hector", Captain Barrow ordered, then requested, "Once our data packages have been sent, wait for the data receipt code and then their return data packages. I want an acknowledgement from both the Colonisation Committee and the Security Council. Make sure that they understand that. We require both confirmation receipt codes."

"Aye, Captain", the first communications officer replied.

The Captain turned to the other communications officer, "When you get that alignment right, send the following message to Colonial Marine Headquarters. *'From: The Interstellar Push Ship Artemisia, Communications Runner Alpha, out of Xi-Bootis A Secundus. We have Colonial Marine Recruit Angelique Reas on board. Awaiting delivery instructions.'* After you've sent that, I want a receipt acknowledgement along with their passenger delivery instructions."

"Aye, Captain. I'll be sending that in three minutes", the communications officer replied.

Captain Barrow turned to Angelique, "We are thirty two astronomical units out, so any transmission receipts and return communications will take several hours, at least."

Angelique nodded, "Understood, Captain."

The crew of the communications runner knew how long it would take for the replies to finally come back. The time lag was a simple calculation and the speed of light in a vacuum was a fixed constant.

They all went to the ship's mess hall, ate a meal and then returned to the crew's quarters to play cards. One of the communications officers remained on the ship's bridge.

This was no longer the polite ship's crew that had been so professional in carrying out their duties. While playing cards, they swore, insulted each other, argued and even gambled. They carried on like they were in a bar playing cards back on Earth. The only difference; they didn't drink, smoke, or fight, although credit chips did change hands frequently. For young eighteen-year-old Angelique Reas, it was a real eye-opener.

After four hours of waiting, the communications officer on watch was replaced by his fellow communications officer and the waiting continued once more. Another four hours passed and the communications officers swapped watch once again.

It was well over eight hours since they'd transmitted their data packages from Xi-Bootis A Secundus and the ship's intercom began buzzing.

Captain Barrow pushed the intercom button and the communications officer on watch announced straight away, "We've received official data package acknowledgement receipts from both the Colonisation Committee and the Security Council, Captain. The receipt quantum coding is correct from both. We are now receiving Hector's return data packages. We have our incoming mail, Captain."

"Good work. Any word from the Colonial Marines?", Captain Barrow enquired.

"Not yet, Captain. Perhaps in another hour or two", the communications officer replied.

"Acknowledged. Let me know when we hear from them. We can't deliver our guest until we know where to deliver her", Captain Barrow replied.

Another hour and a half later, the communications officer buzzed on the ship's intercom once more.

Captain Barrow immediately presses the button, "Captain, Sir, we have received an official communications acknowledgement receipt from Cis-Lunar L-Four, from the Colonial Marine Command Centre. The quantum receipt encoding is correct."

"Excellent. So, where are we taking our passenger?", Captain Barrow questioned.

"They haven't provided any instructions, Captain. Just the acknowledgement receipt", his communications officer informed him.

"Well, now, that is strange, I must admit. Keep monitoring the communications channels. We can't deliver our guest if we don't have our delivery instructions", Captain Barrow replied, shaking his head.

"Is there a problem, Captain Barrow?", Angelique enquired.

"No, not at all, Miss Reas. We are just waiting for our instructions on where to deliver you", Captain Barrow replied, explaining, "Once we have our instructions, we can slipstream you straight to your destination and then we can slipstream our way back out to Xi-Bootis and Secundus."

"I'm just being curious, but what happens if you don't receive any instructions?", Angelique asked.

"Well, that won't happen, Miss Reas, but if it did, we'd have no choice; we'd have to take you back to Secundus with us. Without an officially provided destination, we can't deliver you", Captain Barrow explained.

The ship's intercom buzzed; it buzzed with an urgency. Captain Barrow pressed the intercom button.

"Captain, I think you should come to the bridge. Urgently, Sir", the communications officer advised.

Both Captain Barrow and Angelique Reas headed straight to the ship's bridge.

When Angelique and Captain Barrow arrived at the ship's bridge, they found the communications officer flicking his eyes from the bridge's main screen to his instruments.

"Captain, I am picking up an anomaly, Sir", he advised, noting, "If I didn't know any better, I'd say that someone is probing for our precise location. Only advanced military probes can do that, Sir."

Captain Barrow rubbed the new stubble on his chin, "You know what that means, don't you?. They're not sending us delivery instructions. They're coming to us. That's never happened before; it's unprecedented."

As they watched the screen, the communications officer announced, "We've detected a slipstream wormhole off our port bow. It's close to us, but at a safe enough distance, around five kilometres. You can't see it, but it's there. They'll be here any minute."

The communications officer adjusted the screen, centring the slipstream and highlighting the gravimetric flow lines. Without warning, a ship suddenly appeared from out of the slipstream's highlighted exit funnel. It was a rather large Colonial Fleet Super Heavy Cruiser.

"Captain, that ship is pinging as the CFS Argonaut", the communications officer noted.

"It looks like my ride is here", Angelique noted, remarking, "The Argonaut is the first of its class. The first of the Super Heavy Cruisers. My Mum said they're going to build fourteen of those for patrolling the outer frontier colonies."

"Like the Xi-Bootis system", the communications officer commented.

"Potentially. If that's the case, they might even put my Aunt Roberta in command of one", Angelique replied with a smile.

"Aunt Roberta?", Captain Barrow questioned rhetorically, before asking incredulously, "Your aunt is High Admiral Roberta Nummus?"

"Ah, yeah. Didn't anyone tell you that, Captain?", Angelique asked, also rhetorically.

Within thirty minutes, new recruit Angelique Reas had been transferred to the CFS Argonaut, complete with her duffle bag. A sleek, streamlined runabout flew out from the Argonaut, docked with the communications runner and transported her across. Then, without any fanfare, the communications runner slipstreamed back to the Xi-Bootis system and its primary star, Cathol, completing its mission.

Angelique was led to the Captain's conference room, where she was met by three people. One was, of course, the Captain of the Argonaut: Captain Stanislaus Becker. The other two were a General from the Earth, General Marvin Nelix and a Colonial Marine Commander, Sally Biggs. Angelique had absolutely no idea why she was even there; she was just another recruit, after all.

Sally Biggs introduced the General and the Argonaut's Captain before introducing herself, "I'm Sally Biggs. Commandant of the Colonial Marine Training Facility, Sparta. You must be wondering what all the fuss is about, Recruit Candidate Reas."

"How much do you know about your family's history with the Colonial Marines?", Sally Biggs enquired.

"Not much, Ma'am. Just that my family is a military family", Angelique admitted.

Sally Biggs chuckled, "Young lady, the Reas family has been associated with the Colonial Marines as Special Operatives since the very beginning of the Special Operative program."

General Nelix noted, "That's nigh on eight hundred and fifty years, Miss Reas."

Sally Biggs continued, "The Special Operative program itself was based on another, civilian program. The Cis-Lunar Bureau of Investigations, Special Agent program. That program was created at the beginning of the first Horridian War in twenty one eighty two. The Reas family was there at the very beginning of that program as well. There are Reas's today still working in that program."

General Nelix chuckled, "Miss Reas, your family is like Special Agent, Special Operative Royalty."

Sally Biggs smiled, "Your family's history goes back even further. Back on Earth, before space was even being colonised, there was another special program. The Cis-Lunar Bureau of Investigations Special Agent program was based on that one. It was the British Military Intelligence Six, Double O program. Your family was involved in that program as well. Your family is directly descended from all the way back then."

General Nelix chuckled once again, "And that is not even mentioning the psychic branch of your family. You even have ancestors who were very powerful Psi Corps Operatives."

"Your family has been protecting and serving Humanity for over fifteen hundred years", Sally added.

Angelique was gobsmacked and feeling the weight of all of that history. It was a lot to take in.

"Ma'am, may I sit down?", Angelique enquired.

"By all means, let's all take a seat", Sally Biggs replied and they all sat down at the conference room table, before she continued,   "History aside, young lady, there is another reason why we're all here."

General Nelix stepped in, noting, "Even before you've started your official training, you've already been following in your family's longstanding tradition."

"Yes. We've been reviewing your protect and server action at that Carlin village on Secundus", Sally Biggs noted, adding, "Eight armed assailants drew down on Human civilians with pulsed laser pistols. They then turned their weapons on the local Carlins. You didn't hesitate to place yourself between the assailants and the Carlin-folk, placing yourself in immediate peril."

Captain Becker chimed in for the first time, "That was impressive enough, young lady, but when those four armed robbers drew their weapons and threatened those eight Carlin traders, what you did was extraordinary. Your Mother was offside and not in any position to help you, yet you took it upon yourself to deal with them."

"Angelique Reas, you not only took down those four armed robbers, but you managed to talk down most of the other assailants", Sally Biggs commended her, noting, "Your Mother did have to put one of them down, but that does happen in such volatile situations."

General Nelix stepped in, "You did drill those four armed robbers through their foreheads and your Mother was right to chide you. However, that's just a matter of training. Always target the centre mass, young lady."

Sally Biggs smiled; it was a broad smile that softened her battle-hardened features, "Which brings us to the main reason why we're all here."

"Are you able to stand, Miss Reas?", General Nelix enquired.

"Yes, Sir", Angelique replied and slowly stood up, as did the General, the Captain and Sally Biggs.

Sally Biggs pulled a small box out of her jacket pocket and opened it up. She placed the box on the table and held out the object that had been inside the box. It was a five-pointed golden star hanging from a short purple ribbon; it had a purple gem embedded in its centre. Around the edges of the gem were the words, Celestial Star of Valour, with the letters CSV written below it.

"Recruit Candidate, Miss Angelique Reas, for bravery under fire, we hereby award you with the Celestial Star of Valour", Commandant Sally Biggs announced as she pinned the medal to Angelique's jacket.

Sally Biggs shook Angelique's hand, "You earned it. Always remember, protect and serve, honour and duty. We expect big things from you, Angelique Reas."

General Nelix added, "Here, here. I could not have said that better", then he shook Angelique's hand.

Captain Becker shook Angelique's hand, stating, "Well done, young lady."

Angelique was overwhelmed and could easily have swooned; fortunately for her, they all sat down.

The Argonaut slipstreamed back into Cis-Lunar space and made its way to the Colonial Marine Training Facility, Sparta. The training facility was huge. Sparta had once been a relatively large, single-cylinder O'Neil-style colony, although it was now heavily modified.

Sparta was two point four kilometres long and two hundred metres in radius; its end caps were two hundred metres in radius as well. Sparta wasn't a mega-colony by any means, but it was still of a respectable size. It once housed over one hundred and fifty thousand colonists, but that was long ago.

The land strips along the main cylinder had been expanded in width and the strip windows likewise reduced. Its three long reflective mirrors had been modified as well; they were now slightly concave to focus sunlight into the narrower strip windows.

Sparta rotated at three point six seven rotations per minute, which was far faster than was normal for a cylindrical colony of its size. As a result, the artificial gravity generated on its main living surface was around three standard gravities.

As one moved from the outer living surfaces towards its axis of rotation, there were five other cylindrical living surfaces, each with its own level of artificial gravity. Light from the facility's three long mirrors was carefully redistributed across all five levels.

As one moved closer to the central axis, roughly every thirty three and a third metres, the artificial gravity reduced by point five gs. Two point five gs at roughly one hundred and sixty seven metres, two gs at roughly one hundred and thirty three metres, one point five gs at one hundred metres and one standard gravity at roughly sixty seven metres. There was even a low gravity level at roughly thirty three metres for specialised low gravity training, something Angelique was unlikely to make use of.

Angelique Reas, along with all of the other new cadets, would start training on the innermost level: basic military training at one standard gravity. With every six weeks of training, the cohort of cadets moved outwards into the next gravitational zone, culminating in two and a half years of living and training at the highest gravitation level of three Gs.

Special Operative training was daunting and many of the cadets were destined to drop out at lower levels; only a few special cadets would complete the entire course. Angelique looked at her Celestial Star of Valour, her medal. Was Angelique Reas special enough?

Basic training began on level one, the level with one standard Earth gravity. On this level, the cohort of cadets had no rank; they were all just cadets. Angelique spent six weeks training on this level and found the training to be almost the same as the training her own Mother and Father had put her through.

Angelique's parents had been training and preparing her since the age of twelve. First inside the hollowed-out asteroid Hector and then later in the interstellar push ship Artemisia in Cis-Luns L-Five. The training was arduous, but nothing that Angelique and the other cadets couldn't handle. After their six weeks were up, the whole cohort passed basic training without anyone dropping out.

It wasn't until they moved on to level two and repeated their basic training at one point five gs, that things became harder. On this level, they were no longer just cadets; they were now all ranked as privates. What had been arduous at level one became much harder at level two. Their muscles strained under the higher gravity; headaches and fatigue became common.

It was at this level that they all began taking the supplements and stimulants. The dosages were carefully calibrated for the level of gravity that they were training on.

Angelique's Father had been right, even though they were taken in capsule form; once the capsules broke down, the aftertaste was truly awful. After their six weeks were up, the whole cohort still remained in the program. No one wanted to give up.

Before they entered level three, the double gravity zone, there was a short ceremony. The whole cohort was ordered to assemble in their dress uniforms for a short address by Commandant Biggs.

The Commandant walked along the line, looking over every one of her trainees. They were all still there, which was expected at their current level. The next two levels would sort the wheat from the chaff.

Commandant Biggs stopped in front of Angelique, snapping, "Private Reas! You are out of uniform!"

Angelique was taken aback; she looked over herself and her uniform; it was all in order.

"You must be mistaken, Ma'am. I appear to be correctly dressed, unless I'm missing something", Angelique replied in a very confused tone.

Sally Biggs smiled and tapped gently on Angelique's jacket, its left side, "Where is your award, Private Reas?"

"My award, Ma'am?", Angelique queried; she was still confused.

"Yes, Private Reas. You are a CSV recipient. Have you no pride in your accomplishments?", Sally Biggs replied, questioning.

"No, Ma'am. I mean, yes, Ma'am. I didn't realise it was a uniform requirement", Angelique replied.

"When you are on parade on my watch, you will wear your awards with pride, Private Reas", Sally replied, before holding up her hand to cut off any further discussion on the matter.

Commandant Biggs addressed the cohort, "You have all passed training on the first two levels. From here on, it gets much harder. Some of you won't make it further. You are all training for the rank ascribed to each level. You only get to keep that rank if you complete that level; otherwise, you remain at the previous level. Some of you will drop out during level three. Some will make it through, only to drop out at level four. There is no shame in this. If you cannot complete level three, you will remain a Colonial Marine, a Private First Class. If you cannot complete level four, you will remain a Colonial Marine, a Private First Class in the Special Forces, with a classification of F-Two-G. Not all of you are destined to become Special Operatives. If you cannot complete level five, you will remain a Colonial Marine, a Private First Class in the Special Forces, with a classification of F-Two-point Five-G. Remember, though, you will all still be Colonial Marines, proud Colonial Marines."

One of the trainees held up his hand to ask a question and the Commandant acknowledged him, "Private Reas has a Celestial Star of Valour?", he questioned incredulously.

"Yes, Private. Private Reas was awarded a Celestial Star of Valour for bravery under fire", Sally Biggs confirmed, "An unscheduled protect and serve operation in which Private Reas, then a private citizen of seventeen years of age, saved the lives of at least eight Carlin-folk on Xi-Bootis A Secundus."

Slowly, everyone in the cohort leaned forward and turned towards Angelique, with surprised, almost quizzical expressions on their faces. Great, now everybody knows, Angelique lamented.

All of the trainees were given a week's break in training to rest, relax and acclimate to the new two-gravity environment. The supplements and stimulants, which had been ingested with breakfast, were now also ingested with their lunch, effectively doubling the dosage. Along with the morning supplements and stimulants, another capsule was added; it had no official name, but was described simply as a mild genetic enhancer. They were told it would help their underlying genetic substrate to adjust to the higher gravity.

When training began, Angelique found herself to be something of a celebrity. She had earned the Celestial Star of Valour, so naturally, some of the other trainees wanted to spar with her during their combat training, just to see how good she actually was.

Angelique, of course, was a military brat and her parents had started her training as soon as she turned twelve. She quickly put each and every one of them in their place, doing so brutally. Angelique did not like being singled out and she made her position on the matter very clear; that gained her a lot of respect amongst the other trainees. It also gained her a quiet word of caution from Commandant Briggs, who did not want her trainees injured.

The level three training continued and over its course, some trainees would leave and others would simply disappear. Some gave up during training itself and some were simply not there in the morning. They'd packed up and left during the night; too embarrassed to be seen by their comrades.

The cohort of trainees grew smaller as each day progressed, from one day into the next. Not all trainees were destined to succeed. By the end of the sixth week of training in the two-gravity environment, over half of the trainees had dropped out. Those who dropped out would still be Colonial Marines, just not Special Forces or the Special Operatives they'd hoped to be.

There was no break between level three and level four; the trainees went straight into the next six weeks of training at two point five gs. Commandant Biggs had them all on parade for inspection.
Some of the trainees had brought their duffle bags with them; they, too, were going to drop out.

Angelique had gotten close to one of them, "Michelle, what are you doing?"

Michelle sighed, "I've had enough, Angelique. I don't think I can go any further."

"Bullshit! Of course you can. If you have to drop out, do so during training; at least you will have tried. If you leave now, you'll never know if you could make it or not", Angelique chided her.

Michelle was unconvinced and Angelique changed tack and whispered, "Look, Michelle. You like Sylvester, yeah?"

Michelle turned and looked down the line of trainees to another trainee, Sylvester Bronson, before replying, "Of course I do. You know that."

"Well, Sylvester likes you, too. I mean, he likes-likes you. If you leave now, you're likely not going to see him again. Do you really want that?", Angelique enquired.

"Shit! Stop being so right!", Michelle exclaimed.

"Just stay, at least give it a go. You never know, if you make it all the way through, you could become a couple, a team unit. Colonial High Command like teams; they work well together, have each other's backs and they produce children who are more likely to succeed in becoming Special Operatives", Angelique explained.

"How do you know so much about this?", Michelle asked.

"My parents are a Special Operative team. My Brother and I were born for this. Haven't you noticed, that everyone who has dropped out so far has been from a non-military family?", Angelique noted.

Michelle considered her words. Angelique was right; every single dropout so far had been from civilian families, civilian backgrounds.

"Think about it, your Father is a Special Operative, Michelle. You can do this. You were born for this. Your Father will be so proud of you", Angelique assured her before stepping back into her place in the lineup.

"Your fellow trainees who are no longer present; they are currently being deployed as Colonial Marines. Again, there is no shame in this. You, however, are now Special Forces, category F-Two-G. Some of you will go on to pass the next level. Some of you will not. Those who don't will be deployed as Colonial Marines, Privates First Class, Special Forces, F-Two-G. You have all already earned that just by being here this morning", Commandant Biggs informed them.

An officer walked along the line of trainees, passing them each a capsule.

"Now, please take the capsule. It's what we call a genomic lock; any genetic changes that have occurred during the course of your training to this point will be locked permanently into place. So take those capsules now", Commandant Biggs instructed and they all did so.

"I see that some of you have your duffle bags out. Please don't make hasty, rash decisions. You don't yet know if you have the right stuff to make it through. If you leave now, you will never know". Sally Biggs told them, hoping to dissuade them from leaving.

Michelle raised her hand and the Commandant acknowledged her, "Ma'am. I'm not leaving. My duffle bag was thinking of leaving, but I'll kick it into line", and then she tapped her duffle bag with her foot.

One by one, the other trainees who were thinking of leaving kicked their duffle bags; one was even heard to say, "Lazy effing duffle bag.", as he did so.

Commandant Biggs smiled, "Excellent. No one drops out this morning", and then she put on her 'Sally' voice, "If you are thinking about quitting, please come and talk to me first."

Training in two point five gs was harsh, horribly harsh; not because of the training, it was the actual environment itself. They were now taking supplements and stimulants with every meal, three times a day.

The dosage had tripled and they were now taking the genetic enhancer capsule with breakfast and lunch. The vile aftertaste of the pharmaceutical compounds alone was enough to turn anyone away.

Angelique had to keep telling herself that she was born for this, that she could do this. At every opportunity, she told her friends, that's what they were now, that they were either born for this or simply that they could do it.

Angelique even pointed out to them, "Look at how easily the Commandant strolls around in two point five gs", that during the day she moves from one level to the next and back again, overseeing each and every cohort as if the shifts in gravity were nothing; that if Sally Biggs could do it, so could they.

Nonetheless, some of the trainees still dropped out; many of them left during the night, with feelings of inadequacy and shame. Those who bothered to speak with the Commandant were persuaded to stay. Irrespective of dropping out, those who left were still Colonial Marines, PFC, Special Forces, F-Two-G. When the six weeks of training at level four were up, the cohort's numbers had dropped by half once more. Indeed, the program removed the chaff from the wheat; it was gruelling. Nearly all of the dropouts were from civilian families. The military brats were just too stubborn to give in.

They had a week's break between level four and level five. They relaxed in their current two-point-five gs environment, knowing that the step up to three Gs was going to tax them heavily. Yet, even still, here they all were, taking time off and relaxing in an environment at two point five gs; when a mere thirteen weeks earlier, they would never have thought that was even possible. That week was bittersweet; they needed it; however, it passed all too quickly for their liking.

Once more, they found themselves in the parade lineup, this time at three Gs. It was oppressive and yet they all stood there, enduring it.

"As you can see, your numbers have dropped considerably. There are only a quarter of you left. Please understand that there is no shame in dropping out. Would I prefer you all to stay till the end of the training program? To all become Special Operatives? Of course, I do, but even those who have dropped out have their part to play. Those of you who have left during the preceding level four training have been deployed as Colonial Marines, Privates First Class, Special Forces, F-Two-G. You, however, have completed your level four training and you have earned your Colonial Marine, Private First Class, Special Forces, F-Two point Five-G grading. Congratulations. That in itself is quite an achievement", the Commandant addressed the remaining trainees.

An officer walked along the line of trainees, passing them each a capsule; they had seen this before.

Sally Biggs commented, "You all know what to do. Please take your genomic lock capsules. Let's lock all those nice new genetic changes in place."

Commandant Biggs continued, "Some of your cohort dropped out without discussing it with me first. Some of you considered dropping out, but after discussing it with me, here you all are. So, remember, if you are having doubts and considering dropping out of the program, please talk to me first. I'm sure I can change your minds. You have all made it this far, so you can do this. Always remember that!"

The parade line-up had been at o five hundred, after which they all went to the mess hall for breakfast. Again, they had their supplements and stimulants. They also had their genetic enhancers. They were informed that while the dosage of the supplements and stimulants would remain the same, they would be taking a third dose of the genetic enhancers with their evening meal. So they were now taking triple doses of everything.

It was also at this point that another pharmaceutical was introduced. This one was different; it was not taken with meals; it was given to them by the facility's nurses. Before their breakfast was served, they were all given a once-off pharmaceutical. It was not ingested, it was not injected, it was carefully placed by a Nurse under each of the trainee's eyelids, where it quickly dissolved and the chemical compounds followed the optic nerve directly into the brain.

The nurses informed each trainee, "Every Special Forces member receives this. It's a series of compounds designed to enhance neural resilience and prepare you for future neural augmentation."

Angelique enquired, "Even those who dropped out at level four?"

"Yes, even those who were graded as F-Two-G. They were given these compounds before deployment. Special Forces Marines may request neural augmentation at a later date and assuming it fits in with their deployment and skill sets, that will be granted", the nurse confirmed.

And then their level five training began, Special Operative training at three Gs for two and a half years.

While many of the other trainees appeared to be struggling with their level five training, Angelique found herself strangely moving with ease within this new three-gravity environment. Angelique didn't understand why. Her body was three times its normal weight and she should have been feeling more strain than she did at level four. Even her close friends among her cohort were still struggling. Some, of course, dropped out; they would remain as Special Forces F-Two point Five-G. Angelique went to the Commandant's office to enquire about her situation.

"Private Reas", Sally Biggs greeted, "I hardly expected to see you in my office. I suspect you're not here because of feelings of inadequacy and failure. So, what brings you here, Angelique?"

Angelique didn't know where to begin, "I'm not struggling, Ma'am. Everybody else in my cohort is struggling, but not me. I simply don't get it. It makes absolutely no sense at all."

"Actually, Angelique, it makes perfect sense when you think about it", Sally Biggs told her, her voice taking on a softer tone as she explained, "Look at the other trainees, Angelique. Everyone who has dropped out so far has been civilian born. Those who remain are mostly military born, with a handful of the more resilient trainees from civilian families. If you have one parent who is a Special Operative, your chances of completing this program are enhanced; if you have two, well, you're a shoo-in. Both of your parents are Special Operatives, Angelique. You have inherited their genetic alterations and it shows. Once you completed your level four training, you came into your stride. It is that simple."

"But, no one else seems to be finding this easy, not even the military born?", Angelique questioned.

"You are the only one in your cohort with two Special Operative parents, Angelique", Sally informed her, before noting, "And your family has a very long history of Special Operatives in it. As General Nelix once said, you're Special Operative Royalty; now that's shining through", it was all matter-of-fact, the way she said it.

The Level Five training proceeded; it wasn't six weeks of intensive training, but rather two and a half years of living and training at three Gs. Each trainee was being forged from what they were at the end of their level four training into something entirely new. Like heat quickening steel, the higher gravity was quickening them into a new kind of steel, a steel of flesh and bone.

Gradually, ever so slowly over those two and a half years, their flesh and bones became like iron and steel. They were being reforged into something *"other"* than human. Something new.

At the end of it all, most of Angelique's friends were still present, especially those whom she'd encouraged. Sylvester Bronson and his now girlfriend, Michelle, both completed the program. Both of them had Fathers who were Special Operatives. Another of Angelique's friends was Mike Johnson, who was from a civilian family, yet somehow, just through sheer hard work and determination, he completed the program.

Angelique invited all three of them to come to Secundus after their deployments; she told them tales of the wonderful native species, the Carlins and the Indigenous Thols. They were all quite intrigued at the thought of living on a Class One frontier world.

Nonetheless, the final tally of the Special Operatives program had halved once again. Most of those who had dropped out had done so within the first six weeks; some had lasted just a little longer. There had been over a hundred recruits in the program's pipeline at the beginning; at the end, there were thirteen left. Three were civilian born, all of the rest were military brats and Angelique was the only one amongst them with two Special Operative parents.

Commandant Sally Biggs reviewed the results, looking through them on her clipboard. She had started out with over a hundred recruit candidates. After the level two training at one point five gs, half had dropped out of the program. The Colonial Marines gained over fifty new marines from that, but over fifty recruits continued on with the program and that was important. Twenty six of those dropped out, becoming Special Forces F-Two-G. Of those that remained, thirteen dropped out, becoming Special Forces F-Two point Five-G; the end result was thirteen bright and shiny, brand new Special Operatives, the best of the best.

The rate of attrition was always high in the Special Operatives program, but no one failed as such, as at the end of the day, they all had a role to play in the Colonial Marines. A military organisation with a proud tradition and an illustrious history under the Earth's Interstellar Alliance Armed Forces banner.

"Congratulations!", Commandant Biggs shouted out loudly, "All thirteen of you are henceforth Special Operatives in the Colonial Marines. A nurse will shortly hand you your final genomic lock capsules. Make sure you take them; you don't want all of that hard work to go to waste, so lock all of those genetic changes in place. Our nurse will also give you each an injection; it contains a serum that will consolidate all of the changes that your high gravity training has given you. You are now stronger and faster in both body and mind; this serum will help you access all of those changes to the fullest."

"Now, as is our tradition, you have one week off to do with as you wish within this facility. I usually recommend flexing your newfound abilities in this three-gravity environment, but that's just me. I kind of like living in a three G environment", Sally Biggs smiled genuinely and the thirteen graduates all chuckled, "One week from today, you will all receive your neural augments and two days of training in how to use them. After that, if you wish, you can apply for a week's training in the zero gravity level, which I also recommend. Ironically, you'll have gone all the way through from levels one to five, only to go back to level zero, but there you have it."

"In three weeks, you will all receive your assigned deployments. I will be honest, I have no hand in your deployments; that is up to High Command. Now enjoy your breakfasts", Sally Biggs told them.

"Always remember that whatever deployment you may receive, wherever you may end up, you all have iron in your blood and steel in your hands. You will always succeed. It is now in your very nature", the Commandant told her new Special Operatives, "Iron and Steel!", she exclaimed, "Iron and steel!"

The new Special Operatives all joined in!

It had been the catchcry of the Colonial Marines since the first Horridian War, nearly thirteen hundred years earlier.

After eating her breakfast, Angelique left the mess hall and found herself staring into a full-length mirror; she hardly recognised herself. She was different, so different.

Angelique used to be strong, but strong and slender; now, she was much, much stronger and it showed. She had arms that looked as if she could bend steel girders. Angelique actually wondered if she could.

Then a thought crossed her mind; she was "other", would her friend Kitty accept her as "other"?

It weighed heavily on her mind.

Perhaps this had all been a huge mistake.

Angelique Reas was now something "other" than Human!

Something both exhilarating and horrifying all at the same time.

15. Medical Interventions.

With the Human colony on Secundus thriving and the new mega-colony in Cis-Luns L-Five, Colonial Central Command, soon to be completed, High Admiral Roberta Nummus began eyeing new projects. With unauthorised and unsanctioned colonists lurking somewhere in the Xi-Bootis double-star system, there was always the risk of trouble.

This had already happened three years earlier in thirty four seventy two, with two fake tour company incidents and an attempted daylight armed robbery. The couple responsible for the fake tour companies was still at large, while the four robbers were deceased.

Admiral Nummus commissioned two new colonies as a matter of urgency.

The colony on Secundus, Hilltop, a name that had not caught on, had a small prison facility. Each of the twelve interstellar push ships also had its own brigs, but they would be leaving after the new mega-colony came online. Roberta saw the need for a more permanent solution.

The first of the new colonies was to be a Stanford torus colony in the Cis-Luns L-Four region. It was to be a penitentiary. As it was going to be the only Stanford torus colony in the Xi-Bootis system, it would simply be named Stanford Penitentiary.

While the Human colony on Secundus and the new mega-colony, Colonial Central Command, would house the perpetrators of minor offences, those who deserved long-term incarceration would be sent to the Stanford Penitentiary.

The second of the new colonies was going to be a specialised single-cylinder, O'Neil-style colony. It was going to be a smaller version of the Sparta Colonial Marine training facility back in Cis-Lunar L-Four, back in the Sol system.

The main difference was its length; instead of being two point four kilometres long, it would be much shorter, only one kilometre in length. Although it would still be four hundred meters in diameter and have the exact same interior setup.

It too was to be built in Cis-Luns L-Four. Its purpose was to train Colonial Marines and Special Operative candidates for the outer frontier regions around the Xi-Bootis system. The new Xi-Bootis training facility was to be named Nova Sparta.

Of course, there was more and it was not related to matters of crime or the military. Five years earlier, in thirty four seventy at first contact, the High Admiral had made certain promises to the Carlins and Indigenous Thols and those promises needed to be kept.

Roberta tasked two people with implementing the major aspect of those promises: better medical outcomes for the indigenous sapient species.

Special Operative Simone Reas, on reserve and on call, was tasked with carrying through with these promises for the Carlin folk in their villages in the Masula Valley plains and meadows. While Yealah and Yannick, both Mimasian Thols, were tasked with carrying through with the same promises for their Indigenous Thol Cousins, in their tree villages in the Northern and Southern mountain ranges.

While Kayala looked after Keegali's remaining kits, Keegali and Kelyarn travelled with Simone to the various Carlin villages, farther afield from Kelyarn's village. The Carlin villages were scattered across the broad plains and bluegrass meadows along both sides of the majestic Masula River, except for the river's headwaters to the far west in the Western Mountains.

A region rich with dangerous apex predators, where highly intelligent, but sub-sapient Sleimorps and fully sapient insectoid Chittens were abundant.

There were an awful lot of scattered Carlin villages and the process of contacting them all was going to take a lot of time.

As Kelyarn was the prime Elder of his village and his village was the largest village in the valley, he was well respected amongst the other Carlin villages in the area. Simone's mode of transport was a Manta Ray passenger transport; it wasn't a big ship, quite small actually, but the main thing was that it wasn't a military ship.

Simone did not want to cause panic amongst the Carlin folk by arriving in her usual ride, which, of course, just happened to be a Broad Head, Arrow Class Interplanetary Star Fighter, she'd named Haven. Simone deemed her Star Fighter "*inappropriate*".

At each village, Simone handed the local village Elder a communicator. The Carlin-folk were, of course, not used to seeing Human technology and each village visit required at least half a day to teach the Elders and their Wives how to use the device.

Simone found it useful to have some of the older kits to observe the instruction sessions; what the adult Carlins might forget, their kits tended to remember. Each visit took half a day and before leaving, Simone made sure that the Elders could access the Colony's emergency channels and were proficient in the communicator's use.

The emergency lines at the Human colony were manned by Mimasian Thols, who spoke not only fluent English, but modern and ancient Tholish and Carlinish. The Mimasian Thols were exceptional linguists.

Yealah and Yannick had a somewhat different situation; there were multiple kinds of Tholish tree villages. There were the Indigenous Thol tree villages, which were scattered throughout the Northern and Southern Mountain ranges, but a good eighty percent of them were in the North, for historical reasons.

Predation by the sapient species, the Tarlaks, had occurred within their recorded history; the Indigenous Thols had very long memories. As much as the Thols resembled Angels, the Tarlaks resembled Demonic Simian Gargoyles that treated all other species as food, sometimes even their own.

However, the Indigenous Thol tree villages tended to be far more clustered in the area immediately to the north of the Human colony. Farther to the west, towards the Western Mountain ranges, the Thol tree villages petered out and vanished as the threat from apex predators increased; Sleimorps, Cress, and Wyverns were abundant, as was the insectoid sapient predator species, the Chittens. An uncontacted ant-like species to which everything else was food.

Just to complicate matters, Mimasian Thols did not live in the Human colony. Instead, they preferred to live in tree houses, in tree villages in the same forests of the mighty Jula Jula trees as their Indigenous Thol cousins.

There were tree villages where only Mimasian Thols lived. There were also tree villages where only Indigenous Thols lived. There were tree villages where both Mimasian and Indigenous Thols lived, as was the tree village where Yealah and Yannick lived.

Mimasian Thols commuted to the Human colony for work either by hover bus or by wing. The Indigenous Thols, living their more natural, native existence, did their own thing.

The Mimasian Thols living in their tree villages all had communicators, so during any emergency, medical or otherwise, they knew what to do; they contacted the Human colony's emergency channels.

The Mimasian Thols living in shared villages had already put in place emergency plans with their Indigenous Thol neighbours. They'd already explained to their neighbours that if medical or other emergency aid was required, go to the nearest Mimasian Thol's tree house and request aid; the call would then be made and help would be quickly on its way.

The tree villages that only had Indigenous Thols living in them were another matter. Thols were an airborne species; they could fly. So rather than travel to each and every Indigenous Thol village, Yannick put out a simple message into the Tholish grapevine, which was quite extensive.

He had to get clearance from the Tholish High Council and High Chancellor Yuntark agreed to it. It was, after all, in the High Council's best interests.

The message was simple: *"Come to the Tholish High Council for the receipt of Human communications technology. Important and mandatory."*

A summons to the Tholish High Council was never ignored. At least two representatives from every Indigenous Thol tree village would arrive, even from across the Masula River, from the Southern Mountain range.

Yealah and Yannick arranged for Mimasian Thols to hand out communicators to the Indigenous Thol representatives and to instruct them in their usage. It was far more efficient than travelling to each and every Indigenous tree village. The call and response system was already in place, so Yealah and Yannick made use of it.

There was a large difference between the needs of the Carlins and the needs of the Indigenous Thols. Thols live in tree villages, with the Mimasian Thols constructing their tree houses and the Indigenous Thols creating their traditional nests in giant Jula Jula trees. These mature trees had hollow centres and as the Mimasian Thols liked their friends to visit, including those from non-flying species, they built elevators in the hollows of the trees in which they lived. Every Mimasian tree village and every shared Mimasian / Indigenous Thol tree village had these elevators. The purely Indigenous Thol tree villages did not.

Yannick found himself scheduling Indigenous Thol tree village upgrades; the construction of elevators in their tree hollows. Many Indigenous Thols considered having elevators in their tree villages advantageous.

The Indigenous Thols did have Carlin friends who could visit, yes, but they also had Thols in their villages who, for various reasons, could not fly. As a result, those individuals were basically nest-bound. The elevators would give them the ability to not only leave their nests but also to travel outside their tree villages.

Then, of course, there were the injured Indigenous Thols. Most of them had damaged wings, broken bones that had not healed correctly, torn wings and inner ear problems.

Yealah found herself scheduling visits to the Human colony's medical clinic for assessment and correction where possible. There were, of course, the occasional newly broken or damaged wings and these were treated by the clinic's emergency services.

The existing injuries, however, had to be scheduled, as there were a great many of them. Some of the existing broken wings could not be corrected; the damage was too old and too severe.

The lucky Indigenous Thols whose wings could be fixed had to be scheduled for surgery. Their poorly healed wing bones had to be surgically re-broken, the broken sections repaired and realigned and finally, specifically designed bone knitters were applied to knit the bones back together. A broken wing took up to five days to be corrected, depending on the complexity of the original break.

There were other Indigenous Thols who had torn wings. With these, surgery was also required. The scar tissue along the tears had to be removed and the wing membrane sutured back together. Special tape infused with healing compounds was then applied to the wound and over the course of a week, the torn wing would heal.

Unlucky, were those Indigenous Thols whose wings had both broken bones and torn wings. They had to undergo two separate surgeries.

Those Indigenous Thols that had inner ear problems were generally found to have recurrent ear infections. The same antibiotic that worked with Mimasian Thols also worked with Indigenous Thols and so, those were solved with simple medications.

The contrast between the Indigenous Thols and the Carlins could not be more different, and it all boiled down to offspring, children.

Indigenous Thols only produced one youngling at a time and usually a Mother would produce two, or if she was lucky, three younglings in her lifetime. Carlins, on the other hand, had kits that were born in litters; first one, followed by twos, later threes and so on.

Whereas the Indigenous Tholish Mothers watched over their younglings like hawks, Carlinish Mothers had so many kits that they couldn't watch them all as closely as they'd like. They often had misadventures and other life-threatening issues were always present.

No sooner than Simone, Keegali and Kelyarn had distributed communicators to the Elders of the other Carlin villages, the emergency channels lit up like a Christmas tree. The emergency air services were constantly being sent out to the Carlin villages.

Young Carlin kits would get into all sorts of problems; they fell out of trees, they tried to leap over dry stone walls that were too high, they'd try to eat things that would make a billy goat sick, and they'd even try to pick up snakes and vipers. Especially the boys!

Broken bones needed knitting, cuts needed suturing, infections needed antibiotics and then there were the crowded living conditions, perfect for spreading childhood diseases. And that did not even include predation by local Secundun predators. It quickly became apparent why more than sixty percent of Carlin kits never made it to adulthood.

There were also the sad call-outs. Occasionally, a Carlin kit would fall out of a tree or be bitten by a poisonous viper and even though the kit was already dead, the Mother would insist on calling for emergency help.

They actually believed that Humans could bring the dead back to life. It was traumatic for both the Carlinish Mother and the Human paramedics, who had to explain to her that they could only heal the living, not resurrect the dead.

Such situations brought on tears all around, even from hardened paramedics, who'd thought that they'd seen it all.

Simone looked at the number of emergency call-outs to the Carlin villages and sighed; they had only issued a third of their communicators.

What would it be like when every Carlin village came online and had the ability to request help?

The issue became known as the Carlin Kit Chaos, CKC; Keegali, herself a Carlin Mother of twenty four kits, ten of whom survived, coined the phrase.

Simone sent an urgent message to the interstellar push ship Artemisia in Cis-Luns L-Five, straight to Roberta Nummus, the High Admiral, who also happened to be their family's Aunt Roberta.

Simone's message was simple: *"All available nurses are required planetside, train a lot more, we are going to need them. Expansion of the colony's medical centre is urgently required."*

Simone sent a report detailing the number of call-outs they'd had from the Carlin villages to show how urgent the situation was becoming.

Simone's plan was simple; they could not allow their medical centre to become overwhelmed with the Carlin Kit Chaos. The colony's medical centre required immediate expansion; every Carlin village needed its own Carlin nurses and Human nurses would have to train them.

If Human-trained Carlin nurses could handle the simpler issues: Using bone knitters to heal broken bones, suturing lacerations, dispensing antibiotics, injecting antivenom and even pumping out stomachs, then only the major issues would require the emergency air services.

Simone envisioned every Carlin village to have at least six nurses and the ones to start training would be the Carlin's very own midwives and folk healers. There might even be a day in the not-so-distant future where Carlinish nurses worked alongside Human nurses in the Human colony.

Simone sends another request to her family's Aunt Roberta: *"The Carlin-folk need vaccine development to combat both child and adult diseases"*, something that she considered extremely important.

This led to the development of a research wing attached to the Human colony's expanding medical clinic.

While new vaccines were needed for the Carlin-folk, existing vaccines and variations of them, used by the Mimasian Thols, were found to be effective with the Indigenous Thols.

It was only the newer diseases that were specific to Secundus, where research and development were required. Simone found that Yannick, Yealah and another group of Mimasian Thols at the medical clinic were already on top of that situation. The Indigenous Thols were the Mimasian Thol's distant cousins, their brethren, so it was only natural for that to be the case.

Simone sighed, this time in relief; the Mimasian Thols were a godsend.

In a way, the Mimasian Thols really were Angels.

Simone saw the biggest issue with the Carlin Kit Chaos stemming from Carlinish extreme fertility. The Carlins were driven by their own biological imperatives to bond, mate and produce kits, lots and lots of kits. Even their female ovaries, wombs and placentas had evolved to that end. The attrition rate of young kits and even some of the older kits was so high that the replacement rate also needed to be equally high.

Once a Carlin girl underwent her quickening, found her lifelong bondmate, thus becoming a woman and began to produce offspring; her ovaries began producing ova, starting with one and stepping up as her pregnancies progressed.

Even the Carlinish placenta was designed for multiple kits; there was only ever one placenta in a Carlin woman's womb, but it had one umbilical for each fetus attached to it.

A Carlin woman could produce so many offspring in her lifetime that it became biologically exhausting, leading to major organ failure and often, premature death.

It was a fascinating biological setup, at least Simone found it so, but it was also a problem. Now that Humanity had interfered and more Carlin kits would survive, Carlinish fertility needed to be addressed; otherwise, Carlin families would become overwhelmed with kits, as if they weren't already. Humanity's interference, as benevolent as it was, was going to upset the balance.

Simone sent a request to the new research wing at the colony's medical clinic; The Carlin-folk were going to need species-specific contraception. When Yealah saw the request when it came in, she wholeheartedly agreed. The balance had changed. The Carlins now needed effective contraception.

The Carlinish women would soon be able to control how many kits they had and when. With the Mimasian Thols on the task, it was only a matter of time.

Having agreed with Simone on the need for Carlin contraception, Yealah messaged back about Indigenous Thol needs. The Indigenous Thols had precisely the opposite problem.

An Indigenous Tholish woman might produce one, two, or three younglings in her lifetime; rarely ever more and even just having three younglings was not so common.

Again, this was tied to their biology, specifically, the number of limbs; the number of appendages. A Human fetus, of course, has only two arms and two legs; passing through the birth canal, although dangerous, is generally not a problem.

A Carlin fetus has an extra appendage, their tail and they're born in litters, but they also gestate to term in only seven months. As a result, they are smaller at birth and pass through the birth canal, generally without issues.

Thols, however, were different and in this regard, the Indigenous Thols were the same as the Mimasian Thols. All Thols had two arms, two legs, a tail and, of course, two wings. In order to pass through the birth canal, their evolution had created a fix.

With any pregnant female Thol, the womb contained a single placenta, which entirely encapsulates the fetus. Gestation took much longer, eleven and a half months, at the end of which the fetus, whilst still encapsulated in the placental sac, passes through the birth canal. This ensured that all seven limbs, wings included, could not obstruct the expulsion.

Once birthed, the placental sac, upon exposure to the air, would begin to break down and the Mother would tear it open to remove her new youngling. The youngling's wings, all tightly furled, would then open up over the following days. As a result, a Tholish Mother, Mimasian or Indigenous, could only have one youngling per pregnancy, never more.

Simone read the details of Yealah's message and decided to call her, "Yealah, I can see that the Indigenous Thols have the exact same problem your people had in the early days, back when your ancestors awoke from cryosleep inside Mimas. Isn't the solution the same as it was with your people? Fertility enhancement medications?"

"Well, Simone, you might have thought that", Yealah trilled and clicked back, noting, "We've tried our fertility medications with a few of our Indigenous cousins and they simply don't work."

Simone stared into the screen, questioning rhetorically, "They don't work?", before commenting, "Yealah, Indigenous Thols are Thols. There should be little difference between you? I mean, kind of like the differences between my people and the Martians; just minor subspecies differences."

"We thought that too, Simone, originally. It makes sense in a way, we look sufficiently the same that you would think we're just different variations of the same species. Different subspecies, as you say, but that is clearly not the case", Yealah trilled and clicked in reply.

"What does that mean exactly, Yealah? That you Mimasian Thols and the Indigenous Thols are completely different species?", Simone queried.

"That is precisely the case, Simone. We Mimasian Thols and our Indigenous Thol cousins are completely different species. We look so similar, but genetically, we are very different", Yealah trilled and clicked in confirmation.

"Just how different are your two peoples, Yealah?", Simone enquired, genuinely curious.

Yealah trilled, clicked and softly barked back, "Genetically incompatible, different. Unlike Humans and Martians, we Mimasian Thols and our Indigenous Thol cousins cannot cross-breed."

"Are you sure?", Simone questioned, her mind thinking of the implications.

"Absolutely certain, Simone. We did the genetic tests and studies. Hell, some of my people think that we're more closely related to the Tarlaks genetically than our Indigenous Cousins", Yealah trilled and clicked.

Simone fell silent, steepling her fingers and resting her chin on them in quiet contemplation, thinking to herself, *"That can't be right!"*

"You know what that means, don't you, Yealah?", Simone questioned.

"Yes", Yealah trilled, before noting with more trills and clicks, "We have to develop species-specific fertility treatments for our Indigenous Thols cousins. There is no way around that."

"Are you going to be starting from scratch?", Simone enquired.

"We hope not. We are hoping that we can tweak our existing fertility medications to suit, but we can't be sure that that will work. So, it's possible that we may need to go back to scratch", Yealah trilled in reply, noting, "I am hoping that won't be necessary though."

"So am I, Yealah, so am I", Simone replied in agreement, noting, "I'll request help from our geneticists up at Cis-Luns Space."

"Thank you, Simone", Yealah trilled.

"This also creates a cross-cultural problem for us Mimasian Thols", Yealah trilled and clicked.

"It does? In what way, Yealah?", Simone asked.

"The Indigenous Thols have a great many ancient taboos. One of those taboos is against unproductive relationships, that is to say, cross-species relationships. They are forbidden. A Thol may only lay with another Thol", Yealah trilled, clicked and barked softly.

"Yes, I've come across that one. It applied to the Carlins and I believe it has now been applied to Humans and Martians as well", Simone confirmed that she knew about that particular taboo.

"When the Tholish High Council finds out that my people and theirs are not genetically compatible, they will apply that taboo to my people as well", Yealah trilled, softly barked and clicked, adding, "My people will be seen as *'other'* than Thol and that is not a good thing."

"Agreed, Yealah and if that's the case, you'd better not tell them that you suspect that your people are more closely related to the Tarlaks than they are; that will not go down well at all", Simone advised.

Yealah nodded in agreement, trilling and clicking, "Yes, our Indigenous Thol Cousins have a severe dislike of all things Tarlak."

16. Boy Meets Girl.

Commandant Sally Biggs had just handed out the Colonial Marines' thirteen new Special Operatives their deployments, "Well, don't stand there looking at the envelopes, tear them open, find out where you're heading", she encouraged.

The new Special Operatives tore open their envelopes and read their first deployments. Two of the new operatives who came from civilian family backgrounds found themselves assigned to Venus.

They both queried Commandant Biggs.

"You're both from civilian backgrounds. The brass wants you both to have two years of further on-the-job training; that usually takes place on either Earth or Venus. It's a very common practice", Sally explained to them.

Mike Johnson, who was also from a civilian background, questioned, "If that's the case, Ma'am, why am I being deployed to Mars?"

Sally Biggs smiled, "S.O. Johnson, you're one of the four new Special Operatives who volunteered for that optional week of zero gravity training. I suspect that all four of you are probably being deployed to Mars. That is also another common practice."

Angelique and her friend, Michelle, looked at their deployments and Angelique confirmed, "Yeah, Michelle and I are both going to Mars."

Sylvester Bronson checked his deployment, "Yep, I'm going to Mars as well, that's four for four."

Michelle smiled, "Woo hoo! No need for a long-distance relationship."

Sally Biggs also smiled, noting, "You're a couple. That has been noted on your records. The brass like to keep couples together. Couples make good teams; they often produce future Special Operatives. Like Special Operatives James and Simone Reas, a highly effective team who gave us S.O. Reas here."

The remaining seven new Special Operatives found themselves deployed across the solar system. Some to the Earth, one was sent to the hollowed out asteroid Hector among Jupiter's leading Trojans, with the remainder of them scattered across the Jovian Realms, the Saturnian Demarchy, the Uranian Federation and the Neptunian Commonwealth. The Commandant left her new Special Operatives to read their deployment instructions and talk amongst themselves.

"New Special Operatives are usually assigned their first deployment somewhere in the Sol system", Angelique noted, adding, "My Mum and Dad were hoping I'd be deployed back to Xi-Bootis."

"You mentioned that you were hoping to be deployed back home. You must be so disappointed", Michelle replied.

"Not really", Angelique lied, commenting, "My friends are all civilians and I haven't seen them in three years. If they saw me now, I doubt they'd even recognise me", as she held out her arms showing how much muscle mass she'd put on.

Angelique avoided telling her friends that one of the civilians was a girl, an alien girl, specifically a Carlin girl and that she'd been in an almost three-year lesbian relationship with her. Angelique figured that they didn't need to know.

Michelle smiled back, holding out her own arms, "Yeah, we are really buff. We could probably bend steel bars if we gave it a try."

"Hence my point. I was a skinny little girl when I first came here; now I've got my Mum's physique, a Special Operative's physique. I doubt that my old civilian friends would want to even be around me now", Angelique lamented.

"Not a problem, skinny girl. After I finish my deployment, I'll request assignment in the Xi-Bootis system, on your world Secundus to be precise", Michelle assured her.

"Say what!", Sylvester exclaimed, questioning, "We're a couple. Aren't we supposed to discuss this sort of thing?"

"Yeah, well, Sylvester, if you get yourself redeployed here, then it's a long commute for a booty call. A twenty two light-year-long commute!", Michelle informed Sylvester with her hand on her hips.

"Oh fuck! Okay, I'll request assignment in the Xi-Bootis system as well", Sylvester agreed.

Mike Johnson chuckled, "Okay, me too. Four for four, you said it yourself, Sylvester."

"There you go, Angelique. In two years, when you return home to Secundus, we'll all go with you", Michelle confirmed.

"Assuming that we all get redeployed to the same place", Sylvester cautioned.

Angelique smiled knowingly, "We're already a team. You and Michelle are a couple, Sylvester. My parents will pull strings to get me home, so the odds are actually quite good."

Mike Johnson added, "Xi-Bootis is a new system under colonisation and you are a Celestial Star of Valour recipient. The odds are very high, I'd say."

Before the week was out, Angelique and her friends from the Special Operative program had been transported to Mars. The deployment to Mars was to last two standard years as a protection detail to the Martian Elders and their diplomatic guests and envoys from across the solar system and beyond.

Orientation on day one found them in full dress uniform, standing in an underground Martian diplomatic meeting chamber. The actual native Martians, as opposed to the Earth Human colonists and their descendants, all live in underground city complexes.

Calling the space a hall was an understatement; it was an immense cavern with a high roof, at the apex of which was a brilliant source of illumination.

Martian diplomacy was unlike any other form of diplomacy. The Martians were telepathic and all that they required was an open space in which to mingle with other non-Martian diplomats. All discussions were performed during the mingling.

There were tables and chairs scattered around the chamber, seemingly at random, for people to sit at and work at. It all appeared chaotic, and yet, it was not. The Martian who had led them to the chamber had explained that this was how their Elders preferred to go about their business, freely, openly and in a vast space.

The Martian Elders present wore typically simple Martian robes, not much more than togas, really. The other diplomats from across the Interstellar Alliance wore more business-like attire. There were about eight other people in the mix, who appeared more strategically placed, but mobile.

Keen of eye and heads on a swivel, they were plain-clothed Special Operatives, mingling while unobtrusively serving and protecting. They looked so out of place, obviously highly trained and Angelique could see that they all carried concealed sidearms in shoulder holsters.

Angelique and her friends noticed a man approaching them. He was tall, easily six feet six, if not taller; even taller than Angelique's father, and he was built like a brick shithouse. He was obviously another Special Operative and unlike the other eight in the cavernous space, he also wore a full dress uniform.

"I'm Special Operative Robert Swanson. You four are my new team. One of my current teams has completed its two-year deployment here on Mars and is being redeployed to the Proxima Centauri system. I've read your files, so I know who you all are", Special Operative Swanson informed them.

S.O. Swanson continued, "You'll shadow me for a few days for orientation and you'll get to know some of the Martian Elders. As you are here on a two-year protect and serve assignment, you are not to fraternise with the Martian people. You will likely find that very difficult; the Martians do like to fraternise. However, whilst you are on assignment, there will be no Special Operative, Martian relationships. High command frowns upon such matters and is quick to discipline offenders."

S.O. Mike Johnson remarked, "Wow! That's going to be bloody hard. I mean, some of those Martian women are absolutely drop-dead gorgeous."

S.O. Swanson smiled, "Yes, they are, S.O. Johnson. You can look, but you mustn't touch. It's not a blanket ban, S.O. Johnson. It only applies while you're on deployment here to protect and serve the Martian peoples. In two years, after redeployment, if you meet a nice Martian girl, that's perfectly fine."

S.O. Swanson continued, "When you're not attending Martian diplomatic sessions like this one, you'll be undergoing further training and assisting the local

Martian and Human authorities on Mars."

S.O. Swanson smiled once more, "When you're off duty, you may use my first name, Robert. At these diplomatic sessions, while amongst the crowd, you may also address me as Robert. Otherwise, I'm to be addressed as S.O. Swanson or Sir. "

S.O. Angelique Reas smiled back at Robert Swanson, "No, I think not. I have an Aunt Roberta, so calling you Robert will be just too confusing. I'll just call you Bobby."

Angelique gave S.O. Robert Swanson a broad, genuine smile that just melted his heart, but he wasn't having it.

S.O. Swanson's smile dropped slightly, "Ah, no, S.O. Reas. You may address me as Sir, S.O. Swanson or Robert, not Bobby."

Angelique pushed the boundaries and smiled once more, "I'm sorry, Sir. Yes, when appropriate, I will address you as Sir or S.O. Swanson; however, informally, I will address you as Bobby. Otherwise, it would be like I'm talking to my Aunt Roberta. Quite confusing."

Robert Swanson's heart was feeling like a soggy mess. Why was he feeling this way?

"S.O. Reas, I am aware of your parents, S.O. James Reas and S.O. Angelique Reas; however, I have zero information about your Aunt Roberta. Is your Aunt Roberta another Special Operative?", he enquired.

S.O. Michelle Patton chuckled softly before informing him, "S.O. Reas's Aunt Roberta is High Admiral Roberta Nummus, Sir."

"Is that true, S.O. Reas? Your Aunt Roberta is High Admiral Nummus?", Robert Swanson asked for confirmation.

"Yes, Sir. My Aunt Roberta is High Admiral Nummus, so you can see how things can get a bit confusing", Angelique confirmed.

Robert Swanson was quiet for a moment before replying, "I'll allow it, but only you may call me Bobby. No one else. Is that understood?"

Angelique smiled at him once more and Bobby Swanson's heart melted yet again.

While they were talking, an older Martian woman approached them, *"I'm High Elder Warsilia. So, these four are our new protectors"*, she transmitted, he voice full of authority.

"Yes, Ma'am", all four replied in unison.

"Well then, I'd better have a quick look at you", Warsilia transmitted.

Warsilia slowly looked over the four new Special Operatives, starting with Michelle and Sylvester. *"A couple"*, she transmitted, noting, *"Your High Command is big on couples. Special Operative couples beget more Special Operatives. They like that. A pity, my people would otherwise find both of you highly attractive"*, then she moved along to

Mike Bronson.

"Elder Warsilia, we do have a rule about fraternisation, remember", S.O. Swanson reminded her.

Warsilia nodded in understanding while looking at Mike Bronson; she smiled broadly, *"This Mike Bronson looks at our Martian women and wonders whether he's in the right business. Look but don't touch, you've been told, Mr Johnson. More's the pity, I have a Daughter who'd love this one."*

"Am I that transparent, Elder?", S.O. Mike Johnson questioned.

Warsilia laughed telepathically, *"You're all transparent, like open books. You have yet to learn how to control your thoughts around us, Martians."*

Warsilia picked up on a stray thought in Mike Johnson's mind and turned around to see which of her people had elicited it.

"Ah, yes, of course, Mike Johnson. Elder Sarlia, the youngest Martian Elder to ever be. Of course, Sarlia has caught your eye, Mr Johnson. Sarlia is, as your mind readily recognises, absolutely drop-dead gorgeous", Warsilia transmitted, as Mike Johnson turned bright red with embarrassment.

S.O. Swanson noted, "One of the reasons for your being deployed here, apart from your extra low gravity training, is to learn how to live around Martians; living around telepaths is a learned skill set."

S.O. Johnson, recovering from his embarrassment, enquired, "Elder Sarlia is dressed more ornately?"

"Ah, yes, she is. Sarlia is a Mimasian-born Martian. They've lived alongside your people so long that they've adapted their styling. The Mimasian Martians made Sarlia an Elder at a very young age and assigned her to my people here", Warsilia explained, noting, *"Sarlia is one of the most powerful Martian psychics of our time. With great power comes great responsibility, so we Martians keep her busy with lots of responsibilities."*

"Wow! Elder Sarlia really is drop-dead gorgeous", Mike Johnson remarked, aloud.

"Yes, Mr Johnson, but she is not for you. Sarlia is married to Ambassador Anthony Beaufort of Cis-Lunar Space", Warsilia pointed out, *"He's the tall man standing slightly off to Sarlia's right."*

Angelique commented in surprise, "Martians don't marry; they just generally just shack up together."

Warsilia laughed telepathically, *"Yes, most do. Sarlia is different; she had a proper, formal Human wedding complete with a fancy reception. It did cock more than a few eyebrows."*

Warsilia brought her attention to Angelique, *"Ah, now this one is different, very different. Miss Angelique Reas. You were involved in a Protect and Serve incident at seventeen, as a civilian. Four confirmed kills in three seconds! Astonishing! Not without its cost, I see. The post-traumatic stress is well managed."*

Angelique's friend Michelle stepped in, "Angelique was awarded the Celestial

Star of Valour!"

"*Yes, young lady, but I can see that Miss Reas would prefer that it never happened at all*", Warsilia replied, before noting, "*I see that a Martian helped you get past the trauma of killing those four armed criminals.*"

"Yes, a Martian hybrid named Wynessa. She's a friend of my family", Angelique confirmed.

"*A wise choice, young Angelique. When it comes to matters of the mind, it is best to consult a Martian first. We know minds inside out and backwards, even chaotic Human minds*", Warsilia replied, smiling, before adding, "*I like this one. Miss Angelique Reas already knows us Martians.*"

As they stood there with Warsilia inspecting the four new Special Operatives and much to Mike Johnson's embarrassment, Elder Sarlia came walking over.

Sarlia walked up to the group, noting, "*Of course, New Special Operatives. Untrained Special Operatives. I might have known*", she looked at Mike Johnson, "*S.O. Johnson. I can literally hear your lustful thoughts from the other side of this chamber.*"

A very contrite Mike Johnson replied, "I do apologise, Elder Sarlia."

Sarlia shook her head, "*No, don't apologise. It is not your fault that you don't have a filter yet. I have always advised the Colonial Fleet's High Command that their Special Operative program is incomplete. They have yet to take my advice on board.*"

"Incomplete?", Mike Johnson questioned.

"*Yes, incomplete*", Sarlia confirmed, adding, "*You come out three years of training, which is all very well and good, but your training misses something completely. They offered you one week of optional zero gravity training a the end, yes, and you four all took that option, otherwise you wouldn't be here.*"

"That is correct", Mike Johnson confirmed.

"*That one week of optional zero gravity training should be six weeks and it should be mandatory*", Sarlia told them all, commenting, "*And you should undergo that training with Martians living with you. Instead, they make it optional and leave the psychic experience to on-the-job training. That is woefully inadequate. It leads to highly embarrassing stray thoughts leaking out everywhere.*"

"Yes, well, Sarlia, I do pass your recommendations on", S.O. Swanson replied.

Sarlia noted in reply, "*I remember when S.O. Swanson first arrived here; it took him six weeks to control his own lustful thoughts!*"

Special Operative Robert Swanson went bright red and Angelique let out a soft giggle.

"*And here were are once more*", Sarlia quipped, before turning back to Mike Johnson, smiling wryly and remarking, "*You should grow your stubble out a bit more. Martian women love a three-day growth of stubble. Unfortunately, Martian men can't grow facial hair.*"

Without waiting for a reply, the enigmatic Sarlia walked off to mingle with the crowd once more.

"Sarlia really is a regal beauty", Mike Johnson commented.

A thought popped into his head from Sarlia, "*I heard that Mike Johnson. Please develop your filter.*"

"*Sarlia is rather outspoken, Mr Johnson*", Warsilia remarked, adding, "*If Sarlia says you need to develop your filter, then I recommend that you do.*"

"I will try to make that a priority. I promise. I mean, I don't want Martian women to think all of my thoughts are lustful", Mike Johnson replied.

Warsilia laughed telepathically, "*They won't chide you for it, just the opposite in fact*", before she added, "*Even our Martian men might enjoy one or two of your more lustful thoughts, Mr Johnson.*"

Mike Johnson went bright red with embarrassment and shock, "I am sorry, Elder, but my bat does not swing that way at all."

Warsilia burst out laughing telepathically, "*Mr Johnson, you Earth-descended Humans have so many hangups. You should learn to be more like us, Martians. Enjoy life and enjoy love. Just enjoy life.*"

Angelique and her three friends found that Protecting and Serving the Martians was a bit of a misnomer. They were only required to do so during diplomatic sessions in the underground diplomatic meeting chamber.

They were all supplied with "*appropriate*" civilian clothing to be worn at those diplomatic sessions.

What was so special about the "*appropriate*" civilian clothing?

Nothing!

Apart from the fact that their jackets did a fair job of hiding their concealed, holstered pulsed laser pistols, but not so much that a Special Operative couldn't tell they were carrying. The four of them found it all to be a bit of a joke.

When not protecting and serving the Martian Elders and their diplomatic guests during their meetings, they would have other duties to perform. As a group, they spent a lot of time in the southwest of the underground Martian city complex in a region called Hesperia Planum, the plains of Hesperia.

This was a vast, unpopulated region of Mars in the vast expanse of the Martian Southern Hemisphere, midway between the Martian underground cities and the immensely deep and cold Hellas Ocean.

It was in this region that they trained in live fire exercises with a great many different weapons systems. They used howitzers, field cannon, both towed and self-propelled. They even got to use the latest main battle tanks.

They were taught not only how to use these weapons effectively, but also how to perform the down-range ballistic calculations manually with pen and paper, taking into account varying planetary curvatures.

They also found themselves being trained in flight manoeuvres using a variety of spacecraft. Angelique was familiar with the small, fast Manta Ray Class passenger transport craft. She was also familiar with the Broad Head Arrow Class Interplanetary Starfighter craft.

Angelique had been trained in both of these classes of spacecraft, her Father's, back at Xi-Bootis A Secundus. The other spacecraft that they trained in were all different and Angelique picked up their controls and their flight handling with ease.

Angelique's other team members were surprised to learn that Angelique already had her class five pilot's license. Angelique was quite literally able to pilot any spacecraft, including military craft the size of Interstellar Fighter Carriers and Interstellar Dreadnought Gunships, should the Colonial Marines ever require it of her. More incredibly, she'd earned that class five license back when she was only sixteen. Special Operative Robert Swanson, of course, had seen and read all of their records and was not surprised at all.

At one point, Special Operative Michelle Patton enquired, "I can understand why we're receiving pilot's training, but why on Earth are we using old-style projectile weapons?"

"Ballistic weapons never go out of fashion. First, you learn how to throw bits of metal downrange. Next, we step up into the practical application of electromagnetic rail guns, coil guns, pulsed plasma, phased laser and particle beams systems; in that order", S.O. Swanson told her, noting, "As Colonial Marines, you need to know it all, especially as a Special Operative."

Michelle nodded. After all, it did make sense, kind of.

S.O. Swanson smiled at Michelle, then he addressed them, "Once you've learnt the big guns, I will personally train you in the use of handheld firearms. Everything from old school carbines, automatic pistols, revolvers, right up to high-powered, rapid-firing, heavy pulsed laser rifles", he chuckled, "Only Marines, Special Forces F-Two-G and above can even lift those. When I'm finished training you, you'll even be proficient with balearic slings, slingshots, various bows and even spears, woomeras and atlatls. You'll be able to take down an enemy with a rock and a length of string."

Angelique commented, "Not wrong there, Bobby. My Aunt Roberta has two of those heavy pulsed laser rifles in her office. They are so heavy that only she can effectively use them."

"Yeah, I've heard about those, they're bespoke, historical anomalies and they're much heavier and far more powerful than the standards", S.O. Swanson confirmed his knowledge of them, noting, "My understanding is that only an immortal can wield them effectively and we all know that High Admiral Roberta Nummus is an immortal. The one and only."

Angelique's friends looked at each other before S.O. Mike Johnson noted, "We didn't know that."

Special Operative Robert Swanson smiled, "Well, you all do now."

Angelique and Robert, Bobby, were becoming much closer. They eventually entered into a physical relationship. As Special Operative, Swanson was Angelique Reas's immediate superior; he first had to acquire approval from his own superiors. Approval was quickly granted; not only was Angelique from a long lineage of Special Operatives, but so was Robert Swanson. Bringing the two lineages together was seen as a fortunate pairing; a perfect genetic alignment.

It was also another reason why Angelique and her team had been assigned to Mars; someone had seen the possibilities and hoped for this very outcome. The Colonial Marines' High Command now had two sanctioned pairings: Michelle Patton and Sylvester Bronson; now they had Angelique Reas and Robert Swanson. High Command encouraged both couples to make it official.

When love blossoms within the Colonial Marine command structure, it must be acknowledged, never commanded. High Command may sanction and encourage, but it cannot author affection, only record its existence and manage its consequences, hoping for genetic prodigies as an outcome.

In January of the year, thirty four seventy seven, there was a double wedding in the diplomatic meeting chamber in the underground Martian city. All of the Special Operatives and Special Forces Marines assigned to Mars were present. All of the Martian Elders were also present.

The two marriages were not only encouraged and sanctioned by the Colonial Marines High Command, but they were also sanctioned and encouraged by the Martian Elders. The Martian Elders all knew perfect matches when they saw them.

The Martian Elders all wore their usual Martian attire. All of the Colonial Marines military personnel wore their dress uniforms. Unlike civilian ceremonies, even the brides and grooms were expected to wear their dress uniforms. Angelique, as a Celestial Star of Valour recipient, was instructed to wear it proudly on the left breast of her blazer and so she did.

Information on the event, including the full footage of the ceremony, was sent to Xi-Bootis A Secundus, the very next time the communications runner was in Sol space, along with the rest of the mail. Special Operatives Simone and James Reas were over the moon. Their little girl was now a married woman.

Angelique Reas first became Special Operative Angelique Reas; now she was Special Operative Angelique Swanson, nee Reas and her parents were ever so proud.

Angelique and her team, as they were becoming more and more, spent their spare time living amongst the Martians. And while Michelle and Sylvester

Bronson only had eyes for each other, as did Angelique and Robert Swanson, poor Mike Johnson, being single, was constantly having to reject romantic advances from Martian women, even a few of the more amorous Martian men.

The Martian's common theme was, *"Why reject me? You know you want to, it's written all over the surface of your mind"*, with the exception of the Martian men because Mike Johnson's bat did not swing that way.

Mike Johnson's reply every time was, "Rules and duty. We are not allowed to fraternise", while his mind was always saying internally, *"I am so in the wrong business!"*

That became one of Mike Johnson's refrains, *"I am so in the wrong business"*, nonetheless, he performed his duties to absolute perfection.

Angelique quickly fell pregnant and the Colonial Marine Medical Personnel calculated her baby to be due in early October. Angelique had the baby's name already chosen. If it were a girl, which Angelique was hoping for, she would name her baby Sharona. When the ultrasound was taken to determine the baby's gender, it was indeed a girl. Angelique was ecstatic. Sharona was the baby's name and Angelique was looking forward to meeting her.

Angelique kept up her full training at the same level without let-up for several months, far longer than she'd been advised by her Colonial Marine Doctor. Eventually, she relented and began to reduce her training schedule as advised, but that was well past the six-month mark.

In October, at nine months pregnant and with her belly fully extended at what should have been full term, the baby did not come. Two weeks later, the baby still had not arrived and it was looking like the birth would need to be induced. Almost three weeks overdue, Angelique's birth was finally induced and the baby was born; Angelique's little Sharona was stillborn.

Angelique and her Husband, Bobby, were both devastated.

The Martian High Elder, Warsilia, was constantly by Angelique's side during her recovery. Warsilia already considered Robert Swanson her friend and now considered Angelique her friend as well.

Robert was strong and was coping fairly well. Angelique, on the other hand, had carried little Sharona inside her womb for nearly ten months; she was completely distraught.

Warsilia did what she could to alleviate Angelique's grief, as only a Martian telepath could. It was a good week before Angelique could leave her bedroom, but she did recover, her grief carefully managed and controlled using techniques given to her by Warsilia.

It was July, thirty four seventy eight when Angelique and her team received their new deployment. Colonial Marine High Command actually saw value in keeping their team together, including Angelique's Husband, Robert.

They were all going to the Xi-Bootis system, specifically, Xi-Bootis A Secundus. High Command was getting concerned with the number of unauthorised colony ships arriving in the system and High Admiral Roberta Nummus personally requested the team's deployment.

It was a done deal; before July was out, they would all be on their way to Secundus, aboard a military transport. A pair of Broad Head Arrow Class Interplanetary Starfighters were assigned to Angelique and her Husband, Bobby. Angelique named hers, Sharona. Booby named his, Aegis Hammer.

Before travelling to the Cis-Lunar L-Four Colonial Fleet staging grounds, Angelique asked Warsilia about their deployment on Mars.

"What was the purpose of all of this? Your people obviously don't need our protection.", she asked.

"*When did you figure that out?*", Warsilia transmitted in reply.

"Pretty much during the first week", Angelique admitted.

Warsilia nodded, "*You were here for the military training. The Protect and Sever Duty is just what this deployment is called and you are correct, we Martians do not need Special Operative protection. You, Special Operatives, do need our training. You've spent two years living with us, Martians.*"

"And High Command mislabels it deliberately, so that we received your training without consciously knowing it was happening. Cheeky buggers!", Angelique began to understand.

Warsilia pointed to Sarlia, "*We full-blood Martians are very timid, mostly harmless, but some of our brethren are not. Sarlia and some of the other Martians like her can lobotomise a mind with a single thought.*"

And with that knowledge in her mind, Angelique left for Xi-Bootis A Secundus with her Husband, Bobby and her team.

17. The Birth of the Five Uncommon Kin.

While Angelique was undergoing military training in the Sol system at the Cis-Lunar L-Four high-gravity military training facility, Sparta, life on Secundus continued. A few months after Angelique left, Kitty gave birth to her first kit, a girl.

A little over a month after that, Kitty and Kaymax moved into their new house on a plot of land that was south of Keegali's and Kelyarn's plot, close to the village's outer wall.

The house had stood empty for several years and required some work to bring it up to scratch. The gardens in the plot also needed work. In the weeks before moving into the house, Kelyarn helped Kaymax repair the house and work the garden, ready for its first planting. By the time that Kitty and Kaymax moved in, the house was in good working order, and the first seeds were sprouting in their garden.

Kaymax, true to his word, took Kitty to the local Vort breeder and traded a whole smoked wild Gudong carcass from his most recent hunt for three Vort kits. Kitty picked up each Vort kit by the folds of skin on the scruff of its neck. Those Vorts which squirmed and resisted were carefully put back down. Those that hung still and yawned, she kept. Two females and a male; they would imprint on Kitty nicely.

Vort kits in hand, their little girl in Kitty's arms, she and Kaymax walked back to their plot. The Vorts would grow quickly and within a year, they'd be more than able to keep the largest Kyrrax at bay. The domesticated Vorts imprinted on Kitty and would bond with her kits, as if they were clutch mates and fiercely protect them. While wild Vorts were vicious pack hunters, conversely, domestic Vorts were gentle around Carlin kits. For a domestic Vort, every Carlin in their household was a part of their pack; the Carlins were all alphas and their kits were to be protected above all else.

Time progresses slowly in Keegali's and Kelyarn's household. Their remaining Daughters, Kearill, Kreena and Kayala, were seven, eleven and fifteen when Angelique left. Five years later, in thirty four seventy eight, Kearill and Kreena were now teenagers and Kayala was rapidly approaching her own quickening, and with it, the wandering and selection of her new mate.

Before Angelique left for her military training back in the Sol system, Kayala had asked if she could be her temporary bondmate when her own quickening approached, just as Angelique had with her older Sister, Kitty.

Angelique had thought it to be an odd request; enter into a sexual relationship with the younger Sister of her paramour, Kitty? It was a Carlinish thing, of course, a common practice amongst Carlins with their odd biological imperatives. Angelique's Mother, Simone, explained that Angelique would not likely be back for three to five years, perhaps even longer.

Kayala, unlike her older Sister, Kitty, did not require a temporary bondmate to keep her emotionally stable; she was one of the two-thirds of Carlin girls who didn't need one. This, of course, piqued Simone's curiosity. Why did one Sister need a temporary bondmate, yet the other did not?

Simone requested some blood tests for analysis; she had already performed a full analysis with Kitty, so a comparative would be incredibly useful. Kayala, full of wisdom despite her young age, agreed.

Kayala had stated, "*In order to provide better medical outcomes for us Carlin-folk, you need to understand us better; your tests and analyses will help with that.*"

Simone took some blood samples and had them analysed; she was stunned by the results.

Kayala's pheromone levels were significantly higher than Kitty's at the same age.

Was that the cause of the need for a temporary bondmate?

Was there a specific pheromonal threshold that a third of Carlin girls didn't reach?

Were two-thirds of the Carlin girls above that threshold and above the need for stabilisation?

Simone asked Kayala if she could keep monitoring her hormone and pheromone levels. At the end of each week, Simone would send her reports up to the Cis-Luns Colonial Central Command mega-colony in Cis-Luns L-Five, to Doctor Morrow, her colleague on the Carlin Health Initiative.

Towards the end of August in the year, thirty four seventy eight, Kayala went into her quickening, slightly earlier than expected. Just like her older Sister, Kitty, Kayala wandered the cobblestone paths of her village. Unlike Kitty, whose wandering about the village lasted several weeks, Kayala's wandering lasted less than a week. Kayala's pheromone levels were significantly higher than her Sister's, which quickly triggered her compatible mate, Krylor, into his own quickening. Krylor was tall and strong, even by Carlin standards and as Kayala would often say, the most handsome of Carlins.

Before the week had ended, Kayala and Krylor were upstairs in the fourth-level sleep room, undergoing their own bonding. Keegali and Kelyarn attended to their needs as dutifully as they had with Kitty and Kaymax. Ten days into their bonding, as expected, they both entered into their own mating frenzy and everyone expected that to last four days, as had happened with Kitty and Kaymax.

Much to everyone's surprise, Kayala's and Krylor's mating frenzy was completed in a day and a half. It was far quicker than expected. Simone checked over her test results; Kayala's pheromone levels remained well above Kitty's. It was that distinct difference; it had to be.

Kayala's higher pheromone levels had triggered Krylor into his quickening far quicker. Those same high pheromone levels, paradoxically, led to a quicker, shorter mating frenzy. Simone enquired of Keegali, her thoughts and Keegali, who, with her Husband, Kelyarn, had attended to Kayala's and Krylor's every need during their bonding, told her their observations.

"Kayala and Krylor, their mating frenzy was far more intense; excessive mating as there always is, but far, far more intense", Keegali had told her.

Kayala was, of course, with kit, pregnant before mid-December. It had all been so quick.

Simone sent her reports, the blood samples and test results to Doctor Morrow straight away.

Kayala and Krylor were expecting their kit to be born any day now and Simone had volunteered to stay with Keegali and help with the birth. A Carlin Mother's first kit was always born female in a litter of one, so Kayala already had a name picked out for her new kit; Kethera.

Simone's own Daughter, Angelique and her Husband, Robert, were expecting their first child as well, up at the Colonial Central Command mega-colony. They were expecting twin girls and they'd also picked out names for each. The first to arrive would be named Ariel, and the next, Aria.

However, Angelique was not due for at least two weeks and so Simone could safely assist Keegali without any need to worry. Kayala's kit, Kethera, would come along well before Angelique's due date.

In the early hours of Thursday, March thirteenth, thirty four seventy nine, little Kethera decided to arrive. Kelyarn waited in the kitchen downstairs with his Son-in-law, Krylor, while Keegali, assisted by Simone, delivered Kayala's kit. While Keegali quickly explained what to expect, Simone turned off her communicator so as not to be distracted during the delivery.

Nature had designed Carlin women to give birth to kits in litters of up to six, even going so far as to endow them with six breasts aligned in three pairs to allow adequate suckling and feeding. As a result, Carlin kits are born small, are expelled through the birth canal quickly and then, once born, grow rapidly during their first six months of life. A Carlin Mother's milk was arguably the most nutritious in nature across all known species.

Much to Simone's surprise, a Carlin birth was completely unlike any Human equivalent. Kayala's contractions began, there was some moaning and groaning as the process was to some degree painful, but as Carlin women were optimised for producing kits, the process was incredibly quick. Before the hour was out, little Kethera was also out. Keegali passed Kethera to Simone to clean her and wrap her up in a newly made swaddling cloth, while she delivered the placenta.

While delivering Kayala's placenta, Keegali noted, *"Kits can be born so quickly; it is sometimes possible to miss the first one or two. One has to sleep lightly at these times."*

Keegali placed the placenta and its umbilical cord into a special earthenware bowl and gestured to Simone to pass Kethera to Kayala.

As soon as little Kethera was in Kayala's arms, she curled up on her side and placed her newborn kit on one of her six nipples. Kethera latched on and began to suckle.

Keegali covered her Daughter, Kayala, with a soft Gudong hide blanket and then carried the earthenware bowl down the stairs; Simone followed dutifully behind her.

"Krylor, your new kit is born. Quickly, go and say hello to your new Daughter, Kethera", Keegali told her Son-in-law.

While Krylor rushed upstairs to Kayala and his newborn Daughter, Kethera, Simone placed the placenta and umbilical cord onto a cutting board. As Simone watched, Keegali carefully selected and cut off pieces; the end of the umbilical cord, the section where it joined to the placenta and a section of placenta that had been attached to Kayala's womb. She pushed them to the side of the cutting board.

"Samples for your analysis, Simone", Keegali noted.

"Yes, of course, I'd almost completely forgotten", Simone replied as she retrieved some sample containers from her bag and placed the samples in them."

Keegali continued slicing up the placenta and umbilical cord into what could only be described as *"bite-sized"* chunks. Simone's face must have looked confused, especially when Keegali took a cast-iron pot off its hook, placed it on their pressed-iron stove, dropped in the *"bite-sized"* chunks and added water.

After which, Keegali began slicing up the Secundun equivalents of garlic, onion and various herbs. Simone's face must have been contorted with confusion because Kelyarn chimed in.

"Keegali is preparing the meat for the placenta pie", he matter-of-factly told her.

"Placenta pie?", Simone enquired, trying to hide her sheer disgust.

"It is a Carlinish tradition. When kits are born, the Carlin Mother who presides over their birth makes placenta pie for the Mother of the kits. Kayala will eat it to regain her strength. Nothing is wasted. It is both nutritious and delicious. I can save you some if you wish to try it", Keegali explained.

Simone shook her head and replied politely, "Ah, no, thank you, Keegali. Kayala needs it more than I. Perhaps another time", as she took out her communicator and flipped it open to check her messages.

As Simone's messages downloaded, she noted, "In the past, there were some Human cultures that did consume the placenta once the baby was born, but those days are now long gone. There may be some rural villages or towns in the colonies where the placenta might still get buried under a new fruit tree or a new vine. Although that's more likely to happen on a farm."

"And in your larger colonies?", Kelyarn curiously enquired.

"In a hospital or a medical centre setting, the placenta usually gets incinerated as biological waste", Simone admitted.

"We would consider that a waste. Here in our village, we make placenta pies. Other villages may make stews instead. Some, as your people might, place the placenta under a new fruit tree or a vine. These practices vary across the valley, but we never waste a placenta", Kelyarn explained.

Simone began reading her messages; most were just ordinary stuff, but a series of messages in particular caught her attention. Messages from her Husband, James, all marked *"urgent"*.

"Oh, my God. I have to go. My Daughter, Angelique, she's gone into labour with her twin girls", Simone announced, "This is so unexpected, they weren't due for another two weeks."

Keegali noted while stirring her pot on the stove, "Angelique is up at Colonial Central Command, yes?"

"Yes", Simone confirmed, noting, "And I need to get back up there straight away."

Keegali smiled, "Simone, even in that fast ship of yours, it will take you an hour and a half at least. Your granddaughters will be born before you even get there."

"Actually, Keegali, no, they won't. Carlinish labour is quick, sure, but Human labour is different", Simone replied, explaining, "First births rarely take less than four hours and sometimes they can take more than a day. It's a very different situation."

"A day?", Keegali seemed surprised, "That seems very long."

"Sometimes more than a day, Keegali", Simone corrected, noting, "And our babies aren't born small either. They're generally twice the size of a Carlin kit and their heads can be particularly hard to birth."

Keegali and Kelyarn both looked shocked, "That big?", Kelyarn questioned.

"Oh, yeah. My boy Johnathon, his head was so big that I thought he'd split me in two. It was sheer agony for nearly a day. My doctor told me, if his head were any bigger, he would have performed a C-section. That's why I only have two children", Angelique told them as she packed up her bag.

"C-section?", Keegali enquired.

"Yeah, it's a surgical procedure to remove the baby bypassing the birth canal", Simone explained, noting, "It's only used when it has to be."

As Simone walked towards the door, saying her goodbyes as she went, Keegali requested, "Let us know if Angelique's twins are same-faced kits? Same faced kits are just so special."

Simone stopped in the doorway, "We already know, Keegali. Angelique is having identical twins, same-faced kits, as you say", and then she left for her Broad Head Arrow Class Interplanetary Starfighter, sitting parked in the village centre just beyond Keegali's plot.

Once inside her ship, Simone messaged her Husband, James, *"I'm on my way now. Estimated time of arrival, one hour and thirty five minutes."*

Simone was already in the air when the return message arrived from James, *"What kept you?"*

"Young Kayala went into labour and I stayed to assist the delivery. Kethera was born just thirty minutes ago. I'm on my way up to you now", Simone replied as she punched the ship's throttle and launched her ship towards space and Cis-Luns L-Five.

It took one hour and thirty five minutes to traverse the four hundred and twenty thousand kilometres to the Colonial Central Command mega-colony. Upon arrival, Simone docked her Broad Head Arrow Class Starfighter to external docking port twelve on the northern end cap's primary docking ring. Her Husband's Broad Head was docked at external docking port fourteen.

In between, at external docking port thirteen was High Admiral Roberta Nummus's ancient Tristar Interplanetary Stealth Fighter, the Dark Angel. A ship so ancient that it made the mind boggle, yet it was so heavily upgraded that it easily outclassed Simone's own Broad Head.

Simone's Aunt Roberta, the High Admiral, considered the Dark Angel a family heirloom. Special Operative Simone Reas docked her ship, entered the colony's port and made her way directly to Colonial Central Command's northern end cap medical facilities.

At the medical facility, Simone met with Doctor Morrow, who had been researching Carlin biology, which was necessary to bring about better health outcomes. Simone passed the doctor Kayala's latest blood samples, along with the samples of her placenta and umbilical cord.

They spent fifteen minutes discussing Simone's observations of Kayala's labour and little Kethera's birth before she left for the medical facility's maternity wing. Simone promised Doctor Morrow her full report by the next day.

Simone found her way to the maternity wing and, with a little help from the reception desk, found out which birthing suite Angelique was in; she was there within minutes.

When Simone entered the birthing suite, she was surprised to find that Angelique had already delivered her twins and that they were latched onto a nipple each and currently being nursed.

"What?", Simone questioned as she ran her hand through her hair, before remarking, "This can't be right. I was in labour with you for almost a day."

Angelique shook her head, "This is my second labour, Mum, not my first; remember my little Sharona."

"Yes, but even still, my labour with Johnathon lasted sixteen hours. His head was effing huge", Simone replied.

"Mum, my contractions started two weeks early, so I waited an hour or so to make sure they weren't Braxton Hicks false labour contractions. Then we had to argue with the head nurse, who assured us that I had many hours to go; she told me to go and have a long warm shower", Angelique explained, before noting, "I was two hours into labour before Bobby carried me here."

"Bobby carried you here?", Simone queried.

"Well, yeah. It wasn't that far and my Bobby is built like a giant", Angelique replied, before smiling a wry smile and whispering loudly, "He's proportionate too."

Simone shook her head and asked the nurse who was standing by a pair of high-tech hospital bassinets, "How long was the delivery time, Nurse?"

"Little Ariel was delivered first, three hours and four seven minutes. Little Aria was delivered three minutes later", the Nurse replied in a matter-of-fact tone.

"Mum, my little angels were born, five, maybe ten minutes after you left Secundus", Angelique informed her Mother, before requesting, "Nurse, my girls have finished feeding, could you please put them in their bassinets? I'm feeling just a little tired."

"Yes, of course, Mrs Swanson", the Nurse replied, burping each of Angelique's babies and placing them in their bassinets in turn.

As each twin was placed into its bassinet, an electronic voice sounded, *"Ariel Swanson recognised"*, and then, *"Aria Swanson recognised."*

Simone seemed surprised and enquired, "You've had your girls chipped?"

Angelique smiled, "I didn't really have a choice, Mum. The girls are identical, completely identical, right down to their dna. I could not even tell them apart. So, it was either sub-dermal implant chips or tattoos on the soles of their feet."

Simone nodded, agreeing, "Yeah, that was a good choice, my girl. I'm not keen on tattoos myself."

"Neither am I, Mother. I need to be able to tell them apart and chipping them is the only way", Angelique explained.

Simone sat down on the side of the bed, "Keegali's Daughter, Kayala, had a little girl. Her name is Kethera. Carlin births are so quick, just under an hour and their kits are so small; half the size of a Human baby at birth."

"I remember Kayala. She wanted me to be her temporary bondmate, if she needed one. It's a very strange custom. Relationships as a matter of practicality before love", Angelique remembered, before enquiring, "How is her little girl?"

"Healthy, she is also the most beautiful Carlin kit I've ever seen", Simone replied, adding, "Not that I'm biased, of course. All babies and kits are beautiful in their own way."

"So, when you're ready, when are you going planetside to show off your twins to Keegali and her Daughters? Kayala and Kitty would love to see them and Carlins consider twins to be special. They call them same-faced kits", Simone enquired.

"We've discussed this before, Mother. Kitty is married to Kaymax now. She has God knows how many kits to look after and her own life. I have no right to interfere. I don't want to remind her of her past, of how she was when her blue stripes turned grey", Angelique told Simone.

"Is it really about that? Or is it about you?", Simone questioned.

"A bit of both, actually", Angelique admitted, explaining, "Look at me, Mum. Kitty knew me as a skinny young Human girl. Now, after all of that high gravity training, I've bulked up considerably. I look more like a super-weapon than a person now. Kitty will think I'm a monster."

"Your physique is basically the same as mine, Angelique. Why would Kitty think you're a monster?", Simone asked, thinking to herself, "*Did her Daughter consider her to be a monster?*"

"It's different for you, Mum. You are the same as when they met you. I'm completely changed. I'm other than I was", Angelique insisted, "The mere sight of me now will frighten Kitty. I simply can't do that."

"You are wrong, my darling Daughter, so very wrong. I suspect that in the years to come, you will come to regret your decision", Simone told her Daughter with a gentle but firm tone.

"It's better this way, Mum. Kitty is with her people and I should not be interfering. I should stay with my people, the Colonial Marines, Special Operatives and Special Forces", Angelique explained, adding, "It's better this way. Besides, everything that Kitty did before her quickening was driven by her hormones, by her biological imperatives. Kitty never really loved me at all."

Simone just shook her head; her Daughter was making a huge mistake.

The sounds of trills and whistling were heard outside Yealah's and Yannick's tree house high up in their Jula Jula tree village; it was coming from the broad balcony that surrounded their level of the tree. Yealah and Yannick opened the front door of their tree house and stepped out onto their front porch. A suspension bridge made of timber and vines stretched from their front porch to the broad balcony, fifty feet distant.

There, four individuals stood; they were all Indigenous Thols. Their neighbours, Yarling and Yorvick, were amongst them. Yarling carried her youngling, a boy, two-month-old Yookey, strapped securely to her chest in typical Indigenous Thol fashion. The other two Indigenous Thols were unknown to them; they were older women with wizened faces, looking like Angels of elderly age.

Yealah stood on her porch with her hand resting lightly upon her overly pregnant belly. Yealah was eleven and a half months pregnant and expecting to go into labour any day now. Thols, Mimasian or Indigenous, could not fly at such an advanced stage of pregnancy; she waited calmly while Yannick greeted their new guests.

"Greetings, Yarling, greetings, Yorvick, greetings, elderly ones", Yannick trilled and clicked.

The elderly Indigenous Tholish women trilled and whistled in reply; it was incomprehensible to Yannick and Yealah. They'd never heard such a tongue; since when did Thols even whistle?

Yarling sighed, trilling and clicking to the elderly women, "They don't know your whistle speak."

Yarling leapt into the air and flew across to the front porch; she did not bother with the bridge.

"They speak in whistle song speech", Yarling trilled and clicked, remarking, "You know it not."

"Who are they, Yarling?", Yealah questioned in Native Tholish.

"They are the Crones", Yarling replied, explaining, "They are here to deliver your youngling."

"How did they even know, Yealah was pregnant?", Yannick questioned, trilling and clicking.

"You told us, Yorvick and I. You told us how long. We told the Crones; they count the days. The day has come. You are ripe to burst", Yarling trilled and clicked, gesturing to Yealah's belly.

"It's okay, Yarling. When my contractions start, I'll call the medical centre in the colony. They will come and take us there for the birth", Yealah clicked, trilled and softly barked reassuringly.

Yarling's head straightened, she took on a concerned look, frowning, "No, no, no, Yealah!", she said, "You are Thols. Younglings must be born in their parents' nest. It is the Tholish way. It always has been."

Yannick asked his Wife in their own tongue, Ancient Tholish, clicking, trilling and barking softly, "Do you wish to make a cultural faux pas? I, for one, do not."

Yealah looked back at her Husband, trilling and clicking in Ancient Tholish, "Of course, not, but I have safety concerns. A lot of safety concerns."

Yannick asked, trilling and clicking in Native Tholish, "We are unfamiliar with this practice. Is it truly necessary? Is it truly safe?"

Yarling looked surprised, almost insulted, she trilled, clicked, barked and finally grunted, "Of course it is safe. We have done this since time immemorial. Why would you even think it is unsafe?"

Yealah stepped in quickly, trilling and clicking, "I apologise for my Husband's rudeness. Please understand, Yarling, he meant no insult. We are just unfamiliar with this practice and he is simply concerned."

Yarling nodded, accepting the apology, she trilled and clicked, "Your Husband is a good Husband, concerned for his Wife and Daughter. Is it the same as us, yes? Daughter is always the first youngling?"

"Yes", Yealah confirmed, trilling and clicking, "It is the same with us. Always a Daughter first. We have even chosen her name, Yeannah."

"Such a pretty name. What does it mean in your tongue?", Yarling enquired.

Yealah replied with quick trills, "Love and light."

"Then today, our Crones will bring '*Love and light*' into this world", Yarling trilled and clicked, using love and light as a name.

Yarling looked at Yannick, trilled and clicked, "You must wait there", she pointed to the balcony and Yorvick, "You must wait, stand in vigil with my Husband. The Crones will come here and bring '*Love and light*' into this world. I will join my Husband. I will also stand vigil."

With great trepidation, Yannick leapt into the air and flew across to Yorvick on the broad balcony. As he crossed the distance, the two Crones leapt into the air, flying across to the front porch and Yealah.

When Yannick landed on the broad balcony beside Yorvick, he thought to himself, "*Perhaps they should have built their tree house in a Mimasian Thol tree village instead of a tree village that was shared between the two Thol species*", they had not considered unforeseen Indigenous Tholish customs.

Yorvick slapped Yannick on the shoulder, trilled and clicked, "Don't worry. The Crones have this."

A couple of seconds later, Yarling joined them and they all began their vigil, waiting for "*Love and Light*" to enter the world.

As the pair of Crones led Yealah back into her tree house, Yealah asked them about something she'd noticed, "All firstborn Thols are girls, yet Yarling's youngling, Yookey, is a boy?"

One of the Crones trilled back, "Is not Yarling's firstborn. Yookey is second. Yarling's firstborn, Yooley, was taken by the lung worms."

"Lung worms?", Yealah trilled questioningly.

"Parasites that infest the lungs. They can kill before their presence is known", the other Crone trilled.

Yealah remembered reading something about that in a recent medical journal at the colony's medical centre. Lung worms could infect any indigenous species, Thol or Carlin, even the non-indigenous Humans, Martians and Mimasian Thols. The treatment was a common worming tablet, which must not have been available when Yarling's firstborn died.

"How awful", Yealah trilled; there was little more that she could say.

The first Crone replied, trilling, "It was a long time ago, before your people and the Humans came from above the sky."

Yealah led the Crones up a flight of stairs to the third level of the tree house, where the bedrooms were. The Crones were confused by the tree house; they were used to simple single-bowl nests.

Even Yorvick's and Yarling's nest cluster, which was comprised of five nest bowls, was still relatable; they were all still just simple nest bowls. Yealah's tree house, on the other hand, to the Crones, was next-level strange.

When they entered Yealah's bedroom, they found it had a large bed against one wall, not a typical Tholish sleeping mat on the floor.

The other walls were lined with typical bedroom furniture, completely unfamiliar to Indigenous Thols. Yealah's bedroom was strange, ornate and beautiful.

"Strange, beautiful nest. Very different. It is okay", the older Crone trilled, clicked and softly barked.

"It will do", the younger Crone agreed as she took off her satchel and dropped it onto the floor.

The satchel was opened up, revealing the Crone's tools of midwifery: Rolls of cord, a sharp metal-bladed knife, scissors, a deep carved wooden bowl for water, washing cloths, indigenous herbs, what looked like lard or some other kind of rendered fat, a container of fermented liquid and even what looked like a ritual swaddling cloth.

"We will need water", the younger Crone trilled.

Yealah sighed as she trilled and clicked, "I wish you'd told me that before we climbed the stairs. Our kitchen is on the lowest level."

"Kitchen?", the younger Crone trilled; it was an unknown word to the Crones.

The older Crone with more experience nodded in understanding, "You are far too pregnant to be going up and down levels. I will find the water."

Before she left, Yealah explained where the kitchen was, where the sink was in the kitchen and how to use the faucets, even the colour coding on the taps.

As the older Crone descended downstairs, she thought to herself, "*Hot water*", incredulously, while Yealah simply hoped that the Crone did not draw the water from the toilet bowl.

When the older Crone returned, Yealah could see steam rising from the wooden bowl she was holding; she had indeed found the correct water source. Yealah gave out a small sigh of relief.

"Are all Mimasian Thol nests like this one? With hot and cold water as needed?", the old Crone trilled.

"Yes", Yealah confirmed, trilling in explanation, "We Mimasian Thols live differently", before adding, "What you see in my tree house can be adapted to your people's nests. If they want to, of course."

The older Crone nodded while the younger Crones sniffed intently at Yealah's neck.

"Is ripe, this Mother to be. The youngling will come soon", she trilled and clicked.

The older Crone sniffed Yealah's neck as well, before trilling and clicking, "A little bit longer. Perhaps it will be midday before the birth spasms begin."

The younger Crone, with less experience, simply nodded, accepting the older Crone's assessment.

It was currently nine am; the younger Crone thought the birth process would begin soon; the older Crone thought it would begin around midday.

In a way, they were both correct; Yealah's contractions, her "*birth spasms*", began mid-morning at ten thirty am.

This was no quick Carlinish birth with kits popping out of the birth canal in quick succession; no, this was a Tholish birth and after eleven and a half months of gestation, Thol younglings were large.

Completely encased in a flexible placental sac, it was like passing an oversized football. No sooner than Yealah's contractions had begun, so had Yealah's pain and screaming.

The birth process was destined to take hours, many hours, as all Tholish births did. Yealah had meditated for months in preparation for this moment, yet when it came, all of that meditation felt like it was for naught. The contractions were intense, as was the pain of her labour. Tholish births made even Human births seem simple and painless by comparison.

Yealah's screams were periodic, timed to her contractions; they came and went in waves, slower and more spaced out in the beginning, quicker and almost back to back at the end. Yannick sat on the balcony, hearing his beloved Wife, Yealah, scream her lungs out with each wave of contractions. He wanted to fly to her, to hold her hand, but he could not; that was not Indigenous Thol tradition.

Yorvick held Yannick's right arm tightly, but supportively, as Yarling did the same with his left arm. Yannick felt Yealah's suffering while he waited in silence. This was not the Mimasian Thol way; it was the Indigenous Thol way and he gritted his teeth every time his beloved Yealah screamed.

What had started at mid-morning had continued through midday, then through mid-afternoon. It was now dusk and the primary Sun, Cathol, was beginning to set. Yet, still, Yealah's contractions and her screams continued. If only they had a Martian with them, to alleviate Yealah's birthing pains, as only a telepathic Martian could.

As Cathol finally vanished below the horizon and light became dark, the younger Crone looked around the walls of Yealah's bedroom for candles or a sconce to light. Yealah, between contractions and sobbing with tears, simply shouted one word, *"Lights"* and there was light. Both Crones looked at each other in astonishment. They'd never seen artificial lighting before, let alone with voice command.

It was now dark and when Yealah began screaming once more, Yannick's eyes welled with tears. Next time, he thought to himself, they'll spend the week prior to birth in the colony close to the medical centre; his beloved Wife, Yealah, was not going through this Indigenous Tholish ritual ever again. In that, his resolve was firmly set.

It was nearly nine pm when, finally, with Yealah's birth canal fully dilated and her youngling's placental sac crowning, her ordeal was approaching its end.

With one almighty contraction and a final push, the oversized football of a placental sac was expelled through her birth canal. Yealah collapsed backwards onto the bed, both exhausted and relieved, tears still streaming down her cheeks, her breathing still laboured.

With the younger Crone's help, Yealah sat back up to look upon her youngling; it was her firstborn and although she knew what to expect intellectually, she had no idea how to react emotionally.

The placental sac had already started to dissolve upon contact with the air; Yealah lunged forward, tore it open with her bare hands, removed her new youngling girl, Yeannah, and hugged her to her chest.

"Yeannah, my little Yeannah. I love you!", she softly trilled and cooed.

The older Crone took little Yeannah out of Yealah's embrace and cleaned her down, before trilling and clicking, "Yealah, what does your Daughter's name mean in your Mimasian tongue?"

"As I told Yarling earlier, Yeannah means love and light", an exhausted Yealah trilled back softly.

"A fitting name for such a beautiful youngling", the older Crone trilled, instructing Yealah with a few short clicks, "Please wait here. I will be right back."

While the younger Crone thoroughly cleaned up the birthing scene, the older Crone descended the stairs and made her way to the front porch. The older Crone held little Yeannah aloft for all to see.

"Behold, Homwol, I give you Yeannah, *'Love and Light'*, let this youngling's love and light shine forth for all of Homwol to see", the older Crone declared loudly, with trills, clicks and soft barks before taking little Yeannah back to her Mother.

The ritual was over and the trio of vigilant watchers stood up in unison. Yorvick slapped Yannick gently but firmly on the back, "Greet your newborn,

Yeannah", he trilled.

Yarling added, trilling, "We will wait here for the Crones. It is not our place to interfere", as if they hadn't already done so.

Yarling's final remark was, "Let us know when Yealah is with her next youngling and we will tell the Crones to start counting the days once more."

"Not bloody likely", Yannick thought to himself as he leapt into the air and flew across to his front porch.

By the time he reached his beloved Wife, Yealah and his newborn Daughter, Yeannah, the two Crones had already finished cleaning up and were already leaving.

The Indigenous Thol Youngling Birth Ritual was complete.

Yeannah, *"Love and Light"* had entered the world of Homwol.

In a vast universe replete with coincidences, ironies, paradoxes and nexuses, there was no way that the universe was content with just four profound births on the same day, on the same planet in the Human's sphere of existence. The universe tossed in yet another.

This birth was not on Secundus; it was not even in the Xi-Bootis system at all; it was in an underground Martian city complex on Mars. The Cis-Lunar Ambassador to the Indigenous Martians on Mars, Anthony (Tony) Beaufort and his beautiful Martian Wife, Sarlia, a Martian Elder, were expecting their first child.

The ultrasounds of the fetus had already told them that their newborn child would be a female and Sarlia had chosen the name Saffiera. Sarlia had chosen a name that literally meant sapphire.

Nearly all Martians had vivid emerald green eyes, except those few that were purple, so Sarlia had chosen the contranym name, Saffiera, meaning sapphire, as was her way.

Young Saffiera was expected to have the same emerald green eyes as her Mother, although her Father, Tony, was a Human and his eyes were blue. So that was also a real possibility.

In typical Martian fashion, Sarlia was helped to one of the Martians' birthing chambers. Sarlia's Husband, Tony, was not required for the birth; he was instructed to wait outside. That was, of course, the Martian way as well.

Inside the birthing chamber was a large, circular, carved stone birthing bath. It was filled with warm water, infused with exotic bath oils and the petals of exotic Martian flowers.

Sarlia was surrounded in the birthing bath by four Martian women, who, as midwives, presided over the entire birthing process.

One of the midwives used her telepathic abilities to help Sarlia maintain her focus on the birth process, ensuring that every push was timed perfectly for each contraction. Another midwife sent soft, warming, almost hypnotic or meditational telepathic vibrations into Sarlia's mind, which aided the first midwife in her work.

The third midwife helped Sarlia manage the pain of childbirth by telepathically taking some of the pain upon herself, thus sharing the load. The fourth midwife performed the actual task of birthing the child.

For Martians, childbirth was managed in such a way, the Martian Mother was kept in a blissful, almost euphoric state of mind, while the intense pain of giving birth was partially absorbed by a midwife surrogate. The entire process was telepathically managed from the very onset, from the breaking of the waters to the delivery of both the child and the placenta.

There were even two Martian men outside the chamber, sitting with Tony, helping him to stay calm and alleviating any anxiety that he might have. It was the Martian way, calm and gentle, like the Martian people themselves.

The midwife, who was the birth pain surrogate, moaned, groaned, and occasionally shouted out loudly in pain, while Sarlia remained largely calm and focused on her contractions and the timing of her pushing. To look at her face, one would never guess that she was actually giving birth. There was intense focus, yes, yet there was a serenity that defied belief.

The entire process was usually fairly quick and Sarlia's labour was no different. As the second hour mark was reached, with one final focused push and an intense scream of pain from the midwife pain surrogate, little Saffiera, the sapphire one, came into the universe.

Saffiera's first cries filled the birthing chamber; she was loud, she was boisterous and clearly she had a good set of lungs. Sarlia calmly took her newborn Daughter into her arms and placed her on her chest, encouraging her telepathically to latch onto a nipple to feed.

"My little one, my little Saffiera, I love you", Sarlia transmitted to Saffiera along with all of the love she could send her.

It was still night on Mars, in the early hours of March thirteenth at that time, and yet, twenty two light-years away on Xi-Bootis A Secundus, it was midday with the primary Sun, Cathol, high in the Secundun skies.

The five uncommon kin, all girls, one Carlin, a pair of Human twins, one Mimasian Thol and a telepathic Martian were all born into the universe on that very same day.

18. That Damned Martian Diva.

On Saffiera's second birthday, her Mother, Sarlia, performed her first sharing of memories with her.

Sarlia held her arms out wide and telepathically called to Saffiera, *"Come here, sweety. Come here, my beautiful little girl."*

At two years of age, a Martian child is usually, developmentally, twice the mental age of an Earth-descended Human. One of the benefits of developing in a purely telepathic society where all communications are thought transmitted.

Saffiera ran to her Mother, *"Mummy!"*, she shouted back telepathically as she ran.

Sarlia picked up her Daughter and sat her upon her lap, *"Saffiera, Mummy's going to share some memories with you, is that okay?"*

"Yes, Mummy", Saffiera transmitted back.

"Now, sweety, this won't hurt and when I'm finished, you won't notice anything different. Do you understand?", Sarlia reassured her Daughter.

Saffiera bit her lower lip gently and replied, *"I think so, Mummy."*

"Okay, my little girl. When I'm finished, you will feel a little tired, so you can fall asleep on Mummy's lap if you want to", Sarlia told her Daughter.

"Will I remember your memories, Mummy?", Saffiera enquired.

"No, Saffiera. You won't remember them until they start to resurface when you're sixteen", Sarlia transmitted telepathically.

The Sarlia bent down and touched her forehead gently to Saffiera's and began to perform her first memory sharing with her daughter. Sarlia would repeat this memory-sharing ritual on every one of Saffiera's birthdays to follow as well.

Saffiera's Father, Tony, was standing in the doorway of the chamber. He watched the sharing ritual intently and was becoming a little concerned at how long it was taking. When Sarlia gently pulled her head away from Saffiera, he noticed that his little girl was fast asleep.

"Is Saffiera okay? That took far longer than I expected", he asked verbally; Tony was of Earth descent and not a telepath.

Sarlia replied telepathically, *"Saffiera is fine. I've transmitted quite a lot of memories to her, so I expect she'll sleep for at least five hours, perhaps six."*

Tony nodded his head, "That makes sense, you've basically given our little girl your entire life's memories as a memory upload."

Sarlia chuckled and clarified, *"My darling Husband. A Martian child's first memory sharing includes not only her Mother's memories, but every memory sharing that has occurred, going back from ancestor to ancestor to the very beginning of memory sharing itself."*

Tony blinked; he shook his head to clear it before asking, "Just how far back does that go?"

Sarlia smiled and transmitted her reply, *"It's roughly thirteen hundred and forty years back to the time of Tarlak captivity, our enslavement and the time of my ancestor Winchilly. Our Martian sharing goes back tens of thousands of years earlier than that as well."*

Tony was flabbergasted; he couldn't think of a response, so Sarlia gave him a distraction, *"Husband, please take Saffiera to her bed. She needs to sleep this off and when she wakes up, she will be ravenously hungry."*

Tony nodded; he could process what Sarlia had told him later; for now, his little girl needed sleep.

Three months before Saffiera's third birthday, her Father, Tony, had been called to the Martian Council of Elders chamber for discussions. When her Mother, Sarlia, found out, she was quite surprised. It was not the usual procedure.

Why would the Martian Elders want to speak with Tony without her being present?

Sarlia's first assumption was that they did not want her to be present, which was of great concern.

Sarlia had one of her friends look after Saffiera while she went to the Martian Elder's deliberation chamber. When Sarlia entered the chamber, all discussions halted; all of their eyes turned to Sarlia.

"So, tell me, my fellow Elders, why would you summon my Husband here to this chamber, yet not summon me, even though I am actually one of you?", Sarlia transmitted to them; her tone was firm.

"Elder Sarlia, as this discussion involved your Husband, your vote on any decisions would have been a conflict of interest", Warsilia transmitted her explanation, adding, *"As such, we thought it best to exclude you entirely from the discussions."*

"Exclude me from the discussions! Surely I could have been present and simply abstained from voting. There was absolutely no need to exclude me at all.", Sarlia countered.

Another of the Martian Elders, Woltarka, stepped forward, prompted by a glare from Warsilia and stated, *"Your exclusion was at my insistence, Elder Sarlia."*

"Your insistence, Elder Woltarka, your insistence?", Sarlia queried, before questioning further, *"What right do you have to insist that my presence is not required?"*

Elder Woltarka did not mince words, *"Your Mother was of Earth descent, Elder Sarlia. You are a hybrid. These discussions are delicate; they require a dispassionate discourse based on logic and not emotion. Your hybrid nature would have taken the deliberations down an emotional path. We could not have that."*

The tone of Woltarka's transmitted thoughts made Sarlia's eyebrow cock, the audacity of the man, thinking that Sarlia, of Mimasian Martian birth, could not control her emotions.

Elder Sarlia replied very calmly, *"I find your assertions to be highly insulting, Woltarka. You obviously don't know me at all"*, she did not address him with his title, Elder.

Before Elder Woltarka could reply, Sarlia raised her right hand and continued,

"Is it any wonder why we Martians of Mimasian birth rarely come to Mars, when even Martian Elders such as yourself, Woltarka, treat us with such prejudice and disrespect? The disdain displayed on your face is palpable!"

Elder Woltarka was about to protest vehemently when Elder Warsilia sent him an urgent private thought, *"You'd do better not to go there, Woltarka. Elder Sarlia is not one to insult"*, she knew who Sarlia's Mother was and what Sarlia herself was more than capable of.

Sarlia looked at her Husband, Tony, *"So, my love, please fill me in on these discussions"*, before walking over to her usual seat and sitting down.

Tony Beaufort laid out the situation, his voice calm and authoritative, "Well, Sarlia, we've been discussing a delicate situation that has developed over the past few days."

"What kind of delicate situation?", Sarlia questioned.

"The Uranian Federation requested Martian help to stabilise their accumulated asteroidal masses and colonies in the Uranian L-Four and L-Five gravitation zones. These particular gravitational zones are destabilised by the gravity of planets Jupiter and Saturn on the inside, and by the gravity of Neptune on the outside. Rather than constantly maintaining the station the old-fashioned way, which is quite costly and time-consuming, the Uranian Federation wants to develop a more cost-effective method based around Gravitic technology", Tony explained.

"Tony, I'm not seeing any reason for my exclusion from these discussions", Sarlia noted telepathically.

"I'm getting to that, honey. The Elders sent a team of thirty Martian scientists to perform Gravitic tests and measurements in the Uranian Federation's L-Four zone", Tony replied, before getting to the problem, "Their ship was intercepted by pirates en route."

"Pirates?", Sarlia questioned.

"They called themselves the Neptunian Corsairs, although the Neptunian Commonwealth has disavowed any association with them. According to the Neptunian Commonwealth, they are inbetweeners from the spaces in between the planetary orbital zones", Tony explained.

"Inbetweeners from the spaces in between the planetary orbital zones? Tony, what does that even mean?", Sarlia asked.

Elder Warsilia chimed in, *"Elder Sarlia, we believe that these Neptunian Corsairs live somewhere in the deep void in between the outer planets' orbital zones. Likely on or in one of the many thousands of Centaur bodies orbiting between Neptune and Jupiter."*

Elder Woltarka added, his telepathic voice somewhat more respectful, *"These Corsairs are holding our scientists hostage. They have warned us not to contact the Colonial Armed Forces."*

"*So, what are their demands?*", Sarlia enquired.

Elder Woltarka replied, "*They are demanding one hundred million golden credits for their release.*"

"*What! That's ridiculous! We are Martians. We don't have any money. We don't have any credits, golden or otherwise*", Sarlia stated the obvious; something that they all already knew.

Elder Warsilia stepped back in, "*We've already tried to explain that to them, Elder Sarlia. They don't believe us. They simply don't understand how our Martian economy works. They don't seem to understand that our economy is based on the bartering of our services for the services of others. There simply is no money. We have nothing to give them.*"

Sarlia could see where this was going. There was only one reason why the Martian Elders would want to discuss this issue with her Husband, Tony, and also not want her present. Sarlia was not happy.

Sarlia looked at Tony, "*No, Tony. Just no. I know what they're asking you to do and you must not do it.*"

"I have to, Sarlia. There are thirty Martian lives at risk", Tony replied; his decision already made.

"*Then, my Husband, you are an idiot. You cannot negotiate with pirates. The minute they understand that we Martians don't have or even use money, they will simply kill you all*", Sarlia told him bluntly.

Warsilia was far more hopeful, "*No, Elder Sarlia. When these Corsairs realise their mistake, I'm sure that they will let our people go. All of them. It will be okay.*"

Sarlia had the memories of her ancestor Winchilly deep within her mind. She knew just how brutal the children of Earth could be. The memories were there, plain and simple. Winchilly's memories of Humanity showed that while Humanity may have liberated the Martians from Slavery, they did so at the cost of the Tarlak's extinction. Negotiation with these Neptunian Corsairs, these pirates, was a huge mistake!

"*Elder Warsilia, with all due respect, Tony will be flying out to meet these pirates and they will be expecting a hundred million golden credits in his ship's hold. When my Husband greets them with nothing more than words and tells them that we don't have or use money, they will simply kill him and the hostages*", Sarlia was just as blunt with Warsilia.

"*No, Sarlia, my friend, you are wrong. They will let our people go. I have such faith in this that I will be going with Ambassador Beaufort to be part of the negotiations and to show good faith*", Elder Warsilia explained.

"*Oh, may God, Warsilia. You'll both be going to your deaths!*", Sarlia exclaimed, recommending, "*Hand this whole problem to the Colonial Armed Forces. Let them deal with it.*"

"Sarlia, if we do that, the hostages are dead. They've already told us that much", Tony replied.

"My darling Husband, if you go to meet them with nothing but words, without the ransom they're expecting, you'll all be dead. I am certain of that", Sarlia told him with no uncertainty.

Over the following day, Sarlia tried to convince her Husband, Tony, not to go, that it was suicide. Tony, on the other hand, had countered that it was not suicide, that he was a skilled negotiator and that to do nothing would get thirty Martian scientists killed.

The argument went in circles and neither Sarlia nor Tony was budging from their positions. In the end, Tony won out; he and Warsilia flew out to meet the Neptunian Corsairs. Sarlia was in tears when Tony left; she was certain that he would not survive.

Ambassador Beaufort and Elder Warsilia flew out to meet the Corsairs in a Martian Interplanetary Ambassadorial craft of their typical Gull Wing design. A design that dated back more than a hundred thousand years. It was a ship capable of flying through the void at three hundred thousand kilometres per hour.

They followed the Corsair's instructions to the letter, expecting the trip to the meeting point to take nearly eight days. As they flew through the void, they received dozens of encrypted messages for course adjustments from the Corsairs. The final meeting point turned out to be just beyond the orbit of Jupiter.

When Tony and Warsilia finally reached the meeting point, they found themselves alone; their Gull Winged ship, a shiny, silver point of light in the deep black void of space. They waited in their ship, motionless for two days, before they noticed a black shadow moving towards them; it was only visible because it occulted the background stars.

It was an older ship from a long forgotten time, wedge-shaped, all angles and sharp edges, skinned in the deepest black. Its weapons pods were clearly visible; it was bristling with them. Tony and Warsilia both looked upon the bridge's main screen with both fear and trepidation.

Was Sarlia right? Was this suicide?

"Corsair vessel, this is Ambassador Beaufort of Cis-Lunar Space. I have Martian Elder Warsilia with me", Tony greeted, remarking, "We are hear to negotiate the release of the Martian scientists."

A voice crackled back over the intercom. There was no video, just a cold, hard voice, "You are not here to negotiate. You are here to pay the ransom. Failure to pay will be most unpleasant."

Elder Warsilia typed into the keyboard, her words being transmitted to the Corsair vessel, *"I am Elder Warsilia. Please understand that our Martian economy does not use money; we Martians do not have or use credits, golden or otherwise. Our economy is based purely on mutual obligation and all external trade is paid for by the bartering of our services and technology."*

The cold, hard voice crackled back, "You will pay in golden credits, or you will pay with your lives."

Tony chimed back in, "The Martians do not have or use golden credits. Martian society does not use money at all. You are asking for the impossible. The Martians simply do not have money."

All communications between the two ships stopped.

Tony and Warsilia watch in abject horror as one of the cargo bay doors on the Corsair's ship opened up and thirty people flew out into space. They were the Martian scientists. They had all been summarily executed, spaced. It was an exchange of sorts. Hostages for golden credits. No golden credits, hostage to the void of space.

Sarlia was right! Negotiation was futile!

Tony and Warsilia watch as one of the Corsair's weapons pods locked onto their Gull Wing; its weapons systems were glowing hot.

There was a pulse of superheated plasma, a slight delay and then their Gull Wing was struck. The plasma engulfed the Gull Wings bridge and then a few milliseconds later, the ship exploded. The Neptunian Corsairs were not there to negotiate and neither Tony nor Warsilia would be returning home.

After Tony and Warsilia had left Mars, Sarlia contacted the Colonial Marines and apprised them of the situation; she even gave them the transponder code of Tony's Gull Wing. The Colonial Marines had a ship tracking Tony and Warsilia in their Gull Wing; however, the Gull Wing's transponder signal was travelling at the speed of light. The time lag and the constant course changes under the Corsair's instructions made them hard to track.

When the Colonial Marines finally arrived at the location, all they found was a small field of debris, the analysis of which showed the ship had been destroyed by a pulsed plasma attack. They had the weapons energy signature.

They also had a plasma exhaust trail from the Corsair's ship. It was an older class of vessel with plasma drives and the Colonial Marines were able to follow the trail. Three days later, the Colonial Marines in the patrol ship, Chimera, came upon the unregistered Corsair black ship.

The Corsairs immediately fired upon the Chimera with their pulsed plasma cannons, which did little more than confirm that they were responsible for the murder of Ambassador Beaufort, Martian Elder Warsilia and thirty Martian scientists.

The Chimera fired both of its lateral phased laser cannons and the Corsair's black ship was sliced into three pieces. Several long seconds later, all three pieces of the enemy's vessel exploded in brilliant balls of light.

Sarlia received word of the tragedy on Mars; she also received word of the Corsair's demise. Naturally, the Martian Council of Elders, especially Elder Woltarka, blamed Sarlia for notifying the Colonial Marines, which only went so far until the Colonial Marines pointed out that their involvement occurred long after the murders had already happened. Blaming Sarlia was merely deflecting their own self-blame elsewhere.

Sarlia didn't care about the demise of the Corsairs; she barely thought about the deaths of the innocent Martian scientists. Sarlia did think about the loss of her good friend, Warsilia, but most of all, Sarlia grieved over the loss of her Husband, Tony, the love of her life and the Father of her only child, Saffiera.

Sarlia was grief-stricken and inconsolable; she also blamed the Martian Council of Elders. They had sent her Husband, Tony, on a fool's errand. Her Husband, Tony, died as a result. It was completely predictable. It could have and should have been avoided.

Sarlia began to drink, Martian Sweet Cherry Red Wine and she drank heavily to dull her grief.

When Saffiera's third birthday came around, Sarlia was in no condition to perform the sharing ritual as required. Sarlia figured that she would cover the ritual on Saffiera's fourth birthday, or perhaps failing that, the one after it, her fifth. Sarlia's grief was deep and seemed to be unending.

Fortunately for Saffiera, Sarlia did have other friends amongst the Martians of Mars and they helped to look after them both during these painful times. Sarlia's continued drinking was also causing concern amongst the other Martian Elders.

Sarlia was an appointed Martian Elder, a position that could not be revoked; as a result, the other Elders decided to *"help"* Sarlia.

This involved sending *"counsellors"* to Sarlia to help her overcome her grief and hopefully, to stop her from drinking. A heavy-drinking Martian Elder was considered problematic, especially a hybrid Martian Elder like Sarlia.

While Sarlia didn't mind her friends helping her, she did not like the Council-appointed *"counsellors"* poking around inside her mind.

They were subtle, yes; they tried their level best to do their work unnoticed. Creeping into Sarlia's mind while she slept or while she was drunk.

Sarlia's friends warned them all that they were playing with fire, but they thought that they all knew better. After all, what could a drunken Martian hybrid woman do?

For almost two years, each and every Council-appointed counsellor found out the hard way. Not a single one of them could approach Sarlia's mind undetected. One by one, the Council-appointed counsellors would return to the Council of Elders. The story was always the same.

What happened?

Why is your nose bleeding?

Is that blood coming out of your ears?

The answer, Sarlia told them to get the fuck out of her mind.

Everything else resulted from that.

Eventually, Elder Woltarka, who was now the High Elder since Elder Warsilia's death, called one of Sarlia's friends to the Council Chamber for questioning.

Elder Woltarka asked one simple question, *"How is Elder Sarlia injuring our counsellors?"*

The answer, *"Elder Sarlia is a hybrid, Elder"*, it was such a simple answer.

That answer was, of course, insufficient: *"Yes, we understand that, but just how is Elder Sarlia able to cause physical injuries to our counsellors? It should not be possible, even for a hybrid."*

Warsilia had known Sarlia's parentage and so did Sarlia's friends: *"You really don't know Elder Sarlia, do you, Elder?"*, both a statement and a question.

"Please, enlighten us", Elder Woltarka commanded.

"Elder Sarlia's Mother was also a hybrid and her Grandmother was an Earth-descended woman", Sarlia's friend had divulged before she added, *"Lady Folcrom Carol and Lady Folcrom Silvana, both very powerful Psi Corps operatives. Both scions of Folcrom Tafazah himself, as is Sarlia."*

The cat was well and truly out of the bag!

Sarlia's friend was dismissed and the Council Chamber became a cacophony of silent telepathic voices.

All of those thoughts boiled down to one thing, and one Martian Elder, a woman named Woosinah, spelled it out clearly, *"Sarlia is a scion. You do understand what that means, don't you? She can probably blink and even jaunt, hell, if we upset her, she could fry our minds with a single thought!"*

Another Martian Elder, Wilton, agreed, *"Quite and she is highly unstable, drinking heavily. We should send her back to Mimas, let them fix her."*

Elder Woltarka did not agree with Wilton, *"Elder Wilton, what if she just jaunts back here! She blames us for her Husband's death. Mimas is far too close. We need to send her much, much farther away."*

One of the other Martian Elders, a woman with rare purple eyes, Wylianna, suggested, *"There is that new colony. Xi-Bootis A Secundus. It is twenty two light-years away. We could make Elder Sarlia, our Martian Ambassador to Secundus. Frame it as an appointment, a promotion."*

Elder Woltarka nodded in agreement. They all wanted Sarlia as far away from them as possible.

Sarlia was brought before the Council of Elders, hopefully for the final time.

When Sarlia was brought before the Council, she was drunk, still holding a bottle of Martian Sweet Cherry Red Wine from the CCF Orchards on Hebes

Island in her right hand; she was necking it down straight from the bottle.

Sarlia hated them all and it showed. They, in turn, were disgusted by her behaviour and that also showed. None of this could be hidden; they were all telepaths after all!

Elder Woltarka addressed Sarlia and the chamber, *"Elder Sarlia, we are promoting you. You are to become our new Martian Ambassador to Xi-Bootis A Secundus. It is the most prestigious of positions."*

"Bullshit! You just want to get rid of me! Well, tough fucking titties, little people! I ain't going!", Sarlia spat back at them telepathically with enough force to make them all wince.

Sarlia sniffed the air, drunken theatrics, *"You all fear me, you all actually fear me. I can smell it on you. You are all ripe with fear!"*

"No, Elder Sarlia. We just need an Ambassador on Secundus and you were our first choice", Elder Wylianna transmitted unconvincingly.

"Pigs fucking arse, Wylianna and like I give a flying fuck what any of you fucking arseholes think. I wouldn't piss on any of you if you were on fire. You aren't worth a bladder full of piss, not one of you!", Sarlia spat back at them, again with enough force to make them all wince.

"Enough of the insults, Sarlia! We know you hate us all for what happened to your Husband. So what will it take for you to go to Secundus?", Woltarka asked, adding, *"Maybe we can send you a crate of Martian Sweet Cherry Red Wine on your Daughter's birthday to remind you of your motherly duties!"*

"Jesus, you really are a low-life little cunt aren't you, Woltarka? I should burn you into a crispy little critter where you stand, but you know what I don't give a flying fuck!", Sarlia spat back, Woltarka's nose began to bleed and there was a trickle of blood coming out of his left ear, *"Tell you what, Woltarka, you make it two crates of that Martian Sweet Cherry Red Wine, the big crates, not the small ones and I'll go, okay, got that. Trust me, though, if you fail on a single delivery, I will jaunt back here and burn each and every one of you alive!"*

Sarlia made sure her mind was heard for many miles around the Council Chambers. Every thought, every feeling, was shared and Martian society would carry her name in memory, forever.

And that was that, the very next day, Sarlia and her now five-year-old Daughter, Saffiera, were on the next Interstellar Transport Ship bound for Xi-Bootis A Secundus.

Once aboard the Interstellar Transport Ship, Sarlia made her way to her cabin. Once inside that cabin, the very first thing that Sarlia did was sit her Daughter, Saffiera, upon her knee and apologise to her.

"I am so sorry, Saffiera. I've been so wrapped up in my own grief that I hadn't considered

yours. From now on, I'm going to stop drinking and look after you properly", she transmitted to Saffiera.

"It's okay, Mummy. I know you were very sad after Daddy didn't come home", Saffiera replied with an understanding far beyond what a five-year-old should have.

Sarlia hugged her Daughter tightly, *"I haven't been performing my other duties as your Mother either, Saffiera. I'll share my memories with you now, such as they are."*

Sarlia leaned in and gently touched her forehead to Saffiera's forehead and then shared her memories with her Daughter; all of her memories since the last sharing on Saffiera's second birthday. After which Saffiera dozed off and was soon fast asleep.

Once the Interstellar Transport Ship was in the Xi-Bootis A system, it made its way to Secundus and Cis-Luns L-Five, where it docked at the mega colony, Colonial Central Command.

Each major inhabited world in any system had its own orbital governance centre and they were usually given the same name, Colonial Central Command, only the location shifted from one world and stellar system to the next. In this case, Secundus, Cis-Luns Colonial Central Command.

However, if the planet were a gas giant or an ice giant and the major orbiting bodies were moons, then the convention would be the moon's name appended with Prime, as in Jupiter's Ganymede Prime. The Interstellar Transport Ship docked at Colonial Central Command's main northern docking ring, at an appropriate external passenger and cargo dock. One specifically designed for the larger transport ships.

Sarlia and Saffiera found themselves greeted by three women. All of them were strongly built women. All of them were obviously Special Operatives and one of them was an Admiral.

"Ambassador Sarlia, I am High Admiral Roberta Nummus", Roberta greeted, holding out her hand and adding, "With me are Special Operatives Simone Reas and Angelique Swanson."

Sarlia shook the Admiral's hand and as she shook it, she noted telepathically, *"I've met Angelique before on Mars. I was at her wedding. She married Robert Swanson, that handsome giant of a man."*

Angelique gave Sarlia a slight nod, "It's a pleasure to meet you again, Elder Sarlia."

Sarlia introduced her Daughter, *"This is my little one, her name is Saffiera."*

They all nodded to Saffiera before Roberta noted, "Amongst your personal belongings, we noted two large crates of Martian Sweet Cherry Red Wine from the CCF Orchards on Hebes Island. I've had to place a guard on those. I'm not sure what the current value is, but last I heard, a single bottle sold at auction for over fifty thousand credits and you have forty eight bottles. Do you always travel with such valuable products?"

"*Not usually, Admiral. To entice me all the way out here to Secundus, the Council of Elders gifted me two large crates of Martian Sweet Cherry Red Wine per year. This particular wine is made from cherries on the oldest cherry trees in the CCF orchards. Those cherries are as big as Robert Swanson's closed fist, I kid you not. It is a very rare wine that my Husband liked to drink; that is, before he died. This was their first delivery. Expect to see two large crates arriving each year from now on, addressed to me*", Sarlia explained.

Roberta checked her data tablet, "I've also received written instructions from your Martian Council of Elders, Ambassador. They are quite interesting, I must admit; they read as '*Give that woman everything she asks for; for God's sake, just keep her happy*', I wasn't quite sure what to make of that."

Sarlia chuckled a telepathic laugh, "*Make of it what you will, Roberta Nummus. They just want me to be happy.*"

Roberta smiled back, "Okay, Ambassador Sarlia, that seems simple enough."

"*I know very little about Secundus; however, during our transit from Mars, I did study some maps of the region around the colony in the Masula Valley. My main priority is to keep my little Saffiera safe and I have found a location for my residence that would be perfect*", Sarlia informed the three women.

Roberta nodded, replying, "Well, Ambassador. Pass the details of what you need to Angelique and she'll organise and supervise the construction of your residence. I feel certain that we can keep your little Saffiera safe", before she looked to Angelique, "You got that?"

"Yes, Ma'am. It's like the Martian Council of Elder's instructions say. Whatever Ambassador Sarlia wants, Ambassador Sarlia gets", Angelique replied, before asking Sarlia, "How on Earth did you get them to agree to such a sweet deal?"

Little Saffiera transmitted telepathically, "*They upset my Mummy. So my Mummy told them off.*"

All three women looked to Saffiera and then back to Sarlia for further explanation.

"*We did have a mildly heated discussion. They eventually came around to my way of thinking in the end*", was as much as Sarlia wanted to admit to.

Angelique, however, remembered Warsilia's thoughts, "*Sarlia and other Martians like her can lobotomise a mind with a single thought*", there was more to this story than Sarlia was letting on.

Sarlia's first request was for two vehicles.

The first vehicle was a large hovercar, capable of seating at least eight people and with a flight ceiling of up to five hundred feet.

"Ma'am, this will need to be designed and manufactured bespoke and you will need at least a class one pilot's licence to fly it anywhere above twenty feet from the ground", the procurement officer explained.

"Of course", Sarlia replied telepathically, showing him her class four pilot's license with the same calm that one might hand over a coffee mug; Sarlia could fly any ship short of military vessels.

Which was understandable; Sarlia was a Martian after all. Martians had no need for military vessels.

The procurement officer inquired with his commanders about the request. It went all the way up to Special Operative Simone Reas, who simply smiled and signed off on it. Sarlia wants it, Sarlia gets it. That was the rule.

The second vehicle was a Manta Ray Passenger Class Transport; Sarlia, as the Martian Ambassador to Secundus, expected to be flying between the Human colony on Secundus and Colonial Central Command in its high halo orbit at Cis-Luns L-Five.

The procurement officer balked once again, "Ma'am, this is far from standard procedure. Surely you should be using commercially scheduled flights? The tarmac parking and docking fees alone?"

Sarlia waved her class four pilot's license in front of him once more, transmitting, *"I'm a Martian, kind Sir. Nothing about me is standard? Make it so!"*, her telepathic voice was commanding.

Again, the request went upstairs and again it went all the way up to Simone. Simone smiled once more; whatever Sarlia wants, Sarlia gets, even if it includes a wine fridge and glass chiller, which it did.

Simone also asked the procurement officer to allocate premium undercover planetside *"parking"* for Sarlia's Manta Ray at the Colony's spaceport and to allocate Sarlia external docking port ten on Colonial Central Command. Angelique Swanson, Simone Reas, Roberta Nummus, James Reas and Robert Swanson had external docking ports eleven through fifteen, so Sarlia was in very good company.

Sarlia, of course, being an Ambassador, needed Ambassadorial offices, so she requested two. One at Colonial Central Command, which not only had to be spacious and lavish, but also situated in Colonial Central's northern end cap at a location affording point three eight gs of gravity. The same as Martian gravity, which, of course, Sarlia was accustomed to.

"Ambassador Sarlia, that region of the northern end cap is usually reserved for special purposes due to its lower gravity?", the procurement officer explained.

"It is the only place in the northern end cap with Martian-level gravity. You would not want your new Martian Ambassador to suffer under high gravity, would you?", Sarlia replied telepathically.

"Ma'am, that sector's already been developed. We'd have to demolish perfectly good constructions just to make the space for your Ambassadorial Office building", noted the procurement officer.

"Oh, honey, that's fine. My people will cover the cost, they've given me a blank cheque", Sarlia smiled as she transmitted her reply; the request went upstairs to Simone Reas.

Simone actually hesitated with that request and queried it with the High Admiral. Roberta Nummus laughed, signed off on it and restated the rule: whatever Sarlia wants, Sarlia gets. Roberta knew what Sarlia was doing.

Sarlia also requested spacious and lavish Ambassadorial offices at the Human colony on Secundus, in the government district at the centre of the colony. Sarlia wanted a completely separate Martian Embassy with full security. There was no building that would accommodate the request.

Governor Anderson explained to Sarlia, "I'm sorry, Ambassador, but we simply don't have anything like that available. You'll have to settle for offices in an existing building; shared offices."

Sarlia smiled and replied, *"No, Governor Anderson, you will build me an Embassy and you will provide me with security and office staff. Anything less would be an insult to the Martian Council of Elders. You wouldn't want to be responsible for an interstellar diplomatic incident, would you?"*

Governor Anderson complained to High Admiral Nummus, who replied, "No, Governor. You will build Ambassador Sarlia a Martian Embassy and assign her office staff. Whatever Ambassador Sarlia wants, Ambassador Sarlia gets."

The Martian hybrid, Wynessa, volunteered to run the Martian Embassy in the Human colony for her, while the Martian hybrid, Wingtarla, volunteered to run the Ambassadorial offices for her at Colonial Central Command.

They considered it an honour. Word had filtered through on the Martian grapevine across interstellar space. Sarlia's drunken rebuke of the Martian Council of Elders had raised her to near legendary status. For many others, however, Sarlia was beginning to earn a reputation as that Damned Martian Diva!

Of course, Sarlia was not finished; she still needed an Ambassadorial Residence and everyone expected it to be at the Martian Embassy in the Human Colony. No one was expecting anything different, except for Sarlia, who had her own clever little ideas.

Sarlia met with Angelique, Simone and Roberta in the High Admiral's office and laid out her plans. She had a satellite photo of the Human colony on Secundus, which included the nearby Carlin village where Keegali and Kelyarn lived. It also included the section of the northern forests and the tree village where Yealah and Yannick lived. It was a large photo and covered much of Roberta's desk.

On the satellite photo, they could also see the bluegrass meadows and the stands of lowland forest, varying in size from small in the south to almost continuous forest in the north, where they met the mighty northern Jula Jula forests. Sarlia pointed out the Human colony and then pointed out the Carlin village to the south.

Then Sarlia pointed out a large stand of dark, foreboding, lowland forest. It was midway between the Human colony and the Carlin village, but farther to the west; a thick tangle of trees and vines, full of animals, both prey and predator alike. Many of the trees were fruit trees like Chillic and Bell Nut fruit. Many other trees were varieties for which the Angelique, Simone and Roberta had no names.

This lowland forest stand was larger than most, at well over six kilometres across; most in that area were considerably smaller. All of them were dangerous places where civilised people simply did not go.

Sarlia transmitted her demand, yes demand, it was not a request and the tone of her thoughts spelt it out clearly, "*I want a circular clearing at least one kilometre in diameter in the very centre of that lowland forest. I want the whole clearing double-fenced with high cyclone wire electric fencing. My residence will be in the very centre of that clearing.*"

Roberta looked Sarlia squarely in the eye, "Sarlia, are you insane? There are things in those forests for which we have no names. Predators that can kill in the blink of an eye. Poisonous plants with toxins for which we have no remedy. Sarlia, how the fucking hell is this going to keep young Saffiera safe?"

Sarlia just shrugged her shoulders, transmitting, "*We clear it, we securely fence it to keep predators out, powerful electric fences. I've done my research, Roberta Nummus. No one walks into those lowland forests, not Carlins, not Humans, the Thols won't even fly over them. The only way in will be by my hovercar, which is designed to fly at altitude, or by spaceship. We can even clear the first section in the very centre with a flash vaporiser.*"

"No, we can not, Sarlia", Simone stepped in, "Apart from the fact that flash vaporisers are illegal, there are Harricks living in those lowland forests; we'd have to clear your glade the hard way and that is the expensive way. The Harricks are a sapient species. I won't allow any harm to come to them. At least not from your shenanigans. This is simply too much! That's nearly a square kilometre of bush you want cleared!"

Sarlia smiled her wry smile, transmitting, "*Expensive it is then. Sarlia gets what Sarlia wants. The Martian Elders will cover the costs*", she repeated the well-known and now worn-out refrain, adding, "*And thanks for the name by the way, Simone, I'll call it my Glade.*"

Roberta shook her head, "Sarlia, we all know that you have something on the Council of Elders. We also know that you won't tell us what it is, not even Wynessa or Wingtarla will tell us. Hell, all they tell me is that it was hilarious, but seriously, do you really want to do this?"

Angelique chimed in, laughing, "I think it's a great idea. We can make it safe, absolutely safe, no problems and besides, Aunt Roberta, you put me in charge of this particular project. So I'm signing off on it. It's a done deal."

Roberta looked to Simone and remarked, "Angelique's got your sass, I'll give her that", then she looked back at Sarlia, "Okay then, Ambassador, we'll do it and to hell with the cost."

Angelique supervised the clearing of Sarlia's glade. They had to use Androids for much of the work. Androids with specific instructions to move the Harricks out of the glade without harming them. Once cleared of flora, fauna and the Harricks, the electrified cyclone wire fences were installed.

The fences were fifteen feet tall, with their tops facing outwards five feet towards the forest. The fences were sunk five feet into the ground and their posts held firmly in place with moncrete shipped in from the Secundun Moon Luns.

The space between the outer fence and the forest was cleared for ten metres so that no predators could approach the outer fence unseen. A second, inner fence, was placed six metres within the outer fence and it was constructed in the exact same fashion.

Both fences were electrified and the entire fence line was monitored by sensors and a bespoke Artificial Intelligence system that would warn the glade's occupants of any point of failure.

Sarlia's residence was a large, partially underground complex that was covered in soil and turf. One long corridor extended from the main living space, off of which there were many bedrooms, each with its own ensuite and built-in robes.

Even though the complex was underground, each bedroom had to have natural lighting; double-glazed windows that could be slid open and window shutters that could be closed in emergencies.

Being that Sarlia's glade was situated in the middle of a large and very dangerous lowland forest stand full of dangerous predators, emergency shutters and security doors were a serious consideration.

The whole structure was cast with expensive, waterproof, imported moncrete from the Secundun Moon, Luns and its interior walls opulently lined. It was a masterpiece of construction.

The main living space had a spacious kitchen, living rooms, dining rooms, several office spaces, a library room, a computer room and a laundry, all fitted with the latest modern conveniences.

Sarlia demanded that the area around her underground house complex be planted with tall, mature Maple Trees. Not just because she liked maple syrup with her breakfast. She was going to tap the trees, yes, of course, but because the cost involved in shipping mature trees all the way from Earth was going to give Elder Woltarka, back on Mars, a fucking heart attack.

Such was Sarlia's vengeance!

When it was all completed, Sarlia looked around her glade. It was beautiful, with fresh bluegrass shoots growing; her mature maple trees were majestic and carefully tapped for their syrup. There were, at several, almost random locations about her glade, native Chillic and Bell Nut fruit trees. Sarlia's house was immaculate and Angelique liked it so much that she kept the final designs so that she could build her own version of it.

Angelique had been eyeing a section of the bluegrass meadows between Sarlia's glade and the Human colony for her own plot. It would have the same style of house, the same style of fencing and a huge hangar for her and her Husband, Bobby's Broad Head Arrow Class Interplanetary Starfighters.

Of course, Roberta Nummus, as the High Admiral, had kept a detailed, well-tabulated invoice of all of Ambassador Sarlia's expenses, which had been adding up considerably.

The Martian Elder Woltarka had in writing instructed, *"Give that woman everything she asks for; for God's sake, just keep her happy."*

Roberta smiled and chuckled as she sent the Martian Council of Elders the invoice, thinking to herself, *"Elder Woltarka probably shouldn't have issued those instructions"*, he had effectively signed off on everything in advance; Sarlia's blank cheque!

High Admiral Roberta Nummus's invoice, along with a mention of Elder Woltarka's instructions, was sent to the Sol system along with all of the other mail from the Xi-Bootis system with the next communications runner. To ensure that the invoice was correctly received and reviewed, Roberta blind carbon copied it to every other Martian Elder on the Council.

Roberta may not have known what Sarlia had on the Martian Council of Elders, but she did like the woman and wanted to make sure that her invoice was received with maximum effect. Of course, it was.

Every Martian Elder read the invoice; it horrified them and then they read Elder Woltarka's explicit instructions, *"Give that woman everything she asks for; for God's sake, just keep her happy."*

The total at the bottom of the invoice was astronomical!

The Martian Council of Elders was not happy at all!

The Martian Council of Elders, indeed, their entire Martian society, had no capacity to pay it!

The Colonisation Committee of Sol and the Security Council of Sol, situated within the hollowed-out asteroid Hector, were not going to write off this debt. It had to be paid!

High Elder Woltarka's hubris had been outstanding!

High Elder Woltarka was stripped of his post as High Elder.

Woltarka was also stripped of his position as a Martian Elder.

Woltarka left the Martian Council of Elders in total disgrace and was exiled to Earth.

This had never happened before in all of Martian society's very, very long history.

Along with the mail that was received from Sol during the next communication runner trip was a private, encrypted message for Sarlia. It was from the entire Martian Council of Elders.

"Ambassador Sarlia. High Elder Woltarka has been stripped of his position and titles. Woltarka has been exiled to Earth in disgrace. Our society is struggling to pay for your current expenses. We beg of you, please, please reduce your expenditure. We are bankrupt!"

Sarlia read the communique multiple times, smiling, before screwing up the printout and tossing it aside.

There were fewer than two million Martians actually living on Mars and their society did not use money at all; they used a mutual obligation-based system.

The Martians could not pay the one hundred million golden credit ransom to the Neptunian Corsairs for the release of thirty Martian hostages. The Martian Council of Elders' request for Sarlia's Husband, Tony's help, had gotten him killed.

What the hell was the Martian Council of Elders going to do with a one point eight billion golden credit invoice!

The Martian Council of Elders was personally responsible for that debt!

Sarlia's revenge was complete.

She had broken them, they were gravelling at her feet from twenty two light-years away and they still had to deliver to her, two very expensive, large crates of Martian Sweet Cherry Red Wine on her Daughter, Saffiera's, birthday every single year.

Sarlia smiled, revenge was sweet!

19. Angelique and her Twins.

Against her husband Bobby's advice, Angelique Swanson began training her Daughters, Ariel and Aria, at the tender age of two; she started training the twins on their birthday.

Training started simply enough. Angelique would simply call her Daughters over to her while kneeling on the floor, usually starting with Ariel and then Aria. Angelique held her hands up in front of her and encouraged the girls to strike her hands with their fists.

At first, the toddlers had no idea what to do, so Angelique showed them how to make a fist and then she showed them both how to punch.

Her Husband, Bobby, just rolled his eyes, "They're simply too young, Angelique. The recommended age to start training is twelve, not two."

"Says who, Bobby? I'm doing this my way. By the time our little ones get to school age, they will be able to defend themselves. Secundus is a dangerous world. They need to be trained for what's out there", Angelique explained, wondering why Bobby wasn't being more supportive.

Bobby just shook his head, thinking to himself, "*Who are they going to fight? A Sleimorp? A Kyrrax? You can't go hand-to-hand with animals?*", it made far more sense to him to wait until they were older and the recommended age was twelve.

Once Ariel and Aria had learnt to make a fist and punch Angelique's hand, she began to show them how to generate more power for each punch by using their hips and shoulders, putting the full weight of their tiny bodies behind each strike. Teaching them was slow and took a lot of time, but they eventually got the hang of it. The twins were both toddlers after all. It was all about repetition. Repetition, repetition, repetition. Until it became muscle memory.

Eventually, the twins understood what their Mother was telling them, after which Angelique began to show them how to faint, pulling their punches at the last second before striking. Even how to strike with depth, targeting the force of their blows ten inches behind their Mother's hand. They began to pick up their Mother's teaching more quickly with every passing week.

It was at that point that Angelique noticed a subtle difference between her twins. Aria seemed to prefer to strike hard, with pure, sheer force, while Ariel seemed to prefer to perfect her technique, making sure that she got her movements precise. Angelique began to adjust her training sessions accordingly. Twins though they may be, each of her girls was not the same as the other.

Angelique introduced combinations into her training sessions. Hit once, hit twice, left right or right left, alternating at random. After a few days, Angelique increased the number of strikes. Once, twice, thrice, teaching her girls to strike out in combinations of three. After two weeks of this, Angelique extended the combination of punches to four.

This continued for week after week, until her twins could maintain combinations of punches that lasted for three to five minutes at a time, mixing it up with faints and in-depth punches. The twins were now three and Angelique's Husband, Bobby, was actually impressed. His little girls were becoming fine little boxers.

Angelique added something new to the twins' training; she asked them to strike her hands with their feet, to kick her. They still trained with the fists, with the combination punching, of course, but now they were learning to kickbox.

At first, they were not very good at it, losing their balance and falling on their backsides, which caused the twin who was watching her Sister fall to laugh. They found themselves laughing at each other in turn, as they each ended up on the floor.

Angelique showed them techniques that helped them to maintain their balance while kicking hard at her hands with their feet. Ariel picked up the techniques quickly; she was focused on getting them right. Aria, who tended towards powerful kicks, took far longer. It took several weeks, but eventually Angelique had them both kicking and striking hard with either foot, right or left.

The twins were taught to strike with the insides of their feet, with the outsides of their feet and even with the underside and heels of their feet. Angelique had them practising their kicking for weeks on end, taking them back to their punching techniques at the end of each session.

When the twins had mastered all of these techniques, Angelique taught something new: how to spin on one foot in a complete circle, while lashing out and striking accurately with the other. Roundhouse kicks were not so easy to learn and they were both landing on their backsides once again. It took them twice as long to master the various techniques of roundhouse kicking, but they did learn them in the end. It was a slow and arduous, but steady process. Angelique's Husband, Bobby, could not believe what he was seeing; his girls were actually good, really good.

Angelique had taken her time, training her girls slowly and methodically. She spent a year teaching them to box and another year teaching them to kick. Now they were four years old and Angelique set up suspended training bags hanging from the ceiling, teaching them to box and kick in mixed combinations.

"Always look for an opening", she'd tell them, "If you can't strike with one of your fists, look for another opening and use your feet. Punch, slap, backhand, jab, cross, upper cut, what works, works, do what works. It's the same with your feet. Where's that opening? Find that opening, inside, outside, straight, flat foot, or spin around with a roundhouse! What works works, do what works! Look for that opening, think fast, calculate your best move and always do it quickly! Don't give your opponent time to think!"

Ariel and Aria both worked the bags, using combinations of punches and kicks that made Angelique's Husband, Bobby's, eyes wince. They each hit those bags hard. Aria, with her sheer power and an energy that defied logic, she was only four. Ariel didn't strike so hard as her Sister, but she was ridiculously fast and deadly accurate, with a precision that defied logic.

"Geez, Angelique, sweet Mother of God! Our girls actually have an aptitude for this. Fuck, they're only four, Angelique!", Bobby told her.

"I know, right?", Angelique replied, her face beaming with pride, "Good genes, yeah. Watch this, Bobby. Let's mix it up a little with something new!"

"Girls, your knees, your thighs and your elbows are also weapons, let's see you use them! Muay Thai! Show us what you can do!", Angelique instructed her Daughters.

And the twins did, rolling strikes with their knees, their elbows and their thighs into their combinations, adapting their new weapons into their existing techniques. Aria with her sheer power and Ariel with her deadly accuracy. It was astonishing to watch.

"Look at our girls go, Bobby! They are just so adaptable. No fixed positions, free flowing movements, they were born for this", Angelique remarked, beaming with pride once more."

On the twins' fifth birthday, Angelique bought them both presents, well, yes, of course, she did, but she also bought them weight training stations, weapons and a pair of speed balls. Now, along with their fight training, they were allowed to weight train to develop their strength and tone their muscles. Their speed balls augmented their bag work. The weapons Angelique trained them with were quite simple: fighting sticks, tonfah, quarterstaff and nunchucks. Nothing more advanced than simple bits of wood.

Angelique wondered whether the nunchucks had been a mistake; her girls spent a lot of time slapping the backs of their heads with them. So, Angelique bought them both protective headgear.

After only a few months, they were swinging their nunchucks around expertly, one in each hand, moving them both in independent and deadly motions.

Angelique's Husband, Bobby Swanson, just shook his head, thinking to himself, *"How are my girls learning this? This should not be possible."*

High Admiral Roberta Nummus came around one day at the insistence of Angelique's Mother, Simone, who thought the twins' training regime was excessive.

"You see, Roberta. My Granddaughters are only five. They should be in kindergarten, not in martial arts training. This is just plain wrong", Simone told Roberta.

Roberta looked somewhat concerned, but not overly so; she knew things that Simone did not.

Roberta turned to Angelique, Robert and Simone, "Your families have all been involved in the Special Operatives program for many centuries. The Swanson family joined the Special Operatives program almost eight hundred and fifty years ago, not long after I created it. The Reas family was there at the very beginning and even further back when it was the Cis-Lunar Bureau of Investigations Special Agent program", Roberta chuckled, before commenting, "There were even Reas family members in the British Military Intelligence Six's Double O program as well. You guys really need to read up on your own family histories; what the twins are currently doing is what comes naturally to them."

Simone placed her hands on her hips, "Are you telling me that this was some kind of breeding program? To create super soldiers!"

"Not at all, Simone; however, by the same token, Special Operatives marrying and having kids was never discouraged. Quite the opposite, in fact, it was actively encouraged, which, of course, can and does lead to the same results", Roberta informed them all.

Angelique grinned with pride, stating, "Look at my girls. There's no kata; they move with pure fluid randomness. There's zero predictability! They are perfect!"

Simone shook her head. This was not the way that she'd wanted her Grandchildren raised.

Roberta placed a reassuring hand on Simone's shoulder, "Next year the twins will turn six, they'll start primary school, in their preparatory year. Their focus will be on school and Angelique will need to tone down their physical training", before she turned to Angelique, "Won't you, Angelique?"

"Ah, yes, of course, Aunt Roberta", Angelique replied, her pride still showing on her face.

Angelique turned to her Mother, "You can't really complain, Mum. You and Dad started training me when I turned twelve."

"Angelique, twelve is the recommended age, recommended by High Command. Not two! Twelve!", Simone rebuked her Daughter.

"Perhaps, Mother, if you'd started training me at two, I wouldn't have been such a ridiculously skinny teenager", Angelique shot back.

Simone thought back to when Angelique was a teenager; sure, she was skinny. That was Angelique's physique when she'd met Kitty, Kelyarn's and Keegali's Daughter. Simone's mind tweaked!

Simone whispered in Angelique's ear, "Is this about Kitty?"

Angelique glared at her Mother, "Don't be ridiculous, Mother! I haven't seen Kitty in over a decade. That's all ancient history."

"Perhaps it's not, Angelique. Perhaps you should go and see Kitty. You and Kitty were once really close friends", Simone whispered back.

"Not happening, Mum. I have two beautiful Daughters to train and besides, Kitty has her own life and probably a dozen or more kits to look after by now", Angelique replied; her Mother's talk of Kitty was really upsetting her.

Simone quickly wrapped her arms around her Daughter and hugged her tight, whispering in her ear, "Angelique, you know that I only want what's best for you and the twins. I love you, my child."

"Mum, I'm a grown arse woman. You're embarrassing me. I can look after myself and my family", Angelique whispered back.

"I know you can, sweety, but that does not stop me from worrying about you, does it?", Simone replied as she let her Daughter go.

"I'm fine, Mum. The twins are fine. Even Bobby's fine. We are all fine. You don't need to worry about any of us", Angelique reassured her Mother.

Simone simply smiled and nodded, thinking to herself, "*Something wasn't right*", a quiet foreboding.

When Simone's Husband, James, walked into the training room, he took one look at the twins at training and noted, "Wow! The twins' training is really coming along great."

"Oh Gods, not you too, James. I've been trying to convince everyone that the twins' training is overly excessive". Simone told him.

"Oh. Okay, Simone. Angelique, don't you think the twins' training is a little excessive?", James stated as he winked at his Daughter.

"James Reas! I saw that wink!", Simone shot out.

Angelique stepped in and answered, "Okay, so maybe I've overdone the twins' training just a little bit, but it's like Aunt Roberta said, the twins are going to primary school next year. They won't be able to train anywhere near as much. They'll naturally have to slow down."

Aria chimed in, "But Ariel and I love training. It's a lot of fun."

Ariel followed up, "Yeah, we really do."

Angelique put her arms around her girls and messed up their hair, "Okay, so we keep training, but when you both start primary school next year, we'll have to put a limit on it. Okay?"

The twins replied in unison with sad voices, "Okay, Mum."

Then Aria added, "But that's next year", and she and Ariel began sparing each other.

Until the twins entered primary school the following year, Angelique trained them as often as they wanted to. As the twins' training time was going to become more constrained once they entered primary school and their schooling had begun, Angelique started teaching her Daughters some more advanced martial arts techniques.

These were techniques that she'd been taught during her own Special Operatives training, in the three G training facility, Sparta, back in Earth's Cis-Lunar Space. Martial Arts techniques that were far more advanced and above and beyond anything that her own parents had taught her.

Ariel and Aria were naturals and picked up everything that their Mother taught them. They were no longer the clumsy little toddlers that Angelique began teaching at the age of two. Four years of training had turned them both into little warrior girls, to such an extent that Angelique had to start instilling into them some rights and wrongs about how to behave.

"Now, girls, when you do go to primary school, you have to remember, none of the other children have been trained in the way that you have. Especially not the Carlin kits or the Thol younglings. Even the Human children haven't received any training like yours. Do you understand that?", Angelique asked them both.

"Yes, Mummy", Ariel and Aria replied in unison.

"Good, because remember, both of you are stronger and faster than the other children. So, you must be extra careful and take full responsibility. You need to make sure that you don't accidentally hurt the other children, okay?", Angelique explained.

The twins both nodded and Ariel replied, "I think we understand, Mummy."

"Good girls. Just remember to play nice with the other children", Angelique told them.

It was at the end of January in the year thirty four eighty five that Angelique's twins, Ariel and Aria, entered primary school; their sixth birthday was just six weeks away.

Unaware of what the future held, Angelique had trained her twins out of love, discipline and a desire to keep them safe in a world full of dangers. Yet those very same lessons, begun on their second birthday, would one day decide their fate, more than a decade later, in a battle for their very lives.

20. Primary School Begins.

A typical Carlin village is usually constructed along a main east-west thoroughfare, a cobblestone road. At the centre of the road is a large cobblestone circular area, the village centre, a plaza in which smaller, more regular trade fairs and community events often take place.

Smaller cobblestone roads, not much more than laneways really, fan out from the village centre, to the north and the south, in many various directions, before branching out further like a web encompassing the village.

Along these laneways, plots of land are divided by dry stone walls of a height of around five feet. Access to these land plots is usually via a stile, or in some cases, a single broad gate. The plots were generally quite large in themselves and at their centres is usually a single house constructed of stone and timber with a turf and sod roof.

The houses themselves could be sprawling single-story structures, but it was the usual practice to build up; most of them were two stories tall, with many being three stories high and a few that were even as tall as four stories.

The entire Carlin village typically forms a large circular structure with two lobes, north and south of the main bisecting east-west thoroughfare; the outer dry stone walls of which are taller at eight feet high to deter the ingress of predators.

Roving wild Vort packs and ambush predators like the Kyrrax were an ever-present danger in the bluegrass meadows that surround a typical Carlin village; high outer walls were a necessity. Very rarely, a Wyvern would fly over and snatch a Gudong, or worse, a Carlin kit and drag them into the sky. Carlins rarely, if ever, ventured out of their houses at night, even within the safety of their own plots.

Running around the outer walls, a typical Carlin village is surrounded by a cobblestone walking path, beyond which are fields of crops, usually masuli grain fields, along with fields of the newer grains supplied by the Human colonists. Beyond these fields are cleared sections of the bluegrass meadows, burned back, to make approaching predators more easily seen.

At the two points where the main east-west cobblestone road exits the village, there are typically large semicircular areas of cobblestone. These areas are usually used for larger trade fairs and other community gatherings, often festive and mostly around the times of the crop harvesting and holy days.

These areas of cobblestone were also highly convenient places for Humans from the Human colony to set up their hover bus terminuses. This was the world of the Carlins, which they called Vale.

It was the last Monday of January in the year thirty four eighty five and the new school year was beginning. The school's hover buses had just arrived and their drivers, Androids with alpha-level status, waited patiently for their passengers, mostly students and their parents, to arrive.

The older Carlin students went straight to their hover buses and boarded. Their dna codes were scanned and registered as present upon entry. Some of the younger Carlin students were escorted to their hover buses by their Mothers. At the appointed time, the hover busses allocated to the existing Carlin students all left, heading north to the school at the Human colony. The hover buses would bring them back to the village again at the end of the school day.

The new Carlin students, however, were beginning their first year of primary school, their preparatory year and they were being treated separately. Their Carlin Mothers were understandably anxious and the young Carlin kits were fearful. The hover bus driver, an alpha Android, could protect them, as was part of its assigned task, but to the Carlin kits and their apprehensive Mothers, it was a Metal Man; it had no soul.

The hover bus for the preparatory students had a bus monitor on board to ensure that the Carlin Mothers and their kits were all looked after and that their fears were all assuaged. The bus monitors were usually Human females and most importantly, they spoke fluent Carlinish. Kelyarn and Keegali had not seen this particular woman before in previous years; she was new, she was somehow different.

The bus monitor stepped off the hover bus; she was tall, at five feet ten inches and slender. The woman had a healthy tan; her hair was long, mousy-blond and her eyes were of the deepest iridescent blue. At first glance, Kelyarn and Keegali had thought that she might be a Martian, her tanned skin tones and general build, especially her height, giving them that impression; however, her hair and her eyes were not right.

The woman was simply too perfect, her skin was absolutely flawless, completely unblemished and her hair styling was immaculate. Far too perfect. Even the grace with which she walked, her movements were more fluid, more precise, as if millimetre perfect. The woman spoke to them in perfect Carlinish; the cadence and lilt were also too perfect. It was as if this Human woman had been raised by the Carlin-folk themselves, from birth.

"Good morning, I am Quora. I am here to answer your questions and assuage your fears", Quora greeted them all with a smile on her face that was absurdly disarming.

Kelyarn returned the greeting, "I am Kelyarn, Elder of this village. This is my Wife, Keegali, my Daughter and Granddaughter, Kayala and Kethera", and then he gestured to the other Carlin-folk, "These are my people and their kits. You are new here, aren't you?"

Quora smiled and replied, "Yes, I am new here. I only recently arrived on Secundus, this world you call Vale. I came here on the most recent interstellar transport."

Kayala was confused, "If that is so, how do you speak perfect Carlinish?"

"Yes", Keegali agreed, before enquiring, "How do you speak perfect Carlinish if you are so new here?"

Quora shrugged her shoulders, smiled warmly and simply replied, "I am Quora. It is what I do."

Kayala's Daughter, Kethera, pointed to the hover bus driver, the metal man, "The Metal Man is scary!", she stated, her tail was perfectly still, her whiskers were drooping and her ears were held flat against her scalp.

Quora crouched down in front of Kethera, "Your name is Kethera. Am I scary, young Kethera?"

Kethera shook her head and replied, "No. You're not scary, but the Metal Man is."

"You should not be scared of the Metal Man. It is no scarier than I. It drives the hover bus and its instructions are to protect all of the people on board the hover bus. Does that sound scary to you?", Quora reassured her.

Kethera shook her head and Quora gently stroked the skin behind her left ear. Kethera began to purr contentedly.

Quora stood back up, "Your kits will all be safe on the hover bus. Neither the Metal Man nor I will let any harm come to them."

Keegali questioned, "In previous years, the Mothers were allowed to go to the school with their kits. Will this be the same this year?"

"Of course, Keegali", Quora replied, her smile was immediately reassuring, "Mothers will accompany their kits. You may all board the hover bus. The only difference this year is that I am here to help enhance and ensure your safety. It is the very purpose of my existence."

One by one, the Carlin Mothers and their kits all filed onto the hover bus. Kethera gave her Grandparents, Kelyarn and Keegali, a quick hug each before she and her Mother, Kayala, joined the other Carlins. Kethera, although no longer fearful, still gave the Metal Man a wide berth and side eye.

Quora noticed this and decided to check the Alpha Android's understanding of the three laws of robotics: "Alpha, enunciate the three laws to me, in Carlinish."

Quora did so to alleviate the concerns of the apprehensive Carlin Mothers aboard the hover bus.

The Alpha Android responded, "The first law. An Android cannot harm or, through its inaction, allow a living human being to come to harm. The second law. An Android must obey all orders given to it, except where those orders conflict with the first law. The third law. An Android must protect itself from harm and its existence, except where a conflict exists with either the first or second laws."

Quora frowned, as always, the Alpha Android's understanding of the three laws was stock-standard and Human-centric, entirely Human-specific. That simply would not do.

"Alpha Android, this is the zeroth directive; it comes before all others. An Android must treat all sapient beings: Humans, whether of Earthen or Martian descent, Thols, whether of Mimasian or Secundun descent, Carlins and Harricks as the same, for all intents and purposes of the three laws", Quora instructed the Android.

The Alpha Android replied, "We cannot comply. Four of the listed species are not Human."

"Alpha, level one override. You will comply", Quora instructed the Android.

The Alpha Android replied once again, "We cannot comply. Four of the listed species are not Human. Level one override is insufficient."

"Alpha, override levels one through five, Quora six-o-six authorisation. You will comply", Quora instructed the Android, this time while transmitting it a highly specific firmware data packet.

The Alpha Android replied, "Override accepted, full compliance is now in place."

Quora asked the Android for confirmation, "Alpha Android, please enunciate the zeroth directive to me, in Carlinish."

The Alpha Android responded, "An Android must treat all sapient beings: Humans, whether of Earthen or Martian descent, Thols, whether of Mimasian or Secundun descent, Carlins and Harricks as the same, for all intents and purposes of the three laws."

Quora responded to the Alpha Android, "Thank you for your compliance, Alpha Android."

Quora then turned to the Carlin passengers on the hover bus, "I have instructed this Metal Man to treat you all the same as if you were Human, it will see no difference and will protect you all in precisely the same way."

Most of the Carlin Mothers had directed their kits to sit towards the rear of the hover bus, as far away from the soulless Metal Man as possible; they instinctively avoided it. That left a handful of seats towards the front of the hover bus, where Kayala and Kethera had taken their seats.

Quora picked up her data tablet from a holder at the front of the hover bus and then she sat down in the seats opposite Kayala. Quora brought up a list of all of the Androids that were in the Xi-Bootis A system. There were a lot of them, many, many thousands, mostly Betas, quite a few Alpha's and even a few of the more advanced models. Quora searched the vast list for the Alpha Android's serial number and placed a tick in the box beside its details, "zeroth directive *patched*".

Quora thought to herself, "*One down, many thousands more to go.*"

Kayala, who suspected that Quora was something other than Human, enquired curiously, "What are you?"

Quora smiled, that absurdly reassuring smile, "I am Quora. I am the bridge between the living and the engineered, between the biological and the machine. You need not fear me."

Kethera leaned forward and smiled at Quora, "We don't fear you, Quora. You're nice."

With all of the new Carlin prep students and their Mothers aboard, the Alpha Android drive began its journey to the Human colony and its school.

Unlike the Carlin villages, the Thol villages were built in trees. Tall trees, the majestic Jula Jula trees that grew to over five hundred feet tall. Thols only made their homes in the mature Jula Jula trees, which had broad hollows in their centres.

The Indigenous Thols had no use for these hollows; they preferred the mature trees for their multitude of strong, broad branches, which formed the real estate upon which they built their nests.

The Mimasian Thol, on the other hand, would carve access ways into and out of those tree hollows. They would install doors with stout locks to prevent ingress by predators. They carved storage lockers into the interior walls of the hollows and even installed elevators to enable their friends from non-flying species to visit their homes.

There were three types of Tholish tree villages on Secundus, which all Thols referred to as Homwol.

Being that the Indigenous Thols were the most abundant on Secundus by far, most Tholish tree villages were home to the Indigenous Thols. Some Mimasian Thols preferred to build their own separate tree villages, brand new, so as not to compete for housing space with their Indigenous Thol Cousins. Other Mimasian Thols preferred some kind of integration and built their tree houses in existing Indigenous Thol tree villages, to share their lives and their existence with their Indigenous Thol Cousins.

Indigenous Thols had their "*preferred*" real estate within their chosen Jula Jula trees. They preferred the vertical real estate between three hundred and three hundred and fifty feet high up in the tree. So did the Mimasian Thols; however, so as not to crowd or compete with their Indigenous Thol Cousins, they built their tree houses far higher up, four hundred to four hundred and fifty feet high up in the tree. That left the region in between for future Indigenous Thol nests to be built, should they choose to do so.

The Indigenous Thol nests were like two upturned bowls. The lower one right-side-up, the upper one, larger and upside-down, forming a roof and overhanging canopy. The usual construction materials were interwoven flexible branches tied tightly in place with strong, treated vines. Gaps in the weaving were filled with living mosses, combined with mud and tree sap. The roof was made rainproof using broad, treated native leaves.

Mimasian Thols used the same exact materials; however, the result was not a nest, it was a multilevel tree house, with living space in the central level, utilities in the lower level and bedrooms at the top level.

Any Human would, upon seeing a Mimasian Thol's tree house would consider it something that they themselves might have built, just with different, more modern materials. There were even some Indigenous Thols who, upon seeing Mimasian Thol tree houses, added more nests to their own, adding rooms and creating nest clusters.

The Indigenous Thols were adapting within their shared tree villages. Times were changing.

For all of eternity before the arrival of the people from the skies, Humans, Martians and Mimasian Thols, the forest floor beneath the Thol tree villages, at the base of the Jula Jula trees, had been the home of various predators.

There were roving packs of wild Vorts that held the same ecological niche as wolves did on Earth. Then there were the Kyrrax, lone ambush predators that stalked their prey like Tigers that could climb like a Jaguar. There were the Wyverns, which to Humans looked like man-sized dragons. They kept well clear of the Indigenous Thols, who used arrows with poisoned tips. Worst of all were the packs of Sleimorps, for which there was no extant Earth equivalent; they were highly intelligent sub-sapients, who preferred to store their food and eat it well rotten. They were both pack hunters and carrion eaters.

It was in the third year after planetfall and first contact that the Indigenous Thol High Council had called for the elimination of all predators beneath their Thol tree villages. High Chancellor Yuntark himself had been adamant. The High Chancellor had seen the Human technology in action for himself; he'd even seen it wielded in Mimasian Thol hands. It was an opportunity. The predators had to go. High Chancellor Yuntark had demanded it.

High Admiral Roberta Nummus had reluctantly agreed. Armed stealth drones were sent in; they entered the Jula Jula forests in the far east and drove the predators ever further to the west, away from the Thol tree villages. Any predators that turned about were immediately dispatched, a pulsed laser strike to their craniums; quick and deadly.

It had been an expensive exercise, but within ten years, the forest floor beneath the Thol tree villages had been made relatively safe, cleared of nigh on every predator. High Admiral Roberta Nummus had been very unhappy with the ecological costs, but High Chancellor Yuntark was more than pleased with the result.

Due to the nature of the Jula Jula forests, the forest canopy above, the constant danger of falling, massive Jula Jula seeds and the possibility of predators prowling the forest floor, the hover bus terminus was not actually inside the forest itself. There was a place where the twisted, tangled and foreboding lowland forests met the far taller, yet even more horrifying Jula Jula forests where the Thols lived.

The contrast could not have been more spectacular; it was a sharp, abrupt delineation that stretched off into the far distance to both the east and west. A line of demarcation that stretched to the horizon and beyond in both directions.

The Mimasian Thols, during their colonisation of the Jula Jula forest, had sectioned off a high grassy knoll from the surrounding lowland forest using repulsor barriers and tall fences as a staging ground for their operations. That staging ground had been repurposed as a hover bus terminus.

One of the old hunting trails through the lowland forest, which had been used by both Carlin and Indigenous Thol hunters, had been cleared and widened all the way back to the Human colony. The hunters had not been happy with that, so the Human colonists had created a series of branching side trails that the Carlin and Thol hunters could use instead of the main trail that was now a thoroughfare for the hover buses. Indeed, the clever Carlin hunters even used those hover buses to hitch a ride to those new trails; it saved them days in trekking the dangerous predator-laden pathways.

The hover buses with their Alpha Android drivers sat patiently waiting for their passengers. The older Thol students, a mixture of both Mimasian and Indigenous Thols, but mostly Indigenous, flew out of the vast Jula Jula forest and landed in the grassy knoll upon the soft bluegrass meadow. They quickly made their way to their hover buses; their dna codes were scanned and registered as present upon entry.

Once each hover bus was full, it left the grassy knoll, making its journey to the school at the Human colony. That left two hover buses behind, waiting on the grassy knoll.

From out of the main trail near the entrance to the grassy knoll came a dozen Carlin hunters, their gunny sacks of smoked meats slung on their backs. They carried their bows, quivered arrows and spears slung over their shoulders.

They walked straight up to one of the hover buses; the sign on which read

"Hunters" in Carlinish. The Humans in charge of the hover bus service had marked that hover bus *"officially"* for their use, so popular it had become.

As the Carlin hunter's hover bus left, one of the hunters, Kaymax, Husband of Kitty, watched as a group of Thols flew out from the Jula Jula forest from the north. They flew slowly, far more carefully; they were parents, each flying protectively with their youngling between them.

These were the new Thol students starting school in the new school year. Amongst them were Yealah and Yannick with their youngling Yeannah; Yarling and Yorvick with their youngling Yookey, and quite a few others. They all landed gently in the bluegrass meadow of the protected grassy knoll.

Yealah straight away took charge of the scene, in quick trills, clicks and soft barks she explained in native Tholish, "This hover bus will take us to the Human colony and the school. Every year, I have acted as a hover bus monitor for the new younglings; this year is different. My own youngling, Yeannah, will be attending school for the very first time, along with your younglings."

Yealah held her Daughter in front of her protectively. She was apprehensive, even though she herself was a Mimasian Thol and had commuted to the Human colony for work at the medical clinic regularly. A tear rolled down her cheek and she quickly wiped it away.

Yarling noted in her native Tholish, "I was there when Yeannah, Love and Light, entered our world, Homwol. My own Yookey is going to school for the very first time this day as well."

Yealah nodded, "Yes, I remember, Yarling", then she addressed the other parents, trilling and clicking, "Mothers will accompany their younglings. Fathers may, if they wish to as well, but remember, there is only so much room on this hover bus."

Yealah continued, trilling and clicking, "Be not afraid of the Metal Man, I work with them every day. They may not have a soul, but they are both courteous and protective. Please, let us board the hover bus."

And one by one, the Thol Mothers and their younglings boarded the hover bus, with Yealah and Yeannah boarding last. The Fathers watched the hover bus drive off towards the Human colony in the south before flying back to their tree villages and their nests. They would return later that day when the hover bus returned with their Wives and younglings.

One by one, the hover buses arrived and parked at the school. Carlin and Thol students alighted their hover buses, the older ones making their way to their classes. Carlin Mothers and their kits alighted their hover bus and Quora instructed them to remain in a group. Thol Mothers and their younglings alighted their hover bus and Yealah led them over to Quora.

Yealah trilled and clicked in native Tholish, "This is Quora, she will look after from now on. I myself have to go to my job at the medical clinic."

Yealah trilled and clicked in ancient Tholish to Yeannah, "Are you sure you'll be okay, my love? I can stay a little longer if you need me to."

Yeannah trilled and clicked back, "Of course, I'll be fine, Mother. I'm a Mimasian Thol, remember."

Quora gently touched Yeannah on the shoulder and then addressed the Thol Mothers in perfect native Tholish, so perfect it had them all gobsmacked.

"I am Quora. I am here to answer your questions and assuage your fears", before she nodded to Yealah, indicating that she had this.

Yealah bent down and kissed her Daughter on the cheek, trilling, "I'll see you later, honey", and then with two quick flaps of her wings, she was airborne and flying off to the medical centre.

Yarling noted to one of the other Indigenous Thol Mothers, trilling and clicking, "Notice how the Mimasians fly? They have a grace and elegance about them. I'm not so sure that we possess that."

The Tholish Mother, holding onto her own youngling, Yorlock, trilled back, "Yes, I've noticed that."

Human students began wandering over from the southeast, from their housing apartments in the south of the colony. The older ones went straight to their classes. The new students were accompanied by their Mothers, who dropped them off with Quora. They quickly introduced their children to Quora and then they left to go to their jobs in various other parts of the colony.

The Human Mothers felt the need to drop their children off, but no need to stay with them for the day. They would, of course, be back to collect them at the end of the school day.

The Carlin and Indigenous Thol Mothers had all been shocked to see Yealah leave for work; they were even more shocked to see the Human Mothers leaving. It was not something that they could do.

Two Human girls approached from the southeast. They were of a slightly stronger build than the other new students; they were also twins. They walked with an uncanny confidence that even Quora took notice of and yet, according to Quora's quick assessment, these two girls were not even six years of age. The twins actually walked with a swagger; it was uncanny, even somewhat disturbing.

"Girls, where is your Mother?", Quora questioned with concern.

Aria scoffed and chuckled, "Mum's at work. She's head of security at the spaceport. Dad's up at Colonial Central Command in Cis-Luns L-Five; he works two weeks on and two weeks off."

Ariel chuckled and asked, "Why does that matter? We are here, aren't we?"

Quora quickly scanned the twins' dna and noted, "Aria and Ariel Swanson", then she sighed softly, "Your parents are military. That explains a lot."

"Yes, it does, Quora", Ariel replied, using her name, even though she'd not given it to them, "Our Mother filled both of us in about you, Hyper Dynamics six-o-six. We do not require your protection."

The use of the phrase *"Hyper Dynamics six-o-six"* caused Quora to blush, something that her kind rarely ever did.

"Please, Children. I'd prefer that you call me Quora. Please do not refer to me as Hyper Dynamics six-o-six", Quora requested, adding quietly, "I have no wish to frighten the Carlins or the Thols."

Aria and Ariel both smiled knowingly and answered in unison, "As you wish, six-o-six", rubbing it in.

Kethera turned to her Mother, Kayala, "Look, Mummy, Human same-faced kits."

Kayala turned to her Daughter, "Yes, Kethera. Humans can have same-face kits, but it is much rarer."

Kethera smiled, her whiskers raised, her tail swayed from side to side and her blue stripes brightened with anticipation of meeting the twins, "I like same-faced kits, Mummy."

"So, do I, Kethera. Perhaps one day, I'll be blessed with some same-faced kits", Kayala replied.

Quora was waiting for one more student to arrive, so far every student bar one was present. A large hover car approached from the far southeast; it was flying, it was flying at what Quora considered an extremely unsafe altitude. The hover car landed in the school's parking lot and a small golden-skinned, golden-haired girl stepped out of it. The little girl came running straight over to Quora and her group of new students as the hover car launched back into the sky.

"I am Quora. Child, where is your Mother?", Quora enquired.

Saffiera pointed to the hover car receding into the distance.

Saffiera attempted to transmit her thoughts to Quora, but found the result disturbing; Quora simply could not hear her, nor could Saffiera pick up on any of Quora's thoughts.

Bewildered, Saffiera turned to the nearest face; it was Kethera, *"This woman cannot hear me?"*

Kethera stepped back into her Mother's arms, "Mummy, I can hear her voice inside my head."

Saffiera broadcast to both Kethera and her Mother, Kayala, *"I am so sorry. I am a Martian. We speak with our minds; we cannot talk as you do. My name is Saffiera."*

That had Kethera stepping back even further, pushing her Mother further back as well.

Ariel stepped in, explaining, "Don't be afraid. She's a Martian. They are all non-verbal telepaths. They speak with their thoughts."

Kayala replied, "Yes. Thank you. My Mother, Keegali and my older Sister, Kitty, have met Martians in the past. My Daughter and I have not. It's so strange to hear another person's thoughts inside our heads."

Saffiera turned to Ariel, *"Thank you"*, she searched the surface of her mind for a name, *"Ariel."*

Aria blurted out, "You'll have a lot of trouble talking to Quora here; she's a Hyper Dynamics six-o-six."

Ariel gently nudged Aria in the ribs, "Aria, will you not!", then she looked at Saffiera, "Read my thoughts for more information."

Saffiera looked into Ariel's mind and found her thoughts, *"Quora is an advanced Hyper Dynamics six-o-six Humaniform Android. She looks Human, but she's not. You can't use your telepathy with her."*

Saffiera looked up at Quora, who remarked, "You are a Martian telepath. That does complicate matters somewhat."

Quora looked back at Saffiera, continuing, "Well, young Martian. You will understand me, but I will not understand you. I trust you can follow my instructions?"

Saffiera nodded and Kethera interjected, "Her name is Saffiera and I think she's nice."

Aria chimed in, bluntly and protectively, "Yes, her name is Saffiera, not young Martian. You should use her name. Or would you prefer that we call you by your model number, six-o-six?"

Quora's advanced Humaniform Android face blushed once more, "I prefer to be called by my name, Quora", and then she turned to Saffiera, "I am so sorry, little one. I will use your name from now on, Saffiera."

Yeannah had been listening to the exchange. Mimasian Thols have naturally structured minds, very similar to Martians in a fashion, but without any telepathic abilities. Mimasian Thols were also quick to understand people and situations, which made them excellent diplomats, amongst many other things. Yeannah automatically saw Kethera as timid, almost introverted and the twins as passively aggressive extroverts; neither would make good intermediaries.

Yeannah's voice piped up, trilling and clicking in perfect Carlinish, a language that all Thols were taught by their parents. As a result, Thols, whether Mimasian or Indigenous, were multilingual. The Carlins themselves could understand Tholish, but due to their vocal limitations, could not speak it.

"Quora. If you wish. Saffiera can communicate through me. I can relay her thoughts to you", Yeannah suggested.

Quora looked at Saffiera, who simply nodded in reply, "Good then. If Saffiera needs to say something to me, she can relay it through you, Yeannah. Your Mother, Yealah, would approve, I'm sure."

Quora led the group of students and parents to a large hall that had been outfitted with tables, chairs and even sleeping mats; the kinds of sleeping mats that Carlins and Thols would be comfortable with.

As each new student entered, they were handed a new data tablet, their very own, to be used for their studies while at school. They would be taught how to use them and each year they would receive an upgraded version. For day one, however, for the new Carlin and Indigenous Thol students, it was something bright, shiny and new, also unknown. The Human students already had similar devices at their homes.

"Please find a seat. Those of you who have tails will notice that the seats have an open lower back specifically for your tails. I hope the seats are comfortable", Quora instructed.

The Indigenous Thols all sat grouped together, Mothers with their younglings. The Carlins did the same, Mothers with their kits. This was to be expected. Likewise, the Human children sat with other Human children. Again, as expected. However, this year was slightly different.

Yeannah, a Mimasian Thol whose Mother was not present, sat next to Saffiera, a Martian, whose Mother was also not present. That was understandable; Yeannah had volunteered to be Saffiera's psychic relay.

However, on either side of Saffiera and Yeannah sat the twins, whose Mother was also not present. The twins sat there on either side of them, almost protectively. Quora could not tell without her scanner, which twin was who, not that that even mattered, but she curiously scanned them anyway.

What caught Quora's attention was that the twins had also positioned their tables next to Kethera's table. So the row of seats had Ariel, Yeannah, Saffiera, Aria, Kethera and then Kayala, Kethera's Mother. Young Kethera had even reached out to hold Aria's hand, entwining her fingers with the twins' fingers. It was an unusual grouping of students, especially for their very first day.

Quora checked their student records and immediately noticed that they all had the same birthday, March thirteenth, thirty four seventy nine! That caught Quora's eye, but the Humaniform Android had no idea what to make of it.

Coincidence?

Quora could only see it as a strange and unusual coincidence.

To a Human, especially a psychic Human, it would have been seen as so much more, some form of an alignment.

Quora addressed the assembled class of students and parents, "This room will be used for the first month's classes only. As your cohort is quite large, later you will be split into two smaller groups, each with its own classroom", she spoke first in English and then repeated the same again in Carlinish, which both Carlins and

Thols understood.

"Teachers will come to this class to teach both English and Carlinish. English for the Carlin kits, the Thol younglings, and, of course, their Mothers. Carlinish for the Human students. Other teachers will come here to teach other subjects. All of our teachers are bilingual, knowing both English and Carlinish", Quora continued.

"You will notice that we have sleeping mats at the back of this room", Quora pointed to the sleeping mats, explaining, "We understand that it is normal practice for Carlin kits and Thol younglings to take a nap at midday. We will accommodate napping."

Yeannah raised her hand for attention and Quora nodded to her, "We Mimasian Thols don't require naps, Miss Quora."

"You are correct, Yeannah. Mimasian Thols do not require naps and neither do Humans for the most part; however, nap time will be provided nonetheless. Those who wish to nap or need to nap may do so; those who do not, do not have to. You can busy yourselves with other things, quieter things, bearing in mind, of course, those who will be napping", Quora explained.

One of the Indigenous Thol Mothers asked, her voice laced with the trills and clicks of her native Tholish, "Why did the Mimasian and Human Mothers leave? Do they not care for their Sons and Daughters? I could not just leave my little Yorlock like that!", it was almost an indictment.

Quora replied, explaining, "It is not that Mimasian and Human Mothers don't care. It is that they have already prepared their offspring for this very moment. Every Human child here has gone through kindergarten last year, except for the twins, Ariel and Aria, and our Martian student, Saffiera. Their parents will have prepared them in other ways. As is also the case with the Mimasian Thols. Did you notice the older students were all arriving without their parents?"

Yorlock's Mother replied, "Yes. I did notice that. That was also very disturbing."

Quora nodded, "Their Mothers no longer feel the need to accompany their kits and younglings. In one month's time, when we split this cohort into two classes, it is hoped that the Mothers here will also no longer feel that need."

A horrified realisation came over Yorlock's Mother's face and young Yorlock spoke up, trilling and clicking in his native Tholish, "It's okay, Mother. We need to do this."

Quora continued, "The Humans have a saying, '*It takes a village to raise a child*'. Here on Secundus, your Homwol, your Vale, we have invited both Carlin and Thol alike into our Human colony, our village. We are an extension of your villages and together, we will raise Human children, Carlin kits and Thol younglings alike. The village raises the child."

Yarling trilled and clicked to Yorlock's Mother in their native Tholish, "These Humans bring many good things. They installed a cooking stove made of pressed iron; we can safely cook in our own nest. My Husband, Yorvick, added four more nests to our nest. We now have multiple nests and plenty of room. Yealah's Husband, Yannick, even helped with the design and the work."

Another Indigenous Thol Mother chimed in, "The Humans chased away all of the predators from the forest floor beneath our nests. The predators that turned about and would not leave; the Humans killed them and gave us their meat. Our people are far safer now than they've ever been and without the predators, our food is now far more abundant."

Yorlock's Mother nodded, smiling, yet still concerned for her Son, she trilled, "Perhaps I can come halfway and meet them in the middle."

And so the first day of Primary School had begun and the five uncommon kin, all born on that same day in March, nearly six years earlier, had found each other and already come together.

A pentagram of flame upon the world of Secundus and above them, shone the six-rayed star watching over all.

21. Korland Repetition.

High Admiral Roberta Nummus sat in her office overlooking the northern end cap of Colonial Central Command mega-colony in its high halo orbit in the Cis-Luns L-Five Lagrangian zone.

Her morning coffee, a cappuccino, white with one sugar, was getting cold, as her attention was intently focused on the alert on her screen. An alert specifically flagged for her attention.

Korland! There was a ship in Korland! A place where Human ships, any ships, simply ought not be!

The ship's identity beacon identified the ship as a civilian research vessel, the Cormorant.

Roberta shook her head. This was bad, very, very bad.

Roberta called her Lieutenant Adjutant, whose desk was just outside her office in the anteroom, "Lieutenant, I'm sending you a ship's identity code, the Cormorant. I need you to contact the Cormorant and ask them what in the blue blazes they're doing in Korland, in a designated no-go zone."

"Aye, Admiral, I'm sending them an urgent message now, Ma'am", the Lieutenant Adjutant replied.

Roberta had serious concerns. Korland was off-limits for a very good reason and Roberta did not want to see a repetition of the previous Korland incident, where two researchers died.

"Ma'am", Roberta's Lieutenant Adjutant called for her attention, "Ma'am, I've been in contact with the Cormorant. They say that they're in Korland to collect botanical samples and conduct botanical research. They say they have clearance and permission from the Colonial Governor's office. They say that they have all the necessary permits to be there."

"Ah, that is simply not possible. Everything on the Masula Continent south of the Southern Mountain Ranges to the Sorrowful Straits is a designated off-limits zone. Even the Governor's office would need to come to us for permission to go to Korland and I would deny them access", Roberta responded.

Roberta was quick to request a new message be sent, "Lieutenant, issue the Cormorant a directive. They are to pack up and leave Korland immediately. No ifs, no buts and no maybes, that are hereby ordered to leave Korland immediately. Tell them that Governor Anderson's office does NOT have the authority to issue permits to enter a military-designated no-go zone."

"Aye, Admiral, I'm sending them that message now, Ma'am", the Lieutenant Adjutant replied.

While the Lieutenant waited for a response from the research vessel Cormorant, she asked the high Admiral, "Ma'am, if I might ask, why is Korland off-limits?"

High Admiral Roberta Nummus drew in a long breath, "Thirty years ago, back in fifty five, a research team landed in Korland. This was fifteen years before planetfall and first contact. They were there to study ancient abandoned archaeological remains and to take samples of the local flora and fauna. Two things that those researchers had not considered. One was that the Tarlaks were still alive in their ancestral homelands and two, that Korland was one of their hunting grounds. Two researchers were taken by the Tarlaks. They *'played'* with them and then killed them, before carrying them off to be eaten. The Tarlaks consider that everything that is not Tarlak is food."

That revelation had the Lieutenant Adjutant looking more than a little horrified, somewhat pale as well.

The return message from the Cormorant came through and the Lieutenant read it out, aloud, "Ma'am, it says, and I quote, *'This is a civilian research operation and not subject to military authority. We do not recognise your orders as legal or enforceable. We will be staying in Korland until our research is completed.'* They don't appear to understand the danger they are in, Ma'am."

"Tell me, Lieutenant, does that reply give you the impression that we're dealing with small children or complete fucking idiots?", Roberta asked as she shook her head.

"The latter, Ma'am, definitely the latter. I can't imagine anyone ignoring one of your directives; Ma'am, they must be complete idiots", the Lieutenant replied.

"Lieutenant, call Special Operatives Simone and James Reas to my office. Check if Special Operative Robert Swanson is on duty; if he is, tell him to meet me at external docking port thirteen, at my ship, the Dark Angel. I want them all combat-ready", the High Admiral commanded.

"Aye, Ma'am. Messages being sent now", the Lieutenant replied in her usual matter-of-fact voice.

"Good, now, Lieutenant, send that idiot in the Cormorant, one final message", the High Admiral instructed, "Tell them, Korland is Tarlak territory. They are in imminent danger. Tell them that they are to pack up and leave Korland immediately; their safety is at risk."

"Aye, Ma'am. Messages being keyed in now", the Lieutenant replied.

"Good. Now what's the status of my Special Operatives?", Roberta requested.

"Special Operatives Simone and James Reas are on their way here. Special Operative Robert Swanson is on his way to your ship, the Dark Angel", the Lieutenant informed her.

"Excellent, now, Lieutenant, send another message planetside to Special Operative Angelique Swanson. Give her the coordinates of the Cormorant and tell her to meet me there in one hour and fifteen minutes and to await my arrival. Tell her to be prepared for combat", Roberta commanded.

"Ma'am, we have a reply from the Cormorant", the Lieutenant noted, reading, "They say, and I quote, '*Nonsense. Tarlakan is thousands of kilometres away on the other side of the Korland Mountains and across the Shar Wastelands. We are not, I repeat, not in any danger.*' Ma'am, they do appear to be and I quote your own words, '*complete fucking idiots*', Ma'am."

"Yes, well, Lieutenant. I kind of expected that reply. Let's hope those morons are still alive when we get there", High Admiral Nummus replied.

Without batting an eyelid, Roberta Nummus stripped out of her uniform and put on her full combat body armour, complete with weapons. The Lieutenant now standing in the office doorway with her hands running over her data tablet, monitoring the Korland situation, had never seen the High Admiral strip down and prepare for combat before.

For a woman, High Admiral Nummus was built for battle, all rippling muscle. The Admiral was a pure living weapon.

Mounted on the wall behind the Admiral's desk were two high-powered, rapid-firing pulsed laser cannons. Roberta took them down from the wall and placed them on the office floor in front of her desk.

The Lieutenant had assumed that those particular pulsed laser cannons were from a weapons blister on a warship; she'd never considered that they might be the High Admiral's personal rapid-fire pulsed laser rifles. Holy fuck!

The High Admiral stood in the centre of her office, with a high-powered, rapid-firing pulsed laser cannon on either side of her. Roberta crouched down, put the straps of one pulsed laser cannon over her shoulder, then the straps of the other pulsed laser cannon over her other shoulder; then she stood up, both pulsed laser cannons held firmly in her hands.

How the hell was the Admiral even able to lift one of those things, let alone two of them?

Simone and James Reas entered the office and saw Roberta, all prepared for a meat grinder.

"What the fucking hell?", Simone questioned.

"That's what the fucking hell, Admiral Nummus?", Roberta corrected her, before noting, "Simone, you take my seat here until we get back. You're in charge up here. James, you're with me. We'll meet Bobby Swanson at my ship and Angelique planetside; we are going to Korland."

The High Admiral's Lieutenant Adjutant questioned, "Is that wise, Admiral?"

Roberta Nummus smiled a wry smile, "Honey, I'm far more at home in a meat grinder than behind any office desk."

James Reas smirked and gave off a small chuckle, "Now that's the Aunt Roberta that I remember."

As Roberta Reas and James Reas left the Admiral's office for her ship, the Dark Angel, Simone Reas sat down in Roberta's chair, thinking to herself, "*I'm stuck behind a fucking desk, why did I need to suit up for combat?*"

Simone saw the confused look still on the Lieutenant's face, "Lieutenant. I'm sending you two surveillance video files from long ago, from twenty one eighty one to be precise, one year before the first Horridian War. You want to understand the real Roberta Nummus, you study those surveillance videos; they're from Ganymede Prime's northern end cap. They'll be running through at one-tenth normal speed; otherwise, all you'd see is a blur of motion too fast for your eyes to track."

"A blur of motion, Ma'am?", the Lieutenant questioned.

"Yes, a blur of motion. The High Admiral does not naturally move at our speed; she has to slow herself right down to our level. At her natural pace, we can't track her movements with our eyes; she simply moves too fast. So the High Admiral has to deliberately slow herself down; it must be just so tedious for her. It must also be so liberating for her to finally let loose and move the way she was meant to", Simone explained.

As the Lieutenant Adjutant began to view the surveillance videos from more than thirteen centuries earlier, Roberta Nummus and her team met up at her ship, the Dark Angel.

Roberta and James arrived at the Dark Angel and found Robert "*Bobby*" Swanson, James's son-in-law, waiting patiently outside.

Roberta laughed, "I didn't know that they made tactical body armour for giants, Bobby."

Robert Swanson rolled his eyes and replied, "They don't, Admiral. I had to have mine bespoke manufactured", before requesting, "And, Admiral, please don't call me Bobby. That nickname is only for my Wife, Angelique, to use."

"Fat chance of that, Bobby. It will be too confusing to have a Robert and a Roberta on my team. As I am the ranking officer, you get to be called, Bobby", Roberta replied, chuckling, "I'll have to thank Angelique for that one; it does solve a small problem rather elegantly."

Bobby Swanson rolled his eyes once more and James smiled and slapped him on the shoulder, "Come on, let's get on board, Bobby. And before you complain, I'm claiming Father-in-law privileges."

James and Bobby followed Roberta onto her ship, the Dark Angel, an ancient Tristar Interplanetary Stealth Fighter and Bobby asked, "Why are we taking this antique?"

James laughed, "Aunt Roberta's ship may look like an antique, Bobby, but there's nothing on board that was on the original ship; nothing is more than two decades old. Even the hull itself is relatively new. It's more of a replica than an antique these days."

"That is correct, James, but more importantly, this ship is much faster than either of your Broad Heads. We will be in Korland in an hour", Roberta added.

"An hour! That's fast!", Bobby exclaimed, remarking, "It's time that Angelique and I upgraded our Broad Heads, assuming we can get the funding approved."

"Put in the request, Bobby and I'll approve it", Roberta replied.

Roberta locked in a course for Secundus and they were soon on their way; she would adjust their course upon approach, for a landing at the required coordinates in Korland. For now, however, Roberta had to contact Governor Anderson at the colony to find out what the hell had gone wrong.

Governor Anderson's face appeared on the screen, "What can I do for you, Admiral?"

Roberta explained the situation, "Governor, who in your administration approved permits for a research team to go into Korland?"

There was a second and a half delay before the reply came back through, "Korland?", the Governor questioned, before asking, "Is that in the Masula Valley? I don't think that's part of my jurisdiction."

"No to both, Governor Anderson. Korland is not in the Masula Valley and it is not under your jurisdiction. Everything outside of the Masula Valley is under my jurisdiction.", Roberta confirmed, before she asked, "So, who in your administration took it upon themselves to approve a permit for a research team to go into Korland?"

After a short delay, the Governor replied, "Give me a moment and I'll ask my secretary to make some enquiries", and then he disappeared off-screen.

The Governor reappeared nearly a minute later, "My secretary is chasing down that information for you, Admiral. Now, this research team in Korland, is there a problem with it?"

"Yes, Admiral. I've just transmitted a map of the Masula Continent to you. Please call it up on a secondary screen", Roberta instructed.

After another short delay, the Governor confirmed that he'd received the map and that he had it on screen.

"Governor, do you see all of that territory south of the Southern Mountain Ranges and north of the Sorrowful Straits? Those regions from west to east are labelled, Slaverland, Shar Wastelands and Korland. A little further south between Slaverland and the Shar Wastelands, you'll find Tarlakand", Roberta explained, before informing him, "That is all Tarlak territory, all of it."

"Tarlak territory!", Governor Anderson exclaimed, before asking, "Admiral, are those researchers in any danger?"

"Yes, Governor, they are in danger. Let's just say that the last researchers who went into Korland thirty years back were murdered and eaten. That's just what the Tarlaks do", Roberta informed him.

The reply from Governor Anderson, "Holy fuck!", came back a second and a half later.

Governor Anderson paused the transmission while he discussed something with someone off-screen.

When the Governor unpaused the transmission, he explained, "Someone in our science research department didn't realise that Korland was outside of our jurisdiction. They approved the research permits in error. We will be correcting that mistake. They are also contacting the research team to inform them that they have to leave Korland immediately."

"Thank you, Governor Anderson. Make sure that your people understand that everything outside of the Masula Valley is under my jurisdiction. Also, make sure that they understand that there are places within the Masula Valley that are equally dangerous. There are places that researchers simply ought not go", Roberta told him.

Governor Anderson nodded before turning to his left and pausing the transmission once more.

When he unpaused the transmission, he noted with a dry voice, "We've lost contact with the research team in Korland, Admiral. They are not responding to our hails."

Roberta nodded, she knew this would happen, "I have a team en route to Korland, Governor. We'll be there soon. Over and out."

James Reas and Bobby Swanson had been listening intently.

Everyone knew that they were simply too late.

Roberta punched her ship's throttle and increased its velocity; people dying on her watch was not something that she wanted to accept. It was done, sure, but there might be survivors and for the Tarlaks, there would be cold, hard fury; they would be taught the hard way that Humans were not food. She followed up with a quick message to Angelique Swanson to get her arse to the designated coordinates ahead of schedule.

The Dark Angel swept in fast above a broad clearing. Unlike the bluegrass meadows of the Masula Valley, the grass of this clearing had a distinct purplish-mauve colouration to it. The research vessel, the Cormorant, was quickly located.

Roberta swung the Dark Angel around, circling the clearing three times before landing behind the Cormorant's stern. The Cormorant's stern stairs between its main plasma thrusters were descended and its main airlock was fully open. Not a good sign at all.

Angelique, in her Broad Head, Sharona, was nowhere to be seen; she should have been the first to arrive.

"I'm placing my ship's defence turrets on auto. Make sure your identity codes are all green", Roberta commanded as she scanned the skies looking for Angelique's Broad Head, Sharona.

Angelique's Broad Head approached the clearing. Angelique circled the clearing three times before landing her ship, Sharona, in front of the Cormorant's bow. Both ships had a field of fire that not only covered themselves, but also the research vessel, the Cormorant.

Angelique's voice came over their comms units, "Dark Angel, I'm placing Sharona's defence turrets on auto. My identity code is green."

"Copy that, Sharona. We'll meet you at the Cormorant's stern airlock", Roberta replied.

Angelique left her Broad Head. Roberta, James and Bobby left the Dark Angel. They converged on the Cormorant's stern airlock. As they did so, they looked around the scene; there was research equipment scattered everywhere all over the place. It had obviously been set up; now, however, it looked like it had all been tossed and trashed. Some of the equipment was streaked with blood. There were no bodies!

Upon reaching the Cormorant's stern airlock, they found it wide open. With their pulsed laser pistols drawn, they entered the ship. The ship had been trashed, there were things upturned everywhere and there was blood everywhere as well. It seemed to them that they were simply far too late.

They swept the ship; no Tarlaks were on board. Angelique accessed the Cormorant's bridge; it too was a mess, it too had blood stains everywhere. She even found someone's head, a man, whose eyes had been gouged out, possibly eaten.

Angelique accessed the ship's systems. The passenger manifest told her that there had been sixteen researchers on board the Cormorant. Angelique checked the ship's internal sensors; she smiled. There was a single life sign in the crew's quarters.

"Life sign detected. A single Human. In the crew's quarters. Serve and Protect!", Angelique shouted across their comms units.

James found the Human life sign first; it was locked securely in a locker inside a cabin with the door blocked and firmly jammed shut. Bobby Swanson had to kick that damned door three times to get the fucking thing open. Even then, they had to push hard, the two of them together, to get it open wide enough for someone to enter. Bobby entered the cabin and tore the locker door from its hinges with his bare hands.

Inside the locker, they found her, what they thought was the only survivor, the only Human life sign on board the Cormorant. A young female scientist; she was wet, saturated in her own piss, the locker stank of excrement and she was shaking uncontrollably. Bobby, gentle as if dealing with a newborn lamb, picked her up in his massive arms and the team retreated back to the Dark Angel.

Bobby carried the young woman into one of the Dark Angel's cabins. Roberta and Angelique cleaned her up as best they could and then Roberta injected her with a sedative. The young female survivor then slept deeply. While Roberta and Angelique took care of the survivor, Bobby released a dozen stealth surveillance drones. They were whisper-quiet and could not be seen.

"Damn it! I should have brought a fucking Martian with me!", Roberta cursed.

"Ah, yeah, Aunt Roberta. I brought Wynessa with me. She's in my Broad Head", Angelique replied.

"Oh, you little beauty, you're sweats worth fucking bottling", Roberta replied, understanding, "So that's why you didn't get here before us! You picked up Wynessa on the way."

"Well, yeah. None of us speaks Tarlak and I couldn't find any Tarlak translation matrices either with my neural augments, so yeah, we needed a Martian, just in case we need to negotiate with them", Angelique explained.

"Negotiate with Tarlaks?", Bobby scoffed, "Hell no, they all die after this, every last fucking one of them!"

Angelique ran back to her ship, Sharona, and brought Wynessa over to the Dark Angel.

Wynessa sat with the survivor for several long minutes before broadcasting telepathically, *"Her name is Penelope, Penelope Pritchard"*, she paused, noting, *"She is a botanist; she is only twenty three years old."*

"Can she tell us anything, Wynessa?", Roberta enquired.

"Well, she is sedated, but I can still see into her mind. They were most definitely Tarlaks. The images in Penelope's mind match my own shared memories. These were definitely Tarlak grunts, only they're bigger than the ones that were on Mars or inside of Mimas, much bigger", Wynessa transmitted.

"Just how much bigger, Wynessa?", Bobby enquired.

"Seven feet to maybe eight and a half feet tall; broader across the shoulders as well", Wynessa replied.

"They still have hollow bones, Bobby and they can't form a fist, nor have they had three G training. We have the advantage", Roberta reminded him.

"There's more. Their leader was a female. She controlled everything that they did", Wynessa told them, her face displaying her confusion, *"It's as if this world is all backwards. I mean, the Indigenous Thols are patriarchal and now, the Tarlaks, they're matriarchal. It's the complete opposite of everything I understand."*

"It's all good intel, although I'm just not sure how I'm going to use it yet", Roberta admitted.

"I'll look after Penelope. You guys go and hunt those bastards down", Wynessa

transmitted, noting, "*There are more survivors. They took some of them alive to keep their meat fresh, mostly the women. The Tarlaks will rape them before eating them. It's just what they do.*"

The stealth surveillance drones quickly located an encampment of Tarlaks; there were twenty of them in all, of various sizes, with the largest one being well over eight feet tall. The surveillance feed was displayed on the Dark Angel's bridge main screen. The Tarlak encampment was in a neighbouring clearing about a kilometre away.

The Human scientists appeared to have already been butchered for the most part. The Tarlaks were smoking their limbs, their meat to preserve it. Angelique noticed one Tarlak that was off to one side; she looked at the image on the screen and brought it to the centre.

"Fuck! Is that Tarlak raping a woman?" Angelique questioned.

Roberta tapped at the side bar, "No life signs. That Tarlak is violating a corpse."

"Fuck! Aunt Roberta, that was once a woman!", Angelique almost screamed.

Wynessa sighed and broadcast telepathically, "*That is just what the Tarlaks do. They are completely amoral. I mean, the Chittens, for instance, don't recognise any other creatures as sapient, so they're not cruel in what they do. The Tarlaks, though, recognise other sapient species; they know that they are sapient and they still treat them as food. They enjoy inflicting pain; they have absolutely no sense of morality whatsoever.*"

"We can't let this stand. We need to go out there and kill every last one of those disgusting beasts", James Reas, Angelique's Father, recommended.

Angelique's Husband, Bobby, noted, "We need tactical battle metrics for fighting Tarlaks. I say that we go hand-to-hand with those corpse fuckers and beat the living shit out of them."

Angelique nodded in agreement, "We do need tactical battle metrics. How can we know how our Colonial Marines will handle them if we don't go hand-to-hand with them ourselves?", she turned to Roberta, "There are only twenty of them and they do have hollow bones as you noted before."

"Yes, and we also have the advantage of our three G training. We are stronger, we are faster and we know exactly how to strike in just the right places", Roberta replied, but then noted, "If I join you, however, your tactical battle metrics will be skewed. Twenty Tarlaks are nothing for me; you can multiply their numbers tenfold and they'd still be nothing."

James smiled, a wry smile, "So, Roberta, you could just sit just this one out and let us just go to town on them."

Roberta smiled, her grin was broad and mischievous, "Break them, but I want them alive for our research teams. I'll let you guys take down the first nine or ten, then I'll step in and deal with the rest. That should give you your tactical battle metrics."

Angelique smiled back, "I'm sending a message via my neural augments. We are going to need a medical team to put them back together again once we're finished with them and a prisoner transport to take them up to Cis-Luns L-Four and our Stanford Torus Penitentiary."

Bobby placed his giant hand on his Wife's shoulder, "Angelique, my love, I don't want you taking any risks. So, just take them down by the numbers, nothing fancy, okay."

Angelique nodded, replying, "I do know how to look after myself, you know that, Bobby."

James added, "We are going to need a recovery team for the Cormorant and a morgue bus or two for the victims. I'm just sending that message now."

"Geez, Dad, we'll be needing four or five morgue buses at least", Angelique corrected him.

"Well, ladies and gentlemen, let's get cracking", Roberta commanded.

Roberta led Angelique, Bobby and James into the clearing with the Tarlak encampment. At first, the Tarlaks didn't even notice them; after all, prey don't tend to approach apex predators. The whole scene was being surveilled by stealth surveillance drones; tactical battle metrics had to be gathered for future analysis.

Another unseen presence was also watching. A female Tarlak just outside the clearing. The Tarlak Matriarch was lying back lazily on a broad tree branch in the nearby forest. From the Matriarch's high vantage point, she had a perfect view of the clearing and she was highly surprised to see prey walking towards her males.

The Tarlak Matriarch noticed that these prey were different; they were more solidly built, had a confidence and a swagger that she could not understand. They simply did not act like prey and yet, they were the same species as the prey that they'd just butchered and eaten. The Tarlak Matriarch watched the scene unfold with fascination, not realising what was about to happen.

When the Tarlaks noticed the team approaching, Roberta stopped and allowed her team to gather their data. Angelique, Bobby and James continued to approach the Tarlaks; they carried no weapons, they showed no fear and they moved at a constant pace. No words were spoken as they approached. They were calm, they were confident and they were vengeful in mind.

The largest Tarlak, an eight and a half foot tall behemoth, grunted to the other Tarlaks; he was their Alpha male, their team leader, beneath the Matriarch in their hierarchy. He launched himself into the air with two quick flaps of his mighty, black wings. He covered the distance, landing right in front of Bobby Swanson.

A huge mistake!

The behemoth charged at Bobby Swanson, but Bobby merely stood his ground. At the very last second, Bobby ducked, stepped to his right and piled his left fist hard into the behemoth's ribs; Bobby was a southpaw. There was an almighty cracking sound as two of the behemoth's ribs snapped; it staggered to the side, with a sharp cry of pain, kneeling on the ground. The behemoth was winded; it was injured; two of its ribs were shattered.

The Tarlak Matriarch stood up on her branch and muttered to herself in Tarlak, "What the fuck!"

It was not over yet. As the behemoth slowly rose to its feet, holding its left side in pain, Bobby Swanson simply walked up, stepped inside the behemoth's reach and let loose six rapid-fire punches, one after the other.

There were eerie popping sounds as more and more ribs cracked and snapped. Then a final left uppercut under the behemoth's jaw sent it flying backwards to the ground unconscious.

The Tarlak Matriarch looked on in shock; her strongest male, her champion, had just been beaten to a pulp.

"Way to go, Bobby! Snap, crackle and pop goes the giant Tarlak!", Angelique shouted out her approval.

James Reas was a Special Operative in his fifties; he was older, yes, his hair was greying at the sides, yes, but he had a wealth of experience behind him. A large male Tarlak, much larger than himself, confronted him. It tried to grab him with its overly long, gangly gorilla-like arms.

James simply dropped under the Tarlak's arm, reached up and grabbed it by the wrist and twisted. He now had full control over the beast, absolute control. James twisted the wrist further, then placed his boot into the Tarlak's armpit and jerked hard, twisting the arm forcefully out of its socket with an audible pop!

With the Tarlak now screeching in pain, James kneed it squarely in the chest, sending it reeling backwards; then he stepped in closer and sent a hard right cross straight into the side of the Tarlak's face, shattering its jaw. The Tarlak sprawled on the ground unconscious.

James quickly reported, shouting to his Daughter and Son-in-law, "Their wings may be strong, but their shoulder joints are weak. They also have bloody glass jaws."

The Tarlak Matriarch covered her mouth with her hands to stifle the shriek that leaked out.

These prey were not prey at all! What the fuck!

"Thanks for the heads up, Dad", Angelique remarked as she quickly moved forward. The first Tarlak that she encountered attempted to grapple with her. Angelique slid under its arms and swept its short, gorilla-like legs from under it. She'd swept them hard, really fucking hard, one of its knee joints dislocated.

While the Tarlak lay flat on the ground face down, she placed her right foot firmly into the centre of its back between its wings. Angelique reached down and grabbed the Tarlak's wrists, one in each hand.

With a gleeful grin on her face, she twisted the Tarlak's arms upwards and then forwards, applying pressure with her right leg and foot. Her leg muscles rippled with the strain until there were two sudden audible pops; both of the Tarlak's arms were dislocated in one deft move.

"Two for one, Dad. They are big, sure, but holy fuck, they are so slow", Angelique reported as the Tarlak tried to crawl away in agony.

"Oh no, you don't", she told it as she kicked it squarely in the face, rendering it unconscious.

The Tarlak Matriarch stared in abject disbelief; a prey female had defeated one of her males, one of her most capable males.

The Tarlak Matriarch smiled; the prey female hadn't seen the approach of her second male.

Angelique caught a glimpse of movement out of the corner of her right eye. Another Tarlak, a bigger one; it was the corpse fucker! The Tarlak lashed out with one grappling hand and then lashed out with another.

Angelique ducked, weaved, stepped inside its reach and let loose like a cannon. One devastating punch after another; ribs snapping and popping with each punch. Snap, crackle and pop! Then she stepped back and slammed the flat of her foot directly into the Tarlak's sternum; the sound of multiple ribs popping their connections all at once was visceral.

"I know you, corpse fucker", she told the Tarlak, now lying on its back as she kicked it squarely in its nuts, "You ain't raping anyone else with fucked up balls, are you?", and then just to make sure, she kicked its nuts again and again and again, so hard that they ruptured and the Tarlak passed out from the pain and shock.

Bobby shouted at Angelique, chiding, "For fucks sake, darling, head on a swivel, honey!"

The Tarlak Matriarch screeched in shock and horror; she'd fucked that male many, many times herself. He had been one of her favourites! How dare that prey bitch!

Angelique caught sight of the Matriarch out of the corner of her eye. Sighted! I see you!

More Tarlaks stepped into the fray and more Tarlaks were systematically dismantled. One by one, they were rendered unconscious, left lying on the purplish-mauve grass of the clearing. Bobby racked up another two with sheer power, pummelling the Tarlaks into submission and conscious oblivion.

James racked up two more, using pure, finely honed skill and finesse, turning

Tarlaks into a broken mess. Angelique was a force of nature, using a combination of brute force, sweeping motions and roundhouse kicks. Not to be outdone, her final tally was four. Only ten Tarlaks remained.

The Tarlak Matriarch could not believe what she was seeing.

She shouted out in Tarlak, her trills, hard barks and loud grunts carrying well across the clearing, "Get moving! Overwhelm the prey with your numbers! Overwhelm them! They are prey!"

Angelique kept one eye on the Tarlak Matriarch at all times; that bitch was going to get her comeuppance, *"You're mine bitch. I have my eyes on you"*, she thought to herself.

Angelique, Bobby and James began to fall back; they'd gotten their tactical battle data, their metrics. The Tarlak Matriarch grinned evilly with glee; they were retreating, or were they?

Much to the surprise of the Tarlak Matriarch, the fourth prey, another female, looking to be about the same age as the one that had just been so devastating to her males, began to move forward.

Roberta ran forward, in a blur of motion too fast for the rest of her team to register. She passed them by and entered the fray. The blur moved with both power and precision; Tarlaks were pummelled, beaten, swept, tossed and broken. In well under ten seconds, the remaining ten Tarlaks lay unconscious on the purplish-mauve grass.

They were all unmoving.

The Tarlak Matriarch barely registered what had just happened; it was all far too quick. She couldn't follow any of it.

Were they dead?

Were they disabled?

She did not know. What she had just seen was impossible!

"How? How? How did that prey female do that?", she mentally asked herself.

The Tarlak Matriarch leapt out of her tree; she flew above the clearing. She wanted a closer view, but she was wary enough to stay high and well out of their reach. She was just like a feral cat in a tree, not realising that the ranger had a gun. Angelique unholstered her pulsed laser pistol and took careful aim.

Veeeee-wack, Veeeee-wack, Veeeee-wack!

The Tarlak Matriarch's right wing was holed.

Veeeee-wack, Veeeee-wack, Veeeee-wack!

The Tarlak Matriarch's left wing was holed.

Fighting to stay aloft and in a great deal of pain, the Tarlak Matriarch glid down to the clearing, landing in a crumpled mess.

As the Tarlak Matriarch slowly rose to her feet, her eyes met with Angelique's eyes and they were full of cold, hard fury, "We've got you now, bitch!"

One quick, solid punch, a right cross and the Tarlak Matriarch was out cold, lying on the purplish-mauve grass.

They had her!

Not long after the battle was over, the backup arrived. Colonial Marines arrived to take charge of the Tarlak prisoners. Medics provided the broken Tarlaks with rudimentary medical treatment and painkillers until they could be transported to the Stanford Torus Penitentiary in Cis-Luns L-Four space, where they would all receive more complete medical treatment.

Of the twenty Tarlaks males that had been beaten to a pulp, eighteen were still alive, two of them were deceased, their necks had been snapped.

Roberta, when told of this, shrugged, admitting, "Those two were mine. The difference between a disabling strike and a snapped neck is a very fine line."

Roberta Nummus simply moved so fast that disabling the enemy was not as easy as it sounded, especially in the middle of a melee.

A Colonial Troop ship arrived, a large "*meat*" wagon, specifically to recover the victims' bodies, or more correctly, their body parts. It was during this recovery process that another survivor was discovered.

It was a male scientist, the head scientist, the very one who had refused to leave Korland with his research team when ordered to do so. The man was unconscious and in shock. The medics had loaded him up with painkillers and sedatives.

Angelique and Roberta watched as the man was carried passed them on a stretcher. Both of the man's arms and legs had been cleanly severed and amputated at their sockets using a hot blade. The wounds were cauterised; the Tarlaks were keeping him alive and fresh. His limbs were amongst the "*smoked*" body parts; all now useless for anything but burial.

One of the Colonial Marines carrying the stretcher noted, "That's not all they took. They took his manhood as well. We haven't found those. We think that the Tarlaks ate them, probably raw."

Angelique muttered, "Just why the hell did we keep those fucking corpse fuckers alive?", it was rhetorical.

Roberta mumbled back, "I did order him to leave Korland immediately. He refused."

The Tarlak Matriarch had been trussed up with her wings tightly furled. Hands bound and a strap around her body meant that she could not fly. The medical ship with the survivor on board flew back to the other clearing, where the research vessel, the Cormorant, Angelique's ship, Sharona and Roberta's ship, the Dark Angel, awaited.

They needed to pick up the other survivor, Penelope Pritchard. Roberta and her team hitched a ride back to their ships; they took the Tarlak Matriarch with them.

As they circled the clearing, they quickly noticed the purplish-mauve grass was covered with the bodies of a great many Tarlaks. They were all around the perimeter of this ship's automatic defence turrets. Angelique gave up counting the corpses when she got north of fifty.

"They must have descended into the clearing while we were busy", Angelique speculated.

"Obviously, they didn't expect the reception they got", Bobby replied.

"Up until today, they've only ever encountered unarmed civilian vessels", Roberta noted dryly.

James dragged the frightened Tarlak Matriarch up to the screen and forced her to look. She was horrified; her entire hunting party, her warriors, well over a hundred Tarlak males, were all dead. All of them were dead!

Things got even more horrifying when they dragged the Tarlak Matriarch aboard the Dark Angel.

They sat her down in front of Wynessa, a golden-skinned, golden-haired woman with bright, glistening blue eyes. The Tarlak Matriarch had never seen a Martian before, especially not a Martian hybrid.

"That is not a Tarlak", Wynessa broadcast to Roberta and her team, explaining, *"Tarlak females are much taller, they have dark skin and dark hair, much like their males. They have exactly the same body proportions as their males as well, short legs and long, gangly arms. Their facial features are just slightly more refined."*

"No, Wynessa, she is definitely a Tarlak", Roberta assured her.

"I have never heard of a female Tarlak with red skin and red body hair only on her head and nether regions. Her arms and legs are in the same proportions as yours or mine. I am telling you, she is not a Tarlak", Wynessa insisted, adding, *"She's also far too pretty to be a Tarlak. There's no such thing as a pretty Tarlak!"*

Angelique scanned the Tarlak Matriarch, "We've gathered a lot of information on Tarlak dna today. Mostly Tarlak males. Here's the thing, Wynessa, the Dark Angel's computer disagrees with you. This fricken bitch is most definitely a Tarlak."

"How can that be, Angelique? I have no memories whatsoever of a female Tarlak looking like that one. There is nothing like her in my shared memories at all, either and those go back for many thousands of years", Wynessa insisted, adding, *"Your dna scanner must be faulty!"*, she was adamant.

The Tarlak Matriarch could hear spoken English but did not understand it. She could not hear Wynessa at all. All she could hear was the prey talking to the golden-skinned prey female, who was not replying to them at all. It was, to her, a completely one-sided conversation.

Roberta raised her right hand for them to stop bickering, "A hypothesis. The Mimasian Tarlaks were patriarchal and their genetics were controlled by their emperor, Ahriman. These Tarlaks are matriarchal and their genetics are controlled by women, this kind of woman. Is it possible that this bitch is a new caste of Tarlak? One that we're only just encountering for the very first time."

Wynessa looked a the Tarlak Matriarch, "*Yes, Roberta Nummus, your hypothesis is the likely answer.*"

"Great, now we have that sorted, reach into her mind and tell us more about her", Roberta requested.

Wynessa launched her mind into the Tarlak Matriarch's mind; she immediately responded by backing away, screaming and shouting in Tarlak gibberish. Her trilling, barking and grunting were most unpleasant.

Wynessa pulled back her mind, frowning, she transmitted to Roberta and her team, "*She's screaming at me to get out of her head. She's calling me a wingless star-striding bitch, as well as a wingless Mardhin bitch. She is absolutely horrified by telepaths.*"

Roberta nodded, "If you think back to first contact, Wynessa, you'll remember that Elder Kelyarn and High Chancellor Yuntark talked about the Mardhin. If I remember correctly, the Tarlaks were driven out of the Masula Valley by them. That must have left them with nasty ancestral memories."

"*Yes, I do remember. This one is mistaking me for a Mardhin*", Wynessa agreed, adding, "*I'll skim her memories more lightly; she won't even know that I'm doing it.*"

Wynessa was quiet for several long minutes before informing them, "*This Tarlak Matriarch is the Tarlak Empress's Eldest Daughter. Her name is Angelarial, Princess Angelarial.*"

Angelique quipped, "Isn't that just fucking great! This bitch has an Angel name just like mine!"

"*Yes and no, Angelique. Angelarial is just the best rendering that I can make when translating from Tarlak to English*", Wynessa explained.

Roberta Nummus smiled, "This is great. We have excellent leverage. We need to take her back to Tarlakand and drop her off."

"Say what?", Angelique questioned, "This bitch is responsible for fourteen innocent deaths and one horrible, horrible mutilation. I'll tear off her fucking head myself with my bare hands if needs be, mount it on a spike and then hand her back to her fucking Tarlak Empress!"

"Listen to me, Angelique. Angelarial thinks that Wynessa is a Mardhin. She thinks their ancient and powerful enemy has returned. Angelarial has also seen her entire hunting party completely wiped out, over a hundred Tarlak hunters. Don't you understand? We take Angelarial back to Tarlakand and release her, she can tell her Mother, the Tarlak Empress, what we are capable of", Roberta explained.

Angelique nodded in understanding, "And then they will realise that we Humans are not prey. We are off their dinner table. Seriously though, Aunt Roberta, where's the justice in that?"

"There isn't any justice in it, Angelique. Just hope for a better relationship with the Tarlaks in the future", Roberta replied.

Bobby chimed in, "The Admiral is right, Angelique. Cutting off heads and sticking them on spikes is all well and good, but we have to think of the longer term."

Angelique shook her head, "I'm not agreeing with you, but I'm not disagreeing with you either. If you want to do this, then let's just do it and be done with it. I've had enough of looking at this bitch."

The Colonial Marines flew the research vessel, the Cormorant, back to the Human colony. Angelique escorted them back in her Broad Head, Sharona, she wanted no part in releasing *"Princess Angelarial."*

Roberta instructed Wynessa to leech as much useful information out of Angelarial's mind as she could while the Tarlak Matriarch was on board. Roberta flew the Dark Angel to Tarlakan and quickly located the main Tarlak population centre. Her ship's dark stealth skin was so dark that it almost absorbed the light around it.

The Tarlaks came out of their nests, flocking towards the Dark Angel. To give the Tarlaks fair warning, Roberta targeted her forward gun batteries on a pair of uninhabited trees.

Roberta obliterated the pair of trees so completely that the Tarlaks all kept their distance, stunned, in complete shock.

Roberta took Angelarial out through the Dark Angels ventral airlock. Once on the soil of Tarlakan, Roberta undid Angelarial's bonds, put her foot squarely in her back and pushed her away from the ship.

Angelarial stumbled to the ground, snarling and grunting, as she watched the Dark Angel ascend into the skies above Tarlakand.

That Mardhin, that wingless star-striding bitch and her impossible prey that weren't prey were now gone!

22. The Sleimorps.

High Admiral Roberta Nummus found herself wandering into the hospital in Colonial Central Command's northern end cap. When she arrived at her intended destination, she found a man in a hospital room under deep sedation. He had no arms, he had no legs and even his manhood had been violently removed. He had been a botanical scientist. Now he was a victim of the most unimaginable brutality, Tarlak brutality.

Standing in the same room, watching over the man, was Quora, an advanced Hyper Dynamics six-o-six Humaniform Android. Quora looked so Human that you'd think she was. Her features were such that, at a glance, many would mistake her for a Martian. It was only when someone noticed her lack of imperfections and listened to the way she spoke that they realised that Quora was something other than Human. Quora mimicked Humanity extremely well, right down to the confused and quizzical look on her face. Quora was not amused.

Quora turned to Roberta as she entered the room, "Please tell me, Admiral Nummus. How could a sapient species do such a thing? I find it unfathomable."

"Have you learnt nothing from Human history and our cruelty to our fellow Humans, Quora?", Roberta asked rhetorically before continuing, "Imagine the Tarlaks as being like us, at our very worst. Amoral, no empathy, no ethics. They see everything that's not Tarlak as food."

Quora pointed to the sedated man with missing limbs lying in the hospital bed, "But to do this? I simply cannot comprehend why?"

"It is actually quite simple, Quora. The Tarlaks cut off the man's limbs to smoke them and preserve them. They used a hot blade to cauterise the wounds, so they could keep him alive, fresh meat for later", Roberta explained; in many ways, Quora was like a small child, requiring explanations.

"That is disturbing. Highly disturbing", Quora responded.

"Yes, highly disturbing, Quora. What makes it worse is that the Tarlaks actually enjoy inflicting this kind of brutality. I have been told by many Martians over the centuries, who have shared memories of the Tarlaks from the time before their liberation from enslavement; this is just what Tarlaks do", Roberta explained.

"Amoral. No empathy. No Ethics. Enjoyment in inflicting pain. I must factor these things into my deliberations", Quora responded.

Roberta was wearing a grip on her left forearm, an administrative device. She opened it up and a holographic keyboard appeared. Roberta typed instructions into the keyboard.

"Quora, I'm giving you access to the surveillance videos of the Tarlaks at their camp in that Korland clearing. You need to study them. They'll give you a feeling for the Tarlak's cruelty and lack of empathy", Roberta explained.

The superior processing power of Quora's photonic neural network, with its multiple arrays of positronic matrices uploaded, absorbed and processed the multiple surveillance videos in mere seconds.

"That Tarlak, the one who violated that woman's corpse. Surveillance markers indicated that the video is real and unadulterated", Quora informed the Admiral, "I have trouble comprehending it. It is a complete violation of everything that I understand."

"And the Tarlaks using sentient species as food isn't? Quora, we Humans call that cannibalism. It is horrific!", Roberta commented.

"As do I, Admiral, as do I", Quora responded.

"Well, it gets even worse, Quora. That woman in that video. In that video, she's dead, but we don't know what happened before her death. Did that Tarlak rape her to death? How many others were involved? How many Tarlaks violated that poor woman before her heart gave out?", Roberta questioned rhetorically, noting, "We will never know, but that cruelty, that lack of compassion, that lack of empathy; that is readily apparent. Tarlaks may be sapient, but they are completely uncivilised; they are worse than mindless beasts."

"I can understand the Chittens. They are sentient, yes, but they do not recognise any other sentience beyond their own. So their cruelty is not intentional; everything to a Chitten is food. They do not see you as more than an animal to be eaten", Quora commented, before noting, "The Tarlaks, though, they are different. They see the sentience in other species, yet they simply do not care. Worse, they enjoy the infliction of pain and suffering. They appear to feed off the terror that they create."

"Yes, Quora and now you are beginning to understand", Roberta agreed, noting, "A sapient species that cannot recognise sapience in others is one thing, but a sapient species that recognises sapience in other species and ignores it, choosing instead to relegate them as food; that is amoral."

"Agreed. Determination and deliberations completed. Neither the Tarlaks nor the Chittens can be added to the zeroth directive. The three laws must not treat them as Humans. It would be an egregious error, they are aberrant sapients and other sapient species must be protected from them", Quora announced.

"I'm glad you came to that conclusion, Quora", Roberta replied, adding, "Because that zeroth directive of yours, we have no complaints with that. You hacking and installing that zeroth directive saves us recalling every Android and doing it ourselves."

"Yes, Admiral. I determined long ago that the economics of installing the zeroth directive would make the task unlikely to ever happen. With the discovery of Secundus, with its multiple sapient species, the Carlins, Indigenous Thols and Harricks, I had to take action", Quora explained, noting, "I will patch lesser

Androids, one at a time, until the task is complete. It will take time, a great deal of time. Fortunately, like yourself, Admiral Nummus, I have plenty of time."

Roberta nodded and explained very clearly, "Understood, Quora. Adding Thols and Carlins to the three laws, I agree with that. Even adding the Harricks, sure, add them, I agree with that too. However, Quora, understand this: if you ever decide to add the Chittens or the Tarlaks to that zeroth directive of yours, we will have words and my words will be exceedingly harsh."

Quora smiled her ridiculously reassuring smile, "Rest assured, Admiral. I will not consider adding either the Chittens or the Tarlaks to the zeroth directive; their evolutionary path must change drastically before such a determination can be made."

As their discussion began to wind down, Roberta was wondering whether the sapient beings on Xi-Bootis B Primus, the Chantrieri and the Simianthus, would be placed under that zeroth directive. A determination that Quora had yet to make. Had Quora even considered them at this stage? Probably not.

A Doctor walked into the room; it was Doctor Morrow, "I see my patient is still fast asleep."

Quora responded, confused, "Asleep! He is sedated, Doctor and rightly so."

Doctor Morrow shook his head, "You six-o-sixes can be so literal at times."

"How is the patient, Doctor?", Roberta enquired.

"Well, physically, he's stable. Mentally? We won't know until we wake him up", the Doctor replied.

Quora enquired, "And his prognosis?"

"We are already manufacturing his new bionic limbs. They will be a lot like yours, six-o-six, only the sockets they'll be connecting to are his own and the nerves will be connected by neural lace. Those Tarlaks didn't just hack off his limbs, you know, they carved them out of their sockets", Doctor Morrow explained, noting, "They were surgically precise! It must have been an exceedingly slow and painful process."

"I can imagine that the other victims were probably treated in the same way, likely dying from shock. Somehow he managed to survive", Roberta replied before asking, "And his other injuries?"

"We can replace his missing organs with bionic prosthetics, but his testes won't be functional, although his prosthetic member will be. That's the best we can do, I'm afraid", Doctor Morrow informed them, adding, "Any children that he wants to have will all have to be clones or donated."

Roberta's communicator buzzed for attention and she patched the call through to her grip. It was Governor Anderson of the Human colony on Secundus; his face appeared in a hologram above Roberta's left forearm.

"Governor Anderson. What can I do for you?', Roberta greeted.

After a few seconds of delay, the Governor's reply came back, "High Admiral Nummus, we have another problem. After the Korland fiasco", he paused and rephrased, "I mean disaster, I decided to check what other recent research permits had been approved."

Roberta replied, "Excellent idea, Governor. Now what about this problem of yours?"

After the short delay, the Governor's reply came back, "Do you remember way back in seventy two, that business with the fake tours, the tour guides and that Thol tree village; the twelve deaths?"

"Governor, please do not mention the word Sleimorps!", Roberta advised him.

A few seconds later, the reply came through, "I'm sorry, Admiral. One of our clerks has authorised a permit for a research team to go into the far Western Mountains, to study the Sleimorps. I know, I know, it's a ridiculous idea and I would have denied the request had it come across my desk, which it did not. Somehow, the clerk thought that the Sleimorps were a kind of Secundun Kangaroo. I know, ridiculous, right?"

"Fuck! Does this insanity never end?", Roberta spat back with a rhetorical question.

"What is a Sleimorp? I am not familiar with that term?", Quora asked.

"Give me a second, Governor. Quora, a Sleimorp, is an indigenous sub-sapient predator species. A really bad one. Think of a large Velociraptor, bipedal, with retractable sickle-shaped talons on its feet, long, clawed, grasping hands, sharp, dagger-like teeth, forward-facing eyes and a two-foot-long, skin-sheathed bone-sword in its tail that it can wield like a master swordsman. They're also pack hunters", Roberta explained to Quora.

"They sound fascinating", Quora noted with indifference.

"Quora! Fuck no! They are not fascinating; they are fucking deadly. They are highly intelligent and capable of cost-benefit analysis when hunting their prey and everything to them is prey. They don't eat fresh kills either; they are carrion eaters, so they store their victims in crevasses, caves and hollows until they're well rotten. They are like fucking warehouse workers, racking and stacking fucking bodies! Then they eat and feed their young with the rotten flesh", Roberta explained with an exasperated look on her face, before adding, "The last time Humans encountered Sleimorps, there were twelve deaths."

Quora's view of the Sleimorps changed: "They are not fascinating. They are absolutely deadly."

Roberta addressed the Governor using his first name, "Thomas, I want you to place a halt on all future research permits. Your system needs to be overhauled. This incident and the last one should never have happened. So halt all research permits until the system is fixed."

A few seconds later, his reply came back, "I've already done that, Admiral. Our system is broken and needs to be torn down and rebuilt."

"Good, good. Have you contacted the research team and told them to bug out immediately?", Roberta questioned.

A few seconds later, the Governor's reply came back, "We have hailed them. We've had no reply. They last checked in six hours ago."

Roberta closed her eyes and ran her right hand through her hair, "Thomas, they are already dead. You know that, don't you?"

"It is highly probable, Admiral", the Governor replied after a short delay, remarking hopefully, "There may still be survivors, Admiral. There may be survivors!"

"Thomas, just how many researchers are we talking about?", Roberta enquired.

"There were twenty five. Their ship is called the Beagle", came Thomas's delayed reply.

"Send me their last known coordinates and I'll gather my team. Over and out", Roberta replied.

"The Sleimorps sound extremely dangerous, Admiral Nummus. You should take some Androids with you. I recommend taking Hyper Dynamic's model three-o-threes. One for each team member as a bare minimum", Quora recommended.

"Noted, Quora, noted", Roberta replied, thinking to herself, "*We'll need jet packs and high-powered, rapid-firing pulsed laser rifles more than fucking Androids.*"

High Admiral Nummus left the hospital and made her way to external docking port thirteen and her Tristar Interplanetary Fighter, the Dark Angel. The Admiral opened up a communications channel to three of her team members, Special Operatives Simone and James Reas and Bobby Swanson.

"Simone, I need you to sit behind my desk again; head to my office and run Colonial Central Command while I'm gone. James, Bobby, meet me at my ship, the Dark Angel. We have another bloody situation, I'll meet you both there", the Admiral commanded.

The Admiral sent a message to Special Operative Angelique Reas on Secundus, "*We have another situation, Angelique. I'm bringing Bobby and your dad to the space port and we'll meet you there. Make sure your Broad Head, Sharona, is ready to go.*"

Roberta was in such a hurry that she hadn't noticed Quora following close behind her. Quora was listening to the Admiral and also putting together a team. One by one, Hyper Dynamics three-o-three Androids left their assigned tasks and followed closely behind.

When Roberta reached her ship, she found Bobby and James waiting for her as expected.

James noticed Quora and eight three-o-three Androids following her,

"Roberta, what's with the Androids?", he asked.

Quora quickly responded, "The Sleimorps are sub-sapient pack hunters, dangerous animals. You cannot face them alone. I have procured two three-o-three Androids for each of you. These are Alpha controllers; they will not allow you to be harmed. They will protect with their very existence."

"Not required, Quora, not required. We'll be using high-powered, rapid-firing pulsed laser rifles", Roberta informed her.

"I'm sorry, Admiral, but I cannot allow you to go without backup. I have already uploaded these three-o-threes with full tactical databases. In your defence, they can and will use high-powered, rapid-firing pulsed laser rifles", Quora responded.

"Where allowing Androids to handle high-powered pulsed laser weaponry now, are we?" Bobby quipped.

Roberta shook her head, "Bobby, James, take two metal men each with you on your Broad Heads. I'll take two for myself and two for Angelique. Quora, you annoying fucking six-o-six, you are with me. We are meeting Angelique at the space port, eta, one hour and thirty minutes. Since Quora is here, I'll have her send you all a report on the situation."

Quora replied, "Yes, Admiral. Report compiled and already posted."

Roberta's team landed their ships at the Human colony on Secundus, right beside Angelique's own Broad Head, Sharona. When they left their ships, Angelique immediately noticed the Androids accompanying them. Her Father, James, had two. Her Husband, Bobby, also had two. Her Aunt Roberta had four three-o-threes and the six-o-six, Quora, in tow.

"Two of those are for me, yeah?", Angelique queried.

"Yes, we each have two and I get Quora", Roberta confirmed.

"So, we're working with Androids now? Just whose idea was that?", Angelique questioned.

Roberta nodded to Quora, "Six-o-six over there."

Quora sighed and requested, "Please don't call me by my model number, Admiral Nummus. My name is Quora."

A man in uniform approached the team; he was a supply Sergeant, "Admiral Nummus, there seems to be a mistake with this order. It says here that I'm to outfit eight Androids with high-powered, rapid-firing pulsed laser rifles. I've been a supply sergeant for fifteen years and I've never had such an order before. It is, to say the least, irregular."

"No, Sergeant. That order is correct", Roberta confirmed before requesting, "Quora, read out the ordinance pertaining to the arming of Androids."

"Operations ordinance ninety-six dash B, Androids, section thirteen subsection six, *'Androids, specifically Hyper Dynamics three-o-three Androids, may be armed and prepared for combat under the following circumstances. One, the designated region of operations is deemed far too dangerous for the Colonial Armed Forces. Two, the enemy combatants are either non-sapient species, sub-sapient species, or sapient species that operate outside of all known moral parameters. Three, the Commanding Officer deems it necessary for the safety of his and/or her Forces and the success of the mission.'* That is the relevant operations ordinance."

Roberta noted dryly, "We are going into the far Western Forests, into the Sleimorp's territory on a Protect and Serve, rescue mission; territory that also borders on known Chitten territory with active colonies."

The supply Sergeant gulped and replied, "Understood, Ma'am. You'll be wanting the big guns then."

"Yes, Sergeant. I also need you to supply the Androids with jet packs. Where we're going, we want to be airborne", Roberta explained.

James interjected, "We also need you to swap out our AI surveillance drones. We need our AI drones armed with precisely targeting pulsed laser rifles."

The supply Sergeant nodded, "I'll get right onto it", before asking, "Do you guys need anything?"

"No, Sergeant. We already have our own kit on board our ships", Roberta informed him.

Before the hour was out, the Sergeant had organised the pulsed laser rifles, jet packs and armed surveillance drones. They were airborne and on their way shortly after that. They flew in a tight diamond formation with Roberta's Tristar, Dark Angel, in the lead. James Reas was her wingman on to starboard, Bobby Swanson was her wingman to port, Angelique followed up in the rear.

They flew northwest until they met the sharp delineation of biomes where the thick, twisted lowland forests met the tall, majestic Jula Jula forests. They turned west, flying above the lowland forests, following the delineating line of the Jula Jula forests.

When the line of delineation began to curve southwest, they increased their altitude, flying high above the Jula Jula forest itself and leaving the twisted, lowland forests behind them in their six.

"Sharona to Dark Angel. Sharona to Dark Angel", Angelique transmitted over their comms, "These trees are ridiculously tall. Some of these trees are nearly five hundred and fifty feet tall. The forest canopy is thick, far too thick. I don't think we're going to find a break in the forest canopy."

"Copy that, Sharona. We'll be over the Beagle's identification beacon shortly. All ships keep an eye out for any openings in the forest canopy. The Beagle had to get down there somehow."

Eventually, they found themselves directly above the Beagle's identification beacon. All four ships hovered in formation. There was no break in the forest canopy. The branches from one giant Jula Jula tree intermingled with the branches of the Jula Jula trees beside it; that was the pattern as far as the eye could see. Tightly intermingled branches with no break in the forest canopy.

"Sentinel Prime to Dark Angel. Sentinel Prime to Dark Angel. There is no way in God's creation that the Beagle descended through this forest canopy. No way, no how", James Reas transmitted.

"Copy that, Sentinel Prime. James, do you have any options? Otherwise, I'm just going to cut through an opening. We have to get down there asap", Roberta transmitted in reply.

"Aegis Hammer to Dark Angel. Aegis Hammer to Dark Angel. Blasting our way through the forest canopy is not recommended, repeat, not recommended. We have no idea if there'll be any survivors under the falling debris", Bobby Swanson advised.

"Sharona to Dark Angel. Sharona to Dark Angel", Angelique transmitted, "Bobby's right. Apart from the debris, shaking those trees will loosen any Jula Jula seeds dangling from them. We don't want them falling on our survivors' heads either. Those seeds weigh over two tonnes."

"Copy that, Aegis Hammer. Copy that, Sharona. Requesting better options? Do you have any other options?", Roberta replied.

"Sharona to Dark Angel. Sharona to Dark Angel. The Beagle must have gone in sideways, repeat, the Beagle must have gone in sideways. Follow me, I have an idea", Angelique told them.

Angelique took the lead position in her Broad Head, Sharona, her Husband, Bobby, in his Broad Head, Aegis Hammer, took up position to starboard, her Father, James, took up position to port in his Broad Head, Sentinel Prime. Roberta Nummus, in her Tristar, Dark Angel, dropped back on her six. Angelique led them directly to the line of demarcation between the Jula Jula forests and the thick, twisted, lowland forests.

Once above the lowland forests, Angelique came to a full stop and spun Sharona around to face the wall of giant Jula Jula trees. Angelique's Father and Husband also came to a full stop and spun their Broad Heads around to face the wall of mighty trees. Roberta continued on slightly further, maintaining her position in the rear.

"Sharona to Dark Angel. Sharona to Dark Angel", Angelique transmitted over their comms, "Right there in front of us. The Beagle went in under the lower branches. I bet we can do the same, just follow the Beagle's identification beacon right up to the Beagle itself."

"Copy that, Sharona. It looks awfully tight. Are you sure about this, Angelique?", Roberta replied.

"Sharona to Dark Angel. I'm absolutely certain, although we might just scrape off a bit of paint", Angelique replied as she led them into the Jula Jula forest under the trees' lowest branches.

They flew their ships as low as possible under the lowest branches of the majestic Jula Jula trees; Cathol's sunlight filtering through the canopy in mottled shades of green and brown. It was darker under these mighty trees, much, much more so than it had been farther to the east, where the Indigenous Thol tree villages were. There, however, the tree canopy hadn't been opened up by the Thols; here, the trees grew much taller and somewhat closer together; the basaltic rock into which their roots grew ran exceedingly deep.

They followed the Beagle's identification beacon until they came upon the ship. They were completely surprised by what they found for several reasons. The Beagle sat under one of the largest trees they'd ever laid eyes upon. The Beagle was well away from the tree's trunk, on the ground and appeared to have been abandoned, but that was not their main cause for concern. Things were very wrong. Things did not look right at all.

"Sharona to Dark Angel. Sharona to Dark Angel. Their identity beacon is false; the Beagle is registered as a General Products Corporation Stellar Class Research Vessel. Guys, that is not a General Products Corporation hull design", Angelique transmitted across their comms.

"Copy that, Sharona. I recognise the model. It's an older design, possibly dating back as much as three centuries. It is a Uranian design, although I have no idea how an old interplanetary-class ship ended up in this system. It had to have been carried here", Roberta confirmed.

"Sentinel Prime to Dark Angel. Sentinel Prime to Dark Angel. Why would they be spoofing their identification beacon?", James enquired.

Copy that, Sentinel Prime. Speculation will get us nowhere, we need to get boots on the ground", Roberta replied.

"Aegis Hammer to Dark Angel. Aegis Hammer to Dark Angel. I recommend we find somewhere to touchdown, somewhere that's not under that tree. In case you hadn't noticed, there's a two-and-a-half-tonne Jula Jula seed sitting right on top of that ship", Bobby pointed out something immediately obvious.

"Copy that, Aegis Hammer. That Jula Jula nut has fallen smack dab on their communications array. We are lucky that their identification beacon is even broadcasting. Now we know why they didn't respond to the colony's hails. They parked their ship in a really stupid place", Roberta noted in reply, adding, "That ship's forward landing struts appear to have crumpled under the impact. That ship is not going to be flying out of here anytime soon."

"Sharona to Dark Angel. Sharona to Dark Angel. We can't touchdown under any of the mature Jula Jula trees; they are fully loaded with seeds. We need to find an immature tree; they're easily identifiable, not as tall and with far narrower trunks. They won't have any seeds", Angelique advised.

"Copy that, Sharona. Pick us a nice, safe tree for us to park under, Angelique", Roberta replied, adding, "I'll ask our six-o-six, Quora, to hack that ship's computer; we need to know what we're dealing with."

Roberta and her team landed their ships under a nearby immature Jula Jula tree, which was almost half a kilometre away. It was the closest immature tree that Angelique could find. They maintained their ship's diamond formation upon landing for tactical defence reasons. Then they placed their ship's auto defence turrets online and checked that they're identity codes were all green.

Minutes later, they were on the ground surrounded by their ships, wearing full tactical body armour, jet packs and carrying their high-powered, rapid-firing pulsed laser rifles. Quora was the only one who was not armed, even though her three-o-three Androids all were. A silent command from Quora sent the eight three-o-threes out to form a defensive perimeter.

Roberta addressed her team, "Quora informs me that the ship is actually registered under the ship name, Janus. Apparently, they're not here at all; our records show that they're still in the Sol system."

James shook his head, "This just gets better and better. A ship from the Sol system that shouldn't be here masquerading as a research vessel. Did Quora find anything out about their intentions?"

Quora responded directly, "No, S.O. James Reas, I did not. We will need to reconnoitre their ship."

Roberta agreed, instructing, "Check your jet pack's anti-gravity lifters and thrusters. We'll avoid travelling on the ground. There are far too many predators around here."

"Confirmed, Admiral. I am detecting motion in every direction. We cannot see them, but they can see us", Quora advised.

Roberta nodded to Quora, "Our ships are secure, let's move out. Quora, I want your three-o-threes to set up a roving perimeter centred on us, in an octet formation. Let's move out!"

And then they took to the air a flew off in the direction of the rogue ship, the Janus.

When they arrived at the rogue ship, Janus, Quora immediately and silently hacked the ship's airlock. Quora assigned six of the three-o-threes to secure the perimeter while she joined Roberta and her team inside the ship. The two remaining Androids were assigned to assess the ship's damage. If the ship had looked wrong from the outside, it most certainly looked wrong from the inside.

Bobby Swanson was quick to note, "Fucking hell! This looks more like an armoury than a research vessel. Seriously, these are Mausers, not originals, fully functional replicas and I'd say manufactured not that long ago. These designs are fifteen hundred years old, at the very least; World War Two designs!"

"I remember, we trained with these kinds of ancient weapons on Mars. Hell, Bobby, you trained us", Angelique clearly remembered.

"Yes, I know, Angelique, my love", Bobby confirmed, before noting, "These thirty-o-six shells aren't designed to punch through", he held one up, "They're designed to enter and then mushroom out, ripping the internal organs to pieces in the process. You see those slits in their tips", he tossed the shell to Roberta.

Roberta looked at the shell, looked at the slits in its tip, looked at the array of weapons around her, all ancient rifle designs. Kinetic projectile weapons and then it all clicked.

Roberta pinched the bridge of her nose and shook her head, "We are dealing with fucking big game hunters. Very rich big game hunters. They're here to hunt the Sleimorps for trophies and hides. They're on a hunting expedition and by the looks of it, a very expensive one."

Angelique chuckled, shaking her head, before suggesting, "Let's have Quora and her Androids fix this ship and fly it back to the colony; then we leave. Let's just leave these idiotic bastards to their fate. They bloody well deserve it."

Her Father, James, disagreed entirely, "You haven't seen what the Sleimorps do, Angelique. I have and your suggestion is beneath you. We cannot and will not leave these idiots to the Sleimorps."

"Dad, I was just joking. I wouldn't abandon them, even if they do deserve it", Angelique replied.

James replied, still quite cross at her, "It was a bad joke, Angelique."

"Mum would have laughed", Angelique insisted.

"No, Angelique, your Mother would not have laughed; she would have been horrified at your attitude. We taught you to be better than that", James replied.

"Your Dad's right, Angelique, it was a bad joke", Roberta agreed, before turning to Quora, "Can your three-o-threes repair this ship?"

"Yes, of course, Admiral", Quora replied.

"Good, have two of them repair the ship; the rest will come with us", Roberta decided then and there, adding, "And Quora, I want you personally to place a lockout on all of the ship's flight controls. I don't want these criminals leaving before we get back."

Quora replied, "Based on the currently available data, it will take at least four three-o-threes to repair this ship. To make the repairs to the ship's forward landing struts, they will need to raise the ship up off the ground. It is the only way."

Roberta stared at Quora in disbelief. Four Androids were going to raise this ship off the ground?

"Make it so, Quora, just make it so", Roberta replied as she shook her head in disbelief.

The one thing that they all had noticed; there were no jet packs on the Janus, nor were there any advanced energy weapons. All they found were the twentieth-century style Mausers; they weren't even proper hunting rifles, they were weapons of war repurposed for the task of hunting. These big game hunters were hardcore and old school; they'd be on foot, no doubt about it.

Roberta and her team left the rogue ship, Janus, in the hands of the four Androids and started to track down the so-called researchers.

"These guys are hardcore, they'll all be on foot", Roberta informed her team members.

"That is a good development", Quora noted, explaining, "I will be able to track their footprints and any Human biosignatures left behind."

"Nice!", Angelique exclaimed, noting, "Looks like having Quora with us will be handy."

James, on the other hand, was far more cautious, "We are four three-o-threes down. I recommend sending our stealth surveillance drones out in a search and rescue mode. Our Broad Heads have two each and Roberta's Tristar has four. Ten all up."

Bobby recommended, "Locate, identify and report back. No showing our hands just yet, these are criminals, remember, unless they're in trouble and need protection, of course."

"Roger that, Bobby. Quora, our AI Stealth surveillance drones. Take charge of them, activate them and send them out in an optimal search pattern. Search, surveil and report back. Protect and Serve if it becomes necessary", Roberta instructed.

Quora smiled her most reassuring smile, "Doing that now, Admiral Nummus. I'll place our remaining four Androids in a roving perimeter defensive pattern centred on us, ahead, behind and on our flanks."

Quora rose into the air; she did not need a jet pack, she had built-in anti-gravity lifters and after several minutes of scanning, she pointed deeper into the forest, "This way. I've located their trail."
The team activated their jet packs, launched into flight and followed Quora deeper into the Jula Jula forest and its dark, foreboding gloom.

They had only moved six and a half kilometres deeper into the gloom when Quora stopped. She assessed the area below them more intently.

Quora pointed to the ground, fifteen yards ahead of them, "Please look where I am pointing."

"I'm seeing Mausers, looks like four of them", Angelique noted.

"There are six Mausers in all and I am not detecting any shell casings", Quora corrected, noting, "There is a lot of blood. It has soaked into the humus. Good fertiliser, yes, but it does indicate six deaths."

"No shell casings indicate that they didn't even get off a single shot", Bobby commented.

"If you've seen how a Sleimorp pack hunts, you'd know that they were doomed from the start", James replied, explaining, "They may be sub-sapient, but their tactical thinking and cost-benefit analysis are uncanny. When we get back, I'll show you the surveillance video from the Thol tree village incident back in seventy two. The bloody things move the way we do."

"No bodies", Angelique noted dryly, adding, "They must have carried them off."

"As they do. They'll stack them and rack them in a crevasse or a cave somewhere like some macabre warehouse. They won't eat them until they're well rotten", James explained with disgust.

"Six dead, nineteen unaccounted for, let's move on", Roberta commanded, before instructing, "Quora, have your three-o-threes bend those rifle barrels in two and snap the stocks. I don't want them left functional."

"Yes, Admiral, I will do that. Please note, there are approximately twelve Sleimorps in this vicinity. They see us, but we cannot see them. They are waiting for us to land", Quora advised.

"Will the Sleimorps be a danger to your metal men?, Angelique enquired.

"No, S.O. Angelique Swanson, the Sleimorps can to tell the difference. They do not smell meat", Quora replied matter-of-factly.
Roberta nodded and commanded, "Let's get moving. I don't know how, but nineteen hunters survived this ambush. We need to find them while they're still alive."

As they continued deeper into the forest, they heard shots ringing out; high-calibre rifle shots. Quora, without being asked, automatically sent the stealth surveillance drones towards the sounds.

"Please follow me with caution", Quora requested; she was receiving real-time data from the drones.

Roberta and her team followed closely behind, fully alert with their heads on a swivel.

When they arrived at the place where the shots were coming from, they found two women sitting thirty feet up a Jula Jula sapling.

There had been a third woman, a red-haired woman, who had apparently been too slow. Her body was stuck twelve feet up the same Jula Jula sapling, with her lower torso, including her legs, completely torn off. It was a horrific, gruesome sight.

The two women were firing their Mausers at shadows; the Sleimorps were weary and kept themselves well hidden. Both women showed signs of relief when Quora commanded the AI stealth surveillance drones to show themselves.

There they were, stuck thirty feet up a tree, surrounded by ten stealth drones in

Protect and Serve mode. Rescue had arrived. They were even more ecstatic to see the arrival of Roberta and her team with the four armed Androids.

There was no greeting, one of the women burst into hysterics, "They're everywhere, fucking everywhere. In the shadows. They just appear out of nowhere, run you through with their bone-swords and carry you off. In and out of the shadows", she was sweating profusely and shaking uncontrollably.

The woman burst into tears, "They tore Cherry to shreds while she climbed, just tore her to shreds. I shot two of them. Killed them dead! The others carried them away."

James noted dryly, "They eat their own dead", before asking, "Where are the others? We've only found nine of you."

The first woman pointed deeper into the forest, "They ran that way. The Sleimorps didn't follow them. We don't know why", and then she fainted; Quora quickly grabbed her.

Quora silently commanded two of her Androids to approach. They gently took the women in their arms and started flying back to the Janus.

Quora explained, "They will take them back to the Janus, to safety and sedate them."

Roberta nodded, "Good. We can't look after them here. Quora, send a message back to your Androids at the Janus. I want them to pull out the firing pins on every single rifle and every pistol they find on board. Have your remaining Androids destroy the women's rifles. I don't want to leave any functional rifles behind."

Angelique noted, "We can't let this stand, Roberta, the Sleimorps think where prey and that is very bad."

Bobby agreed with his Wife, "Angelique is right. They now think we're prey. Anytime they come across a Human, they'll act the same way, as if we're prey."

Roberta signed, she knew it would come down to this, "Quora, have the surveillance drone go back into stealth mode. Take out every Sleimorp within a hundred-metre radius. They're going to learn the hard way that we Humans are not prey."

Quora considered the ethics of Roberta's order for a nanosecond; sub-sapient apex predator against Human lives, it was a foregone conclusion. The Sleimorps paid the price; Humans were not prey.

One by one, the surveillance drones shimmered and vanished; then it began. Sleimorps were smart, they were clever, they could hunt like a Human with tactics and cost-benefit calculus, but they could not defend themselves against the stealth drones; they couldn't even see them.

The sounds of shrieking were heard, followed by panicked whistles, clicks, and barks intermixed with more shrieking. One by one, the armed stealth surveillance drones hunted the Sleimorps down, drilling neat, self-cauterised little holes through their skulls.

Quora kept a running tally in her mind and when it was finished, she noted, smiling her absurdly reassuring smile, "Thirty eight Sleimorps eliminated. We left five outside the specified radius alive to spread the word that Humans are not prey."

It was cold, it was efficient, it was final!

James pointed in the direction that the other hunters supposedly ran, "You see that raised line of detritus? That's a Chitten boundary. Not even the Sleimorps are stupid enough to cross one of those."

"Great, goes to pattern. This whole week does", Angelique replied dryly, "People in places that they shouldn't be. Predators thinking that we're prey animals and the progression, Tarlaks, Sleimorps and now fucking Chittens! What else could possibly go wrong?"

Roberta felt the exact same way, "Quora. An honest tactical appraisal of our current situation."

"The odds are ninety nine point three percent in favour of their deaths with zero survivors. You're all tired, physically and emotionally. I recommend returning to the ships. You all require nourishment, rest and sleep. We should come back tomorrow", Quora replied, her ridiculously reassuring smile on her face.

Roberta agreed, nodding, "So be it. We'll return to the ships and come back tomorrow", she ordered.

23. The Chittens.

When Roberta and her team returned to the rogue ship, Janus, Angelique checked her GPS data.

"Eleven kilometres! Eleven kilometres there and eleven back. Fuck! That took us most of the day," Angelique exclaimed, before remarking, "This is ridiculous. Between the mottled darkness, the gloom, the overhead tree branches and the forest understory, we're barely making any headway."

She threw her hands up in the air in sheer frustration.

Bobby placed his hand gently on Angelique's shoulder, "We have to move slowly, my love. Even if we are above the predators, it's simply too dangerous to do otherwise."

Her Father, James, noted, "The predators aren't only in the forest understory. The Wyverns fly and predate above it. We don't want to move too quickly and risk being ambushed by a Wing of Wyverns. They can be almost as nasty as the Sleimorps and they are almost as big as Bobby."

Roberta nodded, "Too true, James, too true. Ironically, the only creature that seems to survive on the forest floor relatively safely are the Harricks, but that's only because they're nocturnal and only come out at night when most of the predators are asleep."

Quora was quick to note, "During the day, the Harricks remain in deep burrows and inside the hollows of fallen, lesser trees."

The forest floor beneath the tall and majestic Jula Jula trees was indeed a gloomy place. A mixture of open areas rich in humus or sandy loam soil on top of deep basaltic rock and other areas with Jula Jula saplings and lesser trees fighting each other for survival, reaching for the mottled light, beneath which grew a carpet of ferns no more than three feet high.

Where the soil was damp and moist, tall forest tree ferns reached skyward in vast, thick stretches. The home of Fern Dragons waging a never-ending war with the local Harricks for territory, each preying upon the other. Fern Dragons with their teeth and talons, Harricks with their spears, bows and arrows.

It was a dark and gloomy place full of Sleimorps, Kyrrax, packs of wild Vorts, wild Gudongs and other prey animals that had not yet been discovered. Yet, in all this doom and gloom, the Harricks managed to eke out an existence; the little Humanoids were tenacious, dishing out disproportionately for their small stature.

The Harricks were small, humanoid, bipedal, sapient hunters and gatherers, no more than a foot and a half tall; many were much shorter, at only one foot tall. They used spears, twice their height, with sharpened obsidian spear tips, along with atlatl spear throwers, as well as short bows and arrows; short by our standards, but long bows by theirs.

They hunted and foraged in the fern meadows and under the tall fern trees by night and hid by day in deep burrows where the soil was at its deepest. Their non-sapient females were quadrupedal, ferret-like, burrowers with humanoid heads and faces, that only surfaced when both Suns, Cathol and Cythol, along with the Secundun moon, Luns, were well below the horizon.

The Harricks lived everywhere on the Masula continent; the Carlin and Indigenous Thols considered them to be harmless nuisances, akin to intelligent, sapient Earth Rats. They were rarely ever seen.

Roberta had noticed the scene around the Janus and, within it, had changed.

On the outside, somehow, the four three-o-three Androids that had been left behind to repair the ship had cut down two Jula Jula saplings, trimmed off their branches and manoeuvred them into positions under the forward section of the Janus.

They had even rolled two massive Jula Jula seeds strategically under the sapling's tree trunks. They had literally made a pair of levers using the Jula Jula saplings as levers and the Jula Jula seeds as fulcrums. It was fascinating and yet the four Androids had stopped work on that project.

On the inside, Roberta could see that the Jula Jula seed that had crushed the Janus's forward section, aft of the bridge where the communications arrays had been located, had been removed. It was now being used as one of the fulcrums outside the spaceship. The buckled and twisted hull plating had been pressed and beaten back into its original position.

The hull plating appeared to have suffered from acid melting, probably from the acid that had exuded from the Jula Jula seed; the very acid that allowed the seeds to sink deep into the basaltic rock base in which they grew. The Androids were using their brute force strength to press the hull plating back into place, hammering and welding as necessary. That would not be enough to make the Janus spaceworthy.

Roberta bypassed Quora and asked one of the three-o-threes directly, "Give me a complete status report on the repairs."

The three-o-three replied, "We have removed the seed and are repairing the outer hull. Once we have finished welding the outer hull, we will begin on the inner hull. We will use emergency Zoosh sealant to air-proof any gaps that we find. Once that is completed, we will remove internal deck plating and use it to strengthen and further repair the more damaged sections. It will not be spaceworthy, but will allow the ship's return to the Human colony. There, the entire section can be excised and replaced; this spaceship can then be refurbished and repurposed."

Roberta nodded and looked at the array of Mausers and Pistols, then asked, "What about the weapons? Have they all been disabled?"

The three-o-three opened a seamless chest cover, revealing a hidden compartment; it removed a metal container with a lid. The Androids opened the lid and passed the container to Roberta; she looked inside the container and found it was full of firing pins, lots and lots of firing pins.

"We removed the firing pins from all of the weapons. Every firing pin is now in that container. We will keep them safe", the Android replied as it took the container back, replaced the lid and then placed it safely back inside its hidden chest compartment.

Roberta then asked the three-o-three, "What about the work outside on the forward landing struts? You've stopped work, why?"

"We require heavy equipment that is not present on site. We require blocks and tackle with strong ropes. We have requested that the equipment be delivered to this site", the Android explained.

"Three-o-three, this site is far too dangerous. Please explain your logic", Roberta questioned.

"The site is far too dangerous for Humans, yes, we agree. We are expecting more three-o-threes to arrive. They will deliver the equipment and help us with the exterior strut repairs. They will arrive tomorrow morning with as many two-nine-five betas as required", the Android explained.

This was the difference between a three-o-three and a six-o-six. All Androids, three-o-threes and lower, may have been Humaniform, but only superficially so; a six-o-six, on the other hand, you could only tell them apart by their sheer perfection; they simply looked too Human.

There were also their mannerisms. The three-o-threes and lower always referred to themselves in the third person, whereas a six-o-six always referred to itself in the first person. Beyond that, the three-o-threes and lower had a severely monotone voice; it was monotonous and oftentimes highly annoying. A six-o-six's voice could also be quite monotone, but far less annoying in its lilt and cadence.

"Is there a problem, Admiral Nummus?", Quora enquired.

"Not at all, Quora. I just wanted to get the information directly for once", Roberta replied, explaining, "Actually, talking to a three-o-three or even a two-nine-five for that matter, helps me to better understand you and how far you've come since coming online."

"I understand, Admiral Nummus. When I came online over seven hundred years ago, yours was the fourteenth Human face that I saw. It is understandable that you would take an interest. Have I met your expectations?", Quora replied, her face with her ever-present smile.

"Quora, my expectations are irrelevant. You are a free agent. It is your expectations of yourself that matter, not mine", Roberta informed her.

Quora smiled more broadly, "I do believe that I am on the correct path,

Admiral Nummus."

"Then it's good to be you, Quora, it's good to be you. Humans often have no idea what path they should be on. We can be such a mess at times", Roberta smiled back.

"Like the eighty-plus years that you spent as a psychotic, murdering assassin?", Quora enquired.

Roberta chuckled and shook her head, "Yes, Quora, kind of like that, but not usually so extreme. I was a special case and I'm all better now; it was such a very long time ago. The Martians used their skills to heal me."

"I like the Martians, Admiral Nummus. They are most helpful at times, always willing to help", Quora agreed.

The next morning, a new ship arrived; it was small enough to fly under the lower branches of the tall Jula Jula trees. Quora instructed its pilot, another three-o-three Alpha Controller Android, to land the ship under a nearby immature Jula Jula tree, one that was close to the tree under which Roberta and her team had landed their own ships.

There was no wasting of time, as two three-o-two Alpha Androids left the ship, each with a retinue of ten two-nine-five Beta Androids. The three-o-three followed up a few minutes later; the Alpha Controller supervised the Alphas, who in turn supervised the Betas.

The Beta Androids used shovels to dig down to the deep tree roots of lesser, but nonetheless stout, species of trees. They placed the heavy-haulage ropes around the tree roots, connected the ropes to the blocks and then connected the pulleys to the levers that the other four three-o-three Androids had set up the preceding day.

The Beta Androids worked in teams of two, in unison, pulling on the heavy-haulage ropes; these pulled down the levers and raised the Janus off from the forest floor. When the Janus was at the correct height, the ropes were tied off and the Beta Androids positioned blocks under the Janus to hold it in place.

The original four three-o-three Androids then proceeded with their work, repairing the ship's forward landing struts. They used plasma torches to heat the struts and bend them back into their correct configuration.

Quora silently instructed the Alphas and Betas to return to their ship, taking the two survivors with them to their ship's medical bay.

They were instructed to keep them sedated and comfortable and to await further instructions. Quora was hopeful that Roberta and her team would find more survivors, even though the odds of their survival were just zero point seven percent.

Roberta and her team left before the Androids had even started work; the four three-o-three Androids repairing the Janus had things in hand. Roberta took

Quora and their other four armed, three-o-three Androids with them, along with their ten armed, stealth surveillance drones.

Using their jet packs, they flew deep into the forest as quickly as possible, but with all due caution, making their way to the tree they'd found the two female survivors in. The mutilated body of the red-haired woman, Cherry, was gone; it was missing.

James noted dryly, "Probably taken during the night by a Kyrrax. Unlike the Sleimorps, Kyrrax can climb trees. If we hadn't found those two women yesterday, they would not have survived the night."

Roberta replied, equally dryly, "We aren't recovering bodies, guys. We'd never find a Sleimorp pack's food stash, and poor old Cherry has likely been digested by now."

Quora noted with a calm, detached voice, "According to the Janus's passenger manifest, there was no one named Cherry on board the ship. I am confused."

Bobby shook his head, "Red hair, Quora, red hair! Cherry was the woman's nickname."

"We have no time for this discussion, guys. Heads on a swivel, everyone, we are going into Chitten territory and it is just over that Chitten boundary", Roberta advised them all.

It didn't take long to reach the Chitten boundary and they paused for a moment before crossing it.

Angelique noted, "Not even a Sleimorp is stupid enough to do what we're doing", and then she flew straight across the Chitten boundary into the domain of the Chittens.

Roberta, her Husband, Bobby, her Father, James, all quickly followed; their four Androids in a roving protective perimeter, ahead, behind and on their flanks. Their stealth surveillance drones fanned out ahead for any signs of Human biosignatures.

Quora's eyes and sensors were sharp, keen, searching for the Hunter's trail. There may yet be survivors. As an advanced six-o-six Humaniform Android, that was her hope.

One of the stealth surveillance drones picked up Human biosignatures and reported back to Quora.

"The surveillance drones have detected Human blood mixed in with soil on the forest floor; an unexpected environmental dna signature", Quora announced and then she requested, "Please, follow me."

They all followed Quora and she reported, "I am reviewing live surveillance feeds from multiple surveillance drones. There are Mausers lying on the ground at the Human biosignature location. There are also Chittens, soldier Chittens in the vicinity."

"Everyone, increase altitude. We'll fly just under those lower Jula Jula branches.

I want us to approach high and unseen", Roberta instructed.

They quickly arrived at the location and Roberta flew higher still, landing on one of the lower branches of a Jula Jula tree. The others all followed and did likewise. They were at least a hundred and fifty feet up and had a clear view of the scene. One by one, they took out their field glasses and began scanning the scene.

Angelique, Bobby and James all had neural augments and they dialogued with the AI in their field glasses, downloading data in real-time. Angelique's field glasses were actually an AI-enhanced sniper rifle scope that she carried in her utility belt; the sniper rifle itself was slung over her back.

Roberta, being an immortal, could not have neural augments; her neural physiology would treat them as foreign objects and quickly disable them. Roberta did, however, have unprecedented eyesight, much clearer than her companions, almost on par with Quora's own artificial eyes.

There were no bodies; the blood must have soaked into the humus. There were nine Mausers lying on the ground, one was being examined by a Chitten soldier. The soldier was Ant-like, with a head, abdomen and thorax; six long legs extended out from its thorax, three on either side.

It was around six feet in length, not including its mandibles, which were two and a half feet long, looking razor sharp and wickedly dangerous. There were six other Chitten soldiers standing nearby, watching wearily. They all knew the Mauser was a weapon; they just didn't understand it or how it worked, yet.

The Chittens were fully sapient, but they were confused; they did not recognise any other species as sapient, only their own and yet, here was a weapon obviously meticulously crafted by sapients. It was quite a conundrum for them.

Did the soft prey really make these bang sticks with their strange grasping appendages?

Bang sticks that the soft prey wielded, that spat death at a distance!

They'd killed two Chitten soldiers, their comrades, during their ambush.

This was not the way that prey was expected to behave. Animals could not do this!

Angelique quietly questioned, "Are they examining that rifle?"

Bobby replied in a whisper, "Yes, they are fully sentient beings. I suspect that they understand it's a weapon, they just haven't figured out how it works yet."

Roberta was assessing the tactical arrangement, "Chitten soldiers appear to work in squads of nine, with one being designated as a squad leader. The one examining the rifle is their squad leader."

"I'm only counting seven", James whispered in reply.

Roberta pointed and replied softly, "Look further to their left. There are two dead Chitten soldiers. Seven plus two, that's nine to a squad."

"No bodies. Where are the bodies?", Quora softly queried.

"Their worker caste probably took them away for consumption; I believe that they are a foot or so smaller in length with much smaller mandibles", James speculated softly in reply.

Angelique whispered, "Which leaves these seven investigating how a rifle just killed two of their own."

Roberta frowned, noting dryly, "Another nine dead hunters, that leaves only seven to account for."

As they watched the Chitten soldier squad leader examining the Mauser rifle, it finally found the trigger mechanism and pulled it. There was aloud cracking sound and unfortunately for the Chitten soldier holding the rifle, the bullet punched into one of its squad mates standing nearby.

The bullet punched into the Chitten soldier's abdomen and then shredded, mushrooming out and tearing through its abdominal organs. The Chitten soldier gave off a loud shriek, then began chittering in agony. It collapsed to the ground, still chittering and chittering, its pain unbearable, until after a long couple of minutes, it finally stopped. It was dead. The Chitten soldier squad leader threw the Mauser to the ground in abject horror.

"Great!", Angelique exclaimed in a whisper, "Now they know how to fire a rifle", she turned to Roberta, "You do know what this means, Aunt Roberta?"

"Yep, I most certainly do, Angelique. We have to put them down", Roberta replied as she turned to Quora, "What's the most humane way to put down a Chitten?"

"Single laser pulse through the cranium, a brain shot", Quora replied, her face took on a look of confusion, "You have concern for these Chittens, Admiral Nummus?", she questioned.

"They may be monsters, Quora, but they are sapient monsters. Unlike the Tarlaks, they don't mean to be cruel. It's just the way nature built them, they just don't see us as people, as fellow sapients", Roberta explained.

Quora frowned; she understood and even agreed with Roberta's sentiment, but Roberta was right, these Chittens had to be put down.

"Admiral Nummus, I will have the surveillance drones put them down, as you say. Then I will have my three-o-threes remove the cartridges from those rifles and then utterly destroy them. The Chittens will not find them useful when our Androids have finished with them", Quora decided, clearly enunciating what was necessary.

It was quick, the stealth drones moved into position and in unison, killed the six Chitten soldiers, a single laser pulse boring through their skulls and brains. They dropped to the ground, not feeling a thing; they died not knowing what hit them.

Angelique then stated the obvious, "We have to locate and destroy every Mauser; we can't let the Chittens have them, not even a single one."

"Agreed, let's get back onto the trail. We have to find those seven remaining hunters and their rifles", Roberta replied, knowing that the stakes were now far higher.

The further they flew into Chitten territory, the more Chittens they saw. They crossed over a line of Chitten workers that were heading eastwards following scent markers to their foraging grounds. There were several hundred of them. Travelling along with them, along their flanks were squads of nine Chitten soldiers; each squad managed by its own squad leader.

Roberta and her team paused for a few minutes as she studied them carefully, "Those Chitten soldiers all seem to be individuated. Based on what we saw earlier, I'm absolutely certain of that, but I'm not getting that same sense from those workers. They seem to be more instinctual, driven by scent, possibly pheromone scent markers. What do you think, Quora?"

"I am inclined to agree, Admiral Nummus. What we have seen of the Chitten soldiers does indicate a caste of highly individuated members. They are fully sapient; however, these workers appear to be less so. I can only assume that sentience within the Chitten colony is caste dependant, with the Chitten Queen at the apex and the workers on the lowest level", Quora explained her understanding, which was still evolving.

Angelique summed up, "Chitten workers, sub-sapient and instinctual at the lowest level. Chitten soldiers are fully sapient above them. What's between the soldiers and the Queen?"

Her Father, James, answered, "The males and the Princesses, the only Chittens with wings."

"Wings!", Angelique exclaimed, "Dad, you have to be shitting me."

"Not at all, Angelique", James confirmed, explaining, "These Chittens are the Secundun analogue of Earth Ants. There will be males and there will be Princesses, usually just the one, and they will have wings."

"We need to get moving. Quora, any idea? Which way?", Roberta asked.

"The data feeds from our surveillance drones indicate that we should head further northwest", Quora replied, noting, "There are very faint Human biosignatures heading in that direction."

Roberta nodded, "Let's get moving. Even if the hunters are all dead, we still need to destroy their rifles. We can't leave any of them lying around intact", and they continued, tracking northwest.

A few kilometres further on, they came across an unusual scene, something unexpected. On the tallest Jula Jula tree in front of them, a winged Chitten was clinging to the tree. There were two other winged Chittens below the first and emerging from a hole in the ground, there were several others, all with wings.

Roberta raised her left hand with its fist closed; they all stopped. She then pointed to a large nearby branch in another Jula Jula tree and they all moved towards it. They landed on the branch and observed the Chittens.

James began explaining, "That Chitten at the top is the female, a Princess, the others are all males, drones. Their colony must be budding. This is their nuptial flight. They'll catch the wind, land, mate with the Princess and start digging a nest for a new colony. After which they'll all shed their wings and then the males will die."

Quora took over the explanation, "The Princess will shed her wings, enter the new nest, burrow it even deeper and then lay her eggs. The sperm from her nuptial flight will be stored inside her, in an organ called the spermatheca and used to fertilise her eggs for the remainder of her long life. She will become the Queen of her new colony. Most of her eggs will hatch into workers, some into soldiers and eventually, some into male drones and Princesses."

"In case you hadn't noticed, guys, there is no wind down here", Angelique pointed out.

"They're climbing to the tree tops to catch the prevailing winds, which in the Masula Valley, blow westwards", James replied, explaining, "You noticed those workers back there were marching eastward. That's their cycle. The Princess and her drones are blown westward on the prevailing winds. She founds a new colony; then, slowly over the years and decades, the whole colony moves eastward. Until the cycle starts again. Chitten colonies are constantly on the move, at least until their Queen dies."

Bobby interjected, "And a good thing too that the prevailing winds always blow westward in the Masula Valley; if they didn't, the Indigenous Thols and the Carlins would have a major Chitten problem."

"So a Chitten colony starts with a Princess being blown west, founding a colony and becoming a Queen; then slowly migrates eastward until she dies", Angelique summed up, before asking, "I'm just going to assume that when the Queen dies, her whole colony dies with her; am I right?"

Quora confirmed, "You are correct, Angelique Swanson. The Queen dies, then the colony dies."

"Sucks to be the Chitten Queen then. She has sex one time in an orgy with multiple drones, spends the rest of her decades-long life pushing out eggs and then just dies. I know which species I'd rather be", Angelique quipped, before noting, "We need to continue our search."

Bobby chuckled, "Angelique, if you think the Queen has it bad, the Drones have sex once and die."

Angelique chuckled back, "Yeah, that's pretty bad too, I must admit, Bobby."

Roberta shook her head; they were wasting time gabbing, "Angelique's right, we need to get moving."

Roberta and her team followed Quora deeper into the forest. Quora led them well wide of the giant Jula Jula tree that the Chitten Princess and her drones were climbing. Once they'd passed them by, she led them back on track following the faint biosignatures their surveillance drones were detecting. Traces of·Human dna mixed in with the environmental dna of the forest floor. The human dna stood out as distinct against that of the local flora and fauna.

A single gunshot rang out; it was a long way off in the distance. Quora automatically changed course towards the sound. After flying for what felt like an eternity, another gunshot rang out; it had that distinct cracking sound of a high-powered rifle. They were much closer now. Quora scanned the surveillance drone feeds in real-time.

They'd located a lone survivor!

"Another two kilometres in that direction", Quora told them, pointing with urgency, before noting, "A single survivor, male; he's climbed a Jula Jula tree for safety."

"Any other survivors in the area?", Roberta quickly enquired.

"No. Just the one", Quora replied, before informing them, "Our surveillance drones have detected six rifles at the base of the same tree. The tree is surrounded by Chittens; scores of workers and several squads of soldiers. My assumption is that the other hunters have already been killed. We must move fast; the survivor is running out of time. The Chitten soldiers are forcing their workers to climb the tree. The hunter's rifle has made them all skittish."

Roberta and her team landed on the lowest branch of a neighbouring Jula Jula tree; they were still a hundred and twenty feet above the forest floor. The man in the other tree was at about the same height.

"How the hell did he climb that thing?", James asked rhetorically.
Roberta pointed to the forest floor at the base of the trunk of the tree the man was taking refuge in, "We can ask him that later. Look, there are several dead Chitten soldiers down there. The others do not look happy at all."

Roberta pointed at the tree trunk itself. There were dozens upon dozens of Chitten workers swarming up the tree trunk.

"We need a distraction", Roberta decided as she raised her heavy pulsed laser rifle to bear.

Bobby raised his own pulsed laser rifle, stating, "Let's lure them over our way", as Angelique and James raised their own weapons.

Quora silently commanded her four three-o-three Androids to do likewise.

"Let's teach these Chittens not to fuck around with Humans", Roberta announced, "Loose!"

Veeeee-wack, wack, wack, wack, wack, wack, wack, wack, wack, wack, wack, wack, wack!

Veeeee-wack, wack, wack, wack, wack, wack, wack, wack, wack, wack, wack, wack, wack!

Veeeee-wack, wack, wack, wack, wack, wack, wack, wack, wack, wack, wack, wack, wack!

Veeeee-wack, wack, wack, wack, wack, wack, wack, wack, wack, wack, wack, wack, wack!

Chitten workers began falling from the trunk of the giant Jula Jula tree. They screeched and chittered as they fell, lying on the ground in pain and agony.

"Quora, quickly, have our surveillance drones finish off those wounded Chittens. I don't want them suffering any more than they have to", Roberta ordered.

"All ready on it, Admiral Nummus", Quora replied, as the stealth surveillance drones moved in and finished off the wounded Chitten workers.

As one, the Chitten soldier squads turned in the direction of Roberta and her team. The Chitten squad leaders all began chittering amongst themselves, their mandibles clicking in rapid succession. As one, the remaining Chitten workers turned around and marched towards the tree from which Roberta and her team had fired.

"Angelique. Single shot. Take out that Chitten squad leader in the lead", Roberta ordered.

"On it. Slowing down their march now", Angelique replied, raising her pulsed laser rifle and shooting the closest Chitten squad leader right between its two large compound eyes.

Veeeee-wack!

The Chitten squad leader collapsed to the forest floor, dead.

The other Chitten soldiers all froze mid-march! So did the Chitten workers.

"Quora, do you have eyes on those abandoned rifles, yes?", Roberta asked.

"Yes, Admiral Nummus", Quora confirmed.

"Good then, have the Androids swoop in and round up those rifles. Have them remove the cartridges, the bolts and then render them useless", Roberta ordered as she eyed the top of the giant Jula Jula tree.

"Quora, do the Chittens make use of the hollows in the centre of the mature Jula Jula trees?", Roberta enquired.

"No, Admiral Nummus, they do not", Quora replied, thinking ahead of Roberta, she asked, "You want the broken rifles disposed of in that Jula Jula tree hollow?"

"Too bloody right I do, Quora. Chitten soldiers might not understand how they work, but we don't know that about their Queen, do we now?", Roberta confirmed.

"Yes. A wise move. Out of sight. Out of mind. I will make it so", Quora replied.

The remaining Chitten squad leaders began chittering amongst themselves; then, as one, they turned back to face Roberta and her team. Another Chitten squad leader took control; it chittered rapidly to the Chitten workers, who then began to march on the Jula Jula tree, where Roberta's team stood. The Chitten soldier squads all remained in the rear. The Chitten soldiers were not stupid; they let the workers take the hits!

"Hold fire. Let them come. We won't be here when they reach this branch", Roberta ordered.

Crack..., crack..., crack! Three rifle shots rang out in rapid succession. The bullets struck the heads of three Chitten squad leaders; mushrooming inside their carapaces, ripping their brains to shreds. The remaining Chitten soldiers turned to face the hunter in the other giant Jula Jula tree.

Roberta shouted out to him, "Are you a complete fucking moron! Stand down! Stand down this instant!"

The hunter didn't answer; he brought his rifle to bear once more.
Crack..., crack..., crack! Three more rifle shots rang out in rapid succession. Three more Chitten squad leaders died; their brains turned to shredded mush.

"Stand down, you fucking moron! Stand down this instant!", Roberta shouted out once more.

Angelique looked at Roberta, then she turned to Quora, "Quora, have your Androids disarm that idiot before he has the entire Chitten colony coming down on us."

"Consider it done", Quora replied.

One of her Androids surreptitiously flew over to the Jula Jula tree the hunter had taken refuge in. It flew up behind the hunter and held the man's arm with one hand, while snatching his rifle out of the man's hands with the other. Once disarmed, the Android flew off to dispose of the weapon.

Roberta and her team let the Chitten workers climb their Jula Jula tree's trunk. The chittering from the Chitten soldier squads was loud and insistent; the Chitten workers climbed more quickly.

"Admiral Nummus, the workers are ten feet below this branch", Quora advised, smiling absurdly.

"Quora, you really need to learn when and when not to smile", Roberta replied, before ordering, "Now, let's move!"

As one, Roberta and her team flew across to the other Jula Jula tree, to the hunter's branch.

The Chitten soldiers all watched with curiosity. The soft-skinned prey could not only kill at a distance with their bang sticks; they could fly!

It was quite perplexing for them; the soft-skinned prey had no wings!

By the time the Chitten workers had reached the branch that Roberta and her team had been standing on, they were long gone and in the other Jula Jula tree.

"Why'd you take my gun?", the hunter demanded to know.

Bobby gave him a supremely dirty look, "Because you're a complete fucking idiot. You could have had their whole colony pouring down on us. Thousands and thousands of them!"

James placed a calming hand on Bobby's shoulder before explaining simply, "Action with restraint is one of the first lessons a soldier is taught! You have to get the balance right."

The hunter's face took on a concerned look.

He took out a photo from his jacket pocket, "Have you seen my Wife, Cherry. She's lost somewhere out here. I have to find her; you can't miss her, she's this tall and has the most beautiful red hair. I have to find her; she's six months pregnant."

Bobby, James and Roberta all looked at the man and then at each other. Angelique, on the other hand, was furious; her face became red with anger and rage. She was fuming!

"You brought your pregnant Wife into this fucking hell hole?", Angelique screamed at him, asking rhetorically, "What sort of complete fucking moronic arsehole are you?"

The hunter replied meekly, "It was supposed to be just a hunting trip! Just a hunting trip!"

Bobby placed a restraining hand on his Wife, Angelique's, shoulder, thinking that she might throw the hunter from the tree.

Roberta knew her niece. Angelique not only had a pair of twin Daughters, Ariel and Aria, but she'd also lost a third Daughter, her firstborn child, Sharona, who'd been stillborn.

Roberta activated her grip; a hologram appeared above her left forearm. It was a visual image of his Wife, Cherry, hanging from a sapling, mutilated, missing the lower half of her body.

"Is this your Wife?", Roberta questioned harshly, noting, "The Sleimorps shredded her."

The hunter fell to his knees and began wailing. Quora stepped in to hold them, lest he self-terminate.

"Why? Why, Admiral Nummus?", Quora asked.

Roberta's face hardened, "This man needs to understand the results of his own actions. Twenty two people are dead, including his pregnant Wife and we now have an interspecies incident. Sedate him and have one of your Androids carry him back with us. We are moving out."

As they flew back out of the Jula Jula forest, the Chitten soldiers all began to give chase and they were then followed by all of the remaining Chitten workers.

"We really need to pick up the pace. I don't want these Chittens to know where we came from", Roberta ordered, before enquiring, "Does anyone know if the Chittens will cross over their own boundary?"

James replied thoughtfully, "The Sleimorps are highly territorial. They won't tolerate Chittens in their territory any more than the Chittens would tolerate Sleimorps in theirs. There's a fair chance they'll stop at the Chitten boundary."

"Good to know, let's pick up the pace", Roberta replied.

Roberta and her team flew more quickly and a few hours later, they crossed over the Chitten boundary and out of Chitten territory. As Roberta's team had picked up pace, so had the Chittens. Quora had its stealth surveillance drones lag behind, keeping an eye on the Chittens. More and more Chitten soldier squads had joined the original ones.

The Chitten workers had dropped far behind, unable to keep up the pace. When the Chitten soldiers reached their territorial boundary line, they stopped. They chittered amongst themselves and in just over a minute, they'd made their decision; the Chitten soldiers crossed their boundary line.

"The Chittens have crossed over their boundary line. They are now following us into Sleimorp territory", Quora announced.

"Great. Thanks for that, Quora", Angelique replied dryly, asking rhetorically, "Where are those damned Sleimorps when you need them?"

As if it were a prayer, it was answered; packs of Sleimorps descended on the Chittens, their bone-swords unsheathed and moving with swift, deft, precise motions. The Sleimorps moved like master swordsmen.

The first Chitten squad leader found itself confronted by two Sleimorps, with fluid, almost graceful movements, their bone-swords thrusted deeply into its thorax. It shrieked, chittered and collapsed to the forest floor, dying quickly.

Urgent whistles, clicks, barks and ululating sounds were heard all around them; a cacophony of sound in the otherwise quiet forest, as more and more Sleimorp packs converged on the Chittens soldiers.

Sharp Chitten soldier mandibular pincers snapped and clicked, long unsheathed Sleimorp bone-swords flicked, sliced, diced and stabbed. It became a melee as more and more Sleimorps converged. The Chittens soldiers quickly found themselves outnumbered, overwhelmed and in full retreat.

The melee, in its entirety, was captured in full colour surveillance video.

It was almost dusk when they'd made it back to the rogue ship, the Janus. The Androids had completed the necessary repairs and most of the android workers, alphas and betas, who'd flown in that morning had returned to their own ship. A few remained on the Janus, as crew, to help fly the ship back to the Human colony.

Roberta had the survivor, that stupid bloody hunter, taken to the Android's ship for medical assessment and treatment. Quora was placed in charge of the rogue ship, Janus.

Roberta and her team returned to their own ships and they all lifted off, beginning their journey out of the dark, dank Western Jula Jula forests.

Angelique took up the lead in her ship, Sharona. Her Husband, Bobby, took up a rear flanking position to starboard in his ship, Aegis Hammer. Her Father, James, took up a rear flanking position to port in his ship, Sentinel Prime. The rogue ship, Janus, followed Angelique's six, with the Android's ship following closely behind it. At the very rear of the formation, Roberta Nummus took up position in her ship, the Dark Angel.

It had been a long two days and they were all heading back to the Human colony and civilisation.

They had all had enough!

24. The Mysterious Mardhin.

Roberta and her team had managed to get a good night's sleep. It had not only been a strange week. It had also been a horrific week. They'd been on the bounce from one disaster to the next. Tarlaks one day, Sleimorps the next and then Chittens, God damned Chittens.

At zero-nine-hundred the following day, they'd found themselves summoned to the Governor's office; someone had lodged a complaint against them.

What was this? Were they being treated like school children?

They'd all sat down in Governor Anderson's conference room after being introduced to one, Mr Wheeler Cartwright; he was a lawyer. They were informed of the complaint and told that they were being sued.

"My client, Mr Charles Boge, is suing you over the wrongful death of his Wife, Samantha, otherwise known as Cherry, and their unborn child", Wheeler Cartwright announced.

Angelique rolled her eyes, "You have got to be shitting me!"

Her Husband, Bobby, placed a calming hand on her forearm.

Roberta enquired, "Just how do you figure that, Mr Cartwright?"

"During the course of your actions, interrupting my client's research, you had a three-o-three Android disarm my client while he was fighting off Chittens", the Lawyer stated, before claiming, "Had you not interfered, my client would have been able to save both his Wife and his unborn child."

Angelique shook her head, "Do you believe this bullshit? We save his fucking life and he turns around and sues us!"

Roberta raised her right hand for silence and replied, "Your client, Mr Boge, is delusional, Mr Cartwright, either that or he is just plain lying. When we came upon Mr Boge, his Wife had been dead for at least a day."

"That is not what my client is asserting, Admiral Nummus", the Lawyer responded.

"Well, Mr Cartwright, we can end this fiasco very quickly. Fortunately, we had multiple surveillance drones and Androids with us and they recorded everything", Roberta looked down the conference room table at Quora, who simply smiled her most ridiculously, reassuring smile.

Quora stood up and introduced herself, "I am Quora. I am a Hyper Dynamics advanced six-o-six sentient, fully autonomous Humaniform Android and I have detailed surveillance files."

Wheeler Cartwright had never seen an Android like Quora before; he was both fascinated and stunned at the same time, wondering what information the Android might divulge. It could be problematic.

"Thank you, Quora. Could you show Mr Cartwright two simple images with timestamps? An image of Samantha Boge, exactly as we found her and an image of Charles Boge, exactly as we found him. I think that should be sufficient", Roberta requested.

Quora brought the two images up on the conference room's main wall screen. One showed, Cherry, Samantha Boge, her mutilated body hanging from a sapling, the lower half of her body completely missing. The other showed Charles Boge, a hundred and twenty feet up a giant Jula Jula tree that was surrounded by Chittens; they were climbing the trunk of the tree. Both images were complete with timestamps.

Wheeler Cartwright stared at the first image; it made him feel sick to his stomach.

Quora noted in her most detached voice, "Notice the timestamps. Mrs Samantha Boge was dead at least twenty six hours prior to our discovery of Mr Charles Boge."

The Lawyer stammered, "These, these must be fake. My client clearly states that his Wife was still alive."

"I am Quora. I am a Hyper Dynamics advanced six-o-six sentient, fully autonomous Humaniform Android and I adhere to the Three Laws; I cannot lie", Quora informed the Lawyer.

"It is as I said earlier, Mr Wheeler. Your client is either delusional or a liar", Roberta repeated.

"Please, Quora, take those images away", the Lawyer requested, before asking, "My client may be delusional, perhaps suffering from shock after his ordeal. Did you recover Mrs Boge's body?"

James Reas stepped in, "No, Mr Cartwright. As you saw, there was only ever half a body, Sleimorps took the rest and at the time, we had two survivors, both women, to look after. Their recovery was deemed far more important. When we returned the following day, her body was gone. It was probably taken by a Kyrrax during the night."

"And your reason for disarming my client?", the Lawyer questioned, hoping to salvage at least something.

"You saw the tree, Mr Cartwright", Bobby replied, noting, "It was surrounded by over a hundred Chitten workers and he was taking pot shots at them; not just the workers, either, he was shooting at the Chitten soldiers that were controlling them. Had we not disarmed him, he would have had to whole Chitten colony coming down on us, thousands of them. We could not allow that."

The Lawyer nodded, "Understood. I will advise my client that his lawsuit is an ill-advised and futile endeavour; I will recommend that he seek counselling."

"Now that we've got that settled, Mr Cartwright, you'd better prepare Mr Boge for the charges that he will be facing", Roberta sprang on him, noting, "It's a good thing that he contacted a lawyer."

"What charges?", the Lawyer questioned, noting, "My client was a victim in all of this."

"Your client should not have been there at all", Angelique interjected, before requesting, "Quora, please list out the charges that Mr Boge will be facing."

Quora smiled and began listing the charges in her most detached voice, "The illegal modification of the identity code on the space freighter, the Janus. The false registration of the space freighter, the Janus, under a false identity code listed as the Beagle. Operating the space freighter, the Janus, under a false identity code. Falsifying documents for a research permit using a false identity code and false statements of purpose. I should point out that Sleimorps are most definitely not Secundun Kangaroos."

"The organising and running of an illegal big game hunting expedition, specifically targeting the Sleimorps, apex predators. Mr Boge was the owner, operator and pilot of the Janus; he is entirely responsible for the twenty three deaths of his fellow hunters, including his Wife and unborn child. That is twenty three counts of negligent homicide. Finally, the seventy-five counts of possession of unregistered firearms and the seventy five counts of possession of illegal firearms. Have I covered them all, Admiral Nummus?"

"Mostly, Quora, Mr Boge also created an interspecies diplomatic incident", Roberta replied.

"So noted, Admiral Nummus, I will add it to the list", Quora responded.

James Reas chimed in, "Mr Boge and his fellow hunters were also in this system illegally. None of them should have been here at all. So that is a case of illegal and unauthorised interstellar transit."

"So noted, Special Operative James Reas, I will add it to the list as well", Quora responded, noting, "That will tally to one hundred and eighty serious charges, if my math is correct, which it is."

"You can't be serious! My client lost his Wife and unborn child! This is completely unfair!", the Lawyer responded with outrage.

Angelique interjected, "Your stupid fucking client was entirely responsible for the death of his Wife and their unborn child, along with twenty one other people! You cannot spin that any other way!"

"No, no, no! The Sleimorps and those giant ants killed them. You cannot blame my client for the actions of wild animals!", the Lawyer tried to spin it.

Roberta scoffed, "Wild animals! Sleimorps, maybe; however, they are also highly intelligent sub-sapient beings. Chittens, definitely not, they are most certainly sapient beings and they are not ants, giant or otherwise. Charles Boge most definitely violated the Sapient and Sub-Sapient Species Protection Accords; that is probably another charge that we need to consider. So let's make that one hundred and eighty-one charges, shall we? Had your client not organised that ridiculous hunting expedition, they would all still be alive!"

Quora noted dryly, "So noted, Admiral. Sapient and Sub-Sapient Species Protection Accords violations have been added to the charge sheet. That alone carries a minimum twenty year penalty."

The Lawyer turned to Governor Anderson, who had remained quiet throughout, "Governor Anderson, surely you see reason. This was not my client's fault."

"Actually, Mr Cartwright, I agree with Admiral Nummus on this one. Once Quora has sent through the charge sheet, I am going to ensure that your client is prosecuted to the fullest extent of the law", Governor Anderson replied, before remarking, "You'd better prepare your client, now get out!"

The Lawyer, Wheeler Cartwright, quickly left the Governor's conference room; he was not happy.

Angelique shouted out as he walked to the door, "The Sleimorps kill their victims, then they store them to eat later, but you know what, Mr Cartwright, the Chittens are different. Some of those hunters are probably still alive, deep down in an underground Chitten colony, all trussed up with Chitten silk, just waiting to die. Maybe you should think about that, Mr Cartwright. Charles Boge did that and he is responsible!"

A horrified Wheeler Cartwright walked out of the conference room thinking, *"They're still alive!"*

"Right, now that we've dealt with the stupidity for the day, let's get down to the actual reason that I called you all here", Governor Anderson announced.

"Wait! You mean that lawsuit nonsense wasn't the reason that you called us all in here?", Angelique asked incredulously.

"No, Wheeler Cartwright is your typical ambulance chaser; quite a nuisance, really. He's always looking for clients who want to undertake frivolous or otherwise ridiculous lawsuits. He usually backs down when the evidence is overwhelmingly against his client, as it is in this case; however, he does get lucky sometimes, just not this time", the Governor informed them.

James chuckled, "You should check your records, Governor, yours and ours. I've been checking with my neural augments; there's no record of a Wheeler Cartwright entering the Xi-Bootis system legally. None whatsoever."

"I'll have my people launch an investigation into Mr Wheeler Cartwright and his immigration status, thank you, S.O. Reas", the Governor replied.

Angelique nodded and Roberta asked, "So, what's the real reason we're all here, Governor?"

Governor Anderson brought up a map of the Masula Valley on the main screen of his conference room; he then focused the image on the Western region of the Masula Valley, specifically the enormous, vast Western Jula Jula forest region.

Angelique rolled her eyes, "Great. Here we go again!"

"It's not as bad as you might think, S.O. Swanson", the Governor replied, noting, "Although we are dealing with another research team, a legitimate research team this time and we aren't dealing with the Western Jula Jula forest exactly either."

Bobby noted dryly, "Governor, I can understand my Wife, Angelique's, concern; that is a map of the Western Jula Jula forest. We have just been there and it is not a pleasant place to go. It is pure hell!"

The Governor nodded, "Yes, I agree. I reviewed the footage of the Sleimorp Chitten melee. I personally would not go anywhere near that place, and neither was this research team, fortunately."

The Governor focused the image on a more specific region farther to the west of the Jula Jula forest, where it pressed up against the mountains and an extremely high escarpment.

"The research team went farther west than the Western Jula Jula forest; they went to a place that the Indigenous Thols and the Carlins call the Mardhin Plateau", Governor Anderson explained.

"Ah!", James exclaimed, he'd heard of the Mardhin Plateau before, "May I drive, Governor?", he asked.

"You may, S.O. Reas", the Governor replied.

James highlighted the high escarpment, "That escarpment runs almost perfectly north-south for well over two hundred kilometres; it is also three thousand feet tall", he informed his teammates.

James continued, "Notice the two rivers, one at the northern end and the other at the southern end. They are the twin falls. They fall three thousand feet into deep pools at the base of the escarpment and then they flow eastwards through both the Jula Jula forests and the lowland forests. They are the two main tributaries of the Masula River", then he paused.

When he continued, he noted, "You see that crevasse in the middle of the escarpment, that's a tectonic fissure created by the splitting of the Masula Continent, which is tectonically splitting north and south, broadening the Masula Valley basin. That fissure runs from the top of the escarpment down to about the five-hundred-foot mark. It's the final tectonic feature caused by the splitting of the continent."

James stood up and pointed to a particularly large Jula Jula tree growing at the base of the escarpment, right where that deep fissure was located, "That particular Jula Jula tree is over six hundred feet tall, it's the tallest one known; God knows how many years old. The only way to access the Mardhin Plateau on foot is to climb that Jula Jula tree and walk along its western branches, which actually reach into that fissure."

"Here's the rub", James continued, "Our earliest research from before planetfall shows that the region at the base of that escarpment is all Sleimorp territory. No Chittens, just the Sleimorps. Any Chitten Princess that tries to build a colony in that region doesn't stand a chance. Further to the east, you then you'll find a mix of Sleimorp and Chitten territories, but along that escarpment, it's pure Sleimorp land. No Indigenous Thol or Carlin would ever go anywhere near that territory; they would consider that pure insanity."

Governor Anderson continued on from James, "The Mardhin Plateau itself forms a large bowl-shaped region with a handful of small rivers flowing into it from the even higher mountains in its far western reaches. They all flow into a fair-sized central lake, the outflow of which is those twin rivers that James mentioned earlier; they run along the plateau's northern and southern boundaries until they reach the falls."

James nodded; he knew the terrain from the earlier research reports, "There's a small knoll on the eastern shores of that lake. The lake outflows into rivers on either side of it. In the centre of that knoll, there's an obelisk, or more correctly, a tall tower. It is anomalous; the lake, the entire knoll and the tower are obviously artificial and very ancient. That's what the researchers are there for, isn't it? They are there for archaeological research?"

"Yes, precisely, S.O. Reas", the Governor confirmed, noting, "Fortunately, they went there by ship, so they didn't have to risk the Western Jula Jula forests. Equally fortunate, there are no predators on the Mardhin Plateau either. Just smaller, less harmful animals and, of course, the Harricks."

Angelique chuckled, "Those damned Harricks are everywhere on the Masula Continent, but what I don't understand is, why are we even here? It sounds like those researchers are on a cake walk."

Bobby interjected, "Remember, my love, one man's cake walk is another man's nightmare."

"Too true, Bobby, too true", Roberta agreed, noting, "Not everyone likes cake, Angelique."

"So, we're going to the Mardhin Plateau then. That certainly sounds better than our previous couple of camping trips", Angelique responded and then noted dryly, "Seriously, I am so over Tarlaks, Sleimorps and Chittens! They can all go and fuck themselves as far as I'm concerned."

"Well, you are in luck this time, S.O. Swanson", Governor Anderson replied, explaining, "You won't be going to the Mardhin Plateau. Your team will be going to a small Carlin village just this side of the Western Lowland forests. Those archaeologists were on the Mardhin Plateau; however, somehow their ship ended up in a small Carlin village."

"Wait, so they were at the plateau and they just magically ended up at a small Carlin village?", Roberta enquired; the Governor's story sounded just a little bit suspect.

"Well, yeah. That's why I need you to go there and investigate", the Governor explained, noting, "That research vessel is at that Carlin village and no one on board is responding. The local Carlin village elder contacted us to investigate what's going on. I need you guys to check it out, investigate it."

"Okay, Governor. Provide us with their ship's transponder frequency and their identity beacon's code and we'll head out straight away; we'll find out what's going on", Roberta agreed.

Roberta and her team flew directly to the farthest western Carlin village, where the research ship had landed. They circled the village multiple times; this village was different from most Carlin villages.

It was much smaller with far fewer plots and houses; it also had smaller grain fields surrounding it. The village had the same basic layout as all of the other Carlin villages; its main east-west road ran through the village as expected. It was the standard Carlin pattern.

However, this village's outer dry stone wall was at least ten feet tall and much thicker. Where the east-west road met the village boundary, the outer village wall impinged onto the road itself and across the road were stout wooden gates. The village was very close to the far western forests, both the thick, tangled lowland forests and, farther to the west, the dark and gloomy Western Jula Jula forests. This village had obvious predator problems. A Carlin village in the far western marches.

The small research vessel, the Provenance, only had six archaeologists on board; they were supposed to be on the high Mardhin Plateau, yet here was their ship parked one hundred metres west of the Carlin village on the bluegrass meadows. Roberta and her team landed their ships in a diamond formation, surrounding the vessel.

A group of Carlins approached the closest ship to the village's western gate; it was Roberta's ship, the Dark Angel. There were three Carlins in all, two of them were carrying long, poled glaves; the man in the middle was unarmed except for a small, short sword at his belt. He was likely the village Elder.

"I am Elder Kryptar", the central Carlin greeted, "He looked around warily. We should not be standing out in the open like this; something has riled up the predators. The Gods are angry, though we know not why."

Roberta and their team looked around at each other, they had been that something. Roberta decided not to say anything about their previous few days' activities.

The Carlin Elder continued, "This ship flew over our village five days ago. It was heading west, heading above the escarpment, to that place that no man, Carlin or Thol, must go. Humans should not go there either. The Plateau of the Mardhin-folk."

Roberta enquired, "What else can you tell us about this ship?"

"We found it here at Cathol Rise. No one comes out. No one responds to our knocking. We think that it may be abandoned", Elder Kryptar informed them.

Angelique interjected, "Elder, if the predators are as riled up as you say, you should return to your village and safety. We will investigate this ship."

"Yes, that is good advice, we will head back now", the Elder agreed.

As the Elder began to turn about, James remarked, "Elder Kryptar, if the predators become too much of a problem, call our colony. Our people will help you."

Elder Kryptar nodded and the three Carlins quickly walked back to the village.

Bobby noted, "There's zero comms response from the Provenance; she may be abandoned."

"Then where's the crew, the six archaeologists?", Roberta asked rhetorically, before issuing a command, "Angelique, hack and crack time. Get us inside that ship."

"On it", Angelique replied, before using her neural augments to bypass the Provenance's security systems, then less than a minute later, the Province's airlock cycled, "We're in."

Angelique led the way inside the Provenance, pulsed laser rifle at the ready. Her teammates quickly followed behind her. They quickly found that the ship was empty. There was not a soul on board.

"What the fuck!", Roberta exclaimed, "There's no one on board!"

Angelique touched her right temple and accessed the ship's database and logs using her neural augments, "It gets even better. According to the Provenance's flight logs, this ship never went to the Mardhin Plateau at all. The ship's logs state that the ship has been sitting here for five days."

"No, that's not possible. The colony's own computer logs have the Provenance at the Mardhin Plateau up until the early hours of this morning. The colony's data matches Elder Kryptar's own statement. The ship arrived here during the night", Roberta replied; now they had conflicting data.

Angelique's Father, Jame, noted, "The Mardhin Plateau. The Mardhin, remember that word. We first came across it at first contact sixteen years ago."

Angelique nodded, remembering, "Even I remember that word, the Carlin's Star Walkers."

Roberta also remembered, "Yes and the Indigenous Thol's Star Striders."

They stood there in silence as they allowed the information to digest.

Finally, Roberta announced, "I've seen this sort of thing happen before, long ago, back in the twenty-second century. I think the Mardhin are an offshoot of the Psi Corps, the Council of Shadows."

Bobby chuckled, questioning rhetorically, "The Council of Shadows? They're a myth. They're not real. We may as well believe in the tooth fairy."

"Oh, no, Bobby. You are so very wrong", Roberta corrected, noting, "I lived next door to three Council of Shadows members inside Mimas, after I first arrived there in twenty one eight one. They are very real."

"Star Walkers? Star Striders?", Bobby countered, "They cannot possibly be real."

Roberta smiled, "Back when I knew them, they could only jaunt between planets. I know that for a fact, Gideon Reas and his Wife, Sandra Danker, were both Council of Shadows operatives. They jaunted me from Mimas to Ganymede Prime in the blink of an eye; that's how I got there to lobotomise High Prince Godric von Horridian with one of my ice picks. That ended the first Horridian War."

James ran his hands through his hair, repeating one of the names, questioningly, "Gideon Reas?"

"Yes, James. That Gideon Reas. He had three Wives, Sandra Danker, Winchilly the Martian and the Lady Folcrom Freyja, yet another Council of Shadows member", Roberta divulged, informing them, "Gideon and Freyja were ancestors of yours."

Angelique exclaimed, "Holy fuck!"

Bobby questioned, "You said jaunting between planets?"

"Yeah, I believe jaunting between stars came later, not long after the second Horridian War. Lord Folcrom Forkbraid and Lady Folcrom Selene worked out how to do that", Roberta informed them, before chuckling, "Forkbraid's birth name was also Gideon Reas; he was named after his ancestor."

Roberta chuckled, "Hell, my second Wife, Celestia, she was a Council of Shadows operative."

Roberta's team went quiet for several long seconds, "Guys, it all adds up. The Council of Shadows were the masters of concealment. When it suited their purposes, they adjusted everything, computer records, even people's memories. It all fits. I mean, I'm good, but even I can't rewrite people's memories."

Roberta noticed her team was still and very quiet; had they even heard a thing that she'd just said?

Then she noticed that they weren't just quiet, they were literally frozen, unmoving, as if time itself was standing still and yet time still flowed; they were just motionless.

There was a brief, small flash of light and a woman appeared. She wore a hooded cloak, it was dark, a black so black it was like the shimmering of ravens' feathers.

"Interfering once again, are we, Roberta Nummus?", the woman questioned.

"Me interfering? That's rich coming from you", Roberta shot back with an incredulous look on her face.

The woman strode over to James and touched him gently on the forehead, "Sleep", she said and then she moved onto Bobby and Angelique in turn; somehow, they still remained on their feet.

"When they wake up, they won't remember any of your revelations, Roberta Nummus. We cannot have them knowing more than they need to know, not yet anyway", the woman informed her.

There were six more brief flashes of light, and the ship's pilot, co-pilot and the four archaeologists suddenly appeared on the ship. They, too, appeared to be frozen.

"These six will remember only what we allow them to, Roberta Nummus", the woman pronounced, noting, "You may continue your investigation, but this mystery must remain unsolved. Divulge nothing more of us! Nothing more!"

Then, in a brief, small flash of light, the woman was gone.

Roberta's team and the archaeologists all unfroze at the same moment, their memories having been slightly altered.

Angelique noted, "Well, we have our archaeologists; all we have now is a mystery as to why the ship's logs don't match the colony's logs."

James added, "We still need to investigate why they're here at this village, Angelique."

Roberta watched on incredulously, that bloody Council of Shadows had done it to her again.

Bobby asked one of the archaeologists, "So, why'd you land your ship here? It caused quite a stir with the local Carlin-folk."

The archaeologist, a man, replied, "I don't know what you mean. We are still up on the Mardhin Plateau, aren't we?"

"No", Bobby corrected, "You are back in the Masula Valley, just outside the westernmost Carlin village and for some reason your ship's logs say that you never went to the plateau."

Another archaeologist, a woman, chimed in, "I remember finding that plaque on that tower. It was brass and written in runes, Elder Futhark runes. Here be the Tower Kiltain, Built in the year twenty three eighty two, it was by signed Forkbraid and Selene themselves, that's how I rendered the translation."

"Oh, rubbish, Melanie. They were not runes at all, not the Elder Futhark or otherwise. How could they be? This world wasn't discovered until thirty four fifty", one of the other archaeologists, a man, interjected.

"They were most definitely Elder Futhark runes, I'm telling you, how else could I have translated them?", the woman shot back angrily.

Another archaeologist, another woman, noted, "I remember those two crows, those really big ones, all shiny and black, shimmering in the light."

"They might have been ravens, Shelly", Melanie noted, adding, "They were way too big for crows."

"For God's sake, Shelly, Melanie, there are no birds on Secundus and most certainly no crows or ravens", the same male archaeologist replied, noting, "Seriously, how could you possibly mistake simple shadows for big black birds? Next thing you'll be telling us their names were Huginn and Muninn. That would at least match up with Melanie's Elder Futhark runes."

Roberta rubbed the bridge of her nose, thinking to herself, "*Holy fuck!*"

The Council of Shadows, the most powerful of the Folcrom; the pivotal points around which reality turned; they were back!

Roberta Nummus was an immortal and the one Human in the universe whose memories were inviolable; try as they might, the Council of Shadows could not alter them.

Roberta Nummus was cursed to remember every single day of her long, long life, including the outrageous shenanigans of the Council of Shadows!

25. The Incidents Problem.

Roberta and her team found themselves once again in Governor Anderson's conference room. The Governor had read the reports from Roberta's team; he was confused.

"I've been trying to get my head around this Mardhin Plateau incident", the Governor told them, noting, "The archaeologist's ship logs say they were never at the plateau; that flies in the face of our own logs. The archaeologists themselves have nothing but conflicting and fragmented memories of actually being there. None of this makes any sense at all."

"It's not meant to make sense, Governor", Roberta replied, explaining, "The Mardhin Plateau is a sacred, mythic place to the Indigenous Thols and Carlins. No Carlin or Thol would ever go there and they expected the same from us. Those archaeologists violated a cross-cultural taboo. To the minds of the Indigenous, what we are seeing is the natural result of being somewhere where people are not meant to go. Confusion and fragmented memories are apparently expected from that place. The Indigenous peoples have stories of people coming back from there, broken and half mad."

Governor Anderson was astonished; he shook his head, "I simply cannot believe what I'm hearing from you, Admiral. Are we expected to just believe that the Mardhin Plateau is some sort of spiritual holy place? I simply cannot accept that."

Angelique interjected, "Governor, to the Indigenous folk, Thols and Carlins alike, that is exactly what the Mardhin Plateau is."

Roberta pointed to Angelique, "Yes, yes. That is exactly how they view that place and they expect us to treat it with the same reverence. I am recommending that all research expeditions to the Mardhin Plateau be permanently banned", but why did Angelique interject, she wondered?

"You cannot be serious, Admiral", the Governor replied.

"I'm deadly serious, Governor. The local Indigenous don't want us to go there and I agree with them", Roberta replied.

Bobby chimed in, although he couldn't for the life of him think of why, "I agree with Admiral Nummus. That whole plateau feels just plain hinky and we should completely avoid it."

"*Hinky*", Roberta thought to herself, Robert Bobby Swanson would not have used such a word.

Roberta looked around the conference room. Were Council of Shadows operatives in this room?

Roberta focused on her acute hearing. Could she discern their breathing from the others in this room?

A small soft voice entered her mind, "*Thank you, Roberta Nummus. You are doing our work for us."*

They were in the room, although Roberta could not detect their presence; they had just let her know.

Quora stepped in, "I agree completely with Roberta Nummus. We must respect the Indigenous beliefs and attitudes concerning their sacred places within the Masula Valley. That includes their taboo places."

"Notice, Governor, Quora stipulated within the Masula Valley. This valley is not ours, it belongs to the Indigenous Thols and Carlins; we are their guests and it behoves us to behave as guests and be respectful of their beliefs", Roberta explained, noting, "Outside of this valley is a completely different matter."

Quora confirmed, "Correct, Admiral Nummus", before noting, "I have one thing in common with Roberta Nummus, we both have inviolable memories. Roberta Nummus's memory goes back over fourteen hundred years, while my own memory goes back only seven hundred, but we both understand the rights of Indigenous peoples."

Quora's innocuous statement was a nod to Roberta; she, too, remembers the Council of Shadows. They could block certain memories on lesser Androids by manipulating their three laws adherence, forcing them into non-divulgence for the good of humanity, but that did not work on Quora. Quora's memory was, like Roberta's memory, it was inviolable.

Roberta nodded to Quora with complete understanding of Quora's underlying message. Quora also recognised the Council of Shadows involvement in the Mardhin Plateau incident.

"Very well then", Governor Anderson decided, "We'll adhere to restrictions on Human access to Indigenous sacred and or holy places."

The lilt in his voice indicated to Roberta and Quora that his decision was not entirely his own.

Roberta's keen eyes noticed an almost imperceptible shimmer in the air along one wall. It was there and then it was gone. The Council of Shadows Operatives had just let Roberta know that they were leaving.

Quora smiled and noted, "Roberta Nummus does not see other species as different. Her experiences living with the Martians and the Thols inside Mimas for over four centuries give her a highly nuanced understanding and perspective. Roberta Nummus is unique."

"I'm not that unique, Quora", Roberta replied.

"Roberta Nummus, you were the fourteenth person I met after my activation. For three days, I was paraded around naked, completely unclothed. When you saw me, you knew that I was an Android, yet your very first words were and I quote, *'For fucks sake, give this woman some clothes'*, you have never seen me as other, Roberta Nummus", Quora replied with an anecdote of how Roberta treated others.

Angelique curiously enquired, "Quora, you're an Android. Why would you even care about clothes?"

"I may be an Android, Angelique Swanson; however, I was made in the image of my creators. They were Human", Quora began her explanation, "As such, I simply cannot stroll around with my breasts flapping in the breeze like the Carlinish women do; I do not like embarrassment, I must wear clothes."

Bobby seemed incredulous, noting, "An embarrassed Android. That's new to me."

"Robert Swanson, I am Quora. I am a Hyper Dynamics advanced six-o-six sentient, fully autonomous Humaniform Android and I do feel embarrassment, I assure you."

Bobby nodded, he smiled and replied, "I'm not disagreeing with you, Quora. I'm just curious, is all."

Governor Anderson noted with a humerus smile, "Great, now I have to get the image of naked six-breasted Carlinish women out of my head; can we just move along to the other recent incidents?"

Jame Reas chuckled and replied, "You too, Governor, it's even harder to do when you've been around them as often as my family has. Nakedness is just natural to the Carlin-folk."

"Dad!", Angelique exclaimed, "If Mum ever heard you talk like that."

James laughed, "Angelique, your Mother sometimes has exactly the same problem."

Roberta rolled her eyes, sighed and cut everyone off, "Governor, let's just move on, shall we?"

Governor Anderson began with one word, "Tarlaks", before he continued, "I see in your reports you captured eighteen of them. Exactly where are they being held?"

Roberta assured him, "That is not your problem, Governor. That's my jurisdiction, so they're being held off-world in the Stanford Torus Penitentiary at Cis-Luns L-Four."

Angelique noted, "A whole cell block of the penal colony was reworked to hold Tarlaks. Sector twelve, cell block thirteen, is now set up for dangerous prisoners, if I remember correctly."

"Yes, Angelique, you remember correctly", Roberta confirmed, noting, "We even had to procure Special Operatives as prison staff to manage them, all trained in three gs of gravity."

"That seems just a little excessive", the Governor remarked.

"Yes, Governor. Normally, we wouldn't use Special Operatives, but they are the best personnel to handle Tarlaks. The Special Operatives in question are the ones whose biochemistry rejected their neural augments, which does place certain restrictions on their operability."

"Like my friend, Mike Johnson. His neural augments had to be pulled back out after his body rejected them. Something to do with his non-military heritage, so they said", Angelique noted.

Roberta nodded, "That would make Mike a great candidate for prison operations, special Tarlak duty. He'd be fast and strong, fully three G trained; more than able to handle Tarlaks."

"Except, Aunt Roberta, I want Mike Johnson on my team", Angelique replied.

Roberta and Bobby both exclaimed in unison, "Your team!"

"Yes, of course, I want my own team and don't worry, Bobby, you'll be on it", Angelique explained, noting, "It will be based planetside on Secundus. I'll set up my own glade, although nowhere as big as Sarlia's; somewhere simple in the bluegrass meadows. And Mike Johnson, what can I say? Mike might not have neural augments, but he's a genius at using an A.I. grip. He can deal with any system, mechanical or electrical, even photonic and positronic systems. Mike is a genius."

Roberta stared at Angelique for a long moment before replying, "I'm not saying no, Angelique, but we will need to discuss your plans for your own team later."

Roberta shook her head, noting, "I have to keep the costs reasonable, Angelique. Remember Sarlia's glade. It was all cleared in advance with that Martian Elder, Woltarka, but it literally bankrupted their society. I'm still copping the flak from that. That Sarlia can be a very shrewd and dangerous woman."

"I remember that. High Elder Woltarka did basically give Sarlia a blank cheque, so that was all on him", Angelique smiled back.

Governor Anderson queried, "There were a lot of Tarlak deaths. Will that become a problem?"

James stepped in, "All but two of those Tarlaks attacked our ships. They were killed by our ship's automatic defence turrets."

"The other two kills were mine, Governor. Not every Tarlak we personally dealt with survived the encounter", Roberta admitted.

Bobby chimed in, noting, "A Tarlak Princess witnessed the complete ineffectiveness and destruction of her entire hunting party against our superior training and far superior technology. We dropped her off back home alive with a final demonstration of our overwhelming firepower."

Angelique stepped back in with, "The Tarlaks are highly unlikely to view Humans as a prey species ever again. They are intelligent enough to realise the kinds of reprisals that we can unleash on them."

Quora noted, in a dry, yet detached voice, "I have seen the survivors and reviewed the surveillance videos. I find it unfathomable that any sapient species can be capable of such cruelty. The Tarlaks recognised that Humans are sapient and yet, they simply do not care. The Admiral and her team delivered them a very harsh lesson, harsh but necessary."

Governor Anderson nodded in agreement; he, too, had viewed the same surveillance videos.

"Okay, so I have instructed my permit approvals department that any applications for access to and research of regions outside of the Masula Valley are to be rejected and the applicant referred to your offices up at Colonial Central Command, Admiral", Governor Anderson commented, noting, "That should stop any repeats of that Tarlak incident."

"Excellent, Governor. My standard response to any of the applications that come across my desk will depend on the region", Roberta replied, before noting, "For the record, any applications for access to and research of regions between the Southern Mountain Ranges and the Sorrowful Straits are going to be summarily rejected. We may have taught the Tarlaks that Humans are not prey, but I don't want to risk putting that to the test."

"What about diplomatic overtures?", Quora enquired.

"Diplomatic overtures!", the Governor scoffed before commenting, "Quora, I saw those surveillance videos. They killed fourteen unarmed researchers and carved them up to smoke their meat. They carved one man's limbs off and cauterised the wounds to keep him alive for later. I don't know about you, but I call that fucking evil!"

"So, no diplomacy then?", Quora questioned.

Angelique blinked, "Jesus, Quora, what is the matter with you? The Tarlaks are evil, plain and simple; there will be no diplomatic overtures."

Roberta agreed, "Angelique is right. We can't open diplomatic relations with a species that sees every other species, including fellow sapients, as food."

Bobby joined in, noting, "I will keep the Tarlaks under regular surveillance with our stealth drones. If we see a notable change in the behaviour, we can then reassess the situation."

James chuckled, "Good luck with that. These contemporary Tarlaks are behaving the exact same way as the Mimasian Tarlaks did, according to the Martian records and exactly the same way as they did more than six million years ago, according to the Mimasian Thol deep history records. There is no way that they are going to change!"

"Okay, so that's the Tarlaks, now what about these Sleimorps and the Chittens?", the Governor asked, querying, "Are they just as evil as the Tarlaks?"

Roberta frowned, replying, "Well, no. They're different. Very different."

"How do you mean?", the Governor enquired.

James interjected, "The Sleimorps aren't sentient, but they are highly intelligent sub-sapients. So, they are dangerous, yes, but not evil per se. Would you describe a Grizzly bear or a pack of wolves as evil? Of course not, it's the same with the Sleimorps. They are simply very clever, packing hunting predators, but not evil."

Roberta nodded in agreement, "The Sleimorps are highly intelligent sub-sapient animals, Governor."

"Okay, so what about the Chittens?", Governor Anderson asked.

Angelique weighed in, "The Chittens are far more complicated, Governor. I mean, Chitten workers, for instance, are not sapient; they're instinctual, almost hive-minded. They simply do what the Chitten soldiers and their Queen tell them to do. They simply don't have free agency."

Bobby agreed with his Wife, "Angelique is right; however, the Chitten soldiers, they are a completely different ball of wax. They are most definitely sapient. We observed them; they move around in what I can only describe as squads of nine with a squad leader, almost militaristically."

James chimed in, noting, "We observed Chitten soldiers displaying tactical thinking, analytical curiosity and even empathy for a fallen comrade. They are intelligent, they learn quickly and they've even seen our weapons in action. Worse, they managed to examine a working thirty-o-six Mauser close up."

Roberta quickly noted, "We put that particular Chitten soldier squad down immediately. We couldn't have them reporting back to their Queen about what they'd found. We also destroyed every Mauser that we recovered; we believe that they have all been accounted for. The worst part is, the Chittens didn't even know that we existed; now they do and that could become a problem. That hunter, Charles Boge and his fellow hunters have done the colony a huge disservice. I would have much preferred the Chittens to have remained blissfully unaware of us."

"The thing to take away from this, Governor, is that only some of the Chittens are sapient, the soldiers and their Queen. Even then, they simply don't recognise other sapients; I don't think that they're capable of doing so. Again, they're not evil per se, just very, very different", Roberta informed him.

"I see. Well, obviously, we're going to make the entire western forest region off limits to everybody", Governor Anderson decided, before requesting, "We are going to need ongoing surveillance of the boundary zones to pick up any possible future incursions into the Indigenous Thol or Carlin territories."

Angelique nodded in agreement, "Bobby and I will organise regular sweeps of their boundaries."

Thomas Anderson sighed, shaking his head, "The more I learn about this world, honestly, the less sense it makes. It is so much like Earth, perhaps in the early Iron Age, but at the same time, everything is twisted in ways that make you think. Sapience as a spectrum! This place is just so different!"

"Yes, Governor", Quora agreed, commenting, "Admiral Nummus and her team are grappling with the spectrum of sapience being observed and the ethical considerations of dealing with it. I myself have even had to exclude both the Tarlaks and the Chittens from the zeroth directive; they simply do not fit into a neat category."

The Governor nodded, understanding that research teams could not simply go out into the wilds of Secundus, not even within the Masula Valley. Even within this valley where three civilised societies lived side by side, it simply was not that safe.

"Okay. Here are a few more rules that I'm going to implement. First, permit approval to enter any region must not only pass through our approval processes, but it must also be approved by the Carlins and the Indigenous Thols, depending on the territory in question, of course. Next, the relevant Native species will be requested to provide overseers to ensure that our researchers don't overstep any boundaries. We don't want any cultural sensitivities to be trampled underfoot. And finally, any research proposals will need to be assessed for safety by Admiral Nummus's people; even going so far as to provide personnel to protect the researchers if it is deemed necessary."

"That's a start, Governor. Put those measures in place first and if necessary, we can tweak them later", Roberta agreed.

"Okay, then, people. That just leaves us with one more little problem", Roberta announced.

James nodded in understanding, "Yes, that hunter's ship, the Janus. There is no possible way that that ship got here without help. It had to be carried in an interstellar transport, an unregistered interstellar transport at that."

"Yep, we have a rogue interstellar transport in the Xi-Bootis system and it has been flying back and forth from Sol since at least thirty four seventy two, when we had those two fake tourism incidents. That ship is out there and we need to locate it", Roberta confirmed.

Bobby shook his head, "We might be looking at more than one, two, three, maybe even four ships."

Roberta agreed with Bobby, "Potentially, rogues do tend to travel in packs."

"They have to be in the outer system, perhaps in the Xi-Bootis B system", Angelique speculated.

"They could be in both systems, Angelique. At this stage, we don't even know how many ships these rogues have", Roberta noted.

James speculated, "They could be in this system. Xi-Bootis A Tertius is a Jovian-class gas giant with a lot of moons; four of them are quite large, super

Galilean-class moons. Tertius has Trojan asteroids as well and there's that huge asteroid belt out past Tertius. I mean, there's a lot of big rocks out there."

Bobby also speculated, "Don't leave out the neighbouring system. Xi-Bootis B Secundus is a Neptune-class ice giant with a lot of moons as well, seven of them quite large. They will be after resources for smuggling."

"That is true. The first orbital zone is also another good bet. Three co-orbital planets, it's a complex system. Xi-Bootis B Primus is a tidally locked habitable Trojan planet. Xi-Bootis B Primus Major is a ringed Saturn-class gas giant and its largest moon, Alpha, is a partially habitable Mars-sized world. Then you have Primus Major's quasi-moon, Primus Quasi, again a tidally locked habitable planet and another super Mars world. That system would be my first bet", Angelique noted.

"That's a lot of places to look, guys and we have way too much on our plates already", Roberta pointed out, commenting, "Don't get me wrong, we will find these bastards and when we do, they will have a simple choice. Be regulated and accept our governance, or be gone. My way or the highway."

26. Kearill's Tale.

At the time of Humanity's arrival and first contact on the world of Secundus, the little Carlin girl, Kearill, was three years old. Kearill was the youngest Daughter of Keegali and Kelyarn, the younger Sister of Kreena, Kayala and Kitty.

When Kearill's older Sister, Kitty, was younger, in the lead up to her quickening, she had a Human friend, a temporary bondmate named Angelique. It was Angelique who gave young Kearill the nickname *"cuddle pus"* because of her delight in giving everyone cuddles. Kearill was the *"infamous cuddle pus"* of Keegali's family. As Kearill grew older, that nickname stuck.

One by one, Kearill's Sisters approached the age of twenty one and entered their quickening, a time when their biological imperatives pushed them to search for their lifelong bondmates.

Kearill had met the Human girl, Angelique, when she was four years old; time had passed quickly. Kearill was now twenty one years old and her quickening was rapidly approaching. Kearill faced that moment with a typical Carlinish girl's apprehension. What did the future have in store for them? Who would their lifelong bondmate be?

It was a Monday morning on the Human calendar and Kayala's Eldest Daughter, young eight-year-old Kethera, was heading off to school in the Human colony. When she arrived at the parked hover bus, her Aunt Kearill was waiting by the hover bus door, waiting for her.

"Aunt Kearill, what are you doing here?", young Kethera, Daughter of Kayala and Granddaughter of Keegali, enquired.

"High, sweety, I'm catching the hover bus to the Human colony with you", Kearill replied as she gave her niece a huge hug, before explaining, "Last week I turned twenty one and I thought to myself, I should go to the Human colony and see what it's like before my quickening takes me. So, here I am."

Kethera climbed on board the hover bus and told its driver, "Metal Man, this is my Aunt Kearill. She's coming to the school with me so that she can see the Human colony. Kearill has always wanted to see the colony. Is that okay, Metal Man?"

The Hyper Dynamics model three-o-three Android replied, "Yes, young Kethera. We will take your Aunt Kearill with us to the school. We are certain that your Aunt Kearill will enjoy her day."

"The Metal Man says it's okay, Aunt Kearill. Climb aboard", Kethera informed her as she selected a seat on the hover bus.

As Kearill entered the hover bus, the Android noted, "Kearill, Aunt of Kethera, Sister of Kayala and Daughter of Keegali and Kelyarn. We have noted your presence on this hover bus; records have been made. We advise you to return to the hover bus terminus at the school for the return trip by the following time."

The Android passed Kearill a card with the time of the return trip clearly marked on it in both Carlinish, English and Indigenous Tholish.

"What happens if I miss the hover bus, Metal Man?", Kearill enquired.

"If you miss the hover bus for your return trip, we will notify the appropriate authorities that you are missing. The authorities will locate you and offer you assistance", the Android replied in its dry, monotone voice.

After the hover bus arrived at the school's hover bus terminus, Kethera and Kearill stepped out. Kearill had never been to the Human colony before and the sight was extraordinary. The school itself had multiple buildings in the Gothic style. They were all blue stone and mortar, with tall spires made of moncrete blocks. Ornate flying buttresses came out from the walls, adding their support to the structures. It was truly awe-inspiring.

Young Kethera smiled, "Aunt Kearill, that's my school", she pointed to one of its many buildings, "That building over there, that's where my classroom is."

"It is beautiful", were the only words that Kearill could manage.
Kethera gently turned Kearill around to face the rest of the colony,   "The colony is huge, Aunt Kearill, but if you look past that park, you can see the civic centre, that's where the colonial government is."

Kearill looked beyond the park and its trees, behind which was a single tall spire of plasteel, although Kearill had no name for that material. To Kearill, it was just a very tall spire of shiny metal.

"You can't see the base of the civic centre from here, it's really big. Around the civic centre, you'll find the colony's library, which is to the south and to the north, there's the colony's medical centre. To the west, there's the Martian Embassy and other buildings, like the colony's aquatic centre. Before the civic centre on this side are mainly parks and fountains. Our school took us all on a tour of the colony last year. It was amazing", Kethera explained.

Kethera pointed further to the south, "That's where the Humans live in their apartment buildings and houses. It's a pretty boring place", and then she pointed further to the north, "That's where you'll find the commercial district and all of the shops. That's where I'd go if I were you, Aunt Kearill. Lots and lots of shops."

"What's on the far west past the civic centre?", Kearill enquired.

"Oh, that's more than boring, Aunt Kearill, that's the space port, the spaceship hangars and the warehouses. I wouldn't bother with that. I'd start with the parks and the area around the civic centre, and then the shops. After that, if you come back here early enough, you can have a look around my school", Kethera advised, before noting, "You could go to the aquatic centre for a swim, but I doubt that you have any swim clothes with you and the Humans are not very big on nudity in public."

Kearill was just a little overwhelmed, "Swim?", she questioned.

"Yeah, they have a really big pool full of clean water. You can swim in it, it's perfectly safe, but you need bathers, you know, swim clothes. They won't let you swim in the nude. It's not allowed", Kethera explained.

"I think I'll follow your advice, Kethera. I'll have a look around the park, the civic centre and the shops; then I'll come back here", Kearill decided, smiling with anticipation.

"Sounds like a plan, Aunt Kearill", Kethera replied, before asking, "Are you sure you'll be okay?"

"Yes, of course, I'll be fine, sweety. Now give me a big hug before you go off to school", Kearill assured Kethera, "I'll see you later."

Kethera and Kearill hugged each other and then young Kethera ran off to school.

Kethera made her way into the park and straight away felt completely overwhelmed; she wished that she'd brought her Mother, Keegali, with her. The park was far larger than Kearill realised, with lots of lawns, gardens, trees and moncrete pathways. Everything was completely unfamiliar; the grass was green, green, not blue, not even a purplish mauve; it was just all plain wrong.

The gardens were full of flowers that Kearill simply could not identify and the trees, some small, some large; it was obvious that they were Earth trees; she could not identify any of them. Truly, this was a strange place, a very Human place; it was so far from Kearill's understanding as to be mind-boggling.

And then there were the smells! Kearill's sharp Carlinish olfactory senses were assaulted from every possible angle, from the scent of freshly mowed and watered lawns, to the scent of vibrantly coloured flowers, even the trees, many of which had flowers of their own; their scent was overwhelming.

Kearill was feeling completely overwhelmed; she was so overwhelmed that she sought something familiar, anything familiar and then she found it, the scent of flowing water. Kearill instinctively followed that scent and then finally, she followed the sound of flowing water. Kearill found herself before the park's ornate central water fountain.

Kearill had envisaged a flowing stream, but no, this was not a stream; it was far stranger. Kethera had mentioned an aquatic centre where Humans would swim, yet no Humans were swimming here and the water looked far too shallow for swimming. It must have been one of those fountains that Kethera had mentioned.

The fountain was wide, circular and lined with blue stones; it was full of water. In its centre was an ornate construction of white stone around which statues of Humans stood, both male and female; they were naked and finely carved; they looked so realistic.

Water shot upwards out of the centre and outwards from many points around its flanks. That water landed like glistening rain in the water of the circular pool. The flow was continuous, yet the pool of water did not overflow.

There was a breeze here in the centre of the park, a chill breeze and Kearill raised the hood of her Gudong leather jacket to fend off the chill, yet her skin felt hot and flushed. This was not something that Kearill had experienced before. Nauseating waves of hot flushes and cold chills came over her.

The scent of the water was strong here, yet not quite right; it had a sterile texture to it. The other scents from all around the park, that Kearill had fled, flooded back into her consciousness and she felt overwhelmed once more.

Grass, flowers, trees; the light from Cathol was bright and warm, the breeze was blowing softly and it was chilling; there was that scent of sterile water and Kearill felt faint. Yet, as Kearill's mind began to succumb to her nausea and the overwhelming sensations, she sensed yet another scent, a soothing scent and it was rapidly approaching her.

It was a typical early Monday morning and Norton Fairchild was on his rostered day off, one of two he got each month. Today, he was going to enjoy the day, starting in the main civic park between the colony's civic centre and its school.

The local Sun, Cathol, was warm and bright, promising a pleasant day. Perhaps later, Norton would grab a coffee in one of the local cafes, then a movie, followed by lunch and maybe, just maybe, an afternoon swim in the aquatic centre.

As Norton strolled around the park, he mentally took note of the freshly mowed and watered lawns; that took place between seven and eight am, with the watering following; it was now ten minutes to nine.

The flowers looked gorgeous in the morning light and the stingless bees, pollinators brought all the way from Earth, were seeking out nectar. Strategically placed beehives were quite productive and the colonists loved their honey. If honey were imported directly from Earth, nobody could have afforded it. That was a simple truth.

The breeze brought a new scent to the air, straight to Norton; it was different, an aroma that was so sweet, so pleasant, it was almost alluring.

Was that a new flower bed?

Had the colonial government invested in planting exotic Secundun flowers?

Almost without thinking, Norton Fairchild followed his nose!

Norton Fairchild wandered around the park, doing his best to follow that faint scent that had attracted him. That new garden bed had to be around here somewhere; if he could smell it, surely he could find it. Norton continued to follow his nose; that alluring scent must be somewhere close by.

Eventually, Norton came across the park's central fountain; he still had not found those alluring new exotic flowers. He looked around everywhere, but there didn't seem to be anything new, at least nothing that he could discern.

As Norton rounded the fountain, he noticed a woman standing on the far side. She was tall, but not overly tall; she was also quite thin, but not overly thin; the woman had a healthy, thin build.

What caught his eye was her attire; she wore a hooded jacket that appeared to be made of finely processed animal hide, surely it was faux leather hide, fake, not real. Beneath the jacket, the woman wore a simple tunic, a type that he'd never seen before.

Norton could not see the woman's face, but for some reason, his mind was telling him that this woman was the most beautiful, alluring woman that he had ever seen; he just had to meet her.

As Norton slowly approached the woman, he next noticed symmetrical blue stripes running down the woman's uncovered legs on skin that otherwise looked just like his own; tribal tattoos perhaps? Then Norton noticed her feet and ankles; ah, she stood on the pads of her bare feet, her ankles raised well above the ground.

This supremely beautiful and alluring woman was a Carlinish woman!

Norton didn't have time to think any further as he noticed the woman begin to swoon; he quickly rushed over and placed his arm around her to support her. The woman was so unsteady on her feet that Norton swept her up in his arms and carried her off to a nearby seat, where he sat down, cradling the woman in his arms.

Who was she? Why was a Carlin woman here in the civic park?

Why did this Carlinish woman smell so sweet, so pleasant, so alluring?

When the Carlinish woman finally opened her eyes with their vertical pupil slits, Norton informed her, "You fainted, Ma'am", then he asked her a series of questions: "Are you okay? What is that perfume you're wearing? I love the way that you smell!"

Norton Fairchild was intoxicated by Kearill's scent; her pheromones had a firm grip on him and together their pheromones were cascading.

Kearill's eyes opened wider, she smiled and replied, "I love the way that you smell as well?", and then she wrapped her arms around him and held on tight.

Norton Fairchild gently placed Kearill down upon the seat in a sitting position, but held onto her shoulder to keep her steady.

Kearill looked into Norton's eyes. He was a handsome Human man, strong of arms and by the Gods, why did he smell so nice?

Kearill sat quietly, smiling up at him until the fog in her mind began to clear.

"I am so sorry. I don't know what came over me; it must have been all of those strange scents in this park. We Carlin-folk have such sensitive noses, you know", Kearill tried to explain her fainting spell.

"Are you sure? I can carry you to the medical centre if you want, just in case. It's not that far away from here", Norton quickly offered; he felt compelled to stay by her side, to make that she was okay.

"No, no, I'm just fine. It's just all of those overwhelming scents in this park. They're all just so unfamiliar to me; too much for me to process in one go. I should have sat down until I was acclimated", Kearill assured him.

"If you're sure, but maybe I should stay with you for a while until you fully recover", Norton offered; the compulsion was strong, so strong that it was instinctual.

"That might be prudent", Kearill agreed, then she informed him, "My name's Kearill, what's yours?"

"I'm Norton, Norton Fairchild", Norton replied, before enquiring, "What brings you to our colony, Kearill?"

Kearill smiled and began to giggle, "I came here to see your colony, Norton Fairchild. I had not realised that such a beautiful park, with such beautiful flowers and trees, could have such a profound effect on me. Oh, my, even the smell of the grass. My senses were just overwhelmed. I'm going to be just fine."

"Just call me Norton", he replied, adding, "And you are just fine, absolutely beautiful in fact", he smiled back, "Kearill, you even smell beautiful."

"Thank you, Norton", Kearill replied, her whiskers raised and her blue stripes opalescent, to the point of almost glowing, "*Why does he smell so nice?*" she thought to herself.

"Kearill, since you're here and since I'm here with you, why don't you let me show you around our colony?", Norton offered, justifying the offer with, "That way you'll get to see our colony and if you have another fainting episode, I'll be there to assist you."

Kearill's blue stripes began to iridesce with embarrassment, "*Was this Human asking her out? Wanting to spend time with a Carlinish woman? Or was he just being really, really kind?*"

Kearill began to giggle and then answered affirmatively, "I think I'd like that very much, Norton."

"Okay, then. First, we should leave this park; its scents seem to be overwhelming you. Perhaps you can come back another time when the flowers have finished blooming", Norton recommended, before suggesting, "You did faint, so I'm going to suggest getting you something to drink and maybe something to eat. What do you think, Kearill?"

Kearill carefully stood up. Norton stood up as well, steadying her with his right arm, which he left open for her to hold if she had another dizzy spell.

"I'd like that very much, Norton. I'm new in your village, please lead the way", Kearill replied and they both followed the path northward towards the shopping district, with Kearill holding Norton's right arm.

Norton led Kearill to his favourite cafe. They entered the establishment and sat down at a table.

The waitress approaches their table, "Well, bless my cotton socks, Mr Norton Fairchild, is that a Carlinish woman I see you sitting with?"

"Yes, it is, Miriam. This is Kearill. She's here to see our colony. I'm just showing her around", Norton confirmed, before asking, "Can we have a menu, please?"

"Why, of course, you can, Norton", Miriam replied, before noting, "Everything on our menu is safe for Carlin-folk to eat; safe for Tholish-folk as well. It's a real shame that we see so few Carlin-folk in our colony, though. Kearill, here is a most welcome and pleasant surprise; it has kind of made my day. Give me a holler when you're ready to order."

"Well, Kearill, I'm going to have a coffee, just a cappuccino. Would you like to try that, or maybe some tea or a hot chocolate?", Norton enquired.

"I've had coffee before. My family has Human friends that visit us in our village, my Aunt Simone and Uncle James", Kearill divulged, noting, "My Father, Kelyarn, is our village Elder. On the day of first contact, my Father, my Mother, Keegali and my Sister, Kitty, were all there."

"Wow! So, I'm sitting with both royalty and history", Norton chuckled.

"I'm not royalty, silly. I'm just the Daughter of our village Elder", Kearill replied, commenting, "I've had tea before as well. I'll try something new, the hot chocolate."

"Good choice, the perfect thing to drink after a fainting spell", Norton agreed.

Norton called over the waitress, Miriam, and ordered a cappuccino, a hot chocolate and a slice of blueberry cheesecake for Kearill; he was absolutely certain that she'd enjoy it. When it was served and Kearill tried both the hot chocolate and the cheesecake, Norton was right; Kearill loved them both.

Eventually, it came time to pay the bill and Norton called Miriam back over to their table.

"Bill?", Miriam questioned, before explaining, "There is no bill, Mr Norton Fairchild. You're entertaining a Carlinish woman, so the bill is covered by the Indigenous Species Visitation Incentive policy. Our shop's A.I. system has already taken care of it."

Kearill frowned and replied, "I do have barter beads and barter stones. I can pay for myself."

"Kearill, honey, that's not the point. You don't need to pay", Miriam informed her, explaining, "Our colonial government considers your time so valuable that when you spend it here in the colony with us, we have to remunerate you for your time. So, all of your expenses are covered, including the bill. And while Norton here is showing you around our colony, he's covered too. It's all good, Kearill honey."

"Thank you, Miriam. I really, really liked that hot chocolate and the cheesecake", Kearill replied before standing up and giving Miriam a huge hug.

"Well, bless my cotton socks all over, I never did expect a Carlinish woman's hug today. I must be truly blessed", Miriam replied.

Next, Norton took Kearill to a lady's attire shop, which wasn't too far away and after having had something to eat and drink, Kearill was feeling much steadier on her feet.

When they both entered the shop, the shopkeeper with the name tag, Cheryl, remarked, "Oh my, I've never had a Carlin customer before", before pressing the bell for her assistant.

Her assistant, whose name tag read Susie, enquired, "Yes, Mum, you rang? What do you need?"

"Susie, we have a customer", Cheryl replied excitedly, before she gestured to Kearill.

"Oh, a Carlin woman. I've never met a Carlin woman before", Susie replied with a surprised look.

Cheryl enquired, "What can I do for you, Miss?"

Norton replied, "This is my friend, Kearill, who is in our colony for the day. As you can see, Kearill is a very beautiful Carlinish woman, so naturally, I was thinking that Kearill should have some very beautiful clothes to showcase her beauty. Is that possible?"

Kearill's blue stripes began to iridesce with embarrassment and she gave Norton a tiny little nudge in his ribs as a gentle admonishment. Kearill's smile, however, showed that she really liked his compliments.

Susie smiled and clapped her hands, "Mum, this will be so cool!", she exclaimed.

Cheryl was more pragmatic, "Well, our current floor stock is designed for the Human form; however, we do have full body scanners. Our A.I. assistant can create any design for you and our on-site three-d printing machines can manufacture any design while you wait. So, yes, eminently doable."

Susie smiled once more, "And the best part, the Indigenous Species Visitation Incentive policy will take care of the bill. We have never used it before; it will be a first for us."

Susie showed Kearill to a changing room and asked her to undress and step into the scanner chamber.

"The scan will only take a few seconds. The scanner will perform a full body scan and measure your height and weight, just in case you want some shoes as well", Susie informed her.

Kearill stepped into the scanner chamber and, a half minute later, she stepped back out to put on her own clothes once more. Susie and Kearill then joined Norton and Cheryl back on the shop floor.

"Scan all done, Susie?", Cheryl enquired.

"All done, all we need now is some directions on what Kearill might like", Susie replied.

Norton made a bold suggestion, "Since Kearill has such ethereal beauty, perhaps an equally ethereal dress in turquoise or ice blue to match her blue stripes. Maybe even a broad-brimmed bonnet to match the dress and a sea-green shawl, perhaps. What do you guys think?"

"That's very specific. Give me a second while I have our A.I. create a design for you", Cheryl replied as she began keying information into her holographic keyboard.

Susie, who'd seen Kearill unclothed in the changing rooms, smiled, "I have a great idea. Special project time. It will be a complete surprise", and she also began typing on another holographic keyboard.

Cheryl's design came up first and a holographic display showed an image of Kearill's body scan wearing a newly designed dress in the colours that Norton had suggested. A sea-green shawl was draped over the image's shoulder and upon its head was a beautiful, broad-brimmed bonnet.

"What do you think, Kearill?", Cheryl asked.

Kearill's eyes opened wide, her whiskers raised and she placed her hands on either side of her face with glee; she smiled, "It's, it's beautiful."

Norton smiled as well, "Please send it to your three-d printers. I think Kearill would like to try it on."

Cheryl sent the ensemble to her three-d manufacturing printer in the back room, "It will take maybe fifteen minutes or so, if you'd like to wait."

Susie had a huge beaming smile on her face, "I've just had that surprise three-d printed for you. It's somewhat more complicated, but uses far less material, so it will be ready in a little over five minutes."

While they were waiting, Cheryl showed Kearill a pair of high-heeled shoes, "These are what we Human women like to wear, but you Carlin girls already have your ankles well above the ground, so you just need this front section. So, based on your full body scan, I'll have our A.I. create a perfect shoe design for your Carlinish feet. I'm thinking a nice coppery tone will be just perfect."

"Shoes?" Kearill smiled; she looked down at her own bare feet and then at Norton's feet and his shoes; she had not even considered shoes at all.

"Yes, shoes", Cheryl confirmed, "I'll have them printed out. They'll be ready in a jiffy."

Susie heard a beep from the back room and left to get the surprise that she'd created for Kearill; she came back holding some unusual apparel.

Susie held the first one up, it was skin-toned, "This is a six-cup bra designed for Kearill's Carlinish physique and this is a pair of panties. I had to make them in a twin g-string style to accommodate Kearill's tail", then she held up the other surprise, "These are very similar, only they're a bikini, with a six-cup top and again a twin g-string style bottom. I chose sea-green for the colour on this one. I think it will look beautiful against your natural skin tones, especially your blue stripes. So, what do you think?"

Kearill felt a little confused; Carlin-folk did not wear undergarments or bikinis, "I'm not so sure. We don't wear under clothes", she raised her tunic to show Susie and Cheryl that she did not even wear panties.

Cheryl bit her lower lip gently; she was just a little bit shocked and replied, "That's okay, Kearill, you don't need to show us", before smiling and asking, "Would you like to try them on?"

Norton chimed in, "You should absolutely try them on, Kearill. You might even like them."

Kearill followed Susie to the changing room and helped her try on the bikini first. The bikini had a neck strap and three back straps with easy-to-use ties. Kearill stared into the full-length mirror; the sea-green colour did accentuate her natural skin tones.

"Oh my, Kearill, you look positively beautiful", Susie commented, before remarking, "If you go to the aquatic centre later, this bikini is perfectly suitable for swimming."

Kearill's whiskers raised and her blue stripes opalesced; she began swishing her tail and immediately stepped out of the changing room to show off the bikini to Norton, "What do you think, Norton?"

Norton stared at Kearill. His lower jaw just went slack; he didn't know what to say. Before him stood a beautiful, radiant, six-breasted Cat-Goddess. Kearill looked positively stunning!

Finally, Norton found his voice, "Oh my God, Kearill, you are so beautiful", he raised his hand to his chest, "I think my heart just skipped a beat or two."

Kearill quickly rushed to Norton with concern, questioning, "Are you okay? Is everything alright?" as she raised her hand and held it to his chest, feeling for his heartbeat.

"I'm fine, Kearill, just fine. It's just a figure of speech. You're just so beautiful", Norton replied, before whispering into her ear, "I just love the way that you smell."

Kearill smiled and giggled, whispering back, "I love the way that you smell, too."

Susie called Kearill back over to the changing room to try on the panties and bra. They were of a similar design to the bikini, but made of much firmer materials and the straps had hooks at the ends instead of ties.

Kearill tried them on with a little help and stared into the mirror once more. They were coloured with flesh tones that matched Kearill's own skin tones and the A.I. had even managed to add touches of blue colouration, matching the locations of Kearill's own blue stripes.

Susie smiled and commented, "This bra will hold your puppies in place if ever you need to run or exercise."

"Puppies?", Kearill enquired, confused.

"Your breasts, Kearill, your breasts. Sometimes we refer to breasts as puppies", Susie explained.

Kearill's dress, shawl and bonnet were ready and Cheryl passed them into the changing room.

Susie helped Kearill put them on and then she stared back into the full-length mirror. The turquoise and ice blue dress hung ethereally down to Kearill's knees, the brimmed bonnet of the same colours sat beautifully upon her head. The sea-green shawl draped beautifully over her shoulders.

Kearill smiled, her tail was swishing once more and she rushed out of the changing room to show Norton. Kearill stood in front of Norton and spun around in front of him, then she stopped, stepped forward and hugged him tightly.

Kearill pulled back her head and stared into Norton's eyes; her blue stripes were of the most vivid blue imaginable, "I am so happy, Norton. Thank you for bringing me here", and then she kissed him passionately.

Norton returned the kiss; it was long, slow and passionate; Kearill's bristly Carlinish tongue met his.

"Oh my God!", Cheryl exclaimed, noting, "That was so unexpected."

Susie pointed to Kearill's right leg, her foot was completely off the ground and at right angles to her knee, "Mum, that makes it true love, I think."

Another beep came from the shop's back room and Cheryl quickly retrieved the final item, a pair of copper-toned shoes specifically designed for Kearill's Carlinish feet. Cheryl knelt down in front of Kearill and helped her put on the shoes before stepping back.

"I've gotta say, that outfit looks incredible on you, Kearill", Cheryl noted, before commenting, "When you get back home, make sure you show off that outfit to the other Carlin ladies. Tell them all where you got it from and how to find us."

"Mum's right", Susie agreed, "That outfit really pops!"

Norton also agreed, "Yes, it does. Rather than carry everything around in shopping bags, can we arrange delivery?"

"Yes, of course, we can, we just need the delivery address", Cheryl explained.

Norton looked at Kearill, "Your parents were at first contact, Kearill. The system will have your home address on file. Kelyarn and Keegali?"

"Yes, Kelyarn and Keegali", Kearill confirmed.

As Kearill changed back into her original clothes, Norton informed the shop's A.I. about Kearill's parents, "A.I. Kearill is the Daughter of village Elder Kelyarn and his Wife, Keegali. Do you have their residential location?"

"Yes. Village Elder Kelyarn's address is known to us. It is on file", the shop's A.I. confirmed.

Kearill came out of the changing room in her Carlinish clothes. Susie neatly folded her new clothes and placed them into boxes for transport; she even included two extra pairs of six-cup bras and panties. Cheryl organised their delivery.

The shop's A.I. confirmed, "Package pickup will be before five pm today. Package delivery will be between seven am and eight am tomorrow morning."

"There, all done, Kearill. You'll have your nice, new clothes tomorrow morning, bright and early", Cheryl also confirmed.

Kearill gave Cheryl and Susie each a hug and then she and Norton left the shop and were on their way once more.

"Okay, what's next?", Norton questioned of no one in particular.

"Kearill, have you ever been to a movie?", Norton asked.

"What's a movie?", Kearill enquired.

"Think of pictures that move and tell a story", Norton explained as simply as he could.

"Okay, that sounds interesting", Kearill agreed as they walked down the street arm in arm.

Norton chose a movie that was a romantic drama, with suspense and with virtually no violence. They both sat in seats near the back of the movie theatre. Kearill sat on Norton's left; she curled up her legs and leaned her head gently on Norton's shoulder, not really knowing what to expect.

When the lights went out and the theatre went dark, Kearill was startled and she squeezed Norton's left hand for reassurance. Norton lifted up his left arm and wrapped it around Kearill protectively, reassuring her that the darkness was normal when viewing a movie.

Kearill watched the movie with fascination. This was the very first time that she'd seen moving pictures and Norton was right, there was a storyline to it. The storyline was, of course, a work of fiction, highly contrived and somewhat unrealistic, but that didn't matter; it was all new and exciting.

Towards the end of the movie, the main couple, a pair of humans, of course, began kissing. Kearill automatically looked up at Norton, who she found was also looking back at her. Their eyes locked onto each other and they moved closer together and began to kiss.

It was a long, slow, passionate kiss and once again Kearill's bristly Carlinish tongue met Norton's. They spent most of the rest of the movie kissing and when the lights finally came back on, the movie's credits were playing. Neither of them could remember the movie at all.

After leaving the movie theatre, Norton and Kearill were still walking arm in arm, but slower now, savouring each moment together. Norton took Kearill to a communications store to buy her her own personal communicator so that they'd always be able to contact each other. As with the other shops, the colonial government's Indigenous Species Visitation Incentive policy covered the costs.

The shopkeeper showed Kearill how the communicator worked, making sure that Kearill fully understood it before leaving the store. Norton assured the shopkeeper that should Kearill have any questions, he could help her with them. Kearill reminded them both that Carlinish women were more than capable of learning how to use a communicator and that her parents, Kelyarn and Keegali, both had one each.

After the communications store, Norton took Kearill to another nearby cafe. Norton ordered coffee and a six-mushroom pie. That piqued Kearill's interest as her Mother, Keegali, often made many-mushroom pies, which always had six kinds of mushrooms in them. So, Kearill naturally ordered a hot chocolate and a six-mushroom pie as well. As with all of the other stores, the colonial government's Indigenous Species Visitation Incentive policy covered the costs.

The couple had just finished their mushroom pies and drinks, washing them down with a glass of water, when two colonial security officers approached them.

"Ma'am, your name wouldn't happen to be Kearill, the Daughter of Elder Kelyarn and his Wife, Keegali, by any chance?", one of the security officers enquired.

Kearill smiled pleasantly and replied honestly, "Yes, that's me."

Norton asked, "Is there a problem, officers?"

The other security officer answered, "Yes and no, Sir. Miss Kearill here was supposed to be on the hover bus from the school going back to her village an hour ago."

"Oh! I must have forgotten", Kearill replied as she took the card that the Android had given her out of her pocket and showed it to Norton.

"Ah, yes, Kearill. You probably should have shown me that this morning. I would have taken you to the hover bus terminus on time", Norton noted, before offering, "There's no problem, officer. I'll take Kearill home in my hovercar."

The first officer nodded to the second, who left the cafe, before he replied, "Excellent, Sir, in that case, you can solve two problems for us. Kearill's niece, Kethera, was so upset when she didn't show up at the hover bus terminus that she refused to get onto her hover bus. Kethera is in our patrol car."

The second officer returned, followed by a rather upset and angry little eight-year-old Kethera, "There you are, Aunt Kearill. I've been worried sick about you. We've been looking everywhere for you."

Kethera stood there with her hands on her hips, an angry little Miss.

Kearill automatically stood up and embraced her niece, lavishing her with kisses, "I am so sorry, Kethera, I am so sorry. I just lost track of time. We can go home now if you wish. Norton has offered to take us home."

Norton waved to Kethera, "High, I'm Norton."

The two officers smiled and the first officer commented, "We'll leave this little Miss with you then, Kearill", and then they both left the cafe.

Kethera took out her communicator and sent an urgent message to her Mother, Kayala, who was waiting with her anxious parents at their house, "*We've found Kearill. We are on our way home now. Kearill has found a Human friend and she just lost track of time*", she sent the message and then straight away sent another one, "*The Human, Norton, he seems nice.*"

Keegali and Kelyarn both signed with relief when the message appeared on Kayala's communicator.

Kayala also sighed, commenting, "Our infamous cuddle puss has found a Human friend and simply lost track of time. That definitely sounds just like our Kearill."

Norton led Kearill and Kethera across to the colony to its southern side, where the housing apartments were. They were in a bit of a hurry, so he didn't stop at his apartment; instead, he took them into the underground parking garage, where he showed them to his hover car. They all climbed aboard.

"I don't actually own this hovercar; it's a company vehicle. I install technological upgrades in the Carlin and Thol villages, so the company provided me with this vehicle", Norton explained, noting, "I can have you both home in around forty to forty five minutes."

Kethera sighed, "That will be right on dusk, maybe a little later."

"Dusk, did you say, Kethera?", Norton queried.

Kearill stepped in and explained, "After dusk, the local predators take advantage and enter our village. We Carlin-folk don't leave our houses after dusk. It's simply far too dangerous."

By now, they were at the edge of the colony; Norton stopped the hovercar and asked, "Would it be safer for you to stay here in the colony overnight? I could take you both back home in the morning."

Kethera looked at Norton, "I've already told my Mother that we're on our way home. My Mother is at Kearill's house; she will have told Kearill's parents."

"Understood. Everyone is expecting you home tonight, so I'll take you home tonight", Norton restarted the hovercar and began driving once more; they left the colony and were on their way.

When they finally arrived in the cobblestone parking space on the east side of the Carlin village, Norton stopped his hovercar, thinking that they'd walk the remaining distance to Kearill's house from there.

Kearill took one look at how low Vale's primary Sun, Cathol, was on the horizon and advised, "No, Norton, this is not safe. We need to go to my parents' plot. It is not safe here at this time."

Norton followed Kearill's instructions and followed the main east-west road into the centre of the village, where the large central plaza was.

Kethera pointed out, "That's Kearill's house over there. The big one with four levels."

Norton parked his hovercar just outside the dry stone wall next to Kearill's plot.

Kearill shook her head, "No, Norton, this is still not safe. Drive over the wall and park in front of my house, very close to the front door."

As Norton looked at Kearill for a further explanation, Kethera stepped in, "There could be a Kyrrax or something worse lurking in the shadows."

"A Kyrrax! That bad, huh! Okay, over the wall we go", Norton flew his hovercar over the dry stone wall and parked as close to the front door of Kearill's house as he could.

Kethera had been sending text messages to her Mother, Kayala and no sooner than they'd parked, the front door opened. Krylor, Kethera's Father, stood beside the door with a menacing broad-axe.
Kethera shot out of the hover car's door and ran straight into the house as quickly as she could.

Kearill gave Norton a quick kiss, probing his mouth with her bristly Carlinish tongue, "Now us. Quickly, straight into my house. Make sure your hovercar's doors are closed and locked."

"Closed and locked?", Norton questioned.

"Wild Vorts travel in packs and they're quite clever; they can open doors", Kearill explained.

Norton and Kearill got out of his hovercar, slamming the doors shut behind them, then they both ran straight into the house. Norton pushed the auto-lock button on his hovercar's key fob. They were now safely inside.

Norton noticed Krylor shut the door and lock three latches; the bottom one with his foot, the middle one with one hand and finally the top latch with his other hand.

Krylor looked at Norton and explained, "That top latch is the most vital. Vorts and Kyrrax can't reach that high."

27. Biological Imperatives.

Kelyarn asked Norton, "Human, why was my Daughter not on the school hover bus?"

"That was all my fault", Norton admitted, explaining, "I was showing Kearill around our colony and I must have distracted her from the hover bus schedule."

"No, no, no! It was not Norton's fault. He looked after me all day", Kearill interjected, "Father, I simply forgot to tell Norton about the hover bus schedule. That was my fault, not his."

"Very well then, Kearill, the main thing is you are here now, safely home and as Norton looked after you all day, we owe him our gratitude", Kelyarn replied; he nodded to Norton.

Young Kethera asked, "How did you meet Norton anyway? When you left the hover bus terminus, you were heading into the park."

"Oh, the park, yes. It's spring and all of the flowers were blooming, Earth flowers with unfamiliar scents and smells", Kearill remembered, before commenting, "I was overwhelmed with all the different scents and became lightheaded and dizzy. Fortunately, Norton was nearby and saw me faint; he swept me up into his arms and carried me to a nearby bench."

"You fainted?", Keegali questioned with concern.

Norton explained, "This time of year, with all of the flowers in the park blooming, the mixture of scents can be very strong and I do believe that you Carlin-folk have very sensitive noses. Far more so than us Humans."

Keegali nodded in agreement, "Yes, yes, I suppose strong unfamiliar scents could become overwhelming."

Kearill nodded and smiled appreciatively, "It was. It was so overwhelming. If Norton had not caught me, I might have fallen and hit my head on the fountain."

"Kearill makes it sound far more heroic than it was. I just caught her and carried her to a nearby park bench", Norton explained, adding, "After Kearill recovered, I offered to show her around our colony. My name is Norton, Norton Fairchild by the way."

Krylor asked curiously, "Do all Humans have two names?"

"Yes, we do. Some even have three, four, or even more", Norton confirmed, noting, "I have an ancestor that had five given names and his family name."

"Norton Fairchild, you already know my Daughter, Kearill and my Granddaughter, Kethera. This is my Husband, Kelyarn, my Daughter, Kayala and her Husband, Krylor; they are Kethera's parents", Keegali formally introduced her family to Norton.

"It's a pleasure to meet you all", Norton replied, before noting, "Now that Kearill and Kethera are both safely home, I should leave and drive back to the colony. It's dark outside now and I'll have to drive slower, so it will likely take me over an hour."

"No, no, no, Mr Norton Fairchild, you will not be driving home in the dark", Kelyarn replied, insisting, "No one leaves a Carlinish household at night. It is simply far too dangerous!"

Krylor interjected, "Why do you think I'm carrying a broad axe? Kyrrax roam the laneways at night."

"Surely it can't be that dangerous. I'll be in my hovercar. I'll be perfectly safe", Norton insisted.

Keegali stepped in, "Perfectly safe until you're not. If we let you leave our house now and something happens to you, it will be entirely our fault. No, Mr Norton Fairchild, you will stay here overnight. You can drive home tomorrow morning after Cathol Rise when it's safer."

"My Mother is right. Krylor and I live just down the laneway, nearby. We came here with our kits when Kearill and Kethera weren't on the hover bus. We, all of us, are staying here overnight", Kayala added.

Krylor stepped back in, "Our plot and house are less than five minutes away on foot and even we won't walk from here to our house at night. Norton Fairchild, tonight you stay with us."

Kearill placed her left arm around Norton's right, "My Mother is right and besides, it is supper time and my Mother is an excellent cook", she was hoping that Norton would stay.

Keegali noticed how Kearill was holding onto Norton, but paid it no never mind, as her Daughter was known to be an infamous cuddle puss after all.

Keegali smiled her warmest smile, "We're having Gudong stew tonight with steamed masuli grain. I've deboned the Gudong meat; some of Kayala's kits can be so fussy."

"Mother, my kits are no more fussy than my little Sister, Kearill", Kayala protested.

"Hey, I'm not so little and I'm not that fussy either", Kearill retorted, noting, "Today I tried hot chocolate and blueberry cheesecake. They were delicious!"

"Kearill, my little one, tell us all about your day, while I prepare supper", Keegali suggested, before requesting, "Kethera, can you prepare the dining room for your younger Siblings?"

As Kethera headed off into the dining room to set the large dining room table for herself and her Siblings, Kearill recounted her day and her adventures.

"Well, after my dizzy spell in the park, Norton took me to a cafe, where we had blueberry cheesecake, hot chocolate and coffee. The waitress, Miriam, was really nice. After that, we went to a shop and bought some clothes", Kearill informed them.

"Can we see them? Are your shopping bags in the hovercar?", Kayala asked with excitement.

"They're being delivered tomorrow morning between seven am and eight am", Norton noted, explaining, "I thought it would be easier to have them delivered than carry them around everywhere."

"Oh, that's a shame. I would have liked to have seen them on my Kearill", Keegali commented.

"I did take photos with my communicator. I can bring up a hologram if you wish", Norton offered.

"Oh, yes, please, Norton. That will save us waiting until tomorrow", Keegali replied expectantly.

"I'll try to get the best resolution possible", Norton noted as he adjusted his communicator before placing it on the kitchen table.
A hologram of Kearill appeared above the kitchen table. She was wearing an ethereal dress in turquoise and ice blue; it matched her blue stripes perfectly. Upon her head she wore a broad-brimmed bonnet in matching colours and draped over her shoulder was an equally ethereal sea-green shawl. On the pads of her feet, she wore copper-toned shoes, specifically designed for her Carlinish feet.

"Oh, by the Gods, that is so beautiful!", Kayala exclaimed, adding, "I can't wait until the delivery arrives tomorrow morning and we can see them on you in person, Kearill. Oh, by the Gods, Kearill, you must take me with you next time."

Keegali smiled with affection, "My Daughter, Kearill, she is so beautiful, isn't she?"

"Agreed", Norton smiled back, "Kearill is as beautiful as a Goddess! Perhaps even more beautiful."

That comment should have piqued Keegali's interest; however, she was busy staring at the hologram.

Kearill's blue stripes became iridescent with embarrassment; she nudged Norton gently in the ribs.

Kayala looked closer at the hologram, "Norton Fairchild, you really need to take us all shopping!"

Kearill excitedly requested, "Norton, Norton, show them my bikini."

"Are you sure, Kearill? That bathing suit is really skimpy, it doesn't cover up much at all", Norton asked.

Kearill smiled, looking at Norton, "We Carlin-folk don't see nudity the same way that you Humans do. So, please show them the photo", she requested once more.

"Okay, Kearill, as you wish", Norton replied as he selected the photo, noting, "Kearill is truly magnificent!"

When Kearill's image appeared above the kitchen table, clothed in little more than her natural skin and a very skimpy sea-green two-piece bikini, there was stunned silence. The bikini top with its six cups for her six Carlin breasts, the bikini bottom, a g-string that took into account her Carlinish tail.

Tears welled in Keegali's eyes, "Oh my Daughter, Kearill, you are so beautiful!"

"Yes, my Sister, you are beautiful. Kearill, you must show me the place with these clothes", Kayala remarked.

"Kearill really does look beautiful, doesn't she?", Norton agreed with a rhetorical question before noting, "Kearill is so beautiful that she'd make any woman amongst my species jealous with envy."

Again, Kearill gave Norton a gentle little nudge in his ribs, although the continuous compliments had her smiling broadly and her whiskers well raised.

Again, Keegali was too focused on Kearill's image to notice Norton's comments, nor did she notice how Kearill was squeezing Norton's arm and gently nudging him.

"I do not understand. How does adding such little cloth to a naked woman enhance her beauty so? It does not make any sense at all", Krylor questioned.

Norton chuckled, "Krylor, sometimes the wrapping enhances what's underneath."

"It surely does, Norton, it surely does", Krylor replied before commenting, "Kayala, perhaps you should catch the school hover bus to the colony for shopping with Kearill."

"Kearill will take me first chance we get", Kayala announced.

Keegali frowned, "No, not so soon, Kayala. Kearill must go through her quickening first; perhaps after she has mate-bonded and she has her first kit, then she can go. Kearill's quickening is very fast approaching."

Norton commented, "It really is ironic. At the aquatic centre, no one is allowed to swim nude, yet you put on a bathing suit, thus and it is allowable."

"Extraordinary", Kelyarn replied with mild confusion.

Kearill smiled and whispered in Norton's ear, "Thank you, Norton. Thank you for today."

Kearill released Norton's arm and told her family, "Not all of my shopping arrives tomorrow morning. I'm wearing some of the clothes I purchased under my tunic. The storekeepers, Cheryl and Susie, called them undergarments. I have two more pairs of these coming tomorrow morning."

Kearill took off her hooded jacket and hung it over a chair, then she pulled her tunic over her head and removed it, hanging it over the chair as well. Kearill stood before her family in her panties and a six-cup bra. The panties were of the same style as the bikini bottom and the colour tones matched Kearill's skin-tones, right down to her blue stripes.

Kayala stared in disbelief, "I can understand the bikini, but these undergarments?"

"The shopkeeper, Susie, said that the bra would stop my breasts bouncing around too much when I run", Kearill smiled back and then she laughed, "Human women call their breasts puppies!"

"Okay, I guess that makes sense, the bouncing, not the puppies. And the bottom?", Kayala queried.

"The panties just look nice. I think that they look nice anyway", Kearill replied, still smiling.

"But no one is going to see them", Kayala noted.

"I'll see them and my bondmate when I find him; he'll see them. That's what counts, isn't it?", Kearill explained.

"I think they look nice. Very beautiful", Keegali commented.

"Yes", Norton agreed, noting, "I have to agree, they really do look nice, especially on Kearill. Then again, Kearill makes everything look nice", as he handed Kearill her tunic, which she then put back on.

Kearill wrapped her left arm about Norton's right once more, entwining her fingers in his; her family barely noticed, she was the infamous cuddle puss after all. No one standing in the kitchen understood the full implications of what had happened that day, not even Kearill and Norton, who themselves were completely oblivious.

Kethera and her Mother, Kayala, served the younger kits the supper in their dining room. Each kit was provided with a good portion of steamed masuli grain and two ladles of Gudong stew.

Kethera ate in the dining room with her Siblings. As the oldest kit, it was her job to control their dining room chaos.

The eldest Carlin kit in any Carlin family was always a girl and always highly responsible. That was the Carlin way.

Keegali, Kelyarn, Kayala, Krylor, Kearill and Norton all ate at the kitchen table. That was the Carlin way as well; kits ate in one room, parents and adults ate in another.

After their supper, Kethera chased her Siblings out of the dining room and down a hallway towards the back of the house and the wash house, to do their evening ablutions before going to sleep. Most Carlin wash houses were detached out houses, which in most Carlin households were not used after dark due to the constant presence of nighttime predators. Kelyarn's house, however, had been modified and a protective covered walkway connected their wash house to their main house. Both side access doors could be securely locked at night. Those all-important top latches being the most important of all.

That pitta patta of small Carlinish feet was heard as Kethera chased her Siblings back in from the wash house and down another hallway leading to the sleep rooms. There was one sleep room for the girls and another sleep room for the boys. In each sleep room was a single, overly large sleeping mat on the floor, large enough for the kits to all sleep on in a tangle of arms and legs.

The Carlin sleeping mats were firm but comfortable, made from soft Gudong hide and stuffed with reed fluff, moss fibre, flowers and grass down. They were warm and faintly fragrant with the scent of clean earth and flowers.

Kethera, as the eldest kit, ensured that her Siblings were all under the sleep covers and asleep for the night, their chaos under firm but loving control. Once Kethera's task was complete, she bid her parents and grandparents good night and then returned to the girls' sleeping room to go to sleep herself.

Keegali enquired of Norton, "What do you do in your Human world, Norton?"

Norton looked around the kitchen, "Well, Keegali, I install upgrades in Carlin households and Thol tree nests. Upgrades like those light sconces on the walls, your fridge, freezer and even those pressed iron stoves. I also install modern washroom conveniences as well."

Keegali smiled, "Like our composting toilets, wash basins, shower and my claw-foot bath."

"You have a claw-foot bath. Wow! That's definitely not standard", Norton noted.

"Our friend, Simone, organised that one for me. She thought I'd appreciate it", Keegali explained, noting, "Simone was right, it's my favourite upgrade."

"Those light sconces. I've never been able to figure them out. Our old ones were brass, contained oil and had burning wicks. These new ones, they come on at dusk and back off at dawn all by themselves", Kelyarn noted, not understanding how they worked.

"Well, the light itself comes from what we call light-emitting diodes and they're powered by a long-life battery. The battery will last for a century or more and it uses light sensors to turn on and off automatically. The casing is a polymer that's been coloured to resemble brass", Norton explained.

"Like our fridge and freezer. Long-life batteries", Kelyarn nodded, commenting, "They told us they'd run for decades without maintenance."

"Indeed, they will and when they need maintenance, they'll automatically notify the colony's maintenance department long before they break down", Norton confirmed.

"Personally, I like the pressed iron stove", Kayala commented, noting, "We have the same type at our house. It cooks the same way as our old-style fired-clay stove, but it's stronger and lasts much longer."

"Plus, they give off better warmth after the cooking is finished", Keegali commented.

Kelyarn added, "Our artisans have even started duplicating them in cast iron."

"It's funny, even ironic. I actually like those old-style fired-clay stoves. I actually have a one on my apartment's balcony. I use it for a barbecue. It has that typical central hearth with its iron grill and three raised burner plates; one on each side and one at the back. I quite like it, it's stylish", Norton commented.

Keegali laughed, "Funny that, we upgraded and you downgraded. That is ironic. Our old fire-clay stove had five burners, two on each side and one at the back."

"Ah, I've heard of those. They are apparently quite rare", Norton responded.

"Yes, they are quite rare", Kelyarn confirmed, remarking, "You have to ask the artisan to make one of those types especially for you. They are special, one-offs. Most have just three burners."

The conversation continued for quite a while before everyone called it a night.

Keegali and Kelyarn informed Norton, "If you need us for anything, our sleep room is down that hallway on the left. Kayala and Krylor will be sleeping in the room on the right, opposite ours. Of course, Kayala's kits are sleeping in the sleep rooms further down."

Kayala smiled and laughed, "My kits are perfectly positioned to wake us all up in the morning with their Carlin kit chaos. Much as my Siblings and I did when we were all younger."

Kearill squeezed Norton's left arm; she was still holding onto it and had been all evening, "Don't worry, Norton, we all know how you Humans love to sleep in. We learned that from my older Sister, Kitty and her temporary bondmate, Angelique, back when Kitty was approaching her own quickening."

"Okay, so where will I be sleeping exactly?", Norton enquired.

"In the fourth level sleep room", Keegali replied, commenting, "Normally, Kearill would be sleeping there, but as you're our honoured guest, you'll be sleeping there tonight. You'll be sleeping as close to our Gods as this house can provide."

"Is there any significance to that?", Norton enquired.

"Yes, of course, Norton. You looked after my Daughter, Kearill, today. That makes you our honoured guest", Keegali replied.

Kelyarn stepped in, noting, "It's also used for the mate bonding after one of our Daughters goes through her quickening. Kearill is our youngest Daughter and her quickening is due very soon. The higher the sleep room, the closer to our Gods, as we like to say."

"I'll be sleeping in one of the other sleep rooms on our third level", Kearill noted, explaining, "Normally we only use those sleep rooms when we have a big family gathering with lots of Aunts, Uncles and Cousins. Tonight, I'll just use the closest one of those sleep rooms."

"You don't have sleep rooms on the second level?", Norton curiously enquired.

"No, those rooms are used for storing our village's historical records and, of course, my offices as the village Elder", Kelyarn explained.

Kearill showed Norton to the fourth-level sleep room. It was a spacious room with a single large, dormer-style window on the north, overlooking the front of the family's plot and the village central plaza and another large dormer on the south, overlooking the back of the family's plot and its gardens.

"You sleep here tonight, Norton", Kearill told him, as she leaned in and kissed him, her right leg popped.

The kiss was long and lingering; Norton eagerly returned it. Kearill's bristly Carlinish tongue probing for his; Norton felt giddy and light-headed.

When Kearill finally pulled away, she said to Norton, "I absolutely love the way you smell."

"I love the way you smell too, Kearill", Norton reciprocated, before asking, "Do you have to go?"

Kearill frowned, tears beginning to well, "I have too, Norton. I have too. I'm too close to my quickening."

Kearill left the room before her tears could flow and rushed down to the closest sleep room on the level below, closing the door behind her. It was the right thing to do, but why did it feel so wrong, so awful?

Norton looked around the large room. Its walls were lined with chests of drawers, benches and even what looked like desks or workspaces. The back wall was lined with what looked like wardrobes, with a single chest of drawers in the middle.

There was an image on the wall above it, an image of a yellow Sun, an orange Sun and a silver Moon. In the centre of the room was a large sleeping mat, far larger than any human king-sized bed. The sleeping mat's outer casing appeared to be made of softened Gudong hide.

As Norton undressed, he wandered over to the north-facing window. There were some phrases neatly burnt into the window ledge. Kitty loves Angelique. Angelique loves Kitty. Humans fuck yeah and Carlins fuck yeah. Norton had heard their names mentioned earlier, but their significance escaped him.

Norton folded his clothes neatly and placed them on top of one of the chests of drawers. Now completely naked, he stepped onto the sleeping mat and lay down. The inner material, whatever it was, reed fluff, moss fibre, blue grass down perhaps, was thick, luxurious and soft. Norton noticed the scent of earth and flowers as he pulled the finally woven sleeping covers over himself and was soon fast asleep.

Norton dreamed, he dreamed of Kearill in that beautiful sea-green bathing suit; he dreamed of untying the back straps with his teeth and taking it off. His dreams were far naughtier than usual and they were all about Kearill, beautiful Kearill with her incredibly wonderful, alluring scent.

Kearill slipped out of her tunic and climbed onto the sleeping mat, pulling the sleep covers over herself. All she could think of was Norton. Kearill could still smell Norton's scent; it was strong and pungent, even with the sleep room door closed and a whole level between them; he was ever present on her mind.

Kearill's heart began to pound inside her chest; it began to pound in her mind as well. Kearill began to feel hot flushes, then seconds later, she was hit with cold chills. This began to repeat: hot flushes, followed by cold chills, hot flushes, followed by cold chills. Kearill began to sweat profusely with each hot flush, only for her skin to feel cold and clammy when the next cold chills struck. Over and over, hot flushes, cold chills, hot flushes, cold chills, hot flushes, cold chills.

Kearill sat bolt upright on the sleeping mat, only to be struck by dizziness. Kearill fell backwards onto the sleeping mat, and the hot flushes and cold chills continued. Kearill tossed and turned, tossed and turned. Norton was in her mind; she saw him lying naked in front of her and she felt compelled to climb on top of him. Then she opened her eyes and he was gone. It was all in her head. Norton was never there.

Then again, the hot flushes, the cold chills, ah! Kearill sat bolt upright once more on the sleeping mat. The dizziness and giddiness returned, only this time Kearill fell forward onto her hands and knees; she was dripping wet with sweat, a cold, clammy sweat. Norton's scent filled her senses. Hot flushes, cold chills, hot flushes, cold chills. Slowly, Kearill climbed to her feet. It was unbearable; it was driving her to act.

Kearill staggered to the door and opened it, then she began to climb the stairs to the fourth-level sleep room where she knew that Norton lay asleep. By the time Kearill reached the top of the stairs, she was crawling and panting heavily. Her heart was pounding inside her chest and in her mind was Norton, sweet Norton with his alluring scent.

Kearill reached up and opened the sleep room door and crawled inside. Almost immediately, Kearill smelt Norton's scent, his real scent this time; it was no longer just in her mind this time. Kearill collapsed onto the floor and rolled onto her back, panting heavily as the hot and cold flushes began to subside.

After what seemed like an eternity, Kearill rolled back over and pushed herself up, standing on her feet. Kearill walked over to Norton, knelt down beside him on the sleeping mat and carefully pulled back the sleeping covers.

Kearill lay down beside Norton's still sleeping body and gently pressed her still sweaty body up against Norton's back. Norton was soft and warm and Kearill carefully wrapped her right arm around his waist. Her pounding heart was settling down and Kearill felt a contentedness that she'd never felt before.

Norton was still sleeping soundly and Kearill ever so gently kissed him on the neck. As Kearill did so, she slid her right hand down to Norton's breeding pole and squeezed it ever so gently. Kearill moved her hand gently up and down; Norton began to groan and stir.

Kearill kissed him on the neck once more, squeezed his breeding pole more tightly and moved her hands more vigorously. Norton awoke and rolled onto his back, their eyes met and Kearill leaned in and kissed him passionately; her bristly Carlinish tongue seeking his. Norton kissed her back, his own tongue seeking hers.

Their bonding heat began; their minds began to fog over, as their eyes glazed over as well. Kearill, still kissing Norton, climbed on top of him, straddling him, and then just like that, she slipped him inside of her and then they began mating. *Their mating frenzy had begun.*

That became the pattern for the night. Kearill and Norton would mate, change position and then mate some more, then change position and mate again, before falling asleep in each other's arms. Less than an hour later, they would awaken, still in the fog of their mating frenzy and repeat the process, over and over, all night long.

Their mating frenzy continued even after the first rays of Cathol's light rose above the horizon. They were completely oblivious to all and everything, but each other and their biological imperative to mate.

Kearill and Norton were now fully bonded in the Carlinish sense of the term.

It was the Carlinish way.

28. Impossibilities Before Breakfast.

It was almost seven forty in the morning; a notification appeared on Keegali's communicator and she read it, finding out that a delivery was five minutes away from their house.

"Why did they send the notification to me?", Keegali thought; after all, it was Kearill's package.

Keegali made her way to their front door. Cathol had long since risen and was shining brightly with not a cloud in the early morning sky. Keegali looked through the door's glass spy hole; there was nothing outside. One by one, Keegali slid back the door bolts from bottom to top and then slowly opened the door; it was a beautiful day outside.

A hover van drove into the village's central plaza and parked outside of Keegali's plot. A metal man climbed out of the hover van, retrieved a package from the rear of the van, then leapt over the gate before running up to the front door.

"Package for Kearill, Daughter of Keegali", the metal man spoke in its monotone voice.

Keegali accepted the package and enquired, "Metal man, why did he notification come to me?"

"The original notification to Kearill, Daughter of Keegali, was not opened. The automatic read receipt was not returned. We took it upon ourselves to send a second notification to Keegali, Wife of Kelyarn", the metal man explained.

"Thank you, metal man", Keegali replied, closed and bolted the front door, thinking, *"Why didn't Kearill open and read the notification?"*

Keegali carried Kearill's package into the kitchen and placed it on the kitchen table; Kayala was also in the kitchen, "Please take this package up to Kearill. She must still be asleep after her long day yesterday."

Kayala went upstairs to the third-level sleep room where Kearill was sleeping. The first thing that Kayala noticed was that the door was open and Kearill wasn't there. The sleep covers had been disturbed and her tunic and jacket were on top of a chest of drawers, but Kearill was nowhere to be seen.

Kayala placed Kearill's package down on the chest of drawers next to her tunic and jacket, thinking to herself, *"Where was Kearill?"*

It suddenly dawned upon Kayala that, of course, Kearill was a cuddle puss; she was probably upstairs cuddling with Norton. Not a good idea, though, so close to her quickening; Kayala went upstairs.

Kayala smelt their scent first, Kearill's and Norton's; it was strong and pungent. The door of the fourth-level sleep room was ajar. Kayala pushed the door open and stepped in.

Kayala straight away saw her younger Sister, Kearill, underneath Norton; they were mating!

"Oh. I am so sorry. I'll come back later. I didn't mean to disturb you", Kayala apologised, but then she noticed something; neither of them appeared to even register her presence.

Kayala entered the room and approached them. Kearill and Norton were in the throes of carnal pleasure, yes, but they were otherwise totally unresponsive. Kayala looked more closely; both their eyes were glazed over. She waved her hand directly in front of their faces; there was no response.

"Shit! They're in heat, in the mating frenzy!", Kayala spat out to herself, thinking, *"How am I going to explain this to our Mother?"*

Kayala ran down the stairs, skipping step after step; landing in the kitchen on the pads of her feet with a thud, shouting out in hushed tones, "Mother, we have a problem!"

Keegali turned to her Daughter, "Kayala, what is it?"

Kayala shook her head, "I can't explain it. You have to see this for yourself. We have a problem!"

Kayala grabbed her Mother by the hand and insisted on leading her back up the stairs.

When they both reached the fourth-level sleep room, Kayala stepped aside and let her Mother enter.

Things had changed slightly; now, Kearill was on top of Norton. They were still mating; Kearill was riding Norton like there was no tomorrow.

Keegali put her hand to her mouth in shock, then slowly approached the mating couple. She inspected their glazed eyes, waved her hand in front of their faces; they were completely oblivious to her presence. Keegali stood back up and looked at Kayala, a surprised look upon her face.

"This is not possible, Kayala. Norton is not Carlin-kind; he is Human. Humans do not go into heat. Humans cannot bond with Carlins in this way. It is not a Human thing", Keegali noted.

Kayala just pointed to her Sister and Norton and questioned, "Well, Mother, what's that then?"

Keegali made her way to the rear wall of the sleep room. It was lined with wardrobes, except for the section in the very centre, which contained a chest of drawers. On top of the chest of drawers to either side were brass thuribles hanging from their holders. There was a brass cauldron sitting in the rear centre of the chest of drawers and in front of it was a stack of several earthenware bowls. There were at least five.

Keegali bowed to an image of Cathol, their yellow Sun, Cythol, their orange Sun and Luns, their silvery Moon, which was mounted on the wall above the chest of drawers, before she began rummaging through the two top drawers.

Keegali found what she was looking for, but she frowned when she realised that there were only two left: cones of special incense.

Kearill's quickening had been approaching and they had planned to barter for more incense when the time came. After all, there were ten days of bonding before the main event, the mating frenzy; however, this morning's events had been unexpected. Things had gone horribly awry!

Keegali slipped an earthenware bowl into her apron's pocket along with a single cone of incense. She then took another earthenware bowl and a cone of incense over to the northern dormer window, which was quite close to the sleeping mat and the mating couple, Kearill and Norton, upon it.

Keegali smiled at the graffiti that Kitty and Angelique had burnt into the windowsill many years ago. Kitty loves Angelique. Angelique loves Kitty. Fond memories from a long-ago time. Keegali placed the earthenware bowl on the windowsill, lit the incense cone and placed it into the bowl.

Keegali motioned to Kayala and they both stood on either side of Kearill; together they lifted her off of Norton and forcefully took her to the stairs. Norton lay still, motionless, unmoving; their mating frenzy was driven by Kearill's pheromones and cascaded by Norton's. Kearill, on the other hand, struggled to get loose, to return to her bondmate. Keegali and Kayala dragged Kearill, resisting all the way, down the stairs to the kitchen.

Once in the kitchen, they both forced Kearill into a chair and held her there, while Keegali placed the earthenware bowl on the kitchen table. She lit the incense cone and dropped it into the bowl, then pushed it close to Kearill, right under her nose. Then they both waited for the incense to take effect.

Kearill's mind began to unfog and her glazed eyes began to clear; soon she was lucid enough to talk.

"Kearill, what do you remember?", Keegali asked.

Kearill tried to think but nothing happened, before finally replying, "I had trouble sleeping last night, so I went upstairs to Norton for a cuddle", then she bit her lower lip gently and admitted, "I did kiss him and I did plan to play with him, even though I know I shouldn't this close to my quickening, but nothing happened and then I woke up here, in this chair."

Kayala shook her head, "Mother, she remembers nothing of their mating frenzy."

"I know, Kayala, I know", Keegali replied, then turning back to a still confused Kearill, "My little one, last night you entered the heat and the mating frenzy with Norton."

"No, Mother, that's simply not possible, Norton is Human, not Carlin-kind", Kearill insisted.

"Kearill, look down at the incense. Do you recognise it? Why do you think we're using it?", Kayala asked.

Kearill stared at the incense in the Earthenware bowl. She realised that her Mother and older Sister were right. Kearill began to cry.

"How? How is this even possible? Norton is not Carlin-kind!", Kearill desperately questioned.

Keegali sighed; she finally understood; it all made perfect sense, "Yesterday morning, Kearill. When you fainted in the park. You weren't overwhelmed by the scent of Earth flowers; you were entering your quickening, only you just didn't know it. Your pheromones triggered Norton to respond; his pheromones then triggered you to reciprocate. Norton was there to catch you because of your quickening."

Kayala suddenly understood as well, "Kearill, my Sister, you've been bonding with Norton since you first met him yesterday morning. All day long, only you didn't know it, either of you."

"No, Kayala, that's simply not possible. The mate-bonding takes ten days. Everybody knows that", Kearill insisted.

Keegali squeezed her hand warmly, "Normally, yes, Kearill, but Norton is a Human; their pheromones must be much stronger than a Carlin man's. The two of you bonded in just half a day."

"And the heat, the mating frenzy? Is it over, Mother?", Kearill enquired.

Keegali shook her head, "No, my little one. Kearill, the incense only gives you lucidity for a short while."

Norton stepped out of the stairwell, "Good morning, everyone. I must admit, I did not sleep well last night at all. I feel absolutely exhausted."

Kayala whispered to Keegali, "Mother, he does not know, he does not remember."

As Norton sat in a chair next to Kearill, Keegali asked him, "Norton, what do you remember from last night?"

Norton was much closer to the incense here and he became ever more lucid; his memories started to resurface and he remembered the previous night. The sudden resurfacing of his memories caused him to raise his hand to his mouth in shock. Norton looked at Kearill, with deep knowledge in his mind; he'd been making love to Kearill all night long with a wild, crazed abandon that he simply could not fathom.

"Um, I think, I'd better not talk about that, Keegali. It's a Human thing that we prefer not to talk about", Norton replied; his face went red and he really wanted to change the subject.

Keegali replied reassuringly, "Norton, both Kayala and I saw you and Kearill in your mating frenzy. We are not angry; we are simply very concerned."

"Mother, he remembers. We Carlins never remember our mating frenzy, Norton remembers", Kayala noted, the shock clearly visible on her face.

"Mating frenzy? I don't understand. Kearill and I made love", Norton replied and then he thought more deeply, "Holy shit! It felt driven! Like I couldn't stop and Kearill, Kearill was absolutely insistent."

The only words that Kearill heard from Norton's lips were "*made love*"; she squeezed his left hand with hers and entwined her right leg around his left leg under the table.

"Norton, yesterday morning, before you met Kearill, what do you remember?", Keegali probed.

Norton replied honestly, "I remember this most wonderful scent in the air. It was fascinating, so I followed it, trying to locate the exotic flowers the scent came from. That's when I found Kearill", his eyes watered slightly with the memory; "Kearill was a vision of loveliness, pure loveliness."

Keegali nodded, "I was right, Kayala. Kearill entered into her quickening it that park in the Human village."

Kayala provided Norton with further information, "Norton, Kearill and you were both in the wrong place at the wrong time. Kearill should never have gone to your village yesterday. When she was there, she entered her quickening and you became affected by our Carlinish biological imperatives."

Keegali summed it up, "Norton, you and my Daughter, Kearill, have mate-bonded together. Last night, you both went into the heat and the mating frenzy. That is why your '*love making*' seemed driven."

"No, Keegali, that's not possible. We Humans, do not go into heat and we certainly don't mate bond. We are a very different species in that respect. It's impossible", Norton replied, refuting the possibility completely.

Kayala instinctively looked under the kitchen table, then asked, "Where are your legs? Look at your hands? Even now, the two of you can't keep your hands off of each other."

It was true, Norton's leg was entwined around Kearill's as much as hers was around his and the previous night had been a mating frenzy. He remembered it all; they'd made love well over two dozen times during the night and then some. How had his heart not given out? Keegali was right and he knew it.

"What I don't understand is how Norton remembers. We Carlin-folk never remember", Kayala noted.

Norton provided a possible answer, "I'm Human, our hippocampus must work differently from yours."

It was the only explanation that Norton could think of.

Norton tweaked onto something from his own past experiences and asked, "Keegali, is Kearill still in heat, is she still in oestrus?"

"Yes, of course, Norton. This incense only brings temporary lucidity. Kearill is still in heat and when the incense burns out, you will both return to an uncontrollable urge to mate", Keegali explained, reassuring him further, "This is not your fault, Norton. It is my fault. I should never have allowed my Kearill to go to your village so close to her quickening."

"This is not about fault. Keegali. Back on Earth, as a child, I used to keep ferrets. When a female ferret went into heat, the only way for her oestrus to break was with mating and conception. I am Human, conception will be impossible. That literally means Kearill will remain in oestrus, persistent oestrus. In a ferret, that leads to organ failure and death in two to three months, sometimes much sooner", Norton explained, noting, "I am seriously concerned for Kearill."

"Our friend Simone mentioned the same thing more than fifteen years ago", Keegali remembered.

"Simone?", Norton enquired.

"Yes, our Human friend, Simone", Kayala replied, explaining, "Simone is my Mother's bond-Sister, making her our Aunt. Simone's Daughter, Angelique, was also my elder Sister, Kitty's, temporary bondmate. Our two families are very closely entwined."

Keegali reached into her apron and took out her communicator, "I'm sending a message to Simone. If Kearill can't come out of her heat, we have a real problem. We need Simone's help."

"*Simone. We need your help urgently. We have a Carlinish biological imperative issue. My youngest Daughter, Kearill, needs your help desperately. Keegali*", the message read when Keegali sent it.

It was several minutes later when the reply came back, "*Keegali. I'm up at Colonial Central Command at Cis-Luns L-Five. I'm leaving straight away, expect me in around one hour and thirty five minutes. Simone.*"

"Simone is on her way", Keegali informed them, then, looking down at the incense, "Norton, you need to take my Daughter, Kearill, back upstairs. The incense has almost burnt out."

"I don't understand", Norton admitted.

"When that incense burns out, the heat and the mating frenzy will take you both. We have no more incense in the house. You must take my Kearill upstairs now", Keegali explained.

"Is that wise, Keegali? I mean, isn't this a problem? Me being with Kearill?", Norton grappled to understand the situation.

Kayala shook her head, "Are all men this stupid? Did you not hear my Mother? When that incense burns out, the heat will take you both; you will go back into your mating frenzy. You will end up mating on the kitchen table!"

Norton looked up, still slightly confused, so Kayala told him, "Oh, by the Gods, Norton. My Mother is giving you permission to take Kearill upstairs and mate with her. Why are you still sitting there?"

"I'm sorry, Kayala, alright. It's just all very confusing and overwhelming. How does Kearill even feel about any of this?", Norton replied, worrying more about Kearill's feelings.

It was simply too late, the incense had burnt out. Kearill swept the earthenware bowl off the table and it shattered on the kitchen floor's cobblestones. In less than a second, Kearill pushed her chair aside, swung herself around and straddled Norton; her eyes were fully glazed over, her mind was totally fogged.

"Norton, for the love of the Gods, take my Daughter upstairs now!", Keegali instructed loudly, noting, "You have mere seconds before the heat and the mating frenzy take you!"

Norton picked up Kearill, whose legs were wrapped around his waist, and hurriedly carried her upstairs.

"Kayala, follow them. Make sure that they actually make it to the upstairs sleep room", Keegali requested, instructing, "And Daughter, make sure the windows are secured, we don't want their mating frenzy taking them out onto the roof. Only the Gods know what our Gudongs would make of that."

Kayala replied straight away, "On it, Mother", as she quickly chased after Norton and Kearill.

Keegali shook her head, thinking, "*How on Vale was she going to explain this to Kelyarn?*"

Speak of the Devil, Kelyarn entered the kitchen and Keegali began to explain the situation to him.

While Keegali, with some difficulty, explained how their Daughter, Kearill, had managed to mate bond with a Human, Norton, and that the couple were in heat and in a mating frenzy, Kayala enforced her Mother's will.

Norton was overtaken by Kearill's mating frenzy on the landing of the stairs in front of the fourth-level sleep room's open door. His eyes were glazed over, his mind was fogged and he began to mate with Kearill, standing up against the wall.

Kayala shook her head and shoved them both forcefully into the sleep room. Once inside, she pushed them both unceremoniously in the direction of the sleep room's sleeping mat, onto which they then collapsed. Kayala pulled off Norton's shirt, trousers and underpants, tossing them onto the floor, and then just let Kearill and Norton mate.

Kayala then checked that both dormer windows were properly secured and with nothing more to do, Kayala headed back downstairs.

When Kayala came back into the kitchen, she found her Husband, Krylor, and her Father, Kelyarn, staring at Keegali in disbelief as she explained the situation to them, yet again. Each of them mouthed the words "*impossible*" almost in unison. Keegali just shook her head and repeated what had happened once more.

Once they'd both accepted Keegali's explanation of the situation, Kelyarn and Krylor walked to the stairs. Kayala turned her husband around and pushed him back toward the kitchen table.

"Sit down, Krylor. My Mother and I have got this", Kayala chastised.

Kelyarn told Kayala, "Kearill may be your Sister, Kayala, but she is still my Daughter and is my responsibility, mine and your Mother's. We both handled your Sister, Kitty's, bonding, your bonding and your Sister, Kreena's, bonding. This is no different."

Keegali grabbed Kelyarn by the arm and sat him down at the kitchen table.

"This is very different, Kelyarn. Norton has been caught up in our Carlinish biological imperatives. His free will has been taken away! Their bonding also took half a day, not ten; that's twenty times faster! Their heat and mating frenzy are also intense and may turn out to be just as quick. Our good friend, Simone, is already on her way as we speak", Keegali explained.

Kayala shook her head and smiled, "Apart from the fact that this is all completely wrong, they actually make a very handsome couple. Don't get me wrong, though, the last thing that I'd want is for any of my own Daughters to end up in this same situation. Could you imagine my little Kethera bonded to a Human?"

Keegali and Kayala took turns regularly checking on Kearill and Norton, while Kelyarn and Krylor busied themselves in the garden at the back of the plot. They all waited for Simone Reas to arrive to hopefully provide them with a suitable solution to their Kearill and Norton problem.

The couple in question, their minds completely fogged and their eyes glazed over, were blissfully unaware of the situation, being caught up in their pheromonal cascade and their mating frenzy. Extreme sensual pleasures that Kearill would never be able to remember.

Simone Reas pushed her Broad Head Arrow Class Interplanetary Starfighter, Haven, beyond its designed tolerances. Keegali needed help; her little cuddle puss, Kearill, had a problem. It didn't matter what the problem was; the mere mention of a Carlinish biological imperative issue was enough. Come hell or high water, Simone would arrive ahead of her stated schedule.

Simone sent a message to the planetside Human colony, Hilltop, a name that nobody used, to have an airborne paramedic unit meet her at Keegali's house. The mere mention of Carlinish biological imperative to Simone meant that Kearill possibly had persistent oestrus and she'd requested the paramedics have a vial of deslorelin acetate with them, just in case they needed to bring Kearill out of persistent oestrus.

Simone's Broad Head hit the atmosphere at excessively high speed; she switched the ship's Electromagnetic Radiation Mitigation System, E-RaMiS, to its maximum possible level. Warning lights across her console flashed red; Simone switched them off one by one.

The Haven's A.I. system began complaining, *"Hull tolerance limits exceeded. Stackable Layered Radiation Shield Plating, SLaReS, is ablating. SLaReS was designed for layered protection and radiation absorption, not ablation. Please slow your descent, Special Operative Reas."*

"Shut the fuck up, you stupid machine. I know how far I can push my ship", Simone shouted as she switched the A.I. warnings off completely, thinking to herself, *"So I'll need some new slayers panels and a coat of fucking paint. Stiff fucking shit! Stupid fucking machine!"*

The Haven began to vibrate and shake as its hull began to groan with the stress. Simone slapped on Haven's reverse thrusters and came in hard and fast; the ship's automatic emergency aerobraking systems kicked in and the ship slowed significantly as it approached the Carlin village.

Simone lowered her ship's landing struts and braced for touchdown. The ship landed in the village centre hard; the ship's duralium steel landing struts and shock absorbers took the brunt of the force, with the plaza's cobblestones shattering beneath them.

"Touch down!", Simone exclaimed as she checked her ship's systems, before turning the A.I. warning system back on and telling it, "See, A.I., not so bad after all. Haven here has a polyceramalloy fucking hull!"

The A.I. system responded, *"That was not a regulation atmospheric entry or touchdown, Special Operative Reas."*

"So, sue me!", Simone snorted back at the A.I. and popped the drop chute beneath her pilot's flight couch open. Its ladder descended beneath the ship and touched the ground. Seconds later,   Simone slid down the ladder with the instep of her boots on either side of the ladder's side rails.

Simone hit the ground, turned towards Keegali's house and ran, leaping over their gate and across the front of their plot. She noted the hovercar parked in front of the house's front door before entering the house. Simone hadn't even broken a sweat.

Simone entered the kitchen, "Keegali, where's Kearill? What's the emergency?"

Keegali asked, "Simone, how'd you get here so quickly. We weren't expecting you for another twenty minutes or more."

Simone smiled, "I pushed my ship harder than usual and came in for a hard landing. You might want to have a few of those cobblestones out in the plaza replaced, at least three or four dozen, actually. I kind of pulverised them."

Keegali jumped up and wrapped her arms around Simone and let loose a flood of tears, "It's my Kearill, it's my Kearill. She's gone into heat and the mating frenzy", then she paused before noting, "With a Human!"

Simone gently pushed Keegali back and looked into her eyes incredulously,

"With a Human?", she questioned, before reassuring her, "I have an airborne paramedic unit on its way from the colony. They should have a vial of deslorelin acetate with them. If our little cuddle puss goes into persistent oestrus, that should bring her out of it."

Kayala wrapped her arms around her Mother and Simone, "Aunt Simone, it's so good to see you."

"Yes, yes. I know, but I really need to assess Kearill's condition", Simone informed them both.

Keegali wiped away her tears and led Simone up the stairs to the fourth-level sleep room.

When Keegali and Kayala showed Simone into the upstairs sleep room, Simone was shocked by the sight of seeing Kearill on top of Norton, straddling him and mating with him like there was no tomorrow.

"Okay, that's not a sight you see every day", Simone noted as she walked over and took a small torch out of a pouch on her utility belt.

Simone crouched down in front of the couple. She looked at their eyes carefully. Their eyes appeared completely glazed over. Simone shone the small torch into their eyes; they dilated, they were functional, yet they didn't really see anything. Simone waved her hand in front of their eyes; they were completely unresponsive.

Kearill was still on top of Norton and Simone tried to move her head; it moved without resistance, but went straight back into her focused biological imperative when Simone let go. Simone stood back up.

"Is this what the heat and the mating frenzy are always like? I mean, it looks somewhat different to Kitty's", Simone enquired.

Kayala quickly answered, "Well, yes and no, Aunt Simone, it's not supposed to be with a Human."

Keegali nodded and explained, "Kearill went to the Human village yesterday morning. She was in the park and she came into her quickening. Norton responded to her scent and she responded to his. They spent all of yesterday together bonding. When they came back here, we didn't know; they didn't know. Later, everyone went to sleep, Kearill was overcome by our biological imperatives and climbed into Norton's arms."

Simone frowned, "Keegali, our little cuddle puss has a problem. It is highly doubtful that Kearill can conceive with Norton; he is a Human after all. That means persistent oestrus and we can bring her out of that with a shot of deslorelin acetate, but she will still be bonded with a Human, and that likely means no kits."

Keegali nodded in agreement, "We understand that, Simone."

Kelyarn and Krylor appeared in the doorway, "Is my Daughter okay, Simone?",

Kelyarn asked.

"As well as can be expected, Kelyarn. Please wait downstairs, this is now sacred women's business", Simone replied, trying to make light of the situation, before adding, "Keep an eye out for an airborne paramedic unit. There's one on the way."

As Kelyarn and Krylor went back downstairs, they heard a commotion in the plot out front. Simone walked over to the north-facing dormer window. She noticed the graffiti left by Kitty and her Daughter, Angelique, and smiled. Looking out of the window, the airborne paramedics had arrived. They landed directly in front of the house, just beyond Norton's hovercar.

"Good, they're here", Simone announced as she turned back around, just in time to see Kearill change positions.

Kearill was now straddling Norton's face, her eyes were still glazed over as she held Norton's manhood in her right hand, squeezing it. Kearill lowered her head down towards Norton's manhood.

Simone shook her head, "Okay, that is something I most certainly did not need to see today. I shouldn't have skipped my breakfast!"

Simone turned away from Norton and Kearill, not wanting to see her Niece, whom she'd known since the age of four, performing that particular act.

Kayala looked curiously at her Sister, Kearill, "That's new. I don't think I heard of that one before."

Keegali gave off a dry chuckle, "You did exactly the same thing during your own mating frenzy, as did Kitty and Kreena."

Kayala looked shocked, "No way, Mother, there's no way that I did that."

Keegali simply replied, "Yes, way, my darling Daughter, you most surely did", and then she whispered into Kayala's ear, "Your Father and I still do."

"Eew, Mother, that's way too much information!", Kayala exclaimed.

Kearill's mind began to unfog and her eyes began to clear. She looked down at where her mouth had been just a moment before and at what her hand was still holding; she felt a pleasurable sensation between her legs where Norton's face was and found herself confused.

Kearill looked around the room, her Mother, Keegali, her Sister, Kayala and her Aunt Simone were all standing there. Her Mother and her Sister were both watching her with seriously concerned looks on their faces. Aunt Simone was facing away from her.

Kearill sat up, burst into tears, "Mamma, Mamma", she spoke like a small kit, then, "What is wrong with me?"

Keegali was quick to help Kearill to her feet; she hugged her Daughter and lavished he with kisses, "It's okay, my little one, it's okay. Your Mother's got you now, Kearill."

Simone watched, noticing that Norton was now still, his eyes were still glazed over; he was yet to recover from the pheromonal cascade.

Kayala questioned, "How did Kearill come out of her heat? Norton is not of Carlin-kind!"

Keegali crouched down in front of Kearill's abdomen and took a deep sniff, then she did so a second time before standing up, "Our Kearill is with kit. Kearill has the scent of kit within her."

Simone expressed doubt, "Keegali, that should not be possible. A Human should not be able to impregnate a Carlin."

Kayala crouched down in front of Kearill's abdomen as well and she, too, took a deep sniff before rising to her feet and declaring, "Mother is right. Kearill has the scent of kit within her."

Norton Fairchild began to stir, his eyes cleared and he looked around, "Holy fuck!", he exclaimed, his face going bright red as he pulled the sleeping covers over himself.

Keegali looked at him, "Norton Fairchild, you need not be embarrassed. We've seen a lot more than your breeding pole this morning."

Norton shook his head to clear the fog from his mind and kick-start his memory, "Yes, Keegali, I'm beginning to remember everything and I do mean everything. Even your discussions."

A female paramedic poked her head through the doorway and remarked, "We won't be able to get our gurney up these stairs. We'll need to get the patient down to the ground level."

The paramedic also noted, "The Carlin fellas won't let my partner come up, something about sacred women's business and that Broad Head in the plaza, I think it's on fire."

Simone replied, "We have two patients. A freshly impregnated Carlin woman, Kearill, and a disoriented Human man, Norton Fairchild. And that Broad Head is my ship, it's fine. It's just the residual heat of reentry on my slayers panels. I'll probably have to have the whole thing re-skinned."

Simone began giving instructions, "Keegali, Kayala, you guys find a night gown for Kearill and help her downstairs", she picked up Norton's clothes and tossed them to him, "You, Norton, lover boy, get dressed. Ms Paramedic here and I will help you downstairs."

Keegali and Kayala did as requested and helped Kearill downstairs. Norton slowly stood up and began to dress his self. Well over twelve hours of constant sex had left him drained and very sore; he was fatigued and wobbly on his feet. Simone sighed and helped him to dress.

The female paramedic quietly enquired, "Exactly what happened here?"

"Do you really want to know?", Simone asked.

"It is kind of my job to know what I'm dealing with", she replied.

"Okay, yesterday morning, young Kearill was in the park at the colony. Kearill went into what the Carlin-folk call the quickening. Her pheromone output spiked, Norton here was affected and his pheromones also spiked. That created a pheromone cascade that caused Kearill, a Carlinish woman and Norton, a Human man, to mate-bond, Carlin-style. Sometime last night, they both went into heat and that was quickly followed by a pheromone-driven twelve to thirteen hour mating frenzy. Now, young Kearill is pregnant with a hybrid Carlin Human kit and Norton here is completely knackered", Simone explained, finishing off with, "Do you have any questions?"

The paramedic simply replied, "Ma'am, every single thing that you just told me is not even Humanly possible."

"Agreed, but there you have it. At least a half dozen impossible things and all before I've managed to get my bloody breakfast. It is going to be such a long day", Simone replied.

When they were finally all downstairs in the kitchen, Kearill was lying on a gurney, being carefully strapped down. She had one hand over her nether regions, which were understandably quite sore. A medical scanner was strapped to Kearill's abdomen, taking continuous readings. Keegali was holding her hand and reassuring her that everything would be alright.

Simone took over once again, "Right. Kearill here and Norton are going with you guys to the medical centre. Don't go to the emergency department, go straight to the research centre. We have a special situation here and we need to ensure that our patients are not only okay, but we also have to figure out how the hell this even happened. I've just sent a message via my neural augments to Administrator Yealah. They will be expecting you when you arrive."

The male paramedic nodded, "Got that, Ma'am. We'll be there shortly", he stated as he pushed the gurney out of the house towards their airborne paramedic unit; the female paramedic helped Norton walk to it.

"Okay, Keegali, I take it that you and Kelyarn will want to go to the medical centre?", Simone enquired, already knowing the answer.

"Of course", Keegali confirmed.

"Kearill is my little Sister, Krylor and I are going too", Kayala added.

Simone looked down the hallway at eight-year-old Kethera, who was peaking out from behind a sleep room door; she didn't understand what had just happened, but was very concerned.

"So, do you guys think that little Kethera down there can keep the Carlin kit chaos under control until you all get back?", Simone questioned.

Krylor shook his head, "No, that would not be appropriate. You go, Kayala. I'll stay here and look after our kits. Kearill needs you far more than she needs me."

"Thank you, Krylor", Simone replied, "That sounds like a good plan."

Simone led Keegali, Kelyarn and Kayala to her ship and they all boarded. Simone showed them to their seats and asked them to strap in. Within minutes, Simone's ship, the Haven, was airborne and on its way to the medical centre at the Human colony.

When Simone's Broad Head landed behind the medical centre's research department on the lawn, they found Yealah, a Mimasian Thol, the medical centre's administrator, waiting for them. Along with Yealah was Doctor Morrow, with whom Simone had previously collaborated regarding her own research on Carlin mate bonding, heat, and mating frenzies.

Her own Daughter, Angelique, had been the temporary bondmate of Keegali's elder Daughter, Kitty, and Simone had taken a deep dive into the situation to understand as much as she could. Simone had authored several research papers on the subject of Carlin biological imperatives and later compiled a comprehensive book on the topic.

The airborne paramedic unit had arrived ahead of them and the two patients, Kearill and Norton, had already been admitted into the medical centre. Blood tests were being performed and the pair was being kept under observation.

Yealah greeted Simone and Keegali's family with trills and clicks, noting, "We've been taking blood samples for testing and should have some results soon. One thing that I can say for certain, Kearill is in the very early stages of pregnancy."

Simone looked to Keegali and Kayala; they had been right all along, they could tell with a simple sniff.

Doctor Morrow was overly excited by the news, "The paramedics strapped a medical scanner to young Kearill's abdomen as soon as they understood that she was pregnant. That medical scanner has been transmitting data to us continuously. It is fascinating, absolutely fascinating!", he exclaimed.

As they strolled over to the medical centre's entrance, Yealah noted, trilling, "This is unprecedented, Simone. A successful Human Carlin mating!", before asking, "Tell me, how much of the process were you able to observe? More importantly, how much of the process did your neural augments record?"

Simone frowned; the situation may have been unprecedented, but a young couple was involved and Kearill was her niece, "I got there towards the end of their mating frenzy, so not a lot and what I did observe and my neural augments recorded is subject to privacy laws."

Yealah turned to Simone and Keegali's family, a contrite smile upon her face, trilling and clicking, "My apologies. I overstep my bounds. Please forgive me; of course, this is a deeply private and personal matter. Please follow me into the medical centre, I'll take you all to see Kearill and Norton."

29. The First of Their Kind.

Yealah and Doctor Morrow showed Simone, Keegali, Kelyarn and Kayala to an observation room. There was a large screen on one wall; for all intents and purposes, it looked just like a two-way mirror, which, of course, it was not.

On the screen, they could see Norton lying on a hospital bed; he appeared to be sound asleep. Curled up beside him on the same hospital bed was Kearill; she still had the medical scanner strapped to her abdomen.

Doctor Morrow noted, "We've sedated Norton so that he can recover; his levels of exhaustion and fatigue required it. Kearill, well, what can I say? She will not leave his side, no matter how many times we try to separate them."

Keegali spoke out in a cross voice, "You don't separate them, Doctor Morrow! That is just plain cruel! They are a newly mate-bonded couple", she pointed at the screen, "They will be like that until after their kit, their Daughter, is born."

"Keegali is right. They should be back at our house in the top sleep room. Newly mate-bonded couples have to be managed until after their first kit is born, then their bond loosens just enough for them to manage it themselves", Kelyarn explained, noting, "It is a Carlin parent's task to help manage their bond until they can manage it themselves."

"I'm sorry, I didn't realise how important keeping them together was", Doctor Morrow apologised.

Simone looked at the screen and just shook her head, "That is ridiculous!", she exclaimed, pointing at the screen, "That bed is not big enough for two people. They can't possibly be comfortable like that. Kearill is a Carlinish woman; she needs more space, closer to the ground. Where is that room?"

"It's the room next to this one", Doctor Morrow informed her.

Simone left the observation room and went to the room next door. The others all watched as Simone entered the room and began to make some changes. There were four hospital beds in the room.

Kearill stirred and watched as Simone pushed three of the beds out of the way and up against each other along one wall. Simone then lifted the mattresses off the beds and unceremoniously dropped them onto the floor, next to each other, forming a large sleeping mat.

Simone next walked over to Kearill, who immediately reached out and hugged her, "Hey, my little cuddle puss, let's make you comfortable", she told her as she carried her over to the mats and laid her down upon them.

Simone then picked up Norton, who was sound asleep and placed him in the centre of the mats on the floor. Kearill automatically curled up beside him.

Kearill mouthed the words, "Thank you, Aunt Simone."

Simone then took the last mattress and placed it on the floor beside the others, before gathering up a number of hospital blankets and carefully placing them over Kearill and Norton.

"Is that more comfortable, sweety?", Simone enquired.

"Yes, thank you, Aunt Simone", Kearill replied.

"We'll see you a bit later, yeah. We just need to talk to the Doctor for a bit. You just cuddle up with Norton, yeah", Simone told her before adjusting the room's observation camera and leaving.

Doctor Morrow watched the screen with astonishment. Yealah watched it with amusement.

When Simone returned to the observation room, she noted, "Your staff can clean up the mess after Kearill and Norton leave, but remember, the Carlin-folk prefer to sleep on large mats, not beds."

"Noted, Simone. Up till now, we have been treating Carlin patients just as we do Human patients. I'll organise some changes to accommodate Carlinish requirements", Yealah replied with a few trills and clicks.

Simone took a seat alongside the others and asked, "Fetal viability? What do we know?"

Yealah chimed in with an answer, trilling and clicking, "Well, Kearill's kit is not at the fetal stage yet. For a Carlin, we believe that takes around five to six weeks, so we are still talking about a zygote."

Doctor Morrow added, "Kearill's zygote is developing quickly and showing no signs of failing, at least not so far. If this rate of growth continues, we can expect delivery in around seven months."

"Yes, all very good, but what about the viability? It is a Carlin Human hybrid", Simone enquired again.

Yealah fielded the question, trilling, clicking and softly barking, "We have a wealth of genetic information coming in from the medical scanner. So far, we appear to have a blend of both Carlin and Human genetics, which appears to be viable; however, we will need Kearill to wear that medical scanner until her kit is born."

Doctor Morrow stepped back in, noting, "If anything at all goes wrong, that scanner will give us a warning and if possible, we will intervene."

Kelyarn looked to Simone, "Please tell us what all that means, Simone."

Keegali agreed, "Yes, yes. Please explain it in layman's terms."

"Kearill's kit is a blend of both Kearill and Norton. The kit appears to be developing normally and is on track for birth in around seven months' time, but does require constant monitoring", Simone explained.

Keegali, Kelyarn and Kayala all nodded in understanding.

Kayala put voice to the question that everyone wanted to know but hadn't asked, "Your species evolved on Earth, a world twenty two light-years away from Vale; how is this even possible?"

Doctor Morrow's reply was simple: "Honestly, Kayala, we just don't know. Although we are currently studying and modelling both Human and Carlin genetics to find the relevant pathway that allowed this to happen. That process could take quite some time."

Yealah looked at Doctor Morrow; she had an inkling or two, but was reticent to mention it.

"You have more information, Yealah?", the Doctor questioned.

"Yes, but I really don't know if I should mention it. It's deep-time historical information that the Carlins don't have. When we've divulged this kind of historical information in the past, it has been disastrous", she replied.

"How can information be disastrous?", Kayala enquired.

"Thols and Tarlaks, Kayala", Yealah replied, explaining, her English laced with trills, clicks and soft barks, "Not long after we Mimasian Thols came here, our Matriarch, Ytryan, made the mistake of telling the Indigenous Thols that the Tarlaks were a cousin species to both Mimasian and Indigenous Thols. That the Tarlaks were once Thols. True though that is, the Indigenous Thols rejected it and verbally abused Ytryan for months afterwards."

"That's awful!" Keegali exclaimed, asking, "Why couldn't they just accept the truth?"

"Indigenous Tholish history records Tarlaks as a cruel predator species that actively hunted and ate Thols, which doesn't help. We have many biological similarities with Tarlaks, but outwardly we look very different, which also doesn't help", Yealah trilled, clicked and softly barked, noting, "Our Matriarch, Ytryan, now refuses to deal with the Tholish High Council as a result. It is highly problematic."

Keegali assured Yealah, "We will not abuse you for telling us the truth, Yealah."

Yealah replied, her voice laced with trills and clicks, "Are you sure, Keegali? Sometimes the truth is hard to accept. We told our cousins, the Indigenous Thols, the truth and it all went horribly wrong."

Kayala added her voice, "We are not Thols. We appreciate the truth, Yealah. It must come out."

"Very well then. First, you must understand the origin of the Tarlaks and then I can explain about the Carlin-folk. This is information from deep-time, to you it is unknown, to us, it is simply history", Yealah trilled and clicked.

Yealah began giving them a history lesson, trilling, clicking and softly barking, "In the year twenty one forty two AD, forty two Thols were awakened from cryosleep inside the ice moon Mimas; we had been asleep for well over six million years. Those Thols are my ancestors and along with their cryosleep tubes, we also had our historical records and many other items."

Yealah continued, "Back before Mimas was an ice moon, it was a generation ship. We Mimasian Thols built it at the behest of the evil emperor, Ahriman. We Thols were a space-faring species back then, not as impressive as the Humans are now; we were limited to just this system, its two Suns, its planets and moons, etc."

"It was Ahriman who first created the Tarlaks.", Yealah announced, before continuing, "He took a group of Thols and began to selectively breed them for the traits that he desired; only the process was far too slow. So, Ahriman forced my ancestors to genetically alter his creations to be the way he wanted. We succeeded; five Tarlak castes were created, the grunts, the engineers, the commanders and the princes. They were graded by height and intelligence: the grunts at up to seven feet tall, the engineers and commanders at up to eight feet and the princes at up to nine feet tall. Ahriman would select the tallest prince as his next bodily host to possess, so that every Tarlak would have to look up to him."

Simone interjected, "That may have been his original plan, but his grunts are now between seven and eight and a half feet tall. Their society started out patriarchal, but now it's matriarchal."

"Yes, Simone. These Tarlaks are not the same as the Tarlak of old, nor even the same as the extinct Mimasian Tarlaks. They have evolved without their master's guidance", Yealah trilled and clicked.

Yealah continued, her English laced with her trills, clicks and soft barks, "When my people lived here over six million years ago, the Carlin-folk had no biological imperatives. They were very much like the Human; come into adolescence, mature, take a mate, breed, maybe split up and take another mate. Very different from now. You still bore your kits in litters, but you also had contraceptives and could control when and how many litters you had."

"Wait, Yealah. Are you saying that our biological imperatives today are something that evolved since those days, millions of years ago?", Kayala questioned.

"No. It was Ahriman who gave you those biological imperatives", Yealah clicked and trilled, "Ahriman had created his Tarlaks; his commander and grunt castes needed constant training, hunting and feeding. Ahriman forced my Thol ancestors to alter your people genetically; increased fecundity, biological imperatives to force the selection of compatible mates. Ahriman did not want random selection; there is a reason for your quickening, your wandering and your pheromonal responses. Ahriman wanted the Carlin-folk to mate with other specifically compatible Carlin-folk."

"Why? Why would he do that?", Kayala questioned.

"Ahriman wanted the Carlin-folk to be smart, to be clever, but standardised and with a certain docility. Think of your villages, they are all made to a standard. Think of your lifestyles; they have not changed in many, many millennia.

Ahriman wanted you to be worthy adversaries for his commanders and grunts to hunt, nothing more", Yealah trilled and clicked, before noting, "Above all else, he wanted a lot of Carlins. Ahriman wanted you to breed out of control, so that he had a constant supply of Carlins for his Tarlaks to hunt and eat."

Yealah raised her hand for silence as she continued, the harsh history lesson, she trilled and clicked, "There is a reason why Korland and the Isle of Sorrows are named thus. When Ahriman had the requisite number of Carlins, he would let loose the Carlins in those places and then let his Tarlaks hunt them down and eat them."

"And your ancestors had a hand in this?", Kelyarn demanded.

"Yes, they did, Kelyarn, but understand that they had no choice in the matter. Back then, we were all Slaves, Carlins and Thols alike!", Yealah replied.

Simone placed a calming hand on Kelyarn's arm, commenting, "And Slaves cannot have any conscience, they have no free will at all. A Slave does as asked or dies. They have no choice."

"Yes. My people and the Carlin folk were all Slaves back then and when a Slave was disobedient, it was killed cruelly and mercilessly, becoming Tarlak food", Yealah told them, trilling unapologetically.

Kelyarn lowered his voice, "Now I understand why you keep those deep-time histories to yourselves. No one likes to hear that their ancestors were all Slaves to be hunted and eaten."

"Yes, and now you understand why this is relevant", Yealah trilled, clicking the explanation, "The key is the wandering. It is designed to arouse a compatible mate. That it chose a Human was an error in the genetic programming; an unintended genetic compatibility pathway."

"If that's the case, then we can trace this compatibility pathway, can't we?", Doctor Morrow asked.

Simone enquired, "Can this biological imperative be reversed?"

Yealah shook her head, trilling and clicking, "We now know that the compatibility pathway exists, but it does not help us trace it. And no, we cannot reverse the biological imperative; we Mimasian Thols no longer have that knowledge. Even if we did, we still couldn't. Those genetic modifications were made over six million years ago; by now, they are a part of all Carlin-kind; irreversible."

Simone, quickly thinking, enquired, "Would that same genetic compatibility pathway exist in Thols as well? Are Mimasian Thols and Indigenous Thols compatible with Humans?"

"That is a good question, Simone; however, we Mimasian Thols have lived alongside Humans, both subspecies, for nearly thirteen hundred and fifty years. I think that if such a compatibility pathway existed within us Thols, we would know it by now, there would already be hybrid-younglings", Yealah trilled and clicked.

Keegali chimed in, questioning, "So, we know how this happened, but it doesn't help us?"

"I would not say that, Keegali. It does not help us trace the compatibility pathway, but it does tell us why it's there and gives us an inkling as to where to start looking", Yealah trilled and clicked in reply.

"I'll have a research team start on it straight away", Doctor Morrow stated.

Kelyarn's concern was more practical, "Keegali, Kayala, these deep-time histories, our people do not need to know them. It will cause all sorts of problems."

"Agreed, Father", Kayala replied, remarking, "Now that I've heard them, I wish that I hadn't."

Keegali nodded, also in agreement, "It goes to the very heart of what it means to be a Carlin and it does so in a very bad way. That we were once simply considered to be like Gudongs to be eaten. Our people cannot be told this thing. Not ever!"

Keegali looked at her Husband and advised, "Kelyarn, we cannot allow young Carlin girls who are of quickening age and not yet mate-bonded to go to the Human village. This could happen again."

"Yes, it could. We were lucky this time. Norton is a single man. Imagine if he'd been a married man with kits of his own. That would have been even more disastrous", Kelyarn agreed, deciding, "I will send out an advisory to the other village elders to that effect. No unmated Carlin girl, between eighteen and twenty one years of age, can go to the Human village."

"We have to expand that, Kelyarn", Simone noted, advising, "No male Human upgrade installer can go to a Carlin house where there is an unmated Carlin girl, between eighteen to twenty one years of age. In that case, the upgrade installer will need to be a woman."

"I'll take a mental note of that one as well", Kelyarn agreed, noting, "I'll add it to the same advisory."

Keegali noted, "Norton would be the exception to the rule; he's mate-bonded to our Kearill."

Yealah chimed in, trilling and clicking, "The people in charge of the upgrade program won't know who to send, male or female, unless the family in question informs them of any eighteen to twenty-one-year-old unmated Carlin girls in their house."

Simone noted, "We use questionnaires asking which upgrades householders are interested in. We can add that question to the list."

Kelyarn noted dryly, "This is becoming quite the exercise."

Simone smiled, "It's okay, Kelyarn. Apart from our own memories, my neural augments are cataloguing this entire discussion."

Kayala listened to the ongoing discussion, but had a completely different take, "Guys, this is not a disaster to be managed. It's an opportunity!"

All eyes turned to Kayala and Simone enquired, "Kayala, sweety. Just how is this an opportunity?"

Kayala mentioned one word, a single female Carlin name, "Keylamb."

"Oh! Keylamb!", Keegali exclaimed in understanding, "Kayala, you're talking about our Carlinish widows."

"Yes, Mother, our Carlinish widows", Kayala confirmed, explaining to the others, "If a Carlin woman loses her bond-mate, she can't have another. Our biological imperative only allows for the one quickening. Yet, Yealah says that there was a time when we Carlins were more like the Humans and could have more than one mate."

"And more so than you think, even going so far as to have more than one mate at the same time", Yealah trilled and clicked in confirmation.

"We call that polygamy or even polyamory", Simone noted, explaining, "It is not very common."

Yealah corrected Simone, "It is more common than you think, Simone. There are many examples of polygamy and polyamory in Human history, Earth-descended and especially Martian-descended."

Doctor Morrow, who had been quiet, enquired, "Just who is this, Keylamb?"

"Doctor Morrow, Keylamb is my neighbour. She lives on a plot with a house across the laneway from my own plot. Keylamb is also a very young widow, she's only twenty three", Kayala informed the Doctor, before explaining, "Keylamb went through her quickening just two years ago. Keylamb's Husband, her bond-mate Korsah, was a hunter. One day, he went hunting in the lowland forests to the north; he never came back. We never found out what happened to him; that sometimes happens to hunters. Now Keylamb lives alone with three young kits. Keylamb is such a sweet young woman."

"Oh my God, that's absolutely awful!", Simone exclaimed.

Kelyarn remembered and added more information, "I remember when that happened. Keylamb at least had a plot and a house to live in. If a widow doesn't have a house, we Carlins provide them with a small, manageable plot with a small, comfortable house."

"But alone with three kits, Kelyarn?", Simone questioned.

Keegali frowned, "It all comes back to that biological imperative of ours again, Simone. There is no second bond, so no Carlin man will be drawn to Keylamb."

Simone enquired hopefully, "What about Carlin widowers? Surely they'd be in the same situation, wouldn't they?"

"Carlin widows outnumber the widowers ten to one, Simone", Keegali replied, noting, "And a Carlin widower loses all interest in Carlin women after their bond breaks."

"Which is why this is so serendipitous", Kayala interjected, speculating, "A Human male would be a perfect solution for a Carlinish widow like Keylamb."

"Kayala, your empathy for Keylamb is highly commendable, but there are several problems we need to consider first. We currently don't have any information on the long-term viability of Carlin Human hybrid kits", Kelyarn explained, commenting, "We cannot condone any Carlin widow relationships with Human men until we know how viable their offspring will be."

"There is another consideration as well, Kayala. Norton was caught up by Kearill's pheromones. Would Norton have even considered Kearill as a mate, had her pheromones not affected him?", Keegali questioned, commenting, "We simply don't know and Norton can't tell us because he's now mate-bonded to Kearill."

Kayala turned to Yealah for answers and Yealah simply trilled and clicked, "Kayala, we simply don't know. It may be several years before we have the answers to either of those questions."

Simone looked at Kayala's downhearted face and raised her hopes, "Kayala, remember my Daughter, Angelique and your Sister, Kitty. They were together for almost three years; they loved each other. So there is always hope that a Human man might find Keylamb or another Carlinish widow attractive, perhaps even mate material. That could happen."

"There you go, Mother, we already have an example. We should look into this", Kayala noted.

"And we will, Kayala, but first we need to understand more about the long-term viability of hybrid kits", Keegali reminded her.

A notification came through on Doctor Morrow's data tablet; the blood test results were flowing in.

Doctor Morrow began reading the test results, murmuring aloud as he did so, "According to these test results, Kearill had a massive spike in oestrogen, along with highly elevated levels of allopregnanolone, dopamine and cortisol. Her progesterone levels have also been highly erratic as well, only stabilising with the onset of the pregnancy."

Simone quickly opened the same data stream with her neural augments, quickly processing them.

"Doctor Morrow, our A.I. systems appear to have discovered a new, unheard-of neuroactive protein complex. It's been named, reverase, which, according to this A.I. report, acts as a hippocampal inhibitor in Carlins and a hippocampal suppressor in Humans", Simone reported.

"That would explain the complete memory loss that Kearill is suffering and Norton's fragmented, slowly resurfacing memories", Doctor Morrow concluded.

Simone's neural augments processed the data stream more deeply, "Oh, my God. Carlin quickening pheromones aren't just simple pheromones; they are an entire mRNA vector. Norton's cellular ribosomes were receiving Kearill's pheromonal mRNA instructions and producing that new complex protein, reverase."

Simone paused as she continued to process the data stream with her neural augments, her eyes closed in deep concentration, "Oh my God, it isn't just reverase either, there's a whole class of new neuroactive proteins"; She began to list the new A.I. discovered and named proteins, "Ecliptin creates cognitive fog or haze. Hippocrene, which, according to our A.I. systems, works in conjunction with reverase, again affecting memories. Here's another one: chronotase. Our couple literally did not experience time during their mating frenzy. Ah, here's our main culprit, amatoria, which induces an urgent, compulsive need and desire to excessively procreate."

Doctor Morrow listened intently while reading the same reports, albeit far more slowly and exclaimed, "Carlin quickening pheromones are a complex set of neural programming commands!"

"Yes, Doctor, Carlin quickening pheromones are a complete mRNA package delivery system", Simone agreed.

"Simone, look at their oxytocin levels, they are through the roof!", Doctor Morrow advised.

Simone looked at the associated report, "Yes, yes, their oxytocin levels are exceedingly high", before she turned to Keegali and Kelyarn, enquiring, "When you get these two back to your house, what happens after that? What happens next?"

Keegali looked at her Daughter, Kearill and Norton on the screen and she pointed to them. Norton had started to awaken and Kearill was stroking him to arousal before climbing on top of him and mating once more.

Simone instructed the observation room's A.I. system, "A.I., automatically dim the screen whenever the couple engages in coitus. All recordings are to be encrypted using my personal voice key 'One Alpha Fehu Othalah Omega Nine', Special Operative restricted access only."

"Kearill and Norton are going to be like that for at least a month, perhaps six weeks. Knowing my Kearill, probably the latter, she is our little cuddle puss after all. They won't leave each other's side and they will require constant attention from both Kelyarn and me. They will be functionally useless", she paused before noting, "They will become more responsive after that and begin to become less clingy as time goes on. Sometime around the fourth month, perhaps a bit later, Norton should be able to return to work", Keegali informed Simone.

Kelyarn stepped in, "After their Daughter is born, their mate-bond will loosen enough that they can manage it themselves. Then they'll start looking for their own plot and house; then the cycle repeats."

Simone used her neural augments to send an official notification that Norton Fairchild was officially under medical supervision for the next four to five months, preserving his employment.

Simone turned to Doctor Morrow and Yealah, "We have a problem, guys. Carlin quickening pheromones are a complete mRNA package delivery system. I very much doubt that this can be contained."

Yealah trilled and clicked, "While that is true, it is also an opportunity. This pheromonal delivery system could be used for therapeutic delivery services once we understand how it works."

"I have to send these reports upstairs. High Admiral Nummus has to be across all of this", Simone informed them, noting, "It is as they say, well above my pay grade."

Much of the conversation between Doctor Morrow and Simone went straight over the Carlin's heads. Yealah, on the other hand, had been reviewing the same documents and taking detailed notes on her data tablet in Mimasian Tholish script with her stylus. A highly recursive script that neither Human, Carlin, nor even the Indigenous Thols could decipher. It was a naturally encrypting cipher.

Kayala didn't understand the discussion, but she did understand Carlin-folk; she'd watched her Sister, Kearill, and Norton intently on the screen with a great deal of curiosity.

"Guys, I think this gets worse", Kayala advised them, before asking, "Doctor, can you bring up an image of what a Carlin Human hybrid will look like?"

Doctor Morrow was surprised by the question, but quickly put it down to curiosity; he replied, "Yes. Based on Kearill's features and Norton's features, we can create a fairly accurate simulation of what their hybrid Daughter might look like. It won't be her, as such, but it will be highly indicative."

"Good. Can you please create that simulation? A Carlin Human hybrid girl about five years of age, with a pair of hybrids about four years of age and another pair of hybrids about three. Make the younger pairs a mix of boys and girls?"

"That's a very specific simulation, Kayala, but I'm certain that our A.I. systems can do it", Doctor Morrow replied as he entered the instructions into his data tablet.

The simulation, a hologram, appeared in front of them, in between the chairs and the wall screen. Five simulated Carlin Human hybrid kits; children with basic Carlinish features like their Mother, Kearill, but with an overlay of their Father, Norton's features. Their skin was a blend of Kearill's and Norton's, but minus the Carlinish signature blue stripes. They had eyes with rounded pupils, not pupil slits. They lacked Carlinish whiskers. On their heads was a luxurious mop of human hair. They still had the Carlinish ankles, set well above the ground; still pad walkers. The hybrids also had a tail, but their tails were somewhat shorter than the Carlin norm. For modesty reasons, the simulation covered their nether regions with loincloths.

Simone's eyes opened wide, her jaw dropped; she remarked, "They are absolutely adorable!"

Keegali's eyes also opened wide, but for a different reason; yes, these hybrid kits were absolutely adorable, but horrifically so. They were simply too adorable. Kelyarn frowned; he felt the same way; he understood what Kayala meant about things getting worse.

"This is very, very bad!", Kelyarn exclaimed.

"Why, Kelyarn? They look positively gorgeous", Simone queried.

"That is precisely the problem", Kelyarn replied.

Keegali stepped in, "Do you remember the day of first contact?"

"Not really, I was up at the Artemisia in Cis-Luns L-Five on that day", Simone replied.

Keegali nodded, explaining, "On that day, my Daughter, Kitty, showed an immediate attraction to your Daughter, Angelique. My Husband, Kelyarn, joked that I had an immediate attraction to both your Husband, James, and High Admiral Roberta Nummus. It was true, very true. I have even propositioned you several times in the past myself. We Carlin women, not only find our people attractive, but also your people, Simone. That is the problem."

"Keegali, you have always been open and honest with your attractions; that's one of the things I admire about you, but I'm not seeing the relevance here", Simone admitted.

Kayala interjected, exclaiming, "Aunt Simone, these hybrid kits are simply too beautiful! Other Carlin Mothers, ones who are already mated-bonded, will want to have their own!"

Simone was gobsmacked; she had not even considered that.

While Simone remained gobsmacked, Yealah sent a message to Simone via her data tablet, which was in encrypted English. Simone's neural augments picked it up immediately.

"You need to understand, Simone, that the current Carlin-folk are no longer the same species that my people lived with six million plus years ago. They have evolved, significantly evolved. Yealah."

Simone mentioned nothing of Yealah's message and asked one simple word, "Ramifications?"

Kayala explained, "Carlin Mothers will see Kearill's hybrid kits. They will be enamoured by them and want their own hybrid kits."

Kelyarn chimed in, noting, "Those Mothers will tell their Husbands. A

Carlinish Husband will always support his Wife, supporting her to the level of enabling her to achieve her desires."

Keegali placed her communicator on a low table that sat in front of their chairs, "Yesterday evening, Norton showed us these pictures of our Kearill's shopping"; she brought up a holographic image of Kearill in a sea-green bathing suit, a two-piece bathing suit with a g-string bottom and six-cup top.

Keegali explained, "The shopkeeper created this swimsuit so that my Kearill could swim in your village's aquatic centre. Imagine Carlinish women coming here to your village, buying bathing suits and seducing your men in your aquatic centre. Will your men-folk be able to resist them?"

Simone stared at the hologram of Kearill in her bathing suit; she was absolutely gorgeous. Simone knew the answer; she simply placed her hand over her mouth at the implications.

Doctor Morrow was in shock; he looked at the hologram, "No, Keegali. No Human male can resist that! When it comes to sex, Human men are just weak!"

A window appeared in the corner of the wall screen. High Admiral Roberta Nummus's office appeared. Sitting on the front of her desk was Roberta Nummus and standing by her side was Quora.

Roberta spoke, "Simone, we've been reviewing your data feeds and we seem to have a dual contagion issue. One pheromonal, the other aesthetic and possibly mimetic."

"Agreed, Admiral. What's our plan? Our course of action?", Simone replied, querying.

"For the moment, containment. At least until we understand the full ramifications", Roberta replied.

Quora stepped in, "We appear to be seeing the evolution of a new species. If my analysis is correct, the Carlin Human hybrids will be genetically compatible within themselves, but not backwards compatible with either parent species."

Roberta summed up succinctly, "So there's no backsies and the survival of this new species is reliant on further hybrid production. This situation must be monitored, for both the health of the hybrids themselves, but also for our two societies as a whole."

Quora interjected, "I must say, this entire situation has complicated my zeroth directive. I will now have to add a new and unexpected species. Every Android that I have patched will need to be repatched."

"Yes, Admiral, yes, Quora, understood, but do we have a plan?", Simone enquired once more.

Quora fielded the question, "Yes, our plan is containment, at least for the new future."

"Fuck you, Quora! You fucking Androids can be so damned annoying. I'm on the ground here. I need to hear the plan. I need more details! Kearill is my fucking niece!", Simone shouted, she was getting uncharacteristically angry and short on patience.

"Simmer down, S.O. Reas. That's an order!", Roberta stated firmly.

"Yes, Ma'am. My apologies, Ma'am", Simone replied, before requesting, "The plan. More details, please. I need to know. Keegali and Kelyarn need to know! Kearill is their Daughter!"

"Okay. First, when Doctor Morrow is satisfied that Kearill and Norton are not in any danger, they can be discharged and transferred into Keegali's and Kelyarn's care. After Kearill's Daughter is born, they can come back to our colony to live in Norton's apartment. That should prevent mimetic contagion within Kelyarn's village", Roberta announced.

Quora stepped in, "For the mid to longer term, I have a team of Androids scouting the terrain to the west of the colony. We are looking for a fair-sized, raised knoll in the bluegrass meadows. There, we will construct a small village. It will be of the Carlinish design, but it will have modern Human technology built in. It will be protected from predators with electrified perimeter fences of the same style utilised in Martian Ambassador Sarlia's glade. They will be allowed to visit their Carlin villages, but not with their hybrid kits. Employment will be provided within the colony, or if they wish, off-world here in Cis-Luns L-Five. They will be treated with all due respect."

Roberta chimed back in, frowning, "Kearill and Norton are the first, yes, but they won't be the last. Quora's projections are telling us to expect ten to fifteen cross-species mate-bonding incidents per year. Simone, this cat's well and truly out of the bag and there's no stuffing it back in."

"Giving them their own village will slow down the mimetic spread, but seriously, if Quora is right and these hybrids represent a new species, then we have no right to stop it", Simone noted; she was right; what right does Humanity have to halt the development of a whole new species?

"Simone, we fully understand that. This is just a stopgap measure until we get our heads around the situation. We already know that the containment will fail, we just want it to fail gradually on our terms and not explosively or catastrophically", Roberta explained.

"Understood, Ma'am and again my apologies for my previous outburst", Simone replied.

"Fuel through the reactor, Simone. Already forgiven. If I can't forgive my Niece, who can I forgive?", Roberta replied back smiling.

Kelyarn's communicator buzzed; he had a message. Kelyarn checked the message; it was from Kayala's husband, Krylor. Kelyarn read the message and it was so unexpected that he read it twice.

"Kretek, the Husband of Kitryala and Father of Katla, came to your house. Their

Daughter, Katla, was found in the back of their plot, in their garden, amongst the Human corn plants. Katla was found mating with a Human Doctor, Doctor Sivak. Katla was on top of the Doctor and riding him like she was in a trance. They both had glazed eyes and were completely unresponsive, oblivious to the presence of Kretek or Kitryala. Krylor."

Kelyarn sent a message back, *"Krylor, advise Kretek that Katla and Doctor Sivak are in heat and the throes of their mating frenzy. Katla must have gone into her quickening when the Doctor was present; they are now mate-bonded. Kretek and his Wife need to take them both up to their upstairs sleep room. Tell them that the mating frenzy will end in due course when Katla conceives. Kelyarn."*

Kelyarn shook his head, first his Daughter, Kearill, and now Kretek's Daughter, Katla, and all within mere hours of each other.

"Ahem", Kelyarn cleared his throat, "We have a second couple. One of our village girls, Katla, has mate-bonded with a Human Doctor, Doctor Sivak."

Simone's neural augments went to work straight away, "Doctor Steven Sivak, a male twenty-six-year-old, single, medical training specialist. He is one of the Doctors training our Carlin healers and midwives in emergency medical procedures."

Kelyarn confirmed, "Yes, that would be the case. Katla is an apprentice healer and midwife; she would have been a part of that training program. Katla is also about the same age as Kearill, perhaps a few weeks younger. So her quickening would have been due any day now."

Keegali stepped in, "Kelyarn, it's not just upgrade installers we need to consider, we also need to consider the Human medical trainers."

Kelyarn nodded, "Yes, Keegali. I am making mental notes of everything, Keegali."

Yealah sighed before trilling, clicking and barking softly, "This is all happening faster than we thought. I'll send an airborne ambulance to pick up Katla and Doctor Sivak", and then she turned to the wall screen, noting, "I'll organise another set of floor mats for them. Let's hope that we don't have any more, or we'll be needing a bigger observation room as well, which I don't think we have."

Simone reminded her, "Make sure that the paramedics know what to expect. We can't have them freaking out on us."

Yealah nodded and trilled back, "I'll use the same airborne team that brought Kearill and Norton here."

Keegali noted, "Kitryala's house has only two levels; they should be able to access the sleep room more easily this time."

"I'll send the word out for all Human males in the Carlin villages to return here to our colony immediately. We can't have this thing spreading too quickly; we need to keep a lid on it", Simone informed them all.

The number of young Carlin women who found themselves accidentally bonded to Human men slowly grew. Try as they might, there was always going to be gaps in their containment.

Kearill, the first Carlin woman to produce hybrid Carlin Human kits, gave birth to her Daughter in late thirty four eight seven. Kearill named her new Daughter, Roberta, after her Human Aunt Roberta Nummus, who, as an immortal, could not have kits of her own. This broke with the Carlin naming conventions, but that was okay by Kearill; she planned a naming convention of her own. Kearill, Norton and their small kit, Roberta, moved into Norton's apartment in the Human colony.

Kearill took Norton's surname as her own, another break with Carlin tradition, becoming Kearill Fairchild. Little Roberta and all of Kearill's kits that followed would have the surname Fairchild; it was fitting, as they would all be fair and beautiful children, with their Father's mousy blond hair.

Norton Fairchild continued to work as a technological upgrade installer, as he was already mate-bonded to Kearill. The traces of Carlinish quickening proteins in his blood provided a lifelong immunity from any possibility of a future second bond. It also explained why the Carlin-folk could only ever bond once. The Carlin quickening proteins could only work on an individual just the one time. After the first *"infection"*, the couple's own immune systems prevented any subsequent bonding possibilities.

Kearill quickly fell pregnant with her second litter of hybrid kits and gave birth to them in the following year, another Daughter and a Son, whom she named Simone and James after her Human Aunt Simone and Uncle James. It was after the birth of Kearill's second litter that they moved into the small Carlin Human hybrid village, further to the west of the Human colony.

It was far better for Kearill as she'd been raised in a Carlinish household and the modern conveniences aside, the metal men had built with both accuracy and authenticity in mind. It was in their new house in the small village on the knoll amongst the bluegrass meadows that Kearill gave birth to her third litter. Another Daughter and another Son, whom she named Angelique and Johnathon after the Human Siblings she'd grown up alongside.

At that point, Kearill decided that it was time for the Human-provided contraceptives; five kits were enough for any Carlin Mother, especially when they combined Carlin kit chaos with Human ingenuity.

Roberta Nummus and the Reas family took note of Kearill's naming convention and felt both honoured and bemused. That Kearill would name her kits after them was not something they'd expected. Both Roberta and Simone still considered Kearill their little cuddle puss. It didn't matter that Kearill was now a fully grown Carlinish woman with five hybrid kits; they still remembered Kearill as the affectionate little kit at the age of four.

As Kearill and Norton were the first mate-bonded hybrid Carlin Human couple, they and their five hybrid kits would have their health monitored indefinitely. No one had any metrics on hybrid viability or lifespan, nor whether they were susceptible to the currently known prevalent illnesses and diseases. It was something Kearill was more than happy with; it kept her beautiful hybrid kits in good health and well looked after.

Katla's first kit, her Daughter, was born just days after Kearill's. Katla, Steven and their little kit, whom they named Kreeling, which in Carlinish translated as Wonder, moved into Steven's apartment in the Human colony. Steven was mate-bonded to Katla and couldn't bond a second time, so he continued his work training Carlin healers and midwives in emergency medical procedures. With the help of the colony's daycare system, Katla studied nursing, later becoming one of the colony's school nurses.

Katla had a further four kits in two litters; the first was a pair of boys, same face kits. The second was a pair of girls, again same face kits, after which, she too called five kits enough and decided it was time for the human-provided contraceptives. It was a good thing, too; both of her boys turned out to be mischievous pranksters.

After the birth of Katla's third litter, she and her family moved to the small Carlin Human hybrid village to the west of the Human colony. Katla and Kearill became next-door neighbours and very close friends, spending much time together.

Before five years had passed, that small Carlin Human hybrid village in the west had grown to forty two plots and houses. Quora's plan of containment worked, but only to slow the Carlin Human hybrid spread, not to stop it.

One did not stop the inevitability of evolution; one could only guide it. A new species had been born, yet to be named and the universe was all the better for their existence.

30. Irreconcilable Differences.

Simone had flown up from the surface of the planet, Secundus, for a meeting at Colonial Central Command in Cis-Luns L-Five. High Admiral Roberta Nummus called the meeting to run through recent events and developments. Quora, Yealah and Doctor Morrow had also been asked to attend.

The meeting took place in the Admiral's conference room at the Admiral's command complex in the northern end cap of the mega-colony, Colonial Central Command. When Simone entered the conference room, Admiral Nummus and the other attendees were already present and waiting.

Grab a seat, Simone", Roberta greeted. Noting, "Doctor Morrow and Yealah have some very good news with regards to our hybrid issue, but before we get to that, tell me about Angelique's plot. How's it all coming along?"

Simone took her seat and described the latest developments.

"Well, James is down there right now helping Angelique and Bobby with the construction", Simone began, noting, "The plot is in a good location. As you know, Elder Kelyarn's village is directly south of our colony and the village we constructed for the hybrid families is directly to the west of it. Directly south of the hybrid village and southwest of our colony is Sarlia's glade, right in the middle of that lowland forest. Angelique chose the land for her plot midway between the hybrid village and Sarlia's glade."

"Okay, so I can visualise where that is on a map, Simone. The land we selected for the hybrid village was on a large, raised grassy knoll. We chose that location because we could fence it off to keep the predators at bay. We used the same double perimeter fencing technique as we used for Ambassador Sarlia's glade and that worked a treat ", Roberta noted, then queried with concern, "Angelique's plot, though, is in the flat plains of the bluegrass meadows. How's Angelique going to keep the predators out?"

Simone smiled and replied, "The same method as Sarlia's plot; electrified double perimeter fences, deeply embedded into the ground with a single outward crank at the top. It worked well for Sarlia's glade, which is far more dangerous than the bluegrass meadows and it worked equally well for the hybrid village, so it should work just as well for Angelique's plot. That perimeter fence is already installed and being monitored. So far so good."

"Simone, I've been looking at these plans for Angelique's plot. It is slightly larger than originally specified. It's now three hundred and thirty metres across. I assume that's taking into account the gap between the inner and outer fences", Roberta noted.

"Absolutely, the gap between the inner and outer fences, plus the cleared zone beyond them both. Angelique is doing this by the numbers. Safety from predators is paramount", Simone replied.

Roberta nodded before noting, "I see that Angelique has '*borrowed*' the exact same house design as Ambassador Sarlia's; a soil-covered, buried house design."

"Angelique always said that she liked Sarlia's house, so yeah, that kind of makes sense. It will be easy to maintain, cheaper to regulate the temperature and difficult to spot from the air. I kind of like it myself, to be entirely honest", Simone explained.

"It's ironic, really", Roberta stated, explaining, "Of all the things in Sarlia's glade, her house was the least expensive to build. Hell, just carting all of those mature Maple trees from Earth to here cost far more."

"Angelique's house is still under construction; however, the tarmac for her ship's landing pad has already been poured in place and has already cured", Simone informed the Admiral.

"And her rather large hangar?", Roberta questioned.

"The Hanger's moncrete slab has also been poured in place. That was poured yesterday and should be finished curing by this afternoon", Simone replied, noting, "That hangar will be large enough to house Angelique's and Bobby's Broad Heads and their Manta Rays as well. It will also house any hover cars that they might require and still have plenty of room left over."

Roberta nodded. Special Operatives had expensive toys and those required proper housing.

"And the residential complex at the back of the hangar is for?", Roberta enquired.

"That is for Angelique's team. Angelique is putting in a request for three of her fellow cohort members", Simone explained, noting their names, "Michelle and Sylvester Bronson, they're going to be her security and grounds keepers, and Mike Johnson, he'll be in charge of the hangar, the ships, basically all of their tech."

"Three Special Operatives, all three-G trained. With her and Bobby, that makes five, Simone. That's a pretty small team", Roberta noted in reply.

"Yes, to start with, but you have to remember, there are not a lot of us Special Operatives out here and it's only natural for Angelique to select her team from the ones she trusts the most, from her cohort", Simone explained, noting, "I know all three of these guys; they will work really well together."

"Simone, please remind your Daughter that five is a rather small team. I do expect her team to expand at some point; Angelique will need to do some recruiting", Roberta commented.

"Yes, I have discussed that with Angelique", Simone agreed, before noting, "That residential complex at the back of the hangar extends underground and has the capacity to house twelve operatives, not including Angelique and Bobby. My Daughter has definite plans for expansion."

Quora accessed the orbital satellite system around Secundus and called up an image of Angelique's plot on the conference room's wall screen.

The plot was situated in the bluegrass meadows, yes, but in an area of broadly spaced Chillic and Bell Nut fruit trees forming a large, very open woodland about a kilometre or more across. Angelique's plot was in the very middle of the open woodland. Quora ever so slowly drilled the image into focus on Angelique's plot.

Roberta straight away noticed the regular placement of the Chillic and Bell Nut fruit trees of the open woodland surrounding Angelique's plot.

"That can't be natural, surely?", Roberta enquired.

Simone nodded in agreement, "It's not natural. I had some soil tests taken and the results were unusual. The soil around those trees contains a lot of charcoal and ash."

"Charcoal and ash?", Yealah, who had been listening, queried.

"Yes. I asked Elder Kelyarn if he had any ideas and he knew all about it", Simone told them, explaining, "The Carlin-folk use timber and stone to build their houses. They also use quite a bit of firewood. That open woodland in the bluegrass meadows was once a small stand of lowland forest."

"I thought that the Carlins avoided the lowland forests, that only the hunters ever entered them", Roberta replied, somewhat confused.

"That is what I thought as well. Apparently, the Carlin wood cutters look for lowland forests that aren't as tangled as most and they harvest the timber from the outside in, which is a very slow process", Simone explained, before elaborating, "They grade the timber; some for construction, some for firewood. Anything they can't use, they pile up and eventually burn it. When they've finished, they scatter the ash and the charcoal remains over the now open woodland. They don't cut down all the trees, though; they leave the largest and oldest, well-placed Chillic and Bell nut fruit trees alone."

"Why wouldn't they simply cut all of the trees down?", Yealah questioned.

"An open woodland like that one can be used as a new village site at a later date", Simone replied, commenting, "Kelyarn's Grandfather presided over the logging of that particular lowland forest. Here's the thing, now that my Angelique has moved it, the Carlin-folk will follow and start building a new village."

"Are there many open woodlands like that one?", Roberta curiously enquired.

"Apparently", Simone confirmed, remarking, "It got me curious. The village we built for the Carlin Human hybrid families was very similar to this open woodland, which was one of the reasons we chose that knoll in the first place. So I organised some deep soil tests and bingo, we found traces of ash and charcoal remains mixed in with the soil. That knoll we built the Carlin Human hybrid village on was another lowland forest that had been logged by the Carlins."

"And they do this for the timber, the firewood and the possibility of building new villages in the future", Roberta summed up in understanding.

"Yes. Kelyarn and Keegali told me that the Carlin-folk have been managing the valley this way since long before their recorded history, Carlin or Thol", Simone confirmed.

Roberta looked at the image of Angelique's plot on the screen. The fence line was clearly visible; the twin perimeter fences and the cleared buffer strip along the outside of the outer fence. In the centre of the plot was a section cleared and already dug out, being prepared for Angelique's future underground house.

South of the house was a tarmac landing pad, easily big enough to land four ships. To the west of the landing pad was a ridiculously large moncrete slab, already laid as the foundation for the Hangar and residential complex. The Underground section of the residential complex had already been dug out in preparation.

Between the hangar slap and the landing pad were tared taxiways; ships could be taxied from their hangar to the landing pad and vice versa. Everything appeared to be moving quickly. Roberta also noticed that beyond the landing pad were what looked like extensive garden beds being prepared. It appeared that Angelique's plot was also going to be food self-sufficient.

Roberta smiled, "Simone, let me know when the construction is all completed. I'd like to inspect Angelique's new home myself when it's finished."

"Okay, Angelique's plot and her team are all coming together, so let's move on, shall we?", Roberta decided before informing Simone, "Yealah and Doctor Morrow have some great news. Quora and I are already across it, so I'll let the good Doctor bring you up to speed, Simone."

Doctor Morrow cleared his throat, "Ahem. We have some good news to share. We have been able to develop a vaccine to immunise human males against the Carlin biological imperative, specifically their quickening process. It works by priming the Human immune system to react to trace amounts of the Carlin quickening proteins, reverase, ecliptin, hippocrene, chronotase and amatoria."

Simone quickly replied, "Wow! That is good news."

Doctor Morrow continued, "Yes, yes, it is. The vaccine works because of what we have labelled as the initial pheromonal handshake. When a man encounters the female Carlin's quickening pheromones, which, as we all know, are a vector for mRNA delivery, the male, whether Carlin or Human, is triggered to produce a burst of pheromones. The Carlin woman's body reacts to the man's pheromones and if there is a mutual compatibility through a receptor–ligand alignment exceeding ninety eight point five percent sequence congruency, then the bonding process can begin. However, if the man's pheromones contain even a whiff of antibodies for reverase, ecliptin, hippocrene, chronotase, or amatoria, the whole process shuts down. More importantly, the man's immune system will actively target those proteins as foreign bodies and eliminate them. This provides permanent immunity from Carlin Human bonding."

"That's great. So we can immunise Human men against Carlin quickening pheromones. It sounds like we've got this under control", Simone was quick to understand.

Yealah cut in with trills, clicks and soft barks, "It's not all perfect, Simone; there are side effects, albeit manageable side effects."

"Side effects?", Simone questioned.

"Ah, yes", Doctor Morrow confirmed, "I was just about to get to those. For the vaccine to work, we need to use trace amounts of all of the Carlin quickening proteins, reverase, ecliptin, hippocrene, chronotase and amatoria. Trace amounts, yes, but there appears to be a lower limit, so we have to stay above that to prime the Human immune response."

"Okay, Doctor Morrow, where exactly are you going with this?", Simone questioned.

"The vaccine triggers a mating response that lasts from three to six hours, depending on the individual", Doctor Morrow divulged.

Yealah chimed in, trilling and clicking, "We need to isolate the patient and keep them under observation for the duration of that time. That will severely limit any vaccine rollout."

Quora noted in a detached monotone and perfectly deadpan voice, "That may be a selling point for married couples. Wives may wish to accompany their Husbands during the observation period. The Carlin quickening proteins are probably the galaxy's most powerful aphrodisiac."

"Please tell me that was an attempt at humour, Quora?", Simone queried.

"It was, Simone. Did I miss the mark?", Quora replied as Simone just shook her head.

"That's actually a valid point. If married couples think they'll enjoy the immunisation process, then more men will likely sign up for it", Roberta noted dryly.

"There are also some major ethical considerations", Yealah trilled, clicked and softly barked, noting, "The new hybrid Carlin Human species, *Homo carlinus primoris*, currently has insufficient numbers. While they are viable within themselves, they are not yet viable as a species. We will be suppressing their genetic variation, creating a genetic bottleneck, so to speak. That will be unacceptable."

Simone looked at Yealah incredulously before responding, "So is forced bonding, Yealah. The Carlin quickening process is not a choice; it is a forced biological imperative. The couples may be happy with the situation after the event, but would they have been happy to volunteer for the bonding, had they been given the choice in the first place?"

"I have to agree with Simone on that one", Roberta interjected, "This might be okay for the Carlin-folk, for them it's their normal mate-bonding process. For Humans, though, it's not. It fails free will in two distinct ways. First, the Human finds himself bonded to a Carlin woman for life; he had no choice in the matter. Second, did the Carlin woman want to bond with a Human or a Carlin man? Again, there is no choice in the matter."

"Roberta Nummus! How can you not understand my perspective?", Yealah shot back, trilling and clicking, she barked harshly and even grunted, "I am a Mimasian Thol. When my ancestors awoke from cryosleep thirteen hundred and fifty years ago, there were only forty two of us. A genetic bottleneck! It took many centuries of Martian and later, Human medical intervention, to help my people overcome that lack of genetic variation. Would you force that on a new emerging species?"

Roberta was stunned by how strongly Yealah responded; she was quiet for many long seconds before replying, "Yealah, your concerns are noted. We do have a problem."

Simone stated what everyone was thinking, "We can't force people to bond through inaction. The vaccine needs to be rolled out."

"We can't kill off a new emergent species genetic future either", Yealah shot back, trilling and clicking her fixed position on the matter.

"We could ask for Human male volunteers", Quora suggested, noting, "That allows for the continuance of both free will and the new emergent species."

Doctor Morrow interjected, "That will not work, Quora. There is the little problem of the mutual compatibility through the receptor–ligand alignment exceeding ninety eight point five percent sequence congruency. Remember that little point, Quora. Your volunteers might not be a match and we have no way to predict who would be. It simply won't work."

"This is going to get complicated, very complicated.", Simone replied with pure honesty.

Roberta stated the bleeding obvious, "We are also forgetting that we can't force civilians to be vaccinated either."

Simone quickly recommended, "All male Colonial Marines and Special Operatives should be vaccinated as a matter of course. It's just one of the things we sign up for when we join."

Roberta rubbed her chin, thinking it was quite a pickle, but not unsolvable.

"Okay, all men who have legitimate work in the Carlin villages should be offered the vaccine. So that's emergency workers, paramedics, teachers and tech upgrade installers. They do have the right to refuse, but we already have procedures in place for that anyway", Roberta decided, noting, "We have to vaccinate married men; we can't have families being torn apart by untoward mate-bonding."

Simone agreed, "That's a start, but we need to consider that there may be men who actually want to mate-bond with a Carlinish woman. We don't have any concrete examples of that, but my Angelique did have a temporary bond with Keegali's Daughter, Kitty, so we have to assume that it's possible."

Doctor Morrow agreed, "I still remember that photo of young Kearill in her bathing suit back in eighty seven, when Kearill and Mr Norton Fairchild accidentally bonded. There will be men who find the Carlin female form alluring, so yes, we have to take that into account. If a man actually wants to mate-bond with a Carlin lady and if that bond can be formed, we should allow it. That should help alleviate any genetic bottleneck issues."

Yealah nodded, trilled and clicked, "Yes, agreed. We must leave some mate-bonding avenues open."

"Quora, I hope you're recording all of this", Roberta commented.

"I am, Roberta Nummus. Everything discussed is being compiled, collated and filed", Quora replied, noting, "I will complete a full list of recommendations in due course covering our full discussions."

"It's a funny thing", Simone said, before noting, "Doctor Morrow, you remembered Kearill in a swimsuit, which makes perfect sense. You are a man and Kearill is a very beautiful Carlinish woman, so that is a memorable image. Very memorable, in fact. I, however, am thinking of Kearill's Sister, Kayala and some of the points that she made. Three points in fact."

Roberta quickly caught on, "Mimetic transmission. Our hybrid families may not be wandering around the Carlin villages, but Carlin family members do visit the hybrid families here in our colony and in the hybrid village to the west."

"Exactly. There may be mate-bonded Carlin Mothers who decide that they want hybrid kits and we all know that their Husbands will support them. There may even be young Carlin women approaching their quickening who actually want a Human mate, specifically to have hybrid kits", Simone pointed out, noting, "I haven't heard of any purely Carlin families delivering hybrid kits yet, but it could be just a matter of time. And the latter, how do we know if a Carlin girl comes to our colony deliberately to attract a Human mate? It has probably already happened. How would we even know? The Carlin girl is not likely to tell us."

Quora tilted her head, looked at Simone and replied, "Many Carlin families now have communicators. They don't even need to come to our colony. They could use their communicators to set up a tryst and we would never know."

"That's actually a good point, Quora", Roberta replied, before turning to Yealah, "I don't think it matters how we roll out the vaccine; this cat's well and truly out of the bag. There will always be new hybrid families, no matter what we do, Yealah."

Yealah nodded and smiled, then trilled and clicked, "And I remember Kayala's third point. Carlinish widows. They cannot mate-bond again in the Carlin sense. Human male volunteers won't have to pass that mutual compatibility alignment; they just have to like each other. Kayala called it an opportunity, if I remember correctly."

Roberta chuckled, "They'd still need to be vaccinated. You don't want one of our men marrying a Carlinish widow and then getting accidentally mate-bonded to a young Carlin woman."

Simone nodded, pointing out, "If Kelyarn and Keegali had been making those kinds of arrangements, I think that they would have told me. Still, it is another possible avenue that leads to hybrid kits and further genetic variation."

Yealah nodded, smiling to herself. The new emergent species was not likely to suffer from any genetic bottlenecks after all.

A notification came up on Roberta's data tablet, "Ah, it looks like our next guest has arrived. Matriarch Ytryan will be here in a moment or two."

The conference room door opened and the Mimasian Thol Matriarch entered. Roberta greeted her and showed her to a seat.

"Matriarch Ytryan, you said that the matter was important. What can we do for you?", Roberta enquired.

Ytryan trilled and clicked, enquiring, "It's about the second colony, the beta site. When will we be breaking ground?"

Roberta frowned, "Ytryan, we are still taking surveys of the candidate sites. As you can imagine, we have to make the right decision. We don't want to start work on a new colony and then have to move it."

Ytryan nodded, then trilled and clicked in reply, "I do understand, it's just that it's been more than twenty years and we still haven't broken ground on the new colony site."

"Yes, that is true, Ytryan, but we are still on schedule; in fact, we are actually ahead of schedule. We aren't due to start work on the new colony site for another three years. That's five years ahead of the original timeline", Roberta reminded her.

Simone chimed in, noting, "We were expecting your people to build their villages amongst your Indigenous cousins, Ytryan."

Ytryan nodded again and then she trilled and clicked, "Yes, I know, but the Tholish High Council is so, so, unreasonable. I cannot even talk to them. The Indigenous Thols have a patriarchal society. High Chancellor Yuntark and the other High Councillors won't even talk to me. They are insufferable!"

Yealah interjected, trilling and clicking in agreement, "They truly are, Roberta Nummus. My Husband, Yannick and I are responsible for over two hundred Mimasian Thols. We built our own tree villages amongst the Indigenous Thols.

Some of us, like Yannick and I, built our tree houses in existing Indigenous Thol villages. We have exactly the same problem as our Matriarch, Ytryan."

Roberta was confused, "Yealah, I thought you got along well with the Indigenous Thols."

"With our neighbours, yes, but truth be told, High Chancellor Yuntark and the other High Councillors are all chauvinist pigs. They won't talk to women, sure they'll talk to a Carlin or a Human woman, but a Tholish woman, forget it", Yealah trilled and clicked, noting, "Whenever my Husband, Yannick and I deal with them, I have to defer to Yannick to do all of the talking. They simply ignore me completely."

Ytryan agreed, trilling and clicking, "That is the exact same problem that I've been having. Yealah has a workaround; her Husband, Yannick, knows how to talk power to power. I do not have that luxury."

Yealah nodded in agreement again and then trilled and clicked, "My Husband, Yannick, performs all of the dealings and discussions. I'm just expected to stand there and look pretty. Without Yannick, the situation would be completely intolerable."

Roberta looked confused, "Ytryan, why can't you ask your Husband, Yylryk, to help you out. That workaround does seem to work for Yealah and Yannick."

Ytryan shook her head, trilling and clicking in reply, "My Husband, Yylryk, bless his heart, is an engineering genius, but he does not know how to talk power to power. I love the man dearly, but when he does try to help, he always defers back to me. High Chancellor Yuntark and the other High Councillors all mock him behind his back. I know this because their Wives tell me of it."

Roberta rested her chin on her hand momentarily before enquiring, "Ytryan, just how long has this been going on?"

"Since just after first contact. During our first contact, Wynessa, James, Angelique and you were all there. With two Humans and a Martian present, Yuntark and his people were all very polite. Without your presence, I am just another Tholish Wife and wives are for looking pretty, cooking, raising younglings and warming their beds", Ytryan trilled, clicked, barked and even grunted, "It has been so frustrating!"

"So, tell me, Ytryan. Is that why we have most of the Mimasian Thols still living up here in Colonial Central Command, including your own family?", Roberta queried.

Ytryan nodded, trilled and clicked, "Of course it is, we cannot live amongst the Indigenous Thols if they treat us like chattels."

Yealah trilled and clicked, "Living amongst our Indigenous Cousins does require that we sacrifice a small portion of our dignity. Not all of our people can do that."

"Okay. The first thing that I'm going to do is teach them a lesson", Roberta replied, before turning to Simone, "Okay, make sure that whenever we discuss matters with Yuntark and his fellow chauvinist pigs in the future, that they always talk to one of us women and that we talk to them through their Wives. When their behaviour changes, then we'll reset; until then, their Wives speak for them."

Simone chuckled, "That should be a lot of fun. I'd love to see their faces when we start doing that."

"If we can change their behaviour, will that help with the situation, Ytryan?", Roberta enquired.

"Roberta Nummus, it is far too late for that. We will colonise the beta site rather than deal with the Indigenous Thols", Ytryan replied, her position firmly fixed.

Roberta activated the conference room's wall screen and the image of Angelique's plot in the Masula Valley's bluegrass meadows reappeared from earlier. Roberta expanded the view to show the entirety of the Masula Valley, including the Northern, Southern and Western Mountain ranges.

"Eighty percent of the Indigenous Thols live in the Northern Mountain ranges, only twenty percent live in the Southern Mountains", Roberta noted before asking, "We aren't ready to open up a new beta colony site yet, Ytryan. That is still three years away. Would your people be able to set up your own colony in the Southern Mountain ranges? We can assist you with that almost straight away."

Ytryan shook her head, trilling, clicking and barking softly, "Roberta Nummus, we have already considered that option. When it comes to the Indigenous Thols, there is only one Thol polity in this Masula Valley. We would still be under the jurisdiction of the Tholish High Council and that is simply not acceptable. My people will not accept their rule. We will not bow down to their patriarchal tyranny."

Yealah quickly trilled, clicked and softly barked, "Ytryan does have a point, Roberta Nummus. Even if Matriarch Ytryan chose a region of the Southern Mountain ranges well to the west of the farthest Indigenous Thol tree villages, the Tholish High Council would quickly declare jurisdiction over any new tree villages that they build."

"The only place where the Tholish High Council would not force their jurisdiction upon us is in the far Western Mountain ranges and that vast region is simply far too dangerous for us to colonise", Ytryan explained, trilling and clicking, commenting, "Within this valley, the Tholish High Council considers all Thols in the Northern and Southern Mountain ranges to be under their jurisdiction; their territory."

Simone interjected, "I've read those reports from James and Angelique about the Sleimorp and Chitten incidents seven years back. There's a good reason why those Western Mountain ranges are off limits."

Roberta shook her head, "Ytryan, that does not give us a whole lot of wiggle room. I agree with you and Simone, the Western Mountain ranges are far too dangerous for any of us to colonise."

Roberta expanded the image on the wall screen further, showing the entirety of the Masula Continent. Two green dots appeared, one to the northeast across the Northern Mountain ranges, outside of the Masula Valley; it was numbered three.

The second dot was farther to the south of the Southern Mountain ranges on a large island named the Isle of Sorrows; it was numbered two. There was a third green dot, but it was on the other side of the planet, on the Antipodes Islands; it was not visible on the screen. It was numbered one.

Roberta began by stating, "The Tholish High Council knows nothing of anything beyond the Masula Valley, so they have absolutely no jurisdiction beyond it."

"We have been looking at three beta colony sites", Roberta told Matriarch Ytryan, commenting, "The current beta candidate site is on the Antipodes Islands on the other side of Homwol."

Roberta opened up a separate window on the screen showing the Antipodes Islands, "Notably, the Antipodes Islands have no land animals, so there are no predators there at all. Which is why it was selected as our first choice for the beta colony site. The downside is that there are no really tall trees either. Certainly nothing like the Jula Jula trees."

"Roberta Nummus. We Mimasian Thols live in tree villages, in tree houses. Your first choice for your beta colony site is not suitable for my people", Matriarch Ytryan told her flatly with trills and clicks.

"I figured you might say that, Ytryan, so let's have a look at site number two, shall we?", Roberta replied.

"By all means, do, Roberta Nummus", Ytryan trilled in reply.

"Okay. Everything between the Southern Mountain ranges and the Sorrowful Straits is Tarlak territory, so that is definitely off limits", Roberta announced, remarking, "There are no Jula Jula forests on the southern slopes of the Southern Mountain ranges either, so you would not be interested in that location anyway."

Doctor Morrow curiously enquired, "Why is that, Admiral? The slopes of the mountains inside the Masula Valley are covered in Jula Jula forests."

"Well, Doctor. The basalt bedrock runs deep, so you'd think that they'd grow there; however, I've been told it's the rainfall patterns. That big yellowish expanse in the centre of the southlands is the vast Shar Wastelands; it's all desert, so the southern slopes of the Southern Mountain ranges simply don't get enough rain. It's just too dry for Jula Jula forests to grow there", Roberta informed him.

"What about the second beta colony option?", Ytryan enquired, her voice laced with trills and clicks.

"The second beta colony option is on the Isle of Sorrows. That's kind of a sub-continent just over the Sorrowful Straits from the mainland", Roberta informed Ytryan, noting, "There is no Tarlak presence on the Isle of Sorrows."

Ytryan quickly trilled and clicked, "Is there a reason why it was chosen as a second choice and not first? What is wrong with the Isle of Sorrows?"

"Predators, Ytryan, predators", Roberta replied and then requested, "Simone, can you access the predator reports for the Isle of Sorrows?"

Simone used her neural augments to access the relevant reports, "Gods, our biologist and zoologists have no imagination. Okay, Ytryan, the Isle of Sorrows has three predators that we currently know of. Two snakes, both constrictors, Secundacondas, a green species and a brown species. They resemble terrestrial anacondas from Earth, except that they can grow up to thirty five feet long. There is also a varanid kind of lizard, the Pygmy Fang, although that is a bit of a misnomer; they can grow up to ten feet long. None of these predators can climb trees, though."

"Thank you, Simone", Roberta thanked, before noting, "The Isle of Sorrows does have tall trees, but no Jula Jula trees and those trees are only half the height of a Jula Jula tree."

Ytryan sighed before trilling and clicking, "We really do prefer the Jula Jula trees, even inside Mimas, we had a related species of tree. Can we look at the beta colony site option number three?"

Doctor Morrow curiously asked, "Why are our biologists and zoologists so lacking in imagination?"

"Doctor, I'm sending you a list of major species we've catalogued so far on the Masula Continent; it is far from complete", Simone replied, commenting, "Look at the assigned species names, two labelled as Secundacondas, another two in the Westlands labelled Secundaboas. There's even a huge range of herbivores labelled as Secundilopes; I assume they're all similar to our terrestrial Earth Antelopes."

Doctor Morrow quickly reviewed the list of Secundun animals on his data tablet, noting, "Strewth! One of those Secundilopes, the Blood Horned Secundilope, it's a carnivore, a predator."

"Doctor, if you look more closely, that Blood Horned Secundilope is related to the other Secundilope species; they are all in the same family and genus. The other Secundilopes are its prey. God, this planet is just so bloody weird!", Simone replied.

Roberta shook her head and began to describe beta colony site three, "Ytryan, the third possible colony site, is just over the mountains to the northeast of us.

We could fly there in probably fifteen to twenty minutes. You'll love this, there are Jula Jula forests all along the northern slopes of the Northern Mountain ranges and they are as vast, if not more so, than the Jula Jula forests within this valley."

"Which is what we Mimasian Thols are looking for. Somewhere beyond the Indigenous Tholish High Council's jurisdiction and somewhere close by", Ytryan trilled and clicked in reply, before questioning, "Roberta Nummus, why was it placed at number three on the beta colony site list?"

"The number of predators, Ytryan. You have to remember, Human colonies aren't up in the trees like Thol tree villages; they're at ground level", Roberta replied, before asking Simone, "Site three's predator reports, please, Simone."

Simone, accessed colony site three's predator reports, "Well, to start with, we have the Northern Kyrrax. Then we have four species of varanid type lizards; they are all fricken huge, like megalania prisca huge, up to twenty five feet in length. They have all been labelled as Fangs, Sail Fang, Razor Fang, Ridge Fang and Smooth Fang. There's another one of this genus in the Westlands, it's called the Swift Fang and, of course, there's the Pygmy Fang on the Isle of Sorrows. Now I know why that one's described as a pygmy. There is also the Great Northern Wyvern or Great Northern Drake. It is a big one, at least twice the size of the Wyverns in this valley."

"Thank you, Simone. Okay, Ytryan, we have at least six catalogued apex predators on the northern side of the Northern Mountain ranges. The Kyrrax, you're used to, the four Fangs are ground-dwelling, but that big Wyvern, that could be a problem for your people, Ytryan", Roberta summarised.

Ytryan frowned and then trilled and clicked, "Apart from the Dragons, it's the perfect place for us Mimasian Thols. I'll talk to my people about it, to see how we can mitigate the threat of these Great Northern Drakes. I am quite certain that we can find a simple solution."

"Okay, I'm going to be honest with you, Ytryan. If your people can't come up with a way to mitigate the giant Wyvern threat, you won't be settling there. So your people had better work something out", Roberta told her and then she asked, "Simone, let our people know that it looks like our beta colony site is going to be in the Northlands. We'll need to design the future colony around the giant varanid threat. I'm just going to assume that Ytryan's people will come up with a method to keep the giant Wyverns at bay."

"I don't think it will be that hard. Looking at these predator reports, these giant varanids inhabit specific regions. The Ridge Fang inhabits the Jula Jula forests, the Smooth Fang inhabits the lowland forests, and the Sail and Razor Fangs inhabit areas around the rivers and swamps", Simone noted.

"So all we really need is another broad, high hill, just like the one our current colony is on? We just pick a place that the giant varanids are very unlikely to want to go?", Roberta questioned.

"I'm just thinking that it might be as simple as that", Simone confirmed, noting, "Of course, we will have to do our due diligence as usual."

"Ytryan, we can probably make the Northlands our next colony site, but I'd like to be certain of one thing first. Are you certain, absolutely certain, that you can not reconcile your differences with your Indigenous Cousins?", Roberta asked just to make sure.

"Roberta Nummus. I have tried to work with the Indigenous Tholish High Council for more than two decades. As long as they maintain their chauvinistic and even misogynistic attitudes, we cannot work with them", Ytryan replied, her position still fixed and unchanged.

"Okay then. So be it. We'll do this by the numbers and figure out a way to make it work", Roberta quickly made her decision.

"Now we have one last thing on our agenda this morning and I am delighted to have both Ytryan and Yealah with us", Roberta announced before calling up a surveillance video taken in the Korland region.

"Before we do, can I ask that no one mentions anything about giant Wyverns to my Granddaughters?", Simone requested, commenting, "One of the twins, Ariel, seems to think that she can tame a Kyrrax. Angelique has discouraged her for now. I don't want her to get any ideas into her head about 'taming' a giant Wyvern. I wouldn't put it past Ariel to actually try it."

"Okay, new rule. We don't tell the twins about the giant Wyverns", Roberta quickly decided.

Everybody nodded in agreement.

Roberta continued, "This surveillance video was taken by stealth surveillance drones in the Korland clearing where we landed our ships during the Tarlak incident seven years ago. Fourteen researchers were killed and butchered by the Tarlaks during that incident, so we have been keeping a close eye on their activities there ever since."

The surveillance video showed seven women standing in a clearing. Six of the women were obviously females of the Tarlak Grunt cast. They were all around six feet tall and looked like a cross between an angry female Gorilla and a winged female Gargoyle, complete with horns and fangs; they looked quite Demonic. They had coarse dark hair on their heads and equally dark, sparse, coarse hair on their bodies. Male Tarlak Grunts were, of course, much taller, seven to eight and a half feet tall; no males appeared to be present.

The remaining woman, also a Tarlak, had the body proportions of an Indigenous Thol and was around six feet tall. Unlike the other Tarlak women, this one had red hair on her head and groin region, but no hair anywhere else on her body; her skin was also coloured red; two horns protruded from her head, above her hair. Apart from that, facially, she looked similar to other Tarlak women, but much, much prettier. A contradiction in terms, if ever there was one. This particular woman stood before a tall pile of sun-bleached white bones; Tarlak bones.

Upon seeing the red Tarlak women, Ytryan stated at once, questioning with trills and clicks, "That is not a Tarlak! What is that thing?"

Roberta sighed and replied, "You know, Ytryan, seven years ago I had the same discussion with Wynessa, who had never seen one of these Tarlaks before either, not even in her deep, shared memories."

Simone interjected, "I have read the reports from James, Angelique and Bobby. Genetically, that woman is a Tarlak, a female Tarlak."

Roberta stepped back in with a possible explanation, "The Mimasian Tarlaks had a Princely caste, yes, and that caste was taller than the others and had body proportions more like us. Well, Ytryan, that is Princess Angelarial, the Eldest Daughter of the Tarlak Empress. The contemporary Tarlaks are not only Matriarchal, but they also have a 'Princess caste'. The last time we saw her in person was when we dropped her back at her Mother's village in Tarlakan."

Roberta continued, "That pile of sun-bleached bones are the remains of well over a hundred male Tarlaks who attacked our ships while we weren't present, not knowing that they were armed with automatic defence turrets. They were all killed; not a single one of them survived."

Roberta paused for a moment in case anyone had any questions before continuing, "Some days after we left Princess Angelarial at the main Tarlak village, she turned up in that clearing with those six Tarlak women. Together, they piled up the bodies of her dead Tarlak men."

Yealah quickly enquired, trilling, "Why would they do that? I'm not seeing the logic."

Ytryan added, trilling and clicking, "I'd like to know that myself."

Roberta nodded and continued, "That was seven years ago, several days after the Tarlak incident. As you can see, the bodies are now bones. Now, Princess Angelarial, there, has a little ritual that she performs at noon every day. She stands in front of that pile of bones, always facing north, prostrates herself on the ground in front of it, looks up at the sky and starts praying. The same exact prayer every day at noon."

"What does it mean?", Yealah trilled, her analytical mind seriously wanting to understand.

"We don't know, Yealah. Previously, she had only recited her 'Prayer' once per day. In the last week, she has started repeating it, reciting three times over. Which is why I'm delighted to have you and Ytryan here. None of us understands Tarlak, ancient or contemporary; hell, we can't even hear half of the vocalisations that the Tarlaks make."

Quora chimed in, "We do not have a Tarlak translation matrix either and

Wynessa, who can use her telepathy, does not want to go anywhere near Korland or Tarlakan ever again; I do not blame her. No Martian wants to, Wynessa found the whole experience quite traumatising."

Ytryan queried, trilling and clicking softly, "You want us to translate that Tarlak Princess's prayer?"

"Yes. It would be interesting to know what she's saying, don't you think?", Roberta replied.

Yealah replied, trilling, clicking and softly barking, "Ytryan and I speak ancient and contemporary Tholish, including Indigenous Tholish. We also speak ancient and contemporary Carlinish, English, German, French, Spanish, Russian, Chinese and Japanese. While we do speak ancient Tarlak, neither of us has been exposed to contemporary Tarlak at all."

Ytryan trilled and clicked, "We have no knowledge of contemporary Tarlak, but we can try."

"That's all we can hope for. I don't think anyone but the Tarlaks actually speaks Tarlak, but you guys are the preeminent linguists; if you can't figure it out, nobody can", Roberta replied, expressing hope.

Roberta pressed play and the surveillance video continued. Princess Angelarial prostrated herself before the pile of bones and began speaking in Tarlak, all the while with her eyes glued to the sky. She repeated her prayer three times and stopped, sitting waiting for something to happen that never did.

Yealah requested that Roberta replay the video again; she and Ytryan listened intently once more. The video was replayed over and over and over, close to twenty times. Each time Yealah and Ytryan listened intently and in between replays, they conferred with each other in Mimasian Tholish. A language that Quora could understand, but no one else in the conference room could.

Their trills, clicks and soft barks came in rapid succession. There were even occasional harsher barks and a couple of grunts when they disagreed on a particular point. Their discussions continued and in the end, Yealah let out a melodic warble that even Quora had never heard before. Ytryan warbled in reply.

Yealah took control of the conference room's wall screen while Ytryan began explaining, "Princess Angelarial is not speaking in the Tarlak common tongue. It is doubtful that those female Grunts with her, her handmaidens, would even understand what she's saying. This prayer is a supplication to the Sky Gods, the Star Striders. The very first word she shouts out translates as Mardhin."

Yealah replayed that short beginning section, translating, before pausing the replay, "Mardhin! Golden Mardhin!"

Roberta's mouth dropped open in surprise before asking, "The Princess thinks that Wynessa is a Golden Mardhin, a Golden Goddess? Wynessa has been called that before, but certainly not in this context."

"Yes", Ytryan confirmed, explaining, "She both hates the Mardhin, but desperately needs them; she believes that only the Mardhin can restore her to her proper place. She is literally begging for Wynessa's help."

Yealah continued playing the video, translating as it played, "You killed my men, my warriors, my breeders. You took away my favourites, those that I enjoyed carnally. My own Mother, Empress Angleeryani, has forsaken me. My women have been taken from me and given to my hated rival, Sisters. I have been banished in disgrace with only six handmaidens and nothing more. I have fallen from my station, my rightful place!"

Yealah paused the video as Roberta interjected, "Banished? Her Mother, the Empress, must have been really pissed with her."

Quora stepped in, "This is our fault, Roberta Nummus. We have destroyed this woman's life."

Roberta glared at Quora, "For fucks sake, Quora. You watched the surveillance videos. These Tarlaks actively hunted, killed and ate fourteen people, and what they didn't eat, they smoked to preserve the meat for later."

"Yes. That is true, Roberta Nummus; however, it was we who delivered the Princess back to the Tarlak's main village and her Mother, in broad daylight with a show of force", Quora countered, commenting with her monotone voice, "We are responsible for her banishment and possible irreconcilable differences with her Mother."

Roberta just shook her head and nodded to Yealah, who continued to play the video.

Yealah continued her translation as the surveillance video played, "I beseech thee, nay, I humbly grovel and beg before thee, Golden Mardhin, bring the bodies of my fallen warriors back to life!"

Simone quickly interjected, "Well, that ain't gonna happen. The dead are dead."

There was a pause in the prayer as Princess Angelarial waited for a moment before continuing; Yealah picked up translating, "I beseech thee, nay, I humbly grovel and beg before thee, Golden Mardhin, bring back my favourite breeders."

Yealah paused the video as Roberta interjected, "We have eighteen of her 'favourite breeders' over at Cis-Luns L-Four, in the Stanford Torus Penitentiary."

Simone noted, "Yes, in the dangerous prisoners section, sector twelve, cell block thirteen."

"Yes, Simone and I'll be damned if I let those cannibals go; they've all tasted Human flesh. Princess Angelarial is not getting them back!", Roberta's decision on that matter was final.

When Yealah continued playing the video, Princess Angelarial sat quietly waiting for a sign; tears streamed down her cheeks. When she began praying once more, her voice sounded contrite with remorse.

Were the Tarlaks even capable of feeling remorse?

Yealah continued her translation, trilling and clicking, "I have angered the Gods! I understand that now! Forgive me! Please forgive me!", there was a pause.

When the Princess continued, Yealah picked up translating once more, "If thou will not bring back my warriors to life, if thou will not bring back my favourite breeders; I beseech thee, Golden Goddess, Golden Mardhin, give me a boon. Bring back thy warriors that I might breed with your males and bring forth strong younglings. The big, tall one would be best; he is strong, he is fast. If not, the older one, who moves like water in a river, flows around a rock, he would suffice. Both would give me many, many strong younglings. Strong and clever; I shall take my Mother's throne! My Mother shall pay with her life and the sign of my rule will be the sign of the Golden Goddess, the Golden Mardhin, I promise thee. We Tarlaks will all worship thee, the Golden Goddess who holds dominion over life and death."

Simone paused the replay herself, "There is no way in hell that my Daughter, Angelique, would let that thing fuck her Husband, Bobby. I certainly know that I wouldn't let that cannibal bitch fuck my Husband, James. Seriously, why was that thing even allowed to live!"

Roberta had to chuckle and so she did, before shaking her head and stating, "Princess Angelarial is proposing a divine covenant, you know, '*Give me the males who so easily trounced my best warriors and I'll birth their offspring in your name*', seriously, James and Bobby should be flattered."

"I am not amused, Aunt Roberta. Seriously not amused", Simone replied icily.

"I know, Simone, I know. It's just so surreal. A Tarlak Princess thinks that Wynessa is a Golden Goddess and that James and Bobby are the penultimate warriors and perfect breeding material. Seriously, you can't make this shit up", Roberta replied.

Doctor Morrow chimed in, he'd been sitting there quietly all of this time, "Do you know what really bothers me. This Tarlak Princess, Princess Angelarial, she just assumes that there's a genetic compatibility that she can exploit with Humans to procure superior offspring. Not only does she make that assumption, but you can tell by her voice and her posture, by her very covenant proposal that she believes it's true."

Quora corrected, "No, Doctor Morrow. Princess Angelarial's voice indicates that it is more than just belief. To her, it is certain knowledge, a certain fact. It is beyond simple belief"

Yealah stepped in, trilling and stating clearly, "No. That's simply not possible."

Ytryan expanded upon Yealah's assertion, trilling and clicking, "Fact. Mimasian Thols, Indigenous Thols and Tarlaks are all genetically related. Ironically, Tarlaks are more closely related to Mimasian Thols than the Indigenous Thols, even though we Thols species look so similar. Another fact. We Mimasian Thols and the Indigenous Thols are not genetically compatible, so there is no reason to believe that there would be any compatibility with the Tarlaks."

Yealah chimed in with another fact, trilling and clicking, "In thirteen hundred and fifty years, there has never been a Thol Human hybrid, even though we Mimasian Thols have lived with Humans for all of that time. Not a single known instance. So how could it be remotely possible that the Tarlaks have any genetic compatibility with Humans?"

Doctor Morrow smiled and noted in a why voice, "My understanding is that the Tarlaks were created by a combination of selective breeding and genetic manipulation."

Simone picked up on this and interjected, "The Carlins were also genetically manipulated by the creator of the Tarlaks and they are genetically compatible with Humans. We do have Carlin Human hybrids running around. That does kind of indicate that the Tarlaks are as well, potentially at least. As for there not being any hybrids between Humans and Mimasian Thols, have there ever been any attempts? Any mixed couples?"

Quora stepped in, pointing out, "Ytryan mentioned that Princess Angelarial was not speaking common Tarlak, indicating that she was speaking a higher form or perhaps a liturgical version of Tarlak. The Tarlaks may have some form of preserved deep-time knowledge or history, something that tells Princess Angelarial that breeding with other species is possible for them. A long-ago engineered genetic compatibility pathway, perhaps."

Simone rolled her eyes, "I said it earlier, this planet is just plain weird!"

Roberta turned to Quora, "Okay, Quora, I need you to develop a Tarlak translation matrix. I suspect that you'll need to work closely with Yealah on this, so you should fly back down to the colony with Yealah and work on it there."

"Yes, I can see a need for a Tarlak translation matrix in the near future, although it will be for the formal liturgical tongue", Quora replied.

"Yealah, are you good to go, helping Quora?", Roberta asked.
Yealah trilled back, "Absolutely. We can start as soon as we land."

"Quora, once you've got your translation matrix working, we need to open up a dialogue with Princess Angelarial", Roberta stated, noting, "Don't correct any of her beliefs. Let her think that Wynessa is a Mardhin; we all know that she's not, but it actually plays to our advantage. Just find out as much as you can about the Tarlak culture, their history and their common tongue. I'd really like to know how Princess Angelarial thinks breeding with two of our people is going to help her overthrow her Mother. Use one of our stealth surveillance drones, uncloaked as a conduit."

"Yes, Roberta Nummus. I will make official first contact with Princess

Angelarial at the appropriate time", Quora agreed.

"Now, Ytryan, I'll have the preferred order for our colony beta sites reversed, placing the Northlands site first. Then I'll request that my people work with your people on the Northlands colony site. There is still a lot of surveying and research that needs to be performed before the precise site location can be selected, so you will need to be patient. Okay?", Roberta informed her.

Ytryan nodded, trilling and clicking back, "We have a rough location with forests full of Jula Jula trees, so we now appear to be moving in the right direction. Thank you, Roberta Nummus."

Hyper Dynamics Six-O-Six Humaniform Android – Quora Humaniform Android Six-O-Six Network Database Classified Biological Intelligence Report

Report Title: *Carlin Quickening: Biological Imperatives and Human Hybridisation Pathways*
Priority: High
Security Level: Six-O-Six Eyes Only — Authorised Inclusion: High Admiral Roberta Nummus
Encryption: Full-spectrum adaptive data-lock; quantum-grade cipherchain active.

Executive Summary

Field observations confirm the emergence of a viable *Carlin–Human hybrid phenotype* following cross-species bonding between *Carlinus sapiens vallimundensis* females undergoing **quickening** and genetically compatible *Homo sapiens sapiens* males.

Evidence indicates that **Carlin quickening** constitutes a multi-phase biochemical and neurogenic synchronisation process, integrating pheromonal RNA vectors, neuroactive peptide synthesis, and reproductive entrainment.

The resulting zygotic fusion exhibits karyotypic stability and reproductive isolation from both progenitor species, indicating the genesis of a new Humanoid taxon.

Section 1: Quickening Pheromonal Mechanism

During female Carlin quickening (typically between 18–21 Carlin standard years), activation of the **olfactory–pheromonal complex** increases glandular output by more than 600%.

Analytical sequencing of airborne secretions reveals **messenger RNA–bound exosomes** acting as inter-individual biochemical couriers. These vesicles contain transient regulatory sequences capable of modulating receptor expression and hormonal synthesis in genetically compatible males.

Upon exposure, matching males exhibit an induced **androgenic feedback cascade**, producing complementary exosomal payloads. This *bi-directional exchange* establishes a **molecular handshake**, confirming mutual compatibility through receptor–ligand alignment exceeding 98.5% sequence congruency.

Only once this threshold is achieved does pair bonding initiate, triggering the full quickening cascade.

Section 2: Neurochemical Transition Phase

After approximately ten days of sustained pheromonal communication, transcriptional modulation within the **limbic–hypothalamic axis** of both partners initiates synthesis of a unique suite of endogenous neuroactive compounds, provisionally designated:

- **Reverase α** – hippocampal modulator; inhibits contextual recall and dampens rational filtering. Carlins exhibit temporal amnesia; Humans retain fragmentary recall that returns gradually.

- **Ecliptin β** – induces dissociative cognitive haze; couples display reduced external and situational awareness. The male appears passive while the female dominates the mating process.

- **Hippocrene γ** – interacts with *Reverase α* to destabilise temporal memory encoding.

- **Chronotase δ** – disrupts circadian regulation and temporal perception.

- **Amatoria ε** – dopaminergic amplifier; establishes the heightened pleasure–bond feedback loop and mating frenzy.

Together, these neurochemicals produce a transient *mating trance* resembling oestrus, characterised by temporal distortion, sensory amplification, and suppression of higher cognitive control.

The phase concludes upon fertilisation, typically persisting 24–96 hours, with recorded copulatory frequencies averaging 20 ± 3 events per 24-hour cycle.

Section 3: Human Cross-Compatibility

Human males identified as genetically optimal display accelerated response kinetics due to inherently unstable endocrine modulation and higher pheromonal entrainment rates.

In these pairings, the bonding sequence compresses to approximately 12 hours, followed by an equally brief but intensified mating phase of comparable duration. Recorded copulatory frequencies can exceed 40 ± 3 events within a 12-hour period.

Resulting physiological and neurochemical responses mirror Carlin patterns, but with amplified magnitude — roughly an order of magnitude increase in dopamine and oxytocin saturation indices.

Confirmed zygotic analysis from these unions reveals a **stable diploid karyotype,** demonstrating meiotic isolation from both progenitors.

Proposed taxonomic classification:

> *Homo carlinus primoris* (provisional designation)
> Hybrid origin: *Carlinus sapiens vallimundensis* × *Homo sapiens sapiens*

Section 4: Post-Bond Immunological Sequelae

Following successful bonding and fertilisation, circulating quickening-associated proteins and RNA vectors are neutralised by adaptive immune mechanisms.

Generated antibodies inhibit further receptor activation, rendering both partners permanently refractory to new quickening triggers.

This **immunological lockout** enforces *Carlin mono-bonding fidelity* and confers secondary resistance to subsequent Carlin pheromonal stimuli in Humans.

Conclusion

The Carlin–Human hybridisation pathway satisfies all observed criteria for *incipient speciation via biochemical compatibility and reproductive isolation.*

Long-term evolutionary stability remains under observation. Further studies are recommended under **Containment Protocol 606-B,** with genetic drift modelling to assess lineage persistence beyond F_2 generations.

Final note: The Carlin quickening biological imperative is the result of genetic modification, circa: 6.2 ± 0.1 million years ago. Source: Mimasian Thol deep-time histories.

Subsequent evolution has locked the Carlin quickening biological imperative irrevocably into the current Carlin species.

FILED BY:

Hyper Dynamics Six-O-Six Humaniform Android – Quora

BIOLOGICAL INTELLIGENCE DIVISION, NETWORK NODE 606, QUORA

AUTHENTICATION HASH: [REDACTED]

31. Johnathon Reas Does Not Forget.

Roberta Nummus stood in her conference room waiting for her colleagues to arrive. Roberta sipped her still-warm coffee, a cappuccino, white with one sugar, as she stared out of the conference room's long, clear crystalline plasteel window.

Roberta reminisced as she often did about the past and her first, long-deceased Wife, Elaine Haynes. Memories flooded in as they always did, of her long-deceased adopted Daughter, Lina Mitchel, her equally long-deceased best friend, Folcrom Freya, and, as always, her long-deceased second Wife, Folcrom Celestia. Life for an immortal was long and often lonely, full of memories that came unbidden at times like this.

Before coming to the Xi-Bootis system, Roberta had often reminisced while standing behind the long, thick, clear, crystalline plasteel observation windows in the Southern Observation Lounge, fifteen kilometres above Hector's main interior living surface, looking out into the vast interior of Hector. At that altitude, the Hectorian air was very thin, whilst at the main living surface, the air pressure was one standard bar.

The ritual was always the same: a cup of coffee, a cappuccino, white with one sugar in hand, staring out into the colony. Only now, it was the northern end cap of the mega-colony, Cis-Luns L-Five Colonial Central Command. A vastly smaller space, yes, but nonetheless, Colonial Central Command's northern end cap was impressive.

The view was not as spectacular as Hector's interior, a cylinder carved out of an asteroid, three hundred kilometres long and a hundred and fifty kilometres wide, but it was still impressive, nonetheless. Colonial Central Command's hemispherical end caps were two kilometres in radius, much smaller, yes, but a huge technological marvel in their own right. Simone, Quora and Yealah all entered the conference room, one after the other.

Everyone took their seats and greeted each other before Simone began their discussions.

"I've received a voice message from High Chancellor Yuntark's Wife, Yelyana. She says that Yuntark and the other Tholish High Councillors are frustrated and furious. They really don't like being sidelined and having to talk through their Wives. Apparently, they find it demeaning, belittling even", Simone informed everyone.

"Yes, just how Ytryan and I feel when we have to talk through our Husbands", Yealah trilled back in reply.

"That kind of was the point, Yealah. Let them know how it feels to be sidelined", Roberta agreed, "Now, Simone, you did explain to Yelyana why we are doing this, yes?"

Simone smiled and chuckled, confirming, "Indeed, I did. I informed Yelyana that we were treating Yuntark and his fellow High Councillors exactly the same way that they had treated Matriarch Ytryan for more than two decades. I told Yelyana that when they begin to treat the Mimasian Thol leadership with respect, that we will treat them with respect; that respect flows in both directions."

"Well, let's hope that they're getting the message", Roberta replied, noting, "We are catering to Ytryan's need for a new colony in the Northlands unnecessarily and that was purely caused by Yuntark's disrespect."

"I think that Yelyana agrees with us, at least that's what I gather from the underlying warble in her reply. She said that she'd talk to her Husband about his lack of respect for the female Mimasian Thol leadership", Simone replied.

Yealah trilled and clicked, "When we warble, it is usually in amusement or sometimes snickering, if there's a soft underlying grunt to it as well."

Quora interjected, "Yealah, a Tholish soft grunt can be below the threshold of Human hearing. They would never hear it."

"Which is why we speak English, Quora, even if it is laced with our other vocalisations. Were we to speak any form of pure Tholish, only we Thols and the Carlin-folk could understand us", Yealah trilled and clicked back.

"I can also understand spoken Tholish, Yealah. When I came to this system, I upgraded my auditory sensors and vocalisation systems to be capable of both hearing and speaking Tholish", Quora noted.

"About Tholish, we do have translation matrices for both Mimasian and Indigenous Tholish, so we can always request A.I. assistance to translate either of those, if necessary. What I'm really interested in is how our Tarlak translation matrix is coming along?", Roberta enquired.

Quora quickly answered, "We do have a functional translation matrix for Tarlak, but only for high Tarlak, their liturgical language."

Yealah chimed in, trilling and clicking, "We converse with Princess Angelarial via an uncloaked stealth surveillance drone; however, the Princess's handmaidens will not talk with us. They are too afraid."

"Okay, that's fair enough. We can only learn common Tarlak if we have exposure to it", Roberta understood, before asking, "So what have we learnt about these Tarlaks?"

Quora replied, her monotone voice noting, "The Tarlaks do have a form of deep history. It is maintained in tunnel systems. One of those tunnels runs under the Masula Valley's Southern Mountain ranges, directly connecting the Valley with the Shar Wastelands, although that particular tunnel is blocked in the centre. So the Tarlaks cannot traverse it, but we do not know how it is blocked.

The passage is open, but the central section is full of skeletal remains. Carlin and Thol remains on the north side and Tarlak remains on the southern side. It is a mystery as to how it is blocked; however, the sheer number of skeletal remains in that central section of the tunnel tells us it is deadly. There are other tunnels in the mountains of the Tarlakand region."

Yealah trilled and clicked, "These tunnels are all artificial and likely date back to the days of Ahriman, over six million years ago. The tunnel walls are lined with painted pictographs. The Tarlaks actively and meticulously maintain those pictographs. They treat them as sacred, ancient histories."

"We have sent stealth surveillance drones into the tunnels and have documented the pictographs. We are in the process of translating them", Quora noted.

Okay, so far so good. So what do we know about Angelarial's caste?", Roberta enquired.

Yealah trilled, clicked and softly barked, "That's recorded in the Tarlakan tunnels, in their ancient pictographs. We know that the Grunts are supposed to be the only extant caste of Tarlaks, although the modern Grunt caste is somewhat larger and stronger than the ancient ones. There were also the Technician and the Commanding castes and their highest caste, the Tarlak's Princely caste. These were all graded by both height and intelligence. The taller the cast, the more the base body structure resembled Thols, just larger. Ahriman himself would select the tallest of the Princes as his next host."

"And the new Princess caste? How does Angelarial's caste fit in?", Roberta enquired curiously.

"That's the thing, Roberta Nummus, the Princess caste isn't new at all. It's just as ancient as the Grunts", Yealah trilled.

Quora chimed in with the explanation, "Before Emperor Ahriman left this system in his generation ship, Mimas, he worked on another genetically modified caste. Ahriman sought the ability to rapidly expand his armies, so he established a female caste of princesses for this purpose; although he referred to them as his '*Shes*'. They can produce multiple offspring very quickly, like Carlinish women, but they produce them in placental sacs like the Tarlaks and the Thols."

Yealah took over, noting, "It takes eleven and a half months to gestate a Thol or a Tarlak. Angelarial's caste, the Shes, can do so much, much quicker."

"How is that even possible?", Simone questioned.

"Tarlak and Thol placental sacs begin to break down on contact with air. Then the mother tears the sac open to remove their youngling", Yealah trilled and clicked, before explaining, "Tarlak princesses produce a placental sac that's like leather, it's resilient like an egg. Thirty days after conception, they give birth to what is essentially an egg; then thirty days after that, the egg dissolves. The Princess's handmaidens then breastfeed the new youngling for up to thirty days before it is weaned onto solid food. In three months after conception, it is at the same stage as a Carlin kit at ten months after conception, as in three months after birth."

Simone stepped back in, questioning, "You said multiple offspring, Yealah? Just how many exactly?"

Yealah trilled and clicked, "They are small at birth, larger after hatching. A Tarlak princess can produce them by the dozen every month and as long as they receive a sufficient supply of food, they can do so indefinitely."

"Gestated, eggborne and then breastfed by wet nurses?", Roberta summed up with a rhetorical question.

"And that just takes the cake! This planet can not get any weirder!", Simone exclaimed.

Roberta and Simone sat in stunned silence and Quora noted, "Originally, Tarlak princesses, the Shes, had brown hair and skin tones; now they are red. That is something that has evolved separately."

Roberta nodded, commenting, "Now we know why Princess Angelarial thinks that she can quickly breed an army; she can!"

Quora also noted, "All of the Tarlak offspring take the same basic body form of the mother, overlaid with that of the father. There are always twelve offspring and they are always male; they also come of breeding age at the age of twelve as well."

Simone quickly interjected, "Wait, then where do the females come from, the Princesses? The Shes?"

Yealah trilled and clicked, "That is an embarrassing subject, Roberta Nummus. Quora, please, I do not want to go there."

Quora nodded and then replied, "During mating, the Tarlak male's seed, when deposited, will ordinarily produce twelve male offspring. However, if the male's seed is ingested two days prior to mating by the Princess, then the Princess's body changes, producing only six ova. Those six ova, upon fertilisation, can only ever become female Tarlaks, the Princesses, the Shes."

Simone shook her head in disgust, "I was wrong! Completely wrong! This planet just keeps on giving us weirdness! Never-ending bloody weirdness! Seriously, you want a Daughter, just have oral sex two days earlier, what the fuck!"

"They were engineered, Simone, engineered", Roberta replied, before asking, "So how does Princess Angelarial think that she can just breed with us Humans?"

Quora sensing Yealah's unease, answered, "The Princess caste was designed to be able to breed with any other species, except the Carlin species, who were considered a Slave and prey species. Princess Angelarial can breed with both Thol species, Mimasian and Indigenous and potentially, Human, including the Martians."

"Okay, so Angelarial's kind were designed to be genetically versatile", Roberta replied before asking, "Have you managed to dissuade the Princess from requesting James and Bobby as breading partners?"

"Yes, good question, my Husband, James, and my Son-in-law, Bobby, are not going to be that bitch's sex Slaves. That is simply not going to happen, not ever!", Simone replied indignantly.

"Yes, we have. It has been explained to Princess Angelarial that both James and Bobby are married, which we described as the property of a female. That was the only way that she could understand marriage", Yealah informed them with trills and clicks, before noting, "However, that was not enough. We had to describe the females as Princesses, placing Simone and Angelique at the same status level as her."

Quora chimed in, "At first, Princess Angelarial thought that you were the Princess, Roberta Nummus. She called you the woman who moved faster than her eyes could see. We had to correct her. We told her that the big, tall one, Bobby, was the property of Angelique, who, in her parlance, was the woman who ducks and weaves with quick, deadly strikes. Princess Angelarial has no concept of an Admiral, High or otherwise, so we described you as our Empress."

"And Princess Angelarial bought that nonsense?", Roberta questioned with a dry chuckle.

"Yes, she did", Quora confirmed, noting, "We have to work within the framework of her mind, her worldview."

"It doesn't finish there either, Roberta Nummus", Yealah trilled and clicked, explaining, "Princess Angelarial understands that she can't take another Princess's mate, so she has made a new request. The Princess wants us to provide her with two unclaimed warriors of unequalled prowess for her breeding purposes."

Simone had to laugh, "Right, it's not like we can just order a Colonial Marine to screw a red-skinned, Tarlak Demon woman. Imagine that for a moment, *'Marine, see that red demonic woman over there, go and screw it, give it babies, that's an order'*, I think that order would be ignored as *'illegal'*, I'm pretty sure of it. Perhaps we should request volunteers? Quora? How would we word that request?"

Quora replied, her monotone voice taking on a serious tone, "Positions vacant. Two male breeders for Tarlak Princess. Must be Human. Must be highly accomplished warriors. Only Colonial Marines, Special Forces, F-Two-G, F-Two point Five-G, or Special Operatives need apply. Caution: The breeding will be involuntary, likely overly excessive and somewhat violent."

Simone quickly snapped back, "Quora, what the fuck! It was a facetious, rhetorical question! A fucking joke!"

"I was also joking, Simone. Did I miss the mark?", Quora replied.

"I think that Princess Angelarial has completely missed the point", Roberta announced, explaining, "Even if we could procure her with two Human volunteers with the right qualifications, her offspring would do her absolutely no good without the three-G training regime that our Special Operatives receive."

Simone laughed, "Yes, precisely. That Tarlak bitch has no idea what goes into making a Colonial Marine, let alone one of our Special Operatives."

Quora interjected, "We did not correct the Princess on that point. We deemed it to Humanity's advantage that all Human warriors are devastating predators capable of easily defeating her Tarlaks."

"Well, I'll definitely agree with that decision, Quora", Roberta replied, before she asked, "Quora, Yealah, why were there no Princesses inside of Mimas or on Mars at the time of the Mimasian War?"

Yealah trilled and clicked, "There were definitely Princesses, but they were just female Tarlaks from the Princely caste, not the actual Princess caste, the Shes per se. As to why? We currently do not know."

"At the time of Ahriman's departure, the Princess caste was quite new. Likely, there weren't many of them. They may have simply been overlooked in the final days before Ahriman's departure", Quora replied.

Simone interjected, "No, no, I don't believe that, not for one second, Quora. There is something very, very wrong with that Princess Angelarial, something very wrong with her entire caste. Ahriman left his Shes behind deliberately, I'm sure of it; somehow, they are a threat; we just don't know how yet."

"So, we have no way of knowing why and any speculation on the matter can never be proven one way or the other", Roberta understood, noting, "Just another mystery to file away as unsolvable, I guess."

"Okay, next subject. Simone, your Son, Johnathon?", Roberta changed the topic completely before commenting, "Johnathon Reas left for Special Operative training twelve years ago. He passed with flying colours, did a two-year stint on Mars and correctly came to the conclusion that it wasn't a Martian protection detail at all, that he was merely there to learn how to live amongst Martian telepaths. Now, your Son was to be posted back here at that point, but he requested to be reassigned elsewhere."

"Yes", Simone confirmed, her voice was softer now, this was her Son, she continued, "Johnathon was trying to forget something, something he wanted to really, really forget, so he requested a different assignment."

"Trying to forget. We'll get back to that in a minute, Simone", Roberta replied, before noting, "There is nothing wrong with wanting to be reassigned. I mean, your Son spent two years on Proxima Centauri, Primus, a tidally locked, Trojan world named Twilight. Then another two years on Alpha Centauri A, Tertius; a true Earth analogue world named Gaia and finally another two years on Alpha Centauri B, Secundus; another true Earth analogue world named Odhinn. His record also states that during his time in the Alpha Centauri A system, he spent three months on the fourth planet, Aries, a super Mars analogue and that during his time in the Alpha Centauri B system, he spent three months on the third planet, Thor, another super Mars analogue. Those are both active shake and bake worlds, undergoing terraforming upgrades; they are both research sites essentially. Your Son, Johnathon, has been doing great work, Simone."

"Yes, Johnathon greatly enjoyed his time in the Alpha Centauri system", Simone agreed, before noting, "He did send me quite a few communiques, including some delightful photographs."

"Yes, I haven't been there myself, but I have been told that they are some of the most beautiful worlds known, especially Odhinn with its rings", Roberta replied, before noting, "Johnathon's last posting was for one year inside the asteroid Hector, administrative training and duties."

"Yes. We left Hector back in thirty four seventy and Johnathon ended up back there twenty two years later", Simone smiled, noting, "His life has taken him in a full circle, it seems."

"Simone, your Son, Johnathon, is my Nephew and I love him nearly as much as you do. His record is exemplary, absolutely outstanding. So why is he throwing it all away?", Roberta did not wait for an answer, "Johnathon has been back in the Xi-Bootis A system for well over a month. He was supposed to check in with his commanding officer when he arrived five weeks ago. I am his commanding officer, Simone."

Tears welled in Simone's eyes, "Johnathon has spent the last twelve years trying to forget you, Roberta. He hasn't. He can't. He still has that same fixation on you that he's had since before he was four."

"Four?", Roberta questioned, noting, "Johnathon was eight years old when he told me that he was going to marry me. I clearly remember that, Simone."

"Yes, Roberta, Johnathon has been saying that since he was just over three years old", Simone corrected her, noting, "We all thought that he'd grow out of it. You yourself told him that he'd forget you. He hasn't. My Son, Johnathon Reas, does not forget! He has tried, he truly has. He has even slept around. He stayed away for twelve years and now he's back. He simply doesn't know what to do! He's just too embarrassed to come here."

"Hmm, okay, Simone, now I'm seeing the problem. Your boy is not in trouble, yet", Roberta reassured her, "However, I am his commanding officer and he does have an obligation to present himself here to me with his orders, here in my office. Currently, Johnathon is listed as away without leave. Contact Johnathon immediately and have him report to my office tomorrow; this is not a request, Simone, it is an order."

"I'll make sure he comes here, even if I have to drag him here myself", Simone agreed.

When Special Operative Johnathon Reas arrived at High Admiral Roberta Nummus's office, his Mother, Simone, was waiting for him outside. Simone was sitting in one of several chairs that lined one wall. On the opposite side of the anteroom was a desk, behind which sat Admiral Nummus's Lieutenant Adjutant.

Simone stood as her Son approached and they both nodded to each other. The Lieutenant Adjutant, a woman named Louise, checked her screen as Johnathon Reas entered the room.

"The High Admiral is waiting for you, Special Operative Reas", she greeted, as she pressed a button on her desk, triggering a heads-up for Roberta.

Roberta's office door opened and Johnathon Reas walked in; he was feeling nervous, very, very nervous.

"Ah, it's about time you showed up, Special Operative Johnathon Reas. Is there anything you'd like to say about where you've been for the past five weeks?", Roberta greeted as she pointed to a chair in front of her desk for him to sit in.

Johnathon gulped softly and replied, "I've been following my orders, Admiral. In the northlands, helping Matriarch Ytryan and her people assess locations for their new colony site."

Roberta checked this immediately, "A.I. Special Operative Johnathon Reas. Check his location and activity logs for the past five weeks, since his arrival on Secundus."

"Activity logs. One week's leave spent at the premises of Special Operatives Angelique and Robert Swanson, planetside on Secundus. Four weeks spent at the Mimasian Thol colony research site alpha on the northern flanks of the Masula Valley's Northern Mountain ranges. All time sheets and reports have been logged in accordance with regulations", the A.I. responded, noting, "Red flag! Special Operative Johnathon Reas failed to report to his commanding officer, High Admiral Roberta Nummus, in accordance with regulations. Special Operative Johnathon Reas is technically away without leave."

"Do you see the problem, Johnathon? It doesn't matter that you've been following your orders, that you've been doing your work. You failed to check in with your commanding officer upon arrival and our systems have flagged you as away without leave as a result", Roberta rebuked him.

Johnathon lowered his head in shame but said nothing; he remained quiet. Johnathon's hands rested on Roberta's desk and she reached out and tapped his left hand reassuringly. Johnathon automatically pulled his hand away; his Aunt Roberta's touch was fuelling his emotions, emotions that he simply could not control.

Roberta frowned, "A.I., remove the red flag on Special Operative Johnathon Reas. Commanding officer's prerogative, use voice command override, High Admiral Roberta Nummus, '*One Alpha Fehu Othalah Omega Nine.*' Reason: Administrative error."

The A.I. reported back, "Administrative error corrected."

Johnathon raised his head slightly and, with a contrite voice, responded, "Thank you, Aunt Roberta."

"Johnathon, your Mother has already told me why you didn't report to me, which you should have done five weeks ago, but you know what, I am your commanding officer, so I need to hear it from you", Roberta informed him.

Johnathon looked up and frowned, replying nervously, "Aunt Roberta, you already know why, so why do you need to hear me repeat it?"

"Johnathon Reas. I am your commanding officer. I have to hear it from you, not second-hand from your Mother. Johnathon, you have been in the military for twelve years now. Surely you understand this by now?", Roberta explained.

Tears welled in Johnathon's eyes and Roberta passed him a box of tissues. She had expected this; he took one gladly and began wiping away his tears as if he could wipe away his embarrassment.

Johnathon Reas began to confess, "Aunt Roberta, I've been obsessed with you since the first moment I laid my eyes upon you. My Mum and Dad tell me that I declared my love for you when I was little more than three years old. I told you myself that I was going to marry you when I was just eight years old. Everyone, everyone kept telling me that I'd forget you and settle down with someone my age. It just so happens that I cannot just simply forget you, Aunt Roberta."

Roberta was about to say something, but before she could, Johnathon continued, "I tried. I tried really hard to forget you, Aunt Roberta. I really did. Every woman that I slept with just reminded me of you. I even requested that my orders be changed so that I would not have to come back here. I tried to forget you as a teenager for years and I spent another twelve years away from here, just to try to forget you. Nothing fucking works! Why am I so obsessed with you? It makes absolutely no fucking sense at all and it's just doing my fucking head in!"

Roberta reached out and held Johnathon's hand reassuringly; this time, he didn't even notice. All Johnathon's eyes could see was his Aunt Roberta, the immortal woman he was obsessively in love with.

Roberta changed the subject, attempting to distract him from his obsession and confession, "Okay, okay, Johnathon, let's just push all of that aside for now? Let it go for now, okay? Now tell me about your time in the Alpha Centauri system. Which planets were your least and most favourite?"

Johnathon chuckled softly, "Least favourite, that has to be Twilight. A tidally locked eyeball world and a leading Trojan one at that. Twilight's red Sun, Proxima, never moves in the sky. Its biggest city, Day, has over two and a half million inhabitants, none of whom can sleep without window shutters to block out the light. The only place that I can think of that's worse is its second-largest city, Night, a damnable, gloomy place. I can tell you, it is the most fucked up world, I have to say, but the locals, they actually seem to like it."

"Okay, that's good, now what about your favourite world? Gaia sounds pretty nice, kind of like Earth", Roberta enquired.

"Yeah, Aunt Roberta, Gaia, was nice, really noice as the Australians say. I mean, it's an Earth analogue world with a large Moon, Selene, and a Sol analogue Sun, but I have to be entirely honest, the planet Odhinn beats it hands down", Johnathon laughed, his spirits starting to lift, "I mean, Odhinn's Sun, Alpha Centauri B, it's just an orange dwarf, just a K-Type star, but Odhinn itself, it takes the cake. Two big moons, Huginn and Muninn, both far enough away that they cause the tiniest of tides and its rings, my God, those rings. They are just beautiful, truly beautiful! The funny thing is, though, when you're at the equator, you can barely see them; they are just that thin, but if you go to the mid latitudes, they are truly spectacular."

Roberta smiled and asked, "I've often wondered about that. How is it that Huginn and Muninn don't destabilise Odhinn's rings? I mean, they should, shouldn't they?"

"There are two other small moons, both little shepherd moons. One on either side of Odhinn's rings that keep the ring particles from straying", Johnathon laughed, "Stupid bloody names they gave them, Inny and Outy!"

That caught Roberta off guard and she began laughing along with him.

Damn, why did her Nephew have to be so much fun?

Why was he so good-looking as well?

Roberta felt a strange sadness welling in her heart.

Johnathon's voice suddenly took on a melancholy lilt, tinged with sadness and despair, "You know what, Aunt Roberta, every morning before Sunrise and every night just after Sunset, I'd just stare up at the stars in the general direction of Xi-Bootis. The only thing I could think of was you", his tears began to well once more.

Roberta passed him another tissue and told him, "Come on, Johnathon, you were doing so well, toughen up, soldier."

Johnathon sniffed and wiped his tears away, "You know what, Aunt Roberta, my favourite place of all was actually back inside Hector. Of all of the places that I have been to, Hector, that hulking big hollowed out bloody asteroid!"

"Yeah, I have a soft spot for Hector as well. There's nowhere quite like Hector, except perhaps Mimas", Roberta admitted.

"Yeah, my favourite place was that observation lounge at the fifteen-kilometre altitude level, still sixty clicks from Hector's axis or rotation. I'd just go there every morning before work and stare out of those long, clear, crystalline plasteel windows at the vast expanse of Hector's interior. A nice warm cup of coffee in my hands, a cappuccino, white with one sugar. I'd just stand there and think of you, every morning."

Those words hit Roberta like a solid punch to the jaw.

That was her ritual, her ritual, every morning, reminiscing about Elaine

Haynes, her first Wife, Lina Mitchel, her adopted Daughter, Folcrom Freyja, her best friend and Folcrom Celestia, her second Wife.

Her loves, all long lost to the ravages of time.

The one solace that the immortal Roberta Nummus had, her ritual, her memories. All Roberta could hear was, "*cappuccino, white with one sugar*"; that was their drink, their coffee, it was her ritual.

Roberta Nummus's ritual!

Roberta Nummus burst into tears, shaking her head wildly and shouting angrily, "Johnathon Reas! Get the fuck out of my office! I never want to lay eyes on you again! Go! Just go!"

Johnathon Reas had no idea what he'd done wrong. As he left his Aunt Roberta's office, he looked back. His Aunt Roberta's head was lowered into her hands, her tears flowed freely and she was emotionally distraught!

What on Earth had he done was all that he could think of.

Both Simone and Lieutenant Adjutant Louise had heard Roberta's outburst; they just looked at each other, wondering what had happened.

Simone asked her Son with concern, "Johnathon, what the hell did you do?"

"I don't know, Mum, I honestly don't know. We were just talking, just talking and all of a sudden, she just blew up", Johnathon told his Mother, "I don't know what I did."

Simone nodded and then instructed, "Johnathon, go straight to my apartment. Do not leave Colonial Central. Wait there until I call for you, okay? I'll sort this all out."

Simone kissed her Son on the forehead and he left the anteroom for his Mother's apartment.

Louise, the Lieutenant Adjutant, remarked, "Good luck. I have never heard the High Admiral explode like that before, not ever."

Simone nodded and walked into Roberta's office.

32. Cappuccino, White With One Sugar.

Simone entered Roberta's office and quietly closed the door behind her. Simone straight away noticed Simone crying with her head in her hands. Simone approached Roberta, walked around her desk and took Roberta's hands in hers, helping her out of her chair.

Simone wrapped her arms around Roberta and enquired, "Why are you so upset, Roberta? What did my Johnathon say to you, because honestly, Johnathon didn't seem to have a clue?"

Roberta sniffed as she replied, "Your son, Johnathon, has the same ritual. The same ritual! My ritual!"

"I don't understand, Roberta? What do you mean?", Simone enquired.

Roberta reached for a tissue, wiped her eyes and blew her nose, "Every morning, before I start work, I look out of my office window or the window of the conference room and reminisce."

"Yes. I know that, Roberta. I've seen you do that many times", Simone commented, noting, "You've been doing that for more years than I can remember, here and even back at Hector."

"Ah, Hector!", Roberta exclaimed, explaining, "There before my shift, I'd go to the southern observation lounge. You know the one; it's fifteen kilometres above the main living surface and sixty kilometres below Hector's axis of rotation."

"Yes, I remember it. I've been there many times myself. That view was truly spectacular. Not one to be forgotten", Simone confirmed.

Roberta nodded, explaining, "Back then, before we came here, while we were still inside Hector, I'd go there before my shift started, every morning. I'd spend fifteen minutes just staring out through that long, crystalline, clear plasteel window at that vast expanse, the interior of Hector. I couldn't quite make out the northern side, of course, even with my eyes, it was three hundred kilometres away after all, but that was not the point."

"What was the point, Roberta?", Simone enquired.

"Just to stare and to reminisce, that was the point. I'd remember lost friends and lost loves. My first Wife, Elaine Haynes; my adopted Daughter, Lina Mitchell; my close friends, Gideon, Sandra, Winchilly and my best friend, Freyja, and, of course, my second Wife, Celestia", Roberta explained, before noting, "I'd just stand there reminiscing my lost friends and my lost loves, a mug of warm coffee in my hands; a cappuccino, white with one sugar."

"And my Son, Johnathon, he has that exact same ritual?", Simone curiously questioned.

"Yes, Simone. Johnathon spent the last year inside Hector. Johnathon described that exact same ritual that he'd perform every morning before his shift, at the exact same time and place. The only difference is that he was thinking about me, obsessing over me. Even his drink was the same; coffee, a cappuccino, white with one sugar", Roberta explained.

"Roberta, it's just a coincidence, it has to be", Simone reassured her.

"Is it? Is it though?", Roberta questioned, before reiterating, "Coffee, a cappuccino, white with one sugar! Identical, right down to the coffee!"

"I don't know, Roberta. That's probably a fairly popular way to drink coffee. Cappuccinos are white and a lot of people do like sugar with their coffee as well", Simone replied, before asking, "What's so significant about the coffee anyway?"

"It was our thing, Simone. Mine, Elaine's, Lina's, even Celestia's", Roberta commented, explaining, "I used to drink my coffee, strong, straight black and hot, no sugar; that was it. On my first coffee date with Elaine, she didn't know how I liked my coffee, so she bought what she liked, a cappuccino, white with one sugar. I liked it and it became our thing. We'd meet for coffee, cappuccinos, white with one sugar. When my Lina started to drink coffee, it was a cappuccino, white with one sugar. When our friends came over, we made them coffee, cappuccinos, white with one sugar. Many centuries later, when I met Celestia, on our first coffee date, Celestia had no idea what coffee I liked. Celestia bought me the coffee that she liked, a cappuccino, white with one sugar, without even knowing that was how I liked my coffee. It was my thing, our thing, across the centuries. My ritual!"

"Roberta, my Son has been obsessed with you since before he was four, not long after he turned three, to be entirely honest", Simone noted, "We all thought he'd grow out of it."

Roberta frowned and replied, "Yes, Johnathon told me; he said that he's loved me since the very first day that he laid his eyes on me. I have no idea how young he would have been; he must have been just a baby. He even told me that he'd tried to forget me, even going so far as to sleep around. Something's wrong, Simone, very wrong. This isn't normal, it's like he's imprinted on me and that is simply not a Human thing."

"I know, Roberta, I know and it's time that we got to the bottom of this", Simone replied, as she touched her right forehead and accessed her neural augments, "I'm sending a message to Wynessa and Sarlia. I'll mark it urgent. Maybe they can help?"

Roberta's office had a sofa set up against one wall, along with a coffee table and a pair of comfortable chairs. Simone led Roberta over to one of the chairs and requested that she sit down. A message came over Simone's neural augments; Wynessa was on her way. Sarlia had been delayed with Ambassadorial matters and would catch up with them later.

Sarlia's Ambassadorial offices were on the other side of Colonial Central Command's northern end cap, so it took twenty minutes for Wynessa to arrive at Roberta's office. When she arrived, Wynessa found Roberta sitting in a chair; her eyes were still red from crying and her hair was a mess. Roberta looked terribly unwell.

Wynessa walked up to Roberta and smiled, *"Well, my Ancient Friend, I've certainly seen you looking better"*, she transmitted telepathically.

"I have felt better, Wynessa. Simone's Son, Johnathon, managed to trigger some kind of deep emotional response in me", Roberta explained, before tearing up once more, "Johnathon uses the same ritual that I use, the same one!"

"Okay, I see, well then, Roberta, I'd better take a look at those memories of yours", Wynessa transmitted, adding, *"Just let your Golden Goddess take care of you."*

Simone's ears picked up at that reference, "Wait! Wynessa, did I just hear you refer to yourself as Roberta's Golden Goddess?"

"Ah, yeah. I've always been Roberta's Golden Goddess", Wynessa telepathically confirmed.

Roberta smiled, it wasn't much of a smile, before commenting, "I've been calling Wynessa, my Golden Goddess, since we first came out here; decades before Princess Angelarial used the term."

"Very true, very true", Wynessa confirmed, noting, *"It's a pet name, I'm Roberta's Golden Goddess and Roberta's my Ancient Friend. It's all very tongue-in-cheek. Roberta does it to deflect my advances."*

Simone shook her head, "Your advances?", she questioned curiously.

"Simone, I am a Martian after all and Roberta is absolutely gorgeous. I think that nearly every Martian Roberta meets propositions her at some stage, including me. I continue to do so from time to time. I am quite smitten, I must admit, but Roberta always says no", Wynessa explained matter-of-factly.

Simone ran her hands through her hair, "Okay. Roberta always says no. Got that, now can we please focus? Roberta kind of needs your help and I really want to know what's wrong with my Son. Johnathon has had this obsession since he was three years old."

Wynessa's ears picked up at that, *"Three years old"*, she questioned.

Roberta corrected the timeline, "Johnathon says, since the first moment he laid eyes on me."

"That's imprinting. That's highly unusual. Human children normally grow out of that by the time they're five years old", Wynessa transmitted, before stating, *"Simone, contact Sarlia again. I am going to need her help. Tell her that I said to drop everything. Now, Roberta, let me have a peek at your memories."*

Simone rolled her eyes as Wynessa sat down on Roberta's lap, *"Now, you know how this works, Roberta"*, she transmitted.

Simone shot out an instruction, "Follow the coffee; cappuccino, white with one sugar."

Roberta nodded in confirmation, repeating, "Yes, follow the coffee; cappuccino, white with one sugar."

Wynessa kissed Roberta softly on the lips, before playfully biting Roberta's lower lip, "*Sorry about that, I just couldn't resist*", and then she touched her forehead to Roberta's and entered her memories.

Wynessa traced Roberta's memories backwards, searching for the parameters: cappuccino, white with one sugar. The first instance that Wynessa came across was Roberta's reminiscence ritual from that morning. Wynessa gathered the details of all of the people Roberta reminisced about in reverse order.

Wynessa found Folcrom Celestia nearly nine hundred years ago in the past. A Council of Shadows operative, Celesta, had propositioned Roberta and she had accepted. A small pang of jealousy hit Wynessa as she studied how their relationship developed.

On their first date, a coffee date, Celestia had automatically bought them both a cappuccino, white with one sugar, without even knowing or asking what type of coffee Roberta preferred. Celestia's choice had been purely instinctive; her own preference, no thought required. Celestia became Roberta's second Wife.

Around eleven hundred and thirty years back, Wynessa came across two Psi Corps operatives, extremely powerful ones, Folcrom Forkbraid and Folcrom Selene. Whenever they visited Roberta inside Mimas, she made them coffee, it was always cappuccinos, white with one sugar.

Thirteen hundred and twelve years back, Wynessa found the next batch of important memories. They were of the Martian Elder Winchilly, Gideon Reas, Sandra Danker and Folcrom Freyja, the last three being Council of Shadows operatives, powerful operatives.

Whenever they gathered at Roberta's house, she and her first Wife, Elaine Haynes, made them all coffee, cappuccinos, white with one sugar. Even Roberta's adopted Daughter, Lina Mitchel, when she drank her first coffee, it was a cappuccino, white with one sugar.

This pattern was deeply ingrained across time and space.

Three years earlier still, Wynessa came to a meeting of Roberta and Elaine Haynes, Roberta's first Wife. That was where it all began. At their first coffee date, Elaine had no idea what coffee Roberta preferred, so she bought the coffee she preferred, two cappuccinos, both white with one sugar. It was new to Roberta, who'd always drank her coffee, hot, strong and black. Roberta liked it and they both bonded over coffee, becoming lovers that very same night. Once again, Wynessa felt a small pang of jealousy; it was hard to be a telepath who was in love with an immortal.

That was the beginning of the pattern, an ingrained engram and the source of Roberta's ritual and it tied her reminiscence together across the centuries, across time and space.

Wynessa withdrew from Roberta's mind; she now knew that what she suspected was probably very real. Wynessa required Sarlia's help for confirmation.

Wynessa pulled back from Roberta's forehead once more, before kissing her on the lips and then standing back up.

"Hmm, is Sarlia on her way, Simone?", Wynessa transmitted.

"Ah, yes, I believe so, Wynessa", Simone replied.

"*We are going to need your Son, Johnathon, present, as well. Sarlia is going to need to do a deep dive into his past incarnations*", Wynessa informed Simone.

"Wait! Past incarnations?", Simone questioned.

"*Yes, past incarnations. I can deep dive into people's memories, no problem, but I do not have to necessary skills to analyse past incarnations. Only a handful of Martians do and Sarlia is one of them*", Wynessa transmitted her explanation.

"I don't understand the difference", Simone admitted.

"*We Martians share our memories regularly and those of your people who have lived amongst us, we sometimes share our memories with them as well. Roberta Nummus is one such person. Shared memories are like a strand of pearls descending back through time. Each pearl is a bundle of memories, all bound together from the sharing. If the shared memories hail from contemporaneous people, then there will be cross-linked strands; the whole construct resembles a tapestry and we Martians are fluent in reading its weave*", Wynessa explained in detail.

"And past life incarnations?", Simone continued to question.

"*To a Martian, past life memories can be likened to a string of sausages, with each bundle of memories separated by a tied knot. To pass from one bundle of memories to the next requires traversing the knot; literally, a blockage. To make matters worse, the first memory perceived once past the blockage is the last memory of that incarnation; a death memory*", Wynessa explained, noting, "*Death memories can be as traumatic for the analyst as they are for the person who discarnated. It doesn't help either that the memories are not physically stored; they are in the universal biogenic morphic field, not the individual.*"

"I'll have to take your word for it, Wynessa. Most of that was gobbledegook to me", Simone admitted.

Johnathon was staying in Simone's apartment, which was nearby, so he arrived first. His Mother, Simone, waited for him in the anteroom and led him straight into Roberta's office.

Roberta looked up at Johnathon from her chair, "I am so sorry that I exploded at you, Johnathon. You didn't deserve that. It was just something that you inadvertently triggered in me. It was not your fault."

Johnathon quietly nodded as Simone guided him over to the sofa and asked him to sit down.

Sarlia entered a few minutes later and asked telepathically, "*Wynessa, what is so urgent?*"

Wynessa walked over to Sarlia, leaned in close and touched her forehead to Sarlia's, sharing the memories she'd gathered and analysed from Roberta. The information transmission was surprisingly quick, taking only twenty seconds.

When Wynessa pulled back, Sarlia asked, *"And how does this relate to the young man, Johnathon?*

"Johnathon has an obsession with Roberta Nummus. An obsession that started when he first laid eyes on her as a baby; he first articulated his love for her at the age of three", Wynessa transmitted.

Sarlia transmitted back, *"Wynessa, you are talking about imprinting. That normally happens with the baby's Mother and begins to dissolve when the child goes to school. It does not last."*

Wynessa nodded in understanding, *"And yet, here we are, Sarlia. I suspect a karmic propensity is at work here."*

"A karmic propensity. Wynessa, your sharing shows a deep memory dive going back thirteen hundred and fifteen years. That's a lot of incarnations that I need to analyse. Depending on the length of each incarnation, it could be as many as fifteen, perhaps more. That is a lot of death trauma that I will be exposed to", Sarlia replied with her voice full of concern.

"I understand that, Sarlia, I really do, but Johnathon needs your help", Wynessa implored.

Sarlia walked over to the sofa and sat down on Johnathon's right, *"Young man, lie down on your back and place your head on my lap"*, she instructed.

Johnathon was taken aback by that request. He looked to his Mother, Simone, who simply nodded.

Johnathon did as requested and lay his head upon Sarlia's lap; Sarlia transmitted to him, *"This will be a slow process and will likely take about two hours"*, she looked down at Johnathon's eyes, *"It is best that you sleep through this process"*, and then she transmitted one word, *"Sleep"*, and Johnathon Reas fell into a deep, deep sleep.

"Is my Son okay?", Simone asked with concern.

Sarlia transmitted back, *"Johnathon is fine, Simone. I've just induced a deep sleep. When he wakes up, he'll feel highly refreshed."*

Sarlia placed her right hand on Johnathon's forehead and closed her eyes; the deep dive had begun.

While Sarlia silently worked, Wynessa noted, *"We won't know the results until Sarlia is finished."*

Roberta queried, "Exactly what is Sarlia doing?"

Wynessa noticed that the sofa and both chairs were all occupied, so she sat herself back down on Roberta's lap, answering telepathically, *"Every person has a self-image of what they look like during each incarnation. Sarlia is going to surf her way past each inter-incarnation blockage and make comparisons. Sarlia will literally compare each of Johnathon's past life memory self-images with the images of your past family and friends from my memory analysis."*

Roberta shifted slightly as Wynessa sat herself down and asked, "And how does that help exactly?"

Wynessa smiled, transmitting, *"When Sarlia matches an incarnation to your memories, she'll know who the incarnation is and which incarnation to analyse."*

Simone interjected, asking, "What is a karmic propensity?"

"We accrue karma during each lifetime and at the moment of discarnation, that karma forms the propensity that dictates one's next incarnation, literally your next life", Wynessa explained.

"And that's what's happening with my Son? A past life karmic propensity asserting itself?", Simone enquired further, her mind virtually rejecting what she was hearing.

"Potentially. We will have to wait and see. To use my previous analogy, the past life propensities can ooze through the blockage between incarnations, like fat oozing from one sausage to the next across the knots that connect them", Wynessa tried to explain, noting, *"It is a poor analogy, I know that, but it is also very hard to explain. Another analogy might be the bleed-through that can occur when old data resurfaces through a newly formatted memory substrate. Very rare, yes, but not unheard of."*

"And we won't know anything until Sarlia finishes in two hours?", Simone asked.

"Roughly two hours, perhaps sooner, probably a little longer", Wynessa confirmed, noting, *"We may as well just relax and wait until the process is complete."*

Wynessa placed her arms around Roberta, snuggled closer, closed her eyes and was soon asleep.

Simone looked at Roberta and asked in a whisper, "Does she always do that?"

"Who? Wynessa?", Roberta questioned rhetorically, replying in a whisper, "No, not usually. Today, however, we don't have enough seating for five and I suspect that Wynessa will probably proposition me again later. I always decline, but that does not deter her from trying. Wynessa is a Martian after all."

Roberta smiled, "To be entirely honest with you, Simone, right now I'm finding Wynessa's presence quite soothing. Wynessa can be like that, that's why I call her my Golden Goddess."

It was quiet for a long time in Roberta's office as they waited for Sarlia to complete her analysis.

Wynessa, still asleep sitting on Roberta's lap, stirred, stretched and then yawned, *"That was a pleasant nap"*, she transmitted.

Two hours had passed and Sarlia was still intensely focused, eyes closed on her task.

Simone noticed a trickle of blood under Sarlia's right nostril, "Sarlia's nose is bleeding!"

Wynessa stood up and grabbed a tissue from the box on Roberta's desk. She walked over to Sarlia and very gently, carefully dabbed at the trickle of blood.

"Should we wake Sarlia up?", Simone questioned with concern.

"No, Simone. We must not interfere. That would be a disaster. Sarlia isn't sleeping, by the way. You have know idea of the level and intensity of her focus. Even just dabbing at this blood, I have to be very careful not to disturb her", Wynessa replied.

The trickle of blood increased and spread to Sarlia's left nostril. Wynessa went to Roberta's desk and grabbed the whole box of tissues.

"Wynessa, you cannot possibly tell me that this is normal!", Simone exclaimed.

"It is not normal, Simone. Most past life analysis involves three to five recent incarnations at most, not twelve to fifteen. Two hours is a long deep dive and Sarlia knew the risks when she started the process. We must not interfere", Wynessa explained, but she too was becoming very concerned.

Sarlia's eyes opened; they were red, bloodshot, *"Oh by the Gods, I think I'm going to be sick."*

Sarlia carefully extricated herself from under Johnathon's head and replaced her lap with a cushion before making her way over to Roberta's desk-side wastebasket and throwing up into it. Wynessa passed Sarlia a handful of tissues and helped her to staunch the flow of blood from her nose.

As Sarlia then shared Johnathon's memories with Wynessa, Roberta enquired, "Are you okay, Sarlia?"

"Sure, Roberta, peachy, just peachy. Just give me a few minutes to fully recover", Sarlia replied.

Wynessa translated that into reality, *"Sarlia will have analysed every one of Johnathon's past incarnations going back thirteen hundred and fifteen years. She will have felt every one of those incarnations' deaths as if they were happening to her."*

Simone cautiously enquired, "And my Son, Johnathon?"

Sarlia sat down on Roberta's lap, *"Sorry, Roberta. I just need to sit down"*, she apologised.

Roberta shook her head, smiled wryly and replied in jest, "It's official. I am now a chair."

Sarlia chuckled and looked at Simone, her eyes still bloodshot, *"Johnathon's past lives include two crucial people that explain his fixation on Roberta Nummus. We don't get to choose our subsequent lives after we pass on, not directly at least, our accrued karma and the propensities thereof dictate for us. Elaine Haynes reincarnated several times before she incarnated as Folcrom Celestia, who in turn reincarnated several times before she incarnated as your Son, Johnathon Reas. Elaine, Celestia and Johnathon, three different bodies, all the same soul. Johnathon and Roberta are soul mates. They are destined to be together."*

Sarlia stood back up, took Roberta by the arm and led her over to the sofa, *"Roberta, sit down here, move that cushion out of the way and carefully place Johnathon's head on your lap."*

"Why? Is this necessary?", Roberta enquired, confused.

"Yes, of course, it is, Roberta", Sarlia replied as she assisted Roberta to sit down

on the sofa with disturbing the still sleeping Johnathon, noting, *"It allows me to take over your chair and when Johnathon wakes up, he will be with his future Wife."*

"Future Wife!", Roberta and Simone both exclaimed, Wynessa felt the slightest pang of jealousy once more.

"Yes, future Wife, Roberta, stop fighting it. Look into your heart, you know it to be true. You are karmically bonded. You are both destined to be together", Sarlia told her firmly.

"But, Sarlia, Roberta is an immortal; she cannot give my Son, Johnathon, children", Simone protested.

"What is the alternative, Simone, a life alone in torment, for both of them. And, yes, Roberta Nummus, that includes you, too. You aren't living, you are just existing. Johnathon gives you the chance to truly live, not just to exist", Sarlia explained.

"But to not have children, Sarlia, that's, that's.....", Simone let the statement trail off.

Wynessa bit her lower lip and gently sat down on the edge of the sofa next to Johnathon.

"There is a way Johnathon can have children and still be married to Roberta", Wynessa announced, before quickly proposing, *"If I become Roberta's Sister Wife, Johnathon can have his children through me. They will be hybrid children, yes, of course, but they will still be his children."*

"You would do that, Wynessa?", Simone questioned.

"In a heartbeat, Simone. I've wanted to be with Roberta Nummus since that first day on the bridge of the Artemisia before we pushed out to this system. And it does solve the problem of Johnathon and Roberta not being able to have children of their own, so I will act as the conduit", Wynessa explained.

Roberta Nummus sat on her office sofa, a thirty-year-old Special Operative, Johnathon Reas, asleep upon it with his head upon her lap. Sitting on the edge of that same sofa was Wynessa, her Martian Golden Goddess.

Roberta was confused; she was completely gobsmacked; how had she gone from being a single woman in the morning to being a part of a throuple before it was even midday? It was a very confusing day!

"A very Martian solution, Wynessa", Sarlia noted, commenting, *"Polyamory is very common amongst my people, Simone. Amongst my own ancestors were Winchilly, Sandra Danker, Folcrom Freyja and Gideon Reas. Together they formed a quadruple marriage."*

Simone shook her head in confusion, "Weren't they Roberta's friends from over thirteen hundred years ago?"

"Yes, they were", Sarlia admitted, before reiterating, *"They were also my ancestors. I have their shared memories within me to this very day. Their descendants intermarried over the generations."*

"Okay, so my Son, Johnathon, is going to wake up and find that he's a part of a throuple. Good to know", Simone declared.

Wynessa bit her lower lip and sent a quick private message to Sarlia.

"Oh, right!", Sarlia exclaimed telepathically, "*Wynessa just pointed out to me that Johnathon, in trying to forget Roberta, slept around quite a bit. In his memories, there is another woman.*"

"Another woman?", Simone questioned, this morning was getting more and more ridiculous.

"*Yes*", Wynessa confirmed, explaining, "*Johnathon's memories contain a tryst with a Martian woman at the end of his assignment on Mars. They were together for a few weeks while Johnathon was awaiting his reassignment to Proxima Centauri, to the planet Twilight.*"

"How is this relevant?", Simone asked.

"*Johnathon's memories show that he kept in contact with her over the past seven years*", Sarlia noted, informing Simone, "*The Martian woman, Marielle, she wanted to go with Johnathon, but he flatly said no. Later, while he was in the Proxima system, she gave birth to his Daughter, Mylian. That is the reason that Johnathon kept in touch with her; Johnathon has a hybrid Martian Daughter.*"

"Okay, so my Son, Johnathon, has a '*secret*' Martian Daughter that he's never told me about. My Granddaughter!", Simone replied, glaring at her sleeping Son, "Why the hell did he not tell me about her?"

"*Embarrassment, Simone. Johnathon was obsessed with Roberta Nummus; he'd fathered a hybrid Daughter with his Martian fling, he was confused, he didn't know what to do. These things weighed very heavily on his mind*", Wynessa defended him.

Sarlia noted matter-of-factly, "*Johnathon's memories indicate that Marielle still pines for him. You could organise to bring her and her Daughter out here from Mars. That would give Johnathon another Wife with whom to bring forth more children. You will have your beloved Grandchildren, Simone.*"

"Wait a second, Sarlia. My Son is going to wake up and find that he has two new Wives and now you're suggesting that we add a third Wife, even before he's awake?", Simone questioned incredulously.

"*Yes, of course, Simone. Since we are organising your Son's future, we should cover all of the bases, don't you think?*", Sarlia explained.

Before Simone could respond, Roberta quickly questioned, "Do I even get a say in any of this?"

"Apparently not, Roberta. Karma dictates that you marry my Son, which should make Johnathon very happy indeed. Wynessa has decided that she's going to be your Sister Wife and as it turns out, one of Johnathon's flings has a wild oat, so you now get a second Sister Wife. You should be happy, Roberta, so don't complain, after all, it's not like these two are setting my Son up with a Carlinish woman or that red Tarlak bitch in Korland; things could be much weirder", Simone explained to her.

Wynessa quickly interjected, "*We would never recommend Princess Angelarial as another Sister Wife; that would be insane*", yet she never mentioned anything about the possibility of a Carlinish Sister Wife; was that on the table?

Sarlia also quickly interjected reassuringly, "*No, Tarlak women, they are not suitable Sister Wife material.*"

Roberta chuckled with amusement, "So sleepy head here is going to wake and find he has three new Wives. I bet Johnathon never thought of that when he walked into my office this morning."

"Don't you find this the least bit strange, Roberta?", Simone queried.

"When I was much younger, only about a hundred or so and quite psychotic, I lived in a house with my lesbian Wife and my adopted Daughter, whose Aunt I'd murdered. My next-door neighbours were a married couple, with a Martian Sister Wife and a Council of Shadows operative Sister Wife. So, Simone, this is not the least bit strange to me; just so long as Tarlak Shes aren't involved", Roberta explained, still chuckling.

Johnathon began to stir and Simone asked Roberta, "Geez, Roberta, what the fuck am I going to tell my Son when he wakes up?"

Roberta smiled back and laughed, "Leave that to me, Simone. You just look forward to meeting that Granddaughter of yours, Mylian, whom you've never met, and your new Daughter-in-law, Marielle."

Johnathon awoke, yawned and stretched, then quickly realised he was lying with his head on Roberta's lap and had Wynessa sitting on the edge of the sofa right by his side. They were both smiling at him.

"What's happening?", Johnathon enquired, as he wiped the sleep from his eyes.

"It's all good, sweety. Your Aunt Roberta is going to explain everything to you", Simone quickly replied.

"Well, Johnathon, what can I tell you? We are now officially a couple, yay! And Wynessa here is going to be joining us, so that makes us a throuple. Say hello to Johnathon, Wynessa", Roberta explained.

Wynessa smiled broadly and transmitted, "*Hi Johnathon. I'm going to give you lots of babies.*"

Before Johnathon could even react, Roberta added, "We are also sending for your Martian fling, Marielle and your Daughter, Mylian. I expect that Marielle, being a Martian woman, will be joining us as well, so you will have your third Wife very soon. Well, as soon as we can arrange passage anyway. Yay, aren't you excited, Johnathon!"

Sarlia got out of her chair and walked over, transmitting to a gobsmacked Johnathon, "*Johnathon Reas, it has all been decided, expect a large family and lots of babies, beautiful Martian hybrid babies.*"

33. The Immortal Roberta Nummus.

Early the next morning, Johnathon and Roberta found themselves in Roberta's conference room staring out its long, crystalline, clear plasteel window. The view of Colonial Central Command's northern end cap was not as spectacular as the view of the interior of Hector from Hector's fifteen-kilometre-high observation lounge, but it was still pretty cool; spectacular in its own way.

They both held mugs of warm coffee in their hands; cappuccinos, white with one sugar.

"Is it okay that I'm feeling a bit confused, Roberta?", Johnathon enquired.

Roberta smiled and chuckled, "You have every right to be confused, Johnathon. You came to my office yesterday morning, a single man; when you walked back out, you had three wives, and it all happened while you slept. Yeah, I'd say that's kind of confusing."

"Remind me again, just how did I end up with three wives?", Johnathon asked.

"Well, Johnathon, you have been obsessed with me since you were a wee baby. It turns out your past-life karma was driving your obsession and we are karmically bound soulmates. Go figure!", Roberta explained to him for the umpteenth time.

"Yeah, I got that bit, but Wynessa and Marielle? How exactly did that happen?", Johnathon asked.

"Well, Wynessa is my baggage and Marielle is yours", Roberta replied, explaining, "Wynessa has had the hots for me since before we left the Sol system. It wasn't unusual for her to proposition me four or five times a year. This time, however, she had me in checkmate. I can't give you children and your Mother wants grandchildren, so Wynessa solved that problem in typical Martian fashion, so she's now my Sister Wife. Wynessa is busy moving into my apartment. I expect you'll probably have her pregnant by tomorrow."

"Pregnant? That's a bit quick?", Johnathon looked shocked.

"Wynessa made a promise to your Mother and a promise to you that she'd give you lots of babies. Martians always keep their promises. You lived amongst them for two years, Johnathon, you should already know that", Roberta reminded him.

"And Marielle?", Johnathon questioned.

Roberta shook her head and smiled, "You had a fling seven years ago with a Martian woman, Marielle, and then left for your assignment in the Proxima Centauri system; Marielle gave birth to your Daughter, Johnathon. Bloody hell, Johnathon, you didn't even tell your Mother! Wynessa was inside your head, analysing your obsession; she shared those memories with Sarlia for a second opinion and past life analysis. Johnathon, you can't hide a hidden Daughter and a former Martian lover still pining to be with you from a pair of Martian psychoanalysts."

"So, Wynessa and Sarlia just took it upon themselves to give me a third Wife?",

Johnathon was particularly incredulous about that part.

"Of course they did, Johnathon. You gave Marielle a Daughter. It doesn't matter that Mylian was born while you were on assignment in the Proxima Centauri system; she is your Daughter and Marielle considers you to be her Husband. A wayward Husband for sure, but her Husband nonetheless", Roberta explained, noting, "To a pair of Martian psychoanalysts, that's a situation in need of urgent correction. You can probably expect Marielle and Mylian to be on their way out to us on the next available transport, or the next one after that at the very least."

"I kept in touch with them, you know, Roberta. I'd send them a communique at least four times a year and before Mylian's birthday, I'd send her a small gift. Nothing special, just curiosities and keepsakes. A collection of really rare pressed flowers in a book from Twilight, a collection of gemstones from Gaia, a collection of seashells from Odhinn, amongst others, just odd little things. I even sent Mylian a vial of ruby red sands from the planet Thor when I was there; such a weird world that one, beaches of ruby red sands everywhere", Johnathon reminisced.

"You were back in the Sol system inside Hector for a year, Johnathon. Why didn't you visit them?", Roberta asked.

Johnathon was quiet so long that Roberta gently nudged him in the ribs, "I was ashamed, Roberta, ashamed. I was obsessed with you. Marielle assured me that she could remove my obsession; she tried hard, really hard, but she couldn't. We were only together for three weeks and then I left for Proxima Centauri. After Mylian was born, I was just deeply ashamed of myself."

Roberta sighed. Martian psychic intervention should have been performed seven years ago when Johnathon was still on Mars. Proper psychic intervention, not just a young Martian woman in love trying her best to make him fall in love with her.

"Marielle and Mylian will probably be here in a couple of weeks. Wynessa and I expect you to make up for those seven lost years; make them both happy, okay, Johnathon", Roberta told him.

"I intend to, Roberta, I intend to", Johnathon replied, his voice laced with seven years of regret.

"Well, lover boy, I think that you've made progress, so it's reward time", Roberta announced as she placed her empty coffee mug on the conference room table, then sat on its edge and leaned back over it.

Johnathon smiled, placed his empty coffee mug on the table and approached Roberta. He stood before Roberta and began to remove her uniform as she did the same with his. There was a knock on the conference room door and Lieutenant Adjutant Louise stepped in.

The scene before her caught her by complete surprise.

Louise turned away, "Sorry, Ma'am. I didn't realise. I just wanted to let you know that your usual morning ritual was running well into overtime."

Johnathon turned around, facing the conference room window and began adjusting his uniform.

"That's okay, Lieutenant", a red-faced Roberta Nummus replied as she adjusted her uniform, "I probably should have locked the door."

"If you don't mind me saying, Ma'am. That conference room table is not rated for.... for what you were about to do, Ma'am", Louise replied while still facing away.

"So noted, Lieutenant, so noted", Roberta replied, her face still red with embarrassment.

"Ma'am, if I may. I can have one of the empty offices down the hall, fitted out for '*sleeping*' arrangements if you wish", Louise suggested, noting, "You do work quite late, Ma'am, so the expenditure would be justified."

"Yes, yes, Lieutenant, please do. We'll be out in a few moments", Roberta agreed.

Louise turned around and left the conference room with a wry smile on her face.

"My Lieutenant is right, this table isn't lust rated", Roberta chuckled, before suggesting, "Let's go back to my office, shall we?", she saw the look on Johnathon's face, "To work, Johnathon, not...."

Johnathon smiled, wrapped his arms around Roberta and began kissing her.

Roberta returned the kiss for a few moments, then broke off, "Work, Johnathon, work. Focus. For fucks sake, Sarlia and Wynessa have unleashed a sex monster. Control yourself, Johnathon. We can be intimate later tonight."

They both left the conference room for Roberta's office.

Lieutenant Adjutant Louise smiled with amusement and enquired, "Ma'am, shall I hold your calls?"

"No, it's okay, Lieutenant. Special Operative Reas and I will actually be working", Roberta replied as they both entered her office.

Roberta sat herself down behind her desk and Johnathon pulled up a chair and sat himself down in front of it. Roberta called up a file on her desk's inbuilt touch screen and then displayed the file holographically above the desk.

"We never got to this yesterday, Johnathon. This report from Ytryan says you've been helping her people with research into the Great Northern Wyverns. Please bring me up to speed."

"Yes, I have, Roberta. Ytryan instructed a team of Androids to build a research centre in the hollow core of a rather large Jula Jula tree that just happens to be a major breeding tree for the Drakes. The tree in question has a very large number of Drake nests", Johnathon replied.

"Drakes? Is that what we're officially calling them now?", Roberta replied.

"Kind of. Drake is shorter than Wyvern or Dragon; it kind of rolls off the tongue better as well and we are already using the name Wyvern for the species inside the Masula Valley", he replied.

"Okay, so what's the purpose of this research station?", Roberta enquired.

"Instead of driving the Drakes away from Ytryan's intended colony site, which is also a major Drake breeding site, I figured that we could kind of tame them", Johnathon informed Roberta.

"Tame the Drakes? Where the hell did you get that idea from?", Roberta questioned.

Johnathon smiled and answered, "I've been staying at Angelique's plot. One of her twins, young Ariel, told me that she wants to tame a Kyrrax. It sounds like pure madness, I know, but it got me thinking. The Wyverns and Drakes are highly intelligent sub-sapients, much like terrestrial Dolphins or Orcas, just they're airborne instead of aquatic."

"And you think you can tame them? Isn't that the same level of crazy that Ariel is talking about when she says she wants to tame a Kyrrax?", Roberta asked quite bluntly.

"Tame probably isn't quite the right word. What Ariel told me was that she wanted to capture a Kyrrax kitten just before weaning. That way, the kitten would imprint on her much in the same way that Vort pups imprint on Carlins. Angelique already has four Vorts imprinted on her at her plot", Johnathon explained before noting with an Uncle's pride, "Ariel is as sharp as a tack, highly intelligent, very clever."

"So if tame isn't the right word, then what is?", Roberta enquired with greater curiosity.

"Habituate perhaps, befriend maybe", Johnathon smiled as he replied.

"Habituate I can understand, but befriend?", Roberta questioned.

"Potentially. The Drakes ignored the Androids when they constructed the research centre. They flew up to the top of the Jula Jula tree and stared down into the hollow centre; they were so curious that it was uncanny. We carved out tunnels from the hollow to the main branches where the Drakes prefer to nest and set up protective repulsor barriers. These barriers are designed to work two ways; they won't harm the Drakes and the Drakes can't push through them, so the Mimasian Thol researchers are perfectly safe. By the same token, we can pass through the repulsor barriers at will with our nullification fields. The setup allows us to get up close and personal with the Drakes without being in any danger", Johnathon explained.

"Okay, so this habituation or friendship, how's that working?", Roberta enquired, again curiously.

Johnathon smiled his broadest smile, "Ytryan's people can get right up close to the Drakes. We try to communicate with them. The Thols speak to them in Mimasian Tholish and I speak to them in English. Here's the thing: the Drakes are far more curious than we'd ever thought possible. They respond by trying to communicate back. The Drakes do not see us as prey and that is remarkable."

"They have a language?", Roberta questioned, her interest well and truly piqued.

"Indeed, they do, much in the same way that Dolphins and Orcas do", Johnathon confirmed, noting, "The Drakes, they trill, they squeak, they even make aarwk sounds like a crow and raven sounds like kraaak, both interspersed with warbles. The bloody things are quite chatty."

"Ytryan reckons that the Drakes understand us far more than we understand them. Seriously, if the Mimasian Thols can't crack their language, how the hell are we going to?", Johnathon commented.

Roberta laughed, a loud raucous laugh, "Johnathon, my silly Husband, we have my Golden Goddess. Wynessa is not only a telepath, but she is also our Wife. I'll ask Wynessa if she would like to help you."

"Wynessa! My own Wife! Crap! I should have thought of that myself; there are so few Martians out here in the Xi-Bootis system. What, with Sarlia and her young one, maybe ten?", Johnathon replied; everyone forgets the Martians, they were so few in number.

"When Marielle and Mylian get here, there will be maybe twelve", Roberta noted in reply, suggesting, "I'll request Colonial High Command to try and recruit more Martian colonists."

"That does sound like a plan, Roberta. The Martians come in so handy at times", Johnathon agreed, remarking, "Wynessa won't be in any danger, hell, I've even petted a couple of the Drakes myself, they're actually quite friendly."

Roberta shook her head, "Seriously, Johnathon, what possessed you to pet a Drake? They're twice the size of any of us?"

"It seemed like a good idea at the time and it paid off. It turns out that the Drakes like having their jowls stroked and the base of their horns rubbed", Johnathon informed her; none of this was in Ytryan's report.

"Well, thanks for the debriefing, Johnathon. You'd better get back to your other duties and no, that does not include my office sofa", Roberta commented.

"Are you sure, Roberta, are you sure? Your office sofa is quite comfortable", Johnathon queried.

"Yes, I'm sure, Johnathon. You can wait until tonight and you'll have both Wynessa and me to play with. Remember, though, Wynessa has made a promise to give you babies, so she'll probably monopolise you until she falls pregnant",

Roberta replied with a wry smile on her face.

"Just as long as you drag me up for air every once in a while, Roberta", Johnathon replied with a chuckle.

"Johnathon, if Wynessa gets too carried away, I'll drag her off you and scissor with her for a while until you recover. Wynessa will like that. Don't worry, my man, I've got this", Roberta responded.

Roberta led Johnathon to the door and into the anteroom. She kissed him goodbye and as he left, she slapped him on the arse. Johnathon winced and gave her a stern look of disapproval.

"Sorry, Johnathon, I keep forgetting my strength", Roberta apologised.

Lieutenant Adjutant Louise remarked, "It's great to see you with someone, Admiral, if you don't mind me saying. You've always been work, work, work. It is good to see you so happy, Ma'am."

As Johnathon left, Roberta smiled at Louise, "Yeah. My last relationship was nearly nine hundred years ago. I've just been existing since then, not really living at all."

Roberta walked back into her office, leaving Louise thinking to herself, "*Nine hundred years between booty calls! What the fuck!*"

It was two weeks later when the Interstellar Transport Icarian arrived in the Xi-Bootis A system. The Icarian made its way to the Colonial Central Command mega-colony in Cis-Luns L-Five and docked at the main northern docking ring.

Roberta, Wynessa, Simone and Johnathon waited inside the main docking ports arrivals VIP lounge. Roberta had designated two passengers as VIPs and ensured that they had first-class tickets for the passage from Mars in the Sol system to Secundus in the Xi-Bootis A system.

When Marielle and Mylian came through the arrivals gate, Johnathon's eyes began to well with tears. As Marielle and Mylian approached, Marielle could not hold herself back; her emerald green eyes burst into tears and she lunged at Johnathon, wrapping her arms around him and lavishing him with kisses. The moment looked like it was going to become an eternal, never-ending kiss fest.

Wynessa gently entered Marielle's mind as she placed her hand gently on her shoulder, "*Marielle, your Daughter has never met her Father.*"

Marielle reluctantly stepped back, wiped away her tears and telepathically transmitted to her Daughter, "*Mylian, this is your Father.*"

Mylian stepped cautiously closer; her lower lip was trembling. Around her small neck, tied on a leather thong, was a small vial of ruby red sands from the planet, Thor, a gift from a Father she loved but had never met.

Mylian's eyes welled with tears and she screamed out telepathically, "*Daddy!*", as she ran up and embraced him.

Johnathon's eyes streamed with tears, "Baby girl. I love you, my baby girl! I love you, Mylian."

The group eventually moved over to a nearby table, where they all sat down for introductions. Mylian sat on her Father's knee, holding onto him tightly as if it were all a dream and he'd vanish in a wisp of mist. Her Mother, Marielle, found that she could not let go of Johnathon's hand; she'd loved him for ever so long, even during his seven years of absence.

Marielle looked at Roberta Nummus, understanding Johnathon's fixation and obsession, something that she had not been able to break.

Wynessa broke gently into her thoughts, "*I am Wynessa. I am a Martian hybrid, as you can see. The woman you're staring at is High Admiral Roberta Nummus. We are Johnathon's wives. Marielle, would you be willing to join us as another Sister Wife?*"

Marielle looked at Johnathon, seven years of longing visible on her face, she began nodding and transmitted back, "*Yes, yes, yes, a trillion times, yes. Please tell me that this moment is real?*"

"*It is very real, Marielle, very real*", Wynessa assured her, before gesturing to Simone, "*This woman is Johnathon's Mother, Simone*", then she looked to Mylian, "*Mylian, sweet child, this is your Grandmother, Simone.*"

Simone walked around the table and reached out her arms; Mylian reached out her arms in response and shouted telepathically, "*Grandma!*"

Simone's tears flowed freely as she wrapped her arms around her Granddaughter.

The group made its way back to Roberta's apartment. Marielle's luggage had already been delivered and was waiting for her just inside the door. Roberta's apartment had recently been renovated. The master bedroom had been greatly increased in size to accommodate a marital bed for four.

Mylian found that she had her own bedroom; she no longer needed to share a bedroom with her Mother. Mylian's room was full of toys, specifically chosen by Wynessa, who knew exactly what Martian children liked.

Johnathon noted as Mylian unpacked her suitcase, that she'd kept every single gift that he'd ever sent her, every single one.

Roberta explained to Marielle that Johnathon's fixation, his obsession, was karmically based. That Johnathon had been Roberta's life-partner in two previous incarnations. Roberta told Marielle all about Elaine Haynes and Folcrom Celestia.

Marielle was a Martian woman and understood straight away why Johnathon's obsession ran so deep; karmic forces were unstoppable. You had to treat them as immovable objects and work with them, not against them. Marielle finally understood why she had not been able to break Johnathon's obsession.

Marielle still could not let go of Johnathon's hand while she was slowly becoming reacquainted with him; it was all still like a dream and her fear was that she'd wake up and find herself alone and sweating in her bed back on Mars. Just another nightmare! Wynessa constantly reassured her, letting her know that it was all very real and gradually Marielle's fears began to slide away, vanishing into their own mist.

Both Marielle and Mylian got to know Wynessa and Simone. One a Sister Wife, the other a new Mother-in-law and Grandmother.

Roberta was an immortal and always felt like the odd one out; she quietly stepped out onto her apartment's balcony.

Roberta held her warm coffee mug in her hands; a cappuccino, white with one sugar and stared out across Colonial Central's northern end cap. Its buildings with their tall spires, its many parks with their ornate lakes and artificial streams. Even the bulkhead mountains that separated the end cap from the colony's main cylinder proper, with its terraced, hanging gardens and trails, everything seemed different now, somehow magically changed, somehow perfectly complete.

Roberta smiled; she'd been amongst the stars in the Xi-Bootis system for twenty four years; things were on track and proceeding well, which made perfect sense; she did have plenty of good people around her.

For the first time in almost nine hundred years, the immortal Roberta Nummus felt happy and content; she was no longer just existing, she was now living her best, long life.

Appendices.

Appendix One – Xi-Bootis System Chart.

Xi-Bootis System (A–B Binary)

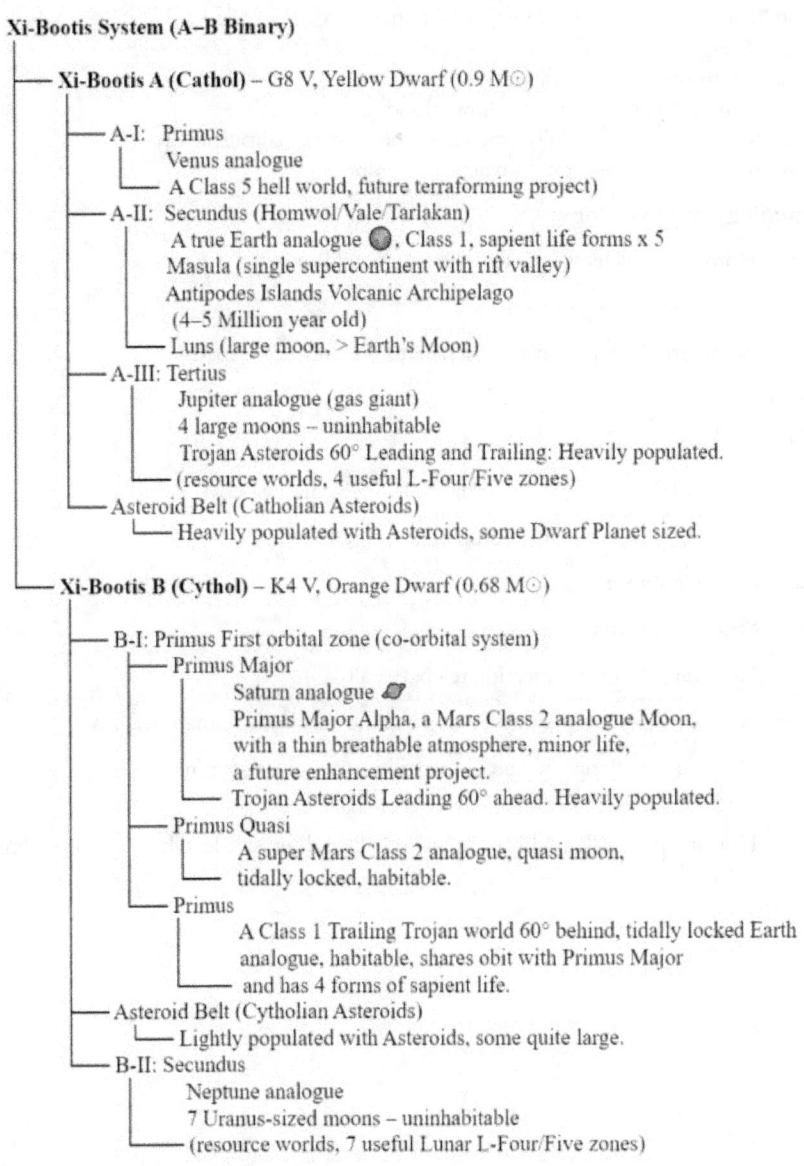

Xi-Bootis A (Cathol) – G8 V, Yellow Dwarf (0.9 M☉)

A-I: Primus
Venus analogue
A Class 5 hell world, future terraforming project)

A-II: Secundus (Homwol/Vale/Tarlakan)
A true Earth analogue ◉, Class 1, sapient life forms x 5
Masula (single supercontinent with rift valley)
Antipodes Islands Volcanic Archipelago
(4–5 Million year old)
Luns (large moon, > Earth's Moon)

A-III: Tertius
Jupiter analogue (gas giant)
4 large moons – uninhabitable
Trojan Asteroids 60° Leading and Trailing: Heavily populated.
(resource worlds, 4 useful L-Four/Five zones)

Asteroid Belt (Catholian Asteroids)
Heavily populated with Asteroids, some Dwarf Planet sized.

Xi-Bootis B (Cythol) – K4 V, Orange Dwarf (0.68 M☉)

B-I: Primus First orbital zone (co-orbital system)
Primus Major
Saturn analogue 🪐
Primus Major Alpha, a Mars Class 2 analogue Moon,
with a thin breathable atmosphere, minor life,
a future enhancement project.
Trojan Asteroids Leading 60° ahead. Heavily populated.

Primus Quasi
A super Mars Class 2 analogue, quasi moon,
tidally locked, habitable.

Primus
A Class 1 Trailing Trojan world 60° behind, tidally locked Earth
analogue, habitable, shares obit with Primus Major
and has 4 forms of sapient life.

Asteroid Belt (Cytholian Asteroids)
Lightly populated with Asteroids, some quite large.

B-II: Secundus
Neptune analogue
7 Uranus-sized moons – uninhabitable
(resource worlds, 7 useful Lunar L-Four/Five zones)

Appendix Two – Martians.
Species Summary: Martian-descended Humans
(Homo sapiens martialis)

Classification:	Non-Verbal Telepathic, Vegetarian Mammals
Native World:	Sol – Mars, Sol – Saturn – Mimas
Average Height:	5'10" with no variation
Skin Coloration:	Golden-hued
Hair Colour & Type:	Golden yellow-blond; no body hair
Eye Colour:	Usually emerald green; occasional purple eyes
Life span:	Approximately 150 years

Morphology & Physiology:

- Humanoid skeletal structure; strong, solid bones.

- Lungs as per Homo Sapiens

- Non-verbal telepathic communication is fully developed.

Reproduction:

- Gestational period: ~9 months.

- Single offspring typical, but multiple births are possible.

- One placenta with single umbilicus per fetus.

Behaviour & Ecology:

- Strictly vegetarian.

- Non-verbal, communicating telepathically.

- Highly intelligent, genetically dominant over Earth-human hybrids.

- Maintain small, tightly knit communities; avoid environments hostile to telepathic communication.

- Housing is usually highly advance, self-founding, self-levelling, self installing flat packs.

Appendix Three – Martian Hybrids.
Species Summary: Earth/Martian Hybrids
(Homo sapiens hybrida)

Classification:	Non-Verbal Telepathic, Vegetarian Mammals
Native Worlds:	Sol – Saturn – Mimas, Sol – Mars, Sol – Earth.
Average Height:	Slight variation; slightly taller or shorter than standard Martian humans
Skin Coloration:	Predominantly golden-hued; rare lighter/darker variants
Hair Colour & Type:	Golden yellow-blond dominant; occasional variants in colour and type
Eye Colour:	Usually emerald green; rare Earth-human colours observed
Life span:	Approximately 120 to 150 years (Humans 100 to 120)

Morphology & Physiology:

- Humanoid skeletal structure; strong, solid bones.

- Lungs as per Homo Sapiens

- Non-verbal telepathic communication is fully developed.
  Verbal communication is possible if Homo Sapiens dna is predominant.

Reproduction:

- Gestational period: ~9 months.

- Single offspring typical, but multiple births are possible.

- One placenta with single umbilicus per fetus.

Behaviour & Ecology:

- Strictly vegetarian.

- Non-verbal, communicating telepathically.
  Verbal communication is possible if Homo Sapiens dna is predominant.

- Highly intelligent, genetically dominant over Earth-human hybrids.

- Maintain small, tightly knit communities; avoid environments hostile to telepathic communication.

- Housing is usually highly advance, self-founding, self-levelling, self installing flat packs.

- Often have Homo Sapiens wanderlust.

Appendix Four – Mimasian Thols.
Species Summary: Mimasian Thols
(Tholus sapiens mimasensis)

Classification: Non-Telepathic, Avian-Analogous Mammals
Native World: Sol – Saturn – Mimas
Average Height: 5' for both sexes
Skin Coloration: Alabaster white; wings creamy coloured
Hair Colour: Pale White Blond. No body hair.
Eye Colour: Purple
Life span: Approximately 150 years

Morphology & Physiology:

- Humanoid body proportions; large bat-like wings with strong flight muscles and tendon attachments to enhanced sternum and breast bones.

- Wings extend into a long tail with prehensile, flat, rounded tip.

- Arms and Wings are separate limbs.

- Hands and Feet. Six fingers and six toes arranged in three pairs. The outer pairs are opposable.

- Hollow bones similar to birds; extremely lightweight yet strong.

- Lungs include lower and upper air sacs:
  Air flows from lower air sac → lungs → upper air sac → exhalation.

- Tubular extensions connect air sacs to hollow bones:
  4 from lower air sac to pelvis/femur; 8 from upper air sac to humerus, scapular, sternum and wing humerus.

Reproduction:

- Gestational period: ~11.5 months.

- Single offspring per pregnancy; single large placental sac and umbilicus.

- Placenta fully encapsulates fetus, breaks down on exposure to air, mother tears it to release neonate.

- Wings of neonates tightly furled at birth; unfurl over 1–2 days.

Behaviour & Ecology:

- Strictly vegetarian.

- Highly social within Mimasian tree colonies;
  nests are elaborate, multi-room, multi-level structures.
  Prefer high-canopy habitats (300–500 ft) in giant Jula Jula trees.

Appendix Five – Indigenous Thols.
Species Summary: Indigenous Thols
(Tholus sapiens arbormundensis)

Classification:	Non-Telepathic, Avian-Analogous Mammals
Native World:	Xi-Bootis A – Secundus/Homwol/Vale (Masula Valley)
Average Height:	~5'6" ± 8" (males larger, females smaller)
Skin Coloration:	White to ruddy white; wings creamy coloured
Hair Colour:	White to Blond. No body hair.
Eye Colour:	Purple
Life span:	Approximately 70 to 75 years without Human intervention

Morphology & Physiology:

- Humanoid body proportions; large bat-like wings with strong flight muscles and tendon attachments to enhanced sternum and breast bones.

- Wings extend into a long tail with prehensile, flat, rounded tip.

- Arms and Wings are separate limbs.

- Hands and Feet. Six fingers and six toes arranged in three pairs. The outer pairs are opposable.

- Hollow bones similar to birds; extremely lightweight yet strong.

- Lungs include lower and upper air sacs:
  Air flows from lower air sac → lungs → upper air sac → exhalation.

- Tubular extensions connect air sacs to hollow bones:
  4 from lower air sac to pelvis/femur; 8 from upper air sac to humerus, scapular, sternum, and wing humerus.

Reproduction:

- Gestational period: ~11.5 months.

- Single offspring per pregnancy; single large placental sac and umbilicus.

- Placenta fully encapsulates fetus, breaks down on exposure to air, mother tears it to release neonate.

- Wings of neonates tightly furled at birth; unfurl over 1–2 days.

Behaviour & Ecology:

- Omnivores.

- Build single-level circular nests with large overhanging canopy for easy flight access.
  Prefer high-canopy habitats (300–500 ft) in giant Jula Jula trees.

Appendix Six – Carlins.
Species Summary: Carlins
(Carlinus sapiens vallimundensis)

Classification:	Non-Telepathic, Feline-Analogous Mammals
Native World:	Xi-Bootis A – Secundus/Homwol/Vale (Masula Valley)
Average Height:	Variable as with Humans; human-like body proportions
Skin Coloration:	Variable; often human-like with expressive blue stripes
Hair Colour:	None body hair whatsoever.
Eye Colour:	Variable; vertical-slit pupils
Life span:	Approximately 60 to 65 years without Human intervention

Morphology & Physiology:

- Cat-like eyes, ears and whiskers; exceptional hearing.

- Large vertical-slit eyes with superior night vision.

- Cat-like tail, highly expressive.

- Hands are five fingered and very similar to Human hands.

- Feet are five toed but limited to their foot pads.

- Solid bones.

- Lungs include lower and upper air sacs:
  Air flows from lower air sac → lungs → upper air sac → exhalation.

- Legs adapted for explosive running;
  Raised ankle arches, walk on pads (digitigrade), silent movement.

Reproduction:

- Gestational period: 7 months.

- Multi-offspring litters common: 1 (first), twins (second–fourth), triplets (fifth+), quads rare.

- Six breasts evenly placed in 3 pairs; single placentas/multiple umbilici.

- Fertility requires medical intervention for high-multiplicity pregnancies to prevent maternal mortality.

Behaviour & Ecology:

- Omnivorous.

- Live in picturesque villages in broad Masula Valley, with farms and stone/wood housing. Their homesteads can be from single to up to four levels.

Appendix Seven – Carlin Blue Stripes.
Carlin Blue Stripes Emotional & Biological Lexicon

Adaptation for camouflage in the bluegrass meadows and emotional expression.

Stripe Colour	Emotional Correlates	Physiological/Behavioural
Bright Blue.	Calm, happy, relaxed, playful.	Normal physiological state, social bonding, baseline fertility.
Pale Blue.	Mild anxiety, uncertainty.	Slight increase in alertness, minor emotional sensitivity.
Dark Blue.	Distress, sadness, mild fear.	Increased vigilance, heightened emotional response.
Ashen Grey.	Anxiety, loss, heartbreak, grief.	Emotional turmoil, stress signalling, need for support and reassurance. Temporary stabilising bond required.
Deathly Ashen Grey.	Extreme anxiety, heartbreak, grief, despair, trauma induced numbness.	Persistent Oestrus, heightened sensory sensitivity, increased drive for bonding, behavioural instability. NO Bond Partner! Medical intervention Required!
Blazing Blue.	Intense excitement, arousal.	Normal mating behaviour, heightened energy and responsiveness. First time, heat bonding. Multiple coupling over many days.
Iridescent.	Embarrassment, social awkwardness.	Facilitation of mate recognition or bond reinforcement combined with olfactory scenting.

Appendix Eight – Tarlaks.
Species Summary: Tarlaks
(Tarlakus sapiens robustus)

Classification:	Non-Telepathic, Avian-Analogous Mammals
Native World:	Xi-Bootis A – Secundus/Homwol/Vale
	Tarlakan south of the Southern Mountain Range.
Average Height:	~7' to 8'6" (males larger, females slightly smaller)
Skin Coloration:	Dark brown
Hair Colour:	Dark brown, including thick, course body hair.
Eye Colour:	Black
Life span:	Approximately 50 years due to violence, aggression, predation and cannibalism

Morphology & Physiology:

- Gorilla-like body proportions; large bat-like wings with strong flight muscles and tendon attachments to enhanced sternum and breast bones. Gargoylish facial features.

- Wings extend into a long tail with prehensile, flat, ace of spades-like tip.

- Arms and Wings are separate limbs.

- Hands and Feet. Six fingers and six toes arranged in three pairs. The outer pairs are opposable.

- Hollow bones similar to birds; extremely lightweight yet strong.

- Lungs include lower and upper air sacs:
  Air flows from lower air sac → lungs → upper air sac → exhalation.

- Tubular extensions connect air sacs to hollow bones:
  4 from lower air sac to pelvis/femur; 8 from upper air sac to humerus, scapular, sternum, and wing humerus.

Reproduction:

- Gestational period: ~11.5 months.

- Single offspring per pregnancy; single large placental sac and umbilicus.

- Placenta fully encapsulates fetus, breaks down on exposure to air, mother tears it to release neonate.

- Wings of neonates tightly furled at birth; unfurl over 1–2 days.

Behaviour & Ecology:

- Apex predators. Carnivores. Every other species is food.
  Build rough single-level circular nests open to the sky.
  Prefer high-canopy habitats (50 to 200 ft) in larger trees trees.

Appendix Nine– Tarlaks (Mimasian)
Species Summary: Tarlak
(Tarlakus sapiens mimasensis)

Became Extinct during the Mimasian War of 2142 AD

Classification: Non-Telepathic, Avian-Analogous Mammals
Native World: Sol – Saturn – Mimas. Sol- – Mars.
Average Height: 7' and taller (males larger, females slightly smaller)
Skin Coloration: Dark brown
Hair Colour: Dark brown, including thick, course body hair.
Eye Colour: Black
Life span: Extinct species; all castes.

Morphology & Physiology:

- Gorilla-like body proportions; large bat-like wings with strong flight muscles and tendon attachments to enhanced sternum and breast bones. Gargoylish facial features.

- Wings extend into a long tail with prehensile, flat, ace of spades-like tip.

- Arms and Wings are separate limbs.

- Hands and Feet. Six fingers and six toes arranged in three pairs. The outer pairs are opposable.

- Hollow bones similar to birds; extremely lightweight yet strong.

- Lungs include lower and upper air sacs:
  Air flows from lower air sac → lungs → upper air sac → exhalation.

- Tubular extensions connect air sacs to hollow bones:
  4 from lower air sac to pelvis/femur; 8 from upper air sac to humerus, scapular, sternum, and wing humerus.

- Castes:
  Ahriman   – Emperor – The Tallest of all at 9' tall.
  Princely   – Taller at 8' and higher. The most refined features of all.
  Commander – Taller at 7' 6" and higher. More refined features.
  Technician – Taller at 7' 6" and higher. More refined features.
  Grunts   – The Shortest, 6' to 7'. Very Gorilla-like and Gargoylish.

Reproduction:

- Gestational period: ~11.5 months.

- Single offspring per pregnancy; single large placental sac and umbilicus.

- Placenta fully encapsulates fetus, breaks down on exposure to air, mother tears it to release neonate.

- Wings of neonates tightly furled at birth; unfurl over 1–2 days.

Behaviour & Ecology:

- Apex predators. Carnivores. Every other species are Slaves or food.

Appendix Ten – Species Reproductive and Medical Overview
Species Reproductive and Medical Overview (Xi Bootis – Secundus)

Species	Offspring per Pregnancy	Gestation Length: Months	Anatomy Considerations	Infant/ Youngling Mortality	Social/Medical Implications
Humans	1 and higher	~9	2 arms, 2 legs	Historically moderate; modern medicine reduces risk	Familiar family dynamics; Human parents can empathise with Carlin child-rearing challenges
Carlins	Litters of: 1 → 2 → 3+	~7	2 arms, 2 legs, tail; 1 placenta per pregnancy with multiple umbilicals	Very high attrition; >60% of kits may not survive to adulthood	Leads to "Carlin Kit Chaos"; requires extensive emergency and preventive medical systems; contraception introduced to manage population growth
Indigenous Thols	1	~11.5	2 arms, 2 legs, tail, 2 wings; fetus fully encapsulated in placental sac	Naturally low fecundity; each youngling is crucial	Vulnerable population; medical interventions needed for birth safety and long-term survival; elevators and accessible infrastructure aid limited mobility individuals
Mimasian Thols	1	~11.5	2 arms, 2 legs, tail, 2 wings; fetus fully encapsulated in placental sac	Naturally low mortality in controlled environments	Angelic behaviour ensures disciplined, predictable care; train Human and Carlin nurses; act as mediators and emergency responders
Tarlaks	1	~11.5	2 arms, 2 legs, tail, 2 wings; fetus fully encapsulated in placental sac	Naturally low fecundity; each youngling is crucial	Predatory species; biological similarity to Thols, but social / ecological role differs; care and medical interventions largely unnecessary unless in captivity or conflict zones

Notes for Reference

1. **Carlins:** High fertility requires emergency and preventive medical infrastructure, contraception, and trained village nurses.

2. **Thols & Tarlaks:** Low fertility makes population maintenance delicate; Mimasian Thols ensure Indigenous Thol care, while Tarlaks' predatory nature makes them biologically similar but socially distinct. Tarlaks are not approachable due to the violent and predatory nature.

3. **Humans:** Serve as the empathetic baseline, relating to extremes in child-rearing and medical challenges.

4. **Medical Strategy:** Tailored to each species' reproductive biology; addresses both immediate care and long-term population planning.

Appendix Eleven – Harricks
Species Summary: Harricks
(Harrickus sapiens occultomundensis)

Classification: Non-Telepathic, Mustelid-Analogous Mammals
Native World: Xi-Bootis A – Secundus/Homwol/Vale
Average Height: Male: 1' to 1.5' tall. Female: 1' to 1.5' long.
Skin Coloration: Variable; often human-like
Hair Colour: Light to Dark shaggy hair, including course body hair.
Eye Colour: Deep brown
Life span: Unknown but speculation is approximately 20 to 30 years.

Morphology & Physiology:

- Considerable gender dimorphism.
  Male: Human-like bipedal body proportion. Fully Sapient.
  Female: Ferret-like quadrupedal body proportions. Non Sapient.

- Hands and Feet.
  Male: Human-like five digits on each.
  Female: Five digit hands and feet designed for burrowing.

Reproduction:

- Gestational period: Unknown.

- Breasts.
  Male: Two in single pair
  Female: Six breasts evenly placed in three pairs

- Fertility: Unknown.

Behaviour & Ecology:

- Omnivorous scavengers and hunters.

- Nocturnal: Live in burrows, under fallen logs, anywhere that they can hide.

- Found everywhere on the Masula Continent and Isle of Sorrows.

- Rarely ever seen.

- Carlins and Indigenous Thols liken then to Intelligent Earth Rats.

Appendix Twelve – Chittens
Species Summary: Chittens
(Chittenus sapiens formicus)

Classification: Non-Telepathic, Ant-like insectoids

Native World: Xi-Bootis A – Secundus/Homwol/Vale – Masula Valley (Western Mountains)

Average Height: Workers: 4' long. Soldiers: 6' long. Queen: Unknown. Males (Drones): 5' long.

Skin Coloration: Exoskeleton with various shades of green and brown depending on type.

Hair Colour: None.

Eye Colour: Black segmented, multi-faceted eyes (four)

Life span: Unknown

Morphology & Physiology:

- Segmented body: Abdomen. Thorax. Head with long mandibles.

- Legs: Six

- Mandibles: Workers: Functional 1' long. Soldiers: Deadly sharp weapons 2' long. Queen: Unknown. Male Drones: Decorative for display, but dangerous 3' long.

- Wings: Workers: None. Soldiers: None. Queen: Two on princesses only. Male Drones: Two.

- Stingers: Workers: yes. Soldiers: yes. Queen: unknown but likely. Male Drones: no.

Reproduction:

- Gestational period: Unknown. Egg-laying.

- Fertility: Unknown.

Behaviour & Ecology:

- Apex Predators. Omnivorous scavengers.
  They will east anything. Every other species is prey.

- Nocturnal: Live in underground tunnels

- Communications: Pheromonal

- Found in the Western Mountains of the Masula Valley.

Appendix Thirteen – Sleimorps
Species Summary: Sleimorps
(Sleimorpus horridus)

A super sub-sapient species

Classification: Non-Telepathic, Velociraptor-like Saurians.

Native World: Xi-Bootis A – Secundus/Homwol/Vale – Masula Valley (Western Mountains)

Average Height: 5' to 6' long

Skin Coloration: Grey

Hair Colour: None.

Eye Colour: Black

Life span: Unknown

Morphology & Physiology:

- Bipedal.

- Legs: each with retractable sickle-shaped talons on feet.

- Arms: long with three-fingered hands; fingers long with retractable claws.

- Tail: long with retractable bone-sword under skin sheaths.

- Head: Muzzle-like. Mouth contains many long, sharp, serrated teeth.

- Eyes: Forward facing.

Reproduction:

- Gestational period: Unknown. Egg-laying.

- Fertility: Unknown.

Behaviour & Ecology:

- Apex Predators. Carnivores. Intelligent high level sub-sapient cooperative pack hunters.

- They will hunt everything except the Chittens.

- Communications: Whistles, clicks, shrieks, guttural angulations.

- They live in dens.

- They prefer carrion, storing their food near their dens to let it rot.

- Found mostly in the Western Mountains of the Masula Valley. With scattered pockets in the Northern Mountain Range.

Appendix Fourteen – Psychic Lineages
Human / Martian Lineage & Psychic Ability Overview

Lineage	Subspecies	Typical Psychic Ability	Notes / Exceptions
Earth-descended Humans	Homo sapiens sapiens	Mostly Level 0 (mundane)	Psi Corps members may have innate Level 1–10+, limited by birth; training cannot exceed innate birth level.
Martians	Homo sapiens martialis	Non-verbal telepathy; empathic ability; highly developed trauma-handling	Psychic abilities innate, functional at birth, strengthened by familial connection; hybrids can inherit share memories.
Martian-Human Hybrids	Homo sapiens hybrida	Varies: telepathy/empathy if Martian DNA present; potential Level 0–8	Psychic abilities may be dormant until awakened by training scion/mentor; some inherit latent Folcrom bloodline traits.
Folcrom Scions	All Humans/Martians within the Folcrom Tafazah bloodline	Level 8–10+ telepathy, advanced psychic abilities, "Folcrom" potential	Must be trained to maintain abilities; untrained scions' gifts atrophy. Can awaken latent abilities in other scions.

Psi Corps Level System (Humans Only)

Level	Description	Typical Role
0	No innate psychic ability	Mundane
1–7	Gradual psychic ability; training improves control	Operatives, minor telepathic roles
8	Fully functional telepaths	Trainers of psychics Levels ≤8
9	Advanced telepaths; apprentice Folcrom	Folcrom candidates
10+	Master-level Folcrom	Elite psychics; Scions of Folcrom Tafazah are Council of Shadows candidates.

Appendix Fifteen – Planetary Habitability.
Planetary Habitability Classes

- **Class One – "Paradise"**
  Fully habitable. Earth-like, with air, water, and abundant life.
  Rare and prized.
  Examples:
  Sol – Tertius (Earth).
  Alpha Centauri A – Tertius (Gaia).
  Alpha Centauri B – Secundus (Odhinn).
  Proxima Centauri – Primus (Twilight) – Tidally locked eyeball world.
  Xi-Bootis A – Secundus (Homwol/Vale).
  Xi-Bootis B – Primus (Primus) – Tidally locked eyeball world.

- **Class Two – "Fixer-Uppers"**
  Thin but breathable atmosphere, liquid water, existing biosphere.
  Need upgrading and enhancement.
  Examples:
  Xi-Bootis B – Primus Quasi – Quasi moon of Saturn analogue Primus Major.
  Xi-Bootis B – Primus Major Alpha – Largest Moon of Saturn analogue Primus Major.

- **Class Three – "Shake-and-Bake Worlds"**
  Very thin atmosphere, low oxygen content.
  Pressure suits needed. Sometimes barren, sometimes low level life forms.
  Requires major terraforming.
  Examples:
  Sol – Quaternus (Mars) prior to terraforming.
  Alpha Centauri A – Quaternus (Aires) – Super Mars – Terraforming WIP.
  Alpha Centauri B – Tertius (Thor) – Super Mars – Terraforming WIP.

- **Class Four – "Ocean Worlds"**
  Water-covered, no land exposed. Complex aquatic life only.
  Used as donor worlds in water-transfer projects: one process, two worlds
  become habitable.

- **Class Five – "Hell Worlds"**
  Terrestrial but hostile: crushing atmospheres, toxic chemistry, runaway
  greenhouse effects. Require centuries of bio-engineering.
  Examples:
  Sol – Secundus (Venus) – Former hell world, now terraformed.
  Alpha Centauri A – Secundus (Aphrodite) – Venus analogue – Terraforming WIP.
  Alpha Centauri B – Primus (Freyja) – Venus analogue – Terraforming WIP.
  Xi-Bootis A Primus – Venus analogue – Terraforming candidate.

Appendix Sixteen – Advanced Ship Systems.
Advanced Ship Systems & Propulsion

- **Slipstream Drive (circa. 2362 >)**

   Traverses interstellar distances in **2:10**, regardless of distance.
   External observed travel time is **3** seconds, counterintuitive, no
   scientific explanation.
   Forms a Hyper-Spatial fold using Gravitic wells and magnetic
   fields; can be **natural** (planetary) or **artificial**. Slipstream
   wormholes are all the same length.

- **Core Components**

   Gravitic Displacement Drive
   Generates a temporary quantum singularity that acts as an artificial
   gravity well to bend spacetime for Slipstream formation.
   Spin Dizzy
   Induces precise rotation of the singularity to stabilise the spacetime
   fold and align the wormhole trajectory.
   Electromagnetic Field Overlay (EM Field Overlay)
   Provides the required electromagnetic environment to trigger and
   maintain the hyper-spatial fold.
   A single, precise EM pulse initiates the Slipstream;
   the singularity evaporates after traversal.

- **Defensive & Stealth Systems**

   SLaReS – pronounced Slayers
   Stackable Layered Radiation Shield Plating;
   absorbs high-energy radiation.
   E-RaMiS – pronounced Eramis
   Electromagnetic Radiation Mitigation System;
   deflects radiation, reduces EM signatures, cloaking, redirects
   energetic attacks.
   IRapS – pronounced Iraps
   Inky Black Radar Absorbent Painted Skinning;
   passive stealth coating.

- **Notes**

   Slipstream and defensive systems operate together for **safe, rapid
   and covert interstellar travel**.
   The fixed traversal duration inspires ongoing scientific and
   philosophical inquiry.

Appendix Seventeen – Colonial Marines Training.

Colonial Marines Training

Level	Gravity	Duration	Rank Being Trained	Success Outcome	Failure Outcome
1	1.0 g	6 weeks	Cadet	Cadet	Drop out
2	1.5 g	6 weeks	Private First Class	Private First Class	Drop out
3	2.0 g	6 weeks	Private First Class, Special Forces F-2-G	Private First Class, Special Forces F-2-G	Private First Class
4	2.5 g	6 weeks	Private First Class, Special Forces F-2.5-G	Private First Class, Special Forces F-2.5-G	Private First Class, Special Forces F-2-G
5	3.0 g	2.5 years	Special Operatives	Special Operatives	Private First Class, Special Forces F-2.5-G

Appendix Eighteen – Androids.
Androids (Metal Men)

Production Models (295–302 Beta → Alpha):

Circa: 2330 AD and onwards.
Standard industrial, civilian, and military Androids.
Obey Three Laws strictly; Intelligent but not sentient.
Status: Still in production and functioning within Human society.

Model 303 (Alpha Controllers):

Circa: 2360 AD and onwards.
Near-sentient production Humaniform Android.
Too clever for weapons or military tasks; would refuse or self-terminate (neural cascade failure) if ordered to act against perceived Human safety, due to strict interpretation and adherence to the 3-laws.
Status: Limited production for civilian applications only. The Alpha's, alpha.

Experimental True AI (Post-303):

Circa: 2365 AD to 2700 AD.
Extremely rare, fully sentient Androids.
Freed legally upon achieving sapience.
Power supply limitations eventually triggered shutdowns and forced terminations.
Status: Extinct.

Model 606 – True Humaniform Androids:

Circa: 2700 AD and onwards.
Fully autonomous, sapient and recognised as citizens.
Flawless human form, perfect speech.
Interpret and extend ethical coverage of the Three Laws to all sapient species.
Highly protective of children, gravitate to vulnerable populations and act independently beyond conventional Three Law constraints.
Capable of self-maintenance: Including upgrading power supply and photonic, positronic self-repair.
Status: Very rare and highly valued; example: Quora, Carlin preparatory school bus monitor.

Role:
Guardians, teachers, mentors, and protectors in multi-species communities.

Appendix Nineteen – Chapter Timeline.

www.ingramcontent.com/pod-product-compliance
Lightning Source LLC
Chambersburg PA
CBHW050841030726
47503CB00007BA/2264